DIFFERENT VISIONS OF HOME

From the moment Maggie Freiler first saw the grove of seven trees on the vast sea of grass that was Kansas in the 1830s, she knew this was where she and her husband should stop and make their home.

Thus Seventrees was founded, and it was here that Schooner, Maggie's daughter, had to find the courage and true grit to triumph over heart-rending tragedy in war and love and to find, at last, fulfillment.

But for young, breathtakingly lovely Victoria, Seventrees meant something else—first, a place to escape from—and then a place that seemed like a paradise forever lost, as she found herself in a gilded cage of corruption far from home. . . .

Seventrees

Sensational Reading from SIGNET

SEVENTREES

by
Janice Young Brooks

A SIGNET BOOK
NEW AMERICAN LIBRARY

COPYRIGHT © 1981 BY JANICE YOUNG BROOKS

 SIGNET TRADEMARK REG. U.S. PAT. OFF. AND FOREIGN COUNTRIES
REGISTERED TRADEMARK—MARCA REGISTRADA
HECHO EN WINNIPEG, CANADA

SIGNET, SIGNET CLASSIC, MENTOR, PLUME, MERIDIAN AND NAL
BOOKS *are published by New American Library,*
1633 Broadway, New York, New York 10019

FIRST PRINTING, OCTOBER, 1981

    4   5   6   7   8   9

PRINTED IN CANADA

PUBLISHER'S NOTE

For

My mother,

Louise Freiler Jones Young,

who came from Pennsylvania
and planted trees in Kansas
more than a hundred years later

I would like to extend special thanks to Mr. Jerry Roy of the Johnson County, Kansas, Library. He helped me find the answers even when I was too lost to be sure of the questions. He was always enthusiastic and encouraging, though I think he suspected (correctly) that I was taking fiction writer's liberties with the information he so generously shared with me.

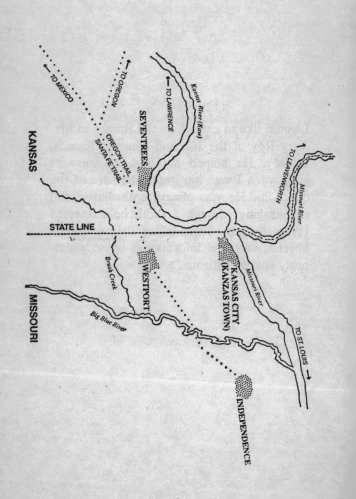

SEVENTREES

Part I

MAGGIE

"In God We Trusted
In Kansas We Busted"

—Sign on back of
an abandoned schooner

1

Germantown, Pennsylvania
1816

Maggie Halleck was fully six years old before she realized she was an orphan. She knew the fact of it before then, but she hadn't felt the heart's truth of it until that spring day in the back garden with Aunt Madlen. That was the day Maggie used the word she'd been hoarding and polishing for months. She'd practiced it, whispering to herself, until it came out with easy magnificence. She had warmed herself to sleep at night for weeks imagining the moment when she would say the word and Aunt Madlen would love her as she loved Luther.

Maggie had hugged the word to herself until the spring cleaning was done for fear it might be overlooked in the frenzy of scrubbing and sweeping that went on every April. When the days began to lengthen, Aunt Madlen always got what Uncle Werner called *housebutz gichtera*—housecleaning convulsions. Until the house was spotless, Aunt Madlen was not aware of anything but soap and brooms and dustrags. When it was done she usually retired to her room with a headache that lasted the rest of the month, but there was always a tranquil moment of transition when one could get her attention.

Now the neat three-story home was so clean it looked raw. Maggie and Aunt Madlen went to the tiny back garden to sit in the shade and have a treat. Madlen Halleck, a hefty blond

3

woman with a perpetually flushed complexion, shed her apron and sat down heavily on the wooden bench built around the old oak tree that shaded the yard. The tree had outgrown the bench and lolled over the wooden planks like Madlen's flesh did at the waist of her dress. She called to Cook to bring out the tray. She spoke now in English, for her husband, Werner, insisted English be spoken on even the most remotely social occasions in the household. Conversations pertaining to work were conducted in German, for German was the language of work.

Maggie found herself trembling with anticipation. It was always an occasion when the spring cleaning was done, but today was even more important because this was the day she would use the word. She had put on a fresh apron and even brushed her honey-colored hair without being asked. Her hands shook as she took the tray from Cook and set it on the bench next to her aunt.

Madlen pried the lid off a tin painted with crimson birds and removed two big crusty pretzels. She put each one on a thick white plate, saying, "With your uncle's people this is a prize for learning prayers. See, the bread has its arms crossed like it's praying." Then, realizing she had touched on a forbidden topic, she crammed the lid back on the tin.

Maggie did not notice her discomfort. Her mouth was dry. Aunt Madlen poured apple cider from a jar into a heavy cup which matched the plate and handed it to the little girl. That was when Maggie said it.

"Thank you, Mother."

Right out. Just like that. *Mother.* She was pleased at how nicely she had pronounced it.

"Don't call me that, Margaret," Aunt Madlen said peevishly.

Maggie felt her face get hot, and something jellylike started happening inside her knees. "Why not? Luther calls you Mother."

"I *am* Luther's mother. I'm not yours. I'm your aunt."

"Then who is my mother?"

Aunt Madlen sighed impatiently, and her forehead creased into a frown. "Your mother passed on when you were a baby. You know that. We've talked about it before."

"Yes, I know. But who is my mother *now*?" Maggie persisted.

"Nobody is your mother now, child. Your mother is dead."

She put chapped, sausage-shaped fingers delicately to her temples, as she always did when the headaches started.

Dead. Finally an explanation she could understand. Before, it had always been "gone to heaven" or "expired" or "passed on." But *dead*? Such an ugly word. Maggie was repulsed at Aunt Madlen saying such a thing. Luther's pet rabbit was dead; the roaches Cook stepped on when she found them in the kitchen were dead; the maggoty bird Maggie had found last week in the bushes was dead. But her mother? Her *only* mother? Dead! Things that were dead were awful, and they never, never came back.

"Margaret! Look what you've done. Now, pick up that cup and rinse out your dress before the stain sets."

"Is . . . is my father also 'dead'?" She cringed at the word.

Madlen made an exasperated noise between pursed lips. "You know he is. Now, go get that dress off."

Maggie dutifully did as she was told. All the while, her thoughts were skidding about on the slick surface of this horrible new reality. She thought mothers were earned somehow, and that Luther, being four years older, had already achieved the right to call Aunt Madlen "Mother." But this was all wrong. Madlen was true mother to Luther, and Maggie had no mother. Worse, nothing could ever change it. The desolation of it made her cold and nauseated. She cried until Cook put her to bed with a tonic and Aunt Madlen's instructions that she was not to have any more cider, since it seemed to make her ill.

As time passed, Maggie began to comprehend that parenthood determined how she and Luther were treated. He was regarded as special simply because he was theirs. Maggie could not genuinely miss having real parents, of course. That would have been like missing the taste of mangoes or the sound of Chinese being spoken—so completely unknown to her that the void could not be defined. But she did miss being loved, and without knowing words to put to the concept, she sensed that her place in her aunt and uncle's hearts was much like her room in the narrow house, small, low-ceilinged, and remote. She wanted them to love her as they loved Luther, and she feared desperately they never would.

Luther was also aware of the difference, and he reveled in it. Not that he disliked Maggie—he felt almost nothing for her, but he discovered that when he was petted and pampered, it was pleasant; when Maggie was not, the contrast enhanced his own pleasure. He fell into habits no one took the trouble to analyze or alter.

Once, when Maggie had done especially well on a sampler, she showed it to Uncle Werner. He was a large crimson-and-gold man with big square hands that would have looked more suitable on a farmer than the owner of a paint company. Apathetically he accepted the sampler, and at that moment Luther said, "I got a perfect spelling paper today." Aunt Madlen squealed with delight and Uncle Werner set the sewing on the side table, unnoticed, while the conversation veered sharply back to Luther's accomplishment.

Maggie stood quietly while he bragged. The words had been very difficult, the teacher had said them very quickly, but only he out of twelve boys got all of them correct. The teacher had complimented him not only on his spelling skill but also on the attractiveness of his handwriting. On and on, he embellished the glory of the spelling test, while Maggie waited. Finally Luther ran out of his own praises to sing and there was a brief lull.

"Uncle Werner. My sampler?" Maggie said quietly.

"What? Oh, yes," he said. As he turned back to her he inadvertently knocked his pipe against the lamp, dumping hot sparks on the sampler.

Maggie snatched up the cloth, frantically brushing it off into the ashstand, but it was already a ruin of little black bites. She burst into tears.

"Stop that wailing!" Werner ordered (in German, for it was also the language of discipline). "You can make another and you'll be more careful of where you put it. Margaret! You'll give your aunt another of her headaches. Stop your noise!"

As Maggie fled, clutching the charred fabric to her chest, she heard Aunt Madlen say wearily, "What shall we ever do with her, Werner? *So* flighty."

Much later, when the tears were dry and the spoiled sampler thrown out, Maggie brooded over her aunt's remark. That Madlen Halleck was utterly in error calling her flighty never occurred to the girl. The facts, as she saw them, were thus: Aunt Madlen and Uncle Werner did not love her. Since adults had mastered their failings, the fault must be hers. If she could be as they wanted her to be, they would love her. So Maggie set out to be as practical and sensible as it was possible for a child to be. The seeds of self-respect in her

6

were still shiny and hard-shelled. The season for germination had not yet come.

Maggie was twelve years old when the letter from Gretta came. It was a freakishly balmy March evening and Aunt Madlen had emerged from a month's confinement with a headache to eat dinner with the family. She felt guilty about neglecting her duties and was being forcefully friendly in an effort to make up for her absence. Werner, ruddy complexion paled to mere pink, was not responding to her charm. Finally she said, "What is that in your pocket? Something to share with us?"

Werner, deep in gloomy contemplation of his plate, was startled by the question and glanced down at the betraying sliver of envelope showing at his breast pocket. "It's nothing," he said, and pushed it out of sight.

But Madlen would not let the matter drop. "Secrets, Werner? You make secrets from us?" She meant to be coquettish, and sounded boisterous.

He looked up at her, a long blue gaze that seemed to chill the food on their plates. "It is a letter from Gretta."

"Gretta! But what . . . has something happened to—?"

"No!" Werner cut her off. "Maggie, pass the dumplings."

The rest of the meal passed in drafty silence. When it was over, Maggie and Luther were excused. She glanced back from the doorway and saw that Madlen had pulled her chair next to Werner's and he had the letter spread out on the table. "Maggie, shut the door," he said.

Maggie asked Luther later if he knew who Gretta was, but he had just turned sixteen and was afflicted with a sophisticated ennui. "Who can say? Who cares?" he replied.

During the next few weeks Maggie sensed a muffled tension in the household. Gradually it began to take shape—a vast, invisible whirlwind of thrumming discontent, with her in the eye. Conversations between Werner and Madlen would cease when she entered the room. There were meaningful glances, whispered discussions, clammy silences.

In late April another letter came. Maggie saw the discarded envelope in the fire grate. It was addressed to Uncle Werner at his Philadelphia office in the overcareful hand of an adult unused to communicating in writing. There was no return address. Two weeks later Aunt Madlen puffed up the narrow flight of stairs to Maggie's tiny room. "We're going to go through your clothes this afternoon," she announced.

7

Maggie knew from Madlen's expression that questions about this break in routine would be met with hostility, so she obeyed without inquiry. Madlen selected a plain brown workdress and a dark blue one with white collar and cuffs. She examined the white trim and muttered about alterations. Then she folded the two dresses, selected some undergarments and a pair of outdoor boots. She clutched the pile of clothing in one arm while fishing around in her bosom for a little scrap of paper. She read it, scowling, nodded several times, and said, "Maggie, when you do your hair in the morning, pin your braids up tightly. You'll wear this brown dress, but it must be washed and ironed first."

Maggie felt a flare of panic. "What is happening?"

Madlen's frown eased a little. She stuffed the little paper back into her bodice and patted Maggie's shoulder in a gesture that was almost affectionate. "You are going visiting."

"Visiting who?" There was a lump of anxiety in Maggie's throat that made it hard to breathe properly.

"Your uncle will explain."

Maggie didn't sleep that night. She was being sent away from the only home she had ever known because of some mysterious letters from someone named Gretta. Where could they be sending her? It must be to work in somebody's house. That would explain why Aunt Madlen had chosen such plain clothing for her to take. If she were truly going visiting, Madlen would not have chosen those drab garments, for she was conscious of fashion and set great store by how people dressed.

In the last few years, Madlen's headaches had become more frequent and more severe. Maggie had assumed increasing responsibility for the running of the Halleck household. Was this, then, to be her reward? She had attempted to become beloved and indispensable and had succeeded in becoming only a commodity. It had been bad enough all these years, being part-time family, part-time servant. What would it be like in a home where no one had any reason whatsoever to care about her?

Maggie was dressed, hair bound as instructed, before the first watery gray light of dawn illuminated her room. If it was going to happen, then let it be done. The reality of where she was going could certainly be no worse than her imaginings. It was still not light when Madlen came to her room. "Ah, you are ready. Good. Your uncle wants to get started right away.

Your clothing is in the carriage, and I've packed some porridge bread and ham. And I've put in some *pfeffernusse*."

Pfeffernusse were Maggie's favorite kind of cookie, and she regarded this uncharacteristic thoughtfulness on Madlen's part as a death sentence. A last gesture to the condemned. *Gott in Himmel*! What were they doing to her? For an instant she considered bolting. She was enraged, insulted, and desperately frightened. Then the practicality she'd been nurturing most of her life took over. Where could she run to? Nowhere. She picked up her shawl and said, "I'm ready to go."

Their departure was ominous. Uncle Werner was already in the carriage, reins clenched in his big square hands. There were no words of farewell between him and his wife. They were angry with each other, and Maggie had a brief hope that at least one of them had wanted her to stay.

Nor did Werner speak after he clucked the horse into motion. Golden morning light washed over the other houses and shops along Rittenhouse Street. Here and there a plump hausfrau scrubbed her front steps. At the corner of Main they did not turn left to drive the six miles to Philadelphia as Maggie had expected, but went the opposite way. Where were they headed? Past the Green Tree Tavern, where Uncle Werner often met with his friends. Past the beautiful big homes where rich Philadelphia merchants spent their summers to avoid the heat of the city. Past the little Mennonite church. The familiar landmarks slid by.

Maggie wanted to memorize each for fear she might never see it again. There was the Concord school, where Luther went to classes. It was set into a corner of the Upper Burial Ground and she had often explored the cemetery while she waited to meet Luther after school. It was a peaceful place, where the past was literally walled off from the present. There was one grave she always visited. It was over a hundred years old, and the stone said that Adam Shisler had died at the age of 969 years. Maggie had often thought about long-dead Herr Shisler and wondered whether it was a blessing or curse to have lived so long. Luther scoffed, saying it was just a stone carver's mistake, but Maggie wasn't sure.

They passed more of the elegant mansions at the north end of Germantown and then they were into the country. Still Maggie waited for her uncle to speak, to explain where they were going. But he kept an iron silence, and before many

9

miles the gentle motion of the carriage and the accumulated tension overcame Maggie and she fell asleep.

When she awoke, they were passing through country so lush the air seemed to vibrate with ripeness. Impenetrably thick stands of walnut stood in the midst of rolling hills so green they shimmered. Here and there, neat white houses dotted the landscape and tidy fences enclosed geometric fields. They passed through a covered bridge, and as the boards thundered under the wheels, Maggie noticed that even the bridge had a fresh coat of red paint and the night lanterns at either end were polished and shiny.

Werner stopped in a small clearing and tied the horse near a thick clump of grass next to a stream while Maggie opened the lunch basket. There was a paper-wrapped box tied with silk ribbon inside the basket with the food. She set it aside and glanced at her uncle. He was standing quite still, gazing out over the stream. He looked so sad it made something twist inside her. She'd never thought of his having feelings. He was either pleased or displeased with the way the house was run. A coldly domineering figure the household catered to, he seemed incapable of sorrow or affection or gaiety. But this place meant something to him, something that touched his heart and showed in his face.

They ate their meal in separate wells of quiet and resumed the incomprehensible journey. In the late afternoon Werner left the main road and turned up a narrow lane. There was a cathedral arch of branches overhead, thick with the companionable twittering of migrating warblers. Do *they* know where they are going and what awaits them? Maggie wondered. Finally Werner called "Whoa" to the horse and got down from the carriage. They were at the gates of a large house that seemed to back into a hillside. She wondered why he had picked this spot to rest.

There were three boys and a man entering the house. The man had a short brownish beard, and the boys were dressed just as he was. They all wore dark pants, collarless blue workshirts, and black flat-brimmed hats. Maggie recognized them as Amish. Such people often brought produce to market days in Germantown. Stern and aloof, they would arrive with a wagon full of turnips, eggs, bushels of apples and potatoes, which they would briskly trade for salt, spices, and coffee. They left the instant their business was finished, never staying to talk or have a beer or sing or visit friends. It was as though they held such activities in contempt. Maggie found their grim self-assurance frightening.

"Get your things," Werner said without looking at her. "And the package."

"Here?" There was a lump of cold ballooning inside her.

"Hurry!" Werner said, urgent now with some distant distress of his own. He opened the gate and gestured Maggie to pass through. "Give the old woman the package." His face was grave, almost frightened, as he got back into the carriage.

Maggie stood in the rutted track and watched him leave. He hadn't said good-bye, hadn't told her where she was or why, hadn't said if he would ever be back. What was she supposed to do? Quickly she moved out of sight of the house and into the shade of a large tree. The muscles in her legs were shaking, and it was hard to breathe. She sat down and buried her face in her parcel of clothes, but she was too frightened and confused to even cry. Something cold and wet touched her hand. She looked up at a lanky yellow dog. He nudged her hand again and wagged his scrawny tail.

She petted him absently and thought about her choices. They were two: she could stay or she could go. It was that simple. But where could she go? Back to Germantown? She didn't know how to get there, and knew she wouldn't be welcomed back. But where else was there? If she were older, more graced or gifted, she might be able to make her way. She could be a teacher or a dressmaker. But she was twelve years old and alone, with no skills, not even beauty to give the illusion of usefulness. She was too tall and regular of feature to be admired for her looks.

The dog flopped down and rolled over to have his stomach scratched. Maggie obliged him and said grimly, "Let's go to the house." She picked up her belongings and trudged up the long drive with the dog shambling along at her heels. There were no people about now, only a flock of fat, sleek ducks who protested her presence and waddled off, muttering raucously. The dog made a halfhearted lunge at one of the stragglers. At least the house appealed to Maggie's sense of order. It was freshly whitewashed wood, built in simple clean lines with two windows set at exact intervals on both sides of the double door.

Maggie tapped gingerly at the closed upper half of the door and waited, her heart beating in her ears. She could hear the murmur of conversation inside. She knocked again, louder this time. The door opened and the man she had seen earlier stood there looking at her blankly. He was slight and had a face that made her think of a hawk in spite of the beard rimming his face. *"Ja?"* he said coldly.

"I'm Maggie Halleck and . . ." Suddenly she had no idea what to say next.

But she was spared the necessity of explaining herself further. The man turned, saying, "Gretta, the girl is here."

Maggie had expected Gretta, whoever she was, to be an ogre, and was surprised when a small, tired-looking woman appeared at the door with a fat baby on her hip. She looked too old and weary to be the child's mother. "You are Margaret? Come in."

Maggie entered an enormous kitchen, unadorned and efficient-looking. Through a doorway ahead there was an equally large sitting room or parlor. The house was built partially into the hillside, giving much more space inside than was apparent from outside. She couldn't imagine anyone having so much living space. But it was extraordinarily plain, bare of any decorative objects whatsoever. A long table was set in the kitchen. It was covered with food and surrounded by children, boys of varying ages and one girl who looked about eight years old. Only the girl was smiling at her; the men were pointedly ignoring her.

Maggie supposed she was expected to begin her work immediately and set her belongings down by the door, but the woman Gretta said, "You may not eat until you cover your head. You have a cap? No? Adelle!"

The girl got up quickly and limped toward another door. Even in her shapeless dress and oversize apron, it was apparent that she was twisted and crippled. Her shoulders were not level, and she dragged one foot with a soft whoosh on the wooden floor. In a moment she was back with a head-hugging pleated cap with long ties. "I put it on you," she said to Maggie with an eager, shy smile.

Maggie had to lean over so the girl could reach. While Adelle fussed with getting the cap over Maggie's thick gold-brown braids, Gretta said, "We are ready. Samuel, John, help Grossmutter to the table." The two older boys rose and disappeared.

Adelle timidly took Maggie's hand in her small warm one and led her to the table. She pushed her stool and plate closer to one of her brothers to make room for another stool and plate for Maggie. Was she really supposed to sit down at the table with them? She might as well do as the younger girl wanted her to. If it was improper, someone would certainly correct her.

The older boys came back then, escorting their grandmother. She was a stout woman who took pained, mincing steps, holding tightly to her grandsons' arms. A lifetime of work and worry lined her face but did not entirely disguise what must have once been awesome beauty. She held her head high, and her bird-bright blue eyes darted quickly, taking inventory of her family, and finally fastened on Maggie, the newcomer. "Gretta, who is this?" she demanded curtly.

"This is Maggie Halleck." Gretta said it placatingly, as if the older woman knew perfectly well what the answer was. "Werner brought her."

The grandmother's eyes narrowed. "I know no Werner," she said.

"Yes, Mama," Gretta answered.

Maggie remembered the package. She slipped back to the door to get it. "My Uncle Werner asked me to give this to you," she said, holding it out to the terrifying old woman.

She glared at Maggie, then at the package. She made a half-gesture as if to touch it, then said, "Put it on the fire, girl!"

"On the fire?" Maggie asked.

"Don't act ferhuddled! Burn it!"

She turned away, and while Maggie stood dumbfounded, the girl, Adelle, gently took the package and set it on the coals in the hearth. They all took their places. There was a long, silent prayer interrupted only by the hissing and sputtering of the gift on the fire. Then the father said amen and they began passing the copious food.

There was a thick milk soup with asparagus in it, bowls of lumpy white schmierkase cheese, pickled pigs' feet, spicy slices of sausage cooked with sauerkraut, boiled eggs that had been pickled in beet juice, smashed potatoes, and crisp pickle spears. There was crusty cornbread with gravy, and when all this had been consumed and the plates cleared away, there were pies: vinegar pie, raisin crumb, and shoofly.

There was very little conversation, none of it directed to Maggie, and when the meal was finished there was another prayer and the men left to finish the evening farm chores. The grandmother was moved to a warm place in front of the fire, where she took up her sewing. Gretta sat at the table feeding the baby a little more porridge while Maggie and

Adelle started washing the dishes. "You don't need to help me," Maggie told the girl as she struggled with a kettle of hot water. "I can manage by myself."

Adelle looked hurt. "Why would I not help?" she asked.

"Because I've been hired to do such chores," Maggie explained.

"What did you say?" Gretta asked from across the room. She was finished feeding the baby now, and set him on a little blanket next to the old woman.

She joined the girls, and Maggie repeated what she'd said.

Gretta stared at her, uncomprehending for a moment. "God forgive Werner! Did he not tell you?"

"Tell me what, ma'am?"

"Come," she said. Maggie followed Gretta outside, and Adelle shuffled along behind. There was a narrow bench by the door where the men sat to remove their boots. Gretta sat down and indicated that Maggie should join her. "We keep apart," she said. "We have no use for *auslanders*. We have no need to hire outsiders for work," she said in halting English.

"Then why am I here with your family?" Maggie asked.

"Because you *are* our family," Gretta answered. "Werner and your father were my brothers. The old one"—she tilted her head toward the door—"she is your grandmother."

"Gretta!" the shrill voice of Grossmutter cut through the green dusk.

"We go in now," Gretta said. "Adelle. Come along."

Adelle clutched Maggie's hand and squeezed it, then followed her mother into the house, leaving Maggie sitting alone in the descending darkness. Maggie's feelings were in chaos. After the first great wave of relief and surprise had passed, there remained shallow tide-pools of unease. The letters from Gretta must have been a request for her to join their household. But why? Only Adelle had shown any sign of welcoming her. Would she be allowed to stay here, or would they someday pack her up and send her back to Uncle Werner? She thought about the fierce old woman who had burned a gift from her own son. Should she be elated at having come to a better place, or in despair at having traded comfortable old sorrows for sharp new ones?

2

The next morning, as Maggie and Adelle did the breakfast dishes, they talked. Maggie was surprised to find that they were almost the same age. "I thought you were younger. You're so small . . ." She stopped, embarrassed at having made reference to the girl's abnormal appearance. She busied herself hanging up a drying cloth while trying to think of a way to retract or modify her remark.

But Adelle took no offense. "That is because you are so very tall. Tall as Mama, I think. I had a fever when I was little. Thanks to God's mercy and Grossmutter's powwowing, I got better and learned to walk again."

"Powwowing?"

"Yes. Grossmutter's pa was the *braucheri*. The healer, you would say. He told her all his cures and hexes. She made me drinks of herbs, and prayers, and turned the hex away. It is a good thing I had the fever, for now I'm not pretty."

"Why is that good?" Maggie blurted out, then cursed herself silently for her tactlessness.

"Because if I were pretty I would be proud, and that would be a sin. A sin inside, the worst kind. Come, cousin, we have much to do to your clothes. Mama will do my chores today so I can help you."

They pulled a table near the window, where the light was good, but before they could begin, Grossmutter, who was once again sitting by the hearth, called Adelle to help her move to another chair. "She had her bad ear this way," Adelle whispered, and winked conspiratorially. Maggie was sorry the old woman was going to listen to them, for she had many questions to ask, and Adelle would be cautious about answering in front of Grossmutter.

For all the drabness of Maggie's utilitarian dresses, they were deemed "Gay Dutch."

"But they're not gay at all. I left my . . ." She almost said "nice," but caught herself. "I left my cheerful clothes in Germantown."

"Not gay, cheerful," Adelle said. "Gay means worldly."

15

Maggie looked down at the mud-colored dress she was wearing. It seemed far from worldly to her. "I don't understand, Adelle. What is wrong with this dress?"

"To start, it has buttons. Soldiers and *Englische* wear buttons. Soldiers are oppressors and *Englische* are frivolous. And it has a flounce at the bottom."

"But if we take off the buttons, how will I keep it on? And without the flounce it will come halfway up to my knees." It was such a pitiful wardrobe to ruin.

Adelle brought out a little wooden box full of metal hooks and eyes. "We sew these on, or you can use straight pins. The dress should not be so long. It will drag in the dirt, and the extra washing will take time from important work. From the flounce we make a *Lepli*."

"A *Lepli*?"

Adelle turned around and indicated a small tab of material at the back waistband of her dress. "This," she said.

Maggie was perplexed. The extra piece of fabric had no apparent use. "What is it for?"

"For?" Adelle asked. The question surprised her. "It is not *for* anything, I think. But it is how our dresses are made. Also we must take the collar off both dresses and the white cloth off the sleeves of the blue dress. Collars and trim are worldly."

After they had completed the alterations on the dresses Maggie had brought with her, they began on the new articles she would need. First a closely woven white shawl, the point pinned at the waist in back, crisscrossed in front and pinned down with a white apron over it. "My buttons wouldn't have shown," Maggie commented.

Adelle was genuinely shocked at this. "But you would have known they were there. *God* would have known!"

Next Maggie had to have caps of her own. Adelle got out a length of organdy and carefully cut enough for two caps, explaining that there were to be six pleats across the back, pointing left. "What if there were seven or they pointed right?" Maggie asked.

She meant it only as an innocent inquiry, but Adelle was upset. "I tell you what is *Ordnung* for our people. The rules are for all, not just for some."

"I will follow the rules," Maggie said. "I just wondered."

"It is best not to wonder," Adelle said softly, and her eyes flicked briefly toward Grossmutter. The old woman, pretending to be doing her mending, was frowning. Maggie realized that to question the rules was to judge them. The girls worked until almost noon, then stopped to prepare the hearty midday meal. Maggie wondered if the vast amounts and excellent quality of the food wasn't worldly, but refrained from sharing this thought with Adelle.

As she ate her dumplings and sausage and cheese, she watched them. The father hardly looked up from his food. He addressed his sons in brusque phrases, questioning them about the work they had accomplished during the morning and were expected to do before evening. They answered him respectfully. There were three boys besides the baby. The eldest son had a beard just like his father's. Maggie had not noticed it when she first saw him because it was fair and sparse. He kept touching it as if to reassure himself it was still there. Later Maggie learned that his name was Samuel and he was twenty-four. The beard signified that he was a married man. "His wife, Rachel, died when the baby was born," Adelle said later. "He brought little John back here to live. We all grieved for Rachel, but it is nice having a baby in the house."

The second son was a boy of nineteen, who was also named John. He was usually called Gretta John to distinguish him from the many others within the community with the same name. It seemed strange that a strapping, robust young man should be called by his mother's name, but Maggie found out that this was common. "His best friend is Mary John Schmid," Adelle told her. "The man on the farm next to the south is Dumpling John Yoder, and his cousins are Plowing John Yoder and John Z. Yoder."

At nine, Benjamin was the youngest of the children of Gretta and Preston Schmid. "Where do you and Benjamin go to school in the winter?" Maggie asked while she and Adelle cleared away the meal.

Adelle rolled her eyes heavenward, as if despairing of ever teaching Maggie anything. "What would we go to school for?"

"Why, to learn things."

"When I am grown, I will be the wife of an Amish farmer," Adelle said, folding her hands and looking quite prim. "I will care for his babies, cook the food, make the clothes, tend to the gardens and accounts. Mama does all this well and is teaching me every day. It is the same for my brothers. Papa is their teacher. They will know farming from him."

"Yes, I see that," Maggie said. "Aunt Madlen has taught

17

me household skills the same way. But what of writing and reading?"

"There are only three books in this house. Grossmutter's hex book, *The Martyr's Mirror*, and Mama's household book. I'm not allowed to read Grossmutter's book yet, and Mama teaches me to read the other two."

"Have you ever seen another book?" Maggie asked.

"No. Other books are—"

"I know. Worldly," Maggie said, and gave Adelle a quick hug. Adelle was pleased and embarrassed. "I've heard you speak two languages, English and Deutsch. You learn them both at home?"

"Yes. When it is time to be baptized into the church, I will be taught High German—so I can read the hymnal better."

At last, Maggie thought. There is one way in which I am prepared for life here. "I have studied High German," she told Adelle. "Our cousin Luther did not do well when he began school, and there was a tutor who came to the house every afternoon. Aunt Madlen let me sit in on his lessons in languages and mathematics if I had done my household chores . . ." Maggie stopped when she noticed how ill-at-ease this admission made Adelle. "I'm sorry. Should I not talk about this?"

Adelle nodded miserably. "Yes. It would be bad if such things were known about you."

What could she do? If she asked the many questions which were mushrooming anew with every answer she got, it seemed she was criticizing or passing judgment. If, instead, she talked about herself, it shocked and disappointed her new family. Best to simply keep quiet, Maggie decided. In time she would learn to fit into this family.

By the end of the day her fingers were a sieve of pinpricks and her eyes felt crossed from all the sewing she'd done, but she was ready to dress properly. Now, if she could just learn to behave and think in the right way. She tossed restlessly on the narrow bed that slid in under Adelle's bed during the daytime. There was so much to learn. Could she ever master it all? She'd tied her apron strings in a bow and had been told by her dear little teacher that bows were worldly, but later in the day she had automatically tied a bow in the strings of her cap, and then again with the apron ties. Poor Adelle had nearly cried the third time.

But Maggie wanted to learn. She wanted desperately to believe that bows were worldly and to pin her apron strings without having to think about it. Where others her age might have chaffed under such restrictions, Maggie welcomed them. Knowing the rules and following them meant belonging. It would make life understandable and orderly to have a rule for everything, a rule that everyone followed and respected, a guideline to stay safely within. The outside world would never trouble Adelle. Maggie wanted to be free of it too. The *Ordnung* would be like a good snug bandage around a sprain. A comfort, a protection against further injury, a way to make a sad life well again.

The next day, Maggie was absorbed into the working life of the women. Besides the meals to cook, there were animals to be cared for; chickens, noisy ducks, and some evil-tempered geese that nipped at her legs and feet when she fed them. Maggie got a lot of exercise trying to keep away from the wicked geese without stepping on the giddy, stupid chickens. As she dodged about, scattering corn and getting *dreck* all over her shoes, she heard Adelle and Gretta laughing good-naturedly. They were standing over the washtub watching her efforts. Even Grossmutter, sitting on the boot bench, wore an expression that might have been a repressed smile.

Grossmutter had declared that it was the day to begin the planting of a new row of lettuce and that it was good to pull weeds by the current phase of the moon, so the women all moved around the side of the house to the garden. Gretta supported Grossmutter on one side, and Maggie rushed to hold her other arm. But as she touched the old woman, she found herself being pushed away. Grossmutter glared at her and called for Adelle to help. Maggie felt her eyes filling with tears and quickly turned away. She would not let this old woman hurt her.

Adelle joined her pulling weeds later. "She is very old and afraid," Adelle whispered. It was a plea.

"Afraid of what?" Maggie asked, her voice still trembling with unhappiness. Grossmutter's dislike of her spoiled everything.

"I cannot talk of it. It is not my place," Adelle answered. She kept her head bent and her face averted so the older women could not tell she was speaking to Maggie.

But Maggie wanted to know more. She would ask about other things and gradually work back to the subject of Grossmutter's fear. When she and Adelle got to the far end of the row, she said, "What is Grossmutter's name?"

Adelle answered this willingly. "Hildy Halleck. Her father was Samuel Halleck. My brother is named for him."

Maggie stopped weeding. What had Adelle said? That Grossmutter was named Halleck as a girl and was still named Halleck after her marriage? "What was our grandfather's name?" she asked.

"The Hessian," Adelle answered. She saw nothing odd in this. It was old, familiar family history to her. "No one knew his true name, so he was just called the Hessian."

"You mean she married a man who wouldn't even tell her his name?" Maggie glanced at the stout old woman at the other end of the field. Could they possibly be talking about the same person?

"Oh, no. Our people didn't want to know his name. He was a deserter from the Hessian army. The *Englische* brought them to fight here in the Revolutionary War. He was hurt, and Grossmutter's father, the *braucheri*, cared for him."

"Was he in the army? The *braucheri*?"

"Maggie! What a question!" Adelle said. "We do not fight—ever. None of our people are in armies. No, the Hessian ran away from the army and was found in the woods suffering terribly from injuries. He was admired for refusing to fight. Our people knew that the other soldiers would come looking for him by name. So, if they did not know his name, they could say they did not know him—without lying. Lying is forbidden by the *Ordnung*."

Maggie smiled to herself. There was something wrong with that reasoning, but for the life of her she couldn't pick which thread unraveled it. "He's dead now, the Hessian?"

"No one knows."

They worked along in silence for a while, Maggie waiting for Adelle to go on and not wishing to prod her. But Adelle said nothing more, and Maggie finally asked, "What happened to him?"

Adelle accidentally pulled up a radish and hastily stuck it back in the loose black soil. "He was *meidung*." She said the word as though even the forming of it with lips and tongue were painful and dangerous.

"What does that mean?"

"It is terrible. It is to be banned. No one may eat or speak with such a one. Not even the family."

"Why was he . . . banned?" Maggie asked. She had meant

20

to use the German word, but found that she, too, was afraid of it.

"Because he was not what he seemed. He said he loved peace and left the army because war was wrong. But he was really only a coward. There were other things, too. He was bad to his wife and sons. He sold a cow to a neighbor, and the cow died. He would not give the money back."

"So he was banned and his sons left with him?"

"Oh, no. The sons had left before the Hessian was banned."

For a moment Maggie was so caught up in the story she forgot that one of the sons was her own father and the other was Uncle Werner. Adelle went on. "Grossmutter was alone then with her daughter when the people put the Hessian under the ban. Grossmutter was very brave and good. She loved him, but she made him leave the house. She would not speak to him or cook his food or share his bed. She did not care for her feelings. She did what was *Ordnung*. She is much admired by our people for that—and for her healing."

"What about her sons? Were they banned too?"

"The older, Werner, was. He showed disrespect for his father. I heard Mama talk of it once. The Hessian drank too much ale. He shouted and struck Grossmutter!" Adelle was speaking in such a low tone now that Maggie had to give up all pretense of work and move closer. "Werner took a knife and held it to his father's throat. Later the Hessian told everyone about it, and Werner was banned. His young brother left with him."

"But couldn't the sons come back after the Hessian was gone?"

"Only if they would admit their sins. Werner came back once, but would not beg forgiveness of the people."

"But he *wasn't* wrong, was he? He was defending his mother."

"He did not honor his father," Adelle said implacably.

"His father was not honorable. You just told me so. Even the people decided so," Maggie said, surprised to find herself pleading Uncle Werner's case.

Adelle was immovable. "He raised his hand in violence."

"But the Hessian was violent first—to Werner's mother."

"First or last, sin is sin. We are peaceable. A man who is not may not be one of us." Adelle's voice was quavering.

Maggie could not agree with this, but she didn't wish to upset Adelle further by arguing about it. "What about my father?" she asked, trying to conjure up a vision of the father she couldn't remember. "Was he banned too?"

"He was not baptized yet, so he could not be banned. That is why you can be here—I think." She had tears spilling from her weak blue eyes now.

"Adelle, what's wrong!"

"I am afraid," the girl sputtered.

"Of what?"

"Of *meidung*."

"You think I will be banned?"

"No. Us!"

"What do you mean? Why would you. . . . you . . . ?" But Adelle had scrambled awkwardly to her feet and was running, scuffing toward the house. "What have I done?" Maggie whispered to herself. Gretta and Grossmutter had watched Adelle's flight and were now staring at Maggie. Grossmutter glared. Gretta wrung her hands.

When Maggie awoke shortly after dawn the next morning, her aunt was already busy making pies, dozens of them. She and Adelle hurriedly dressed, helping each other with the hooks and pins that were so difficult to manage with sleep-stupid fingers. They giggled happily over their mistakes. Maggie suddenly realized what having a sister was like. It was a dream she'd never dared conjure. Both Maggie and Adelle had been dealt somber childhoods, and now, on the precipice of womanhood, they were learning to be girls together. Finally dressed and still flushed with laughter, they went downstairs. Gretta, hair already escaping her organdy cap and sticking to her forehead, said, "Help me get these in the oven and we will fix breakfast while they bake. Oh, dear. Where are the onions?"

"I'll get some from the gardens."

"Let me do it," Maggie offered. She wanted to please them, especially Adelle. Because she was so eager, she got back to the house sooner than anyone anticipated. She skidded to a stop outside the kitchen door. As she reached to open it, she heard loud voices. Preston Schmid's was strident, like metal on metal. "Waste of good food," he was saying, almost shouting. "Will be none to eat them come Sunday."

"They will come," Gretta said.

"We've done no wrong, Preston. The elders said I could write to Werner. It was not to aid him or form a bond. It was allowed."

"It was allowed to bring an orphan child. But she is no child. She is a young woman who speaks out of turn."

"She *is* a child still," Gretta argued.

"As tall as you!"

"It was not an act of free will, to grow tall," Gretta said. Maggie, lurking guiltily by the door, slumped down, wishing she could shrink. She knew she should not be listening, but she was transfixed.

"Even your own mother faults her," Preston went on. "When *that* is known, we will be banned for certain. . . ."

Maggie could not wait to hear what, if anything, Gretta could reply to this. She could not bear to hear more. She tiptoed away, rounded the corner of the house, and then came back, humming loudly, as if to herself. She opened the door, forced a smile, and handed Gretta the onions. Gretta, face blotched with anger, thanked her. Preston turned on his heel and took his place at the head of the table. The sunshine of the morning had dimmed for Maggie.

After breakfast Adelle said, "We have our church services in our homes, Maggie. It will be here Sunday. I must help Mama make pies. Will you work in the garden for me?"

Maggie agreed, wondering whether things would normally have been done this way or Adelle was just avoiding her. Alone in the garden with nothing but the whisper of finches in the woods and the distant lowing of cattle, Maggie thought about what she'd heard. If she was such a danger to them, why had they asked Werner to send her? Upon reflection, she felt sure it had not been Werner's idea. Except for Adelle, they seemed to have no need for her.

But whatever their reasons, they had brought her into their home at the greatest possible risk to their own souls and standing in the community. She had repaid them by prodding at crippled memories and picking at their every belief. Gretta had offered a home, a family, a life. Most important, they had presented her a "sister." Adelle was a gift she could not afford to lose. I've been acting like a hausfrau squeezing the melons, choosing which meets my standards, Maggie thought with disgust. She sat back on her heels, crumbling a clod of dirt. They could be banned, rejected from their church and community, for having her here if she could not mold herself to their ways.

She got up, brushed off her skirts, and marched back to the house. Preston and his sons had not yet left for their work; Gretta and Adelle were making crusts, and Grossmutter was

23

in her usual place, a tray of seeds in her lap. Gathering her flimsy courage around herself like a loosely woven shawl, Maggie went to stand beside the old woman. The light, regular, double thump of rolling pins on dough stopped. The men halted by the door. The room was silent.

Maggie took a deep breath and spoke to her grandmother. "I have asked questions and made everyone unhappy. I will not ask any more. I will accept. Everything."

With knobby fingers Grossmutter went on sorting the tiny seed into the depressions in the tray. The quilted silence was smothering. Finally the old woman looked up as if noticing Maggie for the first time. "Weeds do not stop growing for talk," she said harshly.

The rolling pins thumped simultaneously, the leather hinges on the door creaked. It was over, and Maggie was left wondering desperately if she had made her awesome confession to Grossmutter's bad ear.

On Sunday morning everyone got an early start. When the necessary household chores were done, the men began moving all the furniture back against the walls of the large rooms and the women retired to put on fresh aprons and caps. Gretta and Adelle checked Maggie over carefully. Were her braids done in exactly the prescribed fashion? Her cap was a fraction of an inch too far forward. Were her shoes and fingernails brutally clean and her apron without a single wrinkle or spot? When she had passed their nervous approval, they went back to the kitchen. The men had brought in the many backless wooden benches Maggie had seen stored in the barn. They were set up all over the downstairs rooms in orderly ranks.

They had the pies ready, two dozen of them. Cream schnitz, green tomato, raisin crumb, peach, rhubarb meringue, elderberry custard, onion, lemon sponge, potato, and black bottom. The house was so clean that not even a dust mote dared float in the morning sun as it shone through the sparkling windows.

The family, except for Grossmutter, went to stand by the front door. They kept casting agonized glances at Maggie, who was faint with apprehension. For moments that seemed like generations they clustered there. Finally two identical black wagons turned in from the lane and up the drive to the house. There were three others coming over the next hill. Adelle was standing with her hands clasped and her right foot slightly forward. Maggie imitated her, not knowing whether she stood that way by chance or tradition. Maggie was taking no chances, asking no questions.

The older boys ran to park their neighbors' wagons and unhitch the horses. Gretta and Preston went forward to greet the visitors. Maggie wondered if she would ever, given the chance, learn to tell these people apart. The men were all dressed in long black collarless coats and vests. They wore exact duplicates of Preston Schmid's broad-brimmed flat hat. Their beards were cut in the same style all around their faces, but without mustaches. Their hair was precisely to their shoulders, not a half-inch more or less.

Maggie stood beside and a little behind Adelle on the porch, regretting the difference in their heights. Before long the yard was full of people, and dozens of eyes were on her. She tried to fix her lips into a fractional smile—pleasant, but without a trace of forwardness. It made her face hurt, but she held it until a muscle in her cheek started twitching. They were gathering into like groups now; the bearded married men by the barn, the younger men among the horses with buckets of water, young women with babies in the shade of an oak, a group of young women with black organdy caps by the pump where they could watch the young men tending to the horses.

No one approached the porch. Maggie felt a great rush of love for Adelle. She stayed at Maggie's side, standing as tall and straight as she could and looking into the distance as if no one were there. What price might she pay for her loyalty? Maggie thought. What terrible price?

When the wagons stopped arriving, the groups of people began entering the house. First the ministers, then the older men, the young married men, and finally the boys. Then the women began filing in by age group. Grossmutter had been allowed to take her place earlier because of her bad legs. There was hardly an individual who did not look for a critical moment at Maggie as they passed her.

She and Adelle followed the other young girls and took their places on the back bench in the kitchen. Maggie felt her mind had gone numb. She could not follow the long prayers and endless sermons. A young man stood and sang a long, sad note, and everyone else joined him in the rest of the first line of the hymn. He sang another benchmark note. The song went on for twenty eternal stanzas. Maggie and Adelle shared a hymnbook, and Maggie silently mouthed the words. There was another long prayer, and a second minister stood and began speaking. Several small children fell asleep in their mothers' arms, and others began fidgeting and whining.

Adelle stood and started to move away. Maggie clutched at her skirt, almost crying out—Don't leave me!—but Adelle patted her hand and smiled loving reassurance. She and her mother passed a plate of cookies and a glass of water among the children.

Finally, after nearly three hours, the service was over. A last lethargic hymn was sung, and people began to move about. First the men, then the boys milled around the pie table. Trying desperately to be unobtrusive, Maggie edged away toward the parlor. One by one people stopped talking, and an eager hush came over the room.

They were all looking at her. No. Past her to where Grossmutter still sat on a bench at the far end of the room. Gretta had gone to help her mother walk, but Grossmutter had shaken off her offer. In the crackling silence, the old woman said, "No, I want my granddaughter to take my arm."

Adelle, standing a few paces away, started forward. Grossmutter held out her right hand to Adelle, then, slowly, her left toward Maggie. "Both my granddaughters," she said loudly enough for everyone to hear.

Maggie wanted to jump the benches, to get there before her grandmother changed her mind, but she forced herself to walk sedately. As she and Adelle helped Grossmutter to her feet, one of the ministers stepped forward, his hand extended in greeting. It was not acceptance, and even then Maggie realized it was not for her sake he made the gesture. It was simply a public recognition of the community's regard for Grossmutter and their grudging willingness to let Maggie attempt to prove herself. Still, the crumb had the taste of the cake.

As soon as she was able, Grossmutter shook off Maggie's touch and went back to acting as if she did not exist. Maggie supposed she should feel shocked at this, or hurt, but she was only vaguely disappointed. The fierce old woman had held out her hand and admitted their kinship—once. And "once" was a world away from "never."

Suddenly, as if reading Grossmutter's mind, Maggie knew why she was here. She was kin. Hildy Halleck's blood ran in her veins. She had only two granddaughters, and she hadn't wanted one of them lost to her world without first knowing and assessing her. The old woman's past was antique memory; her future beyond future was her granddaughters', and she'd had to know if Maggie was worthy of the moral strength she'd been bequeathed by blood.

Maggie wondered too.

3

Maggie awoke shivering. In the four years now that she had shared the room with her cousin Adelle, she had never become accustomed to the other girl's constant desire for fresh air. Maggie dangled her arm out from under the bed-clothes and felt for her stockings and drab dress where they they lay folded neatly on the floor. She pulled the clothing back into bed to warm it a little in her own pool of body heat before putting it on. Struggling with the coarse brown stockings, she called, "Adelle? Time to get up. Have you forgotten what today is?"

There was no answer, save the labored breathing that meant Adelle was having another of her "bad spells." If only she would let me close the windows when September comes, Maggie thought, she might not become ill so frequently. "Adelle, get up," she repeated as she slipped the dress over her head and fastened the now-familiar hooks and eyes.

"Yes, yes. I'm awake," Adelle answered. She sounded out of breath.

Maggie leaped from her bed. "You are ill again," she accused, putting her hand to Adelle's sweat-soaked brow.

"No! I'm not!"

Drawing back, Maggie said quietly, "Your face is hot." But she did not pursue the matter. She knew that Adelle felt unreasonably guilty about having frail health and would go out of her way to exert herself in attempts to deny her weakness. Once last year she had insisted on running an errand to the next farm in spite of Maggie's protests. When she did not return, they went out to search and found her unconscious in the woods. She had run most of the way to prove she could easily walk. It had taken Grossmutter's most powerful medicines to save her.

Adelle was thrashing around, dressing under the covers as

27

Maggie had done. When she emerged and bent to put on her shoes, she nearly fell. Maggie rushed to help her. "Adelle, you are sick. Please let me get Grossmutter." This was a figure of speech, since Maggie knew better than to ever address Grossmutter directly. What sparse communication there was between them always passed through a third party, either Gretta or Adelle herself.

Clutching at her temples, Adelle said, "No, I'm just ferhuddled. A bad dream. Nothing."

"You could wait, you know. Be baptized later, when you are feeling better."

"I can't wait. This is the most important day in my life. I won't miss it. Besides . . ."

She didn't go on. She didn't have to. There might not be a day when she felt better, there might not be many days left to her at all. That was why she had been allowed into last summer's baptismal class instead of waiting until she was seventeen like the other girls. Maggie bit back her concerns and hurried away to do her own chores and as many of Adelle's as possible before they left for the neighbor's home where services were being held.

Later that morning, as Maggie watched the baptismal service, she felt a warm tide of relief. Fate had been foiled. Should Adelle be taken now, she would go to her God (my God, too, Maggie reminded herself) as a full member of the church. Perhaps that knowledge would release Adelle from her frantic desire to prove her worth.

The young women, eight of them this year, had filed in at the beginning of the service like shy, mournful birds. They wore stark black dresses, hose, shoes, and the black organdy caps that proclaimed them to be marriageable. Over their dresses they wore white shawls and long white organdy aprons. "How will you keep such an apron clean?" Maggie, ever practical, had asked when Adelle was cutting it out.

"I'll only wear it twice," she had said, smiling sweetly. "For my baptism and my burial." She seemingly had no more fear of one event than the other.

When the regular service was over, the ministers approached the girls, who were honored that day by sitting in the front row. Of each, the questions were asked. "Do you confess that you are becoming united today with the true church of our Lord in heaven?"

"I do," each girl answered in turn. "I do." "I do."

"Do you renounce the devil and the world with its wicked

ways and promise yourself to serve Jesus Christ alone, who died for you on the cross?" The High German, singsong with tradition, echoed through the crowded house. Maggie was overwhelmed. To give up everything one has never known. Renounce the world. The *world*!

"I do." "I do." They answered rapturously.

"Do you promise to keep the laws of the Lord and the church and never to depart from them so long as you shall live?"

Next year they will ask me that, Maggie thought. By then, will I be able to answer with a heart as pure and free of doubt?

"Yes, I do." Adelle's voice, high and breathy, was audible above the others.

Now two other ministers and their wives stepped forward. The first wife removed the girls' caps, and for the only time in their lives, their heads were uncovered in public. One minister poured water from a plain jug into the hands of the other, who dripped it onto the girls' heads. As it ran down their faces, mixing with their tears of joy, he declared that they were hereby baptized into the church. Would I be crying? Maggie wondered. With a chill she realized that she would be—not with joy, but with fear of the enormity of the vow.

Each girl stood, was given the Kiss of Peace by the second minister's wife, who then helped with replacing the caps. As Adelle faced the people in her turn, Maggie felt the surge of affection, almost painful in its intensity, that so often came over her in her cousin's presence. Flushed with emotion and a touch of fever, dressed in the best she would ever wear, Adelle was actually pretty. Maggie no longer noticed her deformities—the way one bony shoulder rose higher than the other in a perpetual shrug, the limp, the manner in which one hand seemed always half-clenched. All she saw now in Adelle was her loving disposition and fortresslike devotion to church and kin.

When the service was over, Maggie and Adelle, by tradition, escorted Grossmutter to their wagon. Then, by tradition likewise, Maggie moved away to ride in the back. Grossmutter was willing to recognize her Gay Dutch granddaughter in public, but not in private—never in private.

"You'll go to bed when we get home," Grossmutter told Adelle as they turned into the drive. "I'll need henbane leaves, Gretta. You will get them."

29

But as Gretta climbed down from the high seat at the front of the wagon, she stepped on a round stone and twisted her ankle. As she limped away, aided by her husband and eldest son, Grossmutter grumbled, "Now I must care for her, too."

Forgetting the unspoken rules of their relationship, Maggie spoke to her grandmother. "I'll get the henbane for you, Grossmutter. I've helped Adelle gather it before. I know what it looks like."

Grossmutter sat stiff and offended. Whether she was shocked at Maggie's idea or at her manner of address was impossible to tell. She was angry, that much was certain. Equally certain was the fact that there was no alternative to Maggie's suggestion. Gretta couldn't hobble about the woods on one leg looking for herbs. Adelle was the patient for whom they were intended; and the men of the family would never be asked to do such a domestic chore. Without deigning to look directly at Maggie, Grossmutter finally snapped, "While you're at it, get some jack-in-the-pulpit root and a handful of *fimffinger graut.*"

Terrible Grandmother had spoken to her—voluntarily and in private. It had taken four years, and absurdly enough, it seemed worth the wait. As soon as the old woman was safely down from the wagon, Maggie hurried off to the woods. The maples were turning, casting blood-crimson shadows; the air was alive with the crackling of leaves as furred creatures scurried away at Maggie's advance. Maggie knew where to find the henbane and the jack-in-the-pulpit roots, but when it came to the five-finger grass, she was not sure. There were many grasses in the shades of the forest, and they looked so much alike. Adelle had always been along before to correct her when she picked the wrong plant.

Maggie hurried back with the henbane and roots. "Grossmutter, I'm sorry, but I was not sure of the grass."

The old woman turned and glared at her. "Get my book, girl!" Book? She had never even been allowed to mention, much less *touch* Grossmutter's hex book. It was the most valued object in the house, possibly in the whole community. Sometimes Gretta was allowed to hold it, just long enough to carry it to Grossmutter's rooms when she wished to consult it for an old hex. Maggie glanced over her shoulder. Surely Grossmutter meant Gretta, not her.

"Be you help or hindrance, girl? Close your mouth and get my book," the old woman ordered.

"Yes, Grossmutter." Maggie took the book down from the

shelf where it stood and handed it to her grandmother. The very touch of it seemed magic and dear.

Grossmutter set the book on the kitchen table and unfolded it, for it was not so much a book as a package. It was wrapped in a thin square of leather the color of acorns and as soft as an infant's feet. It was tied with a narrow braid of something pale amber. Spun honey, Maggie thought.

"My mother's hair," Grossmutter said. "She saved it from her combing." Hex or sentiment? Maggie wondered. The leather was still pliable, but there were ageless crease marks in it. How many times in fifty years had Grossmutter folded it back over in precisely the same way?

Inside, the pages were loose, yellowed with age, and crumbling at the edges. Grossmutter wet her gnarled index finger, and touching the corner of each page, eased it toward herself before grasping it carefully in both hands and turning it over. Maggie tried not to appear curious, but involuntarily moved closer and closer as Grossmutter hunted for the page she wanted. Besides the feathery-fine handwriting, many of the pages were illustrated by beautifully executed ink drawings of the plants. They were the most lovely pictures Maggie had ever seen. Some even had a hint of antique color in the petals of the blossoms.

Maggie suddenly caught at a shred of understanding. It was as flimsy as a cloud at first, but she knew why Grossmutter never let anyone see the book. It wasn't just the magic of it. Grossmutter was proud of the beauty of the book. Pride was unacceptable. Beauty was unnecessary, even wicked. To have pride in the beauty of one's accomplishments was . . . was unthinkable.

"Here it is," Grossmutter said, setting a sheet of paper in front of Maggie. "Make a copy. Take it with you."

Maggie did as she was told, surprised at how easy it was to reproduce the main features of the drawing. She had barely finished a rough sketch when Grossmutter put the book back together and said roughly, "Don't dawdle about, girl."

Maggie returned to the woods and found the grass easily, but before pulling it up, she gave in to an impulse. Flopping down on her stomach, she turned over the sheet of ledger paper and tried drawing the little clump of grass from life. Fascinating, how it flowed with the most imperceptible breeze, how the color and shading changed with the angle. Most amazing of all, she managed to transfer it through her eyes and fingers to the paper. It was not so fine and delicate as

31

Grossmutter's drawing, but it *was* recognizable. Maggie was elated at having accidentally unearthed this talent, however insignificant, in her soul. Perhaps, she thought fleetingly, perhaps there are other secret abilities in me. But on the tail end of that thought there was another. Of what use would a secret talent ever be here? To be able to sketch a pretty picture was more than useless. It was worldly—wicked.

Maggie looked sadly at the paper, then crumpled it and put it in her apron pocket.

Adelle stayed in bed the rest of the day and would eat nothing. Maggie sat up with her all night, listening to her fitful mumblings. The next day she claimed to feel better and insisted on doing some of her household chores, but she still could not eat, even though she tried, and the merest effort made her breathless. She could not be in the kitchen because she panicked and thought there was not enough air to breathe when it became warm.

Incapacitated herself, Gretta was haggard with worry and hobbled around attempting to do the housework. Grossmutter's legs were too feeble to allow her to climb the stairs to Adelle's room, so all the nursing, most of the fall canning, and part of the meal preparation fell to Maggie. She didn't mind the hard labor, the long hours, or the backbreaking sense of responsibility. But she minded horribly that she could do nothing to heal Adelle, only trivial things to ease her discomfort.

By the end of the week Adelle could no longer leave her bed. She tried once and fainted, bruising herself badly. It was decided to move her. Most families had a small house on the grounds for the grandparents, but in the Schmids' case Grossmutter's house was adjoining the main building because of the difficulty she had in walking. Maggie knew that Grossmutter had a small bedroom and a large sitting room, but she had never been invited to see them. Now the boys brought down the beds to set up in the sitting room for Maggie and Adelle so Grossmutter could supervise Adelle's care.

Maggie entered the previously forbidden quarters with a sense of fear and trespass. Certainly Grossmutter would not allow her to stay here! But the fear was quickly forgotten when she stepped past the door. The fragrance was overwhelming, and at first Maggie could not comprehend its source. Then she glanced upward. There wasn't a room above, only a tall peaked roof. There was no ceiling, and the

32

rafters were festooned with bunches of plants drying for use in cures. Peppergrass, skunk cabbage, the purple leaves of henbane, tansy, the red-berried ginseng she and Adelle picked in shady beech groves, thyme, all hanging in softly rustling bunches and emitting the almost tangible cloud of scent which filled the room. Maggie craned her head back, enthralled and mystified.

"Don't gape, girl," Grossmutter snapped. "Make the beds up."

Grossmutter sat by Adelle's side all day, letting Maggie be her legs. "Get the ladder, girl." "Climb up there and cut down some tansy." "Bring me a pitcher of rainwater, girl. Mind that it's clean." "Boil up some cider, girl. Leave the roots in, just so as you can count to twenty."

Maggie climbed and fetched and followed directions, but Adelle steadily weakened. She had a winter-blue cast to her lips and fingernails and started having coughing seizures that left her nearly unconscious. Maggie became frantic herself at such times, though she tried to hide it. She wanted to scream, to curse the cruel Teutonic God who allowed this. She wanted to clutch Adelle to her and drag her back from the icy brink of death. But she controlled herself. Sometimes an agonized whimper would sneak past her clenched teeth or a hot tear would scald a track down her cheek, and the bitterness and resentment boiled inside her until she thought she would burst.

By the end of the second week after her baptism, Adelle could neither move nor summon breath enough to speak. Grossmutter prepared her most powerful hex: a tiny slip of paper with writing that would turn the hex back on the witch who had cast it—if it *was* the doing of a witch rather than the will of God. The paper was folded, creased, and folded again until it was no bigger than a corn kernel. Adelle had to swallow it in rainwater that had fallen during a new moon.

This was done during the early morning, and the family waited anxiously for the result. Adelle became even weaker, and that evening refused to drink the potion Grossmutter had instructed Maggie to prepare. "Please, Adelle," Maggie begged. "Don't turn away. This is good for you. It will make you well." She tried to keep the urgency out of her voice.

Adelle stubbornly refused to open her lips.

"It is almost the time," Grossmutter declared from across the room.

The words chilled and then angered Maggie. "I will not give up. She *can* get well. She *will*!"

"No, girl. Hold her now, and you deny God's will," Grossmutter said. She laced her twisted fingers together, preparing to pray. "Tell Gretta. She will want to say prayers."

To Maggie's utter horror, Gretta began later that night to prepare for Adelle's funeral. "She's not dead!" Maggie protested. "Why are you cleaning house and making pies?" The damned, eternal, inevitable pies! No occasion, large or small, could pass without pies banked up around it.

"She is dying," Gretta said. "People will come."

It was almost dawn with Adelle drifted peacefully into the arms of her God. Sitting at her cousin's side, Maggie heard the last whispered sigh of breath and felt the infinitesimal slackening of the hand she held. And it was over. Over. The only person she'd truly loved was gone. Why did you take her, God? How dare you take her? I've loved so little, asked so little. Why Adelle? Maggie raged silently.

She did not immediately wake Gretta and Grossmutter, who were sleeping in chairs by the small fireplace. She wanted to treasure the moment of peace. Freed of the strain of drawing breath, Adelle looked tranquil. Her lashes lay softly on her pale cheeks, like butterflies taking a brief rest. She looked like the angel she surely was by now.

And Maggie was circled by a many-sided sorrow. Resentment of God, fear of a lonesome life ahead without her only friend, jealousy of the peace Adelle had found, and envy of the courage with which she had faced her death. Not just faced—no, when it became inevitable, Adelle had sought death, embraced it like a husband.

Maggie folded Adelle's hands into an attitude of prayer on her breast and tucked a lock of hair into the cap she'd not been willing to remove through her final illness. She turned to rouse Grossmutter, but the old woman was already awake. "She is gone," Maggie whispered.

"Do you cry for her or for yourself?" the old woman asked. Then she smiled—the first smile Maggie had ever seen on the time-ravaged face. She spoke softly. "It is not fitting to spoil this day. We are strangers and sojourners in this world. We wait to be called back to God. Adelle has gone home today. Rejoice for her."

Later in the day, much later, after Adelle had been dressed in her baptismal clothing, prayed over, and lowered into the dense black earth, Maggie crept away to the place in the woods where the beech trees formed a cage, and cried. Love and laughter and childhood were over. They had died with Adelle. What had Maggie ever done to offend God that he should do this to her? Thy capricious will be done, O Lord. Maggie's outrage was so great she could not express it. She wanted to scream abuses at heaven, throw herself against fate, demanding that the past be given back. But there was nothing she could do. Nothing but learn to accept, and she began to wonder seriously if she ever could.

4

"Can Benjamin help me move the beds back upstairs this morning?" Maggie asked Gretta the day after Adelle's funeral.

"No. Wait for Grossmutter to ask," Gretta replied.

So Maggie waited for her grandmother to put her out of the headily scented sitting room, but nothing was said. When a week had passed, Maggie quietly moved her few extra personal items downstairs. Grossmutter pretended not to notice.

Never loving, affectionate, or even friendly to each other, at least Maggie and her grandmother could be in the same room without the crackling antagonism of the early years. After Adelle's death Grossmutter allowed Maggie to hold her arm and take her into the family kitchen at meals. She said gruffly that it was more efficient than calling for one of the men, since they were busy with the harvest all day and tired when they got home. "Don't be so clumsy with that pan, girl, you'll burn yourself," Grossmutter would grumble, and Maggie tried to read into such remarks some inflection of genuine concern. But if the old woman's heart ever stumbled over her conscience, she gave no outward sign.

Sometimes Maggie wondered why she put up with Hildy Halleck's rudeness and short temper—why she cared what the tough old woman thought of her. But in a way she couldn't put words to, she knew. There was a bond between them that transcended blood and kinship, qualities of endurance and morality that were still tightly furled buds in Maggie and windblown relics in Grossmutter. And there was a terrible strength to the bond—there might never be love between them, nor even friendship, but once having known each other, they could never wholly disentangle their lives and souls.

During the first week of November, a neighbor, Abraham Zook, came to the door before breakfast. Ashen-faced, he explained that his wife was giving birth and something was wrong. Could old Hildy come back with him to treat her?

"My mother doesn't go out anymore, Abe. You know that," Gretta said. "But come in. She will tell you what cures to use."

But Grossmutter had heard, and signaled to Maggie to help her to her feet. "Nora Zook was good to us when Rachel died. I will go," she said. She ordered Maggie to fetch her hex book and certain herbs, then added, "Wear your heavy coat, girl."

"You want *me* to come along?"

"Abe's not fit help. You're better than nothing."

When they reached Zook's farm, Maggie was put to work boiling water for the herbal concoctions, mixing potions, and caring for the little children and the housework while Grossmutter tended to Nora Zook. Maggie was helped with the heavy work by the Zooks' eldest son, Isaac. He was a tall, fair-haired man of twenty-two with the face of a medieval saint and the massive, powerful physique of a pagan god. Carrying in a heavy iron pot of water with one work-corded arm, he said, "May God bless you for your kindness, Maggie Halleck."

"It's nothing," Maggie said with becoming Amish modesty. She found herself tongue-tied and didn't know why. He seemed to carry with him an aura of intense piety that both intimidated and fascinated her. When he spoke in his holy, vibrant voice, she almost felt like saying amen. She'd heard him discussed among the elders of the community as the best choice to replace the current minister when he stepped down. Now, in close contact with Isaac Zook, Maggie could understand why.

By midafternoon Nora Zook had given birth to a healthy baby boy. Nora herself was not well, but Grossmutter assured her distraught husband that she would survive and be back to her work before long. "She'll keep bearing you sons till it kills her," she told Abe bluntly.

Maggie prepared a hearty dinner and was surprised to find

that even in his parents' home, Isaac was deferred to in matters of the soul. He led the prayers at dinner and afterward instructed the small children in a Bible verse before Maggie put them to bed. Later in the evening Grossmutter decided she needed a particular herb they had not brought along. "Isaac has a bachelor buggy, ain't not?" she asked. "He can take the girl to get it."

So Maggie took a moonlight ride with Isaac Zook to fetch something she knew Grossmutter didn't really need. The old woman was obviously matchmaking, and Maggie supposed she should be pleased, but she was merely wary. "You were not in Adelle's baptismal group. How is that?" Isaac asked as they rode through the silent, moonwashed lanes.

"I didn't know the *Ordnung* well enough. Adelle understood," Maggie said defensively.

"That was well considered and most admirable. It is said those who take longest in learning, learn best. . . ." Maggie felt she had passed a test she hadn't known she was taking. He went on, "But the purpose of the baptismal classes is to study the *Ordnung*. You will be baptized next year?"

"Yes, certainly," Maggie replied, and was awarded with a smile and nod of approval.

Maggie and Hildy stayed at Zook's for another day, and when they left, Isaac took Maggie aside for a moment. "May I take you to the Singing?" he asked.

The alternate-week Sunday Singing was the only social activity allowed to the young unmarried people. "I would be pleased," Maggie said, and had a brief worldly thought as to how jealous the other girls would be. Isaac Zook was the most admired bachelor in the community, and though he always attended the Singing, he had never accompanied any girl but his sisters.

That week set the pattern for the winter. Isaac drove Maggie to the Singing twice a month in his bachelor buggy, talking of lofty matters and inquiring with genuine concern into her religious progress. She gradually began to sense that there was a strong strain of teacher in him, and she was a more challenging student than any of the other girls by virtue of the fact that she had come from outside and had a great deal to learn. But whatever his motivation, he was interested in her and liked her company.

It was a curiously proper, almost antiseptic courtship. It was customary for a young woman to invite her escort into her home for an hour's private conversation and perhaps

37

even handholding after the Singing. Parents usually left the hearth fire burning and discreetly disappeared. But Isaac didn't approve of such things. He didn't ever actually say so, but when Maggie offered him a mug of hot cider or suggested he warm himself at the fire before leaving, he respectfully declined and hurried on his way. Maggie was both relieved and disappointed in this; insulted and flattered at once.

The other important change also stemmed from the same week. Grossmutter had not left her home for many years to call upon sick neighbors, but Maggie had proved such a useful helper at Zook's that Hildy resumed this activity. Even those neighbors who had been reluctant to have the *auslander* child join the community four years before changed their minds when her presence meant old Hildy Halleck would come and minister to their illnesses and injuries.

Gradually Grossmutter gave Maggie more responsibility. "You'd best mix that tansy tea, girl. The light's too poor for me to see it proper," she would grumble, and then watch with eagle-sharp eyes while Maggie carefully prepared the concoction. She allowed Maggie to open the hex book sometimes and search for the remedy she needed.

But in spite of Grossmutter's increased confidence and Isaac Zook's flattering attentions, Maggie was suffering a growing unease as invisible and insidious as the far-off scent of skunk. During the winter she was hardly aware of it except when she woke in the night feeling the cloud of some elusive dream weaving its pattern at the edge of her consciousness. By spring it would sometimes come over her during the day and she would have to take a deep breath and assure herself that there was nothing wrong.

But there *was* something wrong. Something inside her which she could not even define, much less fight.

In May there were upheavals in the Schmid household. The oldest son, Samuel, remarried. He and his son, Little John, went to live on a farm several miles away with the new wife. Samuel had never been anything to Maggie but a silent, shadowy figure who was present at meals, but the house seemed big and empty without Little John's cheerful chatter, and Gretta, who had come to think of the child as her own, was dismally depressed. The second-eldest son, Gretta John, was twenty-three years old and was planning to marry in the fall. In preparation, he spent most of his time living in the shell of the house he was constructing some distance away.

Like Samuel, Gretta John had never spoken much to Maggie, nor appeared to take any note of her as a part of the family, but his absence made the rooms and the dinner table seem even bigger and emptier.

Even Benjamin, who had been a pleasant talkative little boy when Maggie first came to Schmid's, was growing up and changing. Almost fourteen, he was becoming a big, square-cut man like his father, and had adopted his austere, flinty manners. Until the last year he had been willing, even pleased, to go for walks with Maggie and Adelle on Sunday afternoons or to sit by the fire and read stories from *The Martyr's Mirror* with them. Now, with Adelle gone and his responsibilities increased, he hadn't the time or the interest in such activities.

The garden the women planted that spring was only half the size of the year before.

In June Maggie began her baptismal instructions. Through her years with the Schmids she had absorbed most of the rules of the *Ordnung*—or so she thought. She soon found that there were even more restrictions than she had imagined. There were rules governing the way a house must be constructed and laid out, clear down to the amount of overhang of the roof. There were well-defined rules about the way a buggy or wagon should be made; specifications as to the exact width of a man's hat brim and the way his suspenders should cross, as well as the number of fasteners his shirt could have, and the length of his beard.

"Why must there be so many rules?" Maggie asked Isaac one afternoon as he drove her home from her class.

"Does it not give you comfort?" he asked, surprised.

Maggie gazed at his handsome, self-assured profile and thought about it. "Comfort? Yes, it does. But . . ." Her voice trailed off. There were things she should not discuss with Isaac. He often seemed vaguely disappointed when she didn't share his religious fervor.

"But what?" he prodded.

Still Maggie didn't answer for a while; then she decided she might as well talk about it. At least this once. "What would really be wrong with wearing a hat with a different width of brim, Isaac? I've studied the Bible and I've never read that God had an opinion on hat brims." It came out more sarcastic-sounding than she meant.

Isaac didn't take offense. He smiled and answered, "It has

39

to do with our kinship with each other in the religious community, not with God's opinion, Maggie."

"But how can an inanimate object like a hat have a right or a wrong? Its purpose is to keep the sun and rain off your head, and it either does that or it doesn't, ain't not?" she said, slipping into one of Grossmutter's phrasings.

They had reached the Schmids' house, and Isaac helped her down from the bachelor buggy before answering. "For a man to wear a different hat would be to assert individuality. It would be a deliberate act of separation, an insult to the judgment of the rest of the community. Such a man would be saying, 'I do not want to be like the rest of you, and this hat expresses my contempt for you.' Do you see?"

Maggie sat down on the boot bench by the door. "Yes, I suppose I do."

Isaac sat down beside her, clasping his work-hardened hands together. "I hope you do. It must be more difficult for you than for the rest of us. Your cousins and I have grown up since birth with the *Ordnung* as our daily guide. To accept is not a matter of choice. With you it is different."

Maggie touched his arm and smiled. "You are the only person in four years who has understood, Isaac."

When he left, Maggie went inside and noticed that Grossmutter was sitting by the door, darning a sock. Maggie thought nothing of her proximity until the next day when Benjamin was loading the wagon with fresh vegetables to take to town to sell. In spite of their reduced garden space, they were still producing more than the family needed, and Preston Schmid had decided that the excess should be sold to city folks and the money used for payments on Gretta John's farmland.

Benjamin came in when breakfast was ready, and Grossmutter said to Preston, "Where is he taking the wagon?"

Preston looked up from his raisin-studded oatmeal. "Germantown. Why?"

"The girl should go with him," Grossmutter declared. There was a moment of thick, apprehensive silence, and she added, "We need pepper. The girl can get it at the market."

No one believed it was necessary for Maggie to go along simply to purchase pepper, but neither were they prepared to argue with the old woman, so Maggie hurriedly gulped her breakfast and accompanied Benjamin and his wagonload of berries and potatoes and lettuce. It seemed a very long ride, but it was actually only late morning when they crested the last hill and Germantown came into sight. Maggie had expected some sense of home to come over her, but it did not. As they rode through the town, she noted dispassionately that there were some new homes, and some old ones were painted a different color, but the place itself did not move her.

The people, however, were a different matter. She watched eagerly for familiar faces and saw a few. Herr Schuller, who used to bring chickens to the Hallecks; Frau Weiser, who went shopping with Aunt Madlen the first Monday of the month; the cobbler's assistant . . . what was his name? Johann something. Astonishingly, none of them seemed to recognize Maggie. They gave her and Benjamin the brief, incurious glances she herself had once given the Plain Folk who came to town with produce. *They regard me as one of "them."* She was shocked by the realization.

She helped Benjamin find a place for the wagon and water for the horse. Then they put the back flap down ("Three leathern hinges only, placed with dull-colored nails . . .") and braced it to act as a sales counter. "You'd best get the pepper," Benjamin said. "These will sell quickly, and I want to get home to finish my work."

He handed her a coin—the first she'd handled since she left Germantown. It felt colder and heavier than she'd remembered. Clutching the money in her hand, she walked down the once-familiar street until she was out of sight of Benjamin.

She would do it.

She'd thought about it during the whole ride, wondering why Grossmutter would expose her to the temptation. Finally she had decided that Hildy Halleck meant for her to succumb. That it was the whole purpose in sending her along to Germantown.

Walking down Main to Rittenhouse, she turned the corner. There it was. The house she'd lived in for so long, which now looked strange and familiar at the same time. It had been larger in her memory. Even the sidewalk and front steps had shrunk in her absence, and the door knocker was lower now. The porch was not as clean as it was when the daily scrubbing was Maggie's job. The door opened, and a buxom woman with untidy hair and a spotted apron said, "Well?"

"I . . . came to . . . to inquire of Herr Halleck's family. Do they still live here?" she finally managed to say.

"Ja." The woman tilted her head warily.

"Are they . . . are they well?" She wanted to ask if they

were in, but her nerve was failing. She could see there were dust balls in the corner of the hall. How could Aunt Madlen allow that? She had always regarded dust balls as almost satanic symbols of a sloppy housewife. "I am family," Maggie explained, since the woman was showing no inclination to answer her.

"Herr Halleck and the son, they are well," the woman said reluctantly.

"And Aunt Madlen—I mean, Frau Halleck?"

"Frau Halleck has not left her bed for a year now," the woman said, as if it were common knowledge. "I must get to my work now," she said, and abruptly closed the door.

Maggie raised her hand to knock again, but stopped. She had no right to know any more.

The ride back seemed interminable. Maggie hadn't meant to make a decision. She kept shying away from it, trying to think of other things. But the decision made itself and rolled over her like a cart heavily laden with memory and need. At one point Benjamin asked if she had bought the pepper, and Maggie found herself crying.

Maggie waited until the rest of the family had gone to bed before she talked to Grossmutter. The old woman was sitting by the window, looking out at the shimmery full moon as if studying it for signs. The rafters were filling with a new supply of freshly cut herbs, and the air was sticky with scent. Standing before her, Maggie said, "Grossmutter. I must leave here. I'm going back to Germantown."

The old woman didn't look at her, and her fierce expression did not alter, but she nodded her head slightly in acknowledgment.

"You knew I would someday, didn't you? That's why you sent me with Benjamin. So that I could see if I had a place to return to?"

Another nod.

"Aunt Madlen is ill. I can be of use in their household. It isn't where I belong, but . . ."—the words seemed to turn gluey and stick in her throat—"but neither is this my place. I thought it was before Adelle died. And I would have stayed if you had wanted me to. . . ."

The old woman looked up sharply, a denial she couldn't voice lighting her eyes.

Maggie quickly corrected her statement. "I would have stayed if you had thought it was right. But you sent me to

Germantown, knowing, before I did, what would happen. Oh, Grossmutter, I'm sorry. I'm so terribly sorry," Maggie said, tears washing down her cheeks.

"To be sorry means nothing. To do right is all."

"Am I doing right?"

Grossmutter sighed, a long, regretful sound like the April wind in a willow tree.

"Yes," she said finally.

"Grossmutter, there is one more thing I must ask of you. I thought once that Gretta had wanted me here, as a companion and helper for Adelle. I was wrong, wasn't I? It was you. You made her invite me, didn't you?" The old woman didn't answer, and Maggie knew the silence was affirmation.

Maggie sat down on the floor beside the old woman's chair. Fighting for composure, she said, "I wanted more than anything to belong here, to share your beliefs. I do share your strength, I think. When I find my place in the world, I will be the kind of person you would approve. I promise. You will not know it, but I will never forget I am Hildy Halleck's granddaughter."

She put the palms of her hands to her eyes, trying to stem the tide of tears, and she thought—though she was never certain—she felt Grossmutter's twisted hand gently touch her head.

Early the next evening Maggie asked Isaac to take her for a walk. He had called on Preston to talk about a horse he wanted to sell just after dinner, and there was still some rosy summer sunset left when they finished their discussion. "Leave? What do you mean?" he said with an edge of anger when Maggie told him of her plans.

"I don't belong here," Maggie said.

"Of course you do. You have become part of the community. Everyone accepts you." He paced angrily, still careful not to tread on the young carrots at the edge of the garden. "Are we not good enough for you?" he asked.

Maggie did not return his anger. "No, you are all too good for me. That is just what's wrong. I cannot live up to the *Ordnung*. I'm sorry, but I can't. Someday I would be *meidung*." Isaac opened his mouth to protest, but she went on, "I shall never truly believe that it is worldly and sinful for a woman's dress to have buttons, but a man's shirt may have exactly four. Five buttons or three buttons are no more sinful than four. There hasn't been a day since I've lived here

43

that I haven't stuck myself on the pins that hold my clothes together."

"Maggie, people can't give up the life they were meant for over something so small."

"But *I* don't consider them important—*you* do. Isaac, I've been thinking—there are few notable events in a person's life. Birth, marriage, children, and death. But I think we are shaped by the hundreds of small things more than by the few large ones. Please, let me say this. I don't want to live out my life without ever sewing a single stitch that is purely decorative. I want to feel a carpet under my feet. I don't need to, but I honestly can't believe I shouldn't. At the end of a hard day of work, I want to sit in a chair that is upholstered. I want to read a newspaper sometimes.

"Isaac, I've grown from child to woman, and I don't know what I look like because I haven't seen a mirror in almost five years. I don't think God will love me more for living the rest of my life without ever once tying a pretty ribbon in my hair or having a petticoat with a bit of lace."

Isaac took her by the shoulders in a grip so powerful it hurt. "These are trifles, worldly things of no significance."

"Yes, but the *Ordnung* makes them significant. I never did think so before I came here. I'm not a light-minded person."

"How can they matter to you?"

"Because I *am* worldly," Maggie answered gently.

"You're not!"

"You don't want me to be—I don't want it either—but I am. I've tried. Truly, I've tried to believe. They *are* trifles. I could do without any of them. I *have* done without all of them. I just cannot believe that I *must*. Beauty and comfort are not necessary perhaps, but neither are they wrong."

"I believe they are," he said, letting go of her shoulders.

"I know you do. I wish I could. I've wanted nothing else since the day I came here. I love and respect everyone in the community. I am awed by your convictions, but I cannot live up to them."

"This is all because you went to Germantown yesterday. I heard about that. Why did Hildy send you?"

"Because she knew me better than I know myself, I think."

"Stay, Maggie. Stay awhile and think about it. Germantown can't be better than your life here."

"I will stay as long as I am needed. But I am needed in town, too. My aunt is ill, and I can help care for her. As for Germantown being better—it's not. I already know that. But there is color there, and laughter and variety. Variety, that's it. Every day here is the pattern for the next, every year the model for the next fifty. Nothing ever changes."

"And that is bad?" Isaac asked bitterly.

"No! It is good. For you, and Preston, and Gretta, and Grossmutter, and Samuel. It was right for me when I came here. I needed the comfort of sameness. I'm frightened to death of what I'm doing, but I must. Please try to understand, Isaac."

"I wanted to marry you."

He said it so softly, with such pain, that it almost took her breath away.

"I am honored to know that," she said simply. "But I must leave."

"Is there no way to change your thinking?"

Maggie shook her head. "I wish there were."

"I will not see you again—ever," Isaac said. There were actually tears in his eyes.

Maggie fought for control of her voice. "I know," she whispered. She could not look at him as he turned and walked away. As she listened to his footsteps fade into the sounds of the woods, she wondered if anything as painful as this could possibly be right. Her fear of the future was suddenly so intense, it was like a physical blow. She was walking down a long, dark corridor, closing door after door behind herself and not seeing anything ahead to light her way to the unknown destination.

5

Uncle Werner didn't recognize Maggie at first. She had spent nearly an hour sitting primly in the front hall enveloped in a rising tide of cold panic while waiting for him to get home from work. What if he wouldn't let her come back to live with them? It was a possibility she hadn't even considered, but it might happen. Then what?

Finally, at the stroke of six-thirty, he came through the door. In the dim light of the hall he didn't notice her at first, and she had a moment to look him over. Like the house, he was smaller and faintly shabbier than she remembered. What was amazing, however, was not any change in his appearance, but a change in the way Maggie regarded him. Whatever quality had inspired a respectful terror in her as a child was gone now. This slightly graying man was merely Hildy's grown son, the middle-aged remnant of the boy who had left his home and life because of the Hessian.

She stood, and he became aware of her presence. "Yes? How may I help you?" he asked. There was disapproval in his voice. What was this strange young woman doing in his house? he seemed to be wondering.

"It's me. Maggie."

His pale eyes opened very wide for a moment. He stepped closer. They were on a level now. "What are you doing here?" he asked.

"I've come back. May I stay? I hear that Aunt Madlen is unwell. I will care for her."

"Yes, very well. I suppose so." Not welcoming arms, but it might have been worse.

"May I see her?" Maggie asked.

Werner led the way up the stairs, and Maggie noted signs of untidiness that made her uncomfortable—the fringe of a rug turned under carelessly, a table in the hall slightly askew, the foggy corners of windowpanes. Werner tapped lightly at the door to Madlen's room, and it was opened by the woman Maggie had met on her earlier visit. Werner and the woman stepped into the hall, and Maggie closed the door behind them.

The room was shaded and dim and smelled abominably of human suffering. Stepping closer to the rumpled bed, Maggie was appalled, thinking for a moment that there must be some horrible mistake. Could this shriveled, ill-kempt wreck be Madlen? Certainly not. Madlen was a hefty, rosy-cheeked woman who smelled of lye soap overlaid with lavender. Maggie looked more closely at the sleeping creature. Yes, she was recognizable in small ways—the way her eyebrows arched, and the lovely oval fingernails, too long now, and dirty. Maggie instinctively straightened the bedclothes before turning away.

She found Werner in his study. "What is it?" she asked, seating herself in the chair opposite him.

"Madlen? The headaches, of course. They got worse and worse, more often. Finally she just didn't get out of bed anymore."

"What does the doctor say?"

"He doesn't know. It might be a growth in her brain—or it might not be." He shrugged defeatedly. "There is nothing to do, he says."

"She could at least be kept clean," Maggie said. "Who is that woman? What do you pay her?"

He named a figure, and Maggie scowled. "You are not getting value for your money, I believe." Werner glanced up sharply, as Maggie had expected him to. She went on. "If you will dismiss her and give me a month, I will have things in much better order. If not, you may replace me and I will leave." It was overly brave, more than she had really meant to say. But there was no taking it back.

Werner didn't answer for a while. He sat staring at the confident young woman sitting across from him and wondering how such a change had happened. Had she merely become brazen of speech, or could she really put his home in better order? Well, so long as he was going to have to feed her anyway—he couldn't put her out, what would people think?—he might as well get value for his money, as she had put it. Never mind that she had become even less like the sort of daughter he would have liked to have. She was certainly more presentable than the slut he'd hired to take care of Madlen. Besides, he had suspected that Luther had been partaking of the dubious sexual charms of the housekeeper, and this would be a good excuse to get rid of the woman while Luther was spending the summer with those friends of his in New York.

Finally he spoke. "Very well. You can start tomorrow."

Maggie thanked him and rose to go, but he called her back. "There is one thing. You will not dress Amish in my home."

At the end of the first month, the house was spotless. Not a drawer, cupboard, or shelf had been overlooked in Maggie's attack. Madlen was scrubbed and fresh as well, and when she was fairly lucid and free of the pain, she sat up in a clean gown with glossy, washed hair up in a tidy bun. When Maggie submitted her accounting of costs—cleaning materials, salary for the twice-weekly cleaning help, new linens and a seamstress to mend old ones—Werner merely glanced at it, nodded, and took from his pocket a like amount for her to manage with the next month. There were no words of praise or encouragement, but Maggie had not really expected such. Still, it would have been nice. ...

During the next month, Maggie had a little more time for herself. The long mirror in her room revealed that she wasn't the knobby, lanky girl who had left this house so long before. She was too tall, and she didn't have the pigeon-plump figure that was fashionable, but her limbs were straight and shapely, her waist nipped in, and her bosom was more than adequate without the added rows of lace across the front of a camisole that many women needed. She was disappointed in her face. She wanted round, pink cheeks and clear blue eyes like Madlen once had. Instead, her face was thin, her eyes were darker, and she thought her mouth much too wide. She'd never heard of such a concept as "classic beauty," so she thought herself merely plain. Her hair was the only feature that remotely pleased her. Not as blond as it had once been, it was still a nice color, like honey, and it fell thick and shiny to her hips when she brushed it out. A shame no one would ever see it that way, she thought, and quickly divided it into thick plaits to braid. How shocked and disappointed Adelle would be at this bit of pride in me, she realized.

She set to work the second month on two improvements—her wardrobe and her mind. She and the seamstress spent many hours sitting by the side of Madlen's bed chatting over the invalid and adapting Madlen's dresses from better times to Maggie's very different figure. Sometimes Maggie would model one of the dresses for her aunt, and if it was one of her good days, she would recognize it and take pleasure in its being worn. "I wore that to Luther's school awards," she would say. Or: "I got a mustard spot on that once when we took Luther for a ride in the country. Where is he today?"

This was a frequent question, and she never seemed to remember the answer. "He is staying with friends in New York this summer," Maggie would tell her over and over, and Madlen's eyes would fill with tears. She never asked what Maggie herself was doing there or why she had come back from the Schmids', and Maggie never mentioned it either.

The previous housekeeper, for some stingy or lazy reason Maggie couldn't fathom, had let newspapers pile up in the basement behind the coal bin. Maggie seized on the yellowed sheets as if they were treasures. She brought them, a bundle at a time, up to Madlen's room, and while the older woman slept, Maggie filled in her years away from "the world."

There were new names, new inventions, and the passing of

48

certain familiar aspects of life. The president of the country since 1825 was a man named John Quincy Adams, the son of an earlier president. France had a new king, and Russia had a new czar. Some people in England had found the fossilized bones of an ancient creature they were calling a dinosaur. Closer to home, the Erie Canal had been completed at the astonishing cost of seven million dollars.

Some of the items were unrelated facts that Maggie noted in passing: Percy Bysshe Shelley had died; so had John Singer Sargent; and a man named Audubon had published a large book of illustrations called *Birds of America*. Other things fell into interlocking networks of information. There were, she learned, steamers operating on the Mississippi River. One made the newspapers by traveling up the vast river as far as Fort Snelling, somewhere near Canada. Elsewhere in the same paper there was an article about the prevalence of malaria in the Mississippi river valley, and a mention of a new factory in Philadelphia that made quinine—a substance that was used to treat the dread disease.

Maggie found this particularly interesting and wished she could share the information with Grossmutter. A wave of longing and loneliness swept over her. She really missed the old woman, who, for all her gruff ways, had cared for her— or at least understood her. Was she any better off here? Not in any external ways, no. She worked nearly as hard, in different ways, caring for her aunt. She was not loved in this house, and she was mature enough now to recognize that she probably never would be. That was a sorrow so severe that it sometimes made her feel like there was something tight tied around her chest.

Still, her mind and soul were her own now. She didn't undergo the daily, hourly conflict of heart and conscience she had at the Schmids'. She didn't have to continuously try to alter her innermost feelings to fit what she should be believing. She no longer had to be on constant watch against revealing her religious "failings."

Here at Werner's home, she was not a failure. She was necessary and competent. She could do nothing to reduce Madlen's suffering, but she was making the healthy intervals, however rare, more pleasant for her. She bought pretty rainbow selections of wool and let Madlen choose colors and patterns for the bedjackets Maggie then crocheted for her. She read stories for her, cared for her grooming needs, and tried to keep her up-to-date with whatever scraps of neighborhood gossip she picked up on market days.

Sometimes—not often, but sometimes—Maggie had a suffocating sense of boredom. A vast liquid fear that *this* might be the rest of her life. Madlen might survive whatever was eating away at her brain for endless years to come, and Maggie would grow old and pale in the darkened room. She was nearly eighteen, the age to be courted and wed and begin her own life, not entombed in a sickroom.

But when such thoughts assailed her, she busied herself with some particularly hard work, turning mattresses or beating rugs, until the fears passed.

In September Luther returned from his visit. He showed no more interest or curiosity about Maggie's unexpected return than his parents had. Maggie was never sure he even knew where she had been, and it was certain he didn't care. He was in his early twenties now; his self-conscious attempts to appear fashionably bored and sardonic did not mask the fact that he was merely lazy and unpleasant. Werner had given him a job in his paint company, and Luther obligingly graced the Philadelphia factory with his presence for as little time each week as he could get away with. The rest of his life was apparently spent in a whirl of socializing.

"I'll need you late at the factory," Werner said on one of the rare occasions Luther attended breakfast.

"Sorry, but I've made plans to go to dinner at the Fasbachers'. Can't disappoint them, you know. Barrels of money," Luther replied. "Maggie, make sure that sewing woman of yours fixes the button on my brown coat."

"Look here, Luther . . ." Werner began.

But Luther forestalled him. "I've been experimenting a bit." He fished a scrap of paper from his pocket and handed it to his father. "I think you'll find this addition to the next lot of paint will make it usable in colder application temperatures."

Werner seized the paper and ignored Luther's exit. From his rapt and obviously pleased attention, Maggie judged that though Luther's work habits and general character were a disgrace, at least he had some aptitude for the business he was theoretically engaged in. Maggie began to collect the breakfast dishes, clattering them angrily. Such offhand accomplishment irritated her. What irritated her more was that Werner allowed Luther to cultivate such aimless habits. Perhaps I'm better off for never having doting parents, she thought. It was a small comfort.

Maggie observed the passing of the seasons from the narrow slit in the draperies in Madlen's room, and began to unconsciously chart the movement of the bar of light on the flowered carpet. Werner lost interest in the invalid who had once been his wife and left the dim, closed room to her as though it were a tiny principality and she the queen of it. Maggie was the only subject in Madlen's twilight world. Luther was a visiting noble. dropping in from time to time, wrinkling his nose at the sickroom smell, and leaving chocolates or feather fans. But it was Maggie who took care of things. She was physician, scrivener, interpreter, servant, courier, diplomat, janitor, palace guard, and more.

Maggie was twenty-two years old when the package came. It was a summer day and she was taking a short respite from her duties to stand on the front steps and breathe deeply of the fresh air. She took little notice of the man coming down the street at first, except to think that it seemed strange to see Plain Folk on this street; in the market or in carriages along the main road, of course, but seldom on side streets. A few passersby gave him a curious second look—much as they must have the time I came to this door in my organdy cap and Amish clothes, Maggie thought. How long ago that seemed.

The man had actually stopped in front of her before she brought her mind back to the present. "Margaret Halleck?" he asked.

"What? Yes, I'm Margaret Halleck. Oh! . . . Benjamin! It is you, isn't it?"

She almost embraced him before she caught herself. She was not one of them anymore. She was an *auslander*.

Benjamin, taller now, more stoic than ever, made no sign of recognition. He merely handed her a parcel, wrapped in a square of brown homespun. "Gretta says give this to you," he said, and started to walk away.

"Wait. How is Gretta? How have you all been? What . . .?"

Benjamin slowly turned back to her. He said nothing, merely gazed at her. There was no affection in the look, nor even the heat of dislike. There was nothing but barely polite disinterest. Maggie's words dried up in her throat. He would tell her nothing. Business talk with an *auslander* was barely permissible. Social discourse, never. "Thank you," she murmured, clutching the parcel tightly.

She watched until Benjamin was gone, then went inside and to her room. She knew what the parcel was—the weight and shape of it were engraved in her memory. In the narrow comfort of her own small attic bedroom, Maggie unwrapped the homespun first and sat staring for a very long time at the hex book. Then gently she untied the amber cord that encircled it and folded back the creased leather. On the top of the stack of pages was a new one. A sheet of ledger paper with a few words in Grossmutter's crabbed hand.

It was dated May 1832—two months earlier. There was neither greeting nor signature.

"I am to die soon. You will have this."

Beneath the top sheet was another addition, a second scrap of ledger paper, wrinkled and older than the other. It was the drawing Maggie herself had once made of the clump of grass. She'd never given it another thought, but Grossmutter had apparently found the little sketch and saved it all these years.

Maggie put her head down on her arms and wept.

Grossmutter's cures could not help Madlen. For another year she steadily declined, then, after two months of repeated bouts of vomiting and partial unconsciousness, she slipped into a deep coma. Maggie sat by the side of the bed for a week, helpless and frustrated. Madlen seemed not so much to die as simply to drift another step away. Maggie didn't quite know when the precise moment of passing ever occurred.

They gave her a funeral that was as parsimonious as Werner could manage without looking bad in front of his friends. Maggie found herself thinking the whole display, stingy as it was, a pointless effort. The florid, hardworking woman the mourners had known had disappeared into a sickroom many years before. She had been lost to them then, not today. The body they were burying was merely that—a body, a poor pain-racked wretch who had finally escaped the pain. Maggie had used up her sympathy in caring for Madlen. The obligation she had felt had been repaid with interest. And love? No, there had never been love between them. Slight affection sometimes, a small degree of mutual respect on occasion, and gratitude on Madlen's part when she was alert enough to be cognizant of her condition.

Gratitude on my side, too, Maggie realized. I needed her to need me. Caring for her gave me a reason to get up each morning with a sense of purpose. This week I will get her room cleaned and aired. I will sort through her belongings, and with Werner's approval, store or discard them. But what about next week? What purpose will I have next week? And next month and next year? That was her real source of grief.

"Poor little savages, running about half-naked, they say. No decent clothes but what good Christian women send out for them . . ." Frau Lieber said emphatically.

Maggie nodded noncommittally and offered her another pink-iced cake. "Where is this mission, did you say?"

"I'm not sure, somewhere out in the West," Frau Lieber said, exhaling a few crumbs, which she frantically pursued among the folds of her skirts. "The point is, my dear, that we're helping to bring decency to them, and we need willing hands and hearts. We get together every Tuesday morning at my house to do our sewing together in Christian harmony. Your Aunt Madlen joined us regularly, you know, before her illness. We would like so much for you to join us when you're able."

"Well . . ."

Frau Lieber fluttered her hands, scattering the recovered crumbs. "No, no need to decide right now. Give yourself some time. It's only a fortnight since your dear aunt passed away, and I probably shouldn't have intruded on your mourning, but I wanted you to know—"

"I will be glad to join you and the other ladies," Maggie interrupted. It was not the kind of activity she had ever imagined herself engaging in, nor was she interested in clothing "poor little savages," but she had to find something outside this tall, gloomy house to do. Accepting this invitation was a measure of her desperation.

She found, to her pleasure, that a number of the ladies brought their daughters along to the meetings, and though most of them were considerably younger than Maggie, their company was indeed refreshing. Silly, all too often, but refreshing. Humor, harmless vanity, and frivolity were strange to Maggie and were like a rich buttery crust to the plain bread her own life had been.

One of the girls, a pretty little eighteen-year-old dumpling named Helga Appel, decided against all reason, and for totally unselfish reasons, to make Maggie over. In her vision, Maggie could be amusing, girlish, and possibly even shorter—or if not shorter, at least less slim. She started inviting Maggie over for visits, and attempted to convince her to curl her bangs or put more lace and ribbons on her bodice, all the while plying her with rich tidbits to eat.

Maggie could not help but enjoy the flattering attention and the tidbits, but she politely rejected the fripperies. The lace and ribbons that had once seemed so appealing to her when they were forbidden, no longer seemed appropriate or even desirable. "I must act my age, Helga," she would say with a smile when the younger girl started talking highly of curling irons or fancy shoes.

"Never say that!" Helga said with horror. "You're almost too old now to catch a husband."

"What makes you think I want to catch a husband?"

Helga's big aquamarine eyes opened very wide. "That's what everybody wants! Certainly you don't want to spend the rest of your life in the dreary old house with your cranky uncle and that awful Luther, do you? Oh, dear, I'm sorry. That was unkind of me."

But Maggie knew it was all true. She didn't want to live out her allotted span in Uncle Werner's "employ." It was becoming obvious that he intended just that. She was a superlative housekeeper and cost him very little, and he disliked it when she went out, even briefly. But she didn't want just a husband, any husband. With most of the men she had met, marriage would simply mean exchanging one employer for another. Besides, they didn't want the likes of her. At the church parties and dinners that Helga dragged her to, Maggie was invariably the wallflower, left to stand tall and alone while the men flocked around the plump, pink little gigglers like Helga.

Ironically enough, it was through Helga—long after Helga had given up on remaking her—that Maggie met the man who would spin her life around and set it on a new course.

6

Maggie had almost resigned herself to being an old maid when she met Gerald Freiler. But he opened a door in her heart, and sunshine flooded into her life for the first time. Later she was to wonder if it had been a mistake, though she always knew if she had it to do over she would still choose the handsome, cheerful man who had offered a way out of spinsterhood and Uncle Werner's house.

She had gone to the Philadelphia Poetry Society's annual Christmas reading with Helga. Poetry was not an important feature in Helga's cultural landscape, but she went in atonement for the many disastrous social affairs she forced Maggie to attend. Maggie liked the Poetry Society. She liked the bright, clever people who spoke crisp, uninflected English. She liked the punch with the paper-thin orange slices and the tart little pastries they served. Most of all, she liked the poetry. She would never try writing poetry herself, for the same reasons she eschewed ribbons and lace—it did not suit a tall, plain woman of twenty-four. She didn't even pretend to understand most of what she heard read, but she reveled in the rich, intellectual wash of words and rhyme.

She and Helga were late to the meeting and Maggie saw Gerald Freiler before he saw her. He was sitting near the front of the hall, turned sideways, talking to his neighbor. His dark hair curled carelessly over the top of his stiff collar, and his light eyes sparked with animation. Maggie surrendered her cloak and bonnet without taking her eyes off him. As the president of the society tapped his gavel on the podium, Maggie and Helga scurried for seats.

"Ladies and gentlemen, welcome to the sixth annual Christmas poetry reading. I have taken upon myself to break with tradition and invite a new member to present the first selection. I think when you hear his poem you will forgive me this little transgression." The speaker, a washed-out young man with a prominent Adam's apple, laughed nervously, and several older women in the audience scowled their disapproval. He persevered. "Good friends, allow me to introduce

55

Mr. Freiler, who has just come to this country. Mr. Freiler has been educated in England and at the University of Berlin."

The young man Maggie had noticed stepped to the podium. As he unfolded the paper he held, he looked over the assembly with a wickedly charming half-smile that hinted they all shared a private joke. Maggie studied him intently as he began to read. Wide, almost Slavic cheekbones, a generous mouth with laugh lines radiating out from moonlight-blue eyes. He was not tall, only about Maggie's height, and there was a wiry youthfulness about his stance. Maggie had never suspected that the mere sight of a stranger could make her heart pound this way. She felt a girlish blush heat her face, and spared a quick prayer to the Hallecks' stern Amish God that no one should notice.

Mr. Freiler began to read. His voice was rich and musical and without a trace of accent as far as Maggie could tell. She could never afterward remember the words, only the sense of optimism, vitality, and gaiety that blossomed in her as she listened. This must be happiness. Pure, undiluted happiness. She had experienced so little of it in the barren years of her life that she hardly dared put a name to it for fear it would melt away under scrutiny.

Polite applause spattered around her. He had finished reading. Helga tapped her arm. "Mr. Freiler is visiting with some cousins of mine in Germantown. Shall we ask him to share a carriage home with us? Isn't he a wonderful-looking man? Maggie? What is the matter? Are you ill—your face is flushed!"

"It's nothing," Maggie said. "Yes, do invite Mr. Freiler to join us."

Maggie was in love.

Mr. Freiler rode back to Germantown with them, warming the December air with his tinder-quick wit and warm laugh. Maggie listened with the same fascination as a child who had discovered how to light matches. He asked permission to escort them to church the following week, and Maggie blurted out a Sunday dinner invitation in return. Helga nudged her, half in anger, half in astonishment. Mr. Freiler cheerfully accepted, and Maggie felt odd and weak.

Walking back from church the following Sunday, he told her a little about himself. An only child, he had been orphaned at the age of eighteen and had used his inheritance getting a good education in languages and literature at several universities in Europe before setting sail for America to make his fortune. "And have you made it yet?" Maggie asked, trying to match his light, bantering tone.

"I'm finding it just a little more difficult than I anticipated," he admitted. "In the meantime, I'm teaching small boys the rudiments of grammar."

"Do you like it in this country, Mr. Freiler?"

"Very well, but I want to see a great deal more of it. I wish you would call me Gerald and let me call you Maggie."

"Yes, that would be nice. I've never known anyone named Gerald. Is it a German name?"

"Irish, I'm told, from my great-grandfather, one lone Celt on the Teutonic tree. He was a sailing man—a captain, the family claims—who swept my German great-grandmother off her feet, married her, then set sail on some unknown venture. He never came back. My mother thought it was very romantic and named me for him."

"I don't think it's romantic," Maggie said bluntly. "I think it's tragic."

Gerald stared at her, unsmiling, for a long moment, and finally said, "You're the first woman I've ever met who had enough sense to realize that. You're quite remarkable."

"Oh, no. I'm not remarkable at all."

"But you are. Talking with most women is like diving into a vat of bubbles. You have to thrash around in the froth endlessly, hoping to find a person in it somewhere. But you . . . you are"—he squinted up his eyes for a minute, conjuring a parallel metaphor—"you are a lake with a calm unruffled surface and great depths where beautiful creatures live in secret." He grinned at her, pleased with the image he had created.

Maggie didn't know what to say to such extravagant and "worldly" (it was the only word her past could serve up) talk. But she didn't need to comment. Gerald went on, "Tell me, Maggie, what do you want of life?"

She almost answered "You," but even he would have been shocked by *that* much bluntness. She thought for a minute, then answered, "I think I want a home. I don't mean a house," she amended hurriedly. "I mean a place that seems like home. I've lived in two places that I can remember, and neither of them seemed to be where I truly belonged. Do you know what I mean?"

"Yes, I do. What would make a place seem home to you?"

"I don't know. But I will recognize it if I am ever there."

Werner was astonishingly rude to Gerald Freiler, and Maggie was desperately worried that he might be scared off by such a reception. But Gerald didn't seem to take very much offense, and when, after a dinner Maggie had agonized over, he took his leave, he kissed her hand gallantly and asked if he might call again. "Oh, yes," Maggie said fervently. "Please do."

She stood at the door, cradling the hand he had kissed against her cheek until Werner barked that he didn't intend to heat all of Germantown and would she please close the door.

Gerald Freiler called frequently during the next two months. He took Maggie for walks or rides in a buggy and brought her small gifts—a lacy handkerchief, a china thimble with painted roses, a tortoiseshell comb—things she had never imagined having or truly wanted. But she treasured them because they came from him. Sometimes they sat in the parlor in front of the meager blaze that was all that Werner would allow, and looked over the books Gerald always brought along. He spoke with such vivacity and imagination of the places he had read about that Maggie found herself almost believing he had been to them.

It was always the frontier. The Great West, he called it. He knew the river valleys, the deserts, the trails. He spoke often of the German communities that had been founded in a place called Missouri—a new state. "We Germans never seem to really leave Germany," he said. "We take pieces of it all over the world." But he didn't want to join any of the small German towns—not yet. "I will make my fortune first," he said.

"How?" Maggie asked.

"Well, it's like your 'home,' Maggie. I'll know the way when I find it."

"I'm afraid you're spending too much of your money on me, then. Please do not buy me any more gifts."

"Nonsense! What is money for, if not to give pleasure? I hope the gifts do that?" He took her hand, and she had to restrain herself to keep from gripping it like a lifeline. She could hear Werner and Luther in the front hall, having one of their arguments about what time Luther had come to work. But when Gerald leaned a little toward her, Maggie forgot about them and moved closer to him.

Their lips met, and Maggie felt dizzy with joy. Suddenly there was a crash of a door behind them. "Herr Freiler, what is meant by this?" Werner Halleck shouted.

Maggie felt the blood drain from her face, and she drew back quickly, but Gerald was not so alarmed. "I beg your pardon? I was kissing your niece. Nothing was meant by it but affection."

"You will leave my house, sir!" Werner said. His face was red, and Maggie could hear from across the room how heavily he was breathing. In other circumstances she would have been concerned for his health—he looked awful.

Gerald calmly picked up his book, hat, and coat and departed, but at the door he turned and winked at Maggie before shutting it.

"What are you smiling at?" Werner demanded of her. "If you see humor in this, there must be something wrong with you. If that young man comes back, you are to tell him never to call again."

"Why should I tell him that?" Maggie asked, trying to remain calm and respectful.

"Because he is not welcome here."

"*I* welcome him." Maggie was astonished at her own courage.

"That much is obvious!" Werner sneered. "But you won't anymore. I shan't have you made a fool of. You're an old maid, Maggie, and he is amusing himself toying with you."

"No, he is not."

"You don't imagine he'd want to marry you! Even if he did, it would only be for your money—he's a penniless schoolteacher."

"My money! I'm as penniless as he is!" Maggie said. It was the first time in her life she'd raised her voice to her uncle.

"My money, then, through you."

"Nobody is half so interested in your money as you are!"

"Well, I can assure you, you'll never get a dollar of it if you see anything more of this man."

"I don't want it," Maggie answered. "And don't think I fail to understand your *real* objection." All the years of carefully controlled bitterness suddenly welled up and spilled over in a scalding torrent. "You just don't want to lose cheap help. I'm quiet and well-behaved and do the work of three people here for nothing but my bread. If I were to marry, you would have to pay someone else your precious pennies!"

"We took you in as a child—"

"Yes, and I had an obligation to you for that. But I've fulfilled it—time and again. I cared for your wife's every need for six long horrible years when you and Luther couldn't be bothered to even ask how she was from one week to the next. I've cared for your house and your clothes and your food since then."

"Look here, young lady—"

But Maggie couldn't be stopped. "I've folded your newspaper and sorted your mail and picked up your slippers hundreds of times. I've sewed and scrubbed and cooked, and I don't remember a single time in twenty-four years that you asked me how I was—how I felt or what I thought. Well, Werner Halleck, I *do* feel and I *do* think, and Gerald cares. He cares! You don't and never will."

"This vulgar talk ill becomes you. I'll not have it. Go to your room. If you don't tell that no-account young man he's not to call here, I'll tell him myself."

Maggie felt faint with spent emotion. She said nothing more, merely stood and walked shakily from the room. She stayed upstairs until she heard the sound of the front door closing. It was Monday evening, and Werner always went to his club meeting on Monday evenings. Gerald knew that, and she felt sure he would come back in a while to find out what had happened after his departure. She combed her hair, freshened her face, and went down to wait in the front hall.

She opened the door before he even had the chance to knock. "Has he calmed down?" Gerald asked.

"No, he hasn't."

"Maggie, what's the matter? You're so pale."

"Please, come sit by the fire. You must be frozen." She waited until Gerald had disposed of his coat and was sitting down before she spoke again. "There is something I must know," she began. "There must be a tactful way to ask this, but I don't know what it is. Gerald, do you ever intend to ask me to marry you?"

The words fell heavily into the dark winter silence in the parlor. Maggie looked down at the cabbage-rose carpet, afraid of what she might see if their eyes met. "Yes, I do," he answered in a soft, almost stunned voice.

Still she could not look up. "Then please ask me now."

He took her hands in his and said, "Maggie Halleck, I love you. You are beautiful and honest and I haven't had you out of my thoughts for a moment since we first met. Marry me and share my dreams. . . ."

60

"I don't understand your dreams."

"You don't need to. Just grace my life by being a part of it."

Maggie informed her uncle the next morning that she was planning to marry Gerald. Werner absolutely forbade the union, saying that he would change his will and eliminate her if she did not discontinue this foolishness by the end of the week. But the next day there was a heavy snow and Werner's horse went lame halfway home. Rather than pay for a hired carriage, he led the reluctant animal the rest of the way home, and in his usual all-or-nothing manner, Werner Halleck dropped dead at his own front steps.

Maggie arranged the funeral, ordered black-bordered stationery, and went to call on the lawyers while Luther drank and wept. Her legacy, for which Werner expected her to give Gerald up, amounted to slightly less than four hundred dollars. All the rest of his surprisingly large estate went to Luther.

They laid Werner to rest next to Madlen, and Maggie wed Gerald Freiler two weeks later. The past was done, and she reached out for the future.

7

1839

Maggie buttoned her coat collar against the damp April wind and checked that the children were properly bundled up. James, a year and a half old now, was trying to climb out of the pram, and Benjamin, a stocky three-year-old, walked alongside Maggie, trying to take steps as long as hers. They were coming home from their usual Monday visit to the bank and the market, and Maggie wondered if she could manage one more week with James in the buggy. He liked walking, tolerated being carried, and despised being pushed along in the vehicle, even though it was the easiest way for Maggie to take him places.

If only I could afford to hire someone to watch the boys

for an hour or two a week while I do the errands, she thought as she stooped to recover the cap James had flung over the side. But if she did that, she would have a little less to tuck away every week, and who could tell when she might need it again, like the time Gerald lost his job teaching literature at the Methodist boys' school. He'd brought her flowers to soften the bad news—an extravagant spray of roses that had made her sneeze.

It hadn't been his fault, of course. The owners of the school had simply demanded more rigid discipline of their students than Gerald was willing to administer, but it was a shame the next job he got paid so much less. Thank heaven Uncle Werner had not had a chance to alter his will before he died. His money, plus what Maggie had carefully saved, had carried them through a bad time, with some left over. *That* bad time—and the next, when Gerald was dismissed for failing to turn in the students who had painted "Privy" on the chaplain's door.

That time he'd brought violets, and it was far longer before he acquired another position. Maggie well remembered the weeks he'd spent at home then—playing with the babies and helping her with the housework until she nearly went wild, and talking about the West. Forever talking. Of Indians, and of gold and farming and furs. He had filled the small parlor of their rented house with books and pamphlets full of pictures and stories of the West. Finally, one of the teachers at the Baptist school died and the principal agreed to let Gerald fill the empty place. He was teaching mathematics, and it gave Maggie an ominous feeling. Gerald knew so little about figures—or at least about money, and that was figures. She often wished Gerald had saved some of his own inheritance instead of spending it on a fancy education that wasn't doing him any good.

"James, your head will get very cold without your hat," she said, and picked the discarded item out of a puddle where he'd thrown it. She brushed off the moisture.

"Nonono!" he screamed when she tried to put it back on him. They were only a block from home now, so she tucked the cap in her pocket, took Benjamin's hand, and hurried across the street. James giggled as the buggy bumped over the bricks.

She got the boys and the buggy inside and put away their coats and hats before removing her own. She took the little black book out of her pocket and glanced at the balance:

$1,207. Not a fortune, but if she could continue to save three dollars a week, by winter they would have almost thirteen hundred dollars.

Of course, the money was her secret. Gerald knew she had "something put away," but he had never asked how much, and she didn't talk about it.

Gerald was happy when he got home that evening. "Kiss me now, my love!" he demanded from the kitchen door, and Maggie happily complied. "Was there ever a woman in the world who kissed so well," he said after a moment. "And to be so beautiful besides! It's a wonder, a true wonder."

Maggie smiled at the flattery and pointed to a rolled newspaper he had in his pocket. "What's that?" she asked.

He yanked it out and spread it on the kitchen table. "Look at this, Maggie my love. There's an article here about Saint Louis—you remember I showed you on the map where that is, don't you? It says here that on a single day last fall two vast wagon trains passed through within a few hours. One carried bales of furs from the Dakota Territory valued at seventy-five thousand dollars, and the other—listen to this!—the other was a heavily guarded wagon train from Mexico bearing almost two hundred thousand dollars' worth of silver. That's almost a quarter of a million dollars!"

"Imagine that," Maggie said, and went back to stirring the stew.

"Yes, imagine! You see, these men got together and went out there with guns and machinery and trinkets that the Mexicans want, and traded it for silver. They made their investment back twenty times over. Just think about it!" He was nearly dancing around the small room in his excitement. Then he noticed Maggie's expression and sobered a bit. "I do think that anyone who wished to make a very good investment would certainly want to consider this seriously."

Does he know how much money I've saved? Maggie wondered, and felt a twinge of guilt. She knew she shouldn't really keep secrets from him, except it was for his own good. She would never use the money on herself, but if he knew about it, *he* would spend it on her. "That certainly is interesting," she answered. "Gerald, would you get the children's hands washed while I put the plates around?"

"For you, my love, I would make sure Philadelphia's hands were washed," he said, and nuzzled a kiss on her neck before leaving.

After dinner Gerald tried to help Maggie bathe the boys in

the tub in the kitchen, but he got them so overwrought with his antics that James slipped and nearly choked on the bathwater, and Maggie had to send Gerald into the parlor. She got the children clean and dry and dressed before sending them in to him for good nights. She watched as he cuddled and tickled them. When she finally had the boys in bed, she went back to Gerald. He had built up a wood fire and was sitting in front of it on the floor reading his newspaper again. "Join me," he said, and patted the carpet.

Maggie sat down, pulled the tortoiseshell pins from her hair to let it fall loose, and snuggled up next to him. "Do you want to read this article?" he asked.

"What article? Oh, about Saint Louis?" Her thoughts had been on the warmth and excitement of his embrace.

"Yes, you might find it interesting. You know, I think this part of the country is getting . . . well, 'used up,' if you see what I mean. It's so crowded, and everyone has a place they're committed to. Out there, in the West, a person could be whatever he wanted. There are riches and freedom and clean open air. Just think, Maggie, a man could be anything he wanted out there." There was reverence lacing his words.

"But, Gerald, you can't be thinking about *us*, can you? I thought you just wanted to invest . . ."

"Maggie—love, I could be anything out there. I could be a rich man and take care of you and the boys. We could build a big house and have servants to spare you the hard work. It's warm all year round in Mexico. You wouldn't forever be fighting the stench and dirt of coal fires, and your hands wouldn't get cold and chapped in the winter. . . ."

Maggie clutched her reddened hands together in her lap and tried to keep her voice even. "Gerald, you can't give up a good job like you have for . . . for a dream like this!"

"It isn't a good job, and besides . . ." He fished around in his vest pocket and brought out a tiny velvet-covered box and handed it to her.

Maggie stared at him in horror.

"Open it," he said, looking away.

Maggie tried to keep the tears from spilling over as she fumbled with the delicate package. Inside was an elaborately scrolled locket on a thin chain. She tried to open it, but her fingers were trembling too much. "Oh, Gerald . . ."

"It will last longer than flowers," he said with a forced smile.

"What happened . . . ? No, don't tell me."

"It wasn't my fault. . . ."

"I know it wasn't. I know, I know . . ." Maggie said, and letting the locket fall to the threadbare carpet, she wrapped her arms tightly around him and cried.

Gerald had never seen her cry. "No, Maggie my love, don't! Please don't. It will be all right." He was obviously more upset at her tears than at the loss of the third job in as many years. He held her close and attempted to kiss away the torrent of tears that frightened him so. Maggie crying! Strong, sensible Maggie, who always knew what to do and told him—crying! It was too much. He sat stunned, feeling her sobs shake him. "Oh, please, please stop," he begged, and held her tightly, fiercely.

Maggie raised her head, recognizing an intensity she had never heard in his voice before. Taking a deep breath, she wiped the back of her hand across her cheek. "I'm sorry, Gerald. It's just that . . . I'm sorry." She feared they were on the brink of a realization that, if molded into words, neither of them could live with. She pulled away and stood up. "I must get a handkerchief."

Gerald sat now with arms around his knees, staring at the flickering luxury of a wood fire in the grate. He had removed his collar, and his hair lay in dark, defenseless curls on his neck. Maggie touched his hair. "Gerald, I love you so," she whispered.

He turned slowly, capturing her hand in his and gently pulling her back down beside him. "Maggie, my love," he murmured over and over between kisses. "I love you, I love you . . ."

Usually Maggie could push her concerns to the back of her mind for a while when she was in Gerald's arms, but now, though his touch caused passion to awaken, her mind could not disengage itself from reality. Disheveled and flushed, Maggie led the way up the narrow stairs to their bedroom, and while her physical self enjoyed making love to her husband, the mental Maggie weighed and judged and considered their plight.

Could it be, she wondered frantically, that success *was* geographical for some men? In a different climate, a different culture, would Gerald find what he liked and was good at? Maggie had no interest in the talk of wealth. Riches were not what she wanted from life—only security. She needed only enough to live comfortably without having to fear real poverty. But she was terrified of the future she was beginning to

65

visualize. Gerald was going from job to job, always for a little less money, with more mouths to feed. What would become of them? Her savings seemed like a lot now, but that would be used up someday. Then what? She couldn't appeal to her cousin Luther. It wasn't just her pride. Luther was rapidly throwing away his inheritance. He'd married a few months after Maggie and Gerald, and, according to neighborhood gossip, had been drinking more steadily than ever.

What would happen to them? What might Gerald become in the face of repeated failure? Tonight Maggie had recognized for the first time that he *was* going to fail again and again, the way they were going. Would he still be happy, generous, loving, as he was now, when he lost the next job and the next after that? There was a melancholy ghost who stood in the shadows behind Gerald, a ghost who sometimes stepped forward and blotted out the cheer. Wouldn't he someday become that "other" Gerald if they stayed here, forever putting off the day of the dream?

Gerald was sleeping now, his arms still around her. Maggie carefully disentangled herself, got up, put on her nightdress, and got an extra quilt from the bottom of the wardrobe chest. Moonlight filtered through the rippled glass window and played on his features. He was so handsome it sometimes made her heart ache to look at him, and she would fling herself at him, needing to taste his lips and touch his glossy hair. He would laugh at her at such times, and tease, "What if old Mrs. Nosy next door saw you? She'd tell the whole neighborhood what a brazen woman you are," and Maggie would smile and breathlessly demonstrate just how brazen she really was.

She was sometimes frightened at the intensity of her love for him.

Maggie spread the quilt over the bedcovers and slipped back into bed. Gerald mumbled something in his sleep and turned over, leaving a warm spot for Maggie to slide into. She stared at a water stain in the ceiling, visible even in the near-darkness, and wondered if the worst that could happen to them in the West would be much worse than what might happen to them here.

It was, she knew, *her* decision. If she indicated to Gerald in the morning that he had to seek another teaching post, he would do so. He would silently drop dust sheets over his dreams and do what she wanted him to do.

But wouldn't he be a different person for it?

66

There were more dangers out there, and few luxuries, but perhaps Gerald was right that there were also more opportunities. Maggie reluctantly got back out of bed, put on slippers, and went downstairs to the parlor. She lit a kerosene lamp and found the locket, lying discarded on the floor. She put it on and shivered a bit at the cold, metallic weight of it resting in the hollow of her throat. She rummaged through the bookcase for the literature Gerald had kept about the West. She finally fell asleep curled in a chair reading about Lewis and Clark's expedition through the Louisiana Territory.

8

"But, Gerald, I don't see any point in going to dinner at Luther's house," Maggie complained. "It's absurd that he invited us, and even more absurd for you to want to go. He's never had a kind word for you—or me either, for that matter."

"Maggie, my love, what your cousin Luther lacks in kind words he makes up for in money," Gerald said as he put her light shawl around her shoulders, "and he might want to invest some of it."

"He only wants to drink it," Maggie scoffed. "I would not have written him that letter telling him we're leaving if I'd known this would come out of it."

"Frankly, love, I don't think it's his idea anyway. I suspect that it's his wife wanting to show off her big new house to everyone, even us, before we get away and she loses the chance."

Sometimes his perceptions surprised Maggie. She hadn't his gift of imagining how other people's minds worked. "Of course, you must be right," she said. They bid the boys good night, and Maggie repeated all the instruction she had already given the neighbor's daughter who was staying with the children. Gerald practically had to drag her out of the house.

It was early June, and they should have been on their way to the West, but there had been unexpected problems. The steamship they had wanted to take from Pittsburgh required advance payment for reservations. When they went to pay, it was already fully booked. That meant setting plans back a bit; then, when it came time for the next ship, James had been suffering a severe cold and Maggie didn't want to start out with a sick baby, so they had to stay on. The landlord had insisted on a full month's rent, and . . .

But now they were ready and due to leave in two days' time. Nothing would go wrong again except the one thing Maggie feared and hadn't yet forced herself to face. She was trying to believe it was the upheaval in her life that had caused her to miss her last menstrual period. But she knew that wasn't the reason. She wasn't going to tell Gerald, however, until it was too late to consider delaying their trip West.

All Maggie had to do now was get through this dinner. In the morning she would withdraw all their money from the bank and Gerald could pay for the trade goods they were taking to Mexico to sell. Now that the time had almost come, Maggie was beginning to share Gerald's excitement about the venture. A new country, new chances, warm weather, and freedom were out there. Gerald, forever dreaming of wealth and adventure, might find what he sought. And she might find the home she had always wanted.

She knew now that the home was not here. It had not been Uncle Werner's house, nor the Schmids', and she certainly had not felt any warmth for the small house they had rented since their marriage. Whereas the unknown seemed to thrill Gerald, make his eyes dance and his spirits fly, it terrified Maggie. Still, the known had become impossible—a long road winding steadily downward into guilt and poverty.

When they arrived at Luther's house in the rich northern end of Germantown, Maggie noted automatically the great size and expensive ornamentation of the house, but her mind was really on how close it sat to the adjoining houses. "Gerald, let's have a yard so big we can't see the neighbors," she said as he pushed the eleborate wrought-iron gate open.

"Why, Maggie, my love, I thought you didn't care about houses."

"I don't. I didn't mention a house. I just want a lot of space that is our own."

He stopped and looked at her seriously. "I'd give you the earth if I could." Running a finger along her cheek, he added, "You know I adore you?"

"I know," she said; then, noticing that the front door was opening, she whispered, "Come on. Let's get this evening over with."

They were greeted by a butler and shown into a drawing room appointed in apple-green silk walls and gold-taffeta-upholstered furniture. Gerald whistled silently. "What did you tell me pays for all this?" he asked.

"The company that Uncle Werner started," Maggie reminded him. "They make paints and varnishes and glue. That sort of thing."

"They must make a good deal of it!"

Further speculation was cut short by the entrance of Luther and his wife. Fritzi Halleck was a tiny woman in her twenties, with froufrou blond hair and fashionably frizzled bangs. Her dress had an enormous skirt of a gold that seemed designed as part of the room. She had a minuscule waistline and a generous bosom, and the overall effect was that of a very feminine pouter pigeon. Luther, in contrast, was thinner and more pasty-looking than ever. Though dressed in the height of masculine fashion, he somehow had a sad, unhealthy appearance that hinted of gin and late nights.

"Welcome, welcome," Fritzi gushed, embracing Maggie, who stood stiffly enduring it and looking down into Fritzi's scented curls. "It's so good of you to spare us your time. I know how *terribly* busy you must be, trying to get ready to make such a *big* change. I'm afraid I'd never be so absolutely *brave*. Do sit down. Be comfortable." Maggie knew that Fritzi tried to be extremely *Englische* and sophisticated, but she was outdoing herself tonight.

She turned her effusive attention to Gerald, and Maggie crossed the room and started to sit on a chair with an intricately carved back and needlepoint cushion. Fritzi noticed and squealed, "Oh, no! Not there. That chair is so delicate, and I'm afraid someone as . . . *tall* as you . . ."

She let the sentence dangle for Maggie to fill in. Maggie felt her face flush with anger and embarrassment. *Someone as big as I might crush it to bits*, she thought. She paused for a moment, considering just walking out the door without a word, but decided since she would never see them again, it was not worth making a scene. She sat on one of the gold sofas.

"Such a cozy room," Gerald said, but the sarcasm went over Fritzi.

"We *do* like it," she pressed. "Of course, we had to do a *great* deal of redecorating when we purchased the house. The people who lived here were *terribly* behind the times, you know. No taste at all. My mother always said that people were just *born* with taste or they weren't." She giggled coyly and waited for someone to say that Fritzi must have been born with taste. No one did.

Gerald strolled across the room, admired some portraits in little silver frames, then quickly, before Fritzi could stop him, sat down heavily in the little needlepoint chair. It creaked in protest. Fritzi gasped and clutched her tiny ivory fan to her bosom. Gerald winked at Maggie, and she smiled back at him.

As the evening progressed, Fritzi forgave Gerald the chair incident and flirted with him outrageously. Luther quietly quaffed everything liquid that came his way and listened with befuddled courtesy to Gerald's inducements to invest in silver, but managed to refrain from committing himself.

They had a clear celery soup, roast pheasant, new carrots in an orange sauce, parslied potatoes, and glazed puff pastries with raspberry-jelly centers served with spiced pears and cheese for dessert. Maggie savored every bit of the un-German dinner, wondering when, if ever, she might dine like this again. No matter what else might be wrong with Fritzi, she certainly knew how to choose cooks.

Fritzi herself ostentatiously picked at her dinner, mentioning at intervals that she certainly wished she had a healthy appetite, but then, people with delicate frames often had poor appetites. Didn't Maggie find that so? Maggie, feeling seven feet tall and sorry about it, said she didn't know. Gerald finally stepped in and said that generally small people with good appetites were known as fat people. After that Fritzi abandoned the subject.

Dinner over, the Halleck children were brought in to be admired. The boy, sullen and tough-looking and only about James's age, glared at them, and the infant girl, Violet, cried. They were whisked out of sight shortly by a very tired-looking nursemaid. The adults then retired to the music room so that Fritzi might entertain them with some mechanically rendered Beethoven while Luther hunched over a brandy snifter.

Finally it was done—the meal, the music, the brandy, were things of the past. Luther blinked a little when Fritzi nudged him and insisted that Maggie and Gerald allow themselves to be taken home in the Hallecks' carriage. Fritzi kissed and hugged Maggie and made her promise to write and give them an address ". . . the very *minute* you get to Mexico!"

Once in the carriage, Maggie started laughing. "Gerald, what if you had broken that chair?" she asked.

"What do you mean, what if? I was *trying* to. When it didn't break, I contemplated setting fire to it." He leaned back expansively against the burgundy leather backrest of the carriage and draped an arm around Maggie's shaking shoulders. "Thank the Lord he didn't send me a silly woman like that! Maggie, my love, don't ever be any other than you are. Promise me?"

"I promise," she said, suddenly sober. What had she ever done, she wondered, to deserve this man's love?

The next morning Maggie went to the bank and withdrew the balance of her money, took it home, and with unspoken misgivings handed over four hundred dollars of it to Gerald to buy the goods they would take along to Mexico to found their fortune. He had studied every trading account he could find and had apparently formulated and ordered his list of goods, though he stubbornly refused to discuss it with Maggie. This apparent practicality and secrecy was so unlike him that she was terrified. Squashing down her fear, she busied herself with last-minute preparations while he was gone. She sewed most of her remaining money in her corset stays and put a few items in the large steamer trunk she had traded all her dishes for. There was another crate of books to be hauled into the entryway. Gerald had insisted on taking all the reading material he could, and Maggie hadn't argued much—after all, the crates would do as chairs or tables, since they had none.

Maggie walked through the house, empty now of all their personal possessions. A shell to be shed like a cocoon. And there by the door was everything of meaning—the steamer trunk, Gerald's books, and two overstuffed carpetbags containing the daily necessities for the first part of the trip. The only furniture they were taking was the beautiful carved walnut cradle Gerald had bought the first time Maggie was pregnant. It was one of the only two things she had insisted on bringing, and she'd carefully crated it with bedding stuffed around it to protect its finish.

The other possession was of more value to her than the rest of it put together. The hex book. She had been afraid even to pack it, for fear a crate might get lost or stolen or damaged. "I will carry it myself," she had told Gerald. "I cannot let it out of my hands."

"Wouldn't you be better off having at least one hand free

for the children?" he had remarked dryly, but with affection, for he sensed what the book meant to her.

"I'll find a way," she said.

So the hex book sat on top of the pile. It was wrapped in a heavy purselike carrier with a sturdy strap. She would *wear* the book and make sure it was never out of her sight. She picked it up for a moment, comforted by the familiar feel, and made one last survey of the house to make sure there was nothing being left behind.

Meanwhile, Gerald spent the morning going from business to business paying for the goods he had ordered. He had devised a policy based on what he had read and on his own personality. People will buy the necessities of life, he had reasoned, because they *are* necessities—but they will try to scrimp on the cost of them when they can. What people are most willing to spend money on (or trade silver for) are the trivialities—the pretty, useless things that enrich the soul and give color to life. He had studied the reports of various trading missions with great care and found this to be true. Shovels sold for three or four times as much in Mexico as they cost in Philadelphia, but satin sold for *twenty* times as much.

As he moved from shop to shop, inspecting his goods, paying for them, and arranging for them to be loaded on the cart he had hired, he thought about Maggie's reaction. She would not understand. He knew that, and that was the reason he had not discussed it with her. No point in upsetting her. Maggie was an exception to this natural weakness of human nature—and thank God she was!

Maggie was sensible. She would never buy a red silk shawl if a drab woolen was available at a better cost. She certainly loved the beautiful things in life as much as anyone, but she wouldn't dream of spending hard-earned money on them. But few people in this world were like Maggie.

By noon he had picked up everything and hired a carter to start immediately for Pittsburgh. "Did you get everything you wanted?" Maggie asked when he got home.

"Yes. It's on its way."

Maggie waited for him to go on, but he didn't. "Gerald, what did you buy?" she finally asked.

He smiled, kissed her playfully, and replied, "I'm not telling."

Nerves frayed, she snapped, "This is quite childish. You are acting as though this trip is none of my business."

"Now, Maggie, don't lose your temper. I'm doing no such thing. I just think it's best if you leave this part of the planning to me. You have so much to think about, and I know this move isn't easy—I'm trying to make it easier by not burdening you."

"Burdening me with what?—that's what I want to know!"

As she spoke, his expression changed. She'd seen it happen before, and it always frightened her—the cheerful, lively Gerald faded and was replaced by the ghost, an unutterably sad man whose sorrows she could not understand or share. "Trust me," he said. "Can't you just trust me?"

She put her arms around him, buried her face in his neck, and whispered, "Come back, come back." She was suddenly terrified that someday the melancholy stranger might replace him permanently.

He stroked her hair. "I'll not leave you, my love. I'll never leave you."

As the hired coach left Germantown, Maggie peered out the window and was assailed by memories of another time she had left. Half a lifetime ago and more. She had been going to the unknown then too, but against her will and without knowing whether she would ever return. This time she was leaving because she wanted to—yes, now that the heady fear of the decision was past, she did want to go West almost as much as Gerald did. There was another difference, she realized as they passed the cemetery. She would never see Germantown again, and instead of sentimental regret, she felt a sort of vindicated courage.

"Where going, Mommy?" little Benjamin asked, stirring sleepily against her side.

She looked at Gerald and felt laughter well up in her. "Home," she said happily, hugging the boy. "We're going home, wherever it may be."

73

9

Maggie's enthusiasm began to dim when they got to Pittsburgh. The point of land where the Monongahela and Allegheny rivers met and formed the Ohio was a swarming mass of confusion. Boats, large and small, were tied up to the bank, and the streets were a beehive, but noisier, smelly and rough. Worst of all, there was all that *water*. Maggie tried to gulp back her fears. So much water. She'd never been on a boat before, not even a rowboat on the Schuylkill that ran picturesquely through Germantown, and the thought was suddenly terrible.

They finally found the sidewheeler *Pride of the Ohio*, and to her astonishment, Gerald's trade goods were there and waiting to be loaded. She tried, and failed, to guess what was in the wooden boxes. Gerald stayed on shore to double-check while Maggie took the boys on board to find their cabin. The main deck was piled high with baggage, boxes, and humanity. This was where the truly poor traveled, finding a place to eat and sleep and tend to personal needs as best they could.

The private cabins were on the second deck, and Maggie struggled to keep herself, the boys, and the hex book together as they squeezed past the other passengers on the narrow steps. Number 16—there it was, a battered door with the number painted crudely and off-center. She pushed it open, herded the boys inside, and stared in shock. Certainly there was a mistake! This was supposed to be a room for four people. There wasn't space for *one* to turn around without bumping the walls. There were two narrow cotlike beds with about a foot and a half space between. There was a small round window in the wall.

They would be on this boat for more than a week, even if it made exceptionally good time to Saint Louis. How would they endure it, cooped up together in this hot, cramped little space? While she was contemplating this dismal situation, there was a loud blast of a horn outside the door. It was repeated a little farther away. Suddenly there was the thundering of feet pounding along the decks and halls. *Be calm*, she told herself. *Don't let the children see your fright!*

She poked her head carefully out the door. A buxom red-haired woman was struggling past with a battered valise. "What is the matter?" Maggie asked.

"Matter? Nothing that I know of. Oh, you mean that horn? Just means we're starting up. Best stay in your cabin till things settle down." The woman's speech held a trace of something guttural and Germanic and soothed Maggie a bit. But where was Gerald? It would be like him to stand around gloating over his trade goods and not notice the boat had gone.

Maggie hung for a moment between panic and anger, but both were short-lived. Gerald pushed his way along the hall. "Maggie, my love, come watch!"

They fought their way through the confusion, up to the top deck. The steamer was already adrift, the engines building up power and the sidewheels beginning their gigantic turning. Maggie watched as the busy bank slipped farther and farther away. So much water. How deep was it beneath them? Deep, dark, dangerous. She felt as though she were suspended above an endless crevasse in the earth. "Gerald," she said, her voice shaking, "hold on to the boys, I'm going back to the cabin . . ." Her voice trailed off as she moved quickly to the stairs. Back in the cabin, she lay down on one of the cots. That was when she became aware of the gentle motion. A few moments later she vomited into the chamber pot.

She had not anticipated this—not in her worst dreams. When Gerald returned and found her ill, he was frantic with worry. She had to tell him: "Gerald, I'm pregnant."

"My God, Maggie, why didn't you tell me? We could have waited . . ."

"No, we couldn't. The baby won't be born until late January. By that time we'll be in Mexico."

"But, my love . . . will you be all right? Traveling?"

Maggie was miserable enough to want him to share in her misery. "I hope so," she said nastily. Another wave of nausea swept over her. When it had passed, she felt guilty about feeling sorry for herself. "Gerald, I'll be fine. You know how healthy I am. Don't worry. It's just the motion of the boat."

But Gerald was concerned, and would not leave her in peace. Every time she managed to drop off into a restless sleep, he would ask how she was feeling. Finally she said, "Gerald, please just leave me alone!"

Even when Gerald left her in peace, the rest of the world wouldn't. Each time they neared one of the miserable little settlements that passed for a city, the fiend with the bugle would start prowling the halls again, blowing ferocious blasts. Every now and then they would come to a shuddering stop and the air would fill with the scraping and thudding and swearing of the roustabouts loading and unloading freight while the pilot and clerk shouted colorful abuses at them. Twice a day they stopped and the stokers were put off the ship in remote wooded areas to cut new fuel for the voracious furnaces that kept the vessel running.

The first night Maggie was introduced to further difficulties. She learned that when the boat traveled at night the pilot had to peer into the darkness for obstacles and was hampered by any light on board. Thus, as dusk faded to blackness, it was *complete* blackness. Not a solitary light was allowed. Gerald and the boys crowded into the tiny cubicle, and the children, frightened by the steamy dark and unfamiliar motion, insisted on burrowing in next to Maggie and whimpering.

Gerald, at a loss without Maggie's guiding spirit, spent most of the first night verbally wringing his hands and asking Maggie what she wanted him to do. When dawn finally came, and with it the greasy odors of breakfast cooking, Maggie could stand no more and asked him to please keep himself and the boys away from her for the rest of the day. He looked vaguely hurt, but obeyed.

Late in the afternoon a new face appeared in the doorway. At first Maggie didn't remember having seen her before; then she recalled. It was the woman she'd talked to in the hallway. The woman with the comforting German voice. "May I come in?" she asked. She was a little older than Maggie, and had a round freckled face and mahogany hair skinned back into a lopsided bun. She wore a striped yellow dress that had probably fit ten years earlier, but was now strained to its limits across an ample bosom and strong shoulders. "No, dear," she said as Maggie struggled to rise. "Don't try getting up just yet. You can be polite to me later, when you feel better." She pushed into the small room, a sturdy pillar of canary efficiency. "I've been watching your man dash around trying to keep one eye on you and the other on the children. Poor man looked ready to drop, so I told him I'd take care of you. I'm Katrin Clay."

"Maggie Freiler . . ." Maggie whispered.

"I know that! I didn't come here to make *you* talk. I can talk enough for any three people, and you don't even need to listen, because I'll get back to everything I said a couple of times, and you can catch it then. Lord! It's hotter than a beanfield in hell in here!" She wrenched open the tiny window and let in what passed for fresh air. "No wonder you're feeling puky in that heavy dress," she said, and before Maggie could protest, she found herself being forcibly undressed. "And *stays*!" Katrin said in horror as she unlaced them. "That's bad for the baby!"

Maggie waved her hands around, ineffectually trying to ward off this friendly invasion of her private life and quell her nausea at the same time, but in a few moments she found herself back in the narrow bunk with fresh sheets and a clean camisole and pantaloons that Katrin had found in the baggage. Maggie's lifelong modesty lay in tatters. Katrin made her sit up, and handed her a cup of lukewarm tea. Maggie attempted to protest this as well, but Katrin was having no objections. "It's not regular tea, it's a potion, and you're gonna drink it."

Maggie took a sip and gagged at the sweet licorice taste.

"Never mind likin' it, just drink it," Katrin ordered, and Maggie somehow managed.

Katrin let her lie back then and washed her face with a cool calico handkerchief. "I moved your man and boys in with my boy John, and I'll stay here with you till you're better. Now, you just close your eyes and rest a bit. I'm going to tell you all about myself, and you can listen or not, as you like."

She was true to her word—her words, rather. Thousands of them. She had a sweet, soft voice with a faint German accent over a Western vocabulary. As Maggie drifted in and out of sleep, she learned that Katrin Clay and her husband, who was an army blacksmith, lived at an army fort on the Missouri ("Cantonment Leavenworth, they call it on paper, but we just call it the fort") with their two sons ("John and Quincy—the next one's gonna be Adams—boy or girl, doesn't matter"). The older boy had recently accompanied her to Pittsburgh to visit some relatives. "Helmut's people, not mine. I was born and bred in Missouri."

"You're not German, then?" Maggie asked weakly.

"Sure I am. 'Least, my folks were. Enough talk for now. You get some rest. We ought to be at Louisville in a day or

77

two, and I want you fit to get up there, so as I can get you out on dry land for a spell of walking."

She was true to her threat. She made Maggie stand out on the deck as they approached the city—if city it could be called. Maggie was sickened at the sight of the water; it had grown immeasurably wider since they boarded. But the air almost made up for it. It was fresh and smelled of green things and land. "Water's low," Katrin said. "Might be here for a while."

"What? You mean we have to wait? Why?"

"Cause of the Falls of the Ohio. See up ahead? That white water. The land drops off here for some reason."

Gerald spotted them and came rushing over with the boys. He was relieved to see Maggie dressed and up, and underestimated the effort it was taking for her to stand calmly at the rail and talk instead of bolting for the stuffy safety of the cabin. Maggie was eager to turn his concerned inquiries about her health to another topic, so she repeated what Katrin had told her.

"Yes, I didn't know when I got us passage on this boat that it's too wide to pass through the canal that passes around the Falls," he said. "I'm told we have to wait until the water's up some, then we run the rapids. That ought to be exciting."

"Exciting?" Maggie said under her breath, and glared at him.

They waited six days. Maggie spent most of the time walking around the muddy ruts that passed for streets in Louisville, but she didn't dare get very far from the river, for it was rising and the captain might decide at a moment's notice to set out. She got to know Katrin better and was rapidly becoming very fond of her. She was different from anyone Maggie had ever known. Blunt almost to the point of inadvertent rudeness sometimes, she was nevertheless kind and concerned. There were only two things that made Maggie uneasy about Katrin. The first was that they had met when Maggie was at low ebb and Katrin mistakenly believed that Maggie was frail, not only of body but of spirit.

"You ought to talk to your man about going back. You won't survive the life out west. It's hard, hard," Katrin said.

"I will survive," Maggie assured her. "I don't want to go back any more than he does. There is nothing to go back to. Nothing at all."

The other thing that vaguely annoyed Maggie was Katrin's contempt for the Indians. "Nasty, filthy savages," she said.

"The white man has come out and tried to help the Indian improve his lot, and they have no gratitude at all."

"Perhaps they didn't want their lot improved," Maggie said mildly. But she didn't want to dispute the matter, knowing so little about the Indians.

Maggie stayed in her cabin being tossed about like a doll while the steamboat ran the rapids. It was a hideous experience, made worse by the fact that Gerald and the boys kept stopping in and exclaiming about what fun it all was. Once out on relatively smooth water again, Maggie was determined to prove to Katrin—and to herself—that she was not a weak, swooning, Fritzi Halleck type of woman. She forced herself to stroll the decks several times a day, in spite of the fact that the murky river grew ever wider and wider and her fear of it grew accordingly.

Toward noon one day Maggie sensed a change in the throb of the engines. "What's happening? Is something wrong?" she asked, alarmed at the increase in noise.

"No, nothing wrong. They're just building up a head of steam to make the bend at Cairo," Katrin said, pronouncing it "*Kay*-ro." Maggie didn't recognize the name for a minute. "You see, we've just been going with the current of the Ohio, letting the engines run for the sake of being able to steer clear of snags and bars. But we're about to meet the Mississippi and turn upstream. The engineer has to have plenty of power ready. Come up, let's watch."

Maggie nearly fainted at the sight of so much water. It stretched endlessly on both sides. Rivers on maps had been innocent networks of blue lines, lacing cities together in a haphazard web. But here the river seemed like an ocean. Most of the passengers were near the front of the upper deck, gesturing ahead and trying to make themselves heard over the straining roar of the engines.

Gerald and the boys, looking mussed but happy, joined her. "Glad you came up. You should have been here a few minutes ago," Gerald said. "We saw a whole flock of cranes fly up from the bank."

"Mommy sick?" Benjamin asked.

"No, dear, not anymore," Maggie answered. "You and the boys . . . ?" Maggie asked Gerald. She was not up to forming entire sentences yet.

"We've been having a grand time. Mrs. Clay's son John has been telling them stories about Indians and bears, and they're learning to eat catfish and stewed beans—"

"Please, Gerald! Not now." Maggie felt her stomach begin to roll.

"Oh, sorry. Come stand up here with us."

"You do that," Katrin said. "Now, watch your steps over those ropes, James," she added as she took charge of the boys and left Gerald to hold on to Maggie.

Maggie went to the edge and got a white-knuckled hold on the rail. Before long they could see a town taking shape downriver—not so much a real town as a collection of rude huts and tents. Everything was a dreary river-mud color. The town had a despondent, temporary look.

"Used to be every boat stopped there," Katrin informed them, "but it's got to be such a wild place that it isn't safe. Ruffians and gamblers and what-not live there. Not many decent folks. Lots of shootings and cholera, but there always seems to be plenty of no-goods to take the places of the ones that die."

They were passing the long tongue of land that Cairo sat on, and were swinging out to the left, away from it. "Government keeps tryin' to set up a city there, but it always gets flooded out," Katrin went on. "Every time that happens, it springs back up, evil as ever. Something cursed about the place, I think. Once there was a big earthquake here, and it shook everything so ferociously that these rivers flowed backward for a spell. But Cairo came back up."

"But we're passing it," Maggie said. "We're supposed to turn here."

Gerald had been soaking up information from sources as voluble as Katrin. "We will turn," he said, "but the Mississippi is turbulent, and especially so where it converges with the Ohio. The boat couldn't manage to cross to the place where they run together just off the point there, so we'll drift on past, then turn and swing across the current."

As he spoke, one of the giant paddlewheels stopped and locked in place. The other continued to chop through the water. Men at the back of the boat swung huge rudders, and the boat began to slew around sideways. When it was crosswise in the Ohio, Maggie could see a frothy ridge of water ahead. The paddlewheel began to turn again slowly, straining against the current, and the passengers chattered excitedly among themselves. The boat rocked and lurched as they reached the line where the two great waterways met and mingled. Behind them, across hundreds of feet of river, were the banks of Kentucky. Farther yet in front, across a muddy expanse, was Missouri, and between was the marshy, snake-invested tip of Illinois.

Maggie finally had to shut her eyes, but the nausea was worse that way. They were going to drown, she was sure of it. The boat turned farther to the right, and the noise of the engines stepped up another notch. Smoke billowed from the chimneys. "What is happening?" Maggie screamed over the din to Katrin.

"Just turning," Katrin said complacently.

"But it sounds like it's going to blow up!"

"Oh, they do. All the time." This didn't seem to Katrin to be a worrisome matter, just a fact. "Look over that way." She pointed to the Missouri bank, which was suddenly a great deal closer.

Maggie could see rubble strewn along the bank, some of the boards still showing dingy white paint, and a charred paddlewheel was half out of the water at a drunken angle where it had snagged on some stumps. Pieces of cloth hung in the trees, and the gold leaf of a splintered harp sparkled incongruously in the midst of the ruin.

"She ran aground last fall, and the boilers overheated. She blew sky-high. Killed nearly everyone on board except those who saw what was happening and jumped overboard in time." Katrin's voice suddenly had an echo of the enormity of the tragedy. She focused pale blue eyes on Maggie. "Life is hard out here. After a year or two, you won't even look twice at something like that. You can't afford to. It gets so even Cairo looks good. You're going to the end of the world —did you know it?"

Maggie shook her head miserably. "I thought I knew, but . . ."

"It'll break your heart if it's fragile. Every man—and every woman—is Job out here. I've seen things . . . oh, things that made me want to close my eyes and die." She put her square, work-roughened hand on Maggie's arm. "Maggie, you can still turn back. There's time."

Maggie looked down at the churning mud-milky water and then back at Katrin. She knew then that the decision had been made to go West and she owed it to Gerald to go through with it, but the decision she had to make now was something utterly different. Who was she going to be? Would she be a Fritzi Halleck or a Katrin Clay?

She was surprised to realize that she had grown to love this woman in the short time she'd known her. She'd never

81

expected to have that sort of warm, deep affection for any-one but Gerald and her children, and yet Katrin's curiosity, strength, and calm ability to accept what life handed her were inspiring. In some ways she was much like Gross-mutter. "No, I can't go back. It's too late for that. But I must change. I can't keep on fearing this world. I'll learn to live with it like you have. But, Katrin," she added, smiling and linking arms with her friend, "I don't think Cairo will *ever* look good to me."

10

After that day, Maggie felt better. The constant asthmatic straining of the engines and the sound of the sidewheels clawing their way through a river that was more mud than water was tiring to listen to, but the motion was different and didn't make Maggie feel quite so ill. Katrin insisted on stay-ing with her nevertheless, and Gerald, sensing that Katrin's presence was soothing to his wife, agreed readily to the ar-rangement.

They made their way slowly up the Mississippi. Where the flood plain was wide and flat, they saw nothing man-made, only lush impenetrable summer growth, for, as Katrin ex-plained, the Mississippi was a flooder, and nothing on low ground lasted long. It was also a reckless, writhing river that would change course at the slightest whim. "I've heard that sometimes folk who live on the riverbank wake up and find the river's gone—moved around on the other side of them in the night and left a loop of lake where it used to be." The vast waterway was full of flotsam, and Maggie once saw a huge tree literally tumbling end over end, the branches still lashing green. "That's a killer," Katrin said as it sank out of sight for a moment, then suddenly shot back up like an oaken geyser a hundred yards farther. "It could come up through the bottom of a boat easy as a hot knife through but-ter, and when the water hit those hot boilers, we'd be knocked into God's lap." Maggie wondered how Katrin could not only accept the possibility of such things happening, but almost seemed to enjoy talking about it. Was that too part of the "western" mentality, or merely a peculiarity of this one woman?

Where the bank was safely higher than the water, or where men were foolhardy enough to defy the river, they saw towns and settlements and forts—Cape Girardeau, Fort de Chartres, Sainte Genevieve—French names given by the fur trappers who had plied their trade on the Mississippi for more than 150 years.

The river was a busy place, full of traffic. They passed other steamboats laden with timber coming downstream as well as flat-bottomed rafts, pirogues, and canoes. Maggie found the shantyboats most interesting and most distressing. They were generally flat, with a little house structure in the middle. Crowded on them were men, women, children, chickens, battered furniture, an occasional pig, and sometimes a splay-legged, swaybacked horse or two. "Do those people have a home somewhere?" Maggie asked.

"That's what you're looking at," Katrin said. "Mostly they just drift. Do a little stealing to keep ahead in the summer, then in winter, when the river freezes up north, they either work for a spell or go on south and sell the raft for firewood."

Maggie felt very sorry for these pitiful families until it occurred to her that everything she owned was on this boat, and it didn't even include anything half so practical as a chicken. Just a baby cradle, books, and all their hopes for the future.

Sometimes Maggie would note brightly painted small shantyboats tied up just upstream or downstream from a settlement, but these boats didn't have livestock aboard. She asked Katrin about them. "Oh, those are whores! Most towns won't let them tie up too close, but they make sure traveling folks know where to find them."

Finally they reached Saint Louis, where they were to change boats. Maggie had expected another slapdash raw-timbered town and was astonished when they approached. There were seemingly miles of boats tied up along the banks of the wide river. Many, including their own, had to wait their turn to get a place. The boats and the street that ran parallel to the water were piled high with every manner of goods—bales of cotton, tools, machinery, wood in both plank and log form, whole dams of food sacks set together like huge squashy bricks, crates marked "Gunpowder."

When finally they docked and left the boat, she was instantly assailed by the most awful smell she had ever experienced. "What is that?" she asked Katrin, trying not to retch.

Katrin lifted her head, tested the air as if previously unaware of anything unusual. "That stink, you mean? Just the fur sheds. Hold your nose and take a look in here."

She pointed toward the nearest warehouse door. Maggie did as she was told. The big building was literally full to the rafters with furs of every animal shade imaginable. Small, lush gray stacks of raccoon pelts, the ringed tails hanging every which way; big coarse buffalo robes, hastily skinned, with the rotten meat still attached; sleek rusty fox furs; pale scratchy possum; squirrel, mink, muskrat, beaver, wildcat.

"Let's get you and the children to the hotel while your husband gets his goods off the boat," Katrin said to Maggie, who had quickly left the building.

As they were pushed and jostled along the busy streets, Maggie became aware of the languages being spoken around her. English of course, but often accented as Katrin's was with German and a western twang. Two magnificently dressed women passed them speaking another version of English that seemed to consist almost entirely of syrupy vowels. "Southern belles," Katrin said, amused at the way Maggie stared after them. There were people in the street speaking German and Gaelic and French—especially French. There were also people talking in undefinable tongues that Maggie thought must be Indian languages.

They finally found an unoccupied carriage and managed to escape the bustle of the riverfront. Saint Louis was not a large city by eastern standards, but it was obviously quite old and, in sections, rich. There were big brick houses with liveried servants and shops displaying European fashions and knickknacks in the windows. But laced through the elegance, there was a disparate crudity, like seeing a fine lady walking down the street arm in arm with a painted floozy.

"Here we are," Katrin announced as they stopped in front of an overgrown log cabin that served as a modest hotel. It was operated by friends of Katrin's. Maggie got the boys inside and thoroughly bathed for the first time in several weeks before putting them down for naps. She wondered if Gerald had finished unloading the trade goods. The contents of that wagon had not yet been discussed in specific terms. They had handled the subject like children playing "hot potato," touching upon it briefly, then hurrying on to a safe subject.

When Gerald did arrive at the hotel, he was so full of excitement over what he had seen in Saint Louis and his plans for the next leg of their long journey, Maggie didn't have an opportunity to ask him anything. She fell asleep to the sound of his voice, and when she awoke in the morning, he was already (or still?) talking.

"You stay in bed this morning, Maggie, my love. Katrin was already by and said she and John would take the boys out with them until noon so you can rest. I'll go buy the things we need to get while we're here. Didn't you have a list someplace?"

"Right here," Maggie said, handing him a slip of paper. "Now, Gerald, *only* buy what's on the list." She got a pair of little scissors and unpicked some of the stitching around one of the packets of money in her stays. She spent the morning resting, doing some mending, and wondering when Gerald would be back. What was taking him so long?

Eventually she heard a commotion outside and went to investigate. She found Gerald directing the unloading of various crates and boxes from a hired wagon. "What is all this?" she asked with alarm.

Gerald looked surprised. "Why, this is what I bought."

"But, Gerald . . ."

"I kept to the list," he assured her, but when they got most of the things to the room and started looking it over, Maggie was crushed.

"Why did you get these porcelain-coated pans?"

"Don't you think they're pretty?" Gerald asked.

"Of course they're pretty, but they're not practical."

Gerald took the pan away from her. "Maggie, I know you didn't want to do this," he said softly, "and I thought if you had some pretty things, it might make it easier for you."

"That was very thoughtful of you," she said, and firmly took back the pan, "but think for a moment—this pan has a wooden handle: it's very attractive and would do nicely on a stove, but we don't *have* a stove. If I would try to cook with this on an open fire, the handle would be burned up in a few minutes." She picked up the frying pan. "And this—the handle is too short and it's welded on."

"What's wrong with that?"

"What happens when the weld comes apart? How would you get it fixed? There won't be anywhere on the prairie to get a new one. The handles have to be bolted on."

"Who told you that?" Gerald asked, clearly impressed.

"Nobody told me. It just makes sense!" Sometimes he was so exasperating.

"Indeed it does," Gerald said, and smiled a little.

But Maggie wasn't to be won with smiles. "Gerald, try to stack these pans up."

"Try to stack them? Why?"

"Because that's how they'll have to be stored. I won't have a kitchen in a prairie schooner, and we've already got more in these boxes than will fit. We still have to buy all our food and weapons and—"

"Now, now! Don't get upset. I see what you mean—I just didn't think of that. I just wanted you to have nice things," he said apologetically.

Maggie set the pans down and sighed. "I know that. But, Gerald, I have all the nice things I want. I have you and the boys, and pretty soon another baby."

There was a knock at the door. Maggie opened it and faced the carter bearing one last box. He brought it in and put it on the floor, then waited expectantly. Maggie looked at him, then at Gerald. He smiled sheepishly and rocked back on his heels boyishly. "Uh, Maggie, my love, we owe the man another thirty-seven dollars. I didn't have quite enough—"

"But I gave you fifty dollars!" Maggie said more harshly than she meant to. She turned to the carter and in a very controlled voice said, "My good man, here is a dollar to pay you to load this all up and take it back. I will follow in a carriage and settle with the proprietor. Gerald, you see to it that the boys get their lunch, and I will be back as soon as I can." With that she picked up her cloak and swept out of the room without a backward glance.

"I'll feed the boys while their ever-practical mother reorders life," Gerald said. But there was no bitterness in it, only amused affection.

By the time Maggie reached the store, her anger had cooled.

She explained to the shop owner in a businesslike manner that she was returning the goods and wished to purchase others in their place. He knew a determined woman when he was face to face with one, and readily agreed. Handsome woman, but had the look of others he'd known who got their way in the end, no matter what obstacles were put in their way. Easier to just go along with her to begin with.

Maggie selected a cast-iron Dutch oven for making bread and found a large frying pan with an ingeniously devised detachable handle. With it removed, the frying pan fitted snugly inside the Dutch oven. She found three pots that nested inside the frying pan, and a small teakettle that went inside a large one that was suitable for making coffee or soup. "Now, I want some serviceable silverware," she told the shopkeeper.

"How about this, ma'am?" he asked, displaying an ugly flat fork. "You could dig through a mountain with this."

"I might have to. How much is it?"

"Ten cents a set," he said, and regretfully restocked the lovely pieces Gerald had selected.

Maggie got a coffee and pepper mill for fifty cents and a set of sturdy plates for ten cents apiece. Then she selected some thick mugs, bowls, knives, and a large ladle. The carter was still bringing in the last of Gerald's purchases. When he put the pile of soft plaid blankets on the counter, Maggie stroked her hand lightly on the top one and was silent for a moment before saying, "I'll need plain ones, please."

"But, ma'am! These are my best. Don't you like them?"

"Yes, but I don't need your best. What about those brown ones up there?"

The shopkeeper pulled down the blankets she had indicated. "You see, they're a bit scratchy. You wouldn't want that."

"But they're thicker than the plaid ones, and I see by your sign they cost only half as much—four dollars a pair instead of four dollars apiece. I'll need five pairs. Now, where are your tools?"

Maggie checked her list and got a lard can, a wooden bucket for water, a shovel, a crowbar, a large and a small ax, a hand saw, chisel, file, and whetstone. When she had checked off the last item on her list, the shopkeeper said, "How 'bout some things for yourself? Perfume? Soap?"

"Soap? I've got enough, thank you, and when I need some more, I'll make it myself."

"You know how?" he asked. Eastern ladies like this *always* bought scented soap.

"Not yet, but I'll learn." Maggie went back to her list. "I think it would be best to buy my tea and pepper here . . . and, oh, yes, a hundred feet of good strong rope. You can lash those tools together with it, and they'll be easier to transport."

"Yes, ma'am," he said with grudging admiration. Why had it never occurred to him to do that? When everything was together, he drew up the bill, reading each item out loud and finishing with, ". . . and two bars of soap and a quart of whiskey."

"I told you I didn't need soap and I didn't want whiskey either," Maggie said.

He ran a distracted hand through his hair. He felt a good deal older now than when she first came in. "With all respect, ma'am, the soap is a gift for you, and the whiskey is for your husband. I figure if he don't already need it, he's gonna!"

Maggie returned to the boardinghouse with everything in three neat bundles and $8.75 back from her fifty dollars.

The stern-wheeler *General Washington*, newly painted and whistle blowing, was almost ready to go. Katrin and Maggie stood on deck watching the last of the passengers arrive. "Katrin, look. There are real Indians taking the boat with us," Maggie said. Three braves stood in a proud knot near the back of the boat. They wore doeskin trousers and had glossy blue-black braided hair with bright feathers woven in. The bare skin of their shirtless torsos glistened.

"Don't you go tryin' to get a close look at them," Katrin warned.

"You mean they're dangerous?" Maggie asked in a hushed voice.

"Lordy, no! But they smell fit to take your nose right off your face. See how shiny they are? They take things like badgers and skunks and skin 'em. They turn the skins inside out and rub the fat all over themselves. Give 'em a rare high odor. But then, I wouldn't want to get downwind of Torchy, either."

"Torchy?"

"Right over there. He's a fur trapper."

A man whose bushy red hair and beard identified him as Torchy stood by the rails. He wore a fringed doeskin shirt and breeches, and, crammed on his wildly flaming hair, a raccoon hat with the animal's ringed tail hanging rakishly over his left ear. Strung casually about his person were his weapons, hanging by leather thongs—a Kentucky rifle, a powder horn, a tomahawk, and a broad-bladed hunting knife. He turned toward them, and recognition lit his face. He strode to where the two women stood. "*Bon jour,* Madame Clay," he said in a language that was obviously several generations removed from its point of origin.

"Don't you take that Frenchy line with me!" Katrin

warned with a smile. "Torchy, this here is Mrs. Freiler. She and her family are going to Mexico."

"*Eh bien*, silver seekers. May I hope for your good fortune," he said; then, noting someone else he knew, he bowed formally and moved away.

"He goes up north every winter for trappin' when the creatures all have thick winter pelts," Katrin said. "Then in the spring, when the beaver and mink and such shed and have their young'uns, he bales up his haul and brings it along to civilization to sell. He always stops at the fort on the way back. He stays drunk for about a month, then goes back to start all over. He's got a wife in Sainte Genevieve, or he used to. French lady she was, but she might be dead by now. Last time he mentioned her, she was ailing."

An ear-splitting whistle cut through the air and was followed by a cloud of orders to start. Ropes were untied, the last parcels and luggage were stowed, and they were off. Traveling the Missouri was pleasanter for a while. The river was not quite so wide nor so turbulent this time of year, and they passed beautiful vistas of bluffs banked by wildflowers. But on the second day they met yet another problem. "Get on your walking shoes," Katrin said at the door of their cabin.

"Walking? But we're on a boat," Gerald protested. He had found a book in one of his crates that he hadn't read before and didn't want to be taken away from it.

"Not for long, we're not," Katrin replied. "River's down, and we're gettin' to some shallows. They'll put the deck passengers off first, but if that doesn't work, the cabin passengers will have to walk as well."

Her prediction was correct. All the passengers ended up wading through the shallow water to the bank and stumbling along for a half-mile while the steamship crew worked the boat carefully through a shallow spot. They were picked up farther along, by which time a great many skirts were ruined, shoes were soaked and muddy, and three of the children who had ventured into the woods were sick from the berries they had found and eaten. One of the Indians had disappeared, which didn't seem to distress either the captain or the Indian's friends. The lady from Albany who had found a water snake in her petticoat was still having hysterics as the ship once again steamed off for the West.

Gerald had found it a great adventure, Benjamin had peed in the woods and wanted to tell everyone about it, and Maggie was exhausted and thoroughly chilled. At least she was fortunate that her pregnancy was no further advanced. She mentioned this to Katrin as they sat around a tiny portable stove drying their stockings. "Yes, you're lucky there," Katrin said. "By the time you take to the trail in the spring, the baby will have a good start in life."

"But we must leave this fall," Maggie insisted.

There was a slightly worried look on Katrin's face, but she didn't pursue the subject. "Are you gettin' off at Independence or Kanzas Town?"

"Which is closer to the beginning of the trail?" Maggie asked.

"About the same, I'd say. It's not like a real road, you know. It fans out at this end and people start from lots of places, then the roads join and follow along the Kaw for a while before turning off south."

"The Kaw? Is that the Kansas River? Why couldn't we take a boat up it?"

Katrin laughed. "Wait till you see it. It's about six miles wide and six inches deep, and five of those inches are quicksand—except when it floods every few years. Then it eats up everything from bluff to bluff. I think you ought to get off at Kanzas Town, though, and go on to Westport. My Helmut is friends with the wagonwright there and says he's a good, honest man. He'll do right by you."

Eventually they reached the end of their water journey. Kanzas Town turned out to be not a town at all. It was simply the landing place for goods and individuals bound for Westport. There was a ledge of rock that jutted out into the water and formed an ideal landing stage. Nearby were a number of large log buildings—warehouses, a Catholic church, a tiny trading post catering to the local Indians, and a dirt track leading to the steep bluffs.

Katrin and Maggie stood silent while the boat tied up to the landing and started unloading goods. Each was trying to blink back tears without the other noticing. Katrin pulled out a large handkerchief and blew her nose. "You write and tell me how you get on," she said gruffly.

"We'll meet again," Maggie said. There was an uncharacteristic catch in her voice.

"Course we will," Katrin answered. "Now, you best get off, or you'll end up going home with me."

They embraced, and Maggie whispered, "God bless you, Katrin. Thank you for everything." Then she quickly took the boys' hands, nodded to Gerald, and the Freilers got off the boat. While Gerald made arrangements to have his family and goods transported to Westport, Maggie stood watching the boat pull away. It was taking with it a woman who Maggie felt might well have been a lifelong friend, had fate not decided otherwise.

"Why Mommy crying?" Benjamin asked.

She put a hand on his little shoulder. "Mommy's not crying, Ben. I've just got a dust mote in my eye." *Will I ever see her again?* Maggie wondered. She felt an overwhelming sense of loss.

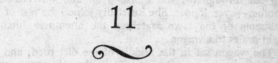

11

It was almost dusk when they arrived at Westport. Maggie had expected a town at Saint Louis and found a city, so she was prepared to discover that Westport was a city as well. She almost laughed when she realized that the collection of a half-dozen raw-looking buildings lining the dirt track was all there was of Westport. The oldest buildings didn't appear to be more than three or four years old. The original purpose of the town was to provide a place for Indians to buy white men's goods—most often whiskey. But, situated as it was on the Santa Fe Trail, a busy little industry was springing up supplying traders heading West to Mexico.

The Freilers and the other family that had disembarked at the Kanzas Town landing were taken to a two-story log house that served as a crude frontier hotel. The men were bedded down in one room along with three other rough-looking types who were already well into a stone jug of something they referred to as "skull varnish." Maggie, the other woman, and the children were given another room with narrow cots, reasonably clean bedding, and one tiny window that let in only a minuscule amount of fresh air.

It was devastatingly hot and stuffy, but Maggie was glad to be on land again even in the July heat. In the morning all the guests sat down to a long, rough-hewn table and had a breakfast of beans, slabs of fried ham, and red-eye gravy. Maggie tasted it and turned to Gerald in astonishment. "What is this?" she whispered.

He leaned close and said, "The way I understand it, they dump the dregs of last night's coffee into the skillet they've fried the ham in. A barbaric thing to do, but I suppose it'll grow on us." In spite of his sarcasm, he finished everything on his plate and took seconds. He was enjoying everything about this trip, even a red-eye-gravy assault on his digestive system.

After breakfast Maggie went back to her room to work on getting the rest of their money out of her stays. She had barely finished when a series of noises erupted from somewhere in front of the building. An awful, bloodcurdling braying cut through the still morning air and was answered by another—even louder. She hurriedly joined the rest of the inhabitants of the town watching the attempted hitching of eight mules to a wagon.

The wagon sat in the middle of the dirt road, and twelve or thirteen men were trying to drag the reluctant beasts into place. Maggie stood well back on the hotel porch next to a toothless old man who seemed to be enjoying the spectacle. "Are they hurting those animals?" Maggie asked in wonder at the intensity of the mules' objections.

"Not yet, they ain't," the man answered. "They's jest full to the eyeballs with green bile, mules is. Hateful critters. Fact is, the onliest thing they hate more than people is each other."

As if to demonstrate, one of the two mules that was already hitched turned and bit a chunk out of its companion. The second mule, a wall-eyed creature with a wild look to begin with, reared up, blood streaming from its shoulder, and crashed its front legs into the other mule's head. Wood splintered as the frenzied creatures thrashed and screamed. The wagon rolled forward and the long wooden tongue rammed through another wagon parked nearby. Men ran around in the streets shouting obscenities and trying to subdue the other mules, which longed to get into the melee. The mules pawed and snorted and brayed. They laid their ears back and rolled their eyes insanely.

The owner of the damaged wagon hauled himself out of the wreckage and grabbed the mules' owner by the shirt and demanded immediate recompense. The muleteer hit him in the mouth. The wagon owner retaliated by butting his head into the muleteer's stomach, knocking him to the ground, where a berserk mule nearly stepped on both of them.

Maggie backed up toward the door of the hotel just as Gerald came out with the boys. "What in the world . . . ?" he asked.

"Jest hitchin' some mules," the old man on the porch said calmly. A woman was screaming somewhere, and there were children crying in siren counterpoint. A crowd had gathered around the fistfight, and several men were waving their wager money in the air and cheering their favorite. One of the mules had gotten loose and was running in circles in the middle of the street.

Somebody fired a gun.

Everything stopped. The muleteer got up out of the dirt, administered a final kick to his foe, spit some blood, and limped over to survey the damage to his livestock. One of the two original combatants stood bleeding and triumphant. The other mule lay in a heap, twisted in the reins and traces, one leg flung out at an impossible angle. The owner scowled. "Broke his leg, son-of-a-bitch!" and with that he pulled a revolver out of his clothing and shot the animal in the head.

Maggie stifled a cry and rushed the boys back into the hotel. James was sobbing, and Maggie herself was trembling. Fortunately there was a back door to the building, and Maggie took them out that way and let them dabble in the tiny stream that ran behind. She was shocked, not only by the scene she had just witnessed but even more so by the reactions of the others. That old man had regarded the mayhem and bloodshed merely as free entertainment. Most of the people in the street had either flung themselves into the fray or stepped calmly out of the way. Would she, would any of them, ever become so hardened? If Katrin had been there, she would probably have chatted brightly about worse acts of violence she'd seen, then commented on the best way to get blood off leather. But Maggie's heart was still beating so wildly she could hear blood singing in her ears.

Gradually the sound of strife from the street diminished, James stopped crying and got interested in a frog, and Maggie felt her own tension easing slightly. She *would* get used to this sort of life. She must! Gerald joined them. "I've located the wagonmaker," he said. "Come on."

It was a large structure, half building, half overgrown shed. "We need a schooner," Gerald told Mr. Heston, the proprietor.

"Going West, huh? Well, long about the end of March I'll have the wagons ready for the spring trade."

"But we need it now."

"Now? Awful late in the year. Thought that bunch other day was the last of 'em. You folks bound for Santa Fe with 'em?"

"If we can catch up," Gerald said.

"Oh, you can catch them, all right. They were just going on out to the missions to meet the army shipment coming from Leavenworth. I hear the shipment ain't left yet. Come on in, let's see what I might have."

They followed him inside. "How long would it take you to build a wagon?" Maggie asked.

"Don't you worry 'bout that. I got one schooner here I'd like to get rid of. You see, I build coffins during the winter and then long about February I start building wagons again. This schooner'll just be in my way. Tell you what, I usually get three hundred dollars for one of these, but you're a friend of the Clays and I was gonna tear this up for the lumber anyhow, so I'll let you have it for two hundred. Now, it ain't calked yet. You'll have to pay for the pitch—that comes to about ten dollars, and my boy'll do the work for another three. Fair enough?"

Gerald glanced at Maggie, who nodded slightly. "Fair enough," he said. "Now, where can I buy the mules?"

"Mules! Oh, Gerald, not mules!" Maggie said.

"Naw, the lady's right. Takes a couple of brawny, rough-tongued men to handle the bastards—'scuse me, ma'am—you'd best get some oxen. Real tractable they are, and you can eat 'em if the going gets bad."

"But I think we ought to get a pair of mules at least," Gerald said. "We could take them along and start raising some to sell when we get to Mexico."

Mr. Heston stared at Gerald for a long moment before a grin spread across his broad face. He started laughing, laughed harder, and ended up wheezing and slapping his knee. "That's a good one, Mr. Freiler," he gasped. "Just a minute . . ." He turned and bellowed to someone in the back. "I got a fella here wants to buy two mules and start a herd." More laughter echoed from behind the shed.

Maggie and Gerald stared at each other, perplexed. "Pardon me, sir," Maggie finally said. "I don't see what's so funny."

Mr. Heston wiped his eyes. "I'm sorry, folks. Don't mean

to be rude to you, it's just that sometimes city folks . . . You see, Mrs. Freiler, mules are . . ." He cast around for a suitably discreet word. "They're barren. Ain't no such thing as a mother mule."

"Then where do baby mules come from?" Maggie asked, then regretted the phrasing. This was a difficult conversation.

"A mule is a cross between a donkey and a horse. That's the only way you get one, so if you were to buy two mules, all you'd ever have would be two mules—and a lot of goddamn trouble!"

Next they had to purchase oxen. They needed six to pull the schooner and six to pull the trade wagon. Then they had to have an additional one to rotate the work load and to replace any animals that might die along the way. In addition, they bought two cows. James, to whom anything larger than a dog was now a mule, kept screaming, "No mool! No mool!" and crying. While Gerald dickered good-naturedly with the man over the price, Maggie attempted to soothe James and inch him up closer to the huge gentle beasts who would be their transportation, companions, responsibility, and (possibly) food for the next seven hundred miles. Maggie looked into the velvet brown eyes of one of the oxen and could imagine she saw her own resignation reflected in them.

While Gerald was getting some information on the care and use of the animals, Maggie took the boys and went to the combination tavern/trading post across the way, where she got out her list. Two hundred pounds of flour for seven dollars, two hundred pounds of bacon for twenty dollars, and fifty pounds of dried beef. "We need a hundred pounds of cornmeal, too," Maggie told the owner.

"And how many eggs in it?" he asked.

"In it? What do you mean?"

The man sighed the weary sigh of a man who has already explained the same thing to a hundred greenhorns. "You see, ma'am, you cain't take yer eggs loose, so you put 'em in the cornmeal barrel as you sifts the meal into it. Keeps the eggs from breakin' and helps keep 'em fresh, too."

They ordered the rest of the foodstuffs—lard, beans, dried fruit, salt, brown sugar, rice, and pickles. "What are you getting pickles for, Maggie?" Gerald asked as he joined her. "Nobody but Benjamin even likes them."

"We'd better learn to. They are supposed to prevent scurvy," she said.

Later in the afternoon, when the wagon was calked, they

pulled up in front of the trading post and loaded the food. Then they took it down the street to the hotel, where their Saint Louis purchases were already packed in the trade wagon Gerald had purchased at Kanzas Town. The boys climbed around inside the four-by-ten-foot schooner, while Maggie supervised getting everything in its place. It was going to be difficult to store everything conveniently and still have room to move around. This was to be their only home for several months, and with two active little boys, there had to be some free space. Large semicircular hoops of wood formed the upper framework, and heavy white canvas stretched over them to form the top. Extra flaps of canvas could be tied at front and back over the openings to enclose the living space and protect them from rain or wind. Other pieces of canvas were supplied to sew to the inside to make pockets for storing small, light items like clothing, soap, or medicine bottles. Running along one side of the interior, from front to back, was a plank of wood called an overjet. This wood was the only bed. Blankets and boxes could be stored underneath it. Their tools and waterproofed kegs of gunpowder, flour, and cornmeal were lashed to various pieces of hardware on the outside. There was even a "butter peg" on the back. Maggie would be able to milk the cow in the morning, hang the covered wooden pail on the peg during the day, and the jolting would turn it into butter for the evening meal.

This information sent Maggie scurrying to the man who had sold them the cow for instructions on how to milk one. He, like the wagonwright, found it vastly amusing that there were city people who didn't know such things. Other townspeople stopped from time to time to watch them work and make comments, which was fortunate, for otherwise they would not have noticed until it was too late that they had forgotten to get candles and nails. Maggie had a sinking feeling that the list she had been going by might have left out other important items. What if there was something important and expensive they'd omitted? They had just a few cents over one hundred dollars left in the world, and where would they buy anything they needed anyway?

Only then did she truly realize that they were going to be entirely beyond the reach of civilization. Growing up in a city, there had been times when she had to do without some items because it was too cold to go out, or because she didn't feel well, or because there was some handy substitute available, but imagine truly needing something and knowing that it simply didn't exist within 350 miles! It was a horrifying idea. What if one of the children was seriously ill? What if the cow were to die and they had no milk products at all? What if . . . ?

Gerald caught her sitting in the wagon staring unseeing at the canvas wall. "Maggie? What's wrong? Are you feeling unwell?"

"What? Oh, no. It's nothing. I was just thinking . . ." She trailed off. No point now in burdening him with her worries. She should have thought of this long before. There was no turning back now.

As the sun rose the next morning, promising a day of searing heat, the Freilers left Westport. The oxen were hitched to the schooner and to the extra wagon—the trade wagon, which seemed to loom up behind them like some horrible family secret. Maggie put the boys, still sleepy and confused, on blankets on the overjet and joined Gerald on the hard wooden seat in front. The tongue of the second wagon was tied loosely to the back end of the schooner, so that Maggie did not have to contend with driving it the first morning out.

Mr. Heston, the wheelwright, came out of his shed to bid them good-bye and give them last-minute instructions. "You just take this road west, it's pretty clear. By this evening you'll be to the Indian mission."

"Indian mission?"

"You know, one of those places the folks from the East come out and teach the Indians religion and farming and such. This one's on the banks of the Kaw, and there's a ferry crossing that lets the Leavenworth road join the Santa Fe Trace there. You'll catch up with the rest of the wagon train there. Then you just follow the trace from there to Mexico. Good luck to you."

Gerald cracked the new whip over the heads of the docile oxen, and they slowly started forward. They had not gotten more than a mile, however, before Maggie found herself shifting around, trying to find a more comfortable position to relieve her of some of the jolting. She got one of the blankets and folded it under her, but it didn't help. Finally she crawled back into the wagon, dropped the flaps, and removed her stays, which, having done admirable duty as their bank, would have to be left off now.

It didn't protect her against the bouncing, but it did make her feel better. She was getting worried. The ache in her back was so much like she remembered just before she went into labor with the boys. Coincidence, no doubt. But still . . .

They stopped at noon to rest for a while. Maggie needed to learn to drive the trade wagon. Gerald instructed her in what he had learned about driving—the reins to the leaders, swings and wheelers must be held just so, with a whip in the right hand. The driver must sit straight and watch for any animal pulling to the side, thus increasing the work for the others. Maggie listened to all this, and when he was finished with his lecture, said, "It is time for you to tell me what I'm driving."

"What you're driving? The trade wagon, of course," Gerald said innocently, and busied himself with readjusting a harness hitch.

"I mean," she said ominously, "what is in it?"

Gerald hesitated, but knew she would have to be told sooner or later. Better to get it over with. "Maggie, my love, you're probably not going to appreciate the reasoning behind this, but I assure you I have given it much study—"

"What's in the wagon?"

Gerald took a deep breath and looked out over the river while he enumerated, "There is a case of opera glasses . . ." Maggie made a strange noise, but he went on as if he hadn't noticed, " . . . and ten bolts of fabrics—crepes, bombazines, silk—and there are mirrors and silverware. Let's see . . ." He glanced at her to see how she was taking this. Her face was frozen in an expression somewhere between surprise and horror. "Let me think . . . perfumed soap, candy, and . . ." He smiled confidently. "Flutes. A crate of flutes!"

Maggie's mouth fell open, and her voice came out a harsh whisper. "Flutes? . . . Flutes!"

"Now, have you got those reins straight? I'll lead, and you just shout if you have any difficulties. I'll keep the boys with me so that you can concentrate on driving until you feel confident about it." He walked briskly to the front of the other wagon and jumped up onto the seat. "Let's go," he said, and cracked his whip smartly over the heads of his oxen.

Maggie sat in the wagon seat, twisting the reins fiercely in her hands. She wanted to scream, to turn back time, to change everything, commit some violence and erase what she had just heard. But Gerald had made sure she would do none of these. She had too much dignity and concern for the children to conduct an argument with him from a distance, and his wagon, the schooner, was steadily pulling ahead. She cracked the whip sharply and stifled a cry as the wagon lurched forward, almost unseating her.

Mirrors. Silverware. Soap. Fabric. Flutes. God in heaven! Flutes!

Had he gone completely mad? They had only one hundred dollars left in the world—everything she had inherited and saved, gone on this venture, and he had bought silly, trivial things. Panic gripped her, and her head ached. Didn't he know that people didn't *need* such things? He should have bought tools and farm implements and practical manufactured goods—good sturdy calico cloth at least—not *flutes!*

Sitting on the high wooden seat, being bounced painfully with every dirt clod they rolled over, sweating with nerves and heat, Maggie passed from panic to despair to anger. How dare he do this to her? What would become of them? Father in heaven, they would starve to death. Everything was gone now—spent on a venture that was foolhardy to begin with. She must have been as much a fool as he was to have gone along with this. The family would be better off in Germantown—even if she had to take in laundry to survive. Damn him!

Gerald turned and peered around the edge of the leading wagon. "How are you doing?" he shouted.

"Fine!" Maggie snapped.

Gerald went back to driving his own team. He would leave her alone for a while. She would never understand his reasons for buying such things, but she would accept that it was done and too late to change. That was another of her good traits: she didn't brood. And when they got to Santa Fe and he made good money . . . well, she would see then. She'd be proud of him. But he was worried just the same. She was red in the face, and her words had a harsh rasp he had never heard before. She was truly angry. He'd seen her irritated, perplexed, and cranky from time to time, but he'd never seen genuine anger in Maggie, and there was something frightening about it.

Maggie, driving the hated wagonload of fripperies, dashed away a tear with her sleeve and tried to think things out. But what was there to think out? It was done.

Gerald had spent almost all their money on pure foolishness. Perhaps someone would be silly enough to buy some of it, and there might be something else he could do in Santa Fe, once they got there. He did seem to have a fine hand with animals; perhaps that was a skill that would prove useful. Of course, he was gifted with both words and music, but those were unappreciated on the frontier, where everyone's primary concern was survival. She *must* try to look on the bright side. If they could dispose of the useless goods for just what they had cost—well, probably less—they could go back to Saint Louis and make some sort of life for themselves.

She tried to tell herself she simply must stop thinking about it. She would not worry about the contents of the trade wagon; she would simply drive it. Neither would she waste any more acid anger on Gerald. He was what he was, and she was married to him—for better or worse. And this was the worse, she thought wryly. But she had realized something that made her very heart hurt. Gerald was flawed. She had looked upon him all these years as someone different from her in every imaginable way and therefore *better*. She had worshiped his dreaming nature, envied his little irresponsibilities, and believed fervently that the things that went awry in his life were not—could not conceivably be—his fault.

It did not make her love him less, but rather more. There was a fire-fringed passion between them that nothing would ever destroy, but some truths had billowed up before her that she could no longer ignore. He was dreams and art and hope; she was reality and craft and caution. Gerald was born to have a wild joyful dance with life, and it was her destiny to keep him—not just him, all of them—from coming to harm.

There was something else blunting her anger as the trail wound through thick stands of trees and shallow creekbeds. Something that had often occurred to her. Where and what would she be if she hadn't married Gerald? If he hadn't flung himself into her life and swept her up in his dance? She would be living, on sufferance, with Luther and Fritzi, and she would certainly be enduring the scalding humiliation of being treated like an employee. Or worse yet, a useless honorary "auntie." A houseful of chairs she wasn't allowed to sit on, and that sullen little boy of theirs instead of her own beautiful children. Unthinkable.

The trail led them briefly along a section of bluffs over the Kaw river valley, and they could see glimpses of the river, wide and dotted with pale sand bars like a milky stream of cocoa poured through a green landscape. Then it was gone again and they were back in the woods.

As they emerged the next time, Gerald leaned over the side of the leading wagon and called back, "I see them ahead. We're here."

We're here, she thought, and sagged a little with relief. A chance to rest—to stand up or lie down or do anything but sit rigidly on the hard wooden seat and clutch the reins. She realized her arms ached to her shoulders with the effort of controlling the oxen.

A wide, flat plain sloped off to the southwest, and in the middle, mere dots growing slowly larger, were the other wagons. There were trade wagons drawn into a rude circle forming an enclosed area for the livestock inside. A man in leather trousers and a plaid shirt noticed them first and called to Gerald, then walked to meet them.

Gerald stopped the wagons and nimbly hopped down to talk to him. Maggie sat silently listening as the boys, freed from the confinement of the schooner, clambered up on the trade-wagon seat with her.

"You folks joining us? Be glad to have you along. The army train ought to get here in a day or two. The reverend is letting us camp by the missions. You just follow that road," he said, pointing toward the bluffs.

"Then what are these wagons?" Gerald asked, indicating the circle.

"Trade goods. No point haulin' 'em down the hill just to haul 'em back up. You take your missus and the schooner on down, and we'll make a space in the circle for your other wagon."

Gerald helped Maggie up into the schooner, lifted the boys in the back, and went back to the trade wagon. He lifted a corner flap and brought a small wooden crate to the schooner. Maggie almost asked what was in it, but thought better. Clucking cheerfully to the oxen, Gerald headed them north along the rutted track. Suddenly the land dropped off and the road plunged down the hill.

Gerald stopped the wagon for a moment, and they sat silently looking over the valley. A blue jay perched above screamed his raucous protest of their invasion of the near-wilderness. The wide, sand-shingled Kaw wound lazily through stands of sycamores and cottonwoods. About halfway down the road there were red tile roofs of the Indian mission showing through the trees, and across the valley a long indentation in the mass of treetops revealed another trail coming from the north—the Leavenworth road, Maggie thought. In every open space there were sunflowers, tall robust plants with their heavy flowers bent of their own weight and nodding their golden heads in the light wind. Nodding a solemn confirmation, a welcome.

As Maggie looked out over the sun-washed valley, she caught her breath. It was so beautiful. But anyone could have seen that. Maggie saw more. The sunflowers, beckoning to her, knew it. The jay, screaming his territorial rights, knew. The sycamores, roots deep in the rich soil, knew. And Maggie knew.

This was home.

12

The Indian mission consisted of three main buildings, stately two-story brick structures that seemed to defy the fact that they were in the wilderness. Scattered around the well-kept grounds were smaller buildings—a smokehouse, spring-house, storage buildings, stables, and such. A stream, almost dry now in the summer heat, wound through the grounds before making a series of small waterfalls on its way to join the Kaw. As the Freilers drew near, a bell was rung somewhere, and Indian children swarmed out of the buildings and onto the grounds. There must have been twenty-five or thirty of them of all ages. Some made their way to other buildings, apparently to do assigned jobs, while the younger ones gathered in happy knots to talk and play games.

A portly well-dressed man stepped out of the front door of the central building, started to walk across the dusty track, then noticed Maggie and Gerald. He approached their wagon. "Reverend Whittacre at your service," he said. Maggie felt sorry for him. He was obviously a man who sorely felt the heat and didn't want to admit it. His heavy dewlapped face was flushed and peeling from a recent sunburn, and his collar was sweat-sodden, but he was dressed as for an eastern Easter service—dark wool suit and vest with a long-sleeved shirt neatly buttoned at neck and wrists. He mopped his forehead with a large, immaculately white handkerchief. "You people joining the other group?" he asked.

"Yes, sir," Gerald answered, then introduced Maggie and

the boys. "May we stay here with the others on your grounds?"

"Certainly. There is a cleared area just over there where the rest of the train is camped. We would welcome you to our evening prayers. I'm sorry my wife will not be able to make you welcome, but she is suffering from the heat. We have lived here for twelve years now, but her constitution does not seem to adjust to August very well." He chuckled mechanically, as if he had made this excuse many times over the years and was a little tired of hearing himself say it.

The Freilers pulled their wagon over to the encampment, and Gerald took the oxen down to the river for water while Maggie began their dinner. There were about forty people there, but only two women. They were both considerably older than Maggie and made no effort to speak to her, busy as they were with their own work. As Maggie dropped the last onion into her stew pot, she heard a man say, "Git that damned Injun outta here. She's just lookin' fer somethin' to steal."

Maggie turned and saw a pretty little girl of about ten hovering at the fringe of the camp. Pointedly ignoring the man's ugly remark, Maggie invited the little girl to come play with the boys. While Maggie tended the fire, the girl kept the boys entertained by demonstrating cat's cradles with her nimble brown fingers. She would not share their dinner, but was thrilled when Maggie got out her knitting and cut off a length of green wool yarn for her. "This will be my Sunday string," she said in strangely accented English. "Thank you, missus."

Evening fell quickly in the river valley, and the woods around them were a discordant symphony of nature. Crickets sung, owls called back and forth to one another, and something—a wild dog? a coyote?—barked his message to a distant comrade. There was the occasional hiss of water being poured over a campfire and the muffled clink of pots and dishes being put back into wagons, and finally the quiet conversations stopped. "The boys are asleep. Come for a walk with me, my love," Gerald said. "I found a pretty place to show you by the riverbank."

Maggie was exhausted, but too excited to sleep. "Yes," she said, gathering a blanket and checking once again on James and Benjamin, "but not for very long."

They walked without speaking to an isolated open grassy area where the only sound was the occasional splash of a fish.

103

"We'll not be alone for a long time when we leave here," he said.

When we leave here. Maggie couldn't imagine ever leaving here. "No, we won't," she said softly, and brushed her lips against his.

He spread out the blanket and she lay down by him, looking up at the cheese-round moon. "This is a nice place, isn't it?" he said as he turned and began to loosen the pins in her hair. "Maybe we can come back here sometime."

Could she tell him how she felt about this moonlit valley? "Gerald . . ." she began, but he silenced her with a tender kiss.

They made love there in the little clearing, all thoughts of Mexico and their disagreements over the trade goods forgotten. Amazing how little I care about the important things in life when I'm in his embrace, she thought as she held him close and ran her hands over his smooth, strong back. It seemed that all the world spun, evaporated, when he held her and whispered of his love for her. Could it be, she wondered, that this *is* the important thing in life and all the rest is insignificant? Loving, being loved, two bodies and hearts responding in perfect rhythm in the milky blue night?

Right now it was. Later she would have to be the real Maggie again—cooking, driving the wagon, caring for the children, worrying about the future. But at this moment she was only Maggie, Gerald's lover, lying in the grass, her limbs entwined with his, skin hot and alive to his touch, the weight of his body heavy and exciting on her, physical satisfaction flooding into every cell of her body. Why couldn't here and now last forever?

The next afternoon the military wagon train began to arrive. Maggie saw them lining up on the opposite bank a little way downstream and watched while the first of the big lumbering trade vehicles were ferried across the river and hauled up the steep hill. Gerald and the boys went to take a closer look. "Want to walk down there with us?" Gerald asked.

"Oh, I think not," Maggie said lightly. She didn't want Gerald to know that she wasn't feeling well. She had meant to go explore the woods—"her" woods—during the day, but had not gotten very far when the gnawing backache had started troubling her again. If only she felt better . . . if only they didn't have to leave this place that had captured her heart . . . if only . . .

Maggie busied herself fixing dinner to keep her mind off her worries. At dusk Gerald returned with two new acquaintances from the military escort. One was the commanding officer, Captain Bruckner. He was a bull-necked man with a florid face and a bone-crushing handshake. "How do, ma'am. Didn't know we were gonna have young'uns along this time. You sure you know the difficulties we're in for?"

"No, I don't suppose I do, but we'll cope with them," she assured him.

"That's the attitude I like. Don't have many eastern ladies on the trail, and when we do, they start out acting like they're going for a Sunday picnic. Awful shock to them when they find out different."

"I'm not expecting a picnic, sir."

"No, ma'am, I don't believe you are," he answered. "You appear to me to be a woman of sense."

The other man was the army doctor who was to accompany the train. Dr. Hutchen looked to Maggie like a hungry crane—thin, beaky, and nervous. He had a faint whiskey aroma, but his overly precise movements denied any drunkenness. Maggie was fascinated at the way he ate his dinner. He took each bit of food apart as if dissecting a particularly interesting specimen, then savored each piece.

"Well, I'd better be getting back to work," Captain Bruckner said when he had finished eating. "Nice to have food with a woman's fine touch. Appreciate it, ma'am. Hate to leave you, but we'll be seeing enough of each other in the next few weeks, and I've got to get the men busy soaking the wheels."

"Soaking the wheels? What for?" Maggie asked.

"So we don't start out with any creepers." Seeing that she didn't understand, he went on. "See how that iron band goes around the outside of your wagon wheel there? When the wood part ages, it shrinks and the iron band 'creeps.' If it gets too loose, it'll come right off and the wheel will wear down to nothing in a few miles."

"Why can't you tighten the band?" she asked.

Bruckner was surprised that a woman was interested enough to ask a reasonable question. "That's what we do at the fort, but we won't be able to out on the trail. You need a blacksmith, and he needs a forge. So all we can do is keep the wheels wet whenever we can so they don't shrink. Takes an awful lot of our time, and farther along it's hard enough to find water to drink, much less enough to soak the wheels."

"There ought to be a better solution . . ." Maggie mused.

"Yes, ma'am, there ought. But there ain't. I figure we waste maybe ten days each way with wheels, what with the time it takes to take 'em off and put 'em back, and the delays when it doesn't work. Come on, you old sawbones," he said to the doctor, who was daintily picking his teeth with his pocketknife. "Let's go back up the hill and see how they're getting along. And don't you go gettin' careless with those stinking cigars of yours. I've got three wagons full of gunpowder sittin' up there safe and sound."

Gerald walked part of the way with Bruckner, but the doctor lagged behind and returned to Maggie. "Forgive me, Mrs. Freiler, I don't often solicit patients, but I'd like to speak to you," he said.

"Yes?"

"Your husband mentioned that you are with child . . ."

"I am, but I'm not due until late January. We'll be in Mexico long before then."

"But I noticed that you walk rather carefully, as if you're in pain."

"Just a slight backache from driving the wagon. When I become more accustomed . . ."

"I don't mean to dispute a mother's instincts, but your color is bad. I would strongly advise you against making this trip now."

"I appreciate your concern and I'm glad for your advice, but it is not a matter of choice. We must make the trip."

"I see. I hope you will see fit to consult me if you do have problems. I am officially an army 'sawbones,' as the captain says, but I've treated a good many wives at the fort too."

She got the boys ready for bed, and as she sat in the schooner singing them an old German lullaby, she wondered if the army doctor was just a fussy old man who was imagining things or whether she should be heeding his warnings. Not that she could stay here until the child was born, as much as she would like to do exactly that. For the first time it occurred to her that it was not just the unborn child's life at stake; it could be hers as well.

No, that was ridiculous. She was turning into a hypochondriac. It was just the unaccustomed activity. In another week she would be used to the wagon rides, the hard physical work, the bending over a fire to cook. It would be easier after a while.

Gerald was sitting by the fire when she came back out of the schooner. As the sky changed from the persimmon glow of sunset to the water blue of night, someone got out a fiddle, and amid much laughter and hasty clearing away of impediments, a dance started up. Somebody had a banjo, and a soldier with a harmonica joined the group. The music was not good, but it was so loud and so good-natured that no one cared about the quality. Those who could recognize the tune and knew the words bellowed them as they danced. About half the men tied handkerchiefs around their heads, which made them look obscenely coy. Thus festooned, they played the women's parts, making clumsy curtsies and pirouettes.

They caught elbows in pairs and swung each other about to the beat of the music. They clapped and sang and laughed as more and more people were drawn into a "dance" that was actually a free-for-all.

She and Gerald were quickly surrounded by men begging a chance to dance with her. "C'mon, Mr. Freiler, don't be selfish," one of them called out.

"I'll give ya five pounds o' bacon for one dance," another shouted.

"Don't take no bacon from him, it's gone bad. I'll give a sack of cornmeal."

"Full of weevils . . ."

"Ain't neither!"

"And my bacon's not rancid either, just a little 'high.' "

Maggie was insulted for a moment, being bargained for like this, but then she remembered all the polite dances she had endured with Helga Appel back home, sitting primly at the sidelines while all the pretty little empty-headed girls were besieged by vapid young men asking for the next dance. Sitting alone, hating every moment because she was not asked and afraid that she might be. Nightmares of being led onto the floor by some gentleman while the other girls whispered, "Look, someone asked that tall girl to dance."

In a sudden jolt of recognition, she realized something about herself. She had always known she was out of place, a misfit, among her Germantown neighbors and certainly among the Schmids' Amish friends, and she had assumed that it meant there was something wrong with her. Now she knew for certain what she had suspected—that she had just been in the wrong *place*. On the frontier, bluntness, a sensible attitude, and a lack of interest in the "frills" of life were not liabilities, they were assets. These people, like her, were tough. She *belonged* where a pregnant woman was not expected to automatically retire with the vapors at the mere thought of

107

physical activity. Out here, if you had a problem, you just solved it—you didn't call in a lawyer or a minister or a seamstress, you took care of it yourself. And when the long day's work was done, you danced—whether you knew how or not didn't matter. It was the fun of it, not the form.

Assuring Gerald that a brief dance would do her no harm, Maggie took a brief turn with two of the men, refusing both their culinary offers. Then she went back to check on the children, straightening their covers and gently pulling James's thumb out of his mouth. Returning to Gerald, she began to wonder how the men could keep up their frantic activity for so long, but after a little while the "dance floor" began to empty. One by one they got too drunk or too tired to dance or pulled some muscle and limped to the sidelines. The volume of the music diminished and the quality increased.

There was a soft, rumbling undertone to the music. Glancing up at the bluffs to the south, Maggie could see an erratic and almost imperceptible lightening of the starless sky. Thunder. They were going to find out right away whether the schooner's canvas was watertight. But until the rain started, Maggie wanted to enjoy the music, there had been so little of music and lighthearted comaraderie in her life.

The frantic exuberance had passed and there was a comfortable sense of well-being throughout the camp, but here and there others glanced up warily at the skyline over the bluffs, and the animals shuffled restlessly, nervous without knowing quite why. The music slowed and a plaintive note crept into it. A young soldier with a clear, sweet tenor voice began to sing a long, lonely song about leaving home. Maggie was so engrossed in listening to his sad voice that she didn't notice at first that Gerald was gone. Then she heard the liquid tones of a flute weave into the song. So *that* was what was in the crate he'd taken out of the trade wagon. He was standing near the central campfire, playing the instrument. Maggie leaned back against the wheel of the schooner and gave herself to the music as the sound of the flute and the boy's voice mingled, interlaced, climbed, glided back down, and throbbed through the camp.

There were a few drops of rain falling now, and the thunder was louder, but the song went on. The boy had asked his love to come with him in his adventure, her parents had refused, and the flute wept crystalline notes of despair. Maggie sensed vaguely that the sadness in Gerald's music was born of some deep sadness in him. Somewhere in the cheerful, loving man she had married there was a yawning pit of sorrow or dissatisfaction or longing—she did not know which, or why.

As the last notes died away, the sky lit up and a vast crack of thunder echoed through the valley. Suddenly the rain started falling in earnest. Great fat blobs of water hurled from the sky hissed in the remaining fires. Hastily gathering up their belongings, the travelers dashed for the protection of their wagons. The soldiers who had left their own encampment to join the dancing and music hurried back to their posts. The horses and oxen and mules pulled tight at their tethers, rearing and snorting.

Suddenly there was a mind-splitting roar from above. The earth was a blaring silver-white, then orange. Percussive pain. Maggie put her hands over her ears and ducked into the schooner. The children awoke screaming, but she could not hear their voices over the reverberations. She gathered them into her arms, trying to shield them from the piercing detonation of God knew what.

The back of the schooner canvas framed a section of the bluffs above them. The crimson sky seemed to pulse, and Maggie thought for a moment that the world had really come to its end. Then, as the sounds diminished, a cacophony of shouted conversations could be heard:

"Get those mules tied up before they run off."

". . . lightning. Never seen the like."

". . . blown to hell and halfway back . . ."

"Shit!"

". . . damned gunpowder . . ."

". . . rain'll help keep it from spreading . . ."

". . . barrels . . . water . . ."

"Hurry!"

Men and animals bumped the wagon. Maggie held the boys tightly. They whimpered. She whimpered.

"Hurry!"

". . . don't dare get close till she's through blowin' . . ."

She could see Gerald standing at the back of the wagon opening. He was staring at the bluff, his eyes dark and appalled. She wanted to reach out and hold him too. He felt her gaze, turned and stared at her. "The lightning hit the gunpowder wagons," he said unnecessarily. His voice was empty and shocked. "Our wagon . . ." He turned away.

In a second he was gone, and the camp quieted as the men pelted up the hill to see what had happened. In a few minutes there was another explosion, and from far away the sound of a man's scream.

Maggie bent her head over the boys. Not Gerald. Dear God, not Gerald. Someone else. Anyone else. Not Gerald. Please, God!

After what seemed like agonized years, she heard raised voices close by. "Dr. Hutchens," she called into the downpour. "Have you seen my husband?"

Hutchens, drenched to the skin, sooty and bedraggled, said, "He's up the hill, trying to . . . Ma'am, your wagon's gone."

"But my husband is safe?"

"He is, but others aren't. Have you any butter? Anything to use as ointment?"

"Yes, I've got burn medicines. Some." She hastily moved things around until she found the small box of herbs and medicines. She handed them to the harried doctor, who thanked her and rushed away.

Maggie slept fitfully, expecting to hear Gerald's voice any moment, but he did not return. At daybreak she heard children's voices. Looking out, she saw the Indian children from the mission, free until classes started, exploring the campsite and watching the soldiers hauling the remaining wagons up the hill. The little girl who had visited them before waved shyly to Maggie. "Could you stay here for a few minutes?" Maggie asked her.

"Please, yes," the child answered, clearly delighted to be invited into the wagon.

Maggie hurried up the long rutted track to the bluffs. Stopping twice to get her breath and let the pain in her side subside, she finally reached the top. There was a vast burned area where the explosive wagons had stood before they were blown apart. Other wagons, burned to silhouettes, stood at the edges of the charred area. The vehicles that had escaped the fire or had been only minimally burned had been pulled away to a safe distance from the still-smoking circle. Maggie picked her way carefully across the field toward Gerald.

He was sitting cross-legged on the ground, head bent and hands outstretched in front. "You've burned your hands," Maggie said softly.

He looked up, startled. He was covered with soot and dirt. His face was darkened and his azure eyes showed like haunted beacons of doom. He started to speak, then shrugged instead and looked back down. Around him were scattered his smoldering hopes. Yards and yards of ruined silk and velvet in black heaps; a box of opera glasses, their lenses cracked by heat; the mirrors in shards; delicately tinted papier-mâché trays now curled charcoal wisps; a crate of fine silverware a twisted puzzle of handles and blades and tines.

"Come rest," Maggie said, and offered him her hand.

He stood, wincing at the effort, and they walked silently down the long hill. The camp was nearly deserted, and as they walked past the campfire from the night before, he stopped. The small crate of flutes was sitting where he had left it. He smiled bitterly. "Flutes," he said. He gave the box a halfhearted kick and turned away, hands jammed into pockets. "Do you think, Maggie, that I can found my fortune on a boxful of flutes?"

Then, after a long crackling pause, he added, "Damn! Damn! Damn!"

"Gerald . . . don't—"

He turned and gripped her arms. "You don't see!"

"See what?"

"Maggie, it's not just losing the things, losing the money. That's not the worst. The worst is that you'll never know that I was right! I *was* right, dammit! We'd have made our fortune on that . . . that reeking mess up there!"

"Gerald, it will be all right . . ."

"*No!*" he was shouting now. "It won't be all right. I failed at teaching because of the way I am—I'll grant that. But this is not my fault! I was right, and fate . . . God . . . whatever . . . struck me down. I'm standing here a goddamn failure again and you're pitying me and you still don't know I was *right!*"

Something cold and hard knocked against Maggie's heart. She had never dreamed of seeing Gerald this way. She searched inside herself and came up wanting. She could not understand him. The words made sense, she shared his sorrow and distress, but in the back of her mind was one diamond-hard belief: he was *not* right about the trade goods. They were trifles—useless trifles. Non-necessities. The loss was theirs entirely. Life would go on forever, for everyone, without silks and mirrors and fancy trays.

And now he was blaming her for it.

She stared back at him, his sense of injustice reflecting hers. The fire had made them adversaries—as passionately dear to one another as ever, but adversaries. Finally he broke the agonized gaze, dropped his hands, and said, "I'm sorry,

111

Maggie, it's not your fault you can't understand." He turned on his heel and walked away, defeated and exhausted.

Maggie did not follow him, nor even watch him go. There was an invisible wall between them now. There were chinks and holes, places where they might reach through and touch one another's souls briefly, but the wall might be there forever. She put her hand to her neck, felt the smooth gold locket he had given her lying in the hollow of her throat, and wondered how they had come to this.

13

It was shortly after noon when the bleeding started. Maggie had been helping Dr. Hutchens tend the injured soldiers when she felt some sharp pains. She sat down for a moment, thinking she had merely overtired herself walking up the long hill for the third time in one morning. Reverend Whittacre had given her some makeshift bandages torn from bed linens, and she put the bundle down just as Dr. Hutchens glanced up from the young man he was tending. "Is there something wrong, Mrs. Freiler? Sit down and rest a minute. You should not be climbing that hill in your condition."

"No, there's nothing wrong," Maggie answered, but she could hear the frightened quaver in her own voice.

So could the doctor. "Lie down," he ordered without looking up from the bandage he was tying.

"No, I'm fine. I think I'll just . . ." She could feel the wet stickiness seeping between her legs now. Voice rising and breaking, she said, "I'll just go back to the schooner . . ." She turned, and the world kept turning. She reached out for support where there was none, and her last thought was that she would dirty her dress falling to the charred grass.

The dreams were horrible. "Freiler! Freiler!" someone calling. Her name. She could answer. But her lips would not move. Her voice was a cheeping whimper. They were lifting her. Who? For a while she thought she was Adelle—such pain, such heat. They lifted her head, tried to make her drink as she had done with Adelle. But her mouth couldn't open.

Then it couldn't close. She sputtered, coughed. The pain bit back.

I'm dying. Do they know? Adelle died. But I'm not ready. She was. I'm not!

Then it was quiet and still for a long time. The pain ebbed, then washed back over and ebbed again. A little farther away each time.

Gradually she became aware of voices again. Hushed, fearful voices. ". . . cannot make any promises, sir . . . blood loss . . . not just the child to consider . . . no movement . . . absolute rest . . ."

"Gerald?" she managed to call feebly.

He was instantly at her side. Another face floated in and out of focus. A vast white canopy. Heaven? No. Her senses began to return. She was inside the schooner. "Dr. Hutchens?"

"Yes, ma'am. I'm here."

"What is wrong with me?"

Hutchens cast a questioning glance at Gerald. He nodded. Thus assured that Maggie could bear the truth, he explained, "You've overtired yourself, and your body is trying to get rid of its extra burden—the baby."

"Did I lose the baby?" Maggie asked.

"No, not yet. If you remain completely immobile for several weeks, we may be able to save the child . . . and you."

"Me?"

"Maggie, my love, the doctor is concerned about the bleeding. I could lose you as well if you don't do as he says." Gerald's face was so pale. That frightened her more than what he was saying. "The wagon train is leaving today—"

". . . and I'm taking the injured soldiers back to Leavenworth," the doctor cut in. "But I will get back here as soon as I can. Unfortunately, my first responsibility is to them. In the meantime, you must stay here, Mrs. Freiler."

"If you're better when the doctor returns, we'll make the trip back to Saint Louis," Gerald said.

"No! Not back. We can't go back!" Maggie said.

"Calm yourself, Mrs. Freiler," Hutchens warned. "There will be plenty of time later to talk about all this. For now you are to do nothing. Don't talk. Don't even think." He smiled.

"But the children?"

"I can take care of them," Gerald said. "Reverend Whitta-

113

cre agreed to let two of the older Indian girls come over and do our cooking."

"That was nice of him," Maggie mumbled. She was already exhausted. She tried to understand what Gerald said next, but the words wouldn't fit themselves into a coherent pattern. Perhaps if she slept a little while . . .

When Hutchens returned a month later, Maggie felt much better. Not well. She couldn't remember what it felt like to be well, but she was able to sit up for as long as a half-hour at a time without becoming faint. She had even persuaded Gerald to help her out of the schooner once or twice and let her walk a few feet. "She can't go anywhere," the doctor declared. "Half a mile in that wagon, and she'd miscarry. You're still spotting sometimes, aren't you?"

Maggie admitted this was true. "But not for several days now."

The doctor was weary too and getting short of temper. "If you people want to make motherless orphans of those little boys outside the wagon, then hitch up your oxen and ride off."

"No, we're staying right here until the baby is born and my wife is well," Gerald said.

After he had gone, Reverend Whittacre and his previously unseen wife came to call. She was a small woman with a flinty, dissatisfied look Maggie had seen before in ministers' wives—women who had to share their husbands with God and his works and resented it. Her dark hair was pulled back into a meticulous and severe bun, and the lines on her face recalled years of scowling disapproval. "Mrs. Freiler," she acknowledged the introduction perfunctorily and crossed her arms across her flat bosom.

Reverend Whittacre bustled into speech to cover his wife's near-rudeness. "Doctor says you're still poorly, Mrs. Freiler. Well, we're here to help people out. We'll do whatever we can for you. Of course, we're a little short of space, but there's an extra room in our apartments—a bit crowded for the four of you, but . . ."

"No." Maggie said the word firmly. Reverend Whittacre looked confused; his wife's scowl deepened.

"Maggie, the doctor said you couldn't be moved to Westport or Saint Louis," Gerald said.

"What I mean is, we won't take your room and incon-

114

venience you. What do you teach these children?" she asked the minister.

"Religion, of course."

"No, I mean what practical things?"

If Reverend Whittacre took offense at Maggie's dismissal of the worth of his religious teaching, he didn't show it. "Why, carpentry, farming, homemaking for the girls . . ."

"Then why not let them work on a practical application of those skills?" Maggie asked. "The boys could help Gerald build a house for us. Not a real house, just something to shelter us for the winter. The girls could help me care for my children until my baby is born." She paused, letting this sink in for a moment before she went on. "We could work out a reasonable trade—our resources for your help."

Mrs. Whittacre looked pointedly at Maggie and her goods—the weather-beaten wagon, tired oxen, helpless children—and came close to a nasty smile. "Your resources?" she asked cattily.

Maggie was not to be put off, not by a woman like this. "Yes, I am a good seamstress. Even in my condition I can teach the girls sewing and relieve you of some of the responsibility. And my husband is an accomplished teacher with years of experience." From the corner of her eye she could see Gerald come to stunned attention.

"A teacher, sir? I had no idea!" Reverend Whittacre said. "Well, this is providential indeed. What do you teach, sir?"

"Grammar, composition, languages . . ." Gerald muttered. Maggie could not bring herself to meet his eyes. Of course he was disappointed, he had never intended to teach again, but these were extraordinary circumstances. They had tried what Gerald wanted to do and it hadn't worked out. He would simply have to do this.

"Wonderful!" Whittacre said. "Our teacher, Mr. Smith, has requested a transfer back to Boston, and I have been attempting to find a replacement for him. It isn't easy to get experienced men to come out here. My, my, my, how fortunate for all of us."

Maggie chanced a glance at Mrs. Whittacre. Her face was a study in conflict. She didn't like having a strange woman take over like this, that was obvious. She was accustomed to making the decisions at the mission, but Maggie had also provided her with a way out of having an extra family camped in her spare room for the winter. "I think that would be a satisfactory arrangement," she said grudgingly.

"Mr. Freiler's teaching will allow him to have a house in

115

spite of the territorial regulations," Mr. Whittacre said. "You see, this land is set aside for the use of the Indians, and no white settlers are allowed unless they are serving the government or the churches."

"There are no settlers here?" Maggie asked. Surely she had seen scattered cabins here and there.

"Well, not officially. Though people do defy the rules, and the army seldom bothers them if they're not creating difficulties. Well, I'm delighted that we've worked this out. Now, Mr. Smith can stay on for another month or so, and you will have time to get some sort of lodgings built by then. Mrs. Freiler, you folks can stay with us until it's ready. I will send some boys over to start bringing your things inside."

"No, that's not necessary. We won't inconvenience you at all. We've spent several weeks living in this schooner, we can spend another month," Maggie said firmly.

"But it's going to get cold soon," Reverend Whittacre objected.

"We can manage. We don't want to be beholden," Maggie answered. It was part of the truth. The rest was that she didn't want to come in any closer contact with Mrs. Whittacre than absolutely necessary. But above all, Maggie knew that if she was tucked away out of sight in the Whittacres' spare room, she would have no control over the house that was to be built for her.

"But the children . . ."

"Could they sleep with the Indian children when the weather is bad?" Maggie asked.

"They could, but it would be highly unsuitable. It's not good to allow white children to mix with—"

"I'm sure you provide adequate sleeping arrangements for the children under your care, Mrs. Whittacre," Maggie pressed on, "and I'm quite capable of deciding with whom my children will 'mix.' "

"Well!" Mrs. Whittacre said coldly. "I can only say—"

Reverend Whittacre cut into the threatened comeback. "We are glad to welcome you folks. Now, if you will excuse us both, there is much to do. Elsie, isn't your homemaking class about to begin?" He quickly shook hands with Gerald and dragged his wife away.

"Oh, my, I'm glad he took her off." Maggie sighed. "I was about to lose our home before we ever got it. What a terrible person."

"Yes . . ." Gerald said absently.

Maggie regarded him steadily for a moment, her heart

aching at the sadness in his face. "Gerald, it's only for a short while—a year or so, until we save enough money to replace the trade goods." She almost made herself think she meant it.

Maggie picked the site of her house with great care. She wanted to be as far as reasonably possible from the main mission building where the Whittacres lived. She wanted a view of the ferry crossing, but well away from the river itself.

"But, Maggie, *this* is a long way back from the water," Gerald protested as she refused yet another suggestion. She had been gently transferred from the imprisoning schooner to a small carriage Reverend Whittacre had lent them.

"But it's on much the same level. The river would only need rise a few feet and this would be flooded."

This was the fifth site he had offered and had rejected, and he was getting irritated. "Look, Maggie, you keep on saying this is only for a short time, and yet you're acting like you are choosing a place to live out your whole life. I'm afraid, come spring, they'll dig us out of a snowbank and you'll still be saying, 'No, not here.' Since you don't like this, how about over there?" He gestured at the slight rise behind them.

Maggie looked back. "Well, there is a nice little stand of trees over there with a sort of clearing in the middle. It would be shady in the summer. What are they? Maples? Seven of them. Pretty in the fall . . ." she mused, ignoring his fidgeting with the reins. "Well, it's not as high as I'd like . . ."

"Maggie!"

"Yes, yes. That will be a good spot, Gerald. Can you move the schooner over near it, though, so I can watch the progress of the building? It's so terribly boring, having to just lie there all day looking at the inside of the canvas."

"You don't want to watch, you want to supervise. I know you, you'd like to be building it yourself. Very well, Maggie, my love," Gerald said, cheerfully himself again now that a decision had finally been reached, "you will be moved, but only if you promise you will do nothing—*nothing*—but watch."

Maggie agreed meekly, but it was an automatic response. In the privacy of her own mind, she was mapping out the dimensions of the house and how the windows should be placed.

Gerald was enthusiastic for a few days. The Indian boys, eager to be outside instead of in a classroom, were glad to help. They took the Freilers' oxen and hauled large stones from the riverbank to make a foundation. Then they and Gerald went to the woods to cut trees to make the house itself. Maggie awoke from a nap one afternoon to the sound of an ax striking a nearby tree. "No, no!" she protested to the startled Indian boy. "Not my maples. I want to keep them." He stared at her, uncomprehending. "Leave my trees alone," she said slowly. "Look, Freilers' trees. One, two, three, four, five, six, seven," she counted them off, pointing to each one.

"Ah! Freilers' seven trees," the boy said, nodding.

For a week they hauled back tall straight oaks they'd cut in the woods. But each day they had to go farther for them, and the work slowed. One morning the ferry operator trudged up the hill to meet them. He was a gaunt young man, all forehead and teeth, but his good nature was apparent from his first words. "Name's Woodren Woodline," he said. "Try and guess what folks call me?"

"Woody?" Maggie said, and laughed at the exaggerated expression of surprise on his long face. "I'm glad to meet you, Woody."

"I been anxious to git up here and make your acquaintance, ma'am, but things been busy on the river. Was hoping to meet yer man, too. He gone?" Maggie nodded. "You folks fixin' to set up here permanent?"

"For a year or two."

"Looks like a mighty big house for a short time. *Two* rooms?" he asked, looking over the foundation and first course of logs.

"It might be longer, and we have, or will have, three children."

"Them yer boys I saw back there by the school? Mrs. Whittacre says you're poorly, ma'am. Beggin' yer pardon, but you don't look poorly to me." Woody appraised her figure as dispassionately as he'd measured up the house. Then he glanced at the beginning of the building and the stack of logs. "You'll make it into that house in time if the weather holds," he said. "But you might could use some help. I can't be away from the ferry, case somebody needs to cross, but I could work around here, cuttin' notches in the logs and such."

"That's very generous of you, but we couldn't ask you to do it," Maggie said. "We have no way to pay you."

He looked at her pityingly, as if she were a slightly simpleminded child. "You ain't been out here long, have you, ma'am? See, that ain't how things work. Everybody got to help everybody out here—whether they get paid or not don't matter. Someday when I need it, you'll help me out."

"But I don't see how . . ."

"I ken think of a way right off the top of my head. You see, I eat my dinners with the reverend and his wife, 'cause I git sick on much of my own cookin' . . ."

He had a strange look, as if he were trying to say something rude in a polite way. Maggie had a feeling she knew what it was. ". . . and you don't like Mrs. Whittacre?"

"It ain't exactly that—she's a good cook and all, it's jest that . . . that . . . No, I don't much take to her, that's the honest truth, ma'am. It ain't Christian of me, I reckon . . ."

"I know what you mean. As soon as I'm well, I'll cook your dinners."

"I have a little vegetable garden, summers. I'll bring food and take you folks on the ferry fer free."

They bargained it all out in a few minutes, and Woody left Maggie to rest while he applied himself to scoring a log in preparation for hewing it square.

When Gerald returned that evening, he and the Indian boys had only two lengths of log. Maggie wondered why it had taken all day to find only two trees, but hesitated to ask for fear it would seem like criticism, and she didn't wish to embarrass him in front of a new friend. She explained to Gerald about her arrangement with Woody, and Gerald insisted that he stay for his first meal.

"Tell Miz Whittacre I'm eating here tonight," Woody told the Indian boy who had been helping him all afternoon.

"You stay? Eat at Freilers' seven trees? Good. I tell missus," he said, and scampered off with the other boys to answer the distant clang of the dinner bell sounding from the mission.

Freilers' Seven Trees, Maggie thought. What a nice sound it had. Imagine a place having their name. A place that really belonged to them. She'd lived in her uncle's house and Schmids' and a rented house and carried all their worldly goods on a riverboat and a prairie schooner, but here, at the very fringe of the civilized world, was a place—a solid piece of land with trees and grass and soon a house—that belonged to them. Maggie felt like one of those airborne seeds attached to bits of fluff and drifting aimlessly. She had landed by chance on a fertile piece of earth and by some miracle had taken root at the sound of that phrase, Freilers' Seven Trees.

How could a name, a mere turn of phrase in the mouth of a child, have that effect?

Gerald and Woody built a fire and stirred together a stew. Gerald objected to Maggie's getting out of the wagon and helping, but she was determined, and after dinner they all sat around the welcome warmth of the coals and entertained one another and the boys. Woody had a packet full of little carved figures that fascinated the children. "Got a lotta time on my hands, between ferry runs," he explained, "and I can't go much of anywhere for fear of leavin' someone sittin' on the other bank waiting for me, so I whittle."

While Woody showed the children how a little piece of wood could turn into a rabbit with a few deft flicks of a knife, Gerald went to the wagon and dug out the box of flutes. He had not played, or even mentioned them, since the fire. He brought one out, rubbed it on his sleeve, and began playing. At first Maggie could think only of his bitter words when they lost the rest of the goods: "Do you think, Maggie, that I can found my fortune on a boxful of flutes?" But Gerald was playing something light and cheerful, the bitterness forgotten or at least put aside.

With darkness came a distance chill. "Winter drawin' in," Woody observed. "Best turn in so's we ken get an early start. You got a long ways to go on this here house."

He gave each of the boys a tiny wood figure and ambled off into the darkness.

Later, when the moon was high and the children were asleep, Maggie asked, "Gerald, why did it take all day to get two trees?"

He stirred sleepily. "We've cut all the good ones nearby, Maggie, my love."

"But, Gerald . . ." She hesitated. She didn't want to nag, and yet . . . "I notice that all the boys came home wearing more beads than they left with."

Gerald didn't take offense; in fact, his eyes lit up as he explained. "Yes, we came to a streambed that had a high clay content in the exposed soil. They showed me how they make beads. It's very interesting, the number of common-looking plants in the woods that you can use for coloring. The yellow color comes from a—"

"Gerald, do you mean that you spent the day playing in the mud!" Maggie said, sitting up suddenly.

"No, of course not. Not all day. Just for a while at lunch. It was so bracing and beautiful, we took a rest. Oh, Maggie,

120

you should have seen the flowers we found in one place. Odd that they'd bloom so late in the year. Of course, the Indian children are so used to nature that they hardly seemed aware of it until I pointed out . . . Maggie, what's wrong? Are you crying?"

"Gerald! Don't you realize, we *need* a house!" she said, brushing away the hateful tears. "It isn't just a whim of mine. We need a house! It's September now, almost October. It gets cold here—it snows, for God's sake! We can't live in a wagon with a little cloth over our heads, and I *won't* live with the Whittacres. I *won't*!" She had an overwhelming urge to slap him or throw something highly breakable.

"Now, Maggie, you're losing your temper. . . ."

"I'm losing my *mind!* Gerald . . ." She took a deep breath, trying to get control. "Gerald, I like flowers, too, and it would be nice some leisurely summer day to learn to make pretty colored beads," she said sarcastically, "but I *must* have a house. How can I make you understand that?"

Gerald wrapped his arms around her. "You're right. I'm sorry. I wasn't thinking of the practical necessities. It was selfish of me to waste time like that—there will be lots of opportunities later for that sort of thing. I'll make up for it tomorrow, Maggie, my love. I promise."

Maggie fell asleep later in the warmth of his arms and the counterfeit comfort of his words. But she dreamed that *she* was building the house.

Maggie was teaching a group of Indian girls how to darn when the pains started. They were slight at first, and she wasn't sure it wasn't just a backache from sitting up all day. After all, the baby wasn't due for more than two months yet, and she had been very careful about following the doctor's instructions as far as possible. She tried very hard not to be alarmed, as much for her own sake as anyone else's. "That's all for today," she told the little girls. "Be sure to anchor your needles carefully so they don't get lost. Leave your work here, and we'll go on with it tomorrow."

"Please, missus, can we take little boys to play?" the oldest girl asked.

Maggie had been uneasy at first about letting James and Benjamin out of her sight, but they had come to adore the attention, and the little girls had proved to be very responsible. "Yes, but bring them back in plenty of time for dinner," she said. "Oh, and tell Mr. Woodline that there's someone across the river waiting for the ferry," she added. The opening at the back of the schooner had been aligned so that she could keep one eye on traffic for Woody while he helped them build the house.

Another contraction took her, sharper this time. She could feel her heart beating faster. Don't panic, she told herself. Just lie down and relax, it isn't time yet. Woody stuck his head in the end of the wagon. "Thank you, Miz Freiler, I'll just run on down there and I'll be back in . . . Miz Freiler, is somethin' wrong? You look real pale."

"No, it's nothing. I'm just a little tired," Maggie said, but the tremble in her voice gave lie to the words.

"I'll send one of the boys for Gerald," he said. "You jest lie down nice and easy. Soon as I git these folks across the water, I'll come back and check on you. You want me to send for Mrs. Whittacre?"

"No! I mean, no need to bother her."

Woody's eyes showed concern and a spark of humor. He repeated what she'd once said to him: "I know jest what you mean . . ." and hurried off. "Git Mr. Freiler back to Seven Trees," Maggie heard him shouting to one of the children as he went.

Maggie curled up on the makeshift bed she'd spent so much of her time in already, and wished she could be out in the sunshine. It was the end of October now, and distinctly cold, even in the middle of the day. And in the mornings there was often a sparkle of frost on the grass and leaves. The maples around the house, the "Seven Trees," had burst into gorgeous array after the first frost, and now the blood-red leaves were slowly loosening their hold and drifting down, making a rustling, colorful carpet. Another contraction crept around from the small of her back and met itself. Not yet painful, only uncomfortable. She shifted a little, took a deep breath, and it faded. Maybe she could will this away if she held perfectly still and concentrated on not feeling it. Unreasonable, she knew, but she could *not* have the baby now, it couldn't survive so early.

The house was almost done—the walls were up, the chimney built and chinked, the windows and doors had been cut in. But there was no roof yet, so it was still a useless shell. Gerald had been begging her to go stay with Mrs. Whittacre, and even the lady herself (under pressure of her husband's orders, no doubt) had come by twice to renew the offer. But Maggie had refused. She had forced herself to be polite to

Mrs. Whittacre, but she had refused nevertheless. She did allow the boys to sleep in the dormitory with the other children, but she and Gerald remained in the schooner. Gerald collected large round rocks, which were set by the campfire during the day. As evening drew on, he would wrap them in blankets and bring them into the schooner for warmth. So far they had been sufficient, but every night was a little colder, and Maggie found herself imagining how nice it would be to be sleeping in a real bed in a real bedroom in a real brick building. She knew, however, as surely as she knew her name, that if she moved in there, her house would not get done this winter—might not ever get done—and she *had* to have a house. Gerald came back from nearly every trip to the woods with something to show her—a branch with particularly colorful leaves, a carpetlike piece of lush green moss, a feather dropped by a bird that soared about for endless minutes without ever flapping its wings.

He wanted to share the beauty around them with her, and Maggie wanted very much to share his appreciation of it, but she could not. Instead of cutting the branch for her, he could have been cutting wood for the house; while he watched the soaring bird, he could have had his sights set lower and been looking for a good straight tree to use as a ridgepole for the house; instead of looking for moss, he could have been finding clay to chink the logs with.

Even Woody seemed distressed with the slow rate at which the house was being built, though he was an outsider and obviously could not criticize Gerald. Neither could he leave sight of the ferry and go into the woods to hurry things.

Maggie closed her eyes against another contraction and tried once again to shut it out. It was beginning to get dark as the sun sank in the autumn sky, and she could hear the sounds that accompanied the end of the day. The school bell rang faintly in the distance, summoning the children to the prayers that always ended the schoolday, and she could barely hear sounds of voices raised in greeting at the ferry landing. Somewhere in the woods Gerald and the Indian boys were urging the oxen on as they dragged back something—the ridgepole, she hoped. She pulled the covers up over her head. Her ears were cold, and she was shivering, but there was no one to ask for a blanket-wrapped rock to alleviate the chill. Dear God, what if she was really having the baby! Gerald would be no help, she could not do it by herself—she would be at the mercy of Mrs. Whittacre's "charity." Abhorrent thought! Another contraction, stronger this time. Definitely painful. Tears squeezed through her lashes. It was no longer a question of "if" she was having the baby. She'd given birth to two children, she recognized the feeling.

She felt the schooner jiggle as Gerald, presumably, got in. "Maggie?" a voice said.

A familiar voice, but not Gerald. A woman's voice. Stunned, Maggie emerged from the covers and stared at the visitor. "Katrin?" she whispered. "Katrin!" The women embraced each other enthusiastically, Maggie sputtering incoherent questions. "Is it really you? But how . . .?"

"Now, calm yourself," Katrin soothed. "Doc told me he was coming down here to see to a Mrs. Freiler who was having troubles with a baby. I asked a few questions and knew it was you he was talking about. Silly old Dutchman finally remembered you'd sent me greetings. I brought my boys along to help out. I see you're gettin' a house of your own here . . ."

Maggie doubled up as another contraction took her. "Oh, Katrin, I'm so glad you're here," she gasped.

"*Gott in Himmel*! You're havin' that babe now, aren't you? Bit early? I'll get Doc in here and we'll just take care of things," Katrin declared calmly.

Maggie could have wept with relief.

She lay snug and warm in the high bed, watching the snow fall past the window. It was thick, rippled glass and it looked like the flakes all made a short detour to the right, then back, as they fell. She was loath to get up, but she had to soon, for this was "moving day." The last shingles and calking had been done the day before, she'd been told; at long last, she was moving into her own house.

She forced herself to stir, very careful not to disturb the tiny baby sleeping beside her. "We're going home today, Mary," she whispered as she tucked the covers snugly about the infant. She stood for a moment, looking at the miniature beauty of the baby. She had not believed for a long time that her daughter could live, she was so very little. More like a china toy than a real infant. In fact, most of her clothing was doll clothes that Mrs. Whittacre had unearthed from a chest. Yet her delicacy had been misleading, for she had thrived after that first uneasy week of constant care.

The birth had been easy enough—probably because the baby was so small—but Maggie had known the moment she saw her that pride must be put aside for the sake of the child's survival. When Katrin announced that Maggie and the baby *had* to be moved to the mission, Maggie had not raised a word of objection. This infinitesimal bit of life couldn't possibly survive the rigors of living outdoors.

Nor had living in Mrs. Whittacre's back room been as bad as Maggie had imagined. The minister's wife, though childless and not at all fond of children in general, was almost idiotically charmed by babies, the littler the better, and Maggie's tiny china doll had completely stolen her heart. Mrs. Whittacre insisted, that first month or so, that the room be kept warm, and would come in several times each day to put extra logs on the fire. It was sometimes so hot that Maggie felt sweat trickling down her sides, and the windows would fog up. She worried that Mrs. Whittacre might burn the building down around them in an effort to keep the baby warm, but perhaps it was the heat that had kept little Mary alive.

Maggie and Mrs. Whittacre were still wary of each other, and both had to make a concentrated effort to be civil, but Maggie was grateful just the same, and had vowed to curb her tongue and temper where the older woman was concerned.

There was a light knock on the door. Maggie opened it to find James and Benjamin outside. "Schooner baby awake, Mommy?" Benjamin asked.

"No, dear, Mary's still sleeping. Do you want to look at her?"

He and James nodded solemnly and came in. They endured Maggie's hugs and kisses, but their real interest was in the little bundle in the bed. Maggie's sons had been the only thing about which she had faced down Mrs. Whittacre. Maggie had insisted that the boys be allowed to visit as frequently as they wanted, and they had spent most nights sleeping in the room with Maggie and their new little sister while Gerald stayed with Woody.

The boys managed to wake the baby, but it was time for her feeding anyway. She came alive, screaming with lusty hunger, and Maggie put her to her breast and sat contentedly rocking in a chair while the boys played a marble game on the floor in front of the fire. Katrin arrived a few minutes later, pink-cheeked from the cold. "It's all ready for you, Maggie," she said. "I just finished the sweeping up, and there's a hot kettle of tea brewing. I've got that pretty cradle of yours all fitted out and ready for the schooner baby."

"What about the hex book?"

"It's safe on the shelf, just like you asked," Katrin assured her.

She bustled around packing up the last of Maggie's meager belongings and keeping up a stream of pleasant chatter. Hutchens had sent word that he would be back to check on Maggie and the baby within the next week or so, and Helmut Clay was sending increasingly cranky messages to Katrin about her plans for returning. "Next time anyone passes through on the way to the fort, I'll be going with them," she said. "I want to be back in time for Christmas. It'll be the last one we spend there."

"Last Christmas at the fort? Why?"

"Helmut's commission is up come spring, and I think he's just weary enough of army life not to renew it."

"What will you do?" Maggie asked. She felt a twinge of panic. What if Katrin moved away—went back east or farther west? How lonely she would be, having her friend too far away to visit.

"Don't rightly know. Settle down somewheres. Watching this house of yours get built has given me a real longing for one of my own. I never minded army life till this past year or so, but folks change, I suppose, even me. My, but that's a hungry child! Boys, you go get your pa and tell him to bring the carriage up to the door. It's time to take your mama and the schooner baby home."

Maggie chuckled. "She's Mary—not the schooner baby," she said.

"No, 'Mary' is a name for a grown-up, like the woman she was named for. Your husband's mother, didn't you say? But this baby was born in a schooner, and she's a schooner baby to me, same as with everyone. 'Schooner' is a right pretty word." She took the now-sleeping infant from Maggie and wrapped her in a couple more layers of blankets. "Now, you get bundled up real good, Maggie. It's time for you to go home to Seven Trees."

14

"Where is Red Deer?" Maggie asked the five little Indian girls who had presented themselves at the door for afternoon sewing lessons.

"Gone now, missus. Chief come for Red Deer and Rushing Water. Time for planting," one of the girls said.

Red Deer and Rushing Water were Delawares, Maggie remembered. That made three tribes now that had reclaimed their children for the spring planting. Fourteen children of the forty at the mission gone. Soon she would have no one to teach. "We shall have our class outside today," Maggie told her students. "We have been inside all winter, and the spring air will do us good."

The girls were too well trained, both by their Indian families and Mrs. Whittacre, to show overt enthusiasm for the plan, but Maggie could tell by their shy smiles that it met with their complete approval. "Schooner baby too, missus?" the youngest, a pretty girl of five, asked.

"Oh, yes, Schooner too. I wouldn't leave her behind," Maggie assured them. She gathered up the baby, who was now sitting up on her own fairly well, and said, "White Flower, you get the quilt and bring it along, please. We will sit in the sun by the ferry landing, and perhaps Mr. Woodline will tell us stories while we work."

But Woody was not available for stories that day. He had just ferried the last of three wagons across the Kaw and got off the ferry swearing colorfully. "Beggin' yer pardon, Miz Freiler," he said sheepishly when he noticed Maggie and the girls.

"What's wrong, Woody?"

"Ain't much. Broken gear is all, wouldn't take a blacksmith half an hour to fix it, but now I gotta spend the time firin' up the forge. It'll take till night nearly, and then this fella's got a creeper," he said, gesturing to one of the wagons he'd just brought across. There were three men standing by it, shaking their heads over a rear wheel. "Here, you," Woody said to an Indian boy who had made the mistake of venturing too close.

127

"You go tell the reverend to get somebody to start up the fires in the forge." He turned back to Maggie. "You see, ma'am, these big wooden wheels have to have an iron band around them so's they don't jest wear away. When the wood shrinks the least bit, the band goes all slippery and comes off."

"I know. Captain Bruckner told me about the problem last fall."

"Well, this fella's a city fella who don't know green wood from cured, and somebody sold him a slapdash wagon. He's got to have that band tightened up now, or he'll never get five miles out, and I gotta spend the day in the damned forge 'cause of it. Like as not, somebody'll turn up wantin' to cross just about the time I got the fire stoked up. I ain't a blacksmith, dammit. I can't do everythin' 'round here."

"Have you talked to Reverend Whittacre about a blacksmith?" Maggie asked, trying to divert his growing anger to a productive line of thought.

"Hell, yes. Beggin' yer pardon, I talked to him. He's sent fer two fellas to come out. One of 'em got in a knife fight in Saint Louis and lost the use of his hand. The other died of dysentery or some fool thing before he got that far. He wants to get the Indian boys to learn the trade, even though the chiefs give him some tomfoolery about fire gods." Woody chuckled in spite of his anger. "Fire gods! Near makes the reverend spit Bibles. They don't believe it, of course, they just don't like jobs that hot—can't say's I blame 'em." He moved off to consult with the men around the wagon.

Maggie got the girls settled with their quilt squares and checked the progress each was making; then she slung Schooner on her hip and went over to the wagon. The men all doffed their hats courteously and then went back to talking while she looked at the bad wheel. Finally she turned to Woody. "I wonder, would there be enough work here for a full-time blacksmith?"

"Enough work! Sure as sure. Specially this time of year. Seems like there's more folk every summer come through here. Why do you ask, Miz Freiler?"

"I just wondered. There might be somebody . . ."

Her thoughts kept going back to the conversation all afternoon. That night, after the children were fed and in bed and Gerald was deep in a book, Maggie went out for a walk. But it was not merely an aimless walk—she went to the forge, where Woody, true to his pessimistic predictions, was still at work. "I'm keeping your dinner warm," she told him.

"Sorry, ma'am. I couldn't leave this, and there weren't anybody around to take you a message," he said, huffing over the bellows.

"It doesn't matter. Have you worked on that wheel yet?"

"Jest gettin' ready to now." He gestured to the dismantled wheel lying in the corner of the tiny shed that served as occasional blacksmith shop.

Maggie went over and took a look. The wheel, like those on the schooner, was almost five feet in diameter. It was made of curved pieces of wood fitted together. Woody had already removed the tire—the piece of iron that went outside, protecting the wood and holding the wheel together, unless it was, like this one, a "creeper." The iron band was like a thick, heavy ribbon, smooth on the inside and outside. Maggie waited until Woody got to a stopping point and was leaning against a bench wiping his face with a handkerchief. "I ken be just as sinful as I want, I figure," he said. "God wouldn't send me to hell, 'cause he's lookin' down now and I know I already ben there. Jesus! This is hot work!"

"Woody, let me ask you something. What if you made this tire, the iron part, with a big ridge along the center—on the inside?"

"That's easy. It wouldn't fit the rim."

"No. I mean make a ridge on the band and a notch to fit it along the outside of the wood rim. . . ."

Woody slowly lowered the handkerchief, crossed his arms, and thought for a moment. "If you were to do that . . . why, Miz Freiler, I think you got a damned good idea there."

"Even if it was green wood and shrank some, the tire would stay in place, wouldn't it?" Maggie asked. "At least it wouldn't slip sideways."

"No, and it can't slip around, 'cause it's bolted on at the weld. You know, I think you got somethin' there. Mighty pretty lady to be so all-fired smart," he said, and smiled.

"Thank you. Could we build one and try it?"

"I don't know enough to, ma'am. Best I can do is jest little repairs and such. You'd need a real blacksmith, and a carpenter maybe to make the wheel special. But you sure got a good idea there, you surely do! Now, you step aside, Miz Freiler, I'm gonna make some sparks here, and I don't want you gettin' burned. I'll be over for my dinner shortly."

So it might work. Maggie went back to the house with a

spring in her step. She had hesitated to ask Woody about it for fear he would tell her some reason why her idea was useless. But he hadn't! That was very encouraging.

Gerald had thrown an extra log on the fire so that he could see to read a little longer. Maggie joined him in front of the blaze and sat rocking gently for a while. The way they were living seemed to suit him—even though he would have disagreed. He taught classroom lessons only in the mornings; most afternoons he took his Indian students outdoors, and he was looking very fit and tanned. Though he protested mildly about having to teach, his heart wasn't in the complaints. Reverend Whittacre dared not attempt to enforce the sort of regulations that Gerald had gotten in trouble with in the past, for the minister had no way to replace him—and they both knew it. And Gerald was a good teacher, when left to his own methods. Reverend Whittacre knew that, too.

Their lives appeared, on the surface of things, very stable now. They had a house, healthy children, worthwhile work to do—and yet they were both dissatisfied in their different ways. The barrier that had sprung up between them was still there. Gerald wanted to get ahead, earn enough money to try their luck trading in Santa Fe, as he had originally intended. Maggie wanted to make money for . . . For what? She wasn't sure. For security, for more comfort for their children, for a hundred small things—a new bolt of dress fabric that wasn't a charitable contribution from Mrs. Whittacre, a new bed for the boys that wasn't handed down from someone else. Mostly because the German blood in her meant that she should earn and save money because it was the Right Thing To Do.

She couldn't tell Gerald it would take many years to earn and save enough to go to Santa Fe. Time enough for facing the truth. Perhaps . . . A diamond flicker of hope sparkled momentarily: perhaps he would find something he was very good at and would lose his interest in going to Mexico.

"Gerald," she said finally, "I need to go to Leavenworth for a few days. To the fort. I'll take Schooner with me. Can you watch the boys?"

He closed his book and set it carefully on a shelf next to the fireplace. "You want to visit Katrin? That would be good for you. The boys are no trouble."

"It's not exactly to visit Katrin, not entirely. I have an idea for a better kind of wagon wheel. I talked to Woody about it,

130

and I need to talk to Katrin's husband, Helmut. He's a blacksmith, you know."

"A better wagon wheel? I adore you, Maggie. Most women spend their lives thinking up new quilt patterns and different ways to bake cornbread, but you think of better wagon wheels!" He took her upturned face in his hands and kissed her long and lingeringly.

But he didn't seem to realize she was quite serious. "Would you rather I came up with quilt patterns?" Maggie asked a little snappishly.

"Dear God, *no*. Leave that to the ordinary women. Do you mind my asking what you're going to do with these special wagon wheels?"

"Sell them, of course. We are living in a complete barter society. We teach the Indians, for which we are provided food. There's no money involved. It's pleasant enough, but not getting us anywhere."

"You're right. But where does Helmut Clay come into this?"

"Katrin told me that Helmut was tired of the army and was going to set out on his own this summer. What better place than here? There is a need for a blacksmith full time in the summers to teach the boys and take care of necessary repairs, and in the winters he could make the wagon wheels. We could sell them for him and make a little on each one in the spring when the wagons start going through." Maggie went on to explain to him what Woody had told her about the ever-increasing traffic and the problems of creepers.

By the time she was through, Gerald was fully as excited about the prospect as she was. "The chiefs are taking all the children back for spring planting anyway, and there won't be much teaching to be done in the spring—no students. The timing is perfect," Gerald said. "But won't it cost something to get started? You can't expect Helmut Clay to buy the materials, build the wheels, and let you make the money selling them, even if he likes the idea."

"Well . . ." Maggie hesitated. She had been rather hoping he wouldn't take quite this much interest. But she could not lie to him. "Gerald, we had a little money left over after we bought our supplies—a hundred dollars, in fact."

"You've been keeping that a secret, eh? Good heavens, you look like you're expecting me to be angry about it."

"You're not?"

"Of course not. It wouldn't have done us any good until

131

now anyway. I'm glad you have it, otherwise I'd have to go over to Westport Landing and rob something."

Maggie tried to picture Gerald robbing someone and ended up in giggles.

There were, as Maggie saw it, two problems. First, she would have to convince the Clays. Second, and far worse in her estimation, she would have to cross the Kaw—twice. Once going and again coming back. But Woody, sensing her unreasonable fear, talked to her all the way across, assuring her that the water was as peaceful as could be and she was in no danger whatsoever. She didn't quite believe him, but white-knuckled and trembling, she was delivered to the far bank with the rest of the train that was traveling between the mission and the fort.

Helmut Clay was a big, silent man with arms like knotted tree trunks and bushy white-blond eyebrows that met in a perpetual scowl. It took Maggie a while to realize that his disposition was not as fierce as his looks. He seldom allowed a smile to mar his forbidding features. His speech, when he said anything at all, was a harsh, guttural mix of English and German. Katrin and Maggie chattered at him for two days about making the move to the mission. Maggie felt like a bird thrashing uselessly against a block of granite, but to her surprise, he finally agreed to the plan.

There were, however, some difficulties. The Clays had saved very little money, and Maggie had to assure them that she would finance the venture as best she could with her pitiful little store of cash. Neither was there anyplace for them to live at the mission. Maggie assured them there would be a house waiting for them, or at least the beginning of a house. How she would manage that, she didn't know, but somehow she would keep the promise.

"But it's illegal for us to settle in the territory," Katrin said. "I had forgotten!"

"It's not illegal if Helmut is willing to teach the Indian boys blacksmithing," Maggie said.

Katrin's lips curved contemptuously at the mention of Indians, but she said nothing. "*Ja*, I vill do that," Helmut said, indicating for the first time his willingness, if not enthusiasm, for Maggie's plan.

The other problem involved the actual construction of the wheels. Helmut was a blacksmith, not a carpenter or wheelwright.

132

"What about Cyrus Vratil?" Katrin asked him. "They left the fort last year to do some farming," she explained to Maggie. "But they aren't doing very well at it. Some sort of blight, then the oldest boy took sick and couldn't help—Cyrus was a good carpenter. Might be willin' to go back to it by now."

Helmut nodded.

"Might want to do his farming down closer to the mission and just work on the wagons part of the time."

Helmut nodded again.

"You think you might ride out there tomorrow and ask him about it?" Katrin asked.

Helmut nodded.

"There's an army train leaving for Santa Fe in a day or two, Maggie. You and me will go along with them, and I can pick out a place for the house. That suit you, Helmut?"

"*Ja*. Suit me," he said, still scowling.

"Then it's settled. Now, Maggie, you hand that baby over and let me cuddle her for a bit. I'm gonna have another of my own before long, you know."

"Katrin! Why didn't you tell me sooner?"

Katrin started making faces at Schooner, who gurgled with delight. "Wasn't sure until lately. Sure will be nice to have our own place to raise a baby. And you and me being so close—it'll be grand, won't it?"

Maggie basked in Katrin's optimism. "Yes, it will be grand."

Unfortunately, things didn't work out quite as well in practice as they had in theory. The Clays' house did get built, mainly through Woody's efforts. He was so glad to have someone coming to serve as blacksmith that he worked far into the night and even managed to get Gerald to work quickly. Reverend Whittacre, too, said a blacksmith would be a welcome addition to the tiny community, and though he wasn't much help, at least he didn't actually hinder them. He even used some of the mission funds to hire some workers from Westport Landing to help with the roof.

Katrin had selected a site for their house a hundred yards or so from Freilers', and she and Maggie were delighted to have each other's company. The difficulty, however, was with the wheel business. Contrary to Katrin's suppositions, Cyrus Vratil had not wanted to abandon his farm and join them, though he had a good stand of trees and agreed to make the wheels and ship them to the mission to be grooved and

133

banded. The first shipment wasn't loaded properly and tilted off the ferry to wash downstream. Only eight of the twenty were recovered. They had already paid Vratil two dollars per wheel, so they had lost nearly a fourth of their investment before even getting started.

They set the recovered wheels out to dry while Woody and Helmut rigged a treadle-powered mechanism that Maggie and Katrin could use to cut the groove around the outside edge. As they finished this job, Helmut affixed the metal bands to each, and they were ready. The first of the military escorts for the wagon trains was forming up and came through the morning after they completed the first eight wheels. They were camping that night at the mission, and Maggie got Helmut to accompany her to talk to Captain Bruckner, who had led the wagon train to Santa Fe.

"Well, if it isn't Helmut Clay!" he boomed. "Ready to sign up for another hitch yet? You've been out of the army a month now. How is everything going, Helmut?"

Helmut nodded contentment.

"But this here isn't your Katrin," he said of Maggie. "Why, you're Mrs. . . . uh . . ."

"Freiler, Maggie Freiler," she prompted.

"Yes'm. I'd have had it in a minute. The Doc told me you'd gotten along all right with that baby. Sure was pleased to hear it, ma'am. After all you folks went through last summer, I'm glad to hear you're doing well."

"I'd be doing better, sir, if you could take a look at something Mr. Clay and I have been working on," Maggie said bluntly.

He seemed taken aback somewhat by this forthright, nongiddy reaction to his small talk. "What's that?" he asked.

"Mr. Clay and I have come up with an idea for a genuinely superior wagon wheel. I'd like for you to come see them and consider giving them a try on some of your wagons."

Bruckner looked a question at Helmut, who nodded. "Might as well, ma'am," he said a little doubtfully, and followed them to where the wheels stood stacked behind the Freilers' house.

"Sure sounds like it ought to work," he said after inspecting them. "And it would cut some time off the trip if we could keep on going instead of having to stop and fix wheels and soak them at every little stream. Don't know, though. Things sometimes sound good and don't work out for one reason or another."

"We've only got eight of them right now," Maggie stepped in before he could think of any more specific doubt. "I'll give them to you. Put them on the back of four of your wagons now. If they work, you can pay us when you get back." Out of the corner of her eye she noticed that Helmut looked somewhat startled, and she added, "If that's agreeable to Mr. Clay—he's my partner in this."

Helmut rubbed his stubbled chin for a moment, scowled ferociously at Bruckner and back at Maggie. Then he nodded agreement.

"Well, ma'am, I can't pass that up. What do you want for 'em?"

"The usual price for a good cured wheel is about three dollars, isn't it? If ours are as good as we think, they'll sell for four dollars. Is that agreeable?"

Now Bruckner rubbed his chin, considering. "Don't suppose that's a haggling price, is it?"

Maggie shook her head. "No. If they work, they're worth it. If they don't, they're not worth anything to you or to us. Four dollars is the price."

He looked at her with a puzzled expression for a moment. He'd never done business with a lady before—not real "business," and certainly not with real ladies, only a few flinty whores peddling their doubtful wares. But this Mrs. Freiler was . . . different somehow. "I'll try 'em. We ought to pass through here going back in five or six weeks. I'll let you know how they work and pay for 'em if they've been better than the ordinary."

For the first time Maggie relaxed enough to smile. "Thank you, Captain Bruckner."

He returned her smile and thought how odd it was. She was damned attractive, really. Wonderful figure, pretty blond hair, alluring smile—*when* she smiled. The only smart women he'd ever known were downright ugly. He'd always thought the two went together. "I'll send some of my men up to get the wheels." He shook Maggie's hand firmly. Turning to Helmut, he said, "I almost forgot to tell you, that Frenchy friend of yours—uh, Torchy?—been lookin' for you at the fort. He's on a terrible binge. Carting around a skinny old lady and two snot-nosed kids and drinking like a parched field. Told him you were down here, and if he ever sobers up, you might get a visit. 'Least I hope so. I don't want him hanging around the fort all summer with that old bitch."

Maggie hardly heard this. She was excited about the prospect of getting her wheels on wagons and finding out if they really solved the problems they were meant to.

15

The next shipment of wagon wheels was overdue, so the next day Maggie took Schooner, James, and her darning down by the ferry dock to wait. Schooner had been cranky for several days, and suspecting an earache, Maggie had the baby's ears covered with wool pads and a cap to protect her from the light wind. Benjamin was with the Reverend Whittacre, studying his numbers, something he'd shown a surprising aptitude for, which the minister was happy to encourage. "Not yet five, and he can do his addition combinations up to twenty and reads as well as a child three years older!" Reverend Whittacre had proclaimed enthusiastically, and took the boy under his special care. Gerald was elated at having a little reader to encourage, and Maggie was pleased too, but she found herself wishing sometimes that her eldest showed a little more of his father—some of his sparkle and gaiety. He was such a serious little boy. More than serious, really—stodgy almost, and downright unfriendly to most of the other children, including little James, who adored him. She consoled herself that he was young yet, it might be just a phase of his development. Still, James was so loving and so much easier to cuddle. He had flashes of Maggie's temper and was easily brought to tears by the most minor slight, but such storms were generally over quickly.

Then there was Schooner—she was Maggie's delight. Maggie didn't even think of her as "Mary" anymore. At seven months, she had more than made up for her premature start in life. She was as large and sturdy as the boys had been at that age. She could sit up by herself for long periods of time without toppling over, and she could make her way from one place to another on her stomach, though not yet on her knees.

The little Indian girls who made such a fuss over her in the spring would certainly be surprised at her progress when they returned to the mission. Reverend Whittacre said that the chiefs would be bringing some of the children back anytime now. Their tribes usually wanted them back for the spring planting and the fall harvesting, but they were allowed to stay at the mission and continue their studies in the winter and the summer. Maggie missed the Indian children, their black eyes bright with secret matters that no "civilized" white man could penetrate, their quiet, intent games, and their bronze beauty. It seemed lonely at the mission with most of them gone.

Her thoughts were interrupted by the sound of voices from the far side of the river. "Woody," she called. "You have passengers over there."

He emerged from his little house, which was more of a shed than a home. "Is it Vratil with the wheels?" he asked, squinting against the sun. "Don't look like it."

By the time Woody was halfway back, Maggie could tell who his passengers were. A tall man in buckskin, with flaming red hair, reeling drunk and swearing in an unprejudiced mixture of French and English. In the center of the flat ferry raft stood an older woman clutching two red-haired children to her rust-black skirts. Maggie gathered her children up and went to tell Helmut that his friend Torchy had arrived, and then followed him back to the ferry landing.

Torchy fell off the raft before it was tied up and waded in. "Helmut! Dear old friend. Observe at what life has done to me. Just look!" he wailed dramatically as he threw himself at a surprised Helmut. "I'm done—done, done, done. *Finis!* *Quelle tragédie!*"

Woody tied up the raft and helped the woman and children up the muddy bank. The woman wasn't much older than Torchy—probably forty-five to his forty, Maggie guessed—but there was something innately aged and grandmotherly in her appearance. Her graying hair was braided tightly and wound in a tiny bun that looked like a rounded rock at the back of her head. Instead of the wide-brimmed bonnet that most women wore to protect them from the sun, she wore a much-mended lace cap and carried a decrepit parasol of silk that had once been black and now matched her faded black dress. Her skin was wrinkled, but as fair as fresh milk. She had thin, pursed lips and snapping black eyes under heavy brows. She glared at Torchy, and her expression was the definition of disapproval.

Maggie stepped forward and took her hand. "How do you do," she said. "I'm Maggie Freiler. Welcome."

137

The woman's bony hand was as cold as her manner. She stared at Maggie critically for a moment and said, *"Je ne comprends pas."*

Torchy managed, through his own loud diatribe, to catch this. He staggered over. "You damn well do *comprends!*" he shouted, nose to nose with her. "You old witch, you think to make me look foolish!"

The woman raised her chin a bit like a good hausfrau who has detected a bad smell and was trying to determine its origin. Maggie nearly laughed. As if this woman, or anyone else, was necessary to make Torchy look foolish. He was doing so well at it without any help at all.

"This wicked old prune is the mother of my wife," he explained to Maggie, some of the slur going out of his voice. "Gran'mère Charron—the grandmother of *mes enfants*. My poor motherless children." With this he began crying again, dramatic Gallic sobs.

The children, about three years old and obviously twins, looked up at him with wide, unfrightened gazes. Perhaps they are accustomed to this, Maggie thought. She knelt down and spoke to them. "Hello, my name is Mrs. Freiler and this is James," she said, pulling him forward. "What are your names?"

The children stared at her, smiling slightly but obviously not understanding her. Maggie pointed to herself, said her name, did the same with James and Schooner, then pointed at the little girl. Her pale blue eyes lit up with comprehension. "Beatrice," she said in a shy, lisping voice. Then she pointed to her brother. "Jacques."

The older woman, Gran'mère Charron, as Torchy had called her, turned to him and shot a spate of French. Maggie had thought French a pretty-sounding language until she heard this woman speak it. She had apparently asked a question. Torchy shrugged elaborately, losing his balance in the process and falling heavily against Helmut. "How am I to know? Go wherever you wish. Leave me my dear little ones is all I ask of you."

Gran'mère Charron spoke again, and Maggie guessed it was pretty strong stuff, for even Torchy looked shocked and the two red-haired children giggled. "Come with me," Maggie said, taking the woman's arm and leading her to Seven Trees. She might not have understood the words, but she recognized hospitality and followed along stiffly.

Maggie got out a bit of her precious tea supply and made

138

a steaming kettle of it. She gave the children cups of milk and some fresh bread, and all the while she kept up a running monologue on the theory that it was more pleasant than silence, even if the older woman didn't understand it. She suspected that she did, however, and was pretending not to, for once Maggie said something wrong—got her words mixed up—and the woman smiled a little behind her hand.

The children soon began to look sleepy, and Maggie spread some quilts on the wooden floor so that they and her own could all take naps. She noticed Gran'mère Charron yawning too, and she managed to convey that she was going out for a while and that the older woman should rest while she was gone. She wished Katrin was here. She had gone with her sons to Westport Landing to purchase some cloth, and wouldn't be back until late in the day. Katrin could deal with this situation so much better.

She walked slowly back down to the ferry. Woody was sitting in front of his house, whittling industriously. "That man was so liquored up you could get drunk just breathin' the same air as him," he said admiringly. "Don't see how he kept upright, and I thought fer sure he was gonna turn my raft over on us."

He pulled a chair out and set it up so Maggie could join him in his shady patch. "What do you suppose has become of Mr. Vratil?" she asked.

Woody shrugged. "Busy time a year on a farm. Might not a gotten time to work on 'em. Wish I could make them wheels fer ya, ma'am."

"I wish you could too, Woody. The whole idea may go to waste if Mr. Vratil doesn't keep up his end of the bargain." She said it lightly, but it had become a very serious concern to her. It had been one thing to go find a blacksmith, but how could she go find a wheelwright? She didn't even know of any, not like she had known Katrin. Perhaps someone in Westport Landing . . .

She sat in the shade with Woody for a while, chatting amiably, and finally decided that the children and Gran'mère were probably awake and she should go back. As she walked up the hill, she heard children's voices.

Were the Indian children coming back? She changed her route and hurried to the mission to alert Reverend Whittacre. By the time he emerged, there was an impressive group approaching the main building. In the center of the group of children was a tall, fierce-looking man on a huge horse. God-like in his dignity and bronzly beautiful, he was shirtless and had long, glossy black hair in thick braids with bright fabric and feathers wound in. But his trousers and boots were those of a white man, as was the saddle on the horse. His skin looked like perfectly cut, unseamed topaz silk. Maggie came as close as she ever had to blushing when she became aware of how carefully she was scrutinizing him.

"Reverend Whittacre," the proud Indian said in amazingly cultured tones, "I have brought the children of my tribe back. I shall return for them when it is time for the harvest."

Maggie was dumbfounded. He spoke better English than most of the people who lived here. "God's blessing on you, Black Feather," Reverend Whittacre was saying. It seemed that he was in awe of the man as well. "I see there are two more children."

The Indian (a chief, it seemed) snapped his fingers and two children climbed off their ponies and stepped forward. "Dancing Bird is not strong. His mother has kept him at her side, for he cannot work well. He must be learned in book matters so that he may serve the tribe with his mind instead of his back." Dancing Bird, a spindly boy of about ten, looked frightened but did not drop his gaze under the minister's scrutiny. "This one," the Indian went on, indicating a girl of seven or so, "is a foundling. She is not of our tribe, but we shall take responsibility for her. She was the only survivor in a village that took the pox."

The rest of the children, ten or more, slid expertly off their ponies and came forward one at a time to greet Reverend Whittacre.

Black Feather got off his massive horse and strode forward, a packet in his hand. "Dancing Bird often has an ear ailment. When this occurs, a mixture of this powder and water will relieve it," he said, and handed it to the minister. Then he remounted and without a word rode off. Maggie was enveloped in a swarm of little girls asking about Schooner and the boys, but while she greeted them, she kept an eye on the retreating figure and was glad to see that he stopped by the Clays' house.

She excused herself from Reverend Whittacre and the girls and hurried to catch up with him. "Pardon me, but what was that you gave him for the child's earache?" she asked.

The Indian did not answer right away, and Maggie had a moment to study his features at close range. His face was like a work of art sculptured from the finest-grain wood. The impassive planes would have seemed lifeless had it not been for the critical intelligence in his dark eyes. It was impossible to guess what he was thinking of her question. Finally he said gravely, "It is a dried, powdered root. Why do you ask?"

"Would it work on a very small child?"

"Probably. Would you like to try it?"

"It's safe . . . ?" she asked, then felt foolish. "I'm sorry, I know it must be or you wouldn't have given it to Dancing Bird."

If the man had taken offense at being questioned, he showed no sign. He reached into the saddlebag and pulled out another, smaller packet and handed it to her wordlessly. Something about him intimidated her. It wasn't fear, though she could imagine him inspiring fear if he so chose. It was his awesome dignity that made her feel strange. His granite eyes were perfectly composed, his posture straight and proud; he seemed to emanate a sense of his own worth. "Are you a medicine man?" she asked.

The corner of his mouth twitched, whether in humor or derision, she could not guess. "If you wish to use such a term, you may," he said.

"You are Shawnee, aren't you?" It was silly to question him, and she sensed that she was somehow belittling herself to do so, but she was intrigued by this handsome red man and wished to draw him out.

But he merely nodded and said, "I am."

Just then there was a commotion in the Clays' house. Torchy burst through the doors and landed at Maggie's feet. Helmut was only a few steps behind, carrying a pail of water. Maggie quickly moved aside as he flung the cold water in Torchy's face. The Frenchman shook, sputtered, swore resoundingly and multilingually, and collapsed. Maggie glanced at Black Feather and caught him in a second of unawareness. His lips were curled in distaste; then suddenly, as if feeling her glance, he was as before—bland, dignified, secretive. She felt the urge to apologize and wondered why. Black Feather dug into the saddlebag again and leaned down toward her. Speaking very quietly, he said, "A spoonful of this in a cup of strong coffee will bring him to his senses," and before she could utter a word of thanks, he was gone.

A week later they were still waiting for the wheels. There had been no word from Cyrus Vratil, and Maggie finished each day angrier and more depressed than the day before.

Black Feather's remedies had proved effective for Schooner's earache and temporarily effective for Torchy's condition, but as soon as they got him sobered up, he had taken Reverend Whittacre's horse and had ridden off to Westport Landing, where he resumed his drinking. Three days later he had returned, bleary-eyed and hung-over, but sober. He was pleasant and painstakingly courteous to everyone, but this didn't seem to soften Gran'mère Charron's heart a bit. She was staying with the Clays, and the children, Beatrice and Jacques, were sleeping at Maggie's house, and every time Gran'mère got anywhere near Torchy, she would hurl a bit of sibilant French venom at him.

"It tears her heart that Jeanne loved me," Torchy explained one evening as he and the Clays and the Freilers sat together over a late dinner. Gran'mère Charron had eaten in silence and departed in invective.

"Your wife?" Maggie asked.

"*Oui*. Her daughter. She had plans for Jeanne to go back to France and be a grand lady. Jeanne preferred to marry me. When Jeanne died these months past . . . well, she blames me for that too, though it was simply the 'delicacy'—it is for this reason I had left her and the children in Sainte Genevieve. Rather they had been with me, but the life, it would have been too hard." The drunken spree seemed to have taken the top layer of the pain from him, but there was still a catch in his voice when he spoke of his dead wife. He sat silently for a while, then said, "The life, it is too hard for me as well. I cannot endure another winter half-buried in the snow wondering if I will starve before it melts."

"I thought you probably enjoyed trapping," Gerald said.

Torchy shook his head. "The trapping, no. The selling, *oui*. All year I think of it—going to Saint Louis, seeing the old friends and new buildings, talking to the buyers . . . Ah, the knowing you have gotten a good price, of having the pockets full of money—this is why I do it. But it is not to be. I cannot leave my children with old Charron all year. She will have them to hate me before they were of enough years to know me. This I owe Jeanne—they have lost their mother, I cannot remove from them their father as well."

"What will you do?" Gerald asked, leaning back in his chair and lighting the foul-smelling pipe he had taken to smoking.

"*Je ne sais pas*. Take them all to Saint Louis? Get work

142

there of some sort? I have no skills but trapping and selling furs. Perhaps there will be something . . ."

"Why don't you sell wagon wheels?" Maggie asked, not really meaning to speak aloud. But the thought had bubbled up with a force of its own and had broken free.

"Wheels?" Torchy asked.

Maggie leaned forward, elbows on table, and explained about the special band on the wagon wheels. "We can probably sell a fair number to people coming through here in the summers, but if we could sell them in Saint Louis to the wagon *makers*—think how many more would be needed!"

"But why doesn't Helmut, or you, Mr. Freiler, take them?"

"I must teach at the mission," Gerald answered, "and Helmut has to be here to work as blacksmith. Besides," he added bluntly, "Helmut doesn't like to talk to anyone, and I'm not exactly a businessman. But you've said that you *like* selling."

Torchy was leaning forward now too, eyes alert. "This is possible. *Oui*. I would only be away for short times. Bea and Jacques could attend schooling with real teachers, not with their Gran'mère. *Bien!* Show me the wheels you speak of. How many are ready now?"

Maggie sagged. "We haven't any. We have been waiting for them to arrive."

"Arrive? From where?"

"A man with a farm near the fort is supposed to be making them, but something has happened . . ."

"But no, you must construct them here. This is better for the making of money," Torchy said.

"I know, but we haven't a wheelwright."

Torchy started laughing. "The trip to Westport was not a waste, then. The companion of my revels was a carpenter who had fallen into disagreement with a neighbor and wished to leave the community. It was his sorrow that he had nowhere to go to make a living without returning to the East. This place, this Seven Trees, would suit him, I think. And his skills would suit us, no?"

Maggie felt some doubts about any "companion of Torchy's revels," but there was little choice. They needed a carpenter or wheelwright, and there were not legions of them to select from.

"Should I speak to him of this?" he asked.

"Yes," Maggie said, "but Helmut and I must meet him before we decide. And Helmut must be consulted about the rest

143

of it—selling in Saint Louis and how much you will make for your efforts and such."

Torchy rose, kissed her hand formally. "Madame, it will arrange itself."

"No. *We* will arrange it."

"*Bien. We* will arrange it."

16

~

"I'll give you my honest opinion, Miz Freiler," Captain Bruckner said. "Didn't have a creeper in the bunch, but the wheels themselves weren't the best. Spokes kept working loose. Might help, too, if you could make 'em a little lighter. Don't know how you'd do that, but I'm glad to pay you what you asked for them just the same. Even the way they are is better than the usual."

Maggie asked him to rest himself over a cup of coffee while she conferred with Helmut. When she returned she said, "We've got a new wheelwright. He's more reliable and more skilled than the man we had before. I've got other wheels here—they're not lighter, but they're made better and I'll give them to you in place of the ones you used on this trip."

"Well, ma'am, that's not necessary," Bruckner said, but it was obvious that he was pleased and impressed at the fairness of this. "I don't see how you're gonna make much money this way, though. You gotta look out for yourself, ma'am, you know."

"I *am* looking out for myself. We've already made one improvement and we'll make more. You bought eight wheels the first time and you can trade them now for eight more. Every time we make them better you can trade the eight to prove to yourself that we're providing the finest-quality wheels in the territory."

"Can't ask for more than that, ma'am. I'll take your eight new ones, all right. I should be making one more trip to Santa Fe through here. Can you supply me with, say, two dozen?"

Maggie thought of the lonely six wheels that Torchy had

left behind after taking a dozen with him to Saint Louis a few days earlier. "Yes," she said, sounding more confident than she felt. Somehow those wheels would be ready, if she had to whittle them herself. "How long will it be until you return?"

"Two, three weeks. I'll be paying cash for 'em this time."

They talked a little longer, drew up an informal contract, and discussed future needs the army might have for wheels. Bruckner was sitting a little too close, held her hand a little longer than necessary when they shook on the deal, and seemed, without saying anything genuinely offensive, to be taking a slightly intimate line. Finally Maggie rose to see him to the door, and he helped her put her shawl over her shoulders. His hand lingered. Then dropped, touching her breast lightly, as if by accident.

She stared down at the bodice of her dress a moment, as if expecting his touch to have stained her clothing. "Captain Bruckner," she said firmly, "I am selling wagon wheels—*nothing* else!"

He didn't even look embarrassed. With an "it-doesn't-hurt-to-try" smile, he said, "Yes, ma'am. Well put."

Maggie paced her little kitchen for a while when he left, trying to work up to righteous indignation, but she couldn't. The truth was, she was flattered. Nobody but Gerald had ever treated her like an attractive woman, not so blatantly. Not even pious Isaac Zook, who had wanted to marry her. Temptation didn't enter into her speculations. She wanted nothing to do with Bruckner, except business, and she was sure he had understood that and would not make any further overtures.

"What are you smiling for? You look like a girl at her first dance," Gerald said.

She whirled around. "I didn't hear you come in." She hoped he didn't detect the embarrassment in her voice. "Captain Bruckner was just here. He wants two dozen more wheels later this summer."

He didn't seem as happy as she expected him to be. "Sounds to me like you are setting up a long-term business relationship with the army," he said.

She should have been warned by his tone of voice, but she was so excited about the sale that she said, "Yes, just think, in a few years we could be making a nice profit from our dealings with the army, not to mention what Torchy may accomplish in Saint Louis and Westport Landing."

Gerald said nothing, just picked up the flute he carried around sometimes and wandered out the door into the fragrant summer night. Maggie followed him. "I thought you would be pleased. What's wrong?"

"Don't you really know?" he asked quietly, sitting on the flat rock that served as a stoop.

"I . . . I . . . No."

"You said in a few years we could be making a nice profit . . ." Gerald parroted. "Are we going to be here in a few years, Maggie?"

Then she realized what she'd done. "Well, for a while yet. That was what we planned, wasn't it? Doing something to make up the money we lost in the fire, so that . . ."—she hesitated a moment over the pronoun—"we could try again."

"And when do you think that's going to be?"

"Well, a year or two. We have to figure out how much we need and by next year we'll know how close we are." This was becoming a conversation she had known was coming sooner or later, but she wasn't ready for it yet. Not now, not when everything was going so well.

"Then what? Will we go to Santa Fe?" There was a mocking tone in his words—or was that her own sense of guilt echoing?

"Of course, if that's what you want." *Please,* she thought frantically. *Not now. I can't talk now about this. It will be easier later. It has to be easier later.*

As if sensing her desperation, Gerald said, "I think I'll walk for a while before going to bed. Good night, Maggie."

She sat for a long time in the dark. At first she could hear the sorrowful melody he was playing on the flute, and as he moved farther away, it became softer and softer, until he was merely a memory replaying in her own mind. Hot tears scalded down her cheeks, but she could not put words to why she was crying. Was it for herself or Gerald that she cried? Both of them, in a way. And she cried for her own confusion.

Why could she not just say: "I am *home* now, I don't want to ever leave this place"? While she sat sniffling in the thick darkness, she knew the answer. If she told him that she wanted to stay, they *would* stay. He would agree to do so because he loved her. But it would be a terrible sacrifice to him, and wouldn't he love her less for having to make it? She could not bear that. Gerald's love was the only thing that made anything else worthwhile.

If they could just not talk about it, things might change, but she knew he never would. Nothing on earth could ever make her *want* to leave her house—her Seven Trees, the friends she'd made, the business she'd started—to pack it all in the hateful wagon, face the dangers of the trail, for someone else's dream, even if the someone else was the man she loved with all her heart.

She had to make Gerald happy enough that he wanted to stay here as badly as she did, but how could she do that? She had no idea what made him happy—she could not understand him that well. But she would try. If nothing else, she must make more time in her life to know him, so that someday she would understand.

The wheels were ready for Bruckner when he came back through. Everyone had pitched in and helped with the work in order to meet the deadline. Torchy had returned from Saint Louis with forty-eight dollars from the sale of the wheels and an order for more the following spring. Maggie, Helmut, and Torchy sat down around Maggie's table and figured it out. They had spent ninety dollars of her original hundred on wheels, the iron for the bands, and transportation. But they had made $176 on the wheels they sold, so even discounting the loss of the first shipment and the subsequent return of the eight wheels that Vratil had made so badly, they were ahead. Not much, but it was a profit and showed a promise. Next year would be better by far. They had the whole winter to build up their supply, they had an army promise to buy more, and wagon makers in both Saint Louis and Westport Landing who had expressed a willingness to buy.

"We will have to keep a few here for people who are passing through," Maggie said. There had been a surprising number of people using the mission as the first-day-out stopping point on their way to Council Grove.

"The wheels require a name as well," Torchy added. "I think we should call them 'Freiler's Wheels.' This would please you?"

"It would please me, but I don't think it would please Mr. Freiler," Maggie said. "We have all come to call this place Seven Trees. Why don't we name the wheels that?"

Torchy scribbled the name on a scrap of paper. "Yes, this has a good sound and looks well. I think we should carve it into the spoke—this way, other travelers in wagon trains will

147

observe that wagon wheels that say Seven Trees do not have difficulties and when next they make such purchase they will remember the name. It has been going round and round before their eyes." He aped a bored traveler reading a name, twisting his head and making faces.

The next day, Helmut turned up at Maggie's door, proudly displaying a branding device for burning the name into the wood. They tried it out on a couple of wheels, then everyone got interested and they branded "SEVENTREES" into the sides of their houses, the seats of a few chairs, and the tailgate of the schooner.

The business and the tiny community had a name.

Seventrees!

Maggie sat turning the letter over in her hands for a long time before opening it. It was fine stationery and the return address—Germantown, Pennsylvania—was written in a delicate hand. But she didn't want to hear from Germantown. She didn't want to hear from her past or from anything outside her world of here and now. But that was cowardly, and Maggie was not a coward. She picked up her darning scissors and carefully slit the top of the envelope.

Dearest Cousin Margaret,

It was *too* wonderful to hear from you, but I confess I don't understand where you are. Silly me, I should have Luther show me on a map or something. Is this Westport Landing address in Mexico? If so, *why* is it called Missouri? Wherever it is, I'm *delighted* to hear that you are all well and have added a daughter to your family.

We are doing well too. Luther doesn't tell me *anything* about the business, of course (I suppose he knows how useless women's minds are in such matters!), but he goes off every morning and tends to things. I busy myself, as usual, with my ladies' groups and shopping. Andrew and Violet are *thriving*.

We are planning a little trip this summer to *Virginia*. Friends of mine (she was a *Cabot*!!!) have invited us to stay for a bit, and I'm so *terribly* excited about it all I can *hardly* sleep at night!

Well, *dear* COUSIN (if I may call you that, in *all* affection), we absolutely must keep in touch now.

Do write and tell me positively everything about Mexico.

Your most loving cousin,
Fritzi Halleck

Maggie folded the letter back up and fanned herself with it. "What a fool!" she muttered.

Katrin was sitting at her side, darning up some of her son Quincy's ten-year-old baby clothes in preparation for the imminent arrival of the next child. "Who is your letter from?" she asked. "Don't mean to pry, but folks so seldom get letters here . . ."

"You're not prying. I don't mind. Here . . ." She handed the letter to Katrin. "Fritzi is my cousin Luther's wife. I wrote and gave them the name of the nearest post—I can't imagine why, except they *are* my only family, and it seemed, in a bad moment, to be the right thing to do." Maggie laughed.

Katrin read the letter, guffawing nastily when she got to the part about how useless women's minds are. "It sounds like *hers* certainly is," she commented.

"Katrin, you look flushed," Maggie said. "Aren't you too hot out here? I'll keep an eye on the children if you want to go inside."

"Hell, no. It's dark as the inside of a vinegar jar in there, and twice as hot. I must get Helmut to cut another window so there's a breeze in the house. It doesn't bother him, of course. He spends all day in the blacksmith shop and thinks the *house* is cool."

So they continued to sit, their sewing in their laps, watching the activities down the hill at the ferry. The army wagon train was preparing to cross the river, and there was a bustle of activity going on. The stock were all to be swum across as soon as the sun moved far enough west to eliminate the glare on the water. If they took them too soon, they would become disoriented if they couldn't see the far bank and would swim around aimlessly in the middle of the Kaw. Meanwhile, Woody was getting the trade wagons pulled onto the ferry, two at a time, and taking them across. The wagons were lined up in pairs up the incline. Each wagon had a strong rope looped between front and back wheels to keep it from rolling.

"John! Quincy!" Katrin called loudly. "Don't you get in the way, now." Lowering her voice, she said, "I swear they'd get themselves run down if I didn't watch 'em every minute. Ten and eleven years old, and their sense is falling out with their milk teeth. They're plain fascinated with the soldiers. Want to be right in the middle of anything that's going on."

Maggie untangled a knot in her sewing. Suddenly she heard Katrin gasp. She looked up. The rope on the end wagon had snapped. The wheels had been turned slightly, so instead of simply crashing into the wagon in front, it had pulled out of line and was slowly rolling down the long incline.

Katrin was screaming to her children and started to run toward the ferry. It seemed, as Maggie watched, that everything was moving slowly, horribly. She ran too. No one below noticed the runaway wagon at first, but at Katrin's shouts several looked up the hill, and the soldiers were scattering in every direction to get out of the way.

But there in the middle, confused and unmoving, John and Quincy Clay stood. Simply stood and looked around, trying to figure out what was happening. As she and Katrin ran, screaming, skirts flying and bonnets lost, Maggie saw one of the soldiers turn back and realize that the young boys were in the path of the wagon. He whirled, ran for the boys, tried to scoop them up, but the runaway was almost upon them. He got hold of Quincy, but lost his grip on the older boy.

"John!" Katrin shrilled.

Suddenly Katrin was no longer beside her. Maggie turned around quickly and saw that Katrin had tripped and fallen. She ran back. Katrin had risen to her knees, grimacing in pain and horror. Hands to her cheeks, she let out one long, chilling wail and collapsed. A second later Maggie heard the splash as the wagon went into the water at the bottom of the hill.

She straightened Katrin's limbs, turned her onto her back, and loosened the top buttons of her dress. Katrin's plump, cheerful face looked like a grotesque gray death mask. Her skin was pale and clammy, her lips flaccid and lifeless. Maggie was frantic. What could she do? She patted Katrin's cheeks and called her name. The eyelids fluttered, and Katrin moaned softly. Thank God, at least she was still alive.

Maggie looked down the hill. Quincy stood alone, head bowed and shoulders shaking with convulsive sobs. A group of soldiers stood and knelt around John. Helmut had heard the commotion and was lumbering down the hill from the shop. The reverend, Gerald, Benjamin, and a flock of Indian

150

children were emerging from the mission buildings and running toward the scene. Maggie shouted at Gerald, who ran to her side. "What on earth happened?" he asked.

"A wagon got away. I think it struck John. Katrin and I were trying to get there, and she fell. Oh, Gerald, I think there's something terribly wrong," she whispered. "Look at her. What can I do?"

"Stay with her," Gerald said. "I'll see if the doctor is down there."

Maggie sat by Katrin for a long time. She held her friend's limp hand and murmured ridiculous reassurances. "Katrin, you're going to be all right. You just took a tumble. You'll be fine," she went on and on, not knowing whether Katrin could hear her or not.

Finally Dr. Hutchens, huffing and pale, came up the hill. Gerald was with him and looked almost the same color as Katrin. He had Benjamin and one of the Indian girls in tow. "Go in the house, please, and keep an eye on James and Schooner," he told the other children.

"John?" Maggie asked.

Gerald and the doctor shook their heads. "Gone," Dr. Hutchens said quietly. "It must have been immediate. He did not suffer. What happened to Mrs. Clay?" He knelt next to her and fastidiously lifted her eyelid.

Maggie explained while Hutchens took her pulse, leaned close, and checked her breathing. Gently he felt her arms and legs and ribs. "There doesn't seem to be anything broken," he said, more to himself than to them.

"I'm going back to Helmut," Gerald said. "Will Katrin be all right, doctor?"

"I don't know. I think it's just shock. Send some men back with poles and blankets. We need to carry her inside very carefully."

Katrin was only half-conscious the rest of the day. Her labor began in the night, and late the next morning, while Helmut and Gerald stood beside Torchy and Woody listening to Reverend Whittacre's funeral prayer over the grave of John Clay, Katrin gave birth to another boy.

Maggie had been by her side every minute and was not sure yet whether Katrin really knew what had happened. She had cried out with the pain of childbirth, had often cried John's name, but Dr. Hutchens primly but firmly declared that she must not be told of the older boy's death until she was through the ordeal of the baby. Maggie washed the infant and wrapped him in a soft cloth while the doctor tended to Katrin. Then Maggie laid the baby in his mother's arms.

Katrin leaned her cheek on the baby's down-covered head and whispered, "John's dead, isn't he?"

Maggie nodded miserably. "Yes, Katrin. I'm so sorry . . ."

When Helmut returned, glassy-eyed and unshaven, Maggie took Quincy home for lunch and left her friends to console each other in their grief and find what rejoicing they could in the birth of a healthy son.

17

The winter came on early and lasted late. Though it was not especially harsh, it seemed interminable. Maggie was never really rested, never warm enough, and found herself longing desperately for spring. Katrin was slow to recover her strength and good spirits, whether from the shocking circumstances of Adams' birth or from some true physical disability, no one could know.

Helmut and the wheelwright worked continuously throughout the winter, and the supply of wagon wheels grew encouragingly. Torchy spent the winter on a building binge. He, more than any of the rest of them, was accustomed to the cold and could work, shirtless, outdoors while the rest of them huddled in blankets in front of fires. He had spent the last twenty years of his existence in the northern wilds, fighting the elements hourly just to survive. Now the "plush" living at Seventrees was hard on him.

He confessed to Maggie that when he got bored, he got melancholy ("sad in the head"), and then he drank. But he had resolved not to drink anymore since he had responsibility for his children, so he had to do something. "Something" was building. He put up a small attractive house for his own family near the Clay and Freiler houses. Then he convinced Woody and the wheelwright, who were bachelors and shared Woody's tiny shack, that they needed a house, and he built most of it for them. Then he started working on Maggie. "You require a place from which to sell the wheels," he said. "A post, an addition to your house, perhaps."

Maggie didn't want him to be "sad in the head," but she didn't think she needed anything built and told him so. "The wheels can stay outside, Torchy."

"Not a post, then, a sleeping room for the children." He threw himself into the construction in spite of her mild objections. When it was completed, Torchy gave up, having failed to convince anyone else they needed a new or enlarged structure. Desperate at the prospect of being cooped up with Gran'mère Charron's wide-ranging complaints, he offered himself to Reverend Whittacre as a French teacher for the balance of the winter.

Black Feather came to the mission around Christmastime to check on the welfare of his tribe's children. Maggie caught up with him before he left. "Mrs. Clay has been ill," she explained. "Your herbal cures were most effective for the children's earaches. Do you know of anything that might help her regain her strength?"

He returned a week later with a leather pouch full of some sort of dried leaves to be steeped in hot water and drunk twice a day.

Maggie held the pouch up to her nose and sniffed. "Ah, *Deshligraut.*" Black Feather gave her a questioning look. Maggie explained: "I don't know the English word. My Grossmutter was the *braucherie* . . . oh, dear, I seem to be having trouble with English today." Where had her usual calm reserve gone? She took a deep breath and started over. "My grandmother was the 'medicine man' in her community. She taught me herbs and cures. But different things grow out here. Let me show you something. Come."

She led the way to her house, but at the door Black Feather stopped. "I will remain outside."

Maggie wondered for an instant if there was an insult implied in his refusal to enter. "Why?" she asked bluntly. "You are welcome here."

"Perhaps by you. Not by the others." He made a slight turning of his head, and past him Maggie could see that he was being watched by several people who had stopped their work to keep an eye on them.

Maggie understood the implications at once and *was* insulted, for both their sakes. But she would not embarrass him further. "I will bring it out, then," she said, carefully taking her hex book down from the shelf Gerald had built especially for it. She and Black Feather sat down on the porch in full view of the neighbors and at a respectable distance from each other, and she showed him her treasured possession. She was gratified that he automatically handled it with the same reverence she always had.

Some of the pages showed plants that were unfamiliar to the Indian, and he asked her to translate the German. Others he recognized. He pointed to one of the first sheets. "This is wild four o'clock," he said. "What purpose do your people use it for?"

Maggie translated: " 'The root is steeped to reduce abdominal swelling.' "

"Yes, but the same root, dried and powdered, can be applied to the gums of infants who are getting their teeth. It helps the pain and digestion. Perhaps you should add that to your page."

Maggie hesitated. It had never occurred to her to violate the purity of Grossmutter's hex book by daring to put a single mark of her own in it. But she should record this information.

Black Feather sensed her dilemma. "This book is sacred to you, is it not?"

"No, not exactly."

"To you, personally, I mean."

"Yes, it is."

"Then you should keep it as it is and compile your own."

Maggie thought about this as they perused the rest of the pages. Yes, she would like to do that. This was a different world, and she was not Hildy Halleck. She should have her own hex book.

When Black Feather left, she prepared the cure as he had instructed and took it to Katrin. "What's this, something from that old German book of yours?" Katrin asked.

Maggie smiled and let her think it an affirmative answer, for she knew Katrin would not put faith in any cure devised by an Indian. Whether it was medicinal value or psychological, Katrin began to improve rapidly.

In the early spring, when the last of the snow had melted and Torchy had taken the first load of wagon wheels to Saint Louis, Black Feather returned. "You're not taking the children so early, are you?" Maggie asked him.

"No. There are things I wish to show you in the woods. Plants you should know about. It would be best if we were accompanied by as many children as possible."

It would not have crossed her mind, but she knew immediately what he meant. To take children meant it was a

154

teaching expedition, not a social meeting between a white woman and an Indian man. What a pity such considerations must be made.

After packing a hearty lunch and gathering about a dozen children, they set out. Black Feather said there were only a few plants of value that came up this early, but they would be gone shortly and Maggie must see them now so she could learn to recognize them. When they returned later, she had several small bunches of moss, bark, and tender sprigs of first spring growth along with detailed verbal instructions on their uses and preparation. "Torchy has gone to Saint Louis, and I asked him to bring me a package of fine paper," Maggie told Black Feather. "When he returns, I shall begin my book. Will you look at it later and make sure I have put things down properly?" She felt like a schoolgirl trying to please a favorite teacher.

"I would be pleased," he answered, his face as stoic and secretive as ever.

By the end of April Katrin was almost back to normal and determined to make up to Maggie for all her care. She bustled about, plump little Adams on her hip in a sling made from an old woolen shawl. She baked, planted, sewed, and kept insisting that Maggie rest for a change.

Torchy returned from Saint Louis, having sold three dozen wagon wheels and taken orders for another three dozen. In his hand he had $144. They paid the wheelwright the money they owed him for his winter's work and divided the balance among the partners—Maggie, Torchy, and Helmut. "While in Saint Louis," Torchy said, "I became knowing of something interesting. I tried to buy the coffee you asked me to get, and found that there was almost none. What has happened to the supply, I do not know. There may be a blockade resulting from this talk of war in Texas. But I was given another drink that was much the same, and I inquired of its contents. It was made of dried sweet potatoes, dried green okra, and wheat that has been browned in a skillet and ground up. Powdered together and cooked, this mixture is a good substitute."

"That's nice to know, but I don't see . . ." Maggie started to say.

"These are all things that would grow themselves here, unlike real coffee," Torchy explained. "If we were to make up such a mixture and give drinks to those who stopped to buy

155

wheels, they would sip and say, 'Voilà! This is good! Where can I buy such a commodity?' would they not?"

Maggie had to smile. She could not quite imagine anyone in the world but Torchy saying such a thing—at least not in the same way—but she took the point. "You think we could sell it along with the wheels?"

"You would raise no objection?"

"Of course not."

Torchy sighed deeply and with melodramatic relief. "Bien, I feared that you would feel disgrace to being a shopkeeper. In that case, I shall share other information with you. In the building that adjoins one of the wagon maker's I visited, is a shop that sells commodities for travelers. Blankets, the tent canvas, sewing needles—these are difficult to be found, you know—and the wagon maker tells me the owner has died and the poor widow wishes to dispose of the business, having no son to continue. Would you wish to put this money back with me to buy what we can of the supplies? With great frequency people stop here their first night out and find that they have forgotten something. We could sell these things."

So by the middle of the summer, Maggie was in possession of a small trading post. Neither Torchy nor her customers ever convinced her that the sweet-potato drink tasted remotely like coffee, but most of the travelers passing through bought five-pound kegs of it because it was better than nothing. The owner of the hotel in Westport Landing even heard of it and came over to buy it for his guests. They called it Seventrees tea and sold it at a reasonable price, but Maggie steadfastly refused to even hint at the recipe when asked.

By July, Maggie sometimes felt she could not continue. She loved being active and busy, but there were limits to her strength. She had the running of the small trading post to attend to as well as the care of the children, the cooking, washing, sewing, and all the bookkeeping for the various aspects of the fledgling business. Gerald offered to help, and sincerely tried, but he never got anything done quite the way she wanted it done, and she was truly more satisfied doing everything herself.

Her only relaxation was working with her cures and when Black Feather visited the mission. She would close the post, pack a lunch for herself, the children, and the taciturn Indian, and they would go off into the woods.

Black Feather showed Maggie how cattail down could be used as a dressing for burns or be rubbed to powder and used as talcum. He taught her how to identify the small iris, the roots of which were powdered and steeped for earache. Pressing the juice out of cornflower stems made a soothing application for burns, and pieces of stem could be chewed to help with mumps. She carefully sketched each plant on the sheets of thick ivory paper Torchy had brought her.

There were many others—blazing star for loose bowels, mint for stomach cramps, licorice for almost everything, the spider-bean leaves for skin rashes. There was so much new to learn. Some plants had useful flowers but poisonous leaves, some looked virtually identical except when they bloomed, and could only be safely selected during a brief period. Maggie's book grew, and before long the rafters of her house and the post were thickly strung with bundles of plants drying for later use in cooking and healing. Sometimes when she walked into the house, the smell brought tears to her eyes. It was so like Grossmutter's sitting room and made her relive the heartache *and* the heart's ease she had known there.

One day, returning from the woods, they were met by a scene of great confusion. A group of travelers had camped at the mission the night before—six wagons of greenhorns on their way to the Northwest, the Oregon Territory. Maggie had found them depressing. They were as ignorant as she and Gerald had been two years before, and this group was planning to go much farther, through more hostile country. Maggie was sure, looking at their stupidly optimistic faces, that they were doomed, and she could hardly keep herself from telling them so. But that would only have offended them, not saved them, so she held her tongue and murmured a few quiet prayers on their behalf.

But as she and the children and Black Feather emerged from the woods, they could hear shouts and see people running about. "Fire," the Indian said. Though Maggie could neither hear, nor see, nor smell anything to confirm this, she knew he must be right. They hurried along, Maggie in terrible fear that it was one of their houses, but it turned out to be one of the settlers' wagons. Fortunately, it had been sitting in a clearing and presented no danger to overhanging trees. Most of the goods had been thrown out onto the ground and the other five wagons hastily moved away from the fiery schooner, but it was lost. Some of the children were still running back and forth from the wagon to the riverbank to bring buckets of water, but it was too late to save it. The men had dug a trench around the area to keep a grass fire from spreading, and the women of the wagon train were huddled, weeping and lamenting.

That evening a lanky, bearded young man came to see Maggie. "I'm sorry for your misfortune, Mr. Veach. Do you know how the fire started?"

"Naw, don't s'pose we'll ever know."

"Is there any way I can help you?" Maggie asked. She felt sorry for him, and yet, in a way, she thought he was fortunate. If such a thing *had* to happen, better here while he could still go back.

"I think maybe you can, ma'am. I notice you got a schooner of your own sittin' out back of your place. Me and my friends put all we had together—two hundred dollars—and we'd like to buy it."

"Oh, no," Maggie said without thinking.

"You on your way someplace with it?" he asked. "I thought you folks lived here."

"No, it's not that I need it now. But . . . don't go west. Stop now. Don't you think this misfortune was God's way of telling you not to go on?"

He stared at her. Confusion, then a hint of determination on his face. "No, ma'am. I don't."

"Please. Don't take offense. You've got a wife and three little children—you don't know what you're letting yourself and them in for. Why don't you go back wherever you came from, where it's safe?"

"You can keep your damned schooner—and your opinions!" he said, and turned to the door.

"Wait!" Maggie said. He was obviously going to buy a wagon somewhere and go on. She could use the money if he was determined to spend it. "Mr. Veach, I apologize. I will sell you the schooner. I'll even put new wheels on it for free, but please, please think very carefully—"

"I been thinkin' 'bout this all my life, ma'am. Here's your money. If you'll show me where them wheels are, I'll put 'em on myself. We gotta be ready to go at daybreak."

Maggie was awake very early the next day. She went to the clearing where the settlers were hitching their teams to the wagons. She shook Mr. Veach's hand and wished him luck. She gave his wife a keg of Seventrees Tea and a little bag of Black Feather's herbal remedies, each wrapped in heavy paper with instructions written on it. "I'll write to you, ma'am," the girl said. "It sure is nice of you to do all this for us."

Maggie had to blink back tears—tears of frustration that

158

she could not stop them and of sorrow for the heartbreaks she knew were ahead of these innocent young people. "Please do," she said, and turned away to discover Gerald standing behind her. Her heart sank. She hadn't told him about the schooner yet.

But he apparently didn't notice their vehicle in the dawn-lit clearing. "Come home now, Maggie, my love," he said, putting his arm around her. As they walked along, he said, "Why do you care so much? You were trying to hang on to that young couple as if they *belonged* to you. You'd never laid eyes on them before yesterday."

"I know. It's just that they have no idea of what they're doing. They've got to cross rivers and mountains, and there are hostile Indians between here and Oregon. It's such a long way and such a hard, hard thing to do for no reason."

He took her face in his hands, tenderly but firmly. "Maggie, you don't *know* what their reasons are. And who are you to warn people against a hard life? Look at the way you work—you're up early every day, you do the work of three people without letting anyone help you, and then you sit up late nights over your bookkeeping. Do you mean to tell me that's not hard?"

"Yes, but it's what I want to do," Maggie protested.

"And this is what *they* want to do. Everyone can't want the same things you do. Believe it or not, my love, there are people in this world who are not Maggie Freiler, and they're happy anyway. You're as close to perfect as a woman can be, but can't you see that other people have different needs, different attitudes and feelings than you have?"

"Gerald, I can't even understand how *you* feel about things, and I love you better than anyone else in the world. I do try, really I do."

He took her hand and kissed her fingertips, one by one. "I suppose trying is all anyone could ask. I wish you would slow down—at least long enough for me to tell you how much I love you."

"Do you?" she murmured contentedly. "Tell me now—the children will not be awake for an hour yet. . . ."

"Maggie, my love, that was nice of you to give that girl that package of cures," Gerald said later over breakfast.

"Ummm," she said dreamily as she cooked Schooner's porridge.

"You like studying that with Black Feather, don't you?"

Maggie came back to earth. "Yes, I do. It's very interesting. You don't mind, do you?"

"Mind what? Improving your skills? Why would I?"

"Because he's a man . . . and an Indian. Katrin says I'm blackening my reputation 'consorting with a savage,'" Maggie answered.

Gerald roared with laughter. "Katrin said *that*? It sounds like the sort of silly, ugly thing your cousin's wife Fritzi would say." Then, seeing that Maggie was not enjoying the joke as much as he was, he added, "No. He's a fine man. As for 'reputation'—that's the sort of nonsense I hoped we could leave behind in Pennsylvania. The Indians—"

"It's not just because he's an Indian."

"Katrin thinks I should be jealous? Is that it? Well, you can tell her to stop wasting her time worrying. I know your love and loyalty and I'd never be jealous."

Maggie felt a small twinge of disappointment. Not that she would like it if he was jealous—in fact, she would hate it, but still . . .

"Gerald, I've been thinking about the cures. There are more travelers coming through here all the time, and none of them seem to be very well equipped to meet sickness along the way. I would like to try making up more of the packets like I gave that young woman this morning and sell them. We didn't see anything like that for sale when we came out, and it would be doing them a favor. Not like taking their money for something useless or shabby."

"I think it's a fine idea, Maggie. But where would you find the time? You're busy from dawn to dusk as it is."

Katrin likes growing and making Seventrees Tea," Maggie answered, almost burning the porridge in her enthusiasm. "If I stepped out of that part of the business, I would have time." She gestured overhead, where her dried and drying material hung. "I have most of what I need here, except . . ." She craned her neck, taking quick inventory of the greenery hung in the rafters. "Yes, I'll need a good deal more wild mint and coneflower root. Would you help me write the instructions, Gerald? You have such a fine hand. And I'll need some small bottles . . ." she raced on.

"I'd be glad to help, Maggie, my love," he said, "on one condition. Don't ever let any more Seventrees Tea in the house. I'll go to Saint Louis with Torchy next week to get your bottles, and I'm going to bring back some real coffee if I have to steal it."

160

When he had finished breakfast, Gerald went out behind the house to get a harness strap that needed mending. In her excitement about the medicines, Maggie had temporarily forgotten about the schooner, until he came back in the house, his face a mask of confusion. "Maggie, the schooner is—"

"Gone. I know. I meant to tell you and forgot."

Gerald leaned on the table. In a sharp voice he said, "Of course! The Veaches. Right under my nose, and I didn't even notice. How amusing that must have been for you!"

"Gerald . . ."

"Damn! I must have become the kind of fool you take me for." His eyes were icy pools of anger. He had become the "other" Gerald—the man whose sorrow and anger frightened her.

"It's just a wagon," Maggie started to justify hurriedly. "It wouldn't have been usable in another year or two. It's been sitting out there in all weather . . ."

He slammed a fist on the table. "Damn! It's *not* just a wagon, and you know it. You can't convince me of things by sheer force of personality. Save that for children and strangers. I know you and I know what selling the wagon means."

"Gerald, it doesn't mean anything," Maggie pleaded. "We would have had to buy a new one anyway. It was old and we needed the money." But she knew she was lying. Selling the wagon meant that she was rooted, like a seed come to rest in a fertile soil, discarding the fluff that allowed it to drift in the wind. Gerald knew it too.

She went to the jar where she'd put the money. "Here, Gerald, take it. Please. Buy a new wagon. If it's not enough, I'll borrow something from Torchy or Helmut. Don't be angry. I didn't think you'd care . . ."

He snatched the money from her hand and walked out the door without another word.

He was gone all day and—for the first time—all night. When he returned in the morning he looked wrung-out, defeated. He was belligerently contrite. "There's no point in having a brand-new wagon sitting out there before we need it," he said, and handed the money back to her. "You'll need it for the business."

"Gerald," she said, putting her arms around his unyielding body, "Gerald, I'm sorry . . ."

His voice sounded like a strum on a tight wire. "Let's

161

don't discuss the things we're sorry about, Maggie. I'm too tired, and there are so many of them."

"Have some breakfast?" she offered. "You look like you need it."

"Stop being so goddamn practical, can't you?"

"I have some porridge made, and there's fresh milk . . ." Maggie said. She must blot out his anger somehow. She was terrified of what she'd done to them.

He suddenly took her arms in a viselike grip. "Maggie, haven't you ever wanted oysters and champagne and toast points for breakfast?"

"But I don't *like* oysters."

He stared at her for a long moment as if he'd forgotten just who she was. "Oh, God!" he finally said. "Oh, my God, you don't *like* oysters!" Then he was laughing, a bitter, edge-of-control laugh. He strode around the room laughing, while Maggie wrung her hands.

"What's wrong?" she finally said in a small voice.

He stopped his frantic pacing, and the spirit suddenly seemed to drain out of him. "Never mind. I don't like oysters either. I'm just tired, love. Keep your money and do sensible, practical things with it."

One day late in September, almost two years from the time Maggie and Gerald had come to Seventrees, she sat at her kitchen table with Torchy, Helmut, stacks of papers, and a small metal box full of money. "Seven hundred and two dollars and thirty-seven cents," she said. "And we are keeping out four hundred of it for purchases for the post over the winter. That makes . . . let's see, one hundred dollars and seventy-nine cents each to keep."

They were all pleased with themselves. It was not a great fortune, but in comparison to the year before, it was a big increase, and they already had a substantial number of orders in for the spring. "I think we can each count on a minimum of five hundred dollars apiece at this time next year—perhaps a good deal more," she said proudly.

In another year, a little voice in the back of her mind said, *you will have enough to go to Santa Fe. What then, Maggie Freiler?*

162

18

When they sat down again a year later, in the fall of 1842, they found that they had exceeded their most optimistic estimates. The partners went into the winter snug and hopeful, but toward Christmas Maggie realized that she had an unforeseen problem. "I'm missing my monthly courses, Katrin," she said one very cold day as they sat over steaming cups of real tea. "Can there be any *other* reason?"

"I suppose there could," Katrin said doubtfully. "But you're only, what, not much over thirty? It can't be that you're stopping because of age, and you haven't had any sort of illness . . . ." She wished she could say something more encouraging, but the truth had to be faced.

But Maggie was having trouble facing it. "Oh, Katrin, I don't want to be pregnant!" she cried. "It was so horrible the last time."

"Maybe it will be easier with this one," Katrin said.

But it wasn't.

During the long interminable winter, Maggie worked at preparing her kit of herbal cures, feeling ever more sluggish and heavy. Sometimes she would have cramps and have to spend a day in bed to make them stop. By April she was having to spend almost every other day lying down. She could not stand the inactivity, but the frequent pain was worse. She grew very thin and often found herself snapping at Gerald and the children. The army doctor came to see her and once again told her that she must cease all activity. Without telling anyone, Maggie also consulted with Black Feather, feeling sure he would have some Indian cure, but to her vast disappointment, he told her the same thing. "Earlier I could have provided you with a means to miscarry," he said in his flawless English, "but it is too late now."

"Oh, no, I wouldn't have wanted that," Maggie had said.

"Why not?" the Indian asked.

"It would be wrong."

He shook his head. "And this is right? This constant illness, taking the ability to work away from a woman who loves to

163

work? I wonder why learning to speak as a white man has not enabled me to understand the thinking of white men . . . and women. You must rest and you must force yourself to eat more," he told her.

Gerald seemed to believe that illness was just God's way of giving a person free reading time, and he piled the bed full of magazines and newspapers he felt sure Maggie would enjoy, and then expected to have long philosophical discussions in the evenings. Maggie tried to take an interest in the fact that the young girl queen of England had married a German prince. She read the fiery editorials advocating annexation of Oregon and Texas from the British and Mexican governments. Gerald brought her a two-year-old copy of a new newspaper, the New York *Tribune*, and read aloud to her about a man named Barnum who had opened an exhibition of freaks. He was also excited about a mental process called hypnosis that a Scottish surgeon had discovered the year before.

Maggie read and listened and tried to share his enthusiasms, but all she really wanted to do was work. Queen Victoria and Santa Anna and P. T. Barnum were all so far away and meant little to her life. Even the "local paper" *Anzeiger des Westens*, a German publication from Saint Louis, was full of political oratory that fascinated Gerald and left Maggie longing for good practical information. If she could have found a book that told her how to make soap last longer, or dyes hold their color, or medicine bottles not leak or spoil—if she had found such a book, she would have devoured it eagerly.

But Gerald meant well, she told herself. Just as she could not understand his intellectualism and was always offering him the comfort of work, he was giving her what he thought was valuable—mental nourishment. And it was good to have his company so much of the time. Occasionally she would sit propped up against her pillows and listen to him read. But she was not paying attention to his words, but the timbre of his voice, the silky gloss of his black hair, the lines of laughter and maturity at the corners of his eyes, and the way his hands looked holding a book.

Reverend Whittacre finally realized that Gerald was going to neglect his teaching duties to be with Maggie and decided to make it official. He gave him leave from his position, but Gerald's use of his free time was not quite what Maggie had expected. He was willing to cook for the family when Maggie was too ill to do so, but his meals were a wretched combination of the children's favorites, not what was good for anyone. He also offered to pick herbs for Maggie's medical kits, but he was careless and haphazard about this as well. If she asked for roots of a particular plant, he would as often as not bring leaves instead because they were so interesting, and sometimes it wasn't even the right plant. He was always very sorry and promised to pay closer attention next time. Often as a token of remorse, he would give her a treasured book to read. German philosophy, usually.

He was supposed to keep the tiny trading post open in the spring when the wagon trains began to come through. When the first customer came and bought a keg of nails, Maggie heard Gerald through the partition that separated the post from their main room. He added up the purchase and finished up by saying, "That'll be twenty-five cents, sir."

"I only got twenty on me," a voice came back.

"That'll be fine," Gerald replied.

Maggie had not slept well and was angry with the world in general. She got out of bed, wrapped a quilt around her shoulders, and went into the other room when the customer left. "Why did you do that!" she demanded.

"Well, he said he only had twenty cents."

"Then you should have only given him twenty cents' worth of nails," Maggie said furiously.

"But, Maggie, you always say you want to run a completely honest business—not cheat people."

"Gerald, that wasn't honest, it was stupid! We pay twenty-two cents for those nails, and you just sold them for twenty. Now, who got cheated? We did! My prices are fair, don't take upon yourself to alter them."

She turned on her heel and went back in the other room, expecting Gerald to follow with his usual apology, but a moment later she heard the front door to the post slam, and when she went to look, he was gone. When another customer came an hour later, she had to get up and serve him herself. It was a long, confused order, and the man wanted advice as much as materials. Maggie nearly fainted before she got him on his way. She hung a sign on the door saying "Closed for the Day" and went back to bed.

Gerald didn't apologize, and Maggie couldn't either. She knew she had spoken harshly, but she'd been right. It was better to close the shop and not make any profit than to have it open and lose money. They hardly spoke all evening, but

165

the next morning Gerald was back at the post. Maggie felt that another course of anger had been added to the invisible wall between them. Would the wall never come down? she wondered desperately.

As spring became summer, things got progressively worse. Gerald hated tending the store and would leap at the slightest excuse to go anywhere. If Maggie needed water to wash the dishes, he would go for it, and sometimes it was an hour or more before he returned, bursting with stories of the interesting things that had held him up along the way. As the wagons began to return from Santa Fe, it was even harder to depend upon him. He was fascinated with the wealth passing through Seventrees—whole wagons nearly full of silver; traders with purses of gold pieces regaled him with stories of how easy it was to make a fast fortune in Mexico, and Gerald would sit up late into the night with them over their campfires playing heartbreaking melodies on his flute and listening to their stories with longing. How much was velvet cloth selling for in Santa Fe? he would ask, and his eyes would light up when he heard the figure; then they would dim again.

Meanwhile Maggie stayed in her bed, racked with physical pain and cursing this pregnancy that had made everything go wrong. If only she'd been well this summer, she could be taking care of the post and Gerald would not be so angry with her and with life so much of the time. His extreme dissatisfaction with life at Seventrees was the one thing she had most wished to avoid. He would never be happy here, and if he wasn't content, she couldn't be, she thought miserably, and wept into the pillow.

Everyone offered to help her, and she was sometimes forced to accept. When Gerald disappeared, Katrin would bring her children to the post and take care of the customers. Gran'mère Charron unbent enough to care for Schooner often and feed the children. Even Reverend Whittacre's wife, who almost never left the mission, came over bringing food.

But Maggie hated taking favors from anyone but Katrin, and she hated more that Gerald left her at the mercy of dogooders like Mrs. Whittacre, who served up huge unwanted gobs of pity along with the help. The only aspect of life that was not utterly depressing to Maggie that summer was that she was at least able to continue with the bookkeeping for the business partnership. The profits were not quite what they might have been if Maggie had been well, but they were encouraging nevertheless.

166

The Clays' oldest son, Quincy, was thirteen years old now and able to help his father in the blacksmith shop, though he was really more interested in what Torchy did and was sometimes allowed to accompany him on trading trips to Westport Landing. Torchy's twins, Beatrice and Jack Q (for the other children couldn't pronounce Jacques properly and had nicknamed him), were only six years old, but they were very helpful to Katrin in the cultivation and drying of the sweet potatoes and okra for Seventrees tea. Woody was very busy with his ferry most of the year, but was always willing to pitch in and help wherever he could. Torchy even built the one thing a predominantly German community could not long exist without—a small brewery. There was beer and singing in the long summer twilight.

All of this community growth and mutual concern warmed Maggie's heart, except that she regretted bitterly that she was lying indoors useless while everyone else worked. "You shouldn't say that," Katrin said when Maggie confided in her. "There's not anyone here who could keep track of the money coming and going like you do. You're doing the one thing that none of the rest of us could, and that's important."

"Katrin, that's dear of you to say. You can always make me feel better."

"You don't look like you're feeling better," Katrin said bluntly. "You look awful, skinny as a wet cat. I think you're going to carry this one full term, though. You're due in about three weeks now, aren't you?"

Maggie nodded, started to speak, then closed her mouth.

"Well, out with it," Katrin demanded. "What you want to say?"

"I have a question, but it's terribly indelicate. . . ."

Katrin laughed heartily. "Since when do you and me have to be 'delicate' with one another? What is it?"

"Well, I . . . I want to know something personal. How is it . . . ?" She hesitated, then went on in a rush, "How is it that you haven't gotten pregnant again?"

"I made Helmut build himself a new bed, that's how. He was old enough and tired enough that he didn't much care, and he was so scared about my being sick when Adams was born that he didn't want me to have any more babies either."

"Build a new bed? You mean . . . ?"

"That's exactly what I mean. There isn't any other way—not that I know of."

167

"But that's awful! You love Helmut. I could never do that!"

"Yes, it was awful, especially at first. But I thought I was dying when Adams was born, and it seemed less awful than leaving Helmut with no wife and a baby to raise. Don't look so worried. Just get some rest and we'll get you through this one just fine." Maggie did go the full term. Her labor started on the hottest night in August and went on all the next day. Her strength was at a low ebb to begin with, it was hot and she was sick, and the pain was endless. As she drifted in and out of a feverish sleep, she heard snatches of worried conversation between Katrin and Gran'mère Charron. "She's gone on much too long for a woman that's borne three already," Katrin whispered. "Better get someone on their way to the fort and get that prissy old Doc Hutchens down here. Don't know what good he'll do, but I sure don't know how to help her."

As the afternoon went on, Maggie kept waking to sudden, sharp contractions that took her breath away and left her shaken, trembling, and shivering. Then, try as she would to fight it, she would fall asleep, only to wake to a nightmare worse than anything she might dream. "He's gone with a wagon train. I'm riding over to Westport Landing to see if there's anyone there . . ." Was it Torchy's voice or Woody's? Maggie wasn't sure.

"I can see the top of the head. That baby's ready, I think. But it needs her help . . ." Katrin again. It was dark now. Katrin and Gran'mère Charron were standing at the foot of her disheveled bed.

"Black Fe . . ." Maggie tried to say.

"Don't talk. Save your strength," Katrin said.

Maggie lifted her head. Her sweat-drenched hair seemed to weigh her down, and flashes of light appeared around the edges of her vision. The pain had taken over her whole body now, replaced Maggie with a shapeless cloud of agony. "Black Feather . . ." she whispered.

"She's just mumbling about that silly old Indian," Katrin said to Gran'mère. "Her mind must be wandering. Poor thing."

Katrin came to the side of the bed and started bathing Maggie's temples in spring water. Maggie feebly grasped her friend's hand, gritted her teeth, and spoke as firmly as she could. "Get . . . Black . . . Feather . . . *now!*"

"Of course, Maggie. If it will make you feel better," Katrin said. It was obvious that she didn't approve. When next Maggie awoke, it was very late. She could hear the singsong insects that made sounds only after the day's heat had cooled all it was going to. "I can't see how this will do any good," Katrin was whispering to someone. "But he seemed sure, and I guess it can't hurt. Now, what did he say? Light this little bunch of twigs, yes. Good heavens, that smells like the dog's dinner! We'll never get that stink out of here. Now, hold it under her nose, but not too close . . ."

Maggie tried to open her eyes, but couldn't. She could detect a smell, but she was not capable of judging what it was. The inside of her nose began to itch, and she tried to raise her hand to rub it, but her hand was too heavy. It itched more . . . more—suddenly she sneezed. It seemed every muscle of her body bunched in splitting agony. She almost cried out, but took another breath instead and sneezed again.

"God in heaven! It's working . . ." Katrin said from the end of the bed. "Keep it burning. Don't let sparks fall on the blanket. . . ." Maggie sneezed twice more, and the last stage of breathtaking contractions resumed.

"Push, Maggie!" Katrin said loudly, and with some last secret reserve of strength, Maggie did do.

"A daughter—a healthy, little girl . . ." she heard Katrin saying as the smell of burning twigs faded. Maggie felt a swirling velvet darkness come closer and envelop her.

Maggie was not herself for a long time. The exhaustion went on for far longer than it should have, and Katrin was finally reduced to asking Black Feather's advice again. Even sitting up to work on the bookkeeping didn't cheer Maggie, and it had been nearly a week after the baby's birth before she would even think about names. Gerald was frantic with worry and guilt over his behavior the past few months and could hardly be convinced to leave her side. Finally Maggie decided on a name—Adelle. They would call her Addie. A good German name, a good courageous frontier name. Gerald had no preference, he wasn't even interested in the child, only in Maggie's welfare. He happily agreed to Addie, since it was the first time Maggie had taken any interest.

But Black Feather's potions and Katrin's cooking had eventually had an effect, and once again Maggie got out her ledger books, her papers, and the little metal money box. Torchy and Helmut came to her house and sat, uncomfortably and a little embarrassed at first, on either side of the bed instead of the big table. Maggie explained all the credits and debits, counted out the money to show that it balanced, then made three piles of bills on the quilt. Twenty-five hundred dollars among the three of them.

"Good, good, good!" Torchy gloated, riffling through his money.

Maggie laughed—the first time in months and months. "What are you going to do with it?" she asked. "I can tell by your face you have something in mind."

"*Oui!* When I take the goods to Saint Louis, I always stay at the miserable boardinghouses. Daytime, I work, I sell, I am happy. Nighttimes I think of my children and am sad—so I drink. This is not good, but I cannot take children to such places. "With this"—he waved the money—"and what I kept from last two years, I can buy a small house there. I have seen it and inquired. Then, when I go on trading trip, I take children and wicked Gran'mère and they stay in a nice house. Others, too—your Benjamin, Helmut's boy Quincy— they can stay there. All my friends here can visit my house there whenever they like."

"Torchy, that's a wonderful idea," Maggie said, wondering if she would ever see the house. Nothing was ever getting her back on a boat again.

"What about you, Helmut?" Torchy asked.

Helmut folded his money and tucked it into his breast pocket. "Save it," he said.

"Save it for what?"

Helmut just smiled and shrugged. "Something."

"And you, Maggie? What will you do with yours?" Torchy asked.

"I don't know for sure . . ." she said. But she knew that it was very soon time for a decision.

Later that same day Dr. Hutchens came to visit her. He checked her over thoroughly. "I'm sorry I couldn't be found when you had this one, though I couldn't have done anything better than the burning-twig business Katrin told me about. Some of these old savage superstitions work, I guess." As he was putting away his instruments, Gerald came in. The doctor sat down and regarded them both with a serious look. "I've got to tell you something. Normally I'd take the husband aside, but you're a different case, Mrs. Freiler. You've got a level head, and I think you're entitled to know the truth," he said in his usual precise, old-maidish manner.

"The truth?" Gerald said. "What's wrong?"

The doctor held up his hand. "One moment, please.

There's nothing wrong—now. Your wife is undernourished and worn out, but she'll be all right so long as she doesn't get pregnant again. I'll be honest with you, Mrs. Freiler. You're not one of these women who can go on putting out a baby every year till you're fifty. To be quite frank, and I think you deserve frankness, I would say if you got pregnant again in the next year or two . . . well, you'd be committing suicide. If you take it easy and eat right, you might be in shape by then, but I doubt it."

"But how . . . ?" Maggie blurted.

He shook his head. "You're not a silly woman. You know how *not* to get pregnant, and I think Mr. Freiler is a considerate enough man to understand that . . . well, desires sometimes have to be put aside for a loved one, for the sake of survival. You must understand that I *am* talking about life and death here. It isn't that you *might* not live through another childbirth—I can almost assure you that you wouldn't. You *do* understand that?"

"Then abstinence is the only way?" Maggie asked, putting a word to what he was trying to say.

The doctor looked disconcerted for a moment at Maggie's forthrightness. He'd never become quite accustomed to Maggie's Teutonic candor. He'd had this discussion before, but always with a husband alone, in hushed terms so the wife's delicate sensibilities would not be offended. But he'd known Maggie Freiler for quite some time, he reminded himself, he should not have been surprised. "Abstinence is the only safe, sure way," he answered. "There is the practice of . . ." he hesitated, trying to think of a proper term suitable to utter in a lady's presence—"of premature withdrawal. I've also heard lately of something called a condom, a protective device, that is made in Europe and sold in this country. In my opinion they are both unreliable. If you and Mr. Freiler simply didn't *want* any more children, it would be a different matter. You could afford to take the risk if it was merely a matter of preference."

"Thank you, Dr. Hutchens," Maggie said miserably. She *had* to survive to raise the children. There was no question in her mind of that. But could the love she and Gerald had for each other survive this stricture? To lose touching, loving, long nights of whispered intimacies? The fire of their physical passion for each other was the only way they could eliminate the invisible wall of conflicting dreams that stood between

171

them. Had their love been condemned by these few curt biological truths?

There was now a fledgling network of roads across Missouri, and when the snows melted the next spring Gerald and Maggie were driving a wagon along one of the raw, rutted tracks. Maggie had once again sewn her money into her stays, and they were on their way to spend a week at Torchy's new house in Saint Louis. Katrin was taking care of the children and Helmut was taking care of the trading post while part of the forge was being rebuilt.

Gerald had little to say along the way. He was still in a mild state of shock, for this trip had been purely of Maggie's devising. It was so unlike her to want to go anywhere that he was a little worried about what was behind it all.

They were both surprised at Saint Louis. When they had seen it on the way west, it had seemed a jumped-up outpost. More civilized than most of the western towns, but nothing like the big eastern cities they were accustomed to. But that had been almost five years ago, and they had not seen any community larger than Westport Landing in the interval. Now Saint Louis seemed like a bustling, confusing metropolis. The Mississippi River was fast becoming the main thoroughfare of the center of the country, and the old city had benefited from the increase in both trade and immigration.

They freshened up and unpacked their clothes at Torchy's modest brick house on Olive Street, then went on a carriage ride through the city. They saw the great Choteau mansion and the house where the illustrious Senator Thomas Hart Benton lived. They watched some of the enlarged and glorified steamers pouring their passengers onto the wharf and wondered at the proliferation of breweries and German name plates on professional establishments. "Six German doctors and eight lawyers in two blocks," Gerald said.

Inadvertently summing up a problem these men had, Maggie wondered, "What would anyone need with eight German lawyers? They had better take to farming."

"But, my love, they are intellectuals. Men of books." He did not add, "like I am." There was no need.

"Speaking of doctors, Torchy gave me the name of a man I wish to consult while we are here. I trust Dr. Hutchens' opinions, but I would still like . . ."

"I know," Gerald said, taking her hand. "I would like to believe he is wrong, too. Who is the doctor?"

"William Beaumont."

"Ah, the man who built a window in a stomach!"

"Torchy said something like that too. What does it mean?" Maggie asked.

"As I understand it, he treated a French trapper in Canada for a gunshot wound in the stomach. The wound would not heal, so he let the man live with him in order to study how his digestive system worked. Very respectable man. He founded a medical school here some years ago, I've heard, but I didn't know he still lived in Saint Louis. I would certainly be interested in talking to him about his experiments—"

"No! I mean, I would rather see him alone," Maggie said. "If you don't mind. . . ."

Gerald took her hand and looked deeply into her eyes. "Maggie, is there something wrong you haven't told me about? It that why we've made this mysterious trip?"

"No, no!" she hastened to assure him. "It's just that if you go along, you and the doctor will get interested in talking about the trapper's stomach, and . . . and I want his full attention. It's selfish of me . . ."

"Not at all. Let's find his office today, then we can do . . ." He grinned at her. " . . . whatever we came here to do."

Unfortunately, Dr. Beaumont agreed with Dr. Hutchens. "I think it would indeed threaten your life to undergo another confinement," he said, "though a healing period of several years might change the situation. Do you want me to explain this to your husband?"

"No, he understands. Visiting you was my own idea," Maggie said.

"Indeed?" He arched his eyebrow, regarding her in a questioning, almost distasteful manner. Was this tall, dignified woman trying to suggest that she actually *wanted* to have sexual relations? Absurd.

Gerald tried to pretend, for Maggie's sake, that the diagnosis meant nothing to him. "Very well, if that's how it is, we'll just have to get used to it," he said with mock cheer. "Now, I'm going to take you shopping. I'm not going to let you near anyplace that sells 'practical' things." He escorted her from one fancy shop to another, even forcing her to buy herself a new hat. She also got a science book for Benjamin, a stuffed elephant for Schooner, and a pretty scrolled harmonica for James. She purchased a length of yellow sprigged cotton for Katrin and a tortoiseshell comb for Gran'mère Charron. But her most serious shopping was for Black Feather, the man she believed had saved her life and Addie's.

She was going to make him a coat—*the* coat. It had to be the warmest and most beautiful coat in the territory. She found a pair of crimson wool blankets to cut it from, mink pelts with which to line it, and real silver buttons.

"Maggie, my love, I'm astonished at you spending so much money on the 'pretty' things for that coat," he said as they sat over a quiet dinner at Torchy's house that night. "I'm very pleased, you know, even though it's being spent on another man."

"But I'm going to spend a great deal more on you. That's the real reason for the trip," Maggie said.

"I wondered when we'd get to the reason. But me? What could you get me? There's nothing I want . . ."

Maggie held up her hand. "Wait here," she said, and went up to the bedroom. She had taken the money out of her stays and hidden it in a drawer. She brought the packet of bills— every penny she had made and saved for four years—just over fifteen hundred dollars. She came back to the table and handed the packet to Gerald. "There *is* something you have wanted for years. To go to Santa Fe. Here is the money to do it. You can purchase your supplies while we are here."

Gerald was speechless with surprise. He just stared blankly at her for a long moment, then got up and folded her in a painfully enthusiastic embrace. When he pulled away, Maggie thought she could detect tears in his eyes. "But why?" he stammered.

"For a hundred reasons," Maggie said, near tears herself.

"Please tell me some of the more flattering ones."

Maggie laughed. "I guess there's only one reason, really. I want you to do this because you want to and I love you."

Something she had said earlier began to come through to Gerald. "What did you mean, 'You can purchase *your* supplies'?"

"Gerald, I am not going with you. I'll wait for you at Seventrees. Don't look disappointed, *please*! You see, we've been thinking about this all wrong. You wanted most of all to go somewhere, and I wanted most of all to stay somewhere, and it seemed like an unsolvable contradiction, but it's not. We don't have to do the same thing. Besides, I need for you to leave. These last months of living together, loving one another, and being unable to . . . to fully express our love,

174

have been hard for both of us. I think it would be easier to get accustomed to if we were apart."

Gerald nodded. "Just knowing that I can't have you has made me desire you more than ever before, and I wouldn't have thought that possible. But, Maggie, this is all your money you've worked so hard for. I haven't been much help. Are you sure . . . ?"

"I've never been so sure of anything. I promised to call on some of Katrin's friends while I'm here to let them know how she is getting along. I will do that tomorrow while you buy your supplies."

"You're not coming with me?"

"I don't think I could stand to," she answered.

Gerald never quite figured out whether she meant his preparations for leaving would be painful to her or whether she meant she could not have viewed his purchases without criticizing them. Either way, she was right. It was time they parted for a while.

19

The loneliness was crushing at first. Maggie felt for months as if the very core of her life had been devastated and all that was left was a feeble mechanical device that caused her to move about involuntarily fulfilling her responsibilities. Her heart was gone, the vital spark of her personality had left for Santa Fe to return—someday.

A week after Gerald's departure a wagon train had come through Seventrees on the way back from Council Grove. A freckled boy brought Maggie a letter. "Man on the trail said give you this, ma'am."

For the rest of the summer Maggie greeted every east-bound traveler, and frequently there were letters from Gerald. He told her at long, literate length of what he was seeing and learning along the trail. The letters were the essence of him: bright-eyed and full of awed wonder at the world. He wrote a delightfully funny account of trying to eat prairie-dog meat and feeling as though his dinner's friends were

175

watching him. Maggie could almost taste the stringy meat and feel the eyes upon her. He told also of an Indian village they had passed which had been burned by an enemy tribe. Everyone in the village except one young girl had been most brutally slaughtered, and the girl herself was on the point of death when they found her. Maggie felt tears welling as she read his heartbreaking description of the burned shell of a community. His letter always ended with an eloquent statement of his love for her, which caused her to cry herself to sleep. "How could anything this painful be the right thing?" she asked herself a hundred times, and yet, something firm and positive in her assured her that it *was* right.

As spring inched into summer, however, her natural resilience began to assert itself, and she found she could smile, even laugh on occasion. In September, when the last trains came back through, Maggie expected Gerald to be with them, but he was not. There was, however, another letter:

Dearest Maggie, my love:

This will probably be the last opportunity I have to write to you this year. I'm staying here for the winter and I hope I can make you understand why. I hardly know where to start, but let me assure you my love and longing to be with you and the children is in no way diminished. Rather, it has grown as the weeks have passed.

But, Maggie, I have given deep and serious thought to the meaning and purpose of this separation. When I return to Seventrees, I mean to return for the rest of my life. I shall never again be parted from you, and I am not yet entirely ready to do this. I ache for the sight of you, but if I were to return now, a part of me would forever wonder what else there might have been to see and do. This is, I know, as selfish and irresponsible as it is possible for a loving husband to be. But although you have never understood me, I do understand myself, and I know if I were to come back now, I would never be content and would, therefore, make you as unhappy as myself.

I must get this to the leader of the wagon train before they leave, so I shall cut short any further news. Be assured, my dearest, that I love you and I will return to Seventrees as soon as I can.

Yours forever,
Gerald

Maggie was angry at first, then deeply sad, but as the winter snows piled up about the house, she finally began to feel a certain understanding, or at least sympathy, with what he said. Sometimes she even found herself feeling relieved to be on her own. It brought on a wave of guilt to think that way, and yet she was entirely in charge of all decisions regarding the house, the children, the way she spent her days, and it was easier not to consider another's feelings in making her decisions.

The first horrible pangs of loneliness were past. She had become accustomed to sharing her big bed with her two daughters instead of Gerald, and the business was doing very well. Gradually the days began to lengthen, the crisp-looking gray-and-white juncos disappeared, and robins took their place. There were only a few patches of snow left in shady corners, and Mrs. Whittacre began her furious spring cleaning of the mission. Maggie discovered that there were whole hours when she didn't think of Gerald at all.

More people than ever began to pass through Seventrees on their way to Oregon and Mexico, and they brought alarming rumors. There was sure to be a war with Mexico, they said. It wouldn't be any time at all. Some said there was already fighting, but there was no confirmation of this. The dispute was over a vast area called Texas, which had belonged to Mexico but had been settled by Americans. The Texans had decided to withdraw from Mexico and sought annexation to the United States. Maggie tried to tell herself that the fighting, if and when it occurred, would be in Texas, far to the east of Santa Fe. But still, with Mexico at war with the United States, Gerald would be in hostile territory.

One of the Oregon-bound settlers brought what was, to Maggie, good news. His brother had gone west earlier and had purchased a kit of cures at Seventrees. It had saved their lives, he wrote back. "Me and my friends all want your kits, ma'am," he said. "I've told everybody about them. You know, lots of folks takes sick afore they even get this far.

177

You ought to sell your kits farther east—like Saint Louis or even Pittsburgh."

Maggie discussed this with Torchy and he agreed that it was a possibility. On his next trading trip to Saint Louis he would take along as many kits as she could spare, and arrange for them to be sold at a post there.

Unfortunately, the first travelers that spring brought along something else. An influenza that was particularly hard on children, and especially Indian children. Katrin kept her own littlest one and Maggie's four as isolated as possible while Maggie tended the mission children. Despite their precautions, the Indian children all got the flu. Classes ceased and Maggie moved into the dormitory. As one exhausting day turned to another and another, Maggie was surprised to find that Mrs. Whittacre, with whom she'd had mercifully little contact over the years, was a competent and untiring nurse in an emergency. But she didn't even pretend affection for her little patients, only a dogged sense of duty. Putting aside their mutual wariness, the two women worked day and night tending the feverish Indian children.

After three interminable weeks, most of them were well on their way to recovery, although several had sustained hearing losses, which Maggie hoped were temporary. But just as Maggie and Mrs. Whittacre thought they could relax their vigilance, the two youngest children suffered relapses. Within a bare hour of each other they passed from feverish lethargy to convulsions and died.

Stunned and weary, Maggie said, "I'll ask Helmut Clay to dig graves up on the bluff where the Clays' son is buried." She was so tired she could hardly speak clearly.

"What!" Mrs. Whittacre roused herself from her weariness. "Bury the Indian *with* the whites?"

"They are all Christian souls and this *is* their land," Maggie said, outraged at the implication that they were not fit to share the earth with the whites.

"But it isn't fitting . . ." Mrs. Whittacre began; then her gaze shifted to the far end of the long, low-beamed dormitory loft.

Maggie turned and saw Black Feather. "I'm so glad you're here!" she said. His presence momentarily lifted her spirits, until she focused on his fierce expression.

The tall Indian strode forward, ignoring Maggie. "The children will be taken home for sacred burial," he said to Mrs. Whittacre. He had obviously heard the conversation.

Mrs. Whittacre had the grace to blush. "That's what I was trying to tell Mrs. Freiler—that you would prefer to bury them among their own. She misunderstood."

Black Feather merely stared at her, unwilling to accept this explanation, yet not arguing. "Mrs. Freiler, I've just come from your house. I believe your own eldest is ill."

Maggie felt a shiver of apprehension. She told herself it could not be—she'd been so adamant about keeping him away from the mission. But she ran all the way home. "Katrin, what is it? Black Feather said Benjamin . . ."

"Calm down. It's probably just a spring cold. That damned Indian shouldn't have scared you that way. I've got the boy in bed, all tucked in."

When she went in to him, Benjamin had already tossed off his covers and was complaining that he was hot. "Ben, you didn't go to the mission after I told you not to, did you?" Maggie asked. "Or go near the travelers' camp?"

"No, ma'am," the boy said. But he didn't lie often enough to do it convincingly. "Well, just once," he added. "I left my arithmetic book at school . . ."

The progress of the infection was fierce. By evening he was raging with fever and shivering convulsively. Maggie wrapped him in layers and layers of blankets, administered all the cures she had used on the other children, and spent the long night holding him in her lap. She knew there was little else she could do. She had seen enough of the illness to know something else—it was nearly hopeless. Even the two Indian children who died had not been consumed by the disease at such a furious pace. She nearly choked on the bitter irony of it all. While she had been caring for the other children, one of her own had been struck a fatal blow. Was this how God repaid honest charity?

All night and all the next day she held Benjamin. Katrin offered to relieve her for a spell, but she would not let him leave her aching arms. By afternoon he had slipped into a mercifully painless coma, and still Maggie held him. At dusk there was a light tap on the door, and Black Feather entered, breaking his own rule about entering her house. He said nothing to her, merely looked at Benjamin and nodded. Then he busied himself building up a fire against the chill of the spring evening and preparing a potion.

"He can't drink," Maggie said.

But Black Feather had some dried grass with the herbs he had brought. The larger stalks were dried and hollow like straws. He sucked the potion up in one, kept his thumb over one end, and put the other end at the corner of Benjamin's mouth. Drop by slow drop he fed it, and the boy's natural swallowing reflexes allowed him to take the medicine without choking.

"It won't help," Maggie said miserably.

"No, it will not," Black Feather admitted. "But you and I are healers. We must try."

Barely an hour later Benjamin began to shake again. He thrashed and gasped hideously for breath. Maggie clutched at him, feeling the bile of fear rise in her throat. Suddenly he went limp in her arms, and with a long, gurgling expiration, he was gone. Maggie was frozen with horror and disbelief. She had known he was dying, but still had not felt in her heart of hearts that it was possible.

She doubled over her lifeless burden and wept with remorse and loneliness and guilt. She'd had too little time for her children in the years since they'd come west. Nine years ago, when Benjamin was a baby, she'd known everything about him; his every mood and whim as an infant had been of consuming interest to her. But coming west, she'd lost him. He'd moved into a world of other people—of teachers and playmates—and Maggie had switched part of her interest to the other children and to the desperate plight of surviving and prospering in their new life. It was inevitable, but agonizingly regrettable. If only she'd had him a little longer, she could have known him better, told him more of her love.

But it was too late now.

Black Feather sat cross-legged in a corner, his own head bowed in respect of her grief for a long while. Finally he rose and said, "You must rest."

Maggie was beyond thinking rationally, but there was such calm authority in his voice, she obeyed. She let the Indian take the boy from her arms and lay him gently on the narrow bed by the door. Then he led her to her own room, careful to stop at the doorway. "I will get Mrs. Clay," he said softly.

"Black Feather, you . . . I . . ." There was so much she wanted to say to him, but the words would not come.

He started to step forward, but stopped in a rare, ungraceful movement. "I will get Mrs. Clay," he repeated grimly.

"Thank you," Maggie whispered between sobs.

They buried him the next day up on the bluff overlooking the valley. It wasn't until Maggie saw John Clay's grave next to the new gash in the earth that she remembered the two dead Indian children. Black Feather must have taken their bodies home to his tribe and returned immediately to her. She'd not seen him again after he left her the night before, and was overcome with a longing to thank him properly for his friendship and support.

As Reverend Whittacre read the service, Maggie looked at the pitifully small coffin and then out over the Kaw Valley. Now, more than ever before, she was home. Her firstborn, the child who symbolized her love for Gerald before there were misfortunes and disappointments, had taken his place in the earth here. His eternal place in the world. Someday it would be hers as well.

A sudden wash of resentment flooded over her. Gerald should have been here to bury his son. Here on the bluff with her, not in Mexico. This was the day of days she needed him. She felt her face growing hot with anger and tried to find her way back to reason. Gerald would not have left her if he'd known that tragedy was going to strike them. Anyway, it had been *her* idea that he go. She had saved the money and insisted that they must live apart. Even before that, years before, when they first met, she'd known that his head was full of the siren call of the West and it was his fate to go farther than this gentle green valley.

But there was still a tight knot of anger in her heart that reason could not unpick.

Black Feather returned that evening. Maggie had put the children to bed and tried to sleep, but the rest she needed so badly eluded her. Flinging a crocheted shawl over her nightgown, she sat on the weather-beaten porch step and looked out over the little community. There was only the sad sliver of a moon, and the darkness seemed cold and infinite. She was dry-eyed now; all the tears were done. They had washed away the knife-sharp edge of first grief. Now there was only the vast, cold darkness.

She didn't hear him approach, but she knew he was near. "Do you need something to help you sleep?" he said in a voice that sounded like the hushed whisper of wind in the oak trees.

She smiled slightly. "No. But I need someone to sit by me. I need *you* to sit by me," she answered with candor.

He took a place on the porch at a respectful distance. It was Maggie who moved closer. "As this day moves into your past, the sorrow will become fainter, though it will always echo in your heart," Black Feather said. "As we grow older, there are many voices crying out from our pasts. But ever more softly."

"You have such voices?" Maggie asked. In all the time she had known this dignified man, she had never heard him speak of his own life, nor had she asked any questions. His family, his exceptionally cultured English, his origins, were an untouched mystery. But tonight she needed to know something about his heart.

"I have a wife and a child who call to me from their graves," he said simply, and Maggie felt ashamed of herself for prodding.

"I'm sorry . . ." she said.

"Do not be sorry," he said, and then, as if it was as natural as the course of the seasons, he put his arm around her shoulders.

Just as naturally, Maggie rested her head against him and blossomed in the warmth and reassurance of his strong arms. She lifted her face, and slowly he turned toward her until their lips met. The merest brushing of soul to soul, culture to culture at first, and then another kiss and another. She twined her arms around him, desperate for the heat and comfort of passion. There was so much they already shared—their interest, their isolation from the whims and prejudices of others, their love of the land and the children of the land. Why should they not share their bodies with each other as men and women were meant to?

Maggie's shawl slipped from her shoulders and a cool breeze touched her through the thin fabric of her nightgown. Astringent nature reminding her to take care. Take care. Take care.

Gradually she realized what she was doing. She was risking her very life: the almost inevitable conclusion to this moment might lead to a pregnancy. She was risking her marriage: when Gerald returned, he would instinctively know of her disloyalty and be destroyed by it. She was, above all, risking her friendship with Black Feather. Unschooled, unsophisticated, unworldly in many ways, Maggie still sensed that the dignity of their friendship could not survive the flame of a clandestine affair. They could have one or the other, but not both.

The measure of their understanding was such that they both began to draw back at the same moment. He smiled

182

sadly at her, and she knew his thoughts had run a parallel path to her own. "You have been my friend," Maggie said softly. "Stay my friend."

He touched her pale hair lightly and held his hand to the side of her face for a moment, then said, "That is how it must be, if you wish it." He made no attempt to apologize, knowing as well as she that the moment had been a mutual lapse and had sealed the bond between them.

The next day Maggie began a long letter to Gerald. She told him about Benjamin's death, but did not mention Black Feather. In closing, she assured him of her love and tried to express in a restrained way her longing for his return. He should, however, stay as long as necessary, she said. "Gerald, there is only one thing I ask of you," she added in a postscript. "Should you decide *not* to return, you must tell me so. I do not mind waiting for your return, but I deserve to know if you are never going to come back."

When the first wagon train bound for Santa Fe passed through Seventrees, she sealed the letter, addressed it simply to Mr. Gerald Freiler in Santa Fe, and gave it to Captain Bruckner with two dollars for his trouble. Then she waited for a reply.

There was none.

June passed. Then July. Black Feather brought the Indian children back to the mission and treated Maggie with the same cool, respectful courtesy he always had. Sometimes she wondered if she had made the right choice, and discovered all over again that reasons of the head and reasons of the heart were sometimes in dire conflict.

In the heat of long August days Maggie would climb the long hill to the top of the bluff where the Santa Fe Trail veered away from the river valley and set out across the plains. She would squint into the blazing summer sun for the first sign of returning wagon trains and meet them with eager inquiries. But there was never a letter for her.

Dear God in heaven, was he dead? she began to wonder. Why else had he not written? Perhaps, she told herself hopefully, he is not in Santa Fe, perhaps he had gone somewhere else and his letters had just not reached her. That must be it, that *had* to be the reason! Finally the last wagon train of the season rolled into Seventrees, and there was, at long last, a letter from Gerald. Maggie clutched it to her heart. At least he was alive, but why hadn't he come back? She didn't dare open the letter. She carried it about for the rest of the day, sealed, in her apron pocket. Was this what she had asked for? Was he writing to say he was never coming back? That his heart now belonged to another place?

"You got a letter from Gerald?" Katrin asked.

"Yes."

"Good, what did he have to say?"

Maggie's hand went to her apron pocket. "I don't know," she said softly. "I can't bear to read it."

Katrin nodded understandingly, patted Maggie's arm, and went about her business.

Maggie waited until the children were in bed, then turned up the wick in the lamp. She sat at the scarred oak table for a long time, looking at the letter, feeling it, trying to guess from the handwriting what it might say. It was not Gerald's usual careful hand, and there was only one thin sheet enclosed. Could that be encouraging? Certainly if it was bad news he would have explained himself in detail and it would be a thick letter. No. He would not be able to prolong the unhappiness. A short letter had to be good news.

Finally she could speculate no longer. Better to face the truth and have done with it. She tore open the envelope and unfolded the single sheet of paper.

> Maggie, my love:
>
> Have just returned from a trip south and find that the last train is leaving. Must hurry, for they will not wait. I intended to go with them, but unforeseen events detained me. I'm coming home, and I wish it were me and not this letter making the journey now, but there are things I have to tie up before leaving, and there simply is no time. Must wait for spring.
>
> How can I possibly tell you of the love I have for you in such short space? I will see you in June—July at the latest.
>
> Your loving husband,
> G.

She read the letter through again, and then a third time, lingering on the final paragraph. She didn't so much come to a conclusion as she was overcome by it. When Gerald returned the next spring, they would live as man and wife. Completely. The doctors meant well with their advice, but time had passed, and if God wanted to take her in childbirth, he would. She wasn't even so afraid of dying now as she had been. Her greatest fear was facing a lifetime without Gerald's love.

20

Maggie set out the plates and had to take one back. It had been more than a year since Benjamin's death, and she still sometimes forgot that he was gone. Deep inside, she still had four children to take care of.

"Oh, Addie, you're such a baby!" Schooner complained, trying to pry the little girl's sticky fist off her paper. "Let go of that!"

The crops planted, the Indian children had been brought back to the mission, and the summer classes had started. Schooner, almost seven now, had been working on an essay at the breakfast table when Addie dipped her fingers first into oatmeal, then into Schooner's schoolwork.

Maggie left the stove and intervened. "Schooner, you must keep your papers farther away from her. She doesn't know how important they are, and she *is* just a baby."

"I know, Mama, but she's got it all sticky now, and I'll have to do it over."

But Schooner could never remain angry with Addie for long, and in a few minutes she was playing pat-a-cake with her. Maggie watched the girls contentedly. Schooner was not a beauty, but she had a fresh, healthy look that was more than pretty. She was a loving child who genuinely liked to get along with people. While other children whiled away long afternoons picking and complaining about each other and seeming to enjoy it, Schooner would try to smooth things over, and if that didn't work, she would find a way to remove herself from the discord.

Addie, in contrast, was astonishingly pretty. Some long-neglected gene had surfaced in her, giving her reddish-gold hair that fell naturally into fat, bouncy curls. Her eyes were blue and huge and heavily fringed with thick lashes. She could not have looked less like her namesake. Even strangers who had no interest in pleasing Maggie invariably commented on the startling beauty of the child. Addie was already spoiled by this, and unless Maggie kept a very sharp eye on her, she tended to prance and pose and be deliberately "adorable." The same strangers were captivated by this, but Maggie found it abhorrent. Maggie wondered sometimes if Schooner didn't mind being put in the shade by her little sister, but Schooner spoiled the younger child as much as anyone and didn't seem to object to the attention she always got.

Maggie was in awe of the mystery of how she had given birth and sustenance to four children, treating each the same (she thought), and how utterly different they had become from each other. Benjamin had been years ahead of other children his age in his studies, but there had always seemed to be an odd lack of fire or joy in what he did.

James, almost nine now, was no student at all. He still read simple English stories ploddingly, one dirty nail-bitten finger under each word as he went along. But he was the one who would say, "You're tired, aren't you, Mama? Do you want some help?" at the end of a hard day, or, "I think Running Deer's feelings were hurt when Mrs. Whittacre told him to wash his face, don't you, Mama?" He was not as cheerful as Schooner, but he seemed to have enough understanding of the human heart for all of them. He brooded and often cried, but he was the one who sang while he did his chores and would take one of Gerald's flutes with him when he went looking for firewood and would fill the woods with music.

"There's the school bell, Mama. I can't find my pencils," Schooner interrupted her thoughts. She scurried about, gathering her things, gave Addie a smacking kiss and Maggie a more restrained one, then bolted out the door. James, typically, had gone for a bucket of water and had not come back. Maggie went to the door and called for him until he sheepishly came running from the opposite direction from the river.

"Do I have to go to school?" he asked plaintively.

"Absolutely," Maggie said, and handed him his books. "Hurry, now. Reverend Whittacre doesn't like for you to be late."

Katrin came by just as Maggie finished cleaning up from breakfast. "Quincy is taking the wagon over to Westport Landing to pick up some things for his father today," she said. "I talked him into taking Adams along for the ride, and he said he'd take Addie along too, if you'd like."

"That's *so* nice of him. He's good to the little ones. Not many boys his age would bother," Maggie said. She was very fond of Quincy. He was sixteen now and taking an ever-greater interest in the business. Torchy had taken him on two trading trips this summer and even let him do some of the actual negotiating, which Torchy reported he'd done exceptionally well.

Maggie cleaned Addie up, combed her hair, and sent her along; then she opened the post and started straightening up the shelves. It was difficult, at the height of the summer trade, to keep everything neat and in order, and she welcomed time to work without Addie clinging to her skirts, demanding attention.

She was so engrossed in what she was doing that she hardly noticed the sounds of a wagon train approaching. The first wagons were already drawing into ranks at the ferry landing before the fact came to her attention. She had anxiously met the first few trains at the beginning of the summer at her favorite place on top of the bluffs, but when Gerald hadn't arrived and business turned brisk, she had abandoned this activity. It only made the disappointment keener, anyway. But she wanted to ask for news of the war that had finally been declared against Mexico.

She folded her inventory pages full of small, neat writing, closed the ledger book, and went to watch the wagons arrive. Most of them were just passing through, continuing along the trail to Westport Landing and points east. Others were dropping out of line and turning down the road to the ferry, where they lined up in pairs to await their turn at crossing the Kaw. But one wagon, a schooner with patched and faded canvas, had pulled off by itself, and a bearded man in black trousers and a faded blue shirt had climbed down.

Maggie's heart seemed to leap into her throat. Even from a distance, she recognized him. Gerald was back—at last. She ripped loose the knot at the back of her apron and ran a quick hand over her hair to smooth it before she ran to greet him. But as she stepped beyond the door, she saw him turn back to the wagon and raise a hand to help someone else down.

It was an Indian girl. Very young. And very pregnant.

No! No! Something inside her screamed. It wasn't what it looked like. She was jumping to conclusions. The girl was certainly some stranger he had given a ride. Yes, that had to be it. Maggie would have run to him, but she did not trust her legs. She walked toward the wagon.

She called his name softly when she got close enough. He turned and looked at her anxiously. Then his eyes flickered toward the Indian girl for an instant and back. "Maggie, my love," he said.

Then she knew.

But she had to ask, to be sure beyond doubt. Without stepping any closer, she gestured to the girl. "Is the baby yours?" she asked in a terrified whisper.

He took a step nearer, eyes and arms beseeching. "Yes."

Maggie crossed her arms, clutching for control. Her throat was constricting. "Betrayal! Betrayal!" voices inside her head shrieked.

"Oh, God, Maggie . . . let me explain—"

"No!" she almost screamed the word. "No! I can't bear . . . Don't explain . . ." She turned and ran.

He was calling to her, but she couldn't hear—wouldn't hear—his voice. She lifted her skirts and with long, stumbling strides sought the privacy of the forest. She had to get away. She could not be seen in this state.

How dare he? Her mind raced and plummeted. *I have loved only him. Only him. Only him. How could he do this to me? Everything gone. A lifetime over.*

Suddenly all the reasoning, all the common sense she'd built and nurtured, drained from her in a gush. Like a wild creature sustaining a fearful blow, Maggie ran for solitude. She was not thinking, hardly feeling, just escaping something she could not accept.

She fled, unseeing, unfeeling of the brambles and thorns tearing at her skirts and flesh, unaware of the spring undergrowth that cushioned the sound of her flight. Suddenly she stopped and collapsed to the ground, waiting for the tears. But they did not come. It would have been a relief, a release, but she sat there on the ground, skirts billowed out around her like a crushed flower, and there were no tears. Only a hot, dry-eyed panic, a sense that her life had crashed down around her and she was left sitting in the rubble of it, not knowing how or why it had happened.

But as she sat, the core of her life crippled and bleeding, anger began to take over. Why did he think he had the right to do this to her? She had given him her life. She'd left everything she knew for *his* dream. She hadn't wanted to go west—*he* had. She'd worked for years for the money for him to go to Santa Fe. She'd worked—at the business, at raising the children—while he enjoyed himself. How dare he. How *dare* he!

She stood. Her whole body was trembling, but it was anger now that moved her. She would not let him drive her off into the thicket of misery. She'd faced bankruptcy, childbirth, harsh winters, and worse. She could certainly face him!

He was at the house when she returned. There was no sign of the girl. As she went in the door, he started to move toward her, but she sidestepped, putting the table between them. For an instant she had a sharp pain of longing to be in his arms, but a fresh surge of anger took her. She sat down on a hard kitchen chair. "Why didn't you write and tell me?" she asked coldly.

Gerald looked older. A few strands of silver glistened in his dark curls. His voice was weary. "I did. I wrote about the village that was burned. Little Smile was the only survivor. She was half-dead. The others wanted to leave her, and I couldn't stand to do that. . . . Maggie, you would have done the same thing," Gerald went on.

I could have done the same thing, but I didn't, she thought. "I wouldn't have gotten her pregnant."

Gerald sat down across from her. "I didn't intend to. Please listen! Please try to understand. I nursed the girl back to health, just like she was a wounded animal, for God's sake! Then I had no way to get rid of her."

"So you slept with her!"

"Maggie, please listen! Just once, hear what I'm saying. I couldn't just put her out to beg or be a prostitute in the streets of Santa Fe. She was just a *child*! She depended on me. Maggie, Maggie, no one has ever depended on me . . . No," he said, raising a hand against her objection. "No, *you* haven't depended on me. With good reason, some of the time. But this one person owed her life to me. She thought I was capable of no wrong. She believed that I could solve any problem in the world."

He reached across the scarred table, captured her white-knuckled hands in his. "Maggie, that's a heady feeling. You must know that. How could I have just thrown her out to fend for herself?"

Maggie pulled her hands away from the rough warmth of his. "But why did you have to make love to her?" she asked briskly, trying to keep the tears at bay. They would not be a relief now, only a further indignity.

He stood, angry and pale. "Goddammit! I don't know. It just happened. She kept telling me of her love. She waited on me. Then one night . . . one night she was in my bed." He leaned forward, his fists clenched. "Maggie, have you never succumbed to any temptation? No, I guess not. It had nothing to do with my love for you. Nothing! It had precious little to do with *me*. I was lonely. It was the middle of the winter—long, lonely nights. Maggie, try to understand. Please try!"

Maggie got up and went to the stove. She poured two cups of coffee that slopped over because her hands were shaking. She set them on the table, careful not to touch Gerald. How dare he say she couldn't understand! She, who had felt the same temptation and resisted it. And it had been harder for her, for she had genuinely loved and respected the other man. But she would not share that knowledge with Gerald. He had forfeited his right to her heart's secrets. She wanted to scream at him, to tell him he could not have been more lonely than she, more unhappy, more in need of comfort and love.

"Maggie, I knew you'd be hurt," Gerald went on. "If I'd known any way to prepare you, I would have done it. But I had to come back. My place is with you. I couldn't face a lifetime away from the only woman I've ever loved." Softly he added, "You *are* the only woman I've ever loved."

Maggie took a sip of scalding coffee, grateful for the physical pain. "What are you going to do now?"

"Dear God! Don't ask me that! I don't know what to do. I'm more obligated to Little Smile than ever now. She's pleasant enough, Maggie. A hard worker. You'll like her . . . I mean . . ."

Maggie gave him a wild look of such offense that he was taken aback. "I shall never like her because I shall never know her. Don't *ever* get her near me! She has stolen the only thing I treasured—my husband's fidelity. She can have no redeeming trait that could make up for that."

"I'm sure she doesn't see it that way."

"I don't care how she sees it! *I* see it that way. Don't try to burden *me* with her—don't try to make *me* feel any sympathy for her. She could drop dead this instant and I would dance in her ashes. Gerald, take your Indian girl to Saint Louis. When the baby is born, bring it back. I will raise it, because it's yours."

"What about Little Smile?"

"I don't care what happens to her."

"You can't mean that."

"I *do* mean that."

"But I have a responsibility to her. She's Indian, an alien in white society. How would she get along if I abandoned her?"

How could he sit here in her kitchen—in the house he would never have bothered to complete had not she and her friends forced him to—and talk about responsibility to another woman? It was the ultimate insult. "Gerald," Maggie said in a terribly quiet voice, "get out."

At first he did not move, did not seem to hear or perhaps to comprehend what she was saying. Then he rose, pale and frightened. "You want me to leave?"

"You must choose. I think you *have* chosen. Get out."

"Maggie, my love, you can't possibly mean this. Do we mean nothing to each other? All the years, the love, the children . . . Maggie, I can't live without you."

An unseen hand had taken hold of her heart and torn it in two. She was shaking with pain. "You have her love."

"I don't want her love! I never did. I don't even like her very well. She whistles off tune, she shuffles when she walks . . . she is a child! But I can't just throw her to life to do with her what it will."

"Then that is your decision. I will care for you and the child when it is born. I will not have her anywhere near me."

"Maggie!"

"There is no point in prolonging this. We've both said what we have to say. I do love you, Gerald, I'll never stop loving you, but your sense of responsibility has developed too late and in a direction I would not have thought." Her voice was beginning to waver and crack. "Please leave now. I cannot bear . . ."

He came around to her, wrapped his arms around her tenderly. She could smell soap and leather and trail dust. Then the tears came. She wept silently, shoulders shaking, hot salt tears burning down her cheeks. He held her tighter and tighter until her breath was almost gone.

But it made no difference. Finally she pulled back, saw that his eyes were red too. "Maggie . . ."

She turned away, brushing at the tears with the back of her hands. "Go away," she whispered.

21

 ～

It wasn't until Gerald was gone that Maggie realized she'd not mentioned Benjamin's death to him. Had he ever gotten the letter she sent? "No, but Helmut told him," Katrin said when Maggie raised the subject. "He met up with them on the road to Westport."

It had been three months now since Gerald had returned and been sent away by Maggie, and she had not yet told the children. He had been away so long that only Benjamin would have remembered him. James thought he did, and Schooner wasn't even interested in the shadowy image in her childish memory that was "Father." Someday she would have to tell them, before someone else did, but she kept putting it off. Someday, when the pain was less acute, she would explain to them. But how?

Black Feather had been to the mission twice since that day. The first time, Maggie had missed seeing him, but he'd left her a packet of some herbs she once mentioned having trouble finding. The second time, they'd met accidentally by the ferry landing, and Maggie had felt, for a moment, such a searing need to touch him that it frightened her. But now she recognized the feeling for what it was—a falsifying of the genuine affection she had for him. A dangerous disguise brought about by her thwarted passion for Gerald. She almost invented an imaginary errand so that she could hurry away, but she forced herself to stay. After a few minutes of friendly talk about medicines and the children Black Feather was responsible for, she felt the tightness in her throat easing and she could speak to him as she always had, treasured friend to friend.

By October, life had returned to normal for most of the fledgling town. There was always an almost audible communal sigh of relief when the last of the wagon trains passed through in the fall. Then everyone could settle into the pleasant domestic flurry of preparing for the winter. The necessities of life helped keep Maggie's mind off the tragedies. For the men, the main concern was with fuel for the harsh months ahead. For the women, it started with food and ended with clothing. Nothing ever seemed to fit the same child as the winter before, and there was an orgy of exchanges as the days grew shorter and temperatures started to drop.

Katrin's little boy Adams was now wearing some clothes that had started with his older brothers, been passed through Benjamin and James Freiler with many patchings, gone next to Jack Q LeSage, and finished up back on a Clay boy. Maggie had helped Gran'mère Charron make dresses for Beatrice LeSage, which then passed back to Schooner and eventually Addie.

This fall, however, James and Schooner didn't fit into anybody's winter coats, and Maggie realized she would have to make new ones. They did not keep fabrics at the Seventrees trading post, and Maggie asked Torchy if she could ride along with him the next time he went to Westport. "Certainly, this would be a great pleasure to . . ." Suddenly he stopped in confusion. "Would it not be just as well for me to pick up the cloth for you and bring it back? I would be most pleased to do so for you."

"That's nice of you, but I'd like to go," Maggie said.

"But there is no need! It is getting brisk weather, and you would not enjoy the ride. It might even snow."

"Torchy, what's the matter with you? Why don't you want me to go?"

The door opened and Katrin came in. Torchy appealed to her for help. "Maggie wants that I should drive her on a shopping expedition to Westport," he said.

Maggie looked from one to the other of them. "It's Gerald, isn't it?" she said. She felt her heart begin to pound as if she'd been running a long distance. In the months since Gerald had gone, she'd forced her heart and mind away from the memory of him whenever she could, but when she was taken by surprise this way, she found it hard to control herself. Just the day before, she'd been cleaning and found one of his flutes, and she'd cried for half an hour. "Is Gerald in Westport?" she asked.

Torchy and Katrin exchanged a quick glance, and Katrin said, "Yes, Maggie. He and the girl live there, and . . ."

"And what? Katrin, you need not keep anything from me. Tell me what you know now. It may save me embarrassment."

"Oh, Maggie, I didn't want you to know they were even near."

"Well, I can't hide here in Seventrees the rest of my life. Do they have a house?"

"That's just it," Katrin said miserably. "They are—or were, last I heard—staying in the wagon. Gerald told Helmut he has no money."

"But he wrote me about selling his goods in Santa Fe. He made a great deal of money on them," Maggie said.

"Yes, so he says, but he was there for some time, and apparently everything is very expensive. Then he was robbed of what he had left just before he returned. I guess he didn't have time to tell you about that the day he . . ." She stopped.

"Yes, we had other things to discuss that day," Maggie said wryly. "You and Torchy are dear friends, trying to protect me. I appreciate it, but it's not necessary. It's unfortunate they're staying this close, but I will just have to learn to live with it. I won't be imprisoned here because of it. Now, Torchy, as I said earlier, may I ride into Westport with you tomorrow?"

Seventrees awoke the next morning to an early snow. By noon it had melted away, but it seemed to forecast a bad winter, and Maggie shivered in her own threadbare coat. She would have a great deal of sewing to do if they were to get through the winter without sickness. She tried to occupy her mind during the ride with the preparations to be made for the long dark winter. She should have some more wood cut. James could miss a day or two of school to do that. He would regard it as a privilege, and it wouldn't do him any harm since he appeared to be almost entirely immune to education anyway. While she was buying fabric, she would get something heavier for curtains. Last year had been overly drafty, and she had meant to take care of that sooner. Try as she would, however, her mind kept imagining what was ahead.

Maybe he was gone by now, she told herself. They might have moved on to Saint Louis. Even if they were in Westport Landing, she might not see them. There was no point in getting distressed in advance. As they rode into the town, she kept her eyes firmly on the building that was their destination. They stopped in front of the wagon maker's shed and Torchy helped her down. The business of signing the contracts was quickly done.

194

"Do you wish me to walk to the trading post with you?" Torchy asked.

"No, thank you. You have things to do, and so has Helmut. I know my way. Shall we meet back here in an hour?"

"This is satisfactory?" he said doubtfully.

She touched his arm and smiled. "Yes. Thank you, Torchy. Be on your way. I am all right."

Maggie saw no one she knew on the way down the street. She tried not to look around at all the new buildings springing up, for fear she might see Gerald or the girl. She greeted the shopkeeper, gave him her list, selected her fabrics and a nice pair of leather shoes for Addie. She waited while he got her things together in bundles to wrap up. In spite of resolve, she found herself drifting toward the windows. She had been watching for only a few minutes when she saw Gerald. He was in shirtsleeves, hurrying against the cold wind. But he was limping slightly, and his hands were red and raw-looking.

It was his hands that did it. He had held her, stroked her skin with those hands. Had held a flute and made it create sad, beautiful music, had touched Benjamin softly in wonder at his infant perfection. Those hands, so ill-suited to the cold and hard work, had held the slim poetry books he had read to her in front of the fire back in Germantown. She raised her head, blinking back tears.

As he drew near, two rough-looking men approached from the opposite direction. As they came even with him, they stopped and let out some contemptuous war whoops; then one of them spat at him. Gerald kept walking, acting as if he had not noticed. But he wore the "other" face Maggie had sometimes seen. This was the miserable, hunted, haunted Gerald. He walked in the door of the dry-goods store and stared at Maggie in shock for a moment. He made a fractional move as if to turn around and leave, but then stopped and straightened and said softly, "Hello, Maggie."

The gentle, defeated tone of it was almost too much to stand. But she forced herself to smile and say hello in a friendly manner. They made strained small talk for a while: strange weather . . . such a surprise so early in the season . . . Westport Landing certainly was growing . . . yes, the German bakery was a welcome addition . . . Finally Maggie said, "Has the baby been born?"

"Yes. A girl."

"May I see her?" Maggie didn't know what had come over

195

her. This was the very thing she vowed she would not do, but she had to see the child.

Gerald led Maggie down the street without speaking, and turned between two buildings. There was a narrow alley, and behind it a wagon. He opened the canvas flap and gave her a hand up. She stooped, crawled in, standing still for a moment while her eyes adjusted to the semidarkness inside. The Indian girl sat huddled in the far end of the wagon. She really was a child herself, no more than sixteen. *Dear God*, Maggie thought, *I could have had a daughter her age if I had married earlier*! She was neither pretty nor ugly, neither thin nor fat. Her hair was tied back with a scrap of ribbon, and she was wrapped in a faded green blanket. She was shivering. A thin mew came from the blanket. Little Smile smiled, a bit of battered pride in the child. She pulled the blanket back and gestured an invitation for Maggie to look.

Maggie took a faltering step forward and peered at the baby. She had downy black hair with a hint of Gerald's curls, a pink little mouth, and enormous dark eyes that seemed to be a deep blue rather than brown. She was a lovely baby, but she was thin and there was a faint bluish cast to her skin. Maggie touched the baby's head, then Little Smile's hand. "You are cold—both of you."

The Indian girl obviously had no idea who this visitor was. She nodded. "Cannot have fire in wagon. Burn down, ma'am."

Without even stopping to think, Maggie stripped off the coat she was wearing and handed it to the girl. "You keep this. I can get another."

Little Smile grasped her hand; tears of gratitude filled her eyes. "Many thank-yous, kind ma'am," she said.

Maggie pulled her hand back, stumbled down out of the wagon. She was unaware of the cold, or of Gerald trying to help her. All she knew was that a helpless girl was going to freeze to death in the wagon this winter if she didn't help her—and the child of the man they both loved. She walked back to the slight protection of the alley, wrapped her arms around herself, and waited for Gerald to catch up.

They stared into each other's eyes, saying what they could not say before in words. Finally Gerald spoke. "You see now, don't you?"

Maggie nodded. "Yes."

"*Gott in Himmel*! I have destroyed myself," he said, looking back at the wagon. "I have destroyed us!"

Maggie was silent for a long time. Then she said, "Torchy will build a house for the three of you. I will pay him, and you can pay me back out of what you can make teaching. Reverend Whittacre would like to have you back."

"A house for the three of us?"

"Yes. She *is* your responsibility now. Gerald, I will do anything for you that you need, but . . . I will not be your 'other wife.' Do you understand? You are still the father of my children, you are welcome to visit them in my house, but you are not my husband anymore."

"I've never touched her again, since that one night," he said.

"Oh, Gerald, why did we ever leave Germantown? What have we come to? Why wasn't love enough? We had so *much* love." She was crying again and wasn't even aware of it.

"I don't know, Maggie, my love. I don't know," he said. "I feel like I'm drowning in regrets for what should have been. I should have come back with my fortune to lay at your feet as an offering of love. I should have dug Benjamin's grave and been at your side. I should have done so many things, and now it's too late. Too late."

Maggie shivered in the cold wind of "should-haves." She had no comfort for him, no convincing denials to salve their wounds. He put his arm around her shoulders and walked her back to the store to pick up her packages. The tiny gold locket at her throat swung coldly against her skin.

No one in Seventrees understood. They thought she was foolish, at best, and Mrs. Whittacre was heard to say things about madness and used the word "besotted"—but not around Maggie. The only one who did not either criticize or pity her was Black Feather. "You have the courage to ignore the closed doors of other hearts," he said to her when he brought the Indian children back for the winter session of school.

"I had to do it, Black Feather, because . . ."

He raised his hand. "You need not explain. You did what you knew to be right. This is all that is necessary for anyone else to know."

Maggie sensed that he referred to the night after Benjamin's death as well as to her invitation to Gerald and Little Smile.

"Thank you. Everyone else here is either trying to rummage in my reasoning or treating me with pity—like someone who has had a death in the family."

"Perhaps they see something about you that you do not see. Is this not a death of a part of your life?"

"Yes, I suppose it is," she said before Reverend Whittacre came and took Black Feather away to discuss the children.

Maggie had selected for Gerald and his "wife" a site well to the west of the cluster of houses that made up Seventrees. They would be close enough to the rest if they needed help, but far enough away that Maggie would not be tripping over them every time she went out her own door. The day before they were to come, she told the children of Gerald's imminent arrival. Little Addie, who had no memory of having a father, was delighted and spent the day telling everyone. "My daddy coming home!" Schooner wasn't terribly interested, but seemed, on the whole, to be pleased. James said little, but sulked when he learned the circumstances—that his father had taken another woman and would not be living with them. "Our father should not live here with another wife! Do you mean our sister is half-Indian?"

"Half-sister," Maggie corrected, almost choking on the word. She had not thought of Little Smile's puny infant in those terms before. Her children's half-sister! And she didn't even know the child's name. Years ago, when she was pregnant with Schooner and feared she might die, she had worried about Gerald having another woman after she was dead, but she had never dreamed it would happen right under her nose—and that she would build them a house! For a moment she wondered if the others were right. Was she mad? *Ferhuddled*, as Hildy Halleck would have said contemptuously. Forgive me, Grossmutter, Maggie thought. You followed your stern beliefs and learned to live with the results. So must I.

She had to do this. Gerald was a dreamer, a poet, a man more interested in the human heart than his own purse. Someone had to watch out for him, and she was the only person who cared enough and was able to do so. The little Indian girl was as helpless against life's harsher aspects as he was. More so.

There was another element in her considerations that no one else could feel. Gerald loved her. No one else would believe that, Maggie thought, but she was sure he loved her in his own way. Just as he was obligated to Little Smile because of the love she bore him, Maggie was obligated to Gerald because of love. To be the object of another's love is in itself a responsibility. Perhaps the children, in time, would come to comprehend this. She hoped so. As for the rest of the community—her friends, her business associates—it would be nice if they respected her decision whether they agreed with it or not, but it could not be a guiding consideration.

Gerald tactfully refrained from visiting the children until Maggie specifically invited him to. James was fascinated with Gerald but was very shy in his presence, as was Schooner. But Addie immediately applied herself to stealing his heart. She climbed into his lap and cuddled, and it was obvious in a very few minutes that he was delighted with her. Maggie invited him often to the noon meal, which he was not required to have at the mission with his students. This seemed somehow less intimate than evening meals, and it allowed Maggie to serve the rest of them and go back to the trading post. It was very painful to her to see the whole family together and know all the while that it was not a family anymore, but only the specter of one. If the children even talked with him about Little Smile, she did not know. It was not mentioned within her hearing, though she did learn the baby's name was Morning Wish. Morning Wish Freiler. In other circumstances, the name might have seemed amusingly incongruent.

Eventually they all became accustomed to this unusual and, according to Mrs. Whittacre, "scandalous" arrangement. James discovered that he and his father had music in common, which broke down the barrier between them; Schooner was James's shadow and came to be very affectionate to Gerald mainly because James was; and Addie—the golden-curled darling of Seventrees—adored her newfound father.

It seemed, as the winter days drew in upon themselves, that life might go on forever this way, but changes were about to occur that would ultimately destroy or strengthen all of them. It began in January with an unexpected letter from Maggie's cousin, Luther Halleck.

"I didn't know you kept up writing to them," Katrin said. She and Maggie were sitting over companionable cups of tea before starting the morning's work.

"I don't really 'keep up,' but about once a year I exchange letters with his wife, Fritzi. I tell her about what we're doing, which doesn't interest her, and she writes silly, frothy letters that leave a sweet taste in my mouth that I'm weeks getting rid of. But this isn't from her—it's from my cousin, Luther."

"And they're coming here?"

"That's what they say."

"Why do they even want to? I thought they were rich city people."

"They are. The letter just says they want to take an extended holiday and thought it would be interesting to see the West. No explanation."

"What are you going to do with them? How long do you think they'll stay?"

"I'm writing to tell them not to come, of course. There's no reason for them to come clear out here and gawk at us. They can take their holiday somewhere else. As soon as this snow melts enough to get to Westport Landing, I'll go to the post office there."

But the snows kept on, and it was the end of February before anyone could get to Westport Landing. The accumulated mail was not put on a boat until the ice melted on the river in March. The steamboat carrying the letter blew up just outside Pittsburgh. The mail bag was blown clear and ended up on the bank, where it was later discovered, but by the time it got to Germantown, the Hallecks were gone. The letter was left lying on the hall table of their old house for many months before the new residents got around to forwarding it.

When Maggie received no response to her letter, she assumed they had taken offense and had not replied for that reason. She gave it no more thought until a rainy afternoon in late May when a bedraggled couple with two children walked in the door of the trading post.

The woman, artificially bright ringlets of hair sodden and sticking wetly to her plump neck, stepped in the door, looked around critically, then shrieked, "Maggie! Cousin! You've hardly changed. I'd have known you anywhere!"

Maggie was almost too stunned to reply. "Fritzi . . ." she said.

Fritzi ran forward, embraced her, and said, "What an adorable little frontier town this is. How amusing it must be to live here. I just know we're going to have a wonderful time."

Maggie looked over the blond head with hints of baby-pink scalp showing between the curls. Luther stepped forward. He looked awful—gray-green skin hanging on a thin frame. He was not yet forty and he looked sixty. His eyes were bloodshot and sunken, and as he came forward to take her hand, she could smell the reek of whiskey on him. "Luther," she said, "how nice to see you again." It was a blatant lie, but what else could she say?

"Thinking about going in a new direction with the business," he mumbled. "Decided to take time out for some visiting first. Wondered how you were getting on. Always wanted to see the West. Land of opportunity, they say."

The little boy at his side saved Maggie from having to answer. He tugged at his father's coat, and Fritzi bustled back into the conversation. "This is Ernest, Maggie. You saw him as a baby, remember? He's ten now, aren't you, darling? What? Oh . . . Maggie, it's been a long trip, and I wonder if you could direct us to your . . . your facilities?"

"There is a latrine in back."

"A latrine? How quaint!" Fritzi said. Luther and the little boy went outside, and Maggie was left with Fritzi and a frail, pale little girl of about eight who was clinging to her mother's damp skirts. "Cousin Maggie, this is our wonderful little Violet. Say hello to your cousin, darling. Maggie, I wonder if there is someone who could take our things in?"

"In?" Maggie said. "Didn't you get my letter?"

"Letter? Why, no. I expect it got lost somewhere. My goodness, such a trip! I had no idea! We had to travel with some of the most outrageous people. This certainly has been an education to all of us. Now, about our trunks . . ."

Maggie did her best to convince them to turn around and go back to Westport Landing, but to no avail. "Oh, it's so dreadfully far away, cousin. We'd hardly get to visit at all. Of course," she pouted, "if you don't want us here . . ."

"No, it's not that," Maggie said wearily.

"But you *don't* want them there!" Katrin said later. "Why didn't you just say so?"

"I don't know. I guess I'd rather put up with them for a while than get into any sort of conflict, and if I told them the truth, Fritzi would have crying hysterics. It would be so embarrassing. She hates outdoor plumbing, though—maybe that will drive her away soon. And that boy—Ernest! He's a terror. Poor James has spent the entire spring taming a little squirrel he found, and Ernest has harassed it back to its wild state in only two days."

"I know," Katrin agreed. "He's taking a big-brother attitude toward my Adams, and you should hear the words the child's learned already. Washed his mouth out with soap twice already today. Adams thinks Ernest is wonderful. How long they staying?"

"I keep bringing up the subject, and they keep changing it, or rather, Fritzi does. I've seen very little of Luther. He spends most of his time off strolling about as if he's the supervisor. He must duck into the woods fairly often, though, because his stagger gets worse as the day goes on, and being confined with him indoors in the evening is almost unbearable. I stay out as long as I can."

"Maybe when his supply of rookus juice runs out, they'll leave," Katrin said hopefully.

But it was not to be. They stayed on. Toward the end of the week Fritzi dashed in, pink-cheeked and alarmed. "Maggie, I thought you said Gerald was gone. I just saw a man I could have sworn was he, walking along with an *Indian* woman with a baby!"

"That was Gerald," Maggie said.

"But the Indian woman . . . ? You must caution him about appearances, my dear. It looked most irregular. Is she a servant or something?"

"She is his wife," Maggie answered.

Fritzi clasped plump, beringed little hands to her heaving bosom. "His *wife?*" When Maggie did not elaborate, she said, "Oh, I see, this is some of your adorable 'frontier humor.' But I hardly consider it amusing."

"It's not meant to be amusing, Fritzi. It's the truth."

"Do you really mean it? You and Gerald are divorced? I had no idea."

"No, we're not divorced. We just aren't married anymore. Sometimes things like that are done in 'adorable' frontier towns, Fritzi."

"But he lives right *here*? Right in the same community as you and the children. How perfectly awful . . . how do you stand it . . . why do you allow such a shocking . . ."

Maggie put her hands on her hips and said, "Fritzi, that is none of your business and I will not discuss it with you—now or ever!"

Fritzi drew herself up, her eyes bulging with indignation. "Well! I never!" she said before turning on her dainty little heel and stomping out.

Now they would leave—wouldn't they?

But they didn't. A week turned to two, then three, and then a month, and the four of them were still crowded into Maggie's house. She had been forced to let James and Schooner go stay with Gerald, partly to make room, more because they both despised Ernest and fought with him constantly. Fritzi never lifted a finger to help with anything

202

unless she was specifically asked; then she fluttered. "My goodness, Cousin Maggie, you mean you'd trust me to make coffee? I don't know a thing about cooking, you know, but it would be such fun to try. Do I put this in here? Ooops . . . Oh, clumsy me, I've spilled some of it. I hope that won't stain."

Maggie did some of their laundry at first, along with her own family's, but quickly caught on. But by that time Fritzi had become "dear friends" with Mrs. Whittacre and started taking the laundry to the mission, where Mrs. Whittacre got the Indian girls to do it. Maggie supposed that Fritzi and Elsie Whittacre enjoyed filling their days with the sort of malicious gossip that appealed to both of them. She knew that she must be their main topic of conversation, and didn't really care much except that Fritzi usually left Violet with Maggie when she went calling. Maggie found a solution to this, too. She let Violet play in the mud with some of the Indian children, and when her mother saw her, filthy, disheveled, with feathers in her hair and beads around her neck, she decided that Violet was really far too delicate to be playing like that.

Finally, when it was getting toward the end of July, Maggie decided that it must be settled. She noticed that Luther managed to get a ride almost once every week with someone or other who was going to Westport Landing, and for the rest of the week he made frequent visits to the woodpile at the back of the yard. Maggie went out late one evening, after everyone else was in bed, and carefully uncorked and poured out all the bottles, than took them down and threw them in the river. Luther came into the trading post in the morning, looking sick and haunted. "Maggie, uh . . . I think someone's been trespassing on your property—signs of thievery, you know . . ."

"I poured it out, Luther."

"But why! I need . . . I mean . . ."

Maggie walked to the door, hung out a sign saying the post was closed, and locked the door. "Sit down, Luther. We're going to talk, and you need to be sober. Now, what are you doing here in Seventrees?" She was hardly aware that she had lapsed into German, though she had spoken it little for years.

"Just a visit."

"Stop that. You seem to have forgotten that I'm not stupid, or maybe you never realized it. What are you doing here?"

The man's long gray face seemed to collapse. Great self-pitying tears filled his bloodshot eyes. "Lost the business . . . unforeseen reverses . . ."

"You drank the profits, you mean?"

He nodded miserably. "Nowhere to go. Friends turned their backs. Thought they were friends, anyway."

"So you thought you'd just move in on me? Whatever made you think you had the right to do such a thing! All those years we lived in a dingy little rented house in Germantown and you never once so much as offered to help us! And you have the gall to just dump your whole family on me!"

"But, Maggie, you're so strong. Never thought you'd take my help if I offered."

"I wouldn't have. But you could have offered. How much money do you have left? What are you buying that whiskey with?"

"Sold the house and furniture. Had to hurry, didn't get much. Used most of it getting here." He staggered into the next room, the living quarters of the house, and returned with a fistful of crumpled bills.

Maggie straightened them and counted. "That's enough to get you back to Saint Louis, but there wouldn't be anything left to live on."

"Don't make us leave, Maggie," he said.

"You are so pitiful . . . so despicably pitiful," Maggie said. She stood up, paced the room angrily. "I'm sick to death of being good old strong, responsible Maggie. I'm tired of bearing the brunt of other people's weaknesses. Why should I solve your problems? *You* created them, *you* solve them."

Luther picked up his money, stuffed it in his pocket, and, head bent, walked toward the door. Maggie got there first. "Give me that money, you fool. You could have a small house built with it here, but you can't stay without being able to do something worthwhile. Do you know anything. Anything at all?"

"Formulas," he muttered.

"What?"

"Formulas—paint, glue, varnish, that sort of thing. Always liked that part of the business. Bookkeeping didn't interest me. Never understood that."

Maggie put the money in her apron pocket and thought for a long time. "Can you actually make those things yourself? . . . You can? I can't see that they're actually necessities, but . . ."

"Maggie, I hear things. You've got lots of respect here. People listen to you. . . ."

"I've *earned* that, Luther. Don't think you can ride on it."

"No. Didn't mean that . . ."

But Maggie was not listening to his protestations. It was true. She had enough influence that a request to the authorities that the Hallecks be allowed to stay in the territory would be honored simply because it came from her, especially if Luther were to be involved with her trading post, which supplied the army with wheels and medicines and other necessities.

"Luther, you can stay here for one year. You will make whatever you can. If it is good quality and sells at the post, I think you will be allowed to stay. If not, you will have to leave. I will take no further interest in you. I will handle your money and supply you enough this winter for food. You will not have another drink—ever. If you do, I'll wash my hands of the entire thing. Is that understood? Your alternative is to take this money back and leave here tomorrow."

"But how will I tell Fritzi?" he whined.

"I don't know or care, but she will have to pay her way. She cannot be a dainty, helpless leech, and you had both better stop raising Violet to be that way. There's not room for weakness here. Fritzi knew the situation all along, didn't she?"

"Yes."

"You had better go find her and discuss this."

Luther did as he was told. He brought Fritzi back—weepy, bleary, and hiccuping—at noon. She said nothing to Maggie, but sank into a rocking chair, dabbing at her eyes and sniffling ostentatiously. Maggie ignored her and went on fixing lunch. She put four plates on the table, and when the children ran in from school, she served her three and sat down herself at the fourth place. Ernest said belligerently, "Where's *my* place? I'm hungry!"

Maggie didn't even look at him—or his family. "Your mother is fixing your lunch. Talk to her about it."

The Freiler children realized that something was wrong, and they ate quickly and left. Maggie rose and spoke to her cousin's wife. "After lunch, I want you to peel the potatoes in that sack, and the floor needs scrubbing. You can bring buckets of water up from the river, and the soap is in the cabinet with the brushes."

"But I don't know how . . ." Fritzi protested tearily.

"Then you have a great deal to learn, don't you?" Maggie said, and left.

22

Another year had passed. Maggie was mending a blanket before putting it away for the summer when the news reached her. Gold, the illusive, intriguing metal that men had always sought with a religious fervor, had been discovered in abundance in California. Torchy and Quincy Clay, a man of eighteen now, had been to Saint Louis on a routine trading trip and returned before they were expected. They had ridden from Westport Landing on horses instead of a wagon, and they pounded into Seventrees in a lather of excitement.

"Gold in California!" Torchy shouted to the crowd that had gathered around the trading post. "The man named Sutter who used to live in Westport has the large landholding out there now. They are gathering it in buckets, it is said."

Maggie looked around the crowd. There was eagerness, anticipation, and unmasked greed on the various faces. Some of them would leave here for the promise of untold riches. Which? Not Helmut or Torchy, she knew. Helmut was neither greedy nor adventuresome, and Torchy had enjoyed life's full measure of adventure already. Besides, he loved the business they had built up, which continued to grow and provide him with homes in Seventrees and Saint Louis, where he could raise his children. But what about Gerald and Luther and young Quincy Clay? Maggie felt an odd shiver of anxiety. She did not like sudden changes, and she knew there would be many.

The crowd was drifting away in chattering knots. She and Torchy were left in front of the trading post with Helmut and Katrin. "We must talk about this," she said to them.

Inside, over cups of Seventrees tea, Torchy voiced what they had all been thinking about. "Many people will hear this news and go west. Some of them will take the sailing ships from the east coast and go around the Cape, but many others will take the land routes. Two most important, the Santa Fe Trail and the Oregon Trail, run together before our community. By next year, next summer, there will be thousands of them passing through here."

"If we are ever to expand, that will be the time," Maggie agreed.

"If we are ready for this, lifetime fortunes could be obtained for all of us."

"Can we be ready, Torchy?" Maggie asked.

"The post requires enlarging, and I cannot do the building, for I must be stocking up on a supply of goods to sell. Quincy should be here—he has been of great help to me, and I fear I cannot do this without him."

They agreed, and Quincy was summoned to join the discussion. He came in shyly. He was a quiet, competent young man whose part in the business had never been discussed. He had simply begun to help out, and had gradually become valuable and necessary to them without anyone taking particular note. Maggie spoke to him calmly. "Quincy, you are at the crossroads, and we wish to tell you something of the roads you may take, as we know them. This story of wealth to be picked up off the ground in California must appeal to you, and I'm sure you have been considering whether to follow the lure of it."

Quincy looked rather apologetically at his parents and nodded. "I have been thinking of it."

"We feel, however, that wealth is to be made here as a result of the many people who will pass through. Less romantic, less exciting, but more chance of success. We are going to expand the post and stock far more goods, and Torchy has just said that he cannot do this without your help."

Quincy smiled at Torchy. "I'm glad to hear you feel that way," he said.

"For my part, I would be glad to make you a full partner," Maggie said.

Torchy nodded enthusiastically. "This has been a thought of mine for some time as well. Even before we heard this news of the gold. I agree."

Katrin had been unusually quiet. Now she spoke. "Maggie, you and Helmut and Torchy are now equal thirds. If Quincy joins and each is a one-fourth partner, the Clay family will own half the business and you and Torchy will have only one-fourth apiece. I'm glad you're offering this to Quincy, I hope he will take it, but is that right? You started this—why should we own half, more than you have?"

Maggie took her friend's hand. "I never wanted to own the whole business, just a fair part. Enough to provide for my family. In fact, I have begun to feel the burden of it sometimes. My interest is in the bookkeeping and my medicines. I'd like to do just these two things. I didn't make the offer lightly, I realized what it meant, and I'd be very happy if Quincy would remain with us on those terms. Quincy?"

"I must think on it," the young man said.

Maggie was pleased. Though she hoped very much he would stay, she respected him all the more for weighing and considering rather than making snap decisions. "Go along, then, and think. We will accept whatever you decide." As he departed, Maggie saw Katrin looking after him and knew what must be in her heart. But she also knew that Katrin would not try to hold him back if he decided to go to California.

"It will mean much investment in goods," Torchy said. "We are possessed of excellent credit, but . . ."

"Yes. We are all inclined to saving. This is a good thing. We must go over books and decide what is needed of our caches."

"We will also have to hire people," Maggie said. "I'm sure some of the young men who assist Helmut in the blacksmith shop as well as those who help with the wheels will leave. We must replace them and get someone to help in the post itself. I'll have far too much extra work with the books and my herbs to do the actual selling all the time."

And so the discussion went on, through the afternoon and evening. Plans were made, figures gone over, supplies weighed and discussed as to reliability. New buildings would have to be built. A larger post, an expanded blacksmith shop, a storage area, a safer place to keep the money—it was heady and exciting, and at first none of them even noticed the quiet tap at the door. Quincy stuck his head in, grinned broadly, and said, "I'm staying." Katrin burst into tears, the first time Maggie had seen her cry in years. Helmut shook his son's hand, then embraced him roughly. Torchy threw his hat in the air and whooped.

Maggie let out a long sigh of relief. She was glad for all of them, but in this as all things, there was one small pocket of sadness. She wished that Gerald were part of her joy. No happiness had ever been complete since the day he'd left for Santa Fe years before. She must, she told herself, stop thinking of him this way. The hurt had to heal. How ironic it was that her medicines were eagerly purchased by travelers, some of whom had written back to her, saying they had saved lives, and yet her own "illness" could not be helped. But that was foolish and melancholy. "Let's celebrate!" she said, pushing away the cobwebs of lost love.

Maggie was behind the house boiling a vat of sunflower heads. The concoction was effective for lung problems and was greatly in demand. She hated doing it under normal circumstances, for it involved constant stirring over a hot fire in the middle of the summer, but this time it was worse because of the smell. She was experimenting with a new idea.

She stood back, gasping with the heat, and quickly beat out a tiny spark that had burned through her skirt. Next time, I wear something else, she thought. Leather pants or something. She chuckled to herself at what a heyday Mrs. Whittacre would have if she had a bit of gossip like that. "I saw it myself! Garbed in trousers, just like a man. Heaven preserve us from such shameful women!" she would probably say.

"You make laughing medicine?" a voice said, startling her.

"Black Feather! I didn't hear you coming. No, I'm trying something new. The last time I bottled this up, about half the bottles got a mold inside and weren't any good. So I thought I'd try boiling them in alcohol instead, and see what happens. I wondered, too, if I put the bottles themselves in here while the liquid is still just at the boil . . ." She rattled on for a while, engrossed in what she was saying. A new supply of bottles, better corks, less breakage. Excellent stand of cattails for making talc this year. Not as much wild licorice as she had hoped. Finally she realized he was not evincing the amount of interest he usually took in talking about herbal cures. "What's wrong? Are you on your way to Westport Landing? You don't often come through, this time of year."

"I've come to take my tribe's children home," he said.

There suddenly seemed to be a chill around Maggie in spite of the blazing July sun and the fire. "Why?"

"Floods."

The chill increased. "Floods?" she whispered. "Oh, Black Feather, no. You mean somewhere else, don't you?"

"No. Here, and before very long."

209

"Certainly not? There's been more rain than usual for mid-summer, but the river isn't even up much."

"Like you, I must abide by my convictions. My tribe believes the children to be in danger here, and they have asked me to bring them back to the reservation. I will do so." He turned and started toward the mission, but stopped before he had gone far. "You should get to higher ground. I would not want yours to be one of the voices from the past," he said, recalling another time.

Maggie could not sleep that night. She tossed and turned, sweat-drenched and frightened. Black Feather's removal of the children had been a topic at Seventrees. "Old fool of an Indian," they had said. "Just goes to show why education is wasted on these savages. Even he is still a superstitious red man, and he's been educated," Maggie had overheard. "He was probably just drunk," a notorious drinker said sanctimoniously. "Them Injuns is alus 'bout skin full of likker. I sure ain't gonna go up the spout on account a talk like that from a goddamned Injun."

Maggie had turned and walked away in disgust. But now, in the dead of a hot July night, she kept thinking of all the other unlikely things Black Feather had told her. Pigs scurry to nest just before sudden cold snaps, he'd said, and Maggie had since noted that it was true. Tight corn shucks predict a bad winter. Cobweb plasters stop bleeding, a ring around the moon predicts rain the next day, cold knife to the back of the neck stops nosebleeds. He'd told her, and all of them had proved to be right most of the time. Her own part of the Seventrees business was founded largely on the herbal cures he had taught her. He had saved her life once before when everyone else had given up hope of her surviving her labor with Addie. Shouldn't she take his word now?

Flooding! The very thought made her panic. She finally fell into a fitful sleep, only to dream of water—swirling around her, dragging at her skirts, driving into her face, choking her. When the children awoke, she was already packing things. "What are you doing, Mama?" Schooner asked, rubbing her sleepy eyes in confusion.

"Black Feather says this lowland is going to flood. We are going to take everything we can up the hill. Wake James and Addie. You aren't going to school today. Tell James to hitch the horses to the wagon."

"But, Mama . . ."

"No 'buts,' Schooner. Black Feather has never lied to me. If it doesn't flood, we'll merely look foolish, and if it does, we will save ourselves and our possessions. Go."

They started loading the wagon shortly afterward. Katrin and Helmut came over to see what was happening. "Maggie, have you gone soft in the head?" Katrin said, half-angry. "It's bad enough to be friends with Black Feather, but this is silly. This river never floods in the middle of summer, and even if it did, how would he know about it beforehand?"

"Katrin, I know you don't like Black Feather, but I think he knows these things. I believe him, I wish you would. Now, I have to pack the dishes. Please, *please* do the same. I'll help you when I'm done, if you want."

"I'm not going to do any such thing, and I'm sorry to see you wasting your time and making mock of your own good sense this way," Katrin answered.

"Katrin, that's up to you. I've never tried to force my ideas on you. But I'm doing what I think I have to do, and I wish, just this once, you would follow suit. But don't be angry with me about it."

Katrin relaxed her scowl a little and walked away, still shaking her head.

Maggie watched her for a moment, then said, "Schooner, go find your father and tell him what we're doing. Say I hope he'll join us. He . . . and his family. Never mind, I'll do it myself. James, you drive the wagon. We'll find a place up on the bluff to unload this, and come back for the rest. What was that?" She stopped, turned her head slightly to listen to a distant rumble.

"Thunder?" James asked.

Maggie noticed that his face was pale and pinched with concern. "Yes, I think it was. Don't worry, James. We'll be all right. Just hurry along with your work."

Maggie put her hand out to pat his shoulder reassuringly, and a raindrop fell on her arm.

23

Maggie and the children made many trips during the long, muggy day. At first everyone just stood around watching them. Maggie was far too respected to be openly laughed at, but she could see smiles behind hands, and hear snickers. Undaunted, she emptied her house and started loading goods from the trading post. The rain kept coming down, sprinkles mostly, but now and then the lightning would flash, the wind would spring up, and the work would have to be stopped while the downpour passed.

About noon she got up to the bluff overlooking the valley and found someone there. A young woman named Nancy whose husband worked for Helmut was sitting in the grass with her two babies and a pile of household belongings. "Hank thinks I'm brooding on another one, and he's lettin' me have my head 'cause of it, Miz Freiler," she explained. "But I heard what you are doing, and I figured if you was comin' up here, I'd do the same. Can't do no harm, I reckon, 'cept to get us a bit wet, and that don't hurt."

Maggie was warmed by the young woman's offhand faith. The two of them used a large canvas meant for a wagon top to erect a temporary shelter from the drizzling rain. Maggie started back down the hill and met Katrin coming up in a heavily loaded wagon. Wisps of her mahogany hair had escaped the calico kerchief and stuck wetly to her neck. Her face was flushed with exertion, and she looked bedraggled and sheepish as she stopped to talk to Maggie. "I guess if my best friend is going to make a fool of herself, I ought to be with her. I still think that Indian friend of yours is crazy, but you're not—not often, anyway."

"Thank you, Katrin. I've got one more load from the post, then I'm going to start bringing up the LeSage's things. Gran'mère Charron can't manage by herself, and Torchy's not back from Westport Landing yet."

Gran'mère Charron, however, was not going to be moved. In rapid French sprinkled with bitter shards of English, she told Maggie she could take Torchy's things—and good riddance, too—but she was staying right where she was until the rain stopped. Yes, the children, Jack Q and Beatrice could take their things if they wished, a holiday would not harm them. She would extend herself to pack a picnic lunch even, but she was not joining in this madness of the head.

By late afternoon the river had begun to rise—not enough to be alarming normally, but under the circumstances, it was being closely watched. Maggie had brought the rest of the canvas from the post, and a tiny tent village had grown up on the lip of the bluff next to the cemetery. Three families had joined the Freilers in bringing all their possessions. Many others had simply brought a few particular treasures and joined for the companionship, not really believing anything was going to happen and yet wary enough to cook their evening meal over a campfire on high ground.

While Schooner made supper, Maggie went down to the mission and asked Reverend Whittacre if she could take the remaining Indian children up the bluff with her. "Your buildings are on higher ground than most of the rest, and probably won't be in danger, but I'd feel better if the children were up on the bluff."

Mrs. Whittacre prevented her husband's reply. "I declare, Mrs. Freiler, this is positively shameful, the way you've frightened everyone just because of some ridiculous Indian superstition. Everything is an uproar because of you, and if you think for one moment that we . . ."

But while she spoke, Reverend Whittacre had been looking out toward the river. It was lapping now at the trunks of a stand of willows that grew well back from the bank. There were branches floating in the water. "That's good of you, Mrs. Freiler," he cut into his wife's lecture. "We'll have the children ready in a few minutes. The Shawnee had gone with Black Feather, but I'll have the rest of them get their things together."

Maggie left the two of them glaring at each other. She didn't want to hear what the minister's wife had to say to him. She went next to the small, run-down house that Luther's family had lived in for the last year. Typical how old and neglected it already looked. Fritzi was mincing about the kitchen, still pretending that she didn't really know how to cook and this was merely a temporary inconvenience. She had hardly exchanged a word with Maggie since Maggie had told her to wash the kitchen floor so long ago. Now she

213

spoke, however. "What do you want here? If it's about the paints, you can go around back and talk to Luther."

"No, I want to warn you that the river is going to flood—"

"That's nonsense! Just another ploy of yours to make yourself the center of attention, to prove what a pillar of the community you are. Go away, go back up there with your friends and let them all pat you on the back and tell you how clever and brave you are. Luther will want to come, I'm sure, he's always telling me that. He can tell you in person. Now, get out of my house."

Maggie tried to keep her temper. "Fritzi, I'm trying to save your life, though God only knows why anyone should. Stay here and drown if you want, but let me take the children."

"Don't you get near my children!" Fritzi shrieked.

"I can't leave her here alone," Luther said when Maggie found him, "but I've got my chemicals on the wagon just ready to take up."

Maggie had one more stop to make—the most difficult. Fortunately, Gerald was outside and she didn't have to see or talk to Little Smile. "Are you coming up on the bluff?" Maggie asked him.

"Yes. We're awfully close to the water here. You're really going out on a limb with this, aren't you? A good many people are going to be upset about the trouble they've gone to if you're wrong."

"I know, and yet I hope I am, but . . ."

"Don't feel apologetic, Maggie, my l— Maggie," he corrected himself. "I'll see you later, it's getting dark, you better get back to the children."

Maggie, my love, he's almost called her.

There was only a handful of the Indian children at the mission, but they were waiting for Maggie when she got back. They had their few belongings in little packs made from blankets, and Reverend Whittacre had put the pack on a wagon along with a few of their own things and several crates of books.

By the time Maggie started up the road with the Indian children, it had begun once more to rain heavily. The much-traveled dirt road was now a river of mud, flowing down the slope to join the Kaw. It was too slick to walk, and Maggie had to take the children into the woods alongside to make any progress. It was getting quite dark, and they were frightened. Maggie kept up a barrage of cheerful chatter as they struggled uphill, while constantly counting and recounting heads to make sure none of them got lost.

Finally she got them to the temporary camp, arranged for them to be fed and sheltered. She checked that her own children were safely accounted for, then walked from tent to tent checking on her friends. Helmut and Katrin Clay were there with their son Adams, but Quincy was not present. He had gone to Westport earlier with Torchy, and the two of them had not returned yet. "Don't worry, Katrin. The roads are probably flooded. I'm sure they won't take any chances," Maggie said.

"I know," Katrin answered. "I'd just feel better if Quincy was here with me. Helmut went down a bit ago to get Gran'mère Charron, but the silly old thing won't come. I suppose if the water comes up much more, somebody'll have to drag her out of the house. It looks like you were right about the flood, Maggie," she admitted.

"No. I wasn't right. Black Feather was."

Katrin just sniffed contemptuously at this idea.

The rain had slowed as Maggie went back to the place where the road to Seventrees come up over the bluff. It was not quite dark. For a few moments the clouds cleared, and a full moon shone down on the community. At least half the houses below were dark and empty. The rest were lighted but oddly quiet. The bluish light illuminated the mission, turning the red tile roofs of the buildings a purple-black. Maggie could see the light in Woody's cabin by the water's edge. Woody had stayed behind to measure the river's level, riding up the hill from time to time to report on it.

Maggie stood in the wagon ruts at the top of the bluff thinking of other times. How long ago had she first been here? Nine years—was that all? It seemed so much longer—a lifetime longer. But she remembered that she had felt even then that there was something about this place that called to her, made her feel instinctively and, against all reason, that this was home. Home. Now home and everything it had come to mean to her and the others was in danger—the hand of God was about to rest heavily on them, and there was nothing they could do about it. She was suddenly tired.

She went back and sat down with the children, not realizing at first that Gerald and Little Smile were there too. Little Smile was holding the little girl and saying something to Gerald. "It's just a small thing," he was saying. "Not worth going back for."

215

"Important to me. Black Feather give. No want float away. I go, please?"

"Oh, very well, but don't dawdle. Schooner, will you hold the baby for a minute? Take a lantern, Little Smile."

"What's she going back for?" Schooner asked.

"A little bag of charms that Black Feather gave her. She keeps it hanging over the door for luck," Gerald answered. There was ill-concealed scorn in his voice. Whether it was for the charms or his Indian wife's belief in them, Maggie could not guess.

Since the rain had stopped, at least for a while, most of the people on the bluff were spreading out blankets and quilts, preparing to sleep in the open. Fires were doused, and sleepy children ceased their cranky crying. "Play your flute, Dad," James said.

"What makes you think I've got my flute?" Gerald asked.

"You never go anywhere without it," James replied.

"How right you are. A man never knows when a flute might come in handy. You can use it in a sword fight if you lose your sword, or put a bullet in it and blow hard, or—"

"Stop it, Dad," James said, laughing. "Just play."

Gerald leaned back against a tree trunk and began to play. Soft, sweet melody filled the air around them. James, too, had brought a flute, and apparently they had practiced together, for James wound a counterpoint melody through Gerald's music. Somewhere close by a woman's voice began to sing—a clear, soft soprano.

> Alas, my love, you do me wrong
> To cast me off so discourteously . . .

Maggie suddenly felt as if something tight was bound around her, catching her breath and making her feel light-headed. She stood suddenly and walked into the darkness. She tried to take a deep, slow breath and force back the wave of emotion that was threatening to engulf her, but it did not help. The tears came in a torrent. It was all her own fault. She should never have encouraged him to go away. He would still be hers if he had not made the trip to Santa Fe and met Little Smile. She could not recapture the tarnished memory of why it had seemed the right thing to do then.

Cocooned in her remorse, she was unaware that the music had stopped. She didn't hear him approach, but when he touched her shoulder, as lightly as the brush of a night moth, and said softly, "Maggie my love . . ." she turned and flung herself into his arms. She cried while he held her, stroked her hair, and tried to soothe her. "It will be all right. Somehow it will be all right. Don't cry. I can't stand to see you cry. I'm sorry. So very sorry. Don't cry, Maggie, my love . . ." He took her chin, lifted her face, and kissed her.

For one sparkling moment they were the whole world. Nothing else mattered. The years, the heartbreaks, the tears—all were erased. They stood, looking into each other's eyes. There was so much to say and so little they could put in words. As one, they turned and looked out over the valley. Gerald put his arm around her shoulders. She could feel the delicious warmth of him through her clothes.

The moonlight glittered in the churning Kaw below them, and they watched it sightlessly for a long time, each wondering about the past and the future. But there was no future for them together—they both knew it. Little Smile and Morning Wish were Gerald's responsibility. If he abandoned them, he would lose both his self-respect and Maggie's. But as long as they lived with him, Maggie would not—could not—share him.

Eventually reality intruded when Maggie noticed that the trees that obscured the bank of the river no longer hid it. Moonlight danced on rushing water closer to them than the trees and their thick shadows. Suddenly, as though an unseen hand had drawn a canvas across the moon, it was dark. It was raining again, and they could hear voices from below, and then the sound of hoofbeats. Woody was riding furiously up the hill, shouting, "Water's rising! We need help down here!"

"Little Smile . . ." Gerald said in the pattering darkness. He grasped Maggie's hand, and they raced to intercept Woody. As they dashed into the road, he reined in, splattering a sheet of mud. "Runoff from the hills. Now it's raining again. Water's coming up fast, and there's a lot of folks still down there!" Then he was gone, up the hill to tell the rest.

Lungs bursting, Maggie and Gerald reached the bluff behind him. They raced to the group of people already scurrying to help down below. Schooner was huddled under a canvas, holding Morning Wish. "Isn't Little Smile back?" Maggie asked her.

"No, not yet, Mama. What's happening?"

Maggie gave quick instructions for Schooner and the older children to keep a close eye on the little ones; then she and Gerald joined the others skidding and slipping down the road to Seventrees. Maggie had to keep hold of Gerald's shirttail to keep from losing him in the crowded darkness.

As they descended the hill, the clouds cleared once again and revealed chaos. The river, not as distant as it should have been, was rising quickly. It was a solid mass of foaming black water tearing through, uprooting trees as it went. There were horses and dogs and cows caught in the water, making pitiful frightened noises as the flood dashed them along.

The water was already past the level of the houses closest to the normal bank, and Maggie could hear, over the roar and hiss of the water, the crack and splinter of wood. They had to claw their way through the people trying to make a last-minute attempt to save their livestock, their favorite dishes, cherished portraits, and clothes. She looked around, drawing back instinctively as they neared the edge of the water. Everything was so changed, it was hard to get her bearings. Then she could see a light—a warm yellow glow out in the water. Little Smile had taken along a lantern. Was that it?

Yes. Maggie squinted her eyes and pushed the wet hair out of her face. Gerald's house was halfway under water, but Little Smile was clinging to the roof, still holding her lantern.

Gerald started to wade into the water. Maggie grabbed his arm. "No, you'll be swept away. That won't help her. Wait. I'll get help." She turned and ran back, shouting for someone to aid them in a rescue. Suddenly there were six men running toward her. She led them to where Gerald still stood at the ever-encroaching edge of the water, shouting to Little Smile to hang on.

"We'll form a chain," Gerald said to the others. "Six of us, hands linked, ought to be able to reach her. I'll go first."

He stepped in, extended a hand. But no one took it. He looked back, a frantic unspoken question in his eyes. "Who's out there, anyway?" one of the men asked suspiciously. "Ain't that Injun woman, is it?"

"What does it matter?" Maggie shouted at him over the roar of the water.

"I ain't gonna risk my life for no goddamn Injun," he said.

Maggie stepped closer, menace in her voice. "You're Karl Boern, aren't you? I spent two nights last spring sitting up with your youngest when he had diphtheria, and your wife never so much as said thank you. *You* can thank me right now. Get in the water!"

The man looked taken aback but still truculent. "Not for no goddamn Injun, ma'am."

"For *me*, Karl. For *me*. Because I ask!" Maggie screamed.

Gerald had turned away and was starting back into the water. Of course he had to. He could not stand on the bank and watch the girl drown. *And neither can I*, Maggie realized. Karl and his friends stood in a frightened knot. There was, Maggie realized, only one way to move them, and she had to do it.

Her stomach heaved inside and her knees grew weak. "Gerald, wait. I'll help," she said, and waded into the water after him. Bile filled her throat, and terror of the water stopped her breathing. Wild images careened through her mind. Even the placid Kaw had always frightened her, but she'd kept the fear at bay, seeing it daily. Now it was a wild thing, berserk and malevolent, reaching out to devour her and everything she loved. She forced herself to turn, hold her hand out to Karl as Gerald kept moving into deeper water.

"Karl," she cried, her voice breaking in the din of rushing water. "Please, Karl!"

Suddenly the man plunged into the water, grasped her hand in an iron grip. He shouted to the others, "Come on. She wants to save her husband's Injun whore, and we gonna help, goddammit!" The others followed him.

Maggie tried to brace herself against the water as they waded farther and farther. She had to consciously remember to breathe. She vaguely heard herself whimpering with horror. The water was little more than waist-deep, but the force was incredible at her back. She had to dig her feet into the ground and lean back against the current. But she dared not lean too far.

Gerald and Karl Boern were holding her hands so tightly that it hurt. Inches at a time, they got closer. Little Smile was screaming incoherently now, and Gerald was shouting above the roaring of the water. "Climb down this side. You can make it. Don't fall. Climb! Stop that damned crying. Climb down here!"

As the line stretched as far as they could, Little Smile lowered her feet over the edge of the roof, got her balance for a second on the top of a window frame, then threw herself into the water toward Gerald. He lunged. The line jerked taut, nearly dislocating eight pairs of shoulders. Gerald called, "I've got her! I've got her!"

All that was left now was to let the line pivot from the

219

bank. The water would sweep the outermost people in an arc toward the bank. What they hadn't planned on was the ragged tree branch drifting toward them from behind.

It missed Gerald, fortunately, and almost missed Little Smile. But her long black hair, streaming out behind her, got tangled in the branches. She slipped underwater for a moment. But Gerald was holding her more tightly than the branch was, and she came back up in a second, choking and coughing in a frenzy of fear.

She screamed, gagged, clutched madly at Gerald, and went under again. He dragged her up with his one free hand and tried to curl both of them in toward Maggie in an attempt to reach the bank sooner.

But it didn't work that way.

Little Smile transferred her frantic grasp to Maggie. As the girl's fingers bit into her shoulders, Maggie leaned back to counteract the extra weight in front of her. But she misjudged. As she leaned back, her feet went out from under her.

She was underwater. Oh, God! She was underwater. She would die and be washed away! Neither Gerald nor Karl had let go of her hands. As she churned her feet wildly for a foothold, they pulled her up and up. It wasn't until she felt air rush into her lungs that she realized the burden around her neck was gone.

Gone.

"Little Smile?" she asked, choking.

No one answered. The line, Maggie and the men, swung slowly toward the bank. Others were there now, pulling them in, shouting encouragement. The water was only to her thighs here. Then her knees. Finally they dropped hands and staggered out. No one spoke for a moment. Then, still panting from exertion, Karl Boern said, "Sorry, Mr. Freiler."

But Gerald didn't answer. Perhaps he didn't hear. He was standing with his back to the rest of them, staring at the muddy water rushing past.

It was a moment no one had the right to intrude on, but Maggie could not just walk away. She touched his arm, feeling the ropy knots tensed under his sodden shirt. He looked at her for a moment, his eyes blank, then went back to his solitary contemplation of the water.

The rest had moved on. Maggie stood for a moment, aching to hold him, to comfort him somehow, but the tight, hunched set of his shoulders warned her not to touch him.

That night seemed to last for years. Others were rescued successfully. Some were not. Maggie did not go back into the water, but worked herself to exhaustion helping from the bank. Torchy's house was gone—they could not even be sure where it had stood. There was no sign of Gran'mère Charron. Maggie knew it would fall to her to tell Beatrice and Jack Q, but she kept hoping the old lady might be found safe somewhere before morning.

Luther's house had toppled sideways and the roof had disappeared, but Luther and his son, Ernest, stood at the bank, trying to comfort a hysterical Fritzi. Her daughter, Violet, had been swept out of her arms as they fled the rising waters. Mad with grief, Fritzi tried to attack Maggie when she saw her, and had to be pinned to the ground until she calmed somewhat.

Woody joined Maggie in searching for others. "Did you get the girl?" he asked. "Mr. Freiler's Indian?"

Maggie shook her head. "Almost."

Woody's dour face lengthened, but he made no further comment. Farther along the bank they heard shouts and discovered Hank, the young man whose wife, Nancy, had been among the first to join Maggie on the bluff. He was clinging to the branches of a tree. Woody and some of the other men formed another chain and got him to safety.

They worked on through the night. All the able-bodied adults of Seventrees were along the bank, ministering to the injured and seeking those who were missing. Maggie kept an eye out for Gerald, concerned for him and not wishing to show it. She sensed this one night he did not want her concern.

As the eastern sky began to lighten, people began to collect the scattered belongings that had washed up into trees along the edge. Maggie, along with many others, dragged herself wearily up the hill to rest for a while. She collapsed in an exhausted, muddy heap next to the makeshift tent where the children were still asleep.

She woke, confused and frightened for a moment, in full sunlight. "Daddy told us not to bother you," Schooner said. "Look at the river, Mama."

Maggie sat up and gazed in horror at her beautiful, beloved valley. The Kaw had obliterated every landmark. No, not every landmark. The mission and its outbuildings still stood, their red tile roofs washed clean by the rain and water lapping about the foundations.

221

But almost everything else was gone. The river was as wide and vast as a great brown lake. No longer churning, but the pace was apparent in the movement of its debris. Dead, bloated animals floated along, rolling lethargically in the water. Trees drifted, caught, formed dams, and broke apart again to reform in endless combinations. There were doors, roofs, wagons, laboriously cut logs.

Maggie put her hand to her mouth as she glimpsed blue-and-red fabric. A body. Tumbling like the animals. Quickly she drew Schooner's attention away from the liquid road of death in front of them. "Where is your father?" she asked, forcing herself not to gag.

"Helping Mr. LeSage look for Gran'mère Charron," Schooner answered.

"Torchy's back? And Quincy?"

"They got here a bit ago."

Katrin rushed up. She was muddy and bedraggled like the rest of them, but her family was intact and she glowed with the knowledge. "You're awake! I heard how brave you were. Everyone is waiting to thank you."

"Thank me?" Maggie asked. She hadn't done anything everyone else hadn't done.

"Yes, for warning us. Even though some of us was a little slow coming around to believing you—about the flood, Maggie. We're all in your debt."

"Katrin! What are you saying? I didn't know it was coming. Black Feather knew. He told *me!*" She was to repeat this many times before the day was out.

"The mission is still standing," Katrin said as they surveyed the scene below.

Maggie felt tears coming to her eyes. "I can't even tell where my house was. Oh, Katrin, everything's gone."

"That's plum silly. Everything's right here. Look around. We're alive. Most of us saved the things most important to us. You've got your hex book and your locket and your family. Only lost houses and such! Just take a little rebuilding, that's all."

Morning Wish started crying at that point, and Maggie busied herself feeding the little brown-skinned girl. *Gerald's daughter*, she told herself. *Gerald's and Little Smile's*. But to her astonishment, it didn't matter when she got the squirming, warm body on her lap. She was *a* child—whose child didn't matter. She was soft and warm and smiled broadly when Maggie smiled at her.

222

The younger children were asleep that evening before the sun had even set, and the older ones had been dragged away from the rapidly receding riverbank and ordered to stay at the temporary camp. There was not enough fresh water to bathe, hardly enough for drinking and cooking, but Maggie had put on a different dress and brushed the dirt out of her hair. She walked along the crest of the bluff, glad of the light breeze and the clear, cheerful meadowlark calls. Glad, most of all, for a little peace and quiet. Away from the overwrought children, the shrill wives lamenting the loss of their best dishes, the mournful laments of the few who had lost loved ones.

She strolled along, the wind whipping her skirts and hair, and thought that her valley would be beautiful again someday. She would build a new house—far from the water. The earth would heal, and so would the community. She stopped and looked out over the river and the scoured land. It was a moment before she realized that Gerald was there.

He was sitting on the grass, just down the slope. He'd not heard her. She stepped carefully down the hill, and when he turned his solemn, bland gaze on her, she sat down beside him. Words bubbled inside her, but she said nothing. He didn't speak either for a long, long while. Finally he spoke, as if completing a shared thought. "The worst of it is—God forgive me—I'm glad. She's gone, and I'm glad, Maggie."

"I know," she said softly, not able to look at him. "So am I."

He turned to face her. "We can't ever go back, Maggie, my love. Too much has happened. But do you think we can go forward together?"

She slipped her arm through his and rested her head on his shoulder. Smiling, she said, "I think we have to try."

Part II

SCHOONER

Bleeding Kansas

1

Schooner didn't get many chances to be all by herself unless she worked at it as she had this morning. Everybody was going to see Mr. Smith's windwagon in a while, so she'd rushed her chores, then gone ahead to wait for the rest of them. She ran up the last stretch of road and kept running until she reached the open spot along the bluffs. She flopped down on the lush spring grass. Later the summer sun would bake it to prickly yellow blades, but now it was soft and cool.

While her heart slowed its racing, she looked out over the busy little town of Seventrees. She'd been at this spot many times before because her mother particularly liked it and brought them here often. This morning Schooner found her mind going back to the morning after the flood. Almost six years ago, it had been. Strange how memory worked; she could remember the smell better than the sight. It was a brown smell. A hot, dead, wet stench that lasted for weeks afterward. Even now, on damp days, you could smell it in one of the mission buildings.

She could squint her eyes a little and look out over the Kaw valley and remember some of what it looked like. The river had seemed like an ocean—vast, black, and churning with itself and all the things caught up in it. Trees, houses, wagons, dead bodies of cows and dogs and wild animals.

Remembering was strange. Like with the flood, some things

227

about it seemed like yesterday, but others—some of the important things—she only pretended to remember. Old Gran'mère Charron's funeral, for one thing. They'd found her body clear down by Kansas Town, and somebody there had recognized it and brought her back to Seventrees to bury. It must have been a fancy funeral, because sometimes people still mentioned it, how there was a real priest and some French praying. But all Schooner could remember of it was her mother taking off her old black bonnet when it was over and saying how strange it was that Torchy, Mr. LeSage, was so upset about his mother-in-law's death, since he'd never liked her much. But funerals were important things. Why didn't she remember it?

The one thing that always stood out in her mind about the flood time was her mother and father kissing. She'd never seen them kiss before, and she'd been so surprised she'd nearly toppled right off the bluff. She'd stayed back, knowing they wouldn't want to talk to her just then, and she had watched. They'd stood there a long time, holding hands and talking to each other. Then Mrs. Clay had come along, and she'd talked to them for a bit; then she'd hugged and kissed Mother and shaken Daddy's hand. After that, Daddy had lived with them.

Schooner was fifteen now and understood about Little Smile and Morning Wish, but back before the flood, she'd just accepted that Daddy lived down by the river with an Indian woman and his baby and it hadn't even seemed strange to her. She'd been glad, though, when they built a nice new house and Daddy came back to live with them. It was wonderful to have him close, even if he did pay a lot more attention to Addie than to her. But it was all right. Everybody paid attention to Addie because she was so very pretty. Everyone except Mother. She was always trying to get Addie to act as nice as she looked, and Daddy would say, "Now, Maggie, my love, let her be."

Schooner stood up and walked over to a better vantage point. Where was everybody? They would miss the wind-wagon if they didn't get started soon. Schooner could see the back of her house from here. It was much farther up the hill than the first house had been. The house they used to live in was taken away in the flood, and Mother hadn't seemed to mind too much, but she had cried because her seven maples were uprooted. One of them was knocked down right where the chimney had been, and Mr. Wooden had cut a big piece and carved Mother a fancy model of the old house out of it. It was in a glass case on the mantel, next to Mother's hex book and great-grandmother's old German one.

Those had been the trees the town was named for, only it hadn't been a real town then, just a few families. The maples must have meant something special to everybody, because when the new house was all built, Daddy and Mr. Clay and Mr. LeSage went out with a big wagon and came back with seven new maples they'd dug up in the forest. "Where do you want your trees?" Daddy had asked her, and Mother had laughed and cried and hugged all three of them.

That summer had been a fearfully busy time. Everybody was clearing land farther up the hill and building houses and new shops. Schooner began to realize her mother was an important person to other people besides her own family. Folks would come to her and say things like, "Do you think this is high enough to be safe, Mrs. Freiler?" and "What sort of winter do you s'pose we're going to have?" and such. Her mother was awfully modest about it, though. She kept telling them it was the old Indian Black Feather who knew about such things, not her. But nobody wanted to believe that.

The same summer, Reverend Whittacre bought a couple of slaves and one of them could bake almost anything so it tasted like heaven. But nobody would even talk to her about recipes except Schooner's mother. Mother had said it was wicked and stupid to be that way, but Schooner hadn't understood. "Do you mean Reverend Whittacre is wicked?" she'd asked.

Her mother had thought it over carefully before she answered. "No, not for the most part. But he's a man of God and he should know better than anyone it isn't right to own another human being. It's a failing in him, just like James not being good at reading but very good at music. Most of Reverend Whittacre is good, but in that one thing he's wrong. It is the opinion that is wicked, not the whole man."

"But there's other people that agree with him. I heard Uncle Luther say he wished he had enough to buy a good strong hand . . ."

"Your Uncle Luther won't ever put it to the test. Slaves are expensive—thank the Lord—and he couldn't afford one. If he could, he might change his mind."

"But other people own slaves. Some here, and lots of them in Westport."

"Not German people."

"Oh, Mother!" Schooner exclaimed. "You think German people can't do anything wrong! What about the Brunings that live out on the mission road? They can't even talk in English, and they have three slaves who have to be taught German to do their work." This was the only point Maggie and her daughter had ever disagreed on, and it made Schooner sad to be in conflict with her mother. She dragged the conversation back to its original base. "Is it illegal to have slaves?"

"Schooner, a great many things are legal and are still wrong, and most of the people we know that own slaves are good to them and treat them kindly. That isn't true everywhere, and someday the wrong of it will be avenged," Mother had said. Schooner had been intrigued by that, but Morning Wish had come in just then with her knee bleeding from falling down, and they hadn't talked about it anymore.

Most people, except Aunt Fritzi, seemed to like Mother even if they didn't agree with her, and they kept her busy that summer of the flood. Mother and Mr. LeSage had sat down right after the water went back and drew up plans and things. Streets all in even lines, and even a park. Schooner heard Mrs. Clay say it was silly to put aside land as a park when it was nothing but wilderness all around, but Mother and Mr. LeSage had talked about gold and all the people that would be coming through the next year and how some of them would be settling. In the end she had her way and there was a nice park.

She'd been right about all the people. Forty-niners, they called them, even though they didn't all come that year. They were folks going out west to make their money finding gold. Somebody had kept track at Kansas Town, down by the river, of the people who had started from there, and in two years there had been over ninety thousand. Ninety thousand! It was such a big number, Schooner couldn't imagine it, but most of them had passed through Seventrees.

Summers and springs those years were strange and exciting. There were people everywhere. They were just starting out and were full of music and hope. They danced and sang and were happy about how rich they were going to get. It seemed to make Mother sort of sad, but Schooner never understood why. By the end of each summer, though, there were always some who stayed on and built houses along Mother's neat, straight streets. Mostly there were German people, who seemed to like being in a place where they could speak their own language. That seemed to please Schooner's mother, though she most often spoke English herself. They had singing societies and drank beer and had a big *Sommernachtfest* every summer and an *Oktoberfest* later on. Daddy found a lot of men who were a lot like him, though Schooner couldn't have said what the common quality was. He and his friends got together and talked about music and all kinds of ideas and books.

Not all the people who stayed were German, though they were just as welcome. Mrs. Woodren was one of them. She'd come to Seventrees as Charity Bloom with her husband and three children. But the husband had taken the cholera and died three days later. Mr. Woodren, the ferryman, who'd always been a bachelor, had fancied her and said the children were goodhearted and obedient, so he'd married her right off, her still wearing the dress she'd worn to bury Mr. Bloom. They had two more children now and were happy as happy.

It was something like that with Mrs. LeSage. She was a French girl passing through with her mother and father and three younger sisters. They'd all talked French with Torchy LeSage, and he'd found out that the oldest daughter didn't want to go with them. He needed someone to take care of his house, since Gran'mère Charron was gone, and he offered to marry the French girl. Now she was Beatrice's stepmother, even though she wasn't much older than Beatrice and Jack Q. Mrs. LeSage was plain and plump and nearsighted, and she didn't seem to be able to bear children, but she got on well with Torchy and the children. She liked working in the trading post and helped Mother with the bookkeeping, since she was good at figures, so it worked out well for all of them. Beatrice said it was like getting a big sister.

Some of the newer people in Seventrees just set down whole families. Didn't marry anyone, just stayed on because they liked it, or their money had been stolen, or the weather turned bad and they changed their minds about California. A few were folks who had gone clear on out or just part of the way and come back this far to settle. They weren't supposed to, because it was Indian Territory, but there were so many of them that the government just seemed to give up trying to keep them out.

Schooner stood up and stretched, raising her arms high in the air. Then she shaded her eyes and looked down the road. Why didn't they get started? They'd miss the windwagon. There was one wagon coming up the hill. Quincy

231

Clay's—and he had Beatrice with him. That was only fitting. Quincy was twenty-four now, and considered the best "catch" in Seventrees. Schooner liked him, with his gentle eyes and soft speech, but he was a large strong man for all that, and Mother said he was a good trader—as good as Torchy LeSage was, maybe better. He had the same sort of dark mahogany hair as his mother, and the sun brought out the red in it in the summers. He and Beatrice made a nice couple, her with her yellowy-red hair like her father's. Everyone knew that Quincy and Beatrice would marry someday, at least everyone thought so except maybe Quincy. Time was getting on, and Beatrice had confided in Schooner that she was getting impatient for him to ask for her hand. She was seventeen now, of marrying age, but he seemed more interested in his business than in getting married.

"Hey, Schooner," Quincy called out when their wagon got close. "Want to ride over with us?"

"Yes, Schooner, do join us," Beatrice called. But she turned so Quincy couldn't see her, and made a comical face that meant, "Don't you dare!"

Schooner almost laughed at her friend. "No, thanks, I'll wait for my folks." She watched them go on and wondered why Quincy didn't want to marry someone as pretty and sweet as Beatrice at the first chance. She was dainty without seeming sickly or anything. She had curly hair and very fair skin and freckles like copper dust, which she hated, but which Schooner thought attractive. Her waist and feet were the tiniest in Seventrees, and all the girls envied her that.

Beatrice's twin brother Jack Q was the same in coloring and build, but he didn't seem "dainty" at all. Wiry—that's what Schooner's mother called him. He traveled most of the time. After the gold rush, one of the adventurers had come back and told the Freilers that he hadn't needed the medicine he'd bought on his way, but that he had sold it for an enormous profit when he got to California, because cures were in short supply. After that, Jack Q had started traveling with the medicines—to the West, down the river system to New Orleans with Quincy, and even to the big cities in the East. He always dressed like his father in the beads and skins of the woodsman, even when he went east. "The city people trust me this way," he explained. "It makes me to look what they call a 'rube,' and the people in the West recognize me as one of them."

So with Jack Q going around the country with the medicines and Quincy traveling in connection with the other business of the trading post, Torchy and the new Mrs. LeSage spent all their time at the big new trading post they'd built the spring after the flood.

Schooner thought it was odd how everybody seemed to date things that way—the old families, anyway. Quincy's older brother, John, had been killed in a wagon accident before the flood. Iris Halleck was born eight months after the flood. The Freilers had come to Seventrees nine years before the flood, the crops had been good the year of the flood. Someday, Schooner supposed, something else important would happen to them all, and a new way of telling when things happened would start up.

"There she is, I told you she was up here," a voice called out. James, driving the wagon for his mother, was just coming up over the hill. Schooner hastily stuffed her brown hair back up under her bonnet. Maggie Freiler was sitting beside James, and Schooner felt a familiar surge of affection and pride. Surely her mother was the most beautiful woman anywhere. She was tall and thin, but not skinny-thin. Her hair was thick and shiny gold and didn't have any gray in it like most people her age. She was forty-four now, and admitted it to anyone who asked. Her face was smooth and "serene" (that was a word Schooner had read once and knew it was a word for her mother) except when she was angry with someone. Not that she was angry very often, but when she was, it was awful. Mostly it happened when Addie started showing off and giving herself airs or went off without saying where she was going. Then Daddy would tell Mother to "leave the girl alone," and he and Mother would argue in polite whispers about it. Those times, Mother was still serene, but it was a cold, black serenity Schooner found fearful.

"Schooner, I'd forgotten you said you'd be here, and I was getting worried about you," Maggie said as Schooner climbed into the wagon.

"I told you . . ."

"I know, but Mr. Spalding's news made me forget."

"Mr. Spalding? From Westport?"

"The Missouri Compromise has been repealed," James said. He took great interest in such things and assumed that Schooner did also.

"Repealed? Does that mean it isn't a law anymore?" Schooner asked. She'd heard people talk about this law before. It said that none of the land above a certain line could

233

come into the Union as a slave state—except Missouri. The line was far to the south of Seventrees, and if this part of the country ever got to be a state, all the slave owners would have to move south or free their slaves.

"That's right. Congress has voted a new law in its place," Maggie said. "It's called the Kansas-Nebraska Act, and I'm afraid it will make some big changes around here."

"Changes? Why?" Schooner couldn't understand how laws made by men clear off in Washington could make much difference to Seventrees.

"You see, the new law says that this part of the country that was given to the Indian is going to be divided into two territories. North of us in the Nebraska Territory, and we're in the Kansas Territory."

"You mean we live in Kansas?"

"The territory of Kansas. It's not a state yet," James said.

"Does this law mean Kansas will be a slave state?" Schooner asked. She didn't much like the idea of slavery, and she knew how much Mother and James would hate such a thing to happen.

"It could be," Maggie said. She was surprised that Schooner was interested. "You see, dear, right now there are as many pro-slavery states as antislavery. Neither side wants the other to have an advantage and unbalance things. The new law says that the voters in Kansas and Nebraska will get to decide for themselves which way they will come into the United States. Nebraska will surely enter as a free state . . ."

"But so will Kansas, won't it?" Schooner asked. This was a worrisome thing. She didn't think her family would want to stay in a place where white people could own black people. Would they have to move away? The thought made her stomach feel cold and awful. She'd rather die than leave Seventrees.

Maggie looked at her daughter, wondering why she had suddenly become concerned about statehood. They'd talked about it before, and Schooner had shown very little interest. The child actually looked pale and frightened. "If the vote were taken today, Kansas would be a free state, but we won't vote for a long time yet. There are a great many people in the East who care desperately about this. Some of them have the power and money to send their friends to live here."

"Oh. You mean so they can vote too?"

"That's right. I'm afraid we might be in for some unhappy times until it's settled—if it's ever settled," she added, more to herself than to Schooner. "It's such a bitter issue, and so unresolvable. Especially out here."

"What do you mean?" James asked.

"People who lived close together in old cities have learned to abide contrary opinions for the most part. They have meetings and elections and make laws in an orderly way. But out here . . . well, it's different."

"Mother, I don't want new people to come here," Schooner said softly. "I like Seventrees just like it is."

Maggie put her arm around Schooner. "I know. So do I. But things have to change. They always do."

Schooner mumbled something so quietly Maggie could hardly hear and had to ask her to repeat it. "I said, we won't have to move away, will we?" Schooner said. Her voice was shaking.

Maggie hugged her close. "No, you'll never *have* to go away. But someday perhaps you'll want to."

"No, I won't," Schooner said fervently. "I'm never going to leave here. I'm going to stay with you and Daddy and James and Morning Wish forever and ever."

Maggie leaned her head against the girl's clover-scented hair and wished she had felt that way as a child. It took her half her life to find home, and Schooner already knew where it was.

Mr. Smith was a swarthy little man who wore a green velvet hat, bushy side whiskers, and an earring on one ear. Someone in Seventrees had said he looked like a whaler, but Schooner wasn't sure what that meant, having lived her whole life hundreds of miles from an ocean. Mr. Smith—or Captain Smith, as he liked to be called—had a mysterious background and elaborately courteous manners. He had been traveling about the area for several weeks, incessantly promoting his windwagon. He needed investors to finance a fleet of these wondrous vehicles, and was staging a demonstration today.

The theory was that the winds that roared across the vast

prairies could be harnessed for the benefit of travelers. The windwagon was a lightweight schooner which lacked the usual canvas hood, but had, instead, enormous sails. There was a rudderlike mechanism attached to the wheels so that it could be steered. There was talk, of course, about what happened when there was no wind. Mr. Smith explained patiently that in that case one simply lowered the sails and used the conventional oxen.

"What have the 'conventional oxen' been doing in the meantime? Running alongside with their tongues hanging out?" Gerald had asked, and even Maggie had laughed at that.

Mr. Smith had pretended not to hear this frivolous remark, but had proceeded to discuss the possibility of obtaining the wheels for the fleet of windwagons from Seventrees trading post. It eventually became clear, however, that he expected the proprietors to *contribute* the wheels as their part of the investment, and at this stage the negotiations had broken down. No one had put a penny from Seventrees into the venture, but they were all turning out for the demonstration anyway. Free entertainment was not to be scoffed at.

There was a sort of unspoken rivalry at work too. The investors Mr. Smith had finally roped into his scheme were all Westport men. The people from Seventrees and the many other little communities which had begun to dot the countryside were rather hoping to see some of the rich gentlemen from Westport be made fools of. There were even families from Kansas Town—or rather, "Kansas City," as it had taken to calling itself.

They were real city people, and Schooner was fascinated with them. They were coming along the road in fancy carriages and wore nice clothes. The men had well-cut coats and tall hats, and some of the ladies wore pastel dresses and carried parasols. Several of them had their servants along—black men in crimson jackets who sat up on the front of the carriage holding the reins, and black women who sat on the projection at the rear carrying hampers of food. Schooner found these people intriguing and a little frightening—like they must know about life and have things that were secrets to her.

How could a lady go around in a pink dress, for example? It wasn't practical. The women of Seventrees would never waste money on a thing like that. Except for Aunt Fritzi, of course. But her pastel dresses always had food spots and torn

236

hems and were ugly. These city ladies had lace and ruffles and were so *clean*.

A few months earlier, Maggie had gone to Kansas City to buy a warehouse to store her medicines while they waited for the boats that took them to Saint Louis. While Maggie was talking over the price of the building, Schooner went out on the street to watch the people. She'd stood close to some of the pretty, rich women at a store. They had smelled just like real flowers, and there weren't even flowers blooming yet. Schooner had been greatly impressed and talked about it when she got home. "Why, that's just bottled scent!" Addie had scoffed, and Schooner wondered how Addie knew about such things. But then, Addie knew, or pretended she knew, all sorts of odd things—mostly from listening in on grown-ups when she wasn't supposed to. She had a way of making Schooner feel like she was a younger sister instead of older.

"What are you thinking about?" Maggie asked her.

"Just wondering where Addie is," Schooner answered.

Maggie's smile tightened a little. "Your father gave her permission to ride along with your Aunt Fritzi."

". . . and Cousin Ernest!" James added disgustedly.

"Now, James . . ."

"Mama, I tell you she's showing far too much interest in Ernest, and he's not good."

"James!" Maggie said, casting a warning glance at him as if to say: "Not in front of Schooner."

"Well, it's true," James muttered.

Just then they came over the last little rise before reaching their destination. A large, flat, treeless area had been selected for the trial run of the windwagon, and there were already forty or fifty people there. They'd brought cold hams and boiled eggs and jugs of cider and whiskey and were settling on blankets to watch and enjoy the outing. The gentlemen from Westport who were the principal investors were all tricked out in their Sunday best and were to be honored passengers on the wagon's "maiden voyage."

Schooner and James went to join Beatrice and Quincy, while Maggie watched for Katrin and Helmut. The younger children ran about getting in everyone's hair; the older boys hung around the windwagon trying to look important. The older women sat in clumps comparing childbirth experiences, while the farmers and merchants talked about crops and politics and passed jugs of potent home brew. All in all, it was a delightful picnic atmosphere. Schooner sat on a scratchy brown blanket with Beatrice, and they ate little sandwiches while they watched everyone. "Look, Schooner, there's your sister," Beatrice said.

Luther Halleck's wagon was as rickety and battered as everything else he owned. His paints and glues were made and packaged meticulously, and he had no interest left over for tending to anything else. One of the front wheels of the wagon was missing a spoke and some of the side boards had been cracked and split for as long as Schooner could remember. Uncle Luther, looking stern and morose, climbed down, leaving the rest of his family to fend for themselves.

Aunt Fritzi dithered until her nineteen-year-old son, Ernest, helped her down. Schooner watched in amazement as he also helped Addie down from the wagon bed. How silly! she thought. Just like Addie was a grown-up lady. How had she made him do that—and why? As far as Schooner was concerned, nobody in their right mind would have anything to do with Ernest. He was a nasty, sly person who was always snickering at the world.

Schooner noticed that her father had also arrived. She called to him, but he didn't hear her. He strolled over to where Maggie was sitting and handed her some papers. They talked for a moment, he made a note on one of the papers, nodded agreement to something she had said, then called to Morning Wish to get out of the wagon. The little half-Indian girl came obediently and sat next to Maggie, who absently re-tied one of her braids while continuing her discussion with Gerald. Schooner noticed some of the pretty city ladies looking at her father. No wonder. He was the handsomest man there. Except for Quincy Clay maybe. That wasn't just a personal opinion, it was a certainty. Even Beatrice admitted that folks said that Gerald Freiler was a fine-looking man. "Aesthetic but virile," she'd said. Schooner hadn't known what either of those words meant, but she liked the sound of it and she liked the way Beatrice used bookish words without seeming uppity.

Schooner's attention was diverted to the windwagon. The gentlemen from Westport had arrived, and Mr. Smith was strutting around all bandy-legged, asking everyone to get out of the way. A space was cleared and the investors climbed aboard, waving and looking dignified. With a grand flourish, Mr. Smith unfurled the sails.

Nothing happened for a moment; then a fresh breeze sprang up, and with a funny sort of lurch, the wagon began to move. Very slowly at first; then it started to pick up speed. Mr. Smith looked proud and busily attended to the rudder while the gentlemen continued to wave and smile at the poor unfortunate bystanders who hadn't the cash on hand to put into such a marvelous machine. The windwagon sailed merrily across the smooth, flat ground, a group of rowdy boys chasing along behind it whooping and laughing. "Westport boys," Beatrice said with the condescending tone they all used in Seventrees when referring to Westport. As she spoke, things began to go wrong with the windwagon.

It was a moment to savor.

Mr. Smith hadn't intended to simply sail off to Santa Fe; he was going to run the windwagon past his audience, then demonstrate its maneuverability by turning it and triumphantly running back past them the other way. As he got to the point he'd selected, he turned the rudder and adjusted the sails. The wagon began a long, slow turn. But the wind had come up, and the wagon started to go faster. About halfway through the turn, the wheels encountered a nest of prairie-dog holes. The wagon jounced, jiggled, and bucked.

The rudder mechanism locked.

Mr. Smith worked frantically to release it. The wagon kept on turning. The investors looked embarrassed, then alarmed. Two of them struggled to help him, but to no avail. The wagon had made almost a full circle.

"Abandon ship! To the lifeboats!" a man standing near Schooner and Beatrice called, and his companions laughed.

The wind increased. The windwagon went faster—still in a circle. The bystanders were roaring with laughter. Even Beatrice, who was normally so refined, was laughing out loud.

One of the investors tried to climb up and loosen the sails, but he lost his balance and toppled overboard, to the loud cheering of the boys who were still running along behind, hollering cheerfully. The discarded investor rose from the tall grass, brushed his sleeves, and walked away, ignoring the catcalls that wafted about him.

As the windwagon neared the audience again on its second pass, the rudder shifted slightly. The wagon was still making a circle, but it was a much bigger circle. Now it was coming—hurtling—toward them. Schooner joined the rest in hastily getting out of the way. She and Beatrice were laughing so hard they could hardly run. There wasn't any real danger, but several women who were inclined to shrieking did so.

Babies were crying and men were trying to save their whiskey jugs, their families, and themselves—in that order.

The wagon flew through the space so recently occupied by the observers. It went over blankets, abandoned parasols, and plates. The wheels squashed through sandwiches, rhubarb pies, bowls of potato salad, and cornbread. Jugs of cider shattered and the contents ran together with jars of milk.

All the while, the windwagon was throwing off investors like a dog shaking off water.

Schooner found herself standing next to her mother. There were tears in her mother's eyes. "It ran over my best plate," Maggie said in a strangely shaky voice.

"Mother, I'm sorry," Schooner said.

"I can buy a new plate, I'll never be able to buy anything this much fun," Maggie said, and Schooner realized she was shaking with laughter. Morning Wish was hanging on her stepmother's skirts giggling.

Mr. Smith had abandoned both the rudder and his dignity and was scrambling about madly loosening the sails as the careening wagon bounced along. One by one the sheets of canvas dropped, slithered over the edges of the wagon, and got tangled in the wheels. Eventually the windwagon came to a halt within a few feet of where it had started. He was the only one aboard. With all the dignity of a captain who has brought his ship safely through dangerous seas, he cleared his throat and said loudly, "Aye, well, the rudder needs a little work, but . . ."

By the time they got ready to go home, Schooner had a stitch in her side from laughing so hard. "Come on, Morning Wish," she said to her little dark-skinned half-sister. The younger girl, eight years old, but small for her age, climbed aboard the wagon and settled down next to Maggie. Schooner sat on the seat with them while they waited for James to find Addie and drive them all home. "Where did Daddy go?" Schooner asked.

"He went to the land office to file our claims," Maggie explained. "Now that the land is officially open to settlement, we have to claim our land. We've never really owned it, you know. We're also claiming some other pieces along the road to Westport—on the Kansas side. It ought to be valuable someday."

"Mama, I'm sleepy," Morning Wish said.

Maggie bunched her skirts up into a sort of pillow for

Morning Wish to put her head on. Schooner had noticed often how her mother did special little things for Morning Wish. The strange thing was, Daddy didn't pay much attention to her, and she was *his* daughter. Schooner had often wondered vaguely how her mother felt about raising her husband's illegitimate child. Schooner loved little Morning Wish in spite of her strange ways, but her existence was sometimes worrisome. Schooner wanted to think of her father as the most perfect man there was, and yet, he had this child by another woman, an Indian woman Schooner hardly remembered. It was a flaw in his perfection, a cruelty to her mother, that Schooner could neither overlook nor justify. Mother never talked about it, and Schooner wished she would sometimes.

It was difficult to wholly accept Morning Wish as a sister. It wasn't so much that her appearance was startlingly in contrast to the rest of them. It was something about the way she was inside. She was quiet and mannerly—almost too much so. As if she were a perpetual guest at their house on her best behavior, but never being one of them. Never wanting to be a Freiler. She spent all her time with the Indian children from the mission, and when they were gone home to their tribes, she simply kept to herself. She would not play with the white children, which was probably just as well, Schooner thought, since some of the children of newcomers were not very kind to her.

There were so many ways she set herself apart. She spoke perfectly good English, and Schooner had heard her jabbering away a mile a minute with the Indian children in their language, but she had never uttered a word of German at home, even though Mother sometimes used it and Daddy insisted that they learn properly how to read the language.

She did lots of other things differently. Once Schooner had taken her fishing down by the river, and as Schooner got one of her father's metal hooks tied to her string, she noticed that Morning Wish had something curved and shiny tied to hers. "What's that thing?" Schooner asked. "You need a fishhook."

"It is the claw of an eagle. It is better," Morning Wish answered, casting her line out.

"Where did you get such an idea?"

"My people have always fished this way," the little girl answered complacently.

"What do you mean, 'my people'? *I'm* your people and I've never heard of that," Schooner had said. For some reason it

241

made her angry, but she had to admit that Morning Wish's way caught more fish.

Schooner moved around trying to get more comfortable in the back of the wagon. She was tired of waiting. "Where have James and Addie gone?" she asked her mother.

Her question was soon answered. As the afternoon sun cast slanting rays in their faces, James and his younger sister were silhouetted against the light. James was walking hard on his heels and had a hand firmly on Addie's sleeve. She was flouncing along angrily, trying to shake his grip loose. "Get in that wagon!" James said, and gave her a rough shove. His face was pale and set. "Kissing boys! That's where she was!" he said to Maggie as he took up the reins and gave a sharp snap of command to the horses.

"What!" Maggie and Schooner said in unison.

"She was over in the grove with a rough bunch of boys from Westport. Playing some sort of kissing game. Mother, she's going on twelve years old—she knows better than that sort of stuff. Those boys were fifteen, sixteen years old. She's gonna get—"

"That's enough!" Maggie said. "We'll discuss this later." She had the black serene look that scared Schooner. Was Addie ever in trouble now!

She had scrunched down at the very back of the wagon and was scowling rebelliously at her mother and brother. Schooner crawled back and sat beside her. "Addie, what did you go and do a thing like that for?"

"Don't be so fancy-mouth!" Addie said. "It was just a game. No harm in that. They said I was pretty and it was a sort of holiday and could they kiss me once. It was nice. Everybody kisses folks. Nothing wrong with it."

"Mother doesn't agree with you," Schooner said. There was something wrong with Addie's reasoning, but she couldn't figure out what. "You must have known you'd get in trouble."

"I wouldn't have if Daddy had been there. Mother's just silly about things," Addie came back.

"Silly" was one word Schooner would never have applied to her mother, and told her sister as much, but she just shrugged it off. Addie could be so irritating. Schooner suddenly felt all the day's laughter and fun drain away. Everybody would be angry now over what Addie had done. But it was more than that. There was a little jealousy in what Schooner felt. After all, she was fifteen, and no one had ever asked *her* for a kiss and said she was pretty.

242

Being pretty had come to mean a lot lately. Aunt Fritzi had a full-length mirror, and Schooner had caught a good long look at herself in it the other day. She was surprised to see that she looked more like a woman than a little girl. She had noticed that her breasts had grown like a woman's, but she hadn't been aware that her hips had gotten wider and her waist seemed to have gone in. She was elated to find that she was "curvy," and had gone around feeling very grown-up for a while. But looking womanish didn't mean pretty.

Her nose was plain and straight, but not little and cute like Addie's. Schooner's mouth and teeth were fine, but Addie had pretty rosebud lips and her teeth almost sparkled. To top it all, Addie had dimples in *both* cheeks. Schooner tried to shake off her envious thoughts as they neared Seventrees. What was it about being fifteen that made her brood on such things?

Addie's behavior at the picnic cast a pall over the family that lasted for days. Maggie was furious when they got home. She sent everyone out of the house and had a long serious talk with Addie, and though Schooner didn't get to hear any of it, she had a pretty good idea that it didn't do any good. When she was finally released from the lecture, she was sullen and rude and Maggie was even angrier. Addie disappeared, and when Gerald returned late that evening, she was with him, hanging on his arm, being adorable and making him laugh. She must have walked down the road and waited for him, Schooner thought. It was typical—she seemed born to make people take sides. The only times Schooner had ever heard her parents disagree or be snappish with one another, it had always concerned Addie. Schooner buried herself in the essay she had to prepare for school the next day and tried not to hear what was being said in the next room. Pretty soon Addie came into the room the girls shared. She was smiling smugly, and Schooner wanted to slap her. Addie undressed and crawled into bed, falling asleep almost immediately.

Schooner had her essay finished except for a word she couldn't spell. She went into the main room to consult her father's dictionary, but couldn't find it. He and her mother must have gone out for a walk, she concluded. She had to have the dictionary. She slipped on her shoes and went out to ask her father where it was.

She hadn't meant to walk especially quietly, nor had she meant to eavesdrop on them, but when she heard her parents speaking, she could not help herself. They were standing by

243

the shed in back of the house, and Gerald was saying, "But, Maggie, I think you're taking this far too seriously. I don't think there was anything wicked in it."

"Sixteen-year-old hooligans don't play kissing games with girls her age *innocently!*" Maggie said.

"But she's just a child."

"Gerald, she's not! She's almost twelve years old. You still think of her as a cute little doll. She's going to be a woman before long, and I'm very concerned about what sort of woman she might become. You've spoiled her into believing that she can do whatever she pleases."

"Well, Maggie, why shouldn't she? She's pretty and bright and has her whole life before her. Why shouldn't she be allowed to enjoy it?"

Schooner knew she shouldn't be listening, and turned to steal away, but her mother's next words and icy tone of voice riveted her. "Gerald, you must allow me the final say in how to raise our daughters. And you must back me up!" She was giving him an order. Schooner could hardly believe her ears. She knew her mother usually got her way, but she'd never heard her mother lay down the law to him as if he was a child.

"Now, Maggie, my love . . ." he said cajolingly.

"Gerald, I mean this. There's already one bastard in this family for me to raise. I'll not have Addie bring home another one."

There was a silence that seemed to reverberate through the still night air. Schooner's first reaction was shock, then a sick realization of how terribly her mother must have been hurt to be able to say such a hurtful thing herself. Schooner did not love her any less for having blurted out those ugly words, but she suddenly knew her parents were not just beloved people who existed only in relationship to her. There was something dark and painful between them that she would never penetrate, nor want to.

Her father was speaking now in a defeated tone she'd never heard before. All the jauntiness was gone. "I deserved that, Maggie, but I never thought I'd hear you say it."

"Gerald, I don't know why . . . I'm sorry—"

But he cut her off. "No, it was my misunderstanding. I've gone along these years thinking because you did not say anything about the past, you did not think about it. That was foolish of me. As for Addie, you try to be more lenient with

244

her and I'll try to be stricter. Perhaps we'll meet in the middle."

Schooner could hear no more. She couldn't bear it. She turned away and tiptoed back to the house and pretended to be sound asleep when they returned.

Schooner first met Henry Grinnell in August 1854, a few months after Kansas became a territory. A group of men in the East who had money to spare for their beliefs felt that Kansas must enter the Union as a free state. They had founded the Massachusetts Emigrant Aid Society to settle the territory. By late summer the selected "emigrants" had begun to arrive. Schooner noticed at first that these people were different from many of those who had passed through over the years. First of all, they were not misfits or failures or scholars who didn't know a plow from a shovel. They were skilled, knowledgeable men and women, craftsmen, farmers, doctors, and lawyers. She mentioned this to her mother.

"That's very perceptive of you," Maggie said. "Most of the people who have gone west have done so because life let them down in the East. But don't be too quick to criticize 'misfits.' Everyone is a misfit somewhere. I was in Germantown, but not here. That isn't the same as failure."

"You couldn't be a misfit anywhere, Mother," Schooner protested.

Maggie just laughed and hugged her.

The other thing that made the Massachusetts Emigrant Aid people different was their faith. This was harder for Schooner to define. It wasn't that they were very religious, not "Bible thumpers." She'd seen plenty of those, people who carried their religion around with them like a torture device. The Emigrant Aid people just had a strong surety in their "moral convictions," as Beatrice put it. Naturally Beatrice could put words to it.

"But why would people leave their homes and businesses just for a 'moral conviction'?" Schooner wondered.

"I think that's what the phrase means," Beatrice said. "Do-

245

ing something about what you think instead of just talking about it. I wish I believed in something that much."

Schooner wished she did too, but as she thought about it more, she wondered. She wouldn't want to leave Seventrees for any reason. Certainly not because slavery was wrong. It *was* wrong, but imagine leaving your home because you thought so. "It must be sort of like being in love," she said to Beatrice. "I think love is a very good feeling that sometimes hurts while it's feeling good," she added. She had thought a lot about the nature of love since that evening in the early summer when she had overheard her parents. "But people can fall in love suddenly. I wonder if you can fall into moral conviction?"

Beatrice laughed, the pretty silver-and-blue laugh that made Schooner feel happy and refreshed. "I think you're going to be a philosopher, Schooner."

"I'm serious," Schooner said, but smiled in spite of herself. She liked talking about things with Beatrice and wanted the conversation to go on.

"I know you are. I don't think people really 'fall' in love. People can form attractions, but love—real love—has to grow over a long time, doesn't it? Think of the people we love, our families and friends. We didn't love our parents to begin with, we just depended on them, and it turned into love."

"But you fell in love with Quincy, didn't you?" Schooner asked. She was fascinated with this subject. She envied Beatrice being in love with Quincy. It was wonderful and grown-up.

"I don't think so. There was one day when I first *realized* it, but it had actually happened over a long period. I guess I started loving him when I was just a little girl—when we first came here. But it isn't always reciprocal . . ." she said sadly.

"Reciprocal?" Schooner asked. Beatrice always assumed that Schooner knew all the lovely big words she did.

"Yes, goes both ways."

"But you and Quincy are going to get married."

"So everyone says—except Quincy. I suppose we will someday, but I'm afraid it will just be because everyone expects it, not because it's what he wants."

"Oh, Beatrice, don't sound so sad."

"I'm not sad, Schooner. Just confused sometimes. Come on, there are wagons pulling in, and we ought to be over

246

helping at the trading post. It's probably some more of the Emigrant Aid people."

"I'll go over. You finish your quilt block," Schooner said, and dashed off.

Beatrice was right. Another group of them had arrived. Schooner hurried around behind the counter and set about marking prices on the new batch of medicines she and her mother had brought over the day before. As she worked, three men came in the door. Two of the men were her father's age, but the third caught her eye. He was only two or three years older than she, but he seemed to have all the self-assurance of someone much older. Even the other men seemed to defer to him. "Henry, what was it you needed?" one of them asked.

"Are you with the Emigrant Aid?" Schooner asked him. It was a pointless question, but she'd felt compelled to ask him something—anything—so that he would notice her and talk with her.

"Yes, ma'am," he said courteously, and stepped forward to shake her hand. "Name's Henry Grinnell. Glad to make your acquaintance."

She stared at him and mumbled her own name. He had sandy hair that curled a little, and slate-colored eyes with lashes that would have seemed feminine on a less robust man. He was quite tall, but there was nothing of the rawboned youth in him. Even in an enclosed room he seemed to stride rather than walk. There was no arrogance in it, just quiet self-assurance.

"I see you have medical supplies," he said. "Do you sell much to veterinarians?" At her questioning look, he added, "Animal doctors."

Suddenly she felt silly and inferior. He had realized right away that she didn't know the word, and it embarrassed her that he could tell. "Is that what you are? A veterinarian?" she said, hoping she was pronouncing it right.

He smiled, a friendly, almost shy smile. "Yes, ma'am. I am. Learned it from my father and took some medical courses in a college to learn more. Chemistry, biology, and such."

"Did you really? My mother would like to meet you. She's very interested in such things. She makes all these medicines herself. I help her some."

"Do you really?" he asked, clearly impressed. "I've seen Freiler's Cures for sale lots of times. Used them myself at home. I had no idea they were made out here. Yes, ma'am,

247

I'd be pleased to meet your mother. I think we're going to be here for a while."

"From the looks of that river, we sure are," one of the other men said.

Schooner hadn't realized that she'd been ignoring the others. "Are you traveling by river?" she asked him. This seemed an odd thing. Nobody traveled on the Kaw; they just crossed it and occasionally floated down to Kansas City on it when it was bank-full and the sandbars weren't such a nuisance.

"We were planning to," Henry Grinnell said. "We're going to a place called Mount Oread. Some of our people were out earlier and decided it would be a fine place to found a city. We're going to call it Lawrence."

"*Found* a city? That sounds strange to me. I thought cities just sort of 'happened.' Our lives are changing a lot out here, you see."

"The country's changing a lot," Henry Grinnell said seriously. "Our aim is to see that it changes in the right ways. Not that we can do much, but we're destined to try."

We're destined to try. Beatrice would have been able to say something fine and poetic back, but Schooner could only stare at him and say, "Oh."

At that point Torchy came out of the back room and took charge. As was the custom, he offered them a friendly cup of Seventrees Tea, only to discover that they were almost out. "Schooner, would you take yourself to Clay's to acquire more tea?" he asked.

As she left, she stopped for a moment where Henry Grinnell stood looking at a harness bit. "Could you have dinner with us?" she asked; then she held her breath and almost prayed.

He smiled again and nodded his head. "I'd like that, ma'am."

"Oh, thank you . . . I mean, good!" Schooner said, and tried to walk out the door instead of dancing.

Almost everyone liked Henry Grinnell. Maggie had been surprised when Schooner announced that she had invited a guest, but was delighted when Henry arrived. She and the young man talked about medicines, about organic chemistry, and about diseases and ailments that people and animals had in common. Maggie agreed to stock certain preparations in larger quantities for Henry's use, and he said he would try to get back to Seventrees every two or three months. He lent her a book from his chemistry course, and Maggie fell on it like a starving person on a loaf of fresh bread.

Gerald discovered that Henry was well read in the classics and managed to get him into an incomprehensible (to Schooner) discussion of Socrates. They talked about translations, fine points of logic, and found themselves in complete and happy agreement. Gerald slapped him on the shoulder and declared him a "fine mind," which obviously embarrassed and pleased Henry.

Henry and James talked all through dinner itself about slavery—the wickedness of it, the political and social justifications and their flaws, the economy of the South. They spoke with fire, and even James used words like "reprehensible," which astonished Schooner.

The only person who did not like Henry was Addie. She did all her usual tricks: she smiled, dimpled, pouted, flirted, and finally gave up. Henry was courteous to her, but seemed completely oblivious of her charms, and it made her angry and sullen. When she tried to push herself into the middle of his discussion with Gerald, even her father said, "Later, Addie." For the first time in her life Schooner felt glad for her sister's misfortune. She was coming to hate the way Addie acted. The traits that had made her such a lovable child suddenly irritated Schooner to the point of rage. Why had she never noticed before that Addie had to have everyone's full attention, and became downright ugly when she failed?

After dinner Beatrice and Jack Q and Quincy stopped by, and the three of them got along with Henry right away too. Jack Q had visited Henry's hometown in his travels for the post, and they compared acquaintances. Quincy talked with him about his trip west, and Beatrice pulled Schooner aside. "He's very mannerly, Schooner. Will he be here for long?"

"For a week or two. If the river doesn't rise enough by then to take rafts, they're going to go ahead with wagons. That's what he told James."

But when the evening was over, Schooner realized that everything she knew about him was from what he had told others. She had brought Henry Grinnell to her family like a treasure she had found, a bright golden prize she considered her own. But he had made himself theirs—not hers. It wasn't that he ignored her, or was rude to her. She'd just had nothing to talk to him about. When he left, he shook Maggie's hand and thanked her for the dinner invitation, forgetting that it was Schooner who had actually invited him. She wanted to sit across the table from him, eyes bright and vocabulary rich and sparkling, and talk about grand ideas—but she had neither the words nor the ideas.

Maggie came to her later that night, as she was crying into her pillow. "Schooner, what's wrong? It was such a lovely evening."

"For everybody else it was, but I'm so dull and stupid!" Schooner sobbed.

Maggie sat on the bed and put her arms around her daughter. "You must never say that about yourself. You're not dull and you're certainly not stupid. Why would you think that?"

"Because Henry talked to everybody but me, and it was my fault, because I'm not interesting."

"We did all take him away from you, didn't we? That wasn't right. But, Schooner, you have the wrong idea of what's 'interesting.' You are fair-minded and inquiring. That's important, and will make you much more interesting when you're grown than people who set their minds in certain tracks early in life and never climb out of them."

"I don't know what you mean."

"Well, for example, when we walk in the woods together, I'm usually looking for plants. Many times I get back home and realize that I've not noticed the sky or the birdsong or anything else. But when you walk in the woods you wonder why some squirrels are red and some gray and where the chickadees build their secret nests. Remember the other day when you were asking what I thought this place would look like a hundred years from now and what people would think it *had* been like?"

"But that was just wondering. That's not knowing things."

"Wondering is more important than knowing. Oh, Schooner, how is it that you don't recognize your own best feature?" There were equal doses of love and frustration in her voice. "I should have been telling you all along, but I thought you knew."

"If I'm as nice as you say, why didn't Henry notice me? He liked everybody else, but he didn't say more than a few words to me."

"Well . . . what did *you* say to him?"

"Nothing much, but . . ."

"No 'but' about it."

Schooner wiped her eyes. "I guess you're right. Mama, you did like him, didn't you?"

"Very much," Maggie assured her. "I hope we will see a great deal more of him. Too bad he's not German."

"Oh, Mother!" Schooner groaned.

"Schooner," Maggie said, taking her hand and looking into her eyes. "Don't try too hard to grow up. You're only fifteen. Enjoy it. You'll never be fifteen again."

"Would you want to be fifteen again?" Schooner asked her. Strange, she'd never thought about her mother being that age.

"Good Lord, no! But I wasn't you."

Schooner still wasn't sure she understood what her mother was talking about, but she felt better about herself and resolved to make some changes. The next morning she cut up some paper into little squares and glued them at the top to make a tiny book. This she slipped into her apron pocket. Later, when she and Beatrice were making soap, Beatrice used a word Schooner didn't know, so she wrote it in the book. When she went home at lunchtime, she got out her father's dictionary and looked it up.

That evening she put some stale pieces of bread in a handkerchief and a tin box full of seeds in her apron pocket and went for a walk, as she often did at dusk. Her path took her by the encampment where the Emigrant Aid people were camping. Henry Grinnell was just pouring water on the embers of a fire.

"Hello, Miss Freiler," he said.

"No, please! Call me Schooner, everyone does."

He set down the bucket and gave the dead fire one more stir to be sure it was out. "Schooner. That's an unusual name."

"It isn't really my name. I was born 'Mary,' but no one has ever called me that. It doesn't seem to mean me at all."

"But why 'Schooner'? Isn't that a kind of wagon?" he asked.

"I was born in one. Our house wasn't built, and that's where my parents and brothers lived—in the wagon."

"I like the name," he said. "It sounds nice. Are you going somewhere?" he asked abruptly.

"Yes, to meet some friends. Would you like to join me?"

"Oh, no. I wouldn't like to impose . . ."

Schooner laughed. "You wouldn't be imposing. They're very friendly folks. Come along." She was surprised at how easy it was to talk to him when there weren't a lot of other people around discussing weighty things. Perhaps some of the nice things her mother had said were right—he liked her name, *that* was something different and interesting about her. As they walked along the riverbank where the trees came down close and the willows wept over the water, she said, "I hope my family didn't intimidate you." There! She'd used the word she learned today, and it came out sounding like she said it all the time.

"No, I found them very congenial," he said.

She couldn't take her notebook out now, but she'd remember "congenial" and look it up later. "Do the same kind of trees grow where you're from?" she asked him. Certainly trees couldn't involve big words.

"Fairly much the same kind, but in different proportions," he said.

Proportions? However would she spell that!

"We have more pines. I miss the smell of them," he said, "and the forest doesn't grow so thickly. The soil was very rocky in my home, and hard to grow anything."

They had come to a big dead elm. Schooner stopped and handed Henry a piece of bread. "Sit down here with me and hold very still," she said. There was a hole at the base of the tree. Schooner whistled a low, soft warble, and there was a rustling sound inside the hollow tree. In a moment a shiny black nose stuck out, then the rest of the animal's face—a black mask, soft white-edged ears. Then, somehow, the raccoon squeezed its fat body out through the small hole and waddled over to Schooner. It sat back and daintily took the bread in its front paws, rolling it around meditatively between it's human-looking "hands" and keeping a wary eye on Henry the whole time.

"Where's your family?" Schooner asked it softly. "Are the babies home?"

About that time the babies appeared. One by one four half-size versions of the mother cautiously came out. They were not as shy of Henry as the older animal, and they scrabbled around chattering with one another, arguing over his piece of bread. "Here, look how smart they are," Schooner said. She took a small lidded tin box out of her other pocket and rattled it. It was full of sunflower seeds. Then she dropped it back into the pocket. The largest of the babies abandoned Henry and came back over to her. He climbed onto her lap and peered into the apron pocket, then fished the box out. "You have to get help, you know," Schooner told him.

Another of the babies came over and got on her lap. The

two little raccoons applied themselves to the box. They had done this before and soon had it open. One held the box while the other pulled at the lid.

"How did you teach them that?" Henry asked in amazement.

"I just showed them once. They're very clever at getting into things. That's why lots of folks don't much like them. But I do."

"I never thought about raccoons as anything but materials for hats and something to keep out of your corn and chicken house."

"That's because you've never been friends with one," Schooner assured him. "I know they're pests, and if anyone knew they were here, they'd be shot. You won't tell anyone, will you?"

"Of course not!" Henry sounded almost offended at the suggestion. "Would I let anyone shoot a friend? Say, aren't they supposed to wash their food?"

Schooner laughed. "No, that's just what folks who don't know them say. They like putting things in the water, but it's not to get it clean. I think they just like the feel of things better when they're wet and slippery. See, they have very soft hands. They don't just eat off the ground like other animals, they pick up everything and get to know it first—including folks' corn and chickens, I imagine."

"How in the world do you know so much about them?" Henry asked.

"Just from watching, and getting to know them," Schooner said. She liked the tone of admiration in his voice. Who would have thought anyone would be impressed with what she knew about something as ordinary as raccoons?

It was getting dark quickly now. Schooner dumped the last of the crumbs out of her pockets and took the now-empty tin box back from the babies who were squabbling over it. She and Henry walked back to the encampment. When they got to the place where a log had fallen across the path, he took her hand to help her over—as if she needed help! She could have jumped it without even hitching up her skirts, but she stepped over carefully and kept hold of his hand for as long as she dared without seeming brazen.

When she got back to her house, Maggie was putting away the last of the dishes from dinner. Schooner put her arms around her mother's waist and hugged her tight. "Do you

know what, Mama? I *like* Schooner Freiler! And I think
Henry Grinnell does too."

Maggie smiled and returned the hug. "Of course he does!
Who wouldn't?"

4

Henry Grinnell and his friends waited a week for the Kaw
to rise, but the river refused to cooperate. Finally they gave
up and put their belongings into wagons and set out to follow
the riverbank. Schooner was not able to talk with him as
much as she would have liked, because it was the busiest time
of year for her. The household chores involved in preparing
for the long harsh Kansas winter took time. The animals had
to be slaughtered, the meat dressed and salted, soap made,
clothing cleaned and repaired, and the blankets brought out to
be aired and patched.

In addition, there was the work of getting the fall shipments of medicines out. The Freilers owned a big warehouse
now in Kansas City and a smaller one in Seventrees, where
the boxing and bottling and labeling were done. Maggie had
hired a German family from Hermann, Missouri, to work for
her. There were four sons who did most of the heavy work,
but there was still a great deal Schooner was required to help
with.

But in her short intervals of free time, Schooner did manage to see Henry several times. Twice during the week, he
joined her on her evening stroll to feed the baby raccoons
and they sat and talked about things that interested them
about animals. Schooner told Henry about the birds, how to
hand-tame the chickadees and titmice, and showed him where
the foxes with their bushy tails and velvet matchstick legs had
a hollow in a rock outcropping. Henry, in turn, told her
things she didn't know about the insides of animals—about
the five stomachs in cows and the appendix which was useful
to animals and sometimes a deadly vestige in humans.

He talked a little about himself, too, but reluctantly and
only when she asked him specific questions. His father had
been a "horse doctor" and had taught him to love animals.

His mother had died when he was an infant. There were no brothers and sisters, and his father had never remarried. The two of them had lived a solitary bachelor existence, and when he was sixteen his father sent him to a real college to take courses in science. It was only a month before he completed his studies when his father suffered a stroke and died.

It was during his years at college that he had developed a loathing for the institution of slavery. When he heard that the Emigrant Aid Society was forming, he applied to them to be included. Because he was young, healthy, skilled, fervent, and unburdened with a family, he was accepted.

"But didn't you hate leaving your home?" Schooner asked.

"It was just a place. The only person who meant a great deal to me was my father, and he was gone," Henry explained.

But Schooner couldn't understand his attitude. To her, places were as distinctly lovable as people. She loved Seventrees—it wasn't just the people, it was the land, the special things that grew there, the animals that made noises at night, the way the heat made a shimmering golden cloud over the horizon in the late summer, when the grasses had all turned yellow, the way the chocolate-brown Kaw rose and fell according to the season. The way the bluffs turned a diaphanous pink in April when the redbuds bloomed made her want to cry for the beauty of it. She could not live where there were no redbuds to bloom and majestic red-tailed hawks to soar above. Surely if you lived where it never got soul-wringing hot in the summer you could not appreciate the breathtaking subzero cold of the winter. And didn't the lush, green, bee-buzzing May make a person love the subtle gray-browns of November all the more? How could anyone think that a place was just the people who lived there?

There was something else she wondered about Henry Grinnell. While he professed that people were more important than places, and felt deeply for people in general, there didn't seem to be any individuals who were dear to him. He spoke about his father, of course, but of the others he had known he said little. He never mentioned any close friends, neighbors, school pals, or other relatives. Schooner wondered how he could be so content, so self-confident, and not be lonely. Beatrice called it "self-reliant."

When they left, Schooner was forced to admit that she had not made any particular impression on him. He liked her well enough, but no more than he liked everyone else in Seventrees. She was merely one unit of a whole. But he was going to be living nearby and would be coming into Seventrees every few months to purchase medical supplies from Maggie, so there was hope. As time went by, perhaps he would come to feel something more for her. Something like what she felt—a fluttery sort of emotion she was reluctant to put a name to.

In the meantime, she was on a determined self-improvement campaign. She had confided in Beatrice that she needed to understand words better, not just love them for their sounds, and Beatrice was happy to help her. Beatrice made a list each week of fourteen new words for Schooner—two per day—that she was to learn and use. Sometimes they were what Beatrice called "concept" words—"integrity," "comprehension," "obsession," "resolution," "harmonious"—and they would talk all day sometimes about the various aspects of the concept. "There is a significant incongruity in your accoutrements," Schooner said one day when Beatrice's petticoat was showing, and Beatrice had clapped her hands and laughed with Schooner until they were both hiccuping.

Maggie and Gerald noticed the improvement in her vocabulary and were both complimentary about it. This pleased Schooner, for it was not always easy to satisfy both of them. So often, what one parent liked, the other ignored or disapproved of.

One day she told Beatrice, "The best thing about knowing words is that you can think about things you can't even comprehend without the words to put to it. Like today's word—'investigate.' It has a nice clean meaning, it's not the same as snooping or prying. I always thought questioning things was one of those, and they're not nice, but now I know the word, it makes a difference. A person can investigate something they want to know without it being a bad thing."

With her new interest in language came increased fascination with her father's books. Gerald probably owned more books than the rest of Seventrees put together. He had them in boxes and crates and on shelves and lying about the house with markers in them. Nearly every time Quincy and Jack Q made a trading trip to Saint Louis or New Orleans, Gerald would hand one of them a slip of paper with the name of a book he wanted and some money to buy it with. Often when settlers came through he would take some books to the wagon train and offer to trade for things they had brought along and already read. Beatrice had called him a "one-man circulating library," and then they'd talked about things that circulate.

Gerald was delighted to help Schooner channel her reading, and selected volumes for her to read that they later discussed. Schooner felt genuinely close to her father for the first time. She had always loved him, but from a distance of age and interest that she had thought unbreachable. During that long winter after she met Henry Grinnell, however, she grew very close to Gerald. They read Wordsworth together and talked about whether John Donne was right when he said "no man is an island." Gerald tried to help her through Milton, but they had to give it up. At Christmas he gave her a book of Shakespeare's sonnets, and Maggie finally had to ask her to stop reciting them all the time. "You'll have us all talking like that in a while," she said, but Schooner knew she was pleased.

"You wouldn't want me to stop, would you?" she asked with a grin. "After all, 'Lilies that fester smell far worse than weeds,' Mother," she added with yet another quote from the sonnets.

Henry made only one short visit to Seventrees that winter, and stayed but two days. It was bitterly cold, and with everyone cooped up together indoors it was impossible for Schooner to get to talk to him alone—not that she had anything secret to say, but she felt more comfortable with him when she didn't have to compete with anyone. It was during his visit that the old Indian Black Feather stopped to see them. He had been gone with other chiefs to Washington to conclude some treaties with the government, and Maggie had been anxious for his return.

Henry had been discussing slavery with Gerald and James while Schooner and Addie helped Maggie with the cooking. Gerald opposed slavery in his usual vague, amiable way, and the younger men were trying to convert him to their fervor. "Kansas must be populated with abolitionists to stop the spread of this immoral institution," Henry said.

"Why must Kansas be populated by anyone?" Gerald asked. "Up until recently the only white people who lived here had very isolated, nonpolitical lives. Aren't you bringing your private battles here to fight out on our soil?"

"Sir! Certainly you can't mean that," Henry said, shocked.

"I'm not sure but what I do," Gerald said, gently weighing his words. "It seems to me that this is, in a political sense, a fight between the North and the South that's been brought to the West for a dress rehearsal."

"Surely you don't condone the practice of a man owning another man's life, Father," James asked.

"No. You know I don't. I merely question whether the issue ought to be brought to a head here. Why Kansas? You see, you may be doing certain members of the human race a great favor by coming out here, but there are others who are suffering for that noble cause."

"What others?" Henry asked. "Your own community has benefited. There is increased business and commerce, is there not?"

"Is that what we are supposed to want in life? Yes, our commerce has benefited. We had enough money brought in that we became worth robbing. Did you know, sir, that some of the ruffians from Westport came in here last fall to rob the trading post? They failed because Torchy was alert and ran them off, but ten years ago we wouldn't have had anything here worth riding out to take. But I wasn't talking about business, or even white men. I'm talking about the Indians."

"Oh, the Indians . . ." Henry said, dismissing them in a word.

"But shouldn't their freedom and their rights be of as much concern to you as the black man's?"

"Perhaps there is something in what you say, sir," Henry answered courteously. But Schooner, eavesdropping from the other end of the room, got the impression that Henry didn't equate the two at all. She hoped that he would not say anything awkward. She didn't know if he had been told that the little Indian girl Morning Wish was a member of the family, not just an adopted orphan.

"I think the roast is done," Maggie said to the men. "Let's have a more general discussion for dinner. Do you think we'll be chosen as a postal station, Mr. Grinnell?"

Schooner breathed a sigh of relief. She should have known that her mother would step in and save the situation from becoming uncomfortable.

Henry was still there the next day when Black Feather returned to Seventrees. Schooner wondered if the coincidence was fortunate or otherwise. Maggie greeted the stern old Indian as always—with a handshake and formal welcome. An outsider could hardly have guessed how much she and the Indian meant to each other; the cool but intense friendship that had been between them for so many years was so restrained and so dignified as to make them seem virtually strangers. But Schooner knew better. She often thought that other than her family and Katrin Clay, her mother loved Black Feather more than the rest of the world put together.

"We are glad to receive you in our home, my friend," Maggie said. "It has been too long, and I'm eager to hear about your travels." There was an almost poetic cadence in her voice when she spoke to him. As if everything they said had its own meaning and a hidden meaning that touched on the core of existence. Schooner had never noticed it before.

Black Feather, tall and bronze, stooped a little entering the door. He was dressed in the coat Maggie had made him after Addie's birth. The coat looked just like it had when she first gave it to him, but the man himself had aged considerably. There were iron-gray streaks in his glossy braids, and his once-smooth face was lined now with age and worry. "I'm afraid I have come to say a final farewell to my friends in this house," he said.

"No," Maggie whispered. "Why?"

"There is much to tell, and I've come a long way in the cold. May we sit by your fire to talk?"

Maggie took his coat and asked him to share their dinner. Gerald introduced him to Henry while the girls hastily set the table. Schooner wondered what Henry thought of this tall, taciturn man who was such a welcome guest at the Freiler table.

While they ate, Black Feather told of his trip, the travel across half the continent, his impressions of the large cities of the East, the long cold trip back. Only when the food was cleared did he get back to his original statement. "My tribe has signed a new treaty with your government. When we left Ohio at the urging of the encroaching white settlement, we were given many hundreds of miles of land here, as you know. At that time it was thought that this was a useless land, fit only for Indians." Schooner felt as though she should hang her head in shame, even though she had nothing to do with the injustice. "The land was given to the tribe as a whole. Now, however, the treaty has been rewritten."

"I know the size of your lands has been reduced," Maggie said, "and I cannot approve of that. But the land has not all been taken away. Why must you leave?"

"Because the land is being given to my people as individuals. The small part left is to be divided up with a set number of acres for each family. It is theirs to do with as they choose. Many of my people, anticipating this, have sold their portions to real-estate speculators before it was even officially theirs to sell."

"But why must *you* go," Maggie asked. It was almost a cry.

"Because I am a chief. I must do what I can to keep some of my people together. We cannot be a tribe here, with white men living among us. I will remove the children from the mission tomorrow. As soon as it is spring, those of us who wish to remain a tribe will move farther west. The day will come, I suppose, when we are backed to the ocean. When that occurs, we shall either fight—if there are any of us left—or become shabby, imitation white men."

Maggie looked at his clenched fists on the table and laid her hand over one of his. She seemed to have forgotten that anyone else was present. Very softly she said, "Please stay."

He turned obsidian-dark eyes to her, and his stern face softened almost imperceptibly. "Maggie, my friend of many years and sorrows, if there was anyone who could change my mind, it would be you. But I know you, above all people, understand that I must do what I must do. Just as you have set your course by your conscience, so must I."

"But, Black Feather, I have done you a wrong myself, and I don't know how to undo it. I too have claimed the lands that were opened. This land and another piece on the road to Westport," Maggie said.

"No. You have earned a place here. You stayed here and loved the land and my people before it became a profitable thing to do. You and your family belong to this valley. You have not driven us away. You have taught our children and cared for them. You have respected the forest and the river. You belong. It is the others who drive us away. The men who have abused their land and abused their freedoms in the East and who now wish to bring their disputes here."

Schooner glanced across the table at Henry. He was staring at Black Feather, his face an expressionless mask. James had risen and was putting another log on the fire. Schooner suspected that he was trying to hide how moved he was by Black Feather's speech. Addie was fidgeting irritably with the ends of her pigtails. Poor Addie, Schooner thought, she cannot understand that this is an important tragic moment in all our lives. Little Morning Wish had climbed into Gerald's lap, and the two of them gazed sadly at the old Indian. Gerald's eyes were full of the understanding he always seemed to feel for the unhappiness of others, and Morning Wish—what was

Morning Wish thinking? Schooner wondered. Morning Wish knew herself to be half-Indian, and the family had taught her to have pride in the fact. What must she think of what he was saying? Was the white half of her driving out the Indian half, or did she feel that she too was fated to be pushed aside? There was enough of the Indian in her that her face showed nothing of her thoughts.

Black Feather rose, and the rest of them, as if drawn by magnets, rose with him. Morning Wish went to the tall, proud man and raised her arms. He stooped, picked her up, and held her in a stiff, formal embrace. Then he said, "Morning Wish Freiler, you must keep in your heart who and what you are. You must select the best of both your worlds and not accept the worst of either."

"I will," Morning Wish said in a clear voice.

Maggie stepped to Gerald's side. She whispered something, and he nodded. She turned her back to him, and he reached up to undo the clasp of the little gold locket she always wore, and handed it to her.

Schooner felt tears come to her eyes.

Black Feather set Morning Wish back down. Maggie took his broad bronze hand in hers and turned up his palm. She laid the locket and its delicate gold chain in his hand. "My dear friend who saved my life and gave me my vocation, I want you to have this. It is the only material possession that I treasure. My husband gave it to me out of love, and we give it to you out of love. Please keep it to remember us."

He made no false protestations, but simply closed his hand over the locket. "In allowing me to know you and your family, the Great Spirit has blessed me. I must go now." He shook hands with everyone, even Henry Grinnell, who was one of those who had inadvertently contributed to his sorrows. Finally he put his hands on Maggie's shoulders and said, "I wish you happiness and long life . . . Maggie."

Schooner saw the tears running down her mother's cheeks and realized with a shock that there was something more than just an old friendship between her and the Indian. Something very close and painful. She glanced at her father and realized by the widening of his azure eyes that he had just realized it too. Some terrifying secret was swimming just below the surface of their lives, rippling the top of their happiness, but not showing itself. Schooner was holding her breath, horrified of what might be said next. A word, a phrase, could wreck them all.

261

But no one said anything. Maggie silently helped Black Feather put on the coat she'd made him, and he left the house without even looking back. Maggie and Gerald were staring at each other in a pained, wordless communication. Schooner couldn't stand it. She ran to the bedroom, grabbed up her coat, and crammed her feet into boots. She went out the back door without speaking, intent on a long, fierce walk in the bitter cold. She had not gone far, however, when Henry caught up. "Wait, Schooner," he said.

But she kept on walking, and he kept pace beside her. Finally the cold began to penetrate her clothes, and she found herself shivering. She stopped and turned back toward the house. "If I learned all the words in the world, I could never say what I feel. Are there words for this, Henry?"

He put his arm around her shoulders and said, "I don't think so, Schooner. I don't think so."

He walked her back to the house. The next morning he was gone, and she did not see him for a long while. She never discussed that evening with anyone again, not even with Henry, but she never forgot the first time she understood what real loss meant.

5

"Said they was gonna to be here long 'bout noon," Ernest Halleck said.

"Do you think they'll really come?" Adams Clay asked.

The two young men were sitting on a couple of stumps near the Seventrees trading post. Schooner had just come out and stood quietly on the porch listening without appearing to. There was something horrible about the two of them that always made her feel it was in everyone's best interests to know what they were up to. She recalled with a slight shudder the time she'd overheard them complaining about Jack Q's dog and how unfriendly it was to them. Not more than a few hours later the dog had been found drowned at the riverbank. No one ever proved they'd done it, but Helmut Clay had given his son Adams a sound thrashing. Uncle Luther hadn't done anything, though, and Aunt Fritzi had carried on terribly about people accusing her "dear baby" of doing such a thing. Being called "dear baby" in public had been a substantial punishment for Ernest, though.

Schooner knelt and pretended to be relacing her high boots. She glanced at them out of the corner of her eye. Her cousin Ernest Halleck was eighteen now, a lanky, sallow, sour-looking man who attempted to dress like a frontiersman in leather and dirt, but because he was sometimes forced to work with his father, his filthy clothing had paint smears on it in places. He had heavy, untidy brows and a wide, thin mouth that he talked out of the side of. Schooner thought of him as a predator, with the rest of the human race as his potential prey.

Adams Clay, on the other hand, was just a dolt. A lumpy, stupid fifteen-year-old who was in the thrall of the older man. Had someone else captured his affection, he might have been cheerful and wholesome. But he'd spent his years growing up in conscious imitation of Ernest. Schooner had a clear, forthright hatred of Ernest Halleck, but Adams made her sad. His parents were such kind, friendly people, his older brother, Quincy, was everything anyone could ask in a friend, neighbor, or business associate, and they all somehow loved Adams and tried constantly to turn him to a better life. But it made no difference. She'd heard folks whisper that there was something "unnatural" about the way they were always together—almost like slave and master—but she hadn't known quite what they meant by that, even though it gave her chills.

"Do you really think they'll come?" Adams repeated.

"If they said they would, they will, you fool," Ernest said. Then, noticing Schooner, he snarled, "Whatcha doin', Miss Snoop? Gettin' yer ears full?"

Schooner pretended not to hear him, but turned instead and called back to Torchy, "Mr. LeSage, I'm going home for a bit to help Mother. Do you need me for anything else?"

"No, everything is in readiness, I believe. The box for the ballots is nailed down as required, and the papers are in order," he answered.

It was March now, almost a full year since the Kansas-Nebraska Act had passed, and today the residents of the new territory were to vote for the first time. Each area would elect its choice of representative for the legislature that would meet and decide laws and rules. More important, the legislature would decide whether the state should come into the Union as slave or free.

Seventrees trading post had been designated as one of the polling places, and even though it was still very early in the morning, people had already begun to arrive. Schooner hoped all of them would know what the choice really was—Quincy Clay was running as an abolitionist representative, and Uncle Luther had surprised everyone (and disgusted a few) by running on behalf of the slave-staters. Certainly no one in the area would have any trouble choosing between the men or the issues. It would be exciting to have a friend who was a member of the legislature.

"I wish Father could have been here to cast his first vote as a Kansan," Schooner said to her mother when she got back to the house.

"So do I," Maggie answered. "But he may be back yet today if he concluded the business early." Gerald had inherited a tiny legacy from a distant cousin, and it had been necessary for him to present some documents to a lawyer in Saint Louis to claim the money.

Schooner forgot all about the scrap of conversation she'd overheard until noon. As they were sitting down to eat, Beatrice rushed in to the house without even knocking. Her hair had come loose and she was so pale that her freckles stood out starkly against her fairness. "Mrs. Freiler, something's wrong! I don't know what to do," she said.

Maggie was instantly on her feet. "What is it? Is someone ill?"

"No, no, not anything like that. But there is a group of men at the trading post from Westport. They came in as if they were buying supplies, then they started picking up voting ballots and marking them. They're drunk, Mrs. Freiler. Drunk and rowdy. My father doesn't dare leave the post to get a gun or anything, and Quincy has gone somewhere to help some people whose wagon has broken down. Oh, what can we do? I'm so worried they'll hurt my father. Please help!"

While listening to this, Schooner was more moved by concern for Beatrice than for the voting process. Her breathing was strained and raspy—like it got when she was sick the winter before—and she seemed to be swaying.

"Beatrice, sit down before you faint!" Maggie ordered. She went to the cabinet where the hunting rifles were kept, took out the guns, and handed one to Schooner. "Stay here, Beatrice. Schooner, come with me. We'll stop this."

"But, Mother!" Schooner said, looking down at the gun in her hands as if it was a snake.

"There isn't time to talk about this. Just hold it as if you knew how to use it and follow me," Maggie said.

Schooner did as she was told, but her heart was thumping so violently she could feel it in her throat. Maggie strode down the road to the post with her skirts and apron ties flying behind. *My God, she looks like an avenging angel*, Schooner thought.

Ernest and Adams were still sitting on the stumps outside the post, but now Addie was with them. "Addie, go home!" Maggie said to her.

Addie whirled around, and the shock of seeing her mother and sister wielding guns wiped the coquettish smile off her face in an instant. She started to move away, but Ernest stood and leered at Maggie. "Aw, Auntie, you don't want to send her away. We're just watching the fun."

Maggie raised the gun and pointed it at his head. "I want her to go home, I said. I did not ask your opinion."

Ernest paled and stepped backward. "I was just jokin' with you, Aunt Maggie. No cause to point that thing my way," he stammered. But there was such hate simmering in his eyes that it made Schooner feel sick to look at him. How could this be happening? Had the world gone mad, or was she—pray God—dreaming it all?

Addie ran toward home, and Ernest turned to walk away, watching Maggie over his shoulder. Adams Clay was right on his heels. "Stay out here on the porch unless I call you," Maggie said to Schooner.

"Yes, Mama," Schooner tried to say, but the words got stuck somewhere and she merely mouthed them.

Maggie went into the trading post. Schooner could hear voices raised inside, but her ears were buzzing and she could not make out the words, only the tone of discord. There was another group of men arriving now, rough-looking young men whom Schooner recognized from her visits to Westport. They too were drunk and were talking loudly and obscenely. They had not realized what was happening, and Schooner prayed that her mother would get the other men out of the post before this gang went in.

Just then Maggie came backing out the door. She had the gun trained on the men inside. "Ain't we got a right to vote, too?" one of them was whining.

"Not if you don't live in the territory," Maggie said.

265

"Mama, there's others . . ." Schooner said, but Maggie didn't hear her.

The other men had figured out what was happening now and were warily getting off their horses and moving toward the door—and Maggie's back.

Schooner glanced down the road. There was a rider coming. She recognized Quincy Clay's red jacket. Quincy was coming! Thank God. But there wasn't time. He was too far away.

Maggie took another step back and got her foot on the hem of her dress. She lost her balance for a fraction of a second, but it was long enough for one of the men in the doorway of the post to lunge forward and grab the end of the rifle. He pushed it up, pointed it to the sky. As if by signal, one of the men who had just dismounted started to move forward.

They would not harm her mother. No one could do that!

Schooner pointed the rifle at him. "Stop!" she shouted.

The man glanced at her and proceeded as if she were of no concern.

There was nothing else to do. In another few seconds he would reach Maggie. They were drunk and ugly, and God only knew what they might do. She started to pull on the trigger—it seemed an enormous effort. "Stop!" she cried again, and the man still ignored her.

At the last second she dropped the sights and squeezed.

The kick of the rifle nearly knocked her down. She felt the corner of the doorway bite into her shoulder blade. The sound was deafening, and her eyes wouldn't focus right for a moment.

Then everything was confusion. People were pushing against her and shouting. Someone—a man—was screaming and swearing, and horses were neighing hysterically. She blinked, put a hand out to steady herself, and blinked again. She had shot a man! He was dancing around in the dust on one foot, holding the other up, blood dripping from his boot. There was no one left on the porch but her and her mother. Maggie had gotten control of her gun again and had it leveled at the men who were hurriedly mounting their horses.

Quincy Clay rode into the group, almost threw himself off his horse, and joined Schooner and Maggie on the porch. He picked up the gun Schooner had dropped. Torchy, who had been behind the ruffians as they exited, took Maggie's gun,

266

and Maggie rushed over to put her arm around Schooner. "Are you all right?" she asked.

Schooner nodded.

"You men go back home, now," Quincy said in a reasonable voice. "We don't want any more shooting here, and we don't want any more of your kind."

"You goddamn Jayhawker bastard!" one of the ruffians said. "You can't get away with this. We're law-abiding folks just wanting to vote."

"Then vote in Missouri where you live," Quincy said. "But don't ever come back here."

They muttered among themselves and got their wounded companion on his horse. As they rode off, one of them shouted, "Ain't no Jayhawkers gonna push us around like this. You'll be sorry—you and that woman with the Injun brat."

Schooner felt like the world was spinning around. It was making her sick. None of this made sense. Her mother was holding her tightly and murmuring soothing words in spite of her own anger.

Quincy and Torchy put the rifles down and hovered solicitously around the two women. Other people had been attracted by the gunshot and were gathering. Quincy put his hand on Schooner's shoulder. "That was about the bravest thing I've ever seen anyone do, Schooner."

"Brave?" she said in amazement. "I was scared to death!"

"That's what made it brave. You're not hurt, are you? You are so pale."

"No, I'm fine," she said, feeling saliva fill her mouth. "Excuse me!" She ran around the side of the building and threw up into a bush. If this was bravery she'd take cowardice.

When it was over, Schooner hoped it would be well and truly over. But she couldn't stop thinking about that awful instant when she shot at another human being. The deafening roar of the gun, the bruising jolt of the recoil, the metallic stench of the moment that seemed to linger in her clothes and hair despite repeated washing. She felt faint and nauseated at the memory. It was some time before she became aware of the echoing repercussions of her action that noon.

There hadn't been another direct confrontation that day with the men from Westport—"Bushwhackers," as people were coming to call them. But neither were there very many

267

more people who came to vote. They found out later that the men had posted themselves along the roads around Seventrees and frightened people into turning back, except for those who were known to favor slavery. The next day, when the votes were counted, Luther Halleck became a territorial representative. Not only did he get more votes than Quincy Clay, he got more votes than there were voters in the district.

"But those were just the ballots that those men had stuffed in the box before you got there," Schooner protested to her mother. "Certainly that can't hold as a legal election!"

"I don't know. I'm afraid it may," Maggie said. "The same thing happened along the length of the border with Missouri."

"But they'll have to hold another election, won't they?"

"It would just happen again. It's already being called a 'bogus legislature,' and the votes haven't all been counted yet. What a sad start for a new state."

Schooner had a shiver of premonition. "It is just the start, isn't it? Mother, I'm afraid of what's going to happen, aren't you?"

Maggie started automatically to soothe, but caught herself. "I am afraid. Yes." Schooner had proved herself an adult—a brave adult; there was no use in continuing to treat her like a child.

That night Schooner couldn't sleep. After the house was dark and quiet, she paced around her room and finally put her clothes back on and went for a walk. It was fortunate that she did so, for as she came back she heard voices and the sound of retreating hoofbeats. She went around to the back door to go in and found a fire smoldering at the corner of the house. The fire was feeble enough as yet that they put it out quickly without having to wake and disturb the neighbors. By morning everyone knew of it, however. The terrifying thing about it was that there was no way to tell if, and when, someone would try again. "We can't live out every day in fear of what *might* happen," Gerald said when he returned. "We must go on like always and hope that God or fate or whatever it was will intervene again."

There was another result of what happened that day at the post that was both flattering and upsetting to Schooner. Quincy Clay suddenly stopped regarding her as simply Maggie's little girl and started treating her like an interesting adult. At first Schooner basked in it. After all, Quincy was an "older man"—twenty-five now—handsome, charming, and one of the most respected members of the community. Schooner, like almost all the other young women, had practically been born with a crush on Quincy, and here he was treating her like she was somebody special.

It would have been wonderful except for one thing.

Beatrice.

Schooner knew that her best friend was in love with Quincy, and that turned the whole thing sour for her. Beatrice had suffered with troubled breathing the rest of voting day, and the next morning Torchy had whisked her off to a doctor in Saint Louis. If Beatrice were to return and find that Quincy was paying undue attention to Schooner, she would be crushed. That just couldn't be allowed to happen. Schooner loved Beatrice like a sister—more, much more, than she loved her real sister. Beatrice could be so easily hurt, she was so fragile and lovely, and Schooner could not bear the thought of doing anything to make her friend unhappy. Perhaps Quincy had just forgotten in Beatrice's absence how wonderful she was.

"Mother got a letter from Mr. LeSage that they will be returning in a few days," Schooner said to Quincy one evening when he had stopped by to visit.

"Is he? Good. I've got an invoice here I'd like him to check before it goes out."

He didn't seem to take the point. "Mr. LeSage says Beatrice is much better now. The treatments were most effective."

"I'm glad to hear that. Beatrice hates going to those doctors in Saint Louis. She'd rather stay here and let your mother give her medicines," he said.

That was better. Schooner waited for him to go on and say some nice things about Beatrice and how happy he would be to see her, but he didn't. "Jack Q tells me he talked to a man in New Orleans who said he was thinking about moving up here—a doctor. We ought to have one in Seventrees. It's a long way to have to send for someone from Westport or Kansas City when there's an emergency."

This wouldn't do. "Quincy, when are you going to marry Beatrice?" Schooner asked bluntly.

He looked at her as if she'd asked when he was planning his trip to the moon. "What?"

"You *are* going to marry Beatrice someday, aren't you?"

"How could I do that? Beatrice's health is so frail—she needs a man who can be home and looking after her all the time. I couldn't do that. I have to be gone more than I'm home."

"Oh, Quincy!"

"What are you upset about?"

"Why have you spent so much time with her all these years if you weren't serious?"

"Because I like her. We get along and enjoy the same things." He was getting defensive. "Why shouldn't we go places together? It's all been perfectly proper."

"Have you ever told her you don't intend to marry her?" Schooner demanded.

"No. Why should I have? We never talked about it." He stared at her belligerently for a moment, then began to look perplexed. "Is this just some idea of yours, or . . . Good God, Schooner! Beatrice doesn't think . . . no, she couldn't . . ."

"Oh yes she does!"

"I never guessed!" He ran his hands through his hair in a strangely boyish gesture. Schooner felt a sudden wave of affection wash over her. She had to restrain herself from touching him. "What a lout I've been," he said. "I'll talk to her about it. I've got to. I don't suppose you . . . ?"

Schooner backed away. "Me? No! I should not have spoken of it at all. It's none of my business."

"But it is," he said softly. Very softly.

She wasn't sure what he'd said. "What?"

Just then the door opened and Addie interrupted them with word that Maggie wanted to see Schooner about something. Quincy quickly excused himself and left.

Schooner was left wondering, as she often did these days, why life was so complex and painful. It hadn't seemed that way to her as a child. Had things changed, or was it only her perception of them? Her mother had warned her last year to enjoy being fifteen because it would never come again, and now she was beginning to understand. So much had happened since then that already, at sixteen and a half, Schooner sometimes found herself wishing to be fifteen again.

6

"It will seem strange without the children," Beatrice said.

"But there *will* be children. They just won't be Indians," Schooner said.

It was one of the first hot days in June, and the two of them were taking a rest on the wide veranda of the Indian mission. They'd been helping the last of the children, a group of five little Delawares, pack their things.

"I think there are more schoolchildren in Seventrees now than there were Indian children when we first moved here," Schooner added. "All that dormitory space will go to waste, though."

"No, it won't. Haven't you heard? The territorial legislature is supposed to meet this summer in the main building. The partitions are to be knocked out, and it will be one long hall."

"Here? Well, of course," Schooner said bitterly. "It's a group the Bushwhackers voted in—they might as well meet as close to Missouri as possible! Where did you hear this?"

"Quincy told me."

"Is he back?" Schooner asked. Since the day she and Quincy had talked he'd been conspicuously absent from Seventrees.

"He was—just for the evening. He's ridden up to Lawrence about something, though."

"So you talked to him?"

"Only for a few moments. I was at the post helping Father with the inventory, and Quincy came by. He acted surprised to see me—as if he hadn't known I was back. He certainly must be busy lately."

So he hadn't had a frank talk with her. Schooner felt an uncomfortable pang. Should she tell Beatrice about Quincy's intentions? No, she couldn't. Whether she should or not didn't matter—she simply *could* not do it. Besides, it wasn't right for her to meddle anymore. Perhaps Quincy had thought it over and changed his mind, and there would certainly be no point in hurting Beatrice with facts that were no longer true.

"What has Quincy gone to Lawrence for?"

"Something about the meeting of the territorial legislature. Not the elected ones—Quincy called that a 'bogus legislature'—but a group of free-staters who have decided to have their own meeting just as though they were truly elected."

"But they'll have no power. Why would they do that? Is Quincy attending as as representative?"

Beatrice shrugged. "I don't know. He didn't stay to talk much about it. I don't think they're holding it for another week or so. He said something about coming back here in the meantime."

Her fine, fiery hair was coming loose tendril by tendril and was sticking to her face and neck. She brushed it back and fanned herself languidly with one hand.

"Beatrice, do you feel well? You look flushed."

"I'm fine, Schooner," she said, rising somewhat unsteadily, "but I am a little tired. I think I better go home and rest for a bit. I'll come back and help this afternoon."

Quincy returned two days later. He had Henry Grinnell with him. "I needed some supplies, and Quincy needed some company," Henry explained when he met up with Schooner at the trading post. "Are you busy or can you come for a walk? We could have a picnic lunch down by the river."

"That sounds wonderful. I put a jug of cider in the springhouse to cool this morning. I'll get it and meet you there."

Schooner dashed home and hurriedly put on a clean dress and washed her face before getting the cider. When she found Henry, he was sitting in the shade of a maple on the riverbank. He watched with obvious appreciation as she approached. She was glad she'd taken the extra time to freshen up.

"I've seen so little of you since last summer," he said. "You've changed, you know."

She smiled shyly. "Have I?"

"Yes. It's not just that you're prettier, though you are, it's something else. Confidence or ease or something. You look sure of yourself and happy."

Schooner had to laugh at that. "I'm less sure of the whole world every day."

"Quincy told me about what happened on election day."

"I wish he hadn't. I want to forget. It was awful." She'd managed to put the horror of that day out of her mind for a while. Now Henry was throwing it back over her like a stinking, suffocating cloak of fright and guilt.

He stopped in the middle of pouring out cups of cider. "You shouldn't say that! It was a remarkably courageous demonstration of your convictions. You shouldn't want to forget that!"

"Oh, Henry, no. You've misunderstood. I'm sorry to disillusion you, but 'convictions' had nothing to do with it. I wasn't upholding freedom or the voting rights of Kansas or any of those high-flown things. I was trying to save my mother from harm. It's as simple as that!"

"But you were also standing against the injustice and illegality of the border ruffians trying to vote in our election," Henry insisted.

This made her angry. "Henry, stop it. You're thinking of masses of people and moral concepts, like you always do. I assure you, not one of those thoughts even crossed my mind. Those men were threatening my mother's safety, and I attempted to prevent it. That is *all*!"

Henry Grinnell looked hurt—or was it disappointment? "There's no need for you to get angry."

She took a deep breath. "No, I guess there's not. I'm sorry. But, Henry, please do me a great favor. Let's don't talk today about voting or slavery or 'convictions.' "

He smiled and took her hand. "You're right. I have the good fortune to be sitting here in the shade with a beautiful girl and a jug of cold cider. The weighty matters of the intellect should be put aside."

"Mrs. Woodren's oldest daughter is getting married tonight to one of the glaziers from Kansas City. There's going to be a big party afterward at the mission. Stay and dance with me tonight, will you?"

"I'd love that," he said.

Henry Grinnell danced as well as he did everything else. He moved with powerful grace and even made Schooner feel that she danced exceptionally well. "You are the envy of every girl here," Beatrice whispered to her while Henry went to get her a cup of punch.

And indeed, Schooner felt that it might be true. Henry had approached the table at the end of the room, and Schooner could see at least four other young women watching him like hungry hawks. It was no wonder. She'd not really appreciated before how handsome he was—wide shoulders, broad chest, and long powerful legs—all of which went perfectly with his sandy hair, already bleached out to a gold cast from his work outdoors, and his strong regular features. The only man she'd ever known as handsome as Henry was Quincy Clay.

As the evening went on, the dancing got more strenuous, the music louder, and the room got hotter and hotter. The young mothers toting cranky, overtired babies drifted away first; then the older people began to mop their brows and protest that they weren't as young as they once were and perhaps they'd better give up dancing for the night.

"Are you tired?" Henry asked.

"No, but I'm going to melt down into a pool in a few minutes," Schooner said. "Could we get some fresh air by the door?"

"Better yet, let's walk for a bit, then we can come back when we've got our second wind. What about your raccoons and their tree?"

"Yes. We could go there, if you want. They've got a new batch of babies, but the mother hasn't been willing to bring them out to meet me yet. Maybe with you along . . ."

They were only a few feet from the raccoon tree when Schooner caught her foot in a vine and stumbled. Henry quickly put an arm around her waist to keep her from falling. Instead of moving away and thanking him as she knew she should, Schooner stood perfectly still, staring into his thickly fringed gray eyes. She turned a little, faced him, and he put his other arm around her as well. "There wasn't a mirror in the room tonight," he said softly in his deep, caressing voice. "So I doubt that you have any idea how beautiful you are."

She said nothing, for she knew she was about to have her first real kiss. He bent his head slowly toward her, looking deeply into her eyes. Then his lips, soft and warm, touched hers lightly. Then again . . . and again. She felt her arms move almost as if by their own volition to hold him. She closed her eyes and shivered at the delicious sensation as he kissed her eyelids. He mumbled something wordless in her ear and buried his face in the hollow of her neck.

She was dizzy and happy. It was a moment before she realized that it wasn't *she* trembling, it was Henry. "Schooner," he murmured, still holding her breathlessly close, "I know this is neither the time nor the place to mention this, but somebody is climbing up my leg." His voice cracked a little with suppressed laughter.

Schooner looked down. There, hanging on Henry's belt loop, was a little bright-eyed raccoon.

"I don't think they have any concept of romance," she said thoughtfully.

Henry burst out laughing. She'd never heard him laugh like that before. They went back to the dance after they gently disengaged the little creature. When Henry walked her home later, he kissed her good night. A long, lingering kiss that made her feel warm and content.

At the end of June the territorial legislature met in Lawrence—not the elected legislature, but the self-appointed one. Quincy Clay attended as representative of his district, but returned discouraged. "Didn't you find yourself in agreement with them?" Gerald asked him one evening shortly after his return, when Maggie had the Clay family to dinner.

"It wasn't that so much—I just felt it was a waste. They took turns lamenting the illegality and immorality of the recent elections—like turning a chicken on a spit until it's burned to a crisp. Around and around and around. They were right, but it doesn't do any good to talk about it at such great length, does it?"

"But what did you expect to happen?" Gerald asked.

Quincy waved his hand in a self-deprecating gesture. "I suppose I thought they were going to plan some large-scale revolution, and I pictured myself as the voice of reason keeping them from doing anything rash. They didn't do what I feared, and yet I'm disappointed."

"What do you think should be done?" Schooner asked while she stacked the plates to clear the table.

"I don't know," Quincy answered. "I really wish I could be more like your firebrand friend Henry Grinnell and be sure I knew where the line was between right and wrong, but I keep seeing elements of wrong in what I think is right, and vice versa."

Schooner nodded. He had put into words what she had often thought herself. In a way she envied Henry's assurance of his moral stand, but it didn't always ring quite true, and sometimes downright irritated her.

"I suppose what I want," Quincy went on, "is to have the past back—everyone just go back where they came from and solve the problem someplace else. But I know that's impossible. Somebody at the convention said that Kansas is previewing a problem that will someday tear the country in half.

That's a terrifying idea, but I think it may be true, and I don't know how it can be averted."

Schooner thought a lot in the next few months about what Quincy had said that evening, and found that she felt much as he did. She *wanted* to agree with Henry. She felt she should: she was in love with him, she kept telling herself. But it was Quincy's cool, curious reasoning that struck a chord in her.

The "bogus legislature," the pro-slavery men, met at the mission as planned, but on the afternoon of the first day, two of the representatives became ill. A doctor was called in from Westport and diagnosed cholera. The legislators didn't even call a meeting to officially adjourn. They simply grabbed their bags and left.

The dread affliction stayed behind and swept through the community. Jack Q whisked his sister, Beatrice, away to their house in Saint Louis immediately, and they were spared, but Torchy and his wife both got it. Torchy survived, but was never entirely robust again. His wife, the Frenchwoman who'd been such a good companion to him and the children, died only a few hours after first falling ill.

The Hallecks were all sick, by turns. Little Iris, the only one in the family that Schooner could abide, was the only one to die. Fritzi and Luther recovered, as did Ernest.

Of the Clays, only Helmut was stricken. Maggie spent all one night nursing him and sitting with Katrin, but when she returned at dawn, the pallor of her tear-streaked face told the truth. "Helmut is dead," she announced in a papery voice. "I left Quincy with his mother. After I change my clothes, I'm going back to help Quincy dress his father for burial. It will have to be this morning. Schooner, go ask your father and James to go up on the bluff and dig a grave."

The ceremony was brief, and at the end of the final prayer, Morning Wish burst into tears. "Morning. Wish, what's wrong?" Schooner asked.

"My stomach hurts and I feel all dizzy."

By the time they got Morning Wish to bed, it was obvious that James was sick as well. All the rest of the day and into the night Maggie and Schooner tended the two of them. They had violent diarrhea and vomiting, along with stomach cramps that had even James crying out in pain. Schooner carried out chamber pots and emptied them into the deep pit that Gerald had dug in the woods. She fetched cool spring water to dip cloths in, and when she was too exhausted to

276

run anymore, she sat between Morning Wish's bed and her own (where James was) and fanned them. Toward evening the patients both fell into fitful, feverish sleeps. "Maggie," Gerald said, "you must get some rest. Schooner and I got some sleep last night. You didn't."

She tried to protest, but he was insistent. "You will get sick too, and *then* where will we all be? I'll stay here with Schooner."

"Very well, but I'll sleep outside," Maggie said. "I don't want to get close to Addie. She is still all right, isn't she?"

"Sleeping soundly. No sign of fever," he assured her. "What about you, Schooner?"

Schooner was so tired she could hardly make sense of what was being said to her. "Yes. I'm fine. Fine."

Any other time, Schooner would have been pleased to have hours virtually alone with her father—to talk with him about books, about nature, about music—but during that long night they hardly spoke. Shortly after midnight Morning Wish woke and asked for a drink of water, but it started her vomiting again, and Schooner had to take the sheets and bedclothes out to the vat of still-simmering water in the backyard and wash them. This done, Gerald told her she must nap for a while. She was willing, but the moment she closed her eyes, James started moaning.

When dawn finally came, Schooner was appalled at how her brother and half-sister looked. In only one day of the devastating illness, they had become gray and wasted. It was as though they had been ill for weeks, not merely hours. Gerald went to find out what had become of the doctor. He was busy, of course, but earlier he had sent a message the day before that he would get to the Freilers as soon as he could. "The doctor died in the night," Gerald said when he returned.

Dear God in heaven! Schooner thought, are you going to take us all? If so, do it quickly and have it over.

The day wore on relentlessly. Addie was sent to the home of a family who had no illness, in the hopes that she could remain unexposed. Schooner and Maggie and Gerald took turns fetching water, boiling sheets, and from time to time looking out the window at the almost steady procession of wagons on their way to the graveyard at the top of the bluff.

Finally, by evening, James showed signs of improvement. There were faint spots of color on his cheeks, and he managed to take a few sips of weak tea without bringing it back up. His sleep now was not the near-coma of illness, but genuine rest. Morning Wish, though no better, was not noticeably worse, which was encouraging. By the next morning they had reason to believe that she too would live. Her color was better, and she had ceased to whimper as the constant muscle cramps racked her body.

When it was over and the cholera had passed, there were twenty new graves on the bluff: Torchy's wife, Helmut Clay, Iris Halleck, three children and the father of a family named Ellison, the Woodlines' infant twin girls, the harness maker's elderly parents, Reverend Whittacre's nephew who had been visiting, six people from a wagon train that had been camped by the river, the doctor, and one of the legislators who had brought the disease to Seventrees.

It was a sad, difficult summer and fall. The community, stunned by their tragedy, grateful for those who had been spared, got back to the business of living. Those who had survived were weak, and many responsibilities had to be shared or neglected for the time being. The trading post, open only part of the time, failed for the first time to exceed the previous year's profits. Many of those weakened by the cholera were easy prey to earaches, bowel complaints, colds, and fevers, and Maggie's household supply of remedies was depleted in spite of Schooner's efforts to help her mother keep up.

Schooner suspected that a new kind of informal "dating" system would grow out of this. Things would be said to have happened the year before the cholera or the summer of the cholera.

As if nature had not dealt them enough blows, their fellowmen were about to deal them more. As the first frosts came, they began to hear reports of ambushings, burned barns, threatening letters, and fights. The victims were always "Jayhawkers"—Kansans who favored the abolition of slavery and had been brash enough to make their views known. So far there had been no retaliation. But retaliation, vengeance, and fanaticism were almost at hand in the person of one man. John Brown.

7

Schooner never saw John Brown, though his presence in Kansas had a profound effect on everyone in the territory. He arrived in October 1855 to join his sons, who were already living in Kansas. He was a self-proclaimed savior of the Negroes. A failure at everything he had ever put his hand to, Brown nevertheless had come from Ohio to resolve the slavery issue. He was a bitter, hate-filled man, at war with the world. "Certainly no one would put faith in the solutions offered by a man like him, would they?" Schooner asked her mother one evening after they had been listening to people talk at the trading post.

"They say he is a fiery and powerful speaker. There are many who have suffered grievously at the hands of the proslavery people. They've had their barns and homes burned, their businesses ruined, and their loved ones threatened, all for the sake of something they believed to be right. It's not hard to imagine that they would like to exact vengeance. John Brown promises them that. Also . . ."—here she hesitated, weighing her words—"there are men who like violence, no matter what the cause. Cruel, dull people who want excitement."

Schooner suspected that her mother was not speaking generally, but had Ernest Halleck and Adams Clay in mind. "Can't someone make Mr. Brown leave Kansas?" she asked.

"No, dear. But perhaps a Kansas winter will cure him of his desire to stay."

If any winter could have discouraged John Brown, it should have been that one. The snows started in November instead of December as usual. It was bitterly cold, below zero for weeks at a time. The Kaw froze so solidly that it was possible to drive heavy wagons across it when the wind was not blowing too hard. The powder snow blew into vast drifts. It had to be shoveled away from the windows and doors.

Several men lost fingers and toes to frostbite, and some people finally gave up and brought the chickens and smaller stock in the house rather than see them all die outdoors. The roads and paths disappeared under several feet of snow. Woodpiles, bushes, landmarks, were gone. Seventrees, still not healed from the summer cholera epidemic, was ill-prepared for the winter. Even a normal winter would have been hard on many of them. *This* was impossible.

The Ellison woman whose husband and children had died of the sickness went mad. She had started screaming in church one morning, and neighbors had taken her in. She became so unruly that they'd had to tie her to her bed, but one night she worked loose, and in the morning she was missing. It was two more days before someone noticed a piece of sprigged flannel in the snow behind the springhouse. When they dug down, they found her frozen—wearing only her nightgown and clutching a child's doll.

Their isolation was relieved once in December when a rider made it in from Westport with the mail, but he could not get out again. They were stranded now, wholly dependent on one another, as most of them had never been before. Those lucky enough to have received a letter read it over and over, then let their friends read it. The newspapers the rider had brought, especially the German-language papers from Saint Louis, were handled to tatters. Gerald's private library became a popular place to visit, and Woody taught many bored young men how to whittle. Some of the women were so desperate for something to do that they unraveled knitted items, traded yarn, and reused it, just to keep their hands busy.

Christmas came and went with forced cheer. They had turkey, chicken, goat, and beef, for the animals might as well be eaten as left to freeze to death. But there were few vegetables and no extra bread, for the canning and milling that normally went on in late summer had not been done adequately because of the cholera.

Presents that year were mainly reknitted items, hand-carved knickknacks, or poems. There was not enough extra grain or sugar for fancy baking, nor was it possible to get into the woods and find enough wood for the sleds, doll houses, and wagons that fathers usually made for their children. Nor was there a Christmas tree for many houses. Schooner missed the warm pine scent and the glow of the little candles they always lighted on Christmas Eve.

But through it all, there was a warm sense of concern for the other members of the community. By January, those who had enough to make it through the winter bundled up their extra food and took it to others who were running low. Some of the families who had lost children or fathers to the cholera moved in together to save valuable fuel and provide the equally necessary companionship. For the first time, Schooner began to feel close to Morning Wish. Confined to the house together, they talked to each other more than before. Never deep talk about how they felt in their hearts about life, but friendly chatter that brought them a little closer.

Addie, on the other hand, took the bad weather as a personal insult, railing against the injustice of being confined with her family. Finally even Gerald found her incessant complaints irritating and told her in the gentlest possible way to keep quiet. After that she fell into a quiet, bitter sulk, which mercifully lasted for weeks.

Maggie set up a quilting frame in her front room, and every morning well-bundled mothers and their children would arrive for a day of sewing and friendly talk. Gerald's friends would come over early to borrow books and end up spending hours sitting around the big kitchen table arguing politics and philosophy.

Schooner found herself wishing for peace and solitude, but for the most part she enjoyed having the house full of people and cheerful conversation.

When the thaws started in late February, the roads were worse than ever. Thick, sucking mud instead of snow. Finally, in March, people were able to travel again. Henry Grinnell and a group of men from Lawrence came to Seventrees for supplies and news. He greeted Schooner affectionately enough, but didn't treat her as though there was anything special between them. Had he forgotten about her? Schooner wondered. Changed his mind? Met someone he liked better? Or had she just spent the winter mentally embroidering something into what had passed between them? Had she reknitted their relationship, taking it apart and making it into something else?

"You look like you've lost your last friend, *liebling*. What's wrong?" Gerald asked when he found her brooding over a pan of burned hominy.

"Not my *last* friend," Schooner said. "It's Henry. I thought he'd come to see me, and he's spent the whole time he's been here talking to people about supplies. When he's not doing that, he's involved in terribly serious conversations with Quincy and some of the others about John Brown."

281

"Ah, Schooner, he's a young man of extremely high ideals and a strong sense of responsibility. That's all very admirable, but people like that tend to put personal affections way down at the bottom of their lists."

"But Mother has those qualities, and she's good to everyone. She's been like a mother to lots of others besides her own children."

"I don't think she ever meant to be," Gerald said softly. "And she doesn't *love* everyone she helps. She does it because it is right and she is able to."

"Don't you think Henry likes me?"

"Of course he does, who wouldn't," Gerald said, giving her a quick hug. "I think he's probably in love with you, but you have to realize that it will be hard to be close to someone like Henry. I don't want you to pin all your hopes on him. He'd never deliberately disappoint you, but I think he'll always care more about what's right than what's kind. It's hard to live with someone whose strengths you can't live up to."

Schooner thought this over for a moment, then said, "Are you talking about Henry or about Mother?"

Gerald smiled wryly. "Both of them, I guess."

"Don't you think I should marry Henry if he asks me?"

"No, I didn't mean that at all. Nor did I mean to sound like I was complaining about your mother. If I had it to do over and could choose between all the women on earth, I'd pick your mother without a second's thought. I'm just trying to tell you that strong people are strong all by themselves. Just be sure that you *want* that."

Schooner thought sure Henry would ask for her hand that summer, but he did not. People began to speak of them as a couple. "When is that young man of yours coming down from Lawrence again?" neighbors would ask; or, "Hope that you and your fella will come to the harvest dinner." She began to understand how Beatrice had felt all these years, and it was an unhappy comparison. Perhaps she, like Beatrice, was pining away for a man who liked her well enough but had no intention of marrying her.

The conflict between pro-slavery and abolitionist forces stepped up that summer. In May a group of free-staters was arrested in Lawrence and the newspaper office was burned. Fortunately, the same day she heard of this in Seventrees, Henry Grinnell had just departed from one of his trips to buy goods from Maggie, so Schooner was spared worrying that Henry had been injured.

In retaliation John Brown and a band of his followers attacked and killed five pro-slavery men at Pottawatomie Creek, only a few miles from Seventrees. Though many of the people in town were not vitally concerned with the conflicting political positions, there was a great deal of interest in this. The murdered men seemed to have been random victims, all unarmed, and one of them had a brother in Seventrees. Even people who had opposed slavery were appalled at the vicious manner of Brown's methods.

It didn't take long for people to notice that Ernest Halleck and Adams Clay had been missing since Brown had massacred the settlers. No one could say for sure they had been part of the band of murderers, but it was widely believed. Schooner heard her parents discussing it. "Poor Katrin," Maggie said. "She's suffered enough tragedy without that boy sullying their name this way. He'll come to a bad end—"

"How do you know he'll come to a bad end!" Addie interrupted, having walked in the door in the middle of her mother's remark.

"I don't care for that tone of voice," Maggie warned.

"Your mother is just concerned about her friend Mrs. Clay," Gerald said to Addie.

"Well, I think it's a mean thing to say about Adams," she said.

"I'm sure your mother didn't mean—"

Maggie's eyes glittered with anger. "Gerald, I don't need you to make excuses for what I say. Addie, go to your room and take care of that darning I told you to do."

Schooner knew she was expected to leave as well, but she was afraid they would continue to argue if she did. The very thought of discord between her parents made her feel a gray-green hurt in the pit of her stomach. So she stayed, chatting about inconsequential things until the threat of argument had passed. Later she asked her father, "Do you think Adams and Ernest are with John Brown?"

He shook his head sadly. "I'm afraid they probably are."

"But remember when I . . . when Mother ran off the men on election day? They were Bushwhackers and were Westport friends of Ernest and Adams. Do you think they've changed sides now?"

"They don't care about sides, Schooner. They're just bullies and want to be in with whoever is doing the most violent bullying. Right now that's Brown and his gang."

283

The next morning, while people were still wondering when the two young men would return and what sort of account they would make of themselves, a farmer from farther west come into the town with tales of further fighting, a skirmish that later would be called the first battle of the Civil War. A Captain Pate, the farmer said, had been enraged by the tales of Brown's murders and had marched out with a group of men who attacked the town of Baldwin and took three prisoners. They camped at Palmyra, a few miles away, in a grove of blackjack oaks. Early the next morning Brown's men attacked Pate's camp. "They was men runnin' all over them woods," he said. " 'Bout half of them didn't 'spect no real trouble, and they was runnin' into each other like a bunch of cats in a sack. I was just passing through with a load of potatoes, and I had to get down under my wagon to keep my hide. Most of my potatoes got buckshot in 'em now."

"Was anyone killed?" Maggie asked.

"Dunno, I 'spect so. There was plenty of shootin'."

"What happened next?" Schooner asked.

He cocked an eyebrow at her. "Do I look like a fool to you, missy? I didn't loiter 'round to find out. Soon as the shootin' died off, I got outta there."

As soon as he left the post, Maggie said, "Schooner, I have to stay here and help Torchy. Go find Quincy and your Uncle Luther. Somebody has to find Adams and Ernest."

They were brought back three days later. Ernest had a bullet-grazed ear and a broken wrist—from hitting a man so hard, he said, but Adams let out it was from falling off a horse. Adams had a clean bullet wound in his thigh and a bruised shoulder. They were not ashamed of their behavior, but rather were cocky and loud. Adams couldn't walk, and so it was not too difficult for Katrin and Quincy to confine him to the house for a few days, but Ernest was mobile and went swaggering about town flourishing his bandaged wrist and telling everyone how he'd never hear anything again like the sound of that bullet shearing through his ear. Schooner had to practically bite her lips to keep from telling him what a vile fool he was, but she remembered the night their house almost burned and kept her temper.

After a while Ernest's ear got infected and he lost some of his assurance. Schooner thought that perhaps they'd heard the last of him for a while, but that was not the case. Addie decided that she would nurse him, and Maggie decided that she would not do any such thing. "You're just being hateful because you don't like Ernest," Addie accused over a dinner that no one could taste.

"My feelings for Ernest have nothing to do with it. He does not need any care that his own mother and the doctor can't provide—"

"I just want to keep him company," Addie interrupted.

"I was not through speaking," Maggie said in an ominously quiet voice. "It would be both unsuitable and unnecessary."

Schooner sat silently, eyes closed, willing her father to keep still. *Please, just once. Don't say anything.*

Gerald cleared his throat. "Ah-hum, I wonder, couldn't she just visit him for an hour or so when Fritzi is there also?"

Maggie said nothing. Just glared at him.

Addie pushed her chair back roughly, making the legs shriek against the wooden floor. "You just don't want me to enjoy myself *ever*. You want me to be perfect and dreary like you! Well, I don't want to be that way. I want to be happy and have a good time. Daddy understands—don't you, Daddy?"

Schooner glanced at her father. He looked stricken, like a man who innocently opened the gate and let the whole herd run loose. Maggie had slowly risen and was speaking in a voice so low and vibrant that it gave Schooner a thrill of real fear. "Addie . . . go . . . to . . . your . . . room."

"Daddy?" Addie whined.

Gerald didn't meet her eye, nor Maggie's. He nodded confirmation of Maggie's order. Addie turned on her heel, tossed her curls, and flounced from the room.

Schooner discovered that she was holding her breath. James and Morning Wish had gone. When? She hadn't noticed them leaving. It was only her now, sitting at the table over her untouched dinner. Maggie standing, petrified with anger, at one end of the table, Gerald sitting at the other end—their gazes locked in sparkling orange fury. There was nothing she could do this time. They didn't even seem aware of her presence.

But she would not listen to them argue. She got up and quickly left the house. She would go to the raccoon tree. It was far enough away she couldn't possibly hear them, and it was a happy place for her. She ran down the narrow dirt road, past Uncle Luther's house, past the carpenter's shop, past the Clays' . . . She was out of breath from running and trying to hold back the sorrow and anger that threatened to spill over.

Someone called her name, but she paid no attention, just kept running through the dark summer night. She ran into the woods. Dodging familiar obstacles, she jumped a tiny stream and finally fell panting and shivering at the base of the tree. She heard footsteps following her, but thought it was the beating of her own pulse in her ears, until a hand touched her shoulder.

"Schooner, what's the matter?" Quincy said.

She couldn't speak. The tears began to wash down her cheeks, and her breath caught in gasps. Quincy sat beside her and spoke in a low, soothing voice. "What is it? Are you hurt?"

She put a trembling hand over her heart. "Only . . . only here," she sobbed, and felt like a fool the way her voice shrilled out of control.

"Your parents?" he asked.

How did he know? Did everyone know? She couldn't talk again, but nodded.

"Now, now, they'll work it out. Don't let it bother you. It's not as bad as you think. . . ." He sat down beside her, put a strong arm around her shoulders. She started shaking, and he pulled her close. "You'll make yourself sick, Schooner. Take a deep breath. That's right. Again." He kept on talking, making soothing sounds, and his voice washed comfort over her. She burrowed against his hard, warm shoulder, and he wrapped her in his arms. "There, you're better now, aren't you? Just relax, don't try to talk. You don't have to. We'll just sit here until you feel better. Are you cold? No?"

Her hair was loose, sticking to her tear-soaked face. He brushed it away gently and took a handkerchief from his pocket. He began to touch her face lightly with it. "That's fine. You'll be fine. Do you want to talk, or shall we just sit here?"

He started to move away. She clutched at his shirt, and he held her more tightly. Suddenly she *did* want to talk. "It's Addie," she said, her voice not yet under control. "They fight over her. Not about other things. Just her. Mother tries to make her behave. Daddy lets her do anything she wants. They don't fight about other things."

Quincy was stroking her arm, murmuring understandingly. "Nobody can agree on everything, Schooner. They love each other. You know that."

286

"I know. But I love them both so much, and they make each other so unhappy. If it weren't for Addie . . ."

"Doesn't everyone have someone in the family who causes problems? Not always the same kind, but problems of some sort."

"I guess so. Adams must make you unhappy. . . ."

"Sure he does. I feel like you do, I guess. I sometimes hate him for the unhappiness he causes my mother."

A mass of conflicting emotions welled up in her. Guilt for her dislike of her own sister, sorrow for her parents, regret that she had made Quincy think about his own unhappiness. But there was something else. Something that made her feel dizzy and caused her to hold tightly to Quincy. She didn't ever really want to move from this place. I could stay here in the green-smelling darkness for eternity, she thought wildly, so long as Quincy was here, holding me. Holding me.

She didn't know quite how it happened, but her arms were suddenly around his neck and she was kissing him. She held him fiercely, bruising her mouth against his, tasting his lips and her own salty tears. She felt herself arching against him, trying to press her body into his—become part of him. Her muscles throbbed and cramped with the effort, and the pain felt warm and good.

He was holding her so tightly she couldn't breathe, crushing her. Suddenly he took his arms from around her, held her face in his hands, and pulled away. "Schooner, you don't know what you're doing. I better take you back." His voice was thick with restrained emotion.

"Not yet . . . not yet," she said breathlessly. "Hold me."

He moved again, putting air and space between them. "You're upset. That's all it is. I can't take advantage of that."

How could she live, breathe, hear, if she were not touching him? The words were careening around in her mind, trying to batter their way out. *I love you, I can't live without being near you. Stay. Stay. Hold me. Let me taste your lips, touch your neck, melt my flesh into yours. Become you. Stay. Put your strong, warm arms around me and fold me inside. Stay. I need to breathe your breath, hear your mind, feel your heart beat against mine. Stay. Please stay.* But when she tried to speak, all she could say was, "Quincy . . . ?"

She reached out to him, and he stood abruptly. She looked up, and he turned away. "Schooner, I'm taking you back now." He sounded like he was far away. "Fix your hair."

"You're angry?" she asked. How could he be?

"Angry? God, no! Another time . . . other reason . . ." He didn't finish.

"Schooner, I can't believe it. Still sleeping?" Beatrice said. "Your mother told me you were still in bed, and I had to see it myself. It's nine in the morning. Wake up."

Schooner stirred, trying to get her bearings. The sun was shining in her tiny window, making a brilliant patch of light on her coverlet. She was so tired. She'd half-slept all night, reliving over and over those few moments of passion with Quincy. Now, here was her dearest friend—the last person on earth she wanted to face.

"Come on, come on, Miss Lazy Bones. There's so much to do, and it's a perfectly beautiful day," Beatrice bubbled. She was radiant, pale cheeks flushed with enthusiasm. How could Schooner tell her? "Here, put on your old dress. We might have to do some climbing. I've got bowls and sacks ready."

"What?" Schooner sat up, and the world seemed to spin about in her confusion.

"The cherries are ripe out behind our house, and the birds are eating them faster than I can shoo them away. We've got to get them picked before they're all gone. Come on." While Schooner dressed, she chattered on. "If we get them all picked this morning, we can spend the afternoon making pies and jam. Your mother said she didn't need you today. Oh, Schooner . . ." She started giggling. "Do you remember the time when we were little that Gran'mère Charron sent us out to pick the cherries and we ate them all? We were so sick, and Gran'mère paddled us anyway." She impulsively hugged Schooner.

Schooner couldn't stand this onslaught of memory, affection, and trust. She burst into tears.

"Schooner! What is it? Did I say something? You were smiling in your sleep when I came in, and now . . . tears? Oh, my dear Schooner, whatever is the matter?"

Schooner just went on crying.

"Now, now. You mustn't do that. Get dressed and come out with me. You'll see, it's such a lovely day, no one could be sad. We'll pick the cherries and make Quincy a pie. He adores cherry pies. Remember the first time we made him one—that summer after the flood—and we left so many pits in? He almost broke a tooth on one, and he thought we'd done it on purpose . . ."

"Beatrice, please. I have to . . . I need a few minutes

alone. Do you mind? Let me meet you in the orchard," Schooner said.

Beatrice looked hurt. "Have I done something . . . ?"

"No, no, of course not. I'm just a little ferhuddled today. Let me just wash my face and I'll be all right," Schooner reassured her. "I'll join you directly."

As she dressed, her mind churned frantically. What had she done? She'd been so obsessed with her newly discovered love for Quincy that she hadn't thought about this—about facing Beatrice. When the facts were faced, she loved Beatrice just as much as she loved Quincy. More, probably. It wasn't the same sort of love, but it had been a mainstay in her life for almost as long as she could remember. She and Beatrice had always been utterly loyal to one another. Best friends. Confiding all their secrets, hopes, worries.

But Beatrice's whole life revolved around Quincy—and around her. If either of them was disloyal to her, it would be a tragedy; but if both of them were to abandon her and for each other! Dear Lord, that would destroy Beatrice.

How had this come about? It was not something she would have ever imagined—and yet, hadn't she always had a crush on Quincy, even as a little girl? She had always gauged other young men by him, without even realizing it. All that time she had merely thought she was seeing him through Beatrice's eyes, but now she knew the truth.

And the truth was ghastly!

Aside from her parents, the two most important people in the world to her were Beatrice and Quincy, and she had to choose. Choosing Quincy would not only ruin her friendship with her best friend but also break Beatrice's heart doubly. Whatever was she to do?

Perhaps it would come to her. Solutions sometimes present themselves to insoluble problems. She would not think about it. She would dress, put on a smile, and go with Beatrice to pick cherries. She'd heard her mother talking about a buying trip Quincy was to go on very soon. Maybe he had already left. That would give her time. Time would show her the way.

She hoped.

She had to force herself to understand what Beatrice was saying as they worked that morning. Her mind kept going back and worrying around her problems. "Schooner, you seem preoccupied," Beatrice observed.

"Do you realize that only two years ago I wouldn't have

known what you meant by that word?" Schooner said. "I have a great deal to be grateful to you for."

Beatrice seemed embarrassed by this. "Isn't it nice that there are so many more things we can talk about now?"

And so many we can't, Schooner thought.

They filled their sacks and baskets with cherries, ate a few, and returned to Beatrice's house. Jack Q was there, packing.

"I thought you and Quincy were going to Louisville," Schooner said uneasily.

"Oh, Schooner. Nice to see you. Yes, we're leaving this afternoon. Quincy'll be by in a few minutes. You girls can tell him good-bye."

"Oh, no. I don't think . . . ah, I've got to be going," Schooner said.

Beatrice looked at her seriously. "What is wrong with you?"

"Me? Nothing. It's just that I've got so much to do—"

Just then there was a knock on the door. "Here he is, right on time. Come in!" Jack Q called.

Quincy stepped in the door, looked at Schooner, and stopped. "I was looking for you," he said.

Schooner felt her skin go cold and her heart beat heavily. She wanted to run to him, throw herself at him, touch the copper-red highlights in his hair. But Beatrice had gone to greet him. She put her arm through Quincy's, looked up at him with adoring eyes. "I was hoping you'd not gone yet," she said. "Schooner and I have been picking cherries all morning to make you a pie. Can you stay a bit?"

"I . . . I can't," he said. His voice was soft, tentative.

Schooner stared at the two of them. Time was not on her side—it was not going to serve up a remedy. Quincy was looking a question at her. She had to answer it. She had to decide.

Schooner cleared her throat. "Actually, Beatrice was going to make the pie for you. I was just keeping her company. I've got things I must tend to. Stay with Beatrice, Quincy, and have some pie." As calmly as she could, she walked to the door. As she passed Quincy, her arm brushed his, and it was like lightning striking her. But she kept on going. The two steps out the door seemed like a hundred.

Quincy turned, watched her go, and was sure of what he had feared—that her affection the night before had simply been misdirected unhappiness. Now she had realized it, and this was her way of telling him that there was nothing between them.

Only Jack Q, knowing them all so well, guessed at the truth.

The trip to Louisville took six weeks. When they returned, Quincy made an excuse to stay in Kansas City. They had to make another trip downriver in a few days, and Quincy told Jack Q he would just meet him on the boat. Jack Q returned to Seventrees and went looking for Schooner. He found her at home, bottling liniment. He pulled out a kitchen chair and sat down on it backward, watching Schooner and Addie work for a while. Finally he said, "Addie, run along. I want to talk to your sister."

She turned her head, dimpled at him seductively. "Secrets? But, Jack Q, I love secrets. Perhaps you'll tell *me* some, another day."

He was unperturbed. "Run along, child. You've got secrets enough of your own."

Schooner waited until Addie was gone, stoppered the last bottle, and sat down across the table from Jack Q. With his wiry frame and uncontrolled mop of red hair, he looked like a puppet ready to fly into action at the jerk of a string. "What is it?" she asked warily.

"I don't want to pry into your affairs, but I think someone ought to thank you on my sister's behalf."

"What do you mean?" Schooner asked.

"I saw the look that passed between you and Quincy the day we left, and Quincy—"

"Did Quincy tell you what happened?"

"No, he didn't say anything the whole trip. And I'm *not* asking. I just thought it might be some comfort to you to know someone recognizes the sacrifice I think you're making for a friend."

Schooner twined her fingers tightly together and stared at her hands as if they weren't a part of her. "I had to. It's selfish in a way. I love Beatrice, and I'm a coward. I couldn't face my own guilt if I hurt her."

They sat in silence for a long moment. Jack Q stood and strolled around the room. Finally, his back to her, he said softly, "If you were to marry someone else . . ." A careful, tentative remark. He couldn't bring himself to turn and watch her expression.

"He hasn't asked me yet," she answered.

"Who?" Jack Q asked, a little too suddenly.

"Why, Henry Grinnell, of course," she answered, perplexed by his reaction. "Who else? Anyway, he might never ask, and I'm not sure now that I could . . ."

"What about someone else?"

"Who else is there? I couldn't marry out of friendship. It has to be more than that, doesn't it?"

Jack Q didn't trust himself to answer. He paced once more across the kitchen, then sat back down at the table. "Let me paint you a future," he said ominously. "Beatrice will never marry anyone but Quincy. Quincy will not marry her while you are free. Are the three of you to grow old and lonely here in Seventrees? Three together, three hearts broken and never having a chance to mend. Watching, waiting, weighing each word and look? Agonizing your lives away? I think not. The other choice is for you to marry. Your Henry"—he could not help the slight sneer that crept into his voice—"or someone else. Otherwise you can just tell Beatrice of your feeling for Quincy. You can't hide it from her forever. You know what that will do to her."

"You don't need to tell me! That's why—"

Jack Q put up his hand. "I know. I know. I didn't come here to anger you. I wanted to thank you. I've done that, and I must leave. I've offered unwanted advice. Forgive me."

Schooner reached out to take his hand, but he pulled back. "I'm sorry too, Jack Q. I didn't mean to sound angry. I value your advice. I'll think on it."

"I hope so," Jack Q said bleakly. He picked up his old fur hat, jammed it over his flaming hair, and left.

Henry Grinnell came to Seventrees the next month. By that time Schooner had given much thought to her situation and was prepared to try hard to rekindle the feelings she once thought she had for Henry. It was not as difficult as she expected. Henry was in particularly good cheer and had even brought her a gift—a little carved box for keeping pins and buttons. "It belonged to my mother," he explained. "I don't remember her, but I always imagine that I do when I see this."

Schooner was touched. Knowing what the little box must mean to him, she could guess something of his feelings for her, though he did not express them in words. "Are you sure you want me to have this, Henry?"

"Yes. I'm sure." He took her hand and kissed her lightly, on the lips.

It was still nice to be kissed by Henry, Schooner discovered. He was handsome, responsible, affectionate in his own restrained way. Perhaps she could convince herself again that she was in love with him. She'd thought so once before—before she knew what the word really meant. She *did* like him—very, very well. And it was pleasant to be courted, if only at rare intervals, by someone her whole family was so fond of. Yes. She could make herself be in love with Henry. It would not be so very hard. I am in love with Henry Grinnell, she told herself. "I am in love with Henry Grinnell," she told Beatrice, as if to make it true.

But Henry went back to Lawrence a few days later without asking for her hand. "I'll be back before long, probably September," he said. "If you're not too busy, maybe we can have another picnic or go to Kansas City for a day."

But when he returned in September, the Freilers had problems and there was no chance for picnics or sightseeing in the city.

"I'm going to marry Ernest," Addie announced at dinner one night.

Maggie didn't even stop to consider this remark. "Don't be ridiculous," she said.

"I'm *going* to marry Ernest."

"Perhaps when you're older you can think about it," Gerald said. "You're only thirteen."

"I'm going to marry Ernest. Right away."

"That is the stupidest thing you've ever said!" James put in.

"Look who's talking about stupid!" Addie came back. "Why don't you read to us or teach us some arithmetic, Mr. Smart."

"Morning Wish, if you're through eating, you may go dress your dolls and put them to bed now," Maggie said.

Clear the arena for the main attraction, Schooner thought in a panic. She knew instinctively there was no way of stopping this argument. It was like the avalanches her father had told her about in his native Germany. Poised, ponderous, and deadly, the dispute was ready to crash down on them, and nothing would prevent it now.

"But I want to know when Addie is getting married," Morning Wish said.

"She doesn't mean it, Morning Wish," Maggie said in a thin gray voice. "She's just making a joke. You run along and I'll come tuck you and your dolls in and listen to your prayers in a few minutes."

But Schooner knew—they all knew, even Morning Wish—that Addie meant every word she'd said.

"I don't want you to marry Ernest," Morning Wish said unexpectedly. "He calls me a half-breed and pulls my hair."

Addie didn't answer. She just looked at the little girl disdainfully.

"If nobody minds, I'll just go along with Morning Wish," James said. "Her dolls are so much nicer than Addie."

Yes, James has the right idea. Get away. We can't stop the avalanche. Escape, Schooner thought. "I have things to do—" she began.

"Please stay," Maggie said to her. It was phrased as a request, but it was an order. Did her mother think *she* could get her sister to see reason? Certainly not. She had no influence whatsoever over Addie. Nobody did.

"Now that you've upset everyone, would you care to explain yourself?" Maggie said to Addie.

"I've explained all there is," Addie said. "Ernest and I are in love and we're going to get married."

Gerald had said little at this point, but his face had an angry flush. "I won't hear of it."

Schooner was shocked. Addie was dumbfounded. She stared in amazement at her father, her reliable support in any argument.

"Aside from everything else, you are only thirteen years old!" he repeated.

"Do you want to wait until I'm an old maid like Mother was?"

"She was not!" Schooner said. Why did Addie think she could save herself by saying something hateful about Mother?

"Girls!" Maggie said. "There is no need for you to fight over *my* age. The point is, you are simply too young to make this decision, Addie."

"You just don't like Ernest. You don't like any of them. Aunt Fritzi told me how you never got along with Uncle Luther and you are jealous of how pretty and rich she was back in Germantown. You're just taking it out on me that I like Ernest. He's really very nice—"

"Addie! How can you say that?" Schooner said. "He is the least 'nice' person in Seventrees! And Mother would never be jealous of a silly, lazy woman like Aunt Fritzi." Schooner was so angry her words tumbled over each other.

"I suppose you know all about what's nice, don't you? Sneaking around with that sour old Henry of yours, holding hands when you think no one is looking. I'll bet you've never been kissed. And what does Mother know about nice? I've heard what people in Westport say about her. That she took that dirty old Indian into her bed while Daddy was away in Mexico. Lots of people think that Morning Wish is hers, not Daddy's."

"My God . . ." Maggie whispered.

Schooner was aware of her father moving across the room toward Addie, but Schooner was there first. She flung herself at her sister, scratching and screaming her crimson outrage. Everyone was shouting, but Schooner couldn't hear the words. Nothing made sense, nothing could penetrate her fury. She wanted to hurt Addie terribly. Her parents were grabbing at her, trying to pull her away, but she thrashed against them. "You should die!" she screamed at Addie. "God should kill you! You are horrible! Horrible! Horrible!"

"*Schooner! Stop it!*" James was shouting at her now. He and Gerald got a hold on her arms and pulled her away. "What happened?" James was asking. "What did the little bitch do this time?"

No one answered him. Addie lay on the floor, crying hysterically. Maggie had her hands over her face, shaking with silent sobs, and Gerald had his arms around her. "Take Schooner outside to cool off," he told James.

Schooner was trembling so violently she could hardly walk. James half-led, half-dragged her outside, over to the pump in the yard. He held on to her with one arm, working the handle with the other. When the water began to flow, he made her bend over and stick her head under. The cold water got up her nose and ran down the back of her neck. Sputtering and shivering, Schooner began to regain her self-control. She was terrified of what had happened to her. She'd become a wild animal, and she had to fight back nausea at the thought.

She stood in the moonlit yard, head back, breathing deeply for a long time. Finally, when she could trust herself to speak, she said, "James, how does she do this to us?"

"What did she say?"

Schooner shook her head, wet hair slapping against her cheeks. "I can't repeat it. I can't even think about it. I wish they would just let her marry Ernest and get her out of our lives. She spoils everything she gets near."

After a while Gerald came out into the yard. His face was starkly pale in the darkness. "Come inside, Schooner. You should get to bed." He put his arms around her, and Schooner could feel that he was still shaking, too. "Are you all right?" he asked.

She nodded. "I'm sorry, Daddy."

He patted her. "Nothing to be sorry for. She deserved it. If you hadn't gone after her so quickly, I would have, and I'd have done her more damage." Then, more to himself than to Schooner and James, he said, "I can't imagine how she got to be the way she is."

I know how she got that way, Schooner thought. I've seen you pamper and pet her and make excuses for her behavior. But she couldn't say so. Her father was as he was. There was such good in him that it would be wicked to point out his mistakes.

Nothing more was said about the matter of Addie and Ernest. In fact, very little was said in the Freiler household about anything for the next week. Fearing another outbreak of rampant emotions, they all kept conversation on a short tether. At the end of the week they rose one morning to discover that Addie was gone. It didn't take long to discover that Ernest Halleck was missing as well.

8

Addie and Ernest weren't to be found.

Search parties were formed and went around the countryside. A couple who looked like them had been seen in Shawnee Town to the west and in Westport to the east. It was several hours before anyone noticed that Adams Clay was missing as well. "Do you suppose they took him along to elope?" people asked in mixed sympathy and amusement. "Don't worry Miz Freiler," they said, "she'll be all right."

Maggie thanked her friends for their concern, but privately she said, "She's ruined her life."

296

Gerald was the one Schooner felt sorry for. He was terribly disappointed that his beloved little girl had done something against his wishes, and he maintained for a while that she must have been taken against her will. But she'd left a note that had fallen behind a chest and wasn't found for a few days. In it she railed against both Father and Mother and said that she was going with the "man she loved." Gerald had to abandon the pose of abduction. Then he started complaining that while she was not physically coerced, it was some sort of mental and emotional witchcraft that Ernest had exerted over her. "After the way we've raised her, she just wouldn't do a thing like this," he said.

"The way *you've* raised her, it is exactly what one would expect," Maggie said coldly.

James made his position clear. Father had let her turn into a whore. He said as much, and he and Gerald didn't speak for days. Schooner couldn't say it. It was true, she thought, but it wasn't the whole truth. She had vague memories of Addie as a tiny girl, strutting, prancing, showing off to anyone who would watch—and Gerald had not been there to make her that way. He had certainly encouraged her worst traits, but he had not created them. Nobody had. She was born as she was—beautiful, headstrong, destined to be spoiled.

Spoiled in several senses of the word.

Schooner refused to take a side and pass a judgment, and because of that she became a valued piece in the desperate game her parents were playing. In subtle ways, each kept trying to win her support. Maggie kept gently recalling ways in which Gerald had undermined her attempts to control Addie. Gerald, when he found himself alone with Schooner, bemoaned the way that Addie's personality had changed so radically and suddenly. Schooner, loving them both, listened, tried to remain impartial, and cursed the memory of how she had once wished they would treat her as an adult and confide in her.

The first frosts came and turned Seventrees into a blaze of color. The chores of preparing for the winter went on as usual. Still there was no word of Addie. They had just been told of a raid by abolitionist followers of John Brown on a farm settlement south of Seventrees when Henry came to visit again. He joined a group of men riding out to see if they could locate the "lost sheep." They returned, cold and wary, four days later. Two of the raiders had been described as resembling Ernest and Adams, but no one knew in what direction they had fled.

In November violence flared again, and it was said that three of the raiders had been captured. "Probably strung up by now," the traveler reported. But Quincy and Jack Q, who had just returned from Cincinnati, saddled their horses and rode out to investigate. They brought Adams back.

"Ernest was with them," Quincy told the Freilers. "But when the intended victims started shooting back, Ernest and the rest fled. Adams was wounded, and they made no attempt to take him with them."

"And what of Addie," Gerald asked.

"She's living with Ernest in whatever abandoned Indian villages or caves they find from day to day. I'm sorry, Mr. Freiler, Maggie, I wish I had better news. Adams says she's as well as you could expect."

"Do you think they'll ever come back?" Schooner asked Quincy as he left.

He glanced around to see if they could be overheard. Lowering his voice, he said, "I don't think they'll live to come back. Ernest is a weak person . . ."

"So is Addie, underneath the meanness," Schooner said. And in a dark, guilty corner of her heart she hoped fervently that none of them would ever see or hear from Addie or Ernest again.

It was a mild winter that year. No one spoke of Addie much, though she was on their minds. Schooner was glad that everyone had given up hope of finding her. Maggie threw herself back into her business. She sent samples and advertising along with Quincy when he made a rare midwinter buying trip. Freiler's Cures increased its orders and extended its territory greatly that winter. Maggie even went to Saint Louis to purchase another warehouse and hire a full-time chemist to work in her new brick building on Tenth Street in Kansas City. There was talk of buying a boat of their own to ply goods along the Mississippi and Ohio, rather than hiring shipping space on other boats.

"Why so much expansion right now—all at once?" Schooner asked.

"Because it's time. I should have done it sooner, but for other things . . ." Maggie said, then paused. "No. That's not the real reason. I need to think about the business. It's the only thing that keeps me from brooding over Addie. Besides, your father is happier when I'm not turning the whole force of my personality on him." She smiled wryly as she said this. Schooner had recognized the truth of this statement in a vague way for a long while, but she was surprised that her mother realized it.

There was talk that winter in the Freiler household about a library for Seventrees. Gerald occupied himself selecting a list of books it should have, and often asked Schooner and Beatrice to discuss the choices with him. During the long winter evenings the family was busy poring over plans, schedules, formulas, blueprints, publishing catalogs. James naturally took little interest in the library plans, but he became more involved in the pharmaceuticals. The transportation of all those delicate crates of bottles and jars fascinated him. He devised a method of double boxing them with a layer of sawdust between the boxes that reduced losses from breakage.

Gradually the gloomy discord which had followed Addie's elopement began to pass. One day in February Maggie was called away from working on her ledgers. Schooner had just brought back the mail and set it down on top of the open page. She stared in surprise at the figures. "Mother, I didn't mean to pry," she said when Maggie returned, "but I notice the page in this ledger . . ."

"Pry? You're welcome to look anytime you want. I never thought you were interested. What's wrong?"

"Nothing is wrong, but . . . you're paying for the library? Is that what these figures mean?"

Maggie smiled. "Yes. I thought you knew that."

"It was stupid of me, but I never even wondered where the money was to come from. It's such a lot of money!"

"To create something very valuable . . ."

"Mother, we're rich, aren't we?"

"I guess we are."

Schooner laughed. "I never knew! It simply never occurred to me at all. I feel very foolish."

"Does it make a difference—being 'rich'?"

"No, I don't think it does. I just always thought of other people being wealthy, and somehow . . . well, I thought it meant they didn't have problems. But we . . ."

"We *do* have problems sometimes, don't we? Speaking of our money, I have to go put some in the bank in Kansas City this afternoon. Do you want to ride along with me?"

They bundled up warmly and hitched up a team. Maggie

put her money in an old sewing basket, under her darning, and they set off. Schooner was bemused by her new discovery. She looked over at her mother, sitting tall and proud as always. Who would guess? she thought. Maggie was dressed, as always, in a clean, neat dress and a heavy coat, her feet in old but well-cared-for boots. She seldom bought anything for herself, certainly not anything showy and gaudy. Their house had always been the same way since the flood. They had what they needed, and a few things they merely liked. Anything that broke or wore out was repaired several times before it was replaced. Not a stingy life, merely careful and modest.

They got to town, stopped by the bank, then walked about a bit in the brisk winter air. The city smelled peculiar to Schooner. It always did. Not bad, exactly, just more of people's interests than God's. Maggie went into a shop to buy some thread while Schooner stayed outside watching the stylish city people hurry along the streets. Suddenly she felt someone touch her arm. She turned to find her mother beside her, staring at something across the street. Schooner glanced in the same direction. All she could see was a farm wagon driven by an old man with a pathetic-looking girl at his side. But Maggie continued to stare at them, an expression of utter horror on her face.

Schooner looked again. The girl was a sad-looking thing, skinny, with a protruding pregnant belly. Her blond hair was matted and snarled, and she held a flimsy shawl around her bony shoulders. Suddenly Schooner gasped. "Mother! It's Addie!"

"Dear God in heaven! It is."

It was days before they pieced together the story from Addie's hysterical ramblings. Ernest had been wounded in the same incident as Adams, but he had managed to ride away. They'd been living in a barn at an abandoned farm. The wound had become infected and his leg had swollen and started to putrefy. There were two other men with them, and they attempted to amputate the leg. Addie didn't know whether he had died of blood poisoning or blood loss, but he *had* died.

She had asked his friends to take her home, but they just laughed. They'd made her stay with them and had used her horribly. They'd traded her off at night as though she were nothing but a piece of property. One night they'd heard

300

noises in the woods, and the two men had gone to see what it was. They'd never come back.

She found her way to a farm, walking through the snow for a day and a half. There she'd been put to work gathering firewood and made to sleep in the loft above the cows. When the farmer made his next trip to town, he'd let her ride in the wagon. That, of course, was where Maggie and Schooner had found her.

Schooner and Maggie had immediately abandoned the business they'd come to Kansas City for and dashed back to Seventrees with Addie, stopping only once along the way. "What are you doing?" Schooner asked as the wagon drew to a stop beside a small stream.

Maggie had dipped the corner of her shawl in the water and was scrubbing Addie's face. "See if you can't get her hair combed, Schooner. We can't let your father see her this way. It would break his heart."

"Why shouldn't he see what she's made of herself?" Schooner said angrily.

"Schooner!"

"Well, it's true. Look at her. She doesn't even act like she hears us or knows who we are. How are you going to hide *that* from him?"

Maggie paused for a moment. "What are you angry at your father for?"

"I'm not," Schooner said, reluctantly attempting to drag a comb through Addie's tangled hair. "It's her. Addie. Why did she have to come back?"

Maggie started to say something, but thought better of it. She put her hand on Schooner's shoulder for a moment in wordless understanding and finally said, "Let's go home now."

Addie was feverish, and lucid only part of the time. They bathed her thoroughly when they got her home, wrapped her in extra quilts, and tried to get some food into her. Gerald was, predictably, devastated by the condition she was in. Outraged, he stormed about seeking to place blame. It was Ernest's fault and Adams' and Luther's and John Brown's. He hung around the sickroom, exhorting Maggie and Schooner to make her well again. Schooner didn't want to help care for her, but did so for her father's sake. She felt sorry for Gerald. He wanted his pretty pride, his golden darling, back as she had been—clean, vivacious, adoring. And Addie was not even a ghost of what she had been. Schooner had once heard the phrase "a broken will" and had not understood what it really meant, but Addie was broken—thoroughly. She had no spirit left, almost no *being*. She slept, she ate, she answered tonelessly when she was asked direct questions. But there was no spark of a real person looking out from those dead-looking eyes. She had no anger, no pride, no remorse, no love. Nothing. She wasn't Addie anymore, just a wrecked human to be tended. Gradually Gerald began to comprehend that his dear Addie of the past was forever lost.

She lost the baby a few days later. She did not cry out, either during labor or after, when they told her the child was dead. It seemed no more important to her than being told what the weather was like outside. It had been a boy, well-formed but not sufficiently developed to survive.

But Addie was in their midst again. Whether alive or dead or in this queer halfway state, she was still a source of trouble. All the old arguments surfaced. Whose fault? Why? But you let her . . . Well, you made her . . . if you'd listened to me . . . I told you so . . . On and on and on. Maggie banged pots, James slammed doors, Gerald disappeared for hours, Morning Wish retreated into a quiet, secret self, and Schooner wondered what sort of poison Addie was that she could do this to them without even trying.

Schooner's only solace during this trying time was Beatrice. She would sometimes think she was going mad at home and would stalk over to her friend's house. Beatrice would listen, soothe, understand, and make Schooner feel better. She had a new book of crochet patterns, and this mindless creativity provided Schooner with a welcome change from real life. They crocheted and talked and read poetry and planned Beatrice's party.

"I think Father believes that by giving me a party for my twentieth birthday it will jolt Quincy into noticing that I'm grown. Father is just investing in getting me out of his hair," Beatrice said with a smile.

"You know that's not true," Schooner said.

"In a way it is. He's not very well, Schooner. His heart. I believe he does worry what will become of me if he doesn't see me safely married. He's excited about the party. He's invited all sorts of people from all over the territory, as well as some particular friends he made in the business before Quincy and Jack Q took over the traveling. How many cakes do you think we'll need to make?"

The party was to be the last week in March, and some of

the guests started arriving days before. Schooner asked Henry to come down from Lawrence. The entire town was invited to the festivities, which were to be held in the dining hall of the mission. Everybody was cooking, and most of the women were busy sewing up until the last day.

Adams Clay came to sit with Addie so Gerald and Maggie could attend. He had been a frequent visitor since her return. He merely sat by her bed for hours at a time, saying nothing. He brought her candy once, and it was the only time she smiled, though she did not eat the little marzipan roses. With Ernest dead, Adams had reverted to what Schooner thought was his true personality. He was as silent as his father had been. There was something clumping and comfortable about him now, like a big gentle draft horse who'd tried to be a cow pony and failed. He obviously lived for those hours of sitting with Addie. He'd probably been in love with her all along, Schooner judged.

Schooner had a new dress for the party, a pale blue flowered print with ruffles around the neck and sleeve. She and Beatrice had spent the day before fixing their hair. Hers had held overnight in an intricately twined bun on top of her head with soft, bouncy ringlets on either side of her face. She'd trimmed a few strands to make a light wisp of bangs. Maggie had let her use a touch of lip rouge, and when she was ready, presented her with a pair of tiny pearl earrings. Schooner had never owned a piece of jewelry. "Thank you, Mother," she said, tears springing to her eyes.

"Now, now, you'll make your eyes all red," Maggie said, blinking a little herself.

Henry Grinnell was frankly and flatteringly astonished when he came to fetch her. "Schooner, is that really you?" he asked. "Mrs. Freiler, your daughter is truly the most beautiful woman I've ever seen in my life."

Schooner got out the new shawl she and Beatrice had crocheted and walked with Henry to the mission. The hall was already filled with people. Beatrice stood at one end receiving guests. She, too, was dressed and coiffed more elegantly than was usual for Seventrees, in the softest of lilac, a taffeta dress with rows of gathered lace at throat and wrists. Her unruly red hair was confined to a large knot at the back of her neck, with flowers laced through it. Tiny tendrils of curls had escaped around her face, and though it was not planned that way, Schooner thought it was charming.

On either side of her were Torchy and Quincy. Torchy was

303

showing his age now, white ribboned through his flaming hair, but he was as erect and energetic as ever, talking excitedly in his own strange English to each guest who greeted Beatrice. Jack Q was merely a younger, slightly shorter version of his father, as brilliant as a rare bird and as elusive. Both of the LeSage men were dressed at the height of masculine fashion, in well-cut coats and vests with expensive silk shirts. They had tailored wool trousers to match their coats, and high leather boots. Schooner had seldom seen either of them in anything but workclothes or skins and furs and beads of the traditional French trapper, and was surprised. Torchy could have passed for a visiting dignitary, and Jack Q's natural grace and vivacity were framed and enhanced. Schooner had never really noticed before how good-looking he was. With them—tall, quiet, and handsome—was Quincy Clay. He was dressed as richly in formal attire, but more somberly. He seemed distracted.

There was a gap in the crowd, and Schooner caught a momentary glance of the four of them, suspended for a fraction of a second as if for a family portrait, smiling, composed, looking as if fate had woven them together for their beauty. Quincy shifted his gaze and looked at her through the corridor of people. In that moment something almost tangible in its force leaped between them, taking Schooner's breath away.

She had successfully avoided any personal private contact with him for almost a year now. He was gone a great deal of the time, and when he was home she invented reasons to keep from seeing him. She had tried not to be obvious in this ploy, but Beatrice, finely tuned to Schooner's behavior, had noticed. "Don't you like Quincy anymore?" she asked.

"It's not that," Schooner said. It's not that! Never that. "I am just impatient with him for not marrying you," she explained. It was weak, and a lie, but it was all she could think of. Beatrice had regarded her oddly and let the subject drop.

But now, in the crowded hall, the year of avoidance was for naught. She knew that when he had looked into her eyes so unexpectedly, he had read her mind's secrets there. She looked away quickly. "What is it, Schooner?" Henry asked.

"Nothing. It's nothing."

They went to Beatrice, wished her happy birthday, talked briefly with Torchy and Jack Q, and Schooner forced herself to nod and smile impersonally at Quincy before moving on. She could feel him watching her as they went.

The party was a huge success. There was loud, happy music, great mounds of food, drinks on a long table in everything from crystal decanters to stone jugs. There were friends of Torchy and Jack Q who had come from far, far away. Men in frock coats and tall hats escorting women in silk dresses and diamonds. There were farmers with manure still fresh on their boots dancing enthusiastically with wives in faded calico. The old were there, and the young—infants being passed from lap to lap while their mothers enjoyed the party. The long room filled with laughter and song, washing away all thoughts of North and South and slavery. Worries over crops were forgotten; the weather, when discussed, was touched on lightly and in pleasant terms. All that mattered for this one evening was the food, drink, music, and pleasure.

Schooner was overwhelmed. This was, to her, the essence of what she loved about Seventrees, compressed into one glorious evening. The rich and the poor, old and young together in a happy babble of French, English, and German. There were farmers, politicians, tradesmen, soldiers, brewers, ministers, and even a professional riverboat gambler and his fancy lady in red taffeta, all elbow to elbow.

Henry scooped Schooner into his arms and whirled her through dance after dance. They tried to talk, but could scarcely hear each other. Finally, breathless, feet throbbing, Schooner said she had to rest for a while. They moved toward the back end of the hall, away from the music and near an open door to the porch, where there was a cool breeze.

"Where is Beatrice?" Schooner asked.

Henry, taller than most of those around them, said, "Just over there, with Quincy. And here are your parents."

Maggie and Gerald joined them. Maggie's face was slightly flushed, as if she, too, had been dancing. Schooner wished she'd seen it. Mother never danced. While they were talking, Schooner noticed Adams Clay come in the door nearby. At first she thought nothing of it; then she realized that he was supposed to be sitting with Addie. Was something wrong? She tapped her mother's arm and pointed at Adams.

He stepped through the door, turned back, and put out a hand to draw someone else in. It was Addie. Somehow he'd gotten her up and dressed. He had apparently tried to fix her hair for her, but lank strands of it had already escaped the hairpins. Her dress hung in awkward folds on her skeleton-like frame. She was looking around in blank confusion, and

305

Adams had put his arm around her thin shoulders in a touchingly protective gesture. He bent, whispered something to her, and her lips formed a thin, mechanical half-smile.

"She's not fit to be here!" Gerald said. "Whatever possessed him to bring her out? And looking like she does now . . ."

Maggie turned to him and said sharply, "She's as fit as she may ever be, and she might never look any better. Gerald, that *is* your dear daughter. She'll not be the beautiful spoiled toy you loved—never again. You might as well . . ."

Schooner clapped her hands over her ears. Why did they do this! Addie's merely walking through a door, unaware of who or where she was, was enough to ignite the old argument. The endless, endless argument. She could not listen to it again, she would not. She darted away, needing to be alone, to clear her mind of this blot on the evening.

But it wasn't just this evening, she thought as she reached the darkness of the porch. Addie would be with them forever, and where Addie lived, discord would erupt. She knew she could not stop it, not even dilute it. She grasped the railing, clenching her fingers around it. She must somehow escape this.

She heard a step on the wooden floor, and without looking, she knew whose step it was. How many things she knew about him—how he walked, what he liked to eat, his favorite melody that he whistled when he was chopping wood, the way he always called his mother "ma'am," how his hair gleamed mahogany in the late-summer sunshine. She clutched the rail tighter.

Quincy said nothing at first, merely took her in his arms. She huddled there against his chest, knowing that the year of remembering how it had felt had not been false. He was warm, strong, and she loved him. "Schooner, we can't go on this way. I wasn't sure until tonight. I thought it had been a mistake, a misunderstanding, but when I looked at you earlier, I knew you felt as I do."

"We cannot betray Beatrice," Schooner said, and backed away a little.

He took her hand, folded it between his. "She would understand. She loves us both."

Schooner shook her head. "No. That's why she wouldn't understand. I do love you, Quincy. I admit it. But I love Beatrice too, and she needs my love more than you do. You're strong and sure and happy."

"Not without you . . ."

"Quincy! Please don't . . ." Suddenly she knew that her resolve was as thin and tenuous as a spiderweb. His love was, acidlike, burning holes and gaps in her private morality. She could not withstand more. Jack Q had been wrong that day. They could not grow old together, never making a move to alter the triangle. Schooner would break sooner or later and betray the heart-friend who would not survive the betrayal. She could not send *them* away—there was only one choice left.

She pulled her hand from between his, savoring the last touch of fingertip against fingertip. "No," she said softly, and walked away.

Before she could change her mind, she went back into the hall. Pushing her way through the crowd, she found Henry. "Schooner! What became of you?" he asked. "I've been hunting everywhere for you."

"I just needed some air. Henry . . . can we talk?"

Henry put his arm around her shoulders and led her to a relatively quiet corner. "What is the matter? What are you upset about?" he asked gently.

Voice quavering, she said, "Henry, talk to me about the future—our future. Do we have a future?"

Henry looked slightly startled by her bluntness. "I have hoped so," he answered. "But I've been afraid to ask . . ."

"Afraid? Why?"

"Because you are so young and so close to your family. I was afraid you would turn me down if I asked you to marry me."

She clutched his hands tightly. "Ask me, Henry. Ask me. I want to make my life with you. It is time for me to leave home."

9

Schooner made the last of her purchases and waited while the shopkeeper wrapped the length of calico into a neat paper parcel. "I'll carry that one myself," she said. "Mr. Grinnell will pick up the rest later."

"You sure, Mrs. Grinnell?" Wesley Savage, the rotund shopkeeper, asked solicitously.

Schooner felt a sliver of anger, but forced it back. He was only showing his concern. So many of Henry's friends acted as though a woman who had one miscarriage was fated to be a helpless frail thing forever. She was tempted to tell them what the midwife had said, that the child had been faulty—deformed. It had not been Schooner's fault for not taking proper care of herself, merely an accident of nature. But, of course, she would not say that. It was not proper to speak of such things. Propriety in Henry's Lawrence counted for a great deal. Even now, when she was due to give birth in another month, the ladies referred to her "condition" or her "imminent confinement," never "pregnancy."

It wasn't that they were prissy people, nor that they shrank from the realities of life, but they were both conservative and well educated and hence put careful emphasis on *how* ideas were expressed. Like the Germans at Seventrees, they had debate clubs, poetry readings, and elocution classes. But they didn't have fests or singing societies or dancing, and Schooner missed the Teutonic heartiness of home. She wrapped a woolen scarf around her neck and tucked the ends in snugly against the cold blast that would assail her when she stepped out.

She walked along the wooden sidewalk, bending her head a little against the gusty December wind. As she walked along, she thought of all the odd things about Lawrence she'd had to adjust to. In her secluded existence at Seventrees, she had come to believe, without ever questioning it, that all communities were like hers. Bigger, perhaps, or older, but much the same. She had quickly learned the error in that thinking. Seventrees had just happened. For twenty years, since Maggie and Gerald built their first house, people had ended up there and stayed. They had not come to that particular place on purpose in most cases, but had settled as a piece of driftwood in the the river settles where it hits a snag in high water.

Lawrence, on the other hand, had not existed seven years before except as a plan. Now it was a large, bustling city. There were some twelve hundred people living here. Wealthy, cultured, dedicated people who had come to the territory for a purpose and intended to see it through. They were organized people—the streets of Lawrence had been named from east to west for the states of the union—in the order in which they had been admitted. There was only one street in

Seventrees that had a name, and it was either Mission Road or Westport Road, depending on which way you were headed.

But the Emigrant Aid people would have none of such nonsense. Their streets were named and planned before they ever left Boston. The businesses and center of town were, naturally enough, located along the length of Massachusetts Street, because that was where most of them had come from. It was an enormously wide thoroughfare with neat wooden sidewalks along both sides. Schooner had often noticed with some amusement that people almost always crossed at the corners, even though there was nothing whatsoever to keep them from crossing mid-block. Organized—oh, they were organized!

And she had tried hard to fit in. It had been especially difficult at first. She was terribly homesick that first summer she'd lived here. Everything was something completely different—even her name. Henry had liked well enough calling her Schooner at Seventrees, but she discovered that he intended that she be known in Lawrence by her proper name—Mary. She hated it. She could not remember to answer to it, and people thought she was rebuffing them when she did not answer to Mary. It had been the first argument she and Henry had.

"Mary is such a nice Christian name, I can't see what you have against it," Henry had said.

"I've never been called Mary. Henry, you met, courted, and wed Schooner. That's who I am. I'll try to change in ways that need be, but don't try to take my name away from me!" she had said.

He had backed down on that and sometimes introduced her as Schooner. But in most other things it was she, not he, who had been forced to change. She learned to serve and partake of proper tea. She'd reluctantly had calling cards printed and enjoyed using them until Henry told her she was simply to leave them at the other ladies' houses without scrawling chummy notes on the back.

She'd learned other things, too. Even in the cold wind of this December day, she could feel her cheeks flush at the memory of one summer night the first week they lived here. She and Henry had been out in the tiny backyard of their house talking about what to plant next to the stables. They'd been standing in the sunset, arms around each other's waists, when a neighbor called hello from the side yard. Henry had moved away from Schooner immediately, almost guiltily. While he and the neighbor chatted, she had stepped close and taken hold of Henry's hand. He pulled it away and gave her a look of such reproach that she had to run into the house to keep from crying in front of them.

She waited, expecting him to come in and apologize for hurting her feelings, but that wasn't what happened at all. He had come in and had said, "Schooner, I'm surprised at you."

"Surprised? But, Henry—"

"One does not make a public display like that in front of other people. I'm sure you know that."

"Public display? Henry, you make it sound as though I was taking your pants off."

"Don't be vulgar," he said, sounding like a disappointed schoolmaster.

Vulgar? Tears came to her eyes again. No one had ever said a thing like that to her. Vulgar? Was that what he thought? "You did not think I was vulgar last night in bed, Henry. As I recall, we both spoke rather frankly."

"That's different."

"Why is it different? Because the sun is shining now and it wasn't then? Are we different people in daylight? Is our love altered by the sunrise?"

That night, when Henry extinguished the lamp and took her in his arms, she was silent. She did not whisper to him how nice it felt to have his body next to hers. Instead, she closed her eyes and was silent. Henry did not seem to notice a difference. If he did, he said nothing of it.

A door had closed.

She suddenly realized that she had married a man she didn't know. He *was* all of the things she had known of him, but he was many other things she had not suspected. She had admired his reserve, not thinking that someday she might feel imprisoned by it. She had made herself a student of language on his behalf many years before, not guessing that her studies would not end with her marriage, but increase. She had respected his devotion to his business, not knowing that she would come to resent the way it took his whole heart.

It had been a moonless night the first September in Lawrence when she had begun her fantasy. It had not been planned. One night, when she was particularly depressed, Henry had turned out the lamp and crawled in bed beside her. He touched her arm, caressed her shoulder, moved closer and nuzzled her neck. This was always how it was. Next he would fumble with the ribbon at the neck of her nightdress and she would sit up and put it over her head. Then he would take her, not brutally, just routinely. As if it were an act as natural and uninteresting as eating or getting a drink of water on a hot day.

But this time, Schooner had been thinking about Quincy when it began. She had been remembering (as she had a hundred times) the night so long before in the woods when she had kissed Quincy and felt the world melt down around her. If only he were Quincy, she thought. If only . . . She closed her eyes, pretending that he was. She smiled in the dark. If he were Quincy . . . She felt herself moving about, writhing with a strange, hot pleasure. He is Quincy. I'm in my marriage bed with Quincy, she thought, and found herself licking and nibbling on his shoulder.

Henry shivered a little and started to mount her, but she wiggled away. "No, not yet," she whispered. Careful, don't say his name. *Don't say "Quincy."*

She took his hand from where it lay at her waist and moved it to her breast. Henry froze for a moment, but she pressed her hand over his, and he began to caress her. She trembled. Don't stop, Quincy, don't stop. She strained against him as she had in the woods that night, and suddenly wanted the hot weight of his body on hers. She drew him closer and whimpered with pleasure as he plunged into her. Oh, *Quincy, Quincy!* she cried silently.

Then it was over and her face was damp with sweat and her own tears. It was wrong—wrong for her and for Henry. Why couldn't she love him this way for himself? He was a good man and loved her in his own limited way. How had things come to this?

"Schooner? What's wrong?" Henry asked her.

"Nothing," she said, trying to keep her voice cool and normal. But he would not question her, she knew that. He would never inquire into the reason for her sudden passion, for Henry did not talk about such things and probably wouldn't risk her speaking "vulgarly." She had gotten out of bed, muttered something about getting a glass of milk, and then gone outside to sit in the stables and cry.

She was convinced that was the night she conceived the first baby—the one doomed to miscarriage at four months. After that she had allowed herself the agonizing pleasure of the waking dream only at rare intervals. Now that she was pregnant again, it was not a problem, for Henry believed that intercourse during pregnancy "in your condition" was harmful, and the miscarriage had convinced him. It had been many months since he'd so much as touched her hand except by accident.

" 'Morning, Mrs. Grinnell. Do you need some help with your package?" a voice said, startling her out of her reverie.

Schooner looked up. It was Eldon Wentworth, their plump, cheerful neighbor from down the street. "Good morning, Mr. Wentworth. Thank you, no."

"Mind if I walk along with you a bit?" he asked courteously. How typically Lawrence, Schooner thought. A public walkway, the man going the same direction as she, but he politely asks if he may walk with her. Sometimes she found herself touched by their niceness; other times, it irritated her. But she liked Mr. Wentworth. He was one of their friends who could, on rare occasions, talk about subjects other than politics.

"Certainly, I'd enjoy the company," Schooner answered. "Did you get your trumpet fixed?"

"Yes'm, I did that. In fact, that's why I wanted to talk to you. A few of us need to brush up a bit on some of the band numbers. I can't have them to my house on account of the baby sleeping, and Henry said we could practice in your parlor. I know what my missus would do if I invited folks without mentioning it to her and I wondered . . ."

"Yes, Henry talked to me about it. It's perfectly fine. I enjoy hearing you play."

The band was one of the few things Schooner had liked about Lawrence to begin with. The members had gotten together before coming west and had played at the embarkation in Boston. Schooner had heard them tell over and over how the poet John Greenleaf Whittier had written a poem for them called *The Kansas Emigrants* and recited it in person. They had put it to the music of "Auld Lang Syne" and played it frequently as a sort of theme. It was a great source of pride to Henry that he was in the band, and it was one interest that he and Schooner shared. Of course, a brass band practicing in the parlor wasn't quite the same as listening to Gerald and James playing their flutes, weaving liquid melody through summer nights, but it was music.

Above all, they couldn't talk politics while they played.

"I was by Mrs. Lane's the other afternoon and could hear

312

that piano going—was that you, by any chance?" Mr. Wentworth asked.

"No, I can't get close enough to the instrument now to play," Schooner said, glancing down at her abdomen.

Mr. Wentworth burst into laughter. "That's a good one, Mrs. Grinnell. I'll have to tell Lucy about that."

Schooner hurried the rest of the way home. She would have to get busy and make some cakes and cookies for the guests tonight. She hung up her coat and scarf, slipped her boots off, and wheezing a little, bent over to rub her cold feet. She must remember to ask Henry to borrow some extra chairs and bring the music stands in from the shed. She stood looking at the tiny front parlor, mentally arranging the absent chairs. Funny how the room, the whole house in truth, had never really become "home" to her. It was where she lived, it was her furniture she kept dusted and polished, but nothing of it seemed "home" or truly hers. She had selected none of it. Henry had just bestowed it upon her along with a new name—Mary Grinnell. She thought about the cradle at her parents' house in Seventrees. Maggie and Gerald had brought it from Pennsylvania. She had slept in it as a tiny baby, as had Addie several years later. She had helped her mother put it in the wagon the day before the flood, and little Morning Wish had slept in it that night under the stars up on the bluff while the deadly water swirled below. Objects in a house should *mean* something, not just function as surfaces and receptacles.

She sat down in front of the tiny fire and held out her hands to the warmth. The mantel here was bare. At home there was a glass case with a lovingly carved model of their first house inside; there was a place beside the Freilers' fireplace where James had once carved his name. (He'd had to do all his own chores as well as Benjamin's for two weeks as punishment.) There was a concave place in the wood just above James's name. Schooner had once tripped and fallen against it and claimed her head had made the dent, even though everyone else maintained it had always been there.

Oh, well, perhaps someday this house would mean as much to her—or at least to her children. She looked at the far wall where she wanted the piano. She'd not mentioned it to Henry yet—that she longed for her own instrument. It was frightfully expensive to have one shipped clear out here, and she was afraid he would say, quite rightly, "Don't you think you ought to practice on Mrs. Lane's and get better at it before we buy our own?" So, rather than giving him the opportunity of turning down her request, she had not made it. Someday. Someday when she could play very well, she would ask.

She busied herself with preparations for the guests, then took a short nap before Henry came home for dinner. He chatted through the meal about his work—a new book he had gotten in the mail about treating certain diseases in pigs, a medicine he had concocted and was trying out on Lucas Smithfield's cows, and so on. Schooner tried, as always, to act interested. He would have been unhappy to know how little she cared about diseases of cows.

"By the way," he said as he rose from the table, "I almost forgot. There was a letter for you in the mail—from your friend Quincy Clay. Addressed specifically to you. Naturally I didn't open it . . ." It hung like a bruised question: Why would Quincy write to you, not us?

Schooner took the letter without offering Henry any reply to his unspoken query. Why would Quincy write to her? She had not heard from him except through Beatrice since she had married Henry and moved to Lawrence. She took a paper knife and sliced carefully into the envelope. It might be the only letter she ever got from him; she must treat it with care. Preserve it as if it were a love letter, which it surely was not. She unfolded the paper, looked for a moment only at the bold, businesslike handwriting. So typically Quincy: neat, straight lines; clear, well-formed letters with an occasional flourish on the tail of a "y" or "g."

She read:

Dear Schooner,

Perhaps I overstep the bounds of friendship in writing this, but I wish to make a request of you. Perhaps I should call it a suggestion, which you may consider. Beatrice has been ill again this winter—nothing seriously injurious, but her spirits are poor and made the more so for not hearing from you, her dearest friend.

She cannot fail to notice that you ceased to write to her with your usual warmth and frequency since she and I were married last spring. She has often mentioned this coincidence and remains convinced, despite my assurances to the contrary, that you have taken offense in some way at our happiness.

Your mother tells me that you are pregnant. I

know that this fact coupled with the bad weather makes a visit impossible, but, Schooner, it would be very nice if you would at least write to Beatrice whenever you have an opportunity. You know how much you mean to both of us and that we wish you the very best in everything.

Give my regards to your husband.

Yours truly,
Quincy Clay

No, not a love letter. A rebuke. A deserved rebuke. She would write to Beatrice this very night. Quincy was right, she had found it almost impossible to write bright, friendly letters to her after she and Quincy had married, and now she suddenly saw how selfish and self-pitying it was. Of course they would marry. How could she have expected otherwise? She married Henry so that she would not endanger Beatrice's chances with Quincy, and it had worked out. What reason did she have to feel sorry for herself? But she did, just the same.

"What does he have to say?" Henry asked in an overly casual voice.

"Just a note about Beatrice's health and my failure to keep up our correspondence," Schooner answered honestly. She laid the letter on the table for him to read if he wanted. There was nothing in it he could not see. "You know how much you mean to both of us" would not say to him what she knew it meant. Quincy was reminding her of his love, but it was phrased as a perfectly respectable remark from a pair of married friends.

But he didn't read it. Her explanation satisfied him.

There was a knock on the front door, and Henry went to answer it. He returned with four of the band members. "Got some papers in today I want to talk to you about, Henry," Mr. Savage from the general store was saying. His big square face was red from the walk in the cold. "The Kansas statehood bill is to be signed later this month—January 29, I believe."

"Before Lincoln takes office?" Schooner asked. Henry smiled at her interest.

"Yes'm," Mr. Savage answered. "Buchanan figures it's going to happen anyway and he might as well have his name to it. Now that North Carolina has withdrawn from the Union,

315

the rest of the southern states are going to follow suit in quick order. It will be a real war in a matter of weeks. Of course, we've been fighting a real war out here for years. Won't make much difference to us, I reckon."

Ephraim Brown, the proprietor of the lumber yard and the band's chief drummer, disagreed. "I think you're wrong there, Wesley. The Bushwhackers are bad enough, but just wait until they have Confederacy troops with them. The South can call up thousands of men to cross over the border and try to wipe out places like Lawrence."

"Yes, but the North can call up just as many to defend us," Eldon Wentworth put in.

The talk swirled around while Schooner cleared away dinner and put cookies out on plates for the men. It was all so complicated—not just a matter of southern slave holders against northern abolitionists, as she had originally thought. The original struggle had attracted a vicious criminal element on both sides. Men who cared nothing for ideals, but looked upon it only as an opportunity for personal gain. The Missouri criminals headed by William Quantrill were called Bushwhackers and the Kansas equivalents were called Jayhawkers, though no one seemed to know where the term came from. These were truly the lunatic fringe, and no reasonable person on either side would have had anything to do with them at first. But in the years since Schooner had shot the Westport Bushwhacker in the foot, things had gotten out of control and distinctly different "parties" had formed within each philosophical camp. Even the people of Lawrence were divided.

Lancaster Drake, a farmer living east of Lawrence, was a good example of how people changed. He was a mild, pleasant man who came to the territory simply to swell the numbers of voters in what he thought a moral issue. He was peaceable, bothered no one, and even once, when a Bushwhacker had been caught setting fire to a neighbor's farm, convinced the neighbor to administer only a strong rebuke and release the young man. But a few months later the Bushwhacker came back and set fire not only to the barn but also to the house, burning the neighbor, his wife, and three children to death. A week later the criminals returned, and while Lancaster was out plowing the fields, they dragged his teenage sons out of the house and shot them to death in front of their mother. She had collapsed and not spoken since.

Lancaster, a peace-loving philosophical man, had left his

316

wife with a neighbor and set out to find the young Bush-whacker whom he'd earlier saved. He located him, cunningly ambushed him, and took him to his mother's house. The mother had pleaded for her son's life—just as Lancaster's wife had pleaded—but Lancaster was a man obsessed. He shot the young man on the front porch of his house and left the mother to bury him. Lancaster had become a Jayhawker, and rather than being shunned by his friends in Lawrence for his cold-blooded murder, was regarded as a fine, honorable man for what he had done.

Nowadays even people like Ephraim Brown, who had never so much as slaughtered a pig or drowned an unwanted cat, proudly called themselves Jayhawkers, meaning simply that they were true Kansans.

"Are you feeling all right?" Henry asked her.

Schooner was standing quite still in the middle of the room. "Yes, I'm fine," she assured him. There would be plenty of time to tell him later what she had felt as she set out plates and thought about Jayhawkers. It had been only a slight pain. Faint and lasting but a few seconds. "Gentlemen, *do* play," she said with a smile. "It's such a cold night and we need the warmth of music in this house."

Nathan Grinnell was born the next morning. An easy birth, a healthy child, though small. Neighbors came to call, bringing thoughtful gifts for both Schooner and her new son. Henry was elated with the baby. He got up with Schooner each time the baby woke during the night and watched besot-tedly as she fed and changed him. He paid Jake Ridenauer, the next-door neighbor's fifteen-year-old son, to take the Grinnell's best horse to Seventrees to deliver the message. The ride nearly killed the horse, and Henry didn't even seem to care. Three days later a wagon pulled up in front of Schooner's house, and the two occupants, so tightly bundled as to be unidentifiable at first, turned out to be Maggie and James.

"See, Ma, I told you she was all right," James said when they got their layers of coats and sweaters off. "I've never seen anyone so downright anxious to get out and ride forty miles in the freezing cold," he told Schooner.

Maggie hugged Schooner and cooed over the baby before sending Henry back out to the wagon. "I brought you some-thing special, little Nathan," she said.

Henry came struggling in with a large, unwieldy object and

unwrapped it. It was the cradle—the one Maggie had brought west and rocked all her own babies to sleep in. All of her own and one half-Indian child who had become hers.

James stayed several days, talking war and politics with Henry and his friends, then went back home. Maggie stayed on for three weeks after. She and Schooner caught up on all the daily news they had missed. Beatrice's illness was nothing serious, Maggie assured her daughter, just the same lung complaint that so often bothered her in the winter. Maggie went on at some length about the wedding before she noticed that Schooner wasn't taking any joy in the recounting. She suddenly stopped talking and went back to kneading some bread. After a long time she said, "Why didn't you come to Quincy and Beatrice's wedding, Schooner?"

"I . . . well, it was a long trip and . . . uh . . ." Schooner couldn't quite remember what excuse she'd used at the time. Illness? No, that wasn't it.

A light seemed to dawn in Maggie's eyes. "I should have seen it sooner," she said softly.

"Seen what?" Schooner said, trying to pretend she didn't understand what her mother meant.

"I wondered," Maggie went on, "but I thought it was only what I *wanted* to think."

"What you wanted . . . ?"

Maggie put a damp cloth over the dough and sat down across the kitchen table. "Of course it was what I wanted. I had hoped from the time you were a child that you would marry Quincy. But I assumed you were never interested in him."

"Interested?" Schooner twisted her hands together and smiled bitterly. "Only so much that I still dream of him at night and imagine conversations with him. He kissed me once, and I sometimes think it's the only thing in my past worth remembering."

Maggie put her hand over Schooner's. "But why . . . ? Beatrice?"

Schooner nodded. "I couldn't betray her, and yet now I wonder if it wasn't more of a betrayal this way. I am sometimes so sick with jealousy I almost think I hate her. And Henry—it's so unfair to Henry, and I can't help it. His only real fault is that he's *not* Quincy."

Maggie said, "Oh, my darling daughter, what can I do? What can I say to relieve your unhappiness? You did what you knew to be the only right choice, and now you are the

318

one paying the price. Does it help any to know that I understand the fierce cost of doing what you believe to be right?"

Schooner forced a smile. "Yes. It helps . . . some."

"Why didn't you ever tell me?"

"I don't know. I guess I just didn't want to burden you with my troubles."

"I would have welcomed *your* confidences. Not that I could have told you anything you didn't know for yourself."

"It doesn't matter," Schooner assured her. "I *am* Mrs. Henry Grinnell now, and so I shall remain. Nathan makes it easier. Much easier. His very existence makes me so proud and happy I often forget everything else. Several times I've had to force myself to let him sleep. I want him awake so I can hold him and talk to him and wait to see his smile. See, you needn't worry about me, I have the cure for my problems right here in my arms. Oh, dear, I'm making speeches about motherhood," she said, embarrassed at her burst of sentiment.

It seemed just a heat rash at first. It was an extraordinarily warm day for May, and Nathan was fretful over getting his first tooth, so Schooner wasn't really alarmed, but she did mention her concern to Mrs. Ridenauer. "I wouldn't worry. They sometimes get loose bowels and a bit of a fever with the first few teeth. And the rash—why, I've got one myself round my neck. It's just the heat. It'll cool down and we'll all be fine," she said.

But Nathan didn't improve. He slept badly, and by morning the rash had covered nearly his entire body, and his temperature was raging. Henry paced and fidgeted while they waited for the doctor, and Schooner rocked Nathan, trying to lower his fever with applications of cool, damp cloths. The doctor identified it as a particularly virulent form of measles. He'd had three other younger children come down with it just this week. He prescribed medicines but offered no false hope.

Nathan Grinnell died just before dawn the next day. He would have been four months old the next week. They buried him in the tiny cemetery on Mount Oread, the large flat-topped hill that overlooked the city. Schooner could barely control herself. She felt the same panicked outrage she'd felt the time she attacked Addie. But there was no one to strike now, no one to blame but God.

She and Henry hardly spoke when they returned home. He was as defeated by their loss as she was, but the spark of love that could have warmed them both was missing from their marriage. There was nothing they could do to console each other. And in cold secret places in their hearts, each blamed the other.

Schooner could hardly bear to get out of bed the next day. Henry had risen early and gone to his office. That was his comfort. But what was hers? Finally she dragged herself out, put on her black dress, and went to work. Each reminder of Nathan was a fresh heartbreak. She folded his baby dresses and linens between sheets of white paper and put them in boxes. She wept over the little silver spoon she'd fed him with, then put it away too.

By midday she had the cradle ready to crate up and send back to Maggie. She would never have another child, she decided. God could not do this to her again, ever. She would survive this agony once—she didn't think she could survive even the fear of it happening again. When Henry came in for his dinner, she said, "Would you help me crate the cradle?"

He stared at her for a long moment, then abruptly sat down on the horsehair sofa and put his hands over his eyes. "I wanted to be the father of a son," he whispered. His voice was on the thin edge of control.

She'd never seen him like this, never believed that his emotions were as real as hers. A wave of something fierce—not love, perhaps, but affection, protectiveness—washed over her. She suddenly felt very sorry for Henry. More sorry for him than for herself. She knelt in front of him and put her hands over his. "I wanted you to be the father of a son, too. And you will be," she said, her earlier resolve to remain childless forgotten. "But we must send the cradle back for a little while. You know Addie and Adams are expecting, and Mother will want them to have it. But we'll have more children. I promise . . ." She went on, soothing him as she would a child.

Drawn out of her own grief and into his, Schooner realized something. She'd been lamenting the loss of a love that meant lightning and sigh-stricken embraces. All the while, she had been on the verge of a love that was less exciting, but possibly more reliable and enduring. Perhaps this was what she was meant to reclaim from the tragedy of losing her child. No, not my child, she thought. Our child.

She would try—really try—to see things differently. Now that Henry had allowed her a glimpse of his true self through

320

his armor of reserve, there was a chance for them, a basis upon which to build a genuine mutual love. Perhaps even the sort of love Schooner had felt for Quincy.

10

Schooner closed the oven door, and gasping in the stifling heat of the kitchen, stepped to the back door. If God wants people to know what hell is like, He should send them all to Kansas in August, she thought. She unbuttoned the top two buttons of her dress and fanned herself. Why had she volunteered to bring cakes to the picnic? Cakes, of *all* things. She could have cooked nearly anything else out in the yard over an open fire. It was midafternoon. As soon as the baking was done, she could bathe and put on fresh clothing.

"Schooner?" she heard Henry calling from inside.

She turned as he came to the door. "What are you doing home so soon?" she asked.

"Nobody needed me today, and I was going to work on some formulas I'm experimenting with, but it's just too hot to even think," he said. "What are you cooking?"

"Cakes. I promised Mrs. Lane. She had so much to do with all those railroad men in town to be entertained, and I thought I ought to help out."

"Are you sure you should . . . ?" Henry asked tentatively.

"Oh, Henry, don't fuss. I'm not pregnant, and treating me like I am won't make it happen," Schooner said. She was weary of this subtle nagging, and yet she couldn't blame him. It had been over two years now since Nathan died, and they were still waiting for signs of another child.

He dropped the subject. Taking a handkerchief from his breast pocket, he mopped his face. "Say, Luke Sweeney came by my office this morning and told me something surprising. Do you remember that fella named Charlie Hart who lived here a while back?"

"Charlie Hart? Oh, yes!" How could she forget? The man had come to the door one day looking for the Lanes' house and had frightened Schooner badly. It wasn't anything he said or did, just his sly appearance. He had wheat-white hair and the sort of blue eyes that were so extraordinarily pale as to appear completely colorless. He had been slim, almost delicate of feature, but there was nothing effeminate about him. Rather, he seemed coldly neuter. He had spoken properly enough, but his voice was sharp-edged and sneering. Schooner had told him he had the wrong house, that General Lane and his wife lived next door, and she'd quickly closed her door in his face. She watched through the side window as the man stood staring at the Lanes' house with narrowed eyes. Then he had gone down the walk and turned in the opposite direction. Schooner had told Henry about the incident and the unreasoning fear she had of the man. He had not taken it very seriously until later. Hart had come in to talk to Henry about trouble with his horse, and Henry had become almost as unnerved as Schooner by the man's presence. Shortly afterward Hart had mysteriously left Lawrence.

"Yes," she repeated, "I remember Charlie Hart."

"Well, Sweeney's been in Kansas City this week and found out who 'Charlie Hart' really is. His real name is William Quantrill."

"Quantrill! The same Quantrill? The infamous Bushwhacker? Do you mean that man lived right here in Lawrence and we never knew it?"

"Appears that he did. Lots of folks upset about it. People he had fallings-out with are awfully worried now. Quantrill's not a man you'd want to personally offend."

"But he's gone somewhere, hasn't he? Texas, I've heard."

"Yes, but he's back in Missouri now."

"I wish he would stay there," Schooner said, going back in the house to check on her cakes.

The line between Kansas and Missouri was invisible, but might as well have been painted on the very soil in blood. The midafternoon sun beat down through the trees, dappling the horses and their riders. More than four hundred of them, many of the men sporting the red bandanna that characterized their leader. They rode quietly, not talking much among themselves. There was little to say. They knew what they were doing; they were on their way to a mass murder. Some of them had long since forgotten just how many people they had killed. When someone did speak, it was often in a deceptively soft southern drawl.

As they emerged from the woods, their leader stopped, waited for the rest to join him, and said in a voice like a newly honed knife, "We're in Kansas now." A subdued cheer went through the ranks. The man frowned, shaded his pale blue eyes, and looked about. "Find Frank James and Cole Younger for me," he said to his lieutenant.

"Yes, sir, Colonel Quantrill."

"We'll rest here for half an hour," Quantrill ordered. "We'll be in Lawrence by tomorrow."

Schooner stuck the last pin in her hair, glanced around to make sure she hadn't forgotten anything, then set out for the picnic. Henry had to practice once more with the band and had left early, taking the cakes and their own supper hamper with him so she would not have to carry it. As Schooner stepped out the door, Mrs. Lane emerged from her house. "Are you going to the park?" the older woman asked.

"Yes. Will you walk with me? Where is General Lane?"

"He's having a drink with the Union Pacific men," Mrs. Lane said, falling in step with Schooner. "I'm meeting him at the park." Mrs. Lane carried a parasol and tilted it to provide Schooner with some shade. "Have you talked to Mr. Grinnell about the piano?" she asked.

"Not yet. I thought I would wait until the heat breaks and he's feeling more . . . more benevolent!"

"I do wish you would speak to him about it. You are really quite gifted and should have an instrument of your own."

"Someday, perhaps," Schooner said. She couldn't tell Mrs. Lane why she didn't ask Henry—the almost superstitious feeling that she was not entitled to ask for a piano without first providing the son he so desperately wished for. "Did you hear that talk that Quantrill is back from Texas?" Schooner asked, changing the subject. General Lane was one of the leaders of the abolitionist cause, and his wife naturally took a great interest in the war and border disputes.

"Yes, I did. The general is most concerned, especially in light of those women being killed—"

"Women? What do you mean?"

"Oh, haven't you heard? There were ten or eleven women who were associated with Quantrill's men arrested two weeks ago. They'd been acting as spies, it was said, and they were brought in for questioning. The authorities had them in a ramshackle brick building in Kansas City. On Grand Avenue—you might be familiar with it—the building collapsed and the women were buried in the catastrophe. It was a terrible thing. No one's fault, of course, but word is that Quantrill's men are enraged over it. I'm sure they'll take some sort of vengeance, and I'm worried . . ."

"Worried about what?" Schooner asked, alarm creeping into her voice.

Mrs. Lane was not one to mince words. "About us, of course. Lawrence symbolizes the abolitionist cause in this part of the country. Any retaliation is likely to be directed at us."

"But we're well guarded, aren't we? The Fourteenth Kansas Cavalry and the Second Colored Regiment are stationed here to protect us for that very reason."

"My dear, the Second Colored are runaway slaves and dirt farmers—honest-enough men, but hardly soldiers. And the Fourteenth is a gaggle of raw recruits and is on the other side of the Kaw . . ."

"But when the bridge is completed . . ."

"That's just it. When *will* that bridge ever be completed? It seems like they've been working on it since Ezekiel saw the wheel. General Lane is going to talk to the commander of the Fourteenth again about the guns tonight. That would help, if we could get them out of that warehouse."

This was a subject Schooner had often heard discussed. The commander of the Fourteenth Cavalry, knowing how important Lawrence was, had ordered hundreds of rifles and an extra supply of ammunition, but when it arrived, he had locked it all away. The citizens of Lawrence had asked, begged, cajoled, and demanded that the guns be turned over to them, but he had refused to let them be distributed to civilians. There was a great deal of bad feeling about it. "Do you think he can convince the army?" Schooner asked.

"Who can guess? I hope so. Not that I relish the idea of firearms in the home, but I believe with Quantrill back in this part of the country we should be prepared for the worst. What's the matter, dear? You're so pale."

Captain J. A. Pike of the Ninth Kansas Volunteers was commander of a small post thirty miles west of the border. He had eaten an early supper and was leaning back in a chair with his feet propped on a hitching rail. The hot, humid air was so heavy it was almost tangible. He was wishing he had eaten a little less cornbread with his meal as he idly watched a pair of hawks circling near the horizon. Suddenly one of the birds somersaulted, flapped wildly, and dropped to the earth. A second later he heard the rifle report.

He put his feet down, and leaning on the rail, shaded his eyes. They were a long way off, but he could see the men. Too far to identify, but close enough to count. Four columns, possibly three crossing between two rises on the horizon. He squinted, whistled at a passing soldier. "How many are there, you reckon?" he asked.

The soldier watched silently for a while. "Two, maybe three hundred. Could be more. Who do you figure they are, sir?"

Pike shook his head. "Couldn't say, but they ain't Union or I'd know." Where, he wondered, were they heading? Lawrence? Fort Riley? Olathe? No telling, but somebody ought to be doing something about it, and he didn't have enough men. "Take the fastest horse we've got here," he ordered the soldier, "and ride over to the next fort. Report what we've seen and let their commander decide what to do. Tell him I've got forty men I can spare."

The young soldier, overeager and uninformed as to what a horse can do on a hot August evening, set out hell-for-leather. He got nearly two-thirds of the way when the horse collapsed, a lathered, trembling wreck. He had to walk the rest of the way, which took an extra two hours. The commander of the next small post was also understaffed. He sent riders to Fort Riley and Fort Leavenworth and sent a message to Pike to bring his men to join whatever reinforcement could be found. "Ought to be able to set out by dusk," he said.

The band looked wonderful. Governor Robinson and General Lane, the leading citizens of Lawrence, had begun the subscription campaign last spring that earned the money for the new instruments. They were all silver-plated, and the drums matched one another. The men had dressed in light blue coats and dark trousers, and they looked wonderfully impressive.

Schooner sat with Mrs. Lane and they chatted between numbers, all the while fanning away the mosquitoes and the flies. Unfortunate place for a park, Schooner thought, so near the river. The Kaw did not have an odor in the summer which was conducive to picnics. But it was the only open place suitable to the occasion. The half-finished bridge would someday connect to this spot, and some of the soldiers from the opposite bank had ferried across and joined the citizens. It was also quite close to the hotel where the important railroad men were staying, and Lawrence wanted to impress them, for they needed a railroad to pass through the town. It had been proved in other places that cities on railroad lines flourished, while others, only a few miles distant, often withered away.

Schooner wondered why, even on a peaceful evening like this, people couldn't stop talking about the war. She would have thought for one evening they could simply talk about crops and babies and discuss their favorite songs or books or quilt patterns or kinds of dogs—any harmless domestic topic. People did talk about such things, she remembered. But here even the women talked of little but troop movements, supply lines, recruitment figures, and presidential proclamations.

"What's wrong, Mrs. Grinnell?" Emmaline Harper, one of Mrs. Lane's lady friends, had joined them. "You look bored."

Schooner failed to detect the faint note of hostility in the remark and answered honestly, "It's just that I long for more pleasant talk sometimes."

"Well, I suppose to those who are not involved in the war effort, that's a simple request. I personally have a son fighting in this war, and I find it a worthy subject," Mrs. Harper said.

Schooner's temper flared. "I personally have a brother fighting in this war," she mocked. "And he is staying in his own state, not causing trouble halfway across the country!"

"Just what do you mean to imply by that?"

"Only that if you people had not come here, Kansas would not be involved in the war," Schooner said. She had spoken far too frankly; she knew it as soon as the words were out of her mouth, but it had been something she'd thought often and bitterly about.

The band had finished a number, and the audience broke into loud applause, preventing Mrs. Harper from replying to this insult. Schooner rose quickly and walked away. What she had said would be the scandal of Lawrence in a few hours, and Henry would be furious. Why hadn't she just kept quiet? She should have learned by now that she was an "outsider"—one of the few native Kansans in Lawrence and a resident of the town for almost five years, but doomed to be a perpetual outsider among these people.

She found a grassy spot to sit near the riverbank. She could hear the band playing their last number. It was now quite dark, the last streaks of sunset fading to a faint line along the horizon. Someone would tell Henry immediately what a disgraceful thing his wife had said, and they would have to discuss it at length when they got home. Poor Henry would be embarrassed, and she hated being the cause of any unhappiness for him.

Perhaps she would suggest that she wanted to visit Seventrees for a while. She had been home only four or five times since they'd been married, but if she went now, it would give Lawrence time to recover from her blasphemy. Yes, she would do that. Tell Henry that she wanted to go home tomorrow for a short visit. Perhaps by the time she got back her outspokenness would be forgotten.

Tomorrow she would go to Seventrees.

The farmer had been taken from his solitary dinner to guide them. He rode at the front of the columns, glancing back uneasily at the three men behind with their rifles trained on him. It was dark now, and he had never been this far from his home. There was no chance of stealing away in the night, not as closely as they were watching, but certainly they would let him go now. Wouldn't they? He could just ride back along the same road.

He tightened the reins. "What are you stopping for?" the man they called Frank asked.

"Crossroad ahead," the farmer said. "Never been this far."

"You don't know the way?" the man with the pale hair asked. His tone was flat and emotionless.

" 'Fraid not," the farmer answered, trying to sound jovial.

"Well, boys, I guess he can't help us anymore," Quantrill said. "We'll have to find someone else." Then, with a languid motion of his hand, he signaled the man's execution. Three rifles barked at once, and the farmer fell. "Cole, your horse is having some trouble with a shoe. Why don't you take that horse instead? Our guide doesn't need it anymore." He smiled nastily, and several men around him snickered.

"But Emmaline Harper of all people! Why did you have to get into an argument with *her*?"

"It wasn't an argument, Henry. I just lost my head and spoke a little more honestly than I should have."

"A little more honestly? Telling Mrs. Harper she ought to go back where she came from—"

"Now, Henry, that's *not* what I said. You see what the gossips have already done? Look, I was hot and tired and sick to death of hearing about the war all the time. Then she started talking about how I had no stake in it even though my brother is in the army . . . and, well, I just said that if the people hadn't come to settle here from the East, Kansas wouldn't be involved at all. It's true, Henry. It may not be a polite thing to say, I'll admit that, but it *is* true." But one look at his face told her she wasn't doing herself any good. He was as offended by this sentiment as Mrs. Harper had been.

"Henry, I'm sorry I said it. I don't apologize for thinking that way, but I do regret having embarrassed you. I've thought it over, and I want to go away to Seventrees tomorrow for a week or two. By the time I get back, everyone will have forgotten about it."

She had half-expected some disclaimer that this was not necessary, but Henry just thought for a moment and said, "Yes, I think that would be wise. I promised Louis Hunsicker I would ride out and look over his stock in the morning, but I can drive you in around noon. We ought to be able to get there by dark."

She put her arm around his waist. "Thank you, Henry. Let's go to bed now. You look tired. Everything will be all right tomorrow. You'll see."

A little after midnight, Pike and his twenty men assembled with others from surrounding forts and set out in pursuit of Quantrill. They were at least eight hours too late.

11

It was almost daybreak, and the faint predawn light let Quantrill's men pick their way carefully around the city. They circled Lawrence—450 men prepared to avenge the Southern cause. At each street leading out of town, two or three men stopped. No one would get away. They reached the river, where ferry ropes connected a feeble military force to the city. Quantrill dismounted. Eight other men, his commanders, followed suit and surrounded him. He spoke in a low hissing voice as he passed out hand-drawn maps. "Each of you will take your men to the area shown. The marked houses *must* be burned. See to it. The names at the bottom are those who must be killed. Burn or kill anything else you want, but make sure you get the ones on the list. Don't hurt any of the women if you can help it, but get all soldiers and all men and boys over ten."

"Ready to cut the ferry lines?" one of his men asked.

"Yes. Station four men here to shoot anyone who tries to get across the river. Now we'll ride in. That damned nigger regiment is on the way. Kill them first, and make it as quiet as you can."

The first group set out. The Second Colored was assembled in tents just outside of town. Few of them even had time to wake and look out the flaps of their tents before fifty knife-wielding madmen literally rode over them. Within a few minutes they were dead—all but one, a boy of fourteen who had awakened early and had gone into a nearby grove to relieve his bladder. He watched helplessly from behind a tree as his comrades were massacred. No guns were fired, and none of the victims even had the chance to cry out.

It was becoming lighter. Quantrill's men assembled in front of the Eldridge Hotel, which they planned to use as a fortress should any Union troops catch up with them. There were a few whispered last-minute instructions, and then, with a signal from Quantrill himself, the killers erupted in wild rebel yells and began to spread through the city.

Schooner had not slept well in the heat. She kept dreaming of the women in the town talking about her, and even, in one sweat-drenched nightmare near dawn, throwing things at her. She rose sluggishly, put on a light wrapper, and went to get some fresh cold water from the pump in the backyard. As she stood there sipping from the battered cup that hung from the pump by a long chain, she listened to the early-morning bird calls in the still, hot air.

Then she heard a muffled "pop." Then another. She turned her head, trying to tell where the sounds came from and what they were. When she heard the third, she knew with a bone-chilling certainty what it was. She gathered up the skirt of her wrapper and ran into the house. "Henry!" she called. "Henry. Wake up. I hear gunshots."

The words were hardly out of her mouth before Henry had leaped from the bed and was hastily jamming his legs into his trousers. "Where are they coming from?" he asked.

"I don't know. It sounded like they were everywhere. There! Hear those?"

"Damn! I've got only knives in the house. No guns. I'll get one," he said.

"Henry! You're not leaving me? Where are you going?"

"To the armory. Schooner, don't leave the house. No matter what. There might be fires. Start filling buckets with water. I'll be back as soon as I get a gun and some ammunition."

"Henry, don't leave me. Please!"

"I can't protect you and the house with my bare hands. I've got to have one of the guns that idiot locked up. I'll come straight back. I promise."

Schooner was dressing as quickly as he was. She pulled her dress over her head as he disappeared. She dashed to the kitchen, fumbling with her buttons as she went. She pulled buckets and jars and bottles from the shelves and went to the backyard with them. She pumped madly at the reluctant handle. When she looked up for an instant, she saw General Lane next door. Still attired in his nightshirt, he came out his front door and hastily wrenched the nameplate off. He flung it into some bushes as he ran around the side of the house and into the waist-high weeds in a vacant lot behind their houses. He crouched and disappeared.

Just then a group of Quantrill's guerrillas came down the street. Ten or twelve men in broad-brimmed hats, red kerchiefs tied at their necks and carrying guns in both hands. They reined in at Lane's house, consulted a piece of paper, then dismounted and went to the door, trampling Mrs. Lane's flowerbeds.

Mrs. Lane was standing on the porch, her graying hair in disarray. She was wringing her hands and shouting, "What do you ruffians want? Go away, I say. Get out of my yard!"

"We're lookin' for General Lane. You his wife?"

"The general is not here."

"Well, then, I don't suppose you'll mind if we just have a look around."

"I most certainly do mind," Mrs. Lane said in a surprisingly strong voice. "You have no business here—"

But she got no farther, for the men had pushed her aside and entered the house. Schooner stood transfixed. She could hear the men shouting obscenities and overturning furniture as they went through the Lanes' house. One of them had carried a torch, and flames were soon licking at the curtains in several windows. Mrs. Lane had given up trying to stop them and now came outside again. Schooner didn't even need

330

to think about whether it was wise to interfere. Wise or not, she must. "Mrs. Lane, here. Quickly, I have water. Take this. I'll bring more." She lifted a bucket over the picket fence that separated their yards. Mrs. Lane ran over and took the bucket, then disappeared inside the house. Schooner picked up two of her larger containers and followed. The two women ran through the house, past the jeering men and up the steps, where they flung their water at the flames. But it was hopeless. The men had broken up Mrs. Lane's beautiful furniture and tossed it into heaps before setting fire to it.

Mrs. Lane was hurriedly dumping pictures and small personal possessions into a valise. Schooner tried to help her, and suddenly both of them thought at once of the same thing. "The piano!" Schooner shouted above the crackling of flames.

They ran back down the steps. Except for them, the house was empty now. The marauders were in the front yard. Schooner and Mrs. Lane pulled and tugged at the heavy piano, but could not budge it. Mrs. Lane ran out in the front to plead with the men to help her. Amazingly enough, four of them, though killers and arsonists, actually tried to aid in bringing out the piano.

They got the instrument as far as the front door, but the carpet had bunched up underneath and the piano would not fit through without being lifted and tilted on its side. They were not willing to brave the encroaching fire to do this. The ceiling was beginning to burn through, and as sparks began to scorch tiny holes in their clothing, Schooner and Mrs. Lane left the house.

Outside was chaos. Groups of Quantrill's men had been busy setting fires to other houses, and the smoke drifted black and thick through the street. Schooner left Mrs. Lane berating the men in her yard and went back to her own house, which was still untouched. Was Henry back? She ran through the house, calling. But there was no response. She went back out on the front porch, wondering what she should do, for she could not simply stand in the middle of this nightmare and do nothing whatsoever. She heard a commotion at the Ridenauer house on the other side of hers. There were horses prancing nervously where they were tied at the front gate.

Then she saw old Mr. Ridenauer come through the front door. Nightshirted and clearly terrified, he was followed by his son Jake, who wore only a pair of riding trousers. Behind them were four ruffians with guns. Mrs. Ridenauer was clutching and pulling at the arm of one of these men and pleading. "We've done nothing. Nothing. Please leave us alone. We've done nothing to you."

The man pushed her aside roughly. "You're goddamn Yankees, that's enough. Leggo of me. Stand the old bastard up there by that tree," he ordered his men.

The others dragged Mr. Ridenauer across the yard and threw him against the trunk of a sycamore. Mrs. Ridenauer ran toward him, as did her son, but she was stopped and held, arms behind her back, as the men took aim and shot father and son. The two clung together and fell in a bloody heap on the foot of the tree.

Schooner's vision blurred, and she felt hot bile rising in her throat. This was a nightmare. Dear God, it could *not* be real. People couldn't do this. She felt her knees giving out and sat down quickly, turning away from the awful sight in the next yard and covering her ears with her hands. But she could not stop the sounds of gunfire, Mrs. Ridenauer's screams, the crackling of the fires, the neighing of frightened horses. *God in heaven, let me wake. Let this be a dream.*

She had to find Henry. Why wasn't he back? How long had he been gone? Time had lost all meaning. Already it seemed like days, since a lifetime ago, that he had left to get a gun. What if he was dead? What if he, like the Ridenauers, was in a blood-soaked heap somewhere? Or injured? She had to find him. He had told her not to leave the house, but what difference did it make? She could not save the house if they chose to burn it.

"What's your name, lady?" a voice said.

Schooner looked up. It was one of the men who had killed the Ridenauers. He was looking at a paper in his hand. Without knowing quite why, Schooner sensed that a lie would be better than the truth. "Mary Freiler," she said quickly.

He looked down his list, shook his head. "Where's your husband?"

"I haven't got a husband. He died last spring."

The man looked at her for a minute, consulted his list again. Would he believe it? Did he have a name for each house, or only for certain people? "Well, ma'am, you best stay inside, then," he said with courtesy so completely at odds with his recent action that it made Schooner start trembling. "Now, get inside."

Schooner did as she was told, but as soon as he had left, she ran down the walk and toward the business district where

Henry would have gone for the guns. She was no longer reasoning, hardly thinking, just acting out of a primitive sense that she must do *something*. As she turned the corner to Massachusetts Street, the sight was like a vision of hell. Quantrill's men were riding wildly through the streets. Many of them had United States flags tied to the tails of their horses and rode with the reins held in their teeth, freeing them to shoot with both hands.

There were bodies everywhere. Men and boys, many wearing the clothes they had been sleeping in or hastily donned when they heard the noise. Here and there a wounded man tried to crawl or limp away before Quantrill's men, with wild rebel yells, rode them down as if it were a sport. Schooner tried not to see it, but there was nowhere to look away. Buildings were burning everywhere, people in upper windows screamed for help or jumped, crashing onto the sidewalks or landing on bodies.

Just before she got to the tailor's shop, two of the ruffians came swaggering out the front door wearing all new clothes. With them were a pair of clerks who had been forced to help them. One of the men turned, said, "What do we owe you for these, gentlemen?" Then he laughed, a shrill, bone-chilling laugh, pulled a gun out, and shot one young man in the head, the other in the abdomen.

Schooner leaned against a post, bent, and vomited until she was faint. She must not look. She must find Henry. *Find Henry. Find Henry. Find Henry.*

Emmaline Harper was coming toward her. Mrs. Harper and another woman. A tall, heavy woman in a calico bonnet, holding a handkerchief to her face. Dress straining at seams. It wasn't a woman, though. It was Mr. Harper in a dress.

Schooner staggered past them, past the window of a saloon. A shot hit the glass, and the window shattered around her, but she hardly noticed. *Find Henry. Find Henry.* She had to step over a body in front of the dry-goods store. Westley Savage, her friend, Henry's friend, lay face-up, a vast hole in his neck, his dead eyes open in an expression of terror.

Across the street the hardware store was burning fiercely. A man ran out, his clothes aflame. As he threw himself on the ground to smother the flames, some of Quantrill's men picked him up, one to each leg and arm, and heaved him back into the burning building. He screamed once, but did not come back out.

A nightmare. It isn't real. Dear Jesus, it isn't real.

Two of Eldon Wentworth's sons ran toward Schooner. She tried to step out of their way, but her mind no longer had very much control over her body, and she fell heavily against a watering trough. As the older boy neared her, he suddenly flung out his arms and was thrown backward into his brother. At the second shot his head flew apart and a shard from his skull pierced the younger brother's eye. The younger boy screamed but suffered only a moment before another bullet ripped through his chest.

Home. She was supposed to go home this morning. Why hadn't they all gone home while there had still been time? Now they couldn't. The principled Easterners lay bleeding and scorched in the dirt. What good were their high ideals doing them now? *Dead. Dead.*

Schooner backed away from the wreckage of human flesh which had been two healthy boys only seconds ago. Behind her were three men lying in a vast pool of blood in the street. One of them opened his eyes and blinked. He was alive. She must help. She ran to him, knelt, and tried to pull him out from under another body that was across his legs. "No," the man whispered. "Leave me. Let them think I'm dead." He closed his eyes again.

"What are you doing?" A horse and rider cast their shadow over her. A wild-looking man with greasy shoulder-length hair looked down on her.

"It's my husband," Schooner lied. "He's dead. I must take him home."

The man dismounted. He didn't even seem to question her diagnosis. "Why don't you put him into that hand cart?" he said, indicating a wheelbarrow up against the side of the nearest building. "Then get out of here before you get the same."

Schooner got the cart, and with a strength she didn't know she possessed, she managed to get the wounded stranger into it. She lifted the handles and began to push the cart down the middle of the street. Another guerrilla saw her and began to follow her. "We are Fiends from Hell. Fiends from Hell," he chanted maniacally. "Get out of here you goddamn nigger-thievin' Yankee bitch, or the Fiends from Hell will get you."

Schooner's heart was in her throat. She pushed the laden wagon faster while the man continued to dog her steps, chanting obscenities. Finally he lost interest in her, and a thin blond woman in a flowered nightgown ran toward her. "Melvin! Melvin!" the woman shouted, and threw herself on the man in the cart.

Schooner grabbed the woman's arm in a firm grip and pulled her away. "Keep quiet," she said. "He's alive, but you mustn't let them know."

The woman quickly got herself under control. "Thank you, ma'am," she said, and took up the handles of the cart.

Suddenly Schooner realized that she'd gotten turned around and was back where she'd started. Thick black smoke was filling the street, and timbers were falling everywhere. The roar of a hundred fires boomed in her ears. Something in a store near her was exploding in the heat, sending glass and debris flying. Everyone who could run was doing so. Everywhere the air was thick with the screams of the dying and bereaved. A high, thin keening from a hundred throats laced through the bass booming of the fires. The rebel yells, demonically gleeful, went on and on.

She couldn't find Henry in this. She knew that now. She must go home, so he could find her. She ran back to a neighborhood barely recognizable, so many of the homes were glaring infernos. But her house still stood. She went to the pump again and with her last bit of strength she worked the handle. As the cool water began to flow, she stuck her head under the stream. She hardly knew why she did it, but it worked. Her mind cleared some, her ragged breathing slowed a little.

She glanced around. On one side the Lanes' house was nearly gone. The roof and floors had collapsed and the walls were blackened shells, still glittering orange in places. On the other side, Ridenauer's house was still blazing and bits of burning material were drifting down around her. She felt a hot sensation on her shoulder and slapped at a spark. Some of the buckets she had filled earlier were still sitting there, and she dumped them over herself, wetting her dress against fire.

She thought she noted a movement. A flutter in a window. She squinted into the smoke-filled air. Yes. An upper window. *Henry!* Then a face appeared.

Henry!

She almost shouted it, but stopped herself. She dashed into the house. He met her at the foot of the steps and folded her into a crushing embrace. "I couldn't get a gun. I got back through the field behind. You weren't here . . ."

"I was looking for you. Henry, go away from here. They won't harm me, but you must get away."

She urged him toward the back door, but she could see men now in the field. Men in red bandannas riding back and forth through the tall grass to flush any men who might be hiding there. "The cellar," she said.

"I couldn't fit," Henry protested. The summer before, Henry had dug out an area under one corner of the kitchen so that Schooner would have a place to store potatoes in the winter. It was only three feet deep and a little wider, but they had laughingly called it the cellar.

"You have to," Schooner said, pulling away the table that sat on top of the trapdoor.

"I don't like leaving you alone," Henry said as he stepped down into the hole.

"I told some of them I was a widow. They believed me. As long as they think there is no man associated with this house, I'll be safe. Please, Henry, get your head down. The men out back are getting closer."

Someone shouted something in the backyard. Henry ducked as Schooner slammed the trapdoor down and hastily pulled the table back over it. She yanked a cloth from a drawer and covered the table. The draped fabric helped conceal the line of the door.

Just then the back door was flung open. The man she had once known as Charlie Hart stood there. His ice-blue eyes glittered insanely. "Where's Grinnell?"

"Grinnell?" Schooner asked stupidly.

"Yeah, that horse doctor. Goddamn horse went lame after he fixed it up."

Was he wanting to kill Henry just because his horse went lame? The man was mad—but of course he was mad. The whole world had gone mad with blood lust.

"He's dead," Schooner said, recalling her earlier lie. "Last spring—a fever."

But it had worked on the other man because he still possessed a shred of reason. Quantrill had lost all touch with reality long before now. Truth, seeming truth, and lies were indistinguishable to him. "Search the place," he ordered the men standing outside, and they flooded in. They went through the house like an evil whirlwind, overturning furniture, yanking open closets and flinging the contents onto the floor. They ripped the doors off the kitchen cabinets and swept the dishes to the floor. They tore the drapes from the windows, toppled the cabinet where Henry kept his drugs, and even took the pictures from the walls.

Schooner edged back toward the kitchen table. She sat down, folded her arms on the table, and put her head down as if weeping. She prayed desperately that she could keep them from removing the cloth and seeing the door underneath.

One by one the men came back to the kitchen. "Cain't find him, but there's still a man's clothes in the bedroom. She ain't no widow, or if she is, she got a man friend," one of them said. Schooner did not look up. She began to cry in earnest.

"I reckon if he's in here we'll have to smoke him out, eh, boys?" Quantrill said. His voice was like cold grease.

They'd left a torch stuck in the ground outside. Now they brought it in. Schooner could hear them throwing furniture into a pile, and in a moment smoke began to come into the kitchen. The men went outside, leaving her in the house.

She watched through the window as Quantrill left. But three or four others stayed in the yard behind, watching presumably for Henry to come out. Schooner bent, whispered, "Henry?"

A muffled reply.

"I'm all right. They've set a fire, though. Stay there. I'll try to put it out."

She went outside. "What are you doing?" one of the guards asked.

Schooner walked to the outside pump. "Putting out your fire," she said.

"No, ma'am, you ain't. We got our orders."

Dear God! She couldn't leave Henry to burn in there. She turned to go back inside. "What you going in there for?" the man asked.

"I want to save some things," she said as calmly as she could.

"Well, I reckon you can do that."

She went back to the kitchen. It seemed safe enough to assume that the men had no intention of coming back inside. She pulled away the table and opened the trapdoor. Henry emerged, filthy and pale. "I told them I wanted to save some things. They won't let me get water to put out the fire. They're waiting to see if you're hiding in here. Oh, Henry. How can you get out? There are men front and back now. Wait! I think I know . . ." A brief memory of something that had happened earlier flashed through her mind. When the men were pushing Mrs. Lane's piano toward the door, the parlor rug had ruched up into heavy folds. "Wait! I think perhaps . . ."

Within a few minutes Schooner was backing out the kitchen door, struggling to pull a carpet. Henry was underneath it, crouched down and crawling. One of the men in the yard started forward. Schooner turned, and a moment of panic turned her blood cold. "No!" she shouted. "You've done enough damage. This belonged to my grandmother. Keep your filthy hands off it!" She was screaming as if she'd lost her senses, and the man stepped aside and merely watched as she strained and tugged at the heavy rug. Every inch of progress took a terrible toll. Her muscles burned and cramped with the effort, and her fingernails bent and split to the quick as she yanked. But she kept on. Into the yard now. Pulling, pulling, pulling.

She could see Henry's form. It was a wonder that they didn't discern why the one great fold in the center of the carpet kept its shape. But they had lost interest in her attempt to save her "grandmother's" carpet.

Pull.

Pull.

Finally she reached her destination—a clump of bushes at the side of the yard that were safely out of the way of the fire. She dropped to the ground, whimpering with exhaustion. The house was fully in flames now, orange tongues of fire licking from the windows, filling the sky above with another black cloud. It was a sunny morning somewhere, but it looked like night in Lawrence.

Apparently the men were satisfied that anyone who might have been in the house was dead, and without a backward glance they strolled away to where they'd left their horses. "They're leaving," Schooner whispered to Henry under the rug.

She did not move or speak again for a long time. Finally the sound of their voices faded and she said, "I think it's safe now."

Henry crawled out carefully and crouched beside her. "If I can get across the field . . ."

"Hey! Here he is! Under the goddamn rug!"

They'd returned. Schooner and Henry stood.

"You must think you're pretty damned clever, lady. Well, this is what clever'll get you." The man leveled his gun, trained it on Henry, and fired.

Schooner was holding her husband's arm when the bullet struck him. The force knocked them both back, and Schooner fell into a black pit of unconsciousness.

She must get up early and pack some things to take along to Seventrees. She'd stay a week or so, and when she came back, everyone would have forgotten about what she'd said to Emmaline Harper. She'd take her new blue dress and maybe she could get some shoes in Kansas City while she was so close. She'd get something nice for Henry, too. A surprise.

It was so hot already. Terribly hot. It must be morning. She'd get up without disturbing Henry. She turned toward him. Just a few more minutes' sleep, then she'd get up. She put her arms across his chest.

Sticky.

There was something hot and sticky on his chest.

She opened her eyes, squinting against the glare of sunlight. Henry was on the ground beside her, his mouth open, his eyes open. How could he sleep that way? What were they doing outside?

Then for one agonizing moment the whole morning unfolded again and she realized the truth. Henry was dead. They'd killed him. Was she dead too? She hoped so.

She moved a little, rolled away from Henry's dead embrace. No. She was in pain—she couldn't quite tell where—but she was alive.

It was too much to bear. Doors and windows in her mind slammed shut. All the horror, the pain, the sorrow—all of it must be safely locked away where it couldn't hurt her. What was left was a small, sensible shadow of Schooner.

She walked uncertainly to the pump, repeated the earlier ritual of pouring water over herself, and watched calmly as Henry's blood bled down her dress, making a pink puddle in the dirt. Then she walked to the shed and got out a sturdy shovel and began to dig a grave. She would bury Henry.

It was over now. The rebel yells no longer sliced the hot air, only distant sobbing. No gunshots, no hoofbeats. No one left to dig the grave but her.

She dug for nearly three hours, unaware of the blisters that formed and broke on her hands. She stopped only twice to get a drink and pour cool water over her sweat- and blood-soaked dress. People passed in the street. People as numbed and inhuman as she was. Weeping women carrying babies and searching for the bodies of their men.

The church bells were ringing as Schooner finished her grim task. She knelt and patted the dirt down firmly over Henry's grave. There were no flowers except the sunflowers growing in the field. She picked some of these, noticing impersonally that the palms of her hands were bleeding.

Mother would have a cure for that, she thought. She would have to remember to ask about it when she got home. She laid the sunflowers on the mound of earth and whispered, "Good-bye, Henry."

She walked away without looking back at the black shell of the house she had lived in with Henry. She went along Massachusetts Street toward the Kaw. The bodies were gone now, as were all the buildings. No, there was one store left standing, and one of the five hotels.

She could hear the shrieks of grief coming from the Methodist church on the next street, where dozens of men and boys were laid out. Dead now, all of them. Merely waiting to be identified and buried. Who would put flowers on all those graves? Were there enough flowers in this world—or the next—for such an excess of graves?

There had been almost two hundred men and boys slaughtered in Lawrence, but none of Quantrill's "Fiends from Hell" had died. People would say later that there were no women killed. But Schooner knew better. Mary Grinnell had died that hot, bloody August morning.

A woman passing her on the street spoke. "You're the one who saved Melvin, aren't you? He's going to live, thanks to you. I don't even know your name."

Schooner stared at her, not quite sure what the woman was talking about. But she must be polite. If she were rude, people would remember it when Mrs. Harper told what she'd said last night. "Schooner Freiler," she answered.

"Where are you going?"

Schooner turned a vacant smile on her. "Home," she said, pointing toward the Kaw. "I'm going home."

12

A rider got to Seventrees at noon. He was immediately surrounded by crowds of citizens alarmed by his lathered horse and horrified demeanor. He collapsed in front of the trading post. In broken phrases between gulps of whiskey he told them of the devastation of Lawrence. "Terrible, terrible!" he kept repeating, as if saying it might make it less so.

"What of the Grinnells?" Maggie asked, her voice shaking with dread.

He shook his head. "I don't know, ma'am. But the town needs help. They need food and shelter and strong backs to dig the graves."

Torchy LeSage, stooped and white-haired now, opened the doors of the post and began boxing up provisions. Maggie rushed home and got down bottle after bottle of her precious coneflower juice to treat burns. Gerald helped her bag all of her supply of cattail down for dressing wounds. Quincy Clay, who had said nothing while he listened to the rider's account, rushed home, where Beatrice met him on the front steps. She had baby Ned on her hip. "Quincy, what is it? Why are all those people at the post? What's happened?"

"Lawrence has been attacked and burned," he said, dashing past her. "Where's Jack Q?"

"Burned! Schooner? What of Schooner?"

"I don't know," he said, voice rising. "We're going to Lawrence to find out. Where's Jack Q, I asked!"

"Eating breakfast," Beatrice answered just as her brother came out of the kitchen.

Quincy quickly repeated what he'd heard, and in a very few minutes the two shaken men were on their way. Beatrice stood on the front porch watching them ride out of Seventrees with a large group of others intent on helping the stricken town upriver. In those few minutes she realized something she'd never noted before. Desperate anxiety in Quincy's voice when he spoke of Schooner that said more than his words. Perhaps she was wrong, she told herself. Jack Q had sounded just as worried. But that was small comfort,

341

for Beatrice had long suspected that Jack Q was in love with Schooner. *Please, God, let me be wrong about Quincy*, she thought as she stood on the porch with tears coursing down her cheeks and spilling on Ned's hair.

Maggie insisted on going with the men. Gerald tried to stop her, but she was adamant. "They need help. I am able to help," she said simply. To the everlasting shock of several of her neighbors' wives, she donned a pair of Gerald's trousers, a blue plaid shirt, and the broad-brimmed hat she wore to work outside. Mounted on their best horse, her medicines packed into bulging saddlebags, she was a handsome sight. She was in her fifties now, but still slim and straight. Her glossy honey-colored hair was only highlighted by the encroaching strands of white and her movements were as lithe and sure as ever. When they were ready to go, she spurred her horse and rode with the energetic grace of a girl for the forty dusty, hot miles of road to Lawrence.

Before they were halfway, they could see shreds of smoke hanging over the burned-out town, and when they were still five miles away they could smell it. The scene that met them when they got to Lawrence was appalling. Maggie had intended to ride straight to Schooner's house, but the destruction was so complete she couldn't even identify where it had been, and she had ridden by it twice before a resident was able to tell her that the blackened shell before her had been the Grinnells' home.

"Where are the Grinnells?" Quincy asked the woman who had pointed out the house.

She shrugged. "Where is anyone?"

The rest of the group from Seventrees had gone directly to the Methodist church to distribute the goods they'd brought. Only Schooner's parents, Quincy, and Jack Q had gone to look for her. They dismounted, tied their horses to a singed post, and walked around the house. In the back there was a heavy rug, a few kitchen utensils by the pump, and a mound of dirt with wilted sunflowers laid on top.

Gerald stood at the foot of the grave. "She must have buried Henry," he said. They'd been meeting people along the road who all told them no women had been killed, and they were eager to believe that this must be Henry's grave, not Schooner's.

They picked their way back through the blackened rubble of Lawrence to the church. But no one knew what had become of Mary Grinnell. Ironically, they spoke to the one person who did know, but she did not recognize the name as belonging to the woman who had called herself Schooner Freiler.

After an hour of fruitless searching and questioning, Maggie said, "She must have started for home. But which way?"

Quincy said, "Maggie, you and Gerald follow the road back. We must have passed her along the way. She might have stepped into the woods to rest. Jack Q and I will follow the river, in case she went that way."

"Quincy's right, Maggie," Gerald said. "We have to be home when she gets there. She could have gotten a ride on a passing wagon or even a boat, if she went by the riverside. She's not here anymore, and there's nothing more we can do in Lawrence."

As soon as Maggie and Gerald left, the two young men began the laborious search along the banks of the Kaw. Jack Q, trained since childhood by his father, knew how to read the bending of a twig, the tiny puddles that seeped into footsteps at the bank, or a leaf turned the wrong way. He soon had them on the trail of someone who had walked along the riverbank only hours before. "Was it Schooner?" Quincy asked.

"I can't tell that unless she's stopped and carved her name in a tree trunk along the way," he answered, attempting a lightness neither of them felt. "But it *is* a small woman whose hands are bleeding. Didn't you see the print on those leaves back there where she'd slipped and fallen?"

"Hurry!" Quincy said.

"Calm down. Your mental state has to be better than hers if we're to help her," Jack Q replied.

It was dark when they saw the faint flicker of candlelight coming from a ramshackle cabin set among some willows. There was a bony goat tethered by the door, and some dingy clothes hung on a line between two trees outside the one oil-papered window. Their pistols drawn in case there were Bushwhackers inside, Quincy and Jack Q knocked at the door.

There was no response at first, only a breathless silence. They knocked again and a woman's voice called nervously, "Who's there?"

"We mean no harm," Jack Q answered. "We're looking for a woman who might have come this way today. We're her family," he added, not thinking this was not true.

The door opened a crack and the muzzle of a hunting rifle

343

showed. They were carefully scrutinized for a moment before the door opened farther. The interior of the cabin was as shabby as the outside, and in the corner, on a filthy pallet on the floor, was a huddled lump the men knew must be Schooner. "Oh, my God!" Quincy muttered, and quickly knelt beside her.

She would have been unrecognizable to any but her closest friends. Her dress was tattered and singed and had blood caked on the sleeves and skirt. She was filthy and sweat-soaked, and her fair hair in such a wild tangle that it almost concealed her face. She was sleeping on her side with her burned, blistered hands balled into tight knots under her chin.

"I done what I could for her," the woman whined. "But my man's gone upriver and I didn't know—"

"Thank you," Jack Q said. "We're grateful to you. How far are you from the road?"

"It's jest up over yonder hill."

"Do you have a wagon we can borrow? Quincy, don't touch her hands," he added. The woman didn't answer, and Jack Q tried to reassure her. "Do you know the Freilers at Seventrees?"

"Them German folks what makes the potions? Sure, who don't?"

"This young woman is Maggie Freiler's daughter. Please let us use your wagon. We'll bring it right back, along with anything else you want from the trading post."

"I thought you said you was her family," the woman said suspiciously. "You don't sound German to me. How am I to know I'd ever see my wagon again? We're poor folk . . ."

Jack Q nodded. Of course the women had no reason to trust them. He knelt on the other side of Schooner. "She's sleeping so soundly it worries me, but her breathing is regular and she doesn't seem to have a fever. I think it's just as well we don't move her yet."

"You may be right," Quincy said. "But the others ought to be told we've found her. Maggie's probably tearing up the road by now. I'll stay here with her, if you want to ride back."

Jack Q considered this for a moment. "I think my horse has a rock in his hoof. I can't see to get it out tonight. Maybe you better go instead."

Quincy was reluctant to leave Schooner, and he hadn't noticed Jack Q's horse favoring a hoof, but he'd never known his brother-in-law to say anything that wasn't strictly true, so he agreed. "You don't mind sitting with her for a few hours?"

"No," Jack Q said grimly. "I don't mind. Bring a woman with you. Maggie, preferably."

Jack Q sat by Schooner the long night, his eyes never leaving her face. He rested his hand on her forehead from time to time, checking for fever. He held her tightly in his arms when she cried out and flailed at the demons who invaded her dreams. Once she woke, looked up at him, and sobbed, "Help me, Jack Q, help me." By dawn he was exhausted with the effort of wanting to help her and finding nothing he could do. He could not even treat her injured hands until he had salve. He certainly could do nothing for her tortured mind except to be near her and whisper meaningless comfort.

The sun was barely up when Quincy returned. He had Schooner's half-sister, Morning Wish, with him. "I couldn't find Maggie," he explained. "She'd gone back out looking."

Morning Wish ran everyone out of the cabin, then removed Schooner's wretched clothing and checked for other physical injuries. There were none of lasting consequence. Blisters, a few burns, and a bad scratch on her leg. Schooner, weary and disoriented, made no objections when Morning Wish gently pried open her fingers to examine her hands. "How did you do this, Schooner?" Morning Wish asked. She didn't want to answer as much as she wanted to know if Schooner was aware of what had happened and where she was.

"I don't know. Digging, I think. Henry's grave . . ." Tears started running down her dirty cheeks.

"You did the right thing," Morning Wish assured her. "Do you know where you are?"

Schooner shook her head negatively, wincing at the pain it caused.

"Do you know who I am?"

"Morning Wish," Schooner mumbled.

Morning Wish wanted to keep her talking, but not about the events of the past day. "How old am I, Schooner?" she asked as she began to gently dab at the dirt on Schooner's hands.

Schooner cringed at the pain, took a long shuddering breath, and said, "Sixteen. Seventeen this month."

"Good. Now, hold very still. I have to pour some water over your hands. I've got it warm, so it will hurt only a little. Then we'll put some of Mother's medicine on and go home.

She's waiting for you. No . . . don't pull back. She went back out looking for you, but she'll be back by the time we get there." Morning Wish chattered brightly while she carefully dried Schooner's hands and put a soothing salve on the palms. Every now and then she would ask a question. "Do you remember the day of the windwagon? What fun we had then. What was that man's name? The funny captain." She was determined to keep Schooner alert, but concentrating on things other than the recent tragedy.

"Do you want me to comb your hair and wash your face?" Morning Wish asked. "Jack Q and Quincy are with me, and everyone will want to see you when you get home."

Schooner shook her head. "It doesn't matter," she said numbly.

"It *does* matter. Do you remember the day Addie came home? After Ernest was killed?" Morning Wish had a small hand mirror in the pack of medicines. She held it up to Schooner. "Look at yourself," she said brutally. "Is this what you want me to take home to Mother?"

Schooner gazed at the bedraggled being in the mirror for a long moment before she recognized it as herself. For the first time she began to cry in earnest—long, dry, racking sobs. "They killed Henry. I almost saved him. They shot him. He didn't even have a gun. I buried him. I . . ."

Morning Wish put her arms around Schooner until she was calmer. "It's over now. You did all you could. You did the right things, Schooner. We're going home now. Everything will be all right at home."

Outside the cabin, Jack Q paced restlessly. His hair, the brilliant orange-red his father's had been twenty years earlier, caught the early shards of sunlight and flamed. He had a great deal on his mind. Schooner, of course, but there was nothing he could do for her. He might spare his sister some pain, however. But that meant speaking frankly to Quincy, and part of the bond between them rested on the things they did *not* talk about.

"Do you think she'll be all right?" Quincy asked.

"Who?"

"Schooner, of course. Who else would I be thinking of?"

Jack Q debated with himself for a moment, then answered, "Beatrice."

"Just what do you mean by that?" Quincy bristled.

"If you two are going to argue, do it later," Morning Wish

cut in from the door of the cabin. "Help me get Schooner into the wagon and we'll go home."

As they rode slowly along the bumpy track to Seventrees, Jack Q and Quincy did not speak. Jack Q wondered whether, in all honesty, he had been trying to protect his sister or his own interests.

The Freilers had seen the mental near-destruction of a family member before, and they'd learned from it. Years before they had, with loving sympathy, allowed Addie to become a self-sorrowing vegetable. Only the dull-witted Adams Clay had sensed what should be done. From the night he dressed her and brought her to Beatrice's birthday party, she had improved. She'd never regained the sparkling rebelliousness she'd been born with, but she had become a happy person. Wife to Adams and subsequently contented mother to three children in five years, she was a testimony to what could happen to a woman forced to live life rather than grieve for it.

Maggie, therefore, welcomed Schooner with tears and sympathy and put her to bed for a week. She and Morning Wish and Gerald took turns sitting by her, listening when she cared to talk, handing her handkerchiefs when she needed to cry, and providing companionable silence when it was required. But after a week, it was over.

"We're going to have a memorial service for Henry," Maggie announced. "We will put up a tablet on the bluff. You must have a decent dress to wear."

"No, Mother. I can't go out. I don't want this—"

"You can go out and you will. It won't be any easier next week than tomorrow. A service in memory of Henry is the least he deserves. He had other friends here in Seventrees. Now, get up. I have a dress of Morning Wish's that might fit, with some alterations."

Schooner was too angry to notice the tears in her mother's eyes. But the anger itself was a hot, clean emotion that began the long process of diluting her grief and horror.

Morning Wish had another idea. "Draw what it was like," she told Schooner, placing some pieces of charcoal and sheets of paper by the bedside.

Schooner protested this was both morbid and ridiculous. "I can't hold anything with my hands bandaged this way. I have no talent, and besides, who would want to see such pictures?"

"Nobody," Morning Wish said. She left the paper and charcoal.

Another darned Indian superstition, Schooner thought crankily. Wouldn't Morning Wish ever just be one of them and stop working at being an outsider? But late that night, when the images of Quantrill and the flames and the bodies were most intense, Schooner blotted her tears on her bandaged hands and got out of bed. She sat up until dawn, painfully drawing the pictures that haunted her mind. They were childish, clumsy drawings of no artistic merit. Not pretty pictures, certainly, some not even recognizable, but they transferred the horror to paper. When Morning Wish came in with a breakfast tray, Schooner showed her the pictures.

"Tell me about them," Morning Wish said with the enigmatic calm she'd inherited from her Indian forebears. "Is the burning house yours? This must be Henry's grave, isn't it? Is this one a piano?"

Schooner told her all of it, and later in the morning they borrowed a boat and went out on the river. Sitting in the middle of the Kaw, Schooner took the pictures one by one, tore them to tiny bits, and threw them in the water. Her hands throbbed with the effort. "Help me tear them, Morning Wish," she asked.

"No. *You* must do it."

When it was done, the daughters of Gerald Freiler, so different and so completely in accord for the first time, sat for a long while on the placid river watching the little white pieces of paper drift and tumble until none of them remained.

"The pictures are gone now," Morning Wish said.

Schooner looked at her dark-skinned half-sister and thought: *She looks like a high priestess, and so she should. Her magic has power.* "Yes," Schooner agreed. "The pictures are gone."

They stood again on the bluff overlooking Seventrees. Reverend Whittacre, an old man now and still refusing to acknowledge the heat of a Kansas summer, wore a fine high-collared shirt and read the service. "Take unto your bosom, O Lord, the soul of thy departed servant, Henry . . ."

Schooner, pale and composed, stood between Maggie and Gerald. She looked past the memorial tablet at the others who had come to the service. Beatrice, thinner and more frail than ever, was standing very straight, tears running silently down her pale cheeks. To her left, Quincy dug into his pocket, pulled out a clean handkerchief, and handed it to her. He looked at his wife, at Reverend Whittacre, and at the marble tablet—but he did not look at Schooner. Jack Q was on Beatrice's right, and Schooner thought fleetingly how odd it seemed to see him perfectly still. He seemed to always be in motion, always busy, darting like a water bug. His clear blue gaze caught hers for a moment in silent reassurance. There was something very comforting in his presence.

". . . who gave his life in service to thy works and word, O Lord above . . ."

The tiny cemetery was growing year by year. Once it had been a favorite lookout point, the place where Maggie and Gerald had first seen the site that would become home to all of them. Later, Quincy's brother John, killed as a child in a wagon accident, had been buried here. Then Schooner's brother Benjamin, and a few years later the flood victims. Beatrice and Jack Q's Gran'mère Charron and Morning Wish's mother. Little Smile had a pretty red granite marker, and Morning Wish kept it well tended, planting new flowers around it each spring.

Next to Little Smile's grave were those of the Hallecks. The unlamented Ernest who had nearly destroyed Addie; the little girl Violet who had died in the flood; and the child Iris, who had died of the cholera with so many others. That had been the year the majority of graves were dug. Helmut Clay's, Torchy's second wife, and so many other neighbors.

". . . and help us prepare, Heavenly Father, for the day when we too may join thee. Amen."

"Amen," they all echoed.

One by one they came to Schooner. They patted her shoulder, touched her arm, and tried to express their sympathy before drifting away. "Schooner, I'm so sorry," Beatrice said, hugging her with fierce strength.

Schooner knew Beatrice was imagining how she would feel if she lost Quincy. But Schooner *had* lost Quincy, and now she'd lost Henry as well. "Thank you, Bea," she said.

There was an embarrassed moment when no one knew what to say next. Maggie said sensibly, "Jack Q, how is your father doing? I haven't had time to visit him in the last two weeks."

"I'm afraid he's not well, but he refuses to admit it and talks constantly about building an addition to the house this winter. We suggested hiring a nice, ugly widow woman to

349

nurse him, but he said he'd rather go back to trapping in the Dakotas than endure that."

They all chuckled fondly and turned away from the cemetery to walk down the hill. Schooner went slowly, and Maggie slowed her pace as well. When the others were well ahead, Maggie said, "I'm sorry James couldn't get away from his regiment in time to be here, but I'm sure he could be excused from duty if you'd like."

Schooner was perplexed by this. "Why would he do that?"

"I thought you might like to go away. Go east, perhaps, see things. To Europe, if you'd like. You've never been anywhere, and James could escort you."

"My sorrows are inside me, Mother. You know I can't run away from them. Besides, I love this place as though it were a person. Seventrees is my home and haven. The last thing I want to do is leave. But, Mother, I can't be idle. May I work for you? I remember most of the formulas, I think."

"I can't think of anything I'd like better, but the business has changed, I warn you. We have many new products, and it's much more complex . . ." Her voice trailed off as they came within sight of their house. "There's Woody at the door. I wonder . . ."

Woody hurried to meet them with the news that the caretaker at the Kansas City warehouse had gotten drunk during the night and had staggered into a shelf laden with medicines that were being shipped out at the end of the week. "Nobody wanted to bother you folks," he said, "but somebody's got to go down and straighten things out."

"Schooner, are you ready to start working today?" Maggie asked.

"Yes, I guess I am."

"Good. Then let's get to the warehouse and take inventory."

And that quickly and unceremoniously, Schooner passed from one stage of her life into another.

13

Maggie's suggestion to visit Europe didn't appeal to Schooner, but Torchy heard about it and he took it to heart. By Christmas he had declared that he was going to France in the spring. It was the country of his origin and language, he said, and he wanted to see it with his own eyes before he died. This pronouncement caused quite a stir, but he was determined, and no warnings about the state of his health or his age could change his mind. Jack Q, eventually convinced that this was not just an idle threat, agreed to accompany his father on the long trip. "Quincy can handle the trading by himself," he told Maggie and Schooner. "We've talked for a long time about making some European contacts for the medicines, and I can take care of that."

"You really think we can sell Freiler's Cures in Europe!" Schooner said. She found it quite extraordinary to think that the home remedies they had been making, first at their kitchen stove, then at a small separate building behind the house, and now in the Kansas City factory, should find their way into French homes.

"We can't know without trying. I hear that things American are all the rage. Can you have samples of all your products ready for me by April? You'll have to relabel most of them in French, and we'll design a new label with a buffalo or something wild-westish on it."

Gerald decided to go as far as New York with them. He had distant cousins in Germany with whom he had corresponded sporadically over the years, and had received a letter saying that they were immigrating to America. He decided he would meet their boat and see to it that they got settled without being cheated along the way. "It's an outrage the way newcomers are robbed," he said. "Besides, I've got friends in the East I can introduce them to."

"You *had* friends in the East a long time ago," Maggie warned.

"The old German communities don't change. Why don't you come with me, Maggie? It would be a nice trip."

351

"Yes, Mother. You deserve a rest," Schooner added.

But Maggie shook her head. "When I left, I left for good. There is no one I want to see—no one I could visit, anyway," she added, thinking of her Amish cousins. "Gerald, how will the school function without you?"

Once the Indians left, the mission school had been turned over to the state, and for several years Gerald had run it. "I've got that young mathematics teacher who can oversee things," he said.

The spring seemed to last only days, in the rush of preparations. It was, for a short time, almost possible to forget that the country was in the throes of a civil war. After the destruction of Lawrence, the center of war activities seemed to move away from Kansas and eastern Missouri, almost as if to give the beleaguered residents a respite before the next shattering blow fell. The war was a constant topic of conversation among the residents of Seventrees and those who passed through, but Schooner got into the habit of slipping away from such conversations.

It was hardest for her when her brother, James, was home. Since childhood she had been close to James, but he seemed different to her now that he was a soldier. He was proud of himself, his uniform, his gun and equipment, and he longed for battle. "All this damned training and marching, and we've never been in a real engagement," he complained, and Schooner was appalled. She tried to explain to him what it was like to be surrounded by the madness of battle, but she ended up crying and distraught and he still didn't truly grasp what she was attempting to express.

"You want me to desert or something?" he asked.

"No. I just can't bear to hear you looking forward to battle."

"I've spent two years of my life preparing for it, Schooner. Can't you understand that?"

"I don't want to understand it!" she shouted.

Thereafter they were both careful about what subjects came up, and Schooner was sorry such a barrier had come between them.

At the end of April the travelers and the medicines were ready. Their route was to be overland to St. Louis; then they would swing far to the north to avoid traveling through the border states. Torchy had sold his house in Saint Louis some years before and purchased in its place a grand house with many outbuildings south of the city, overlooking the river. He wanted all his good friends from Seventrees to stay there for a week before departure and see them off. Maggie and Quincy protested that business called; Beatrice objected to making the trip with little Ned; but Katrin Clay took Torchy's side, and between them they brushed away all these practical considerations. Consequently, the leading citizens of Seventrees found themselves enjoying a week of festivities in Saint Louis.

The day after they arrived, Schooner went to explore the woods her bedroom window overlooked. Torchy, old woodsman that he was, had resisted the temptation to "prettify" the natural growth and had insisted that the gardener merely keep the paths walkable and plant a few brightly colored wildflowers where they could be seen easily. The result was nature at its most enjoyable.

Once out of sight of the graceful mansion, Schooner looped up her skirts and gave herself over to an abandonment she'd not felt for a good many years. She went running and skidding down a steep path and leaped the tiny stream that meandered through the woods. She startled a rabbit and laughed as it gracefully bounded away through a thicket of wild phlox. She came to a little clearing where the grass had been cut short and several wooden benches set up in a semicircle overlooking a breathtaking vista of the Mississippi and the distant city of Saint Louis.

She sat down, not on a civilized bench, but on the ground. I'm a twenty-four-year-old childless widow, she thought. How grim it sounded. And yet, to her own surprise, she didn't feel grim. She felt quite youthful and reasonably contented. She'd thrived on the hard work during the winter and spring, and if she still felt pangs of longing and confusion when she saw Quincy and Beatrice together . . . well, that was not the worst pain a person could be afflicted with. She had, in fact, grown almost accustomed to it, like a physical complaint that one learned to avoid aggravating when possible and endure otherwise. Fortunately for her, Quincy spent a great deal of time away from Seventrees, and she and Beatrice had found time to be together without the strain she'd once felt.

As if materializing out of her thoughts, Quincy came along the path and into the clearing. Schooner sensed his presence before he spoke, and whirled around to face him. "You look like a girl, sitting there with your skirts spread out and your hair loose," he said, and she felt herself blushing.

"I feel like a girl. Isn't that silly?" she answered.

Quincy sat down on one of the benches, leaned back, and stretched his arms along the backrest. "You'll never be old, Schooner," he said easily. "I saw you come into the woods, and I followed you. We haven't had a chance to talk alone for years. Do you mind?"

"I'm not sure. What do you want to talk about?"

"Us."

"There is no 'us,' Quincy. There is you and your wife, and there is me."

He ignored this. "Don't run away," he said as she made a motion to rise. "I'm not trying to make you uncomfortable. Quite the opposite. You remember the night of Bea's party? The night you agreed to marry Henry?"

"Oh, yes," Schooner said softly. She could still feel what it was to stand on the porch, wrapped in Quincy's strong embrace, aching with love of him and loyalty to Beatrice. "Yes, I remember. When I'm an old woman, that memory will be with me."

He looked at her for a long time, then turned his head and stared resolutely out over the river valley. "I loved you then. I love you now."

"Quincy, don't tell me that!"

"I have to," he said, his voice thick with emotion. Still without looking at her, he went on. "But I know you've been avoiding me these months since you came back, and I've found myself doing the same. We need to talk about it. That's why I'm telling you how I feel—because I won't be saying it again."

"What do you mean?"

"I'm going to live in Seventrees the rest of my life, and you might also. We will be working together a good deal of the time if Jack Q makes European contracts to sell Freiler's Cures. Our families are friends; *we* are friends, Schooner. I want us to remain so."

"Yes, I want that too," she said, nervously picking apart a thick blade of grass. She had a fleeting memory of Jack Q talking to her at the kitchen table long ago, predicting a bleak and empty future. But it would not be. It would not! They sat frozen in a long silence punctuated only by the "yoo-hoo" call of a chickadee. Neither of them could admit the dread innermost thought: Beatrice was frail. She could not live forever.

Quincy stood abruptly. "Torchy is bringing some English

friends to dinner tonight. Somebody he met in the East years ago. It's getting late. Walk back with me?"

They strolled back along the tree-shaded paths, talking with careful lightness about Torchy's house, about little Ned's progress, about business matters. All the things friends would discuss. But of unspoken accord, they were very cautious to walk at a safe distance so that they might not, even by accident, touch each other.

Torchy's guests that night were a group of adventurers out to see America's "Wild West." There were twenty-five in the company, some from England, others from New York and Boston. They were setting up an outrageous camp on the front lawns. They had their own food—tinned delicacies—camp beds and stoves, and brightly colored tents. It looked like an illustration from a book of fairy tales.

The two principals of this strange group were dining and staying inside the mansion. The older man, a florid-faced giant with a string of titles behind his name, had done this before and had managed to take home to England an impressive collection of heads—moose, elk, antelope, and buffalo. His experiences on the plains and mountains had been the high point of a pampered and useless life, and he was back to relive his previous glories. Glories which he repeated in stupefying detail over the finest dinner Torchy could provide.

The younger man was a distant cousin of his. Schooner was seated next to him, and her first impression was of cleanliness. He had glistening blond hair, pale blue eyes, and was dressed immaculately in a truly white shirt, a cream-colored vest, and a dark chocolate suit that was entirely free of both lint and shine. He was quite tall and broad-shouldered and moved with careful grace. "I'm Elgin Farrington," he said as he poured Schooner a glass of the fine wine that Torchy kept in his Saint Louis cellars. "But I'd like you to call me Elgin."

"I'm Schooner Freiler. Are you a hunter, too? Like your cousin?"

"A hunter, but not like my cousin. I capture my trophies on paper and canvas. I'm an artist."

"For a living?" Schooner asked, astonished.

He threw back his head and laughed. "A living? No, Miss Freiler. It is a hobby which I am free to indulge. God in His infinite mercy saw fit to provide me with an older brother to inherit the family title and responsibility for our estates. All I

355

have to do is spend my share of the wealth and try to stay out of everyone's way. You Americans are so forthright!"

"I'm sorry—"

"No. You misunderstand. I did not mean that as a criticism, rather as a compliment. It is an admirable trait, and very refreshing. Tell me, Miss Freiler, what do you think of the war?"

"Sir, I do *not* think about the war."

He was taken aback. "Then you are indeed a rarity. I have heard little else in the two months since I arrived in your country. Forgive me if I offended you. It was not intentional."

"No, forgive me. That was rude. You see, I lost my husband in the conflict, and it is something I do not wish to discuss."

"Then I have addressed you incorrectly, *Mrs.* Freiler."

"Freiler was my maiden name. I've taken it back. It is easier for the sake of business."

"Business? You are engaged in business? Are you by any chance the Freiler of Freiler's Cures? You are! No wonder you're proud of the name. I took a chill on the crossing and was introduced to Freiler's Fever Pills in New York. They cured me so quickly I threw out all the other remedies I'd brought along. Tell me, are the others at the table your family?"

Schooner told him who everyone was and was delighted with his interest and curiosity. He assessed Maggie as dignified and self-assured, Jack Q as fiery and hardworking, and Beatrice as a frail, sweet-scented rosebud. "Am I correct, Miss Freiler?"

"Remarkably so. Are your paintings so perceptive?"

"I hope so. Would you like to see some of them after dinner?"

"Yes, I would, Mr. Farrington."

"We're going to be good friends, I hope. You must call me Elgin."

"Very well. You must call me Schooner," she replied.

The evening passed quickly. Elgin's drawings and paintings were attractive and interesting. He said he had first been influenced by Mr. Audubon's paintings of bird life in America, and Schooner thought many of his earlier paintings were small masterpieces of English birds and animals. His more recent work, the sketches he had done since his arrival, were charcoal line drawings of people he had seen—a fruit vendor pushing his heavy wagon through the streets of New York; a pair of portly bankers in conversation outside the double brass doors of their bank; a steamboat captain, arm outstretched shouting an order; and a woman at the tiller of a shantyboat.

Schooner was impressed at how he captured the essence of people in such a few quick lines. He and Gerald got into an animated conversation about the Dutch masters, and by the time the evening ended Elgin and his cousin had been invited to visit Seventrees on the next leg of their journey west. Schooner went to bed that night thinking what a pleasant respite this trip had been. She and Quincy had come to an understanding that might make life a little easier. And Elgin Farrington, though a rather odd outsider, had made her feel genuinely feminine again.

Schooner had not anticipated how difficult the actual departure would be. As they stood in the jostling crowd on the wharf next to the weather-beaten stern wheeler *Prairie Queen*, she noted that her mother was chalky-white. She thought it was because of Maggie's intense dislike of boats. But as the captain called the last warning to board, Gerald came to Maggie, took her in a bone-crushing embrace, and kissed her—a kiss to scandalize everyone within blocks. "I'm coming right back, Maggie, my love. Alone."

He said it quietly, only for Maggie's ears, but Schooner heard and wondered for a moment what he meant. Then she remembered—so long ago, she'd been only five or six years old. Gerald had gone on another trip, and when he'd returned from Mexico, he had Morning Wish's mother, Little Smile, with him. No wonder Maggie was distressed and Gerald was making such an effort to reassure her.

Beatrice was also taking things badly as her buckskin-clad father and brother boarded the boat. She feared her father would die during the trip and she would never see him again. "Don't worry," Schooner said, taking Beatrice's arm as they watched the big steamer pull away. "He's tough. He'll be back. I'm sure of it."

"Schooner's right," Quincy added. "Remember, last fall we thought he was so frail he should have a nurse, and he spent the winter building the fanciest structure in town?"

"But . . . but, Quincy . . ." she sputtered, finally giving way to worried laughter, "it was a chicken coop!" Suddenly they were all laughing at the memory of the elaborately gabled, shuttered, gingerbreaded chicken coop Torchy had constructed.

The next morning found them all back at the wharf. A rumor had reached them the night before that General Price was on the move. "Price?" Elgin asked.

"But it's only April," Beatrice said. "You see, Mr. Farrington, people here have taken to saying there are four seasons—winter, spring, summer, and Price's raid."

"General Stirling Price is the Confederate general in charge of the western end of the war," Quincy explained. "He wants to have control of the large cities in Missouri, and several times he's marched up here in the autumn to implement that policy. He's failed before, but we all expect it to happen again sooner or later."

"I thought Missouri was a Southern state," Elgin said.

"It's a border state with strong Southern sympathies, but there are a great many Union sympathizers as well, particularily in the western part of the state and in the cities," Quincy said. "More of them every day, it seems. Even a few years ago the ruffians from Kansas City and Westport were coming across the border to harass us, but the big merchants and newspapermen have begun to realize that the success of the Confederacy would spell doom for them. Most of the founders of those cities are men from Kentucky and Virginia—men whose background made them pro-Southern, but they aren't themselves slaveholders or plantation owners. They are merchants, factory owners, and railroad men whose business is more firmly allied with the North."

"Then they have sacrificed their ideals for their financial interests?" Elgin asked.

Maggie surprised them by getting into the conversation. "No, they haven't, for they had no ideals, except a romantic memory of the gracious, indolent society of the South—a society none of them were a part of. Had they been successful Southern gentlemen, they would not have come out here. Some of the most vociferous proponents of slavery in Kansas City, for example, changed their tune when it came to secession. They were socially Southerners, but politically they found the destruction of the Union unthinkable. When it became necessary to take a side, they stood up for the continuation of the central government."

Elgin was perplexed. "But we read clear back in England about a raid on a Kansas town—Lawrence, I believe it was—by a group of Missourians."

A stunned hush fell over the group.

Elgin glanced around and said apologetically, "Did I drop a brick?"

"Do we have to talk about the war?" Schooner said angrily.

Quincy stepped in. "Regardless of what's happened in the past, this rumor of Price's army has to be taken seriously. It won't be safe to travel by road." He glanced at Maggie, who was sitting very straight and pretending not to hear. "Maggie, we have to go home by boat."

"I'd rather face Price than a river," she said coldly. "I'll just wait here until the danger is past."

"That could be years!" Schooner said. "But I don't see how we'll all get passage at such short notice."

"Allow me, please," Elgin Farrington said. "My cousin and I have a boat chartered for our expedition. We would be more than happy to accommodate all of you."

Maggie stood and said, "Excuse me," in a gray voice.

Between them they managed the near-impossible, and when the steamboat set out the next day, Maggie, lips set in a grim line, boarded and disappeared into her cabin. Schooner found herself much in Elgin's company during the long up-river ride. He was a delightful companion, eager to question her about all the new sights and sounds along the river. She was naturally drawn to him by their mutual interest in the wildlife of the countryside.

Elgin brought out chalk and paints and gave Schooner some elementary art lessons which even he admitted were totally wasted on her. "But I *can* play the piano well enough that people don't pay to get away," she said, laughing over an abortive attempt to capture the lines of a fox they saw along the bank.

"Too bad you haven't got a piano along," Elgin quipped, twisting his head in an attempt to determine which was the top of the picture.

Schooner thoroughly enjoyed his company, but was under no illusions. Beatrice said: "I think he's in love with you."

"Nonsense. We regard each other as pleasant oddities. He's accustomed to silly little women who practice all the 'feminine arts,' and I'm a pioneer who has endured the hardships he's just heard about. I actually help run a business. I'm unique to him, like the different kinds of birds he's seeing. He'd take just as much interest in them if they could talk back like I do."

"You are the least romantic woman!" Beatrice said in despair.

"No, but I'm not soft-headed, either. Besides, I don't want anyone in love with me. It just complicates life. I'm happy as I am."

"Then you really don't care about him?"

Schooner considered this for a moment, then said honestly, "I think he's charming and I'm flattered at his attention. But I'm not going to get all giddy about him. Anyway, he has one great flaw."

"What's that?"

"He's English," Schooner said.

"You sound just like your mother!" Beatrice exclaimed. "What is the matter with the English?"

"Only one thing that I can see. They have a tendency to live in England. I wouldn't leave Seventrees again for any man. So stop trying out your matchmaking on me."

"I just want you to be as happy as I am. You know that. Marriage is a wonderful thing—with the right man."

"And a terrible thing with the wrong one. Stop trying to get me into someone's bed and kitchen. Here, let me hold Ned for a while." She cuddled the child and observed, "Have you ever noticed how nice babies smell in the sunshine?"

"That's another reason you should marry," Beatrice persisted.

"So that I can smell like a baby in the sunshine?"

"Don't be silly and try to change the subject. You spend most of your free time trying to get your hands on someone's baby to hold and rock and talk nonsense to. You should have children of your own."

"I'll just keep on borrowing Ned," Schooner said, but the light bantering tone had gone out of her voice. Beatrice had struck a nerve. It was true—she was getting to be a universal aunt, and she wanted to be a mother instead.

"I'm sorry," Beatrice said quickly. "I didn't mean to make you unhappy. But I still won't be the least surprised if Mr. Farrington proposes, and I wish you'd accept."

Beatrice's prediction came true. The English visitors camped outside Seventrees for several weeks, assembling the last of their supplies and engaging local hunters to accompany them. Before they left, Elgin asked Schooner if he might leave some of his bulkier belongings and formal clothing at Seventrees for the summer. Then, almost as an afterthought, he inquired courteously if Schooner might also consent to marry him when he returned in the fall.

Just as politely, she turned him down.

"I'll ask again," he warned. "Perhaps you'll have changed your mind."

"I'm sorry, Elgin. I won't change my mind."

"I'll be so sun-browned and dashing you won't be able to turn me down," he said with a boyish smile.

"Perhaps," she said. "Now, you better get ready to go, or your cousin might leave without you."

14

The rumors that General Price was coming in April were indeed false, but in September the rumor started up again, and this time it was true. Price, the Confederate general of all the armies west of the Mississippi, had entered southern Missouri with more than ten thousand well-trained soldiers, a baggage train of five hundred wagons, and a herd of cattle to feed the soldiers, as well as a huge arsenal that included a number of twelve-pounder mountain howitzers.

Even Schooner, who was practiced at ignoring talk of war, was unable to discount the panic that this news engendered. James was home for a few weeks during the middle of the month, but a messenger arrived with orders that he was to return to his regiment immediately. "Price was approaching Saint Louis, they say, but now he's veering toward Jefferson City," he explained to his mother and sister.

"And Kansas City?" Maggie asked.

"Probably, unless someone stops him along the way. It's unlikely that they can. I've got to be off right away, Mother. I think you ought to clear your most valuable stock out of the Kansas City warehouse until this is over. If Price comes this far, he'll either take the city or burn it to the ground. Too bad Dad isn't back yet to help. I wish I could stay, but . . ."

"I wish you could too," Maggie answered in a repressed voice.

"James! Don't go!" Schooner finally said. She had kept

silent until the mention of burning the city. It brought back all the memories.

"Schooner, don't start this again. You know I have to go."

By the next morning Schooner and Morning Wish were at the warehouse helping Maggie supervise the packing and transporting of the most valuable supplies of drugs. For two weeks they worked. By the end of the month the rumors had taken on a feverish pitch. Price had taken all the towns along the Missouri, some said. He was only a few miles from Independence. He had been defeated and turned back. He'd burned Saint Louis. For every possibility, there was someone to swear it was true and someone to swear it wasn't.

By October 9 it was officially confirmed that Price was indeed moving toward Kansas City, wishing to take it because the city was a doorstep to Kansas, which he wanted to overrun. That night militiamen rode throughout the state of Kansas with a proclamation from the governor. Schooner was at the trading post getting some thread when one of the men dropped off a stack of the sheets that were to be posted in prominent places all over town. It read:

> The State is in peril. Price and his rebel hosts threaten it with invasion. Kansas must be ready to hurl them back at any cost. Kansans, rally! The foe will seek to glut his vengeance upon you. Meet him, then, at the threshold and strike boldly; strike as one man against him. Let all business be suspended. The work to be done now is to protect the State against marauder and murderer. Until this is accomplished we must lead a soldier's life and do a soldier's duty. Men of Kansas, rally! To arms! The rebel foe shall be baffled and beaten back!

Schooner sat down on the steps of the post, reading the message. Suddenly her shell of reserved, deliberate ignorance cracked and shattered around her. Price's invasion was not an idle threat, not just the alarmist gossip of people who had nothing better to think about. This was a very real threat to her home, her loved ones, everything that meant anything to her. Dear God!—Price's men might do to Seventrees what Quantrill's did to Lawrence. Tears of rage came to her eyes at the thought.

Not *her* town! Not this time!

She hitched up her skirts and ran home to show her

mother the proclamation. Maggie was just coming out the door, tying her bonnet strings. "Where are you going?" Schooner asked. "Have you seen this?"

Maggie took the paper, read it quickly, and said, "I have a message to call on General Blunt in Kansas City."

"Why?"

"I have no idea, but I think we better find out."

Entering Kansas City, they met with an eerie sight. At the east and south sides of the city hundreds of men, soldiers and civilians alike, were busily working on trenches and breast-works to protect the city against invasion. "I have orders to see General Blunt," Maggie told a guard, showing him the papers she'd received.

"Straight down the road, ma'am. Southwest corner of Tenth Street."

"But that's my building!"

"Beggin' your pardon, ma'am, not this month it ain't."

The two women stormed into the warehouse they had so recently emptied of their most important products. The shelving had been pushed back carelessly against the walls, and soldiers lounged, ate, smoke, and slept all over the first floor. Crates of drugs were being used as chairs, and here and there smashed bottles littered the floor. Maggie went to the front office. She found the door barred by a surly sergeant. "You can't go in there, lady. It's the general's office."

"It's *my* office. Get out of our way!"

Schooner was as overwhelmed as the surprised sergeant. She'd never heard her soft-spoken mother talk this way. They walked in and found General Blunt going over some maps, which he hastily turned facedown.

"Ah, Mrs. Freiler, I take it. I'm sorry to have bothered you to make the trip from Seventrees, but I understand your husband is gone just now. I needed to talk to him about drugs for my men."

"General Blunt, this is my company. Not my husband's."

This struck the general as so patently impossible he ignored it. "Nevertheless, I would not have bothered you if he had been available. As you see, we need to use your building to house some of the Kansas troops. The government will no doubt pay you some sort of stipend for the use—"

"These are Kansas troops? What are they doing in Missouri? You can't do that!" Schooner blurted out.

Red flooded the general's face. He was unaccustomed to women speaking out this way. "As you can see, young lady, I *have* done it and I hardly feel that you are qualified to give me advice on the extent of my command. Now, Mrs. Freiler, I'll need drugs in case Price should get this far—"

"General, I'm happy to help in any way I can. My building and my products are yours, but I would rather be asked before the fact," Maggie said firmly.

"That's not how it works," he blustered. "That's the damn trouble. You civilians don't know a thing about war."

"Yet we bear the brunt. My own daughter lost her husband and home to Quantrill's raiders last year," Maggie said harshly.

General Blunt stiffened, and the florid color drained from his face. Maggie had deliberately hit a nerve in the man's pride. It was well known that shortly after the raid on Lawrence, he had been leading a troop of his men into the little town of Baxter Springs. Just outside town they came upon a ragtag group of men whom Blunt assumed were a welcoming committee. He rode, smiling and nodding, into their midst before he discovered that they were actually William Quantrill and his band. The damage to his troops and his military reputation had been severe. "I believe I may have underestimated you, madam," he said stiffly.

"I believe you did. Now, sir, I will be glad to donate the use of my building. If it is damaged by the enemy, we shall all be sorry. However, if it is damaged by you and your men, I'll submit a bill. We'll write up the form now and get your authorized signature. I hope I'll be able to return it to you to tear up once this is over. About the drugs, if you would make a list of what you think you'll need . . ."

By the time they left the office, General Blunt was wiping his brow and muttering to himself. Maggie and Schooner went down the steep incline to the riverbank to hire a boat to bring the required medical supplies from Seventrees. A steamer from downriver was docking as they arrived. "I wonder why anybody . . . ?" Maggie began, but ceased whatever thought she had begun. She suddenly scrambled down from the high wagon seat and called, "Gerald! Over here!"

Schooner watched as her father turned, smiled broadly, and bounded off the steamer. He caught Maggie, swung her around, and kissed her enthusiastically. People around them stopped and stared. Some looked sideways, as if such a display were an unforgivable breach of taste, but most were smiling fondly. Surely homecomings were the happiest, most important moments in life, Schooner thought. At least they

364

should be. Her own homecoming had been tragic, Addie's as bad, and Gerald's return from Mexico years ago had been awful for her mother. But this time it was as it should be. She went to welcome her father.

There was another surprise awaiting Schooner when they got back to Seventrees. Elgin Farrington had returned. "Where is the rest of your party?" Schooner asked, looking around for the flamboyant hunting expedition. They weren't the sort of group that could be easily overlooked.

"They've returned by a more northern route," he replied. "I left them in Omaha."

"You're joining them farther east?"

"I'm not joining them at all. They're going back to England and I'm staying here. Hello, Mr. Freiler," he added as Schooner's parents approached. "How was your trip? Mrs. Freiler, how are you?"

"Mr. Farrington is planning to stay in this country," Schooner said.

"Oh?" Maggie asked coolly.

"There's so much to see, so much to record, and I had very little time," he explained. He gestured to a pack sitting on the ground that was stuffed to overflowing with papers covered with sketches. "I'm stopping right now while all this is fresh in my mind. I'll do my real paintings over the winter and be better prepared to go out west again in the spring."

"You're going to spend the whole winter painting?" Maggie asked, and Schooner hoped Elgin couldn't hear the thread of criticism in the remark.

"What else have I to do?"

"You have no responsibilities?" Maggie asked.

"No, my older brother manages the family estates. I love this country and want to stay as long as I can. By the way, is there somewhere in Seventrees where I can take rooms for the winter?"

"There are some very nice hotels in Kansas City," Maggie answered sweetly, and Schooner turned to her with surprise. Why was her mother behaving this way?

"Mother, you know all the hotels in Kansas City are full of soldiers right now. Perhaps that boardinghouse just to the east of the mission . . ."

When Schooner asked her mother later why she'd been rude to Elgin, Maggie protested, "I didn't know it sounded rude. I just assumed a man like him would be happier in

Kansas City." She refused to be drawn out any further on the subject.

The next day General Blunt's commander, General Sam Curtis, declared martial law in Kansas and ordered all men between the ages of eighteen and sixty to military service. Colonel Thomas Moonlight came to Seventrees to process the volunteers, who started arriving by the end of the week.

Men in farm clothes and hunting clothes and merchants' clothing with packs containing bacon and bread and whiskey poured into town. A tent village sprang up on the banks of the Kaw and in the little park. Gerald declared the school closed so soldiers could be housed in the classrooms. Families doubled up and gave their extra beds to hardware dealers from Topeka, freed slaves from Atchison, farmers from Eudora, a minister and his three sons from Tonganoxie, and a former cavalry officer from DeSoto with his aged father, who insisted that sixty-year-olds were mere boys.

There were also men from Lawrence.

They broke Schooner's heart. A few of them were familiar to her—a clerk from one of the hotels, almost unrecognizable from disfiguring burns; a former neighbor who had learned to load and fire a gun with one arm because he lost the other one to a knife wielded by one of Quantrill's men; the man who used to help Henry with the yard work limped around Seventrees on crutches. Schooner had escaped and blocked out that awful August morning, but these men would carry through life daily reminders, hourly reminders of that day.

Reverend Whittacre, who had reluctantly freed his slaves at the outbreak of the war, went so far as to sign up for duty, even though he was well past sixty. "I lied," he explained simply when questioned. "God will understand."

Schooner's uncle, Luther Halleck, dug a deep trench in his backyard. He buried his bottles and jars and sealed his secret paint and glue recipes into a pack and covered the whole thing up before marching proudly to the school to put his name on Colonel Moonlight's list. "I don't want any damn rebel bastard making my paint if they take the place," he declared, and Schooner recalled how, when she was a child, he spoke so highly of the institution of slavery. How time and circumstance changed people, she thought.

Woody turned the operation of the ferry over to his wife and daughters while he and his sons-in-law practiced drill on the park green with the rest of the volunteers. Gerald,

Quincy, and Adams assembled on the porch of the Freilers' house to go sign up together. They were joined by Elgin Farrington, who insisted that even if he wasn't a citizen of the country, he *was* temporarily a citizen of Seventrees. "You wouldn't expect me to stay back with the women and children when the fighting starts, would you?" he asked.

Colonel Moonlight, unlike his superior, General Blunt, did not underestimate Maggie Freiler. He knew she had authority in the community and he made an effort to keep her informed. "Price is said to have passed Jefferson City, ma'am. Too well-fortified," he reported. Later: "He's on the way toward Kansas City with a long baggage train slowing him down. Pleasonton had a good-sized force trying to catch up to the end of it. We'll get him between the hammer and the anvil, that we will, if Pleasonton can move quickly enough."

For two weeks they waited. More and more Kansans poured into the communities along the length of the Kansas-Missouri border, and the towns were hard pressed to feed and house them. But somehow it was done. The third week of October, Price's armies were almost upon them. Kansas City, with Colonel Kersey Coates at the head of the Home Guards, was well defended, and Price seemed to know it. He was sensible enough to keep from being caught between the armies of Kansas City and Westport, but instead swung his long line of cavalry and foot soldiers to the south of Westport.

"We'll get into position tonight, ma'am," Colonel Moonlight told Maggie. "Make sure the ladies feed the soldiers well. Tomorrow will be a long day."

Tomorrow will be the *last* day for many of them, Schooner thought, and felt a cold, hurting place in the pit of her stomach. She made a fierce mental prayer that at least her own men—Gerald, Quincy, James, Adams, and Elgin—would survive unharmed. What a high price they might all pay! And for what? For a Virginia gentleman's desire to own black people? For a Northern factory owner's unwillingness to compete with cheap labor from the South? For career military men who have no purpose in life unless there is a war going on? Or was it all for something else she could never grasp?

As evening came, the women of Seventrees dug into their precious winter stores of ham and potatoes and onions and spices to make a feast for the soldiers. They filled bowls with steaming buttered turnips, stewed tomatoes, fluffy hominy, and made scalding buckets and kettles of strong coffee and

Seventrees tea. A pit had been dug in the middle of the park to roast two fat hogs. Clean calico cloths covered platters piled to tottering with honey-colored biscuits.

It was well after dark when the sated soldiers retired to their tents and schoolrooms and borrowed beds and the women of the town began the massive cleanup tasks. Schooner, hands wrinkled like white raisins from dishwater, finally, after midnight, crawled into the big bed she shared with Morning Wish, only to be awakened again two hours later. "Moonlight's brigade is falling into position," Maggie whispered, and Schooner was instantly awake and dressing.

There was little time for farewells as the men hastily assembled their weapons, saddled their horses, and rode into the night. Maggie and Schooner opened the Freiler house and gathered in the fearful women of their circle. Addie brought her three children, and Beatrice brought Ned, a sleepy bundle in a pastel quilt. Katrin Clay joined them, and even Fritzi Halleck, who had never been in the house the Freilers built after the flood of 1848, came along.

They put the children back to bed on blankets in front of the parlor fireplace, and the women sat out the rest of the long, long night. They spoke sometimes—vague, worried remarks that weren't directed at anyone.

"I wonder where James is tonight."

"I hope Adams is warm enough. I knitted him some new socks."

"Quincy was worried about his horse."

Most of the time they tried to sleep, but none of them succeeded, and when the pink streaks of dawn began to light the eastern sky, they were as exhausted as if they had already fought a battle.

15

As soon as it was light enough to pick out her way, Schooner threw on a heavy coat and walked up the road to the top of the bluff. Next to the cemetery were signs of men having camped briefly—doused fires, a few belongings left behind in the darkness. But there was no indication of which direction they had gone. She squinted into the pink haze of dawn to the south and east over the rolling hills. It was deceptively beautiful. The maples and oaks had turned color and reflected the tentative morning light. But she knew that, hidden in the forests south of Westport, there were many hundreds, indeed thousands, of soldiers and civilians readying themselves for battle.

She went back down the hill, the frosted grass crunching under her feet. The town of Seventrees was ominously still. The women and children moved about quietly, as if the town was a vast sickroom. There was still a great deal of cleaning up to be done, and Schooner, like the others, busied herself with domestic chores. But she wondered, as she straightened beds and cupboards, whether any of it would exist by the next day. If Price's men managed to overrun the Kansas border armies, Seventrees might just be a smoking scar on the bluffs of the Kaw in a matter of hours.

By seven o'clock they could hear the distant rumble of gunfire, and the women began sensibly to pack their most precious small belongings in preparation for flight. By nine the sounds of battle were closer yet, and Schooner and Morning Wish went back up the road. Standing once again at the cemetery, they could see white puffs of gunsmoke drifting up from the hills south of Westport. When the wind shifted toward them, they could faintly hear shouts, cries, and explosions, as well as the terrified whinnying of wounded horses.

Schooner and Morning Wish stood there for a long while. "If we see anyone coming, we will rush to warn the others," Morning Wish said.

"Warn the others to do what?" Schooner asked bitterly. "To abandon their land and homes and everything they treasure?"

"Other people have been asked to do that," Morning Wish said.

Schooner glanced at her half-sister. Her beautiful dark face was like a disdainful mask. She meant "her people," of course. Schooner sensed for a fleeting moment how this day must feel to her. The Freiler half of her was fearing for her loved ones, but the Indian half of Morning Wish must be gloating at the spectacle of white men slaughtering each other and pouring their lifeblood into the ground they had stolen from the Indians. Schooner wanted to cry out to her, "Can't you love *us* more? We consider you one of us, yet you insist on standing apart, silently judging us." But even as she thought it, she knew what Morning Wish's answer would be. She *did* love her family—her immediate family. But the rest of the community did not accept her as one of them. They were vaguely courteous to her on Maggie's behalf, but Schooner had seen the critical glances, the subtle snubs, and the way they pointed her out to newcomers as a novelty. A German Indian to make jokes about. More than just jokes. Strange men who were automatically polite to white women felt free to make lewd remarks to Morning Wish.

Schooner had never truly sensed things from Morning Wish's point of view, and the despair of it, coupled with her terror of the battle raging just out of sight, washed over her with an almost physical force.

"Look!" Morning Wish said. "I see someone coming!"

The two young women hurried back toward the point where the road started down the bluff, turning frequently to see just who was coming. Shading her eyes, squinting with concentration, Morning Wish suddenly said, "They're ours!"

Two men in civilian clothes were riding toward Seventrees. One of the men had the crumpled body of a Union soldier with him. Schooner and Morning Wish turned and ran down the slope, their only thoughts at the moment to prepare medical treatment. Hair and skirts flying, stumbling in ruts, they were soon overtaken by the riders, who shouted for them to get out of the way.

Schooner veered off toward her house, shouting for her mother to bring medicines as the riders pelted toward the now-empty school. But Maggie was not there; she had anticipated such an occurrence, and when Schooner found her mother, she was already at the school, binding up a rider's swollen ankle. The soldier, a young man from Wisconsin, was lying on a cot, his face gray and pinched with pain. The front of his uniform was drenched with blood from a bullet in his shoulder. An elderly doctor from Atchison who had stayed behind to treat the wounded was carefully cutting away the material in preparation for examining the injury. The second civilian was being given liberal doses of whiskey in preparation for having his broken arm set when the doctor was through with the soldier.

Many of the women had crowded around the school, asking each other in frantic whispers what the riders said about the battle. Finally the man with the injured ankle came out on the porch to explain what he knew. "I only saw a part of it all, you realize, ladies," he said apologetically, "but what I saw looked good for us. We met the advance guard of Price's men across Brush Creek. Us on the north side, them on the south. There was a fierce lot of shooting, and them Johnny Rebs started falling back, going up the hill yonder, into the heavy woods. We was following across the creek when the man riding next to me got it. His horse fell, catching my foot someways. We was trying to help each other up when this here soldier came along and got a shot. He fell smack into the middle of us. Seemed to appear that none of us was doing much good, and the soldier boy was bleeding bad. We grabbed a couple of stray horses that was stamping around scared like, and we rode back here."

"So the Union is winning?" one of the women asked.

"Well, ma'am, I don't know as you could say that, exactly. But we was pushing them back a ways. 'Course, they got the advantage now. Looking down from the hill all along the ridge, and they've got more troops coming in from the east all the time."

"Are there many more wounded?" Beatrice asked, voicing the question they all wanted answered.

The man hesitated, rubbed his stubbly chin reflectively, and finally said softly, "A hell of a lot, ma'am."

A terrible hush fell over the group of women, broken only by the irritable whimpering of a baby in one woman's arms, and the distant rumble of gunfire. "I'm going back, ladies," the man said. "I might not be much good for fighting, but I might could bring some more men back."

As he started to move away, Schooner touched his arm. "Wait, I'll go with you. We'll take a wagon, and some bandages."

"Oh, no, miss! You can't do that!"

Maggie had stepped out onto the porch as Schooner spoke. Schooner knew what her mother would think, but glanced at her for confirmation anyway. Maggie had her hands clasped tightly, and her knuckles were white, but she nodded curtly. "I'll not get close to the fighting. Just help bring back the wounded," Schooner said.

Katrin Clay, almost white-haired now, but still buxom and forceful, stepped forward. "I'll be with you, Schooner. I've still got that heavy spring wagon Helmut used to bring in his forge supplies. Make a right comfortable way for an injured man to travel. I'll need some mattresses for it," she added, turning back to face the group of stricken women.

No one spoke for a moment; then there was a sudden babble of German and English and French, as the rescue effort fell into an organized plan. Within half an hour a line of wagons was making its way up the hill. Driven mostly by older women, since the younger ones had children to look after, the procession made an odd spectacle. Hay wagons, Sunday carriages, milk carts, buckboards, and even a few old prairie schooners and Conestoga wagons struggled up the incline. There wasn't a mattress left in a bedroom in the town. They had all been put either on the wagons or on the floors of the schoolrooms where the soldiers would be brought for treatment.

As Schooner's wagon came to the top of the hill, she could see other men hobbling, riding, and some nearly crawling toward Seventrees. "Do you want me to take you in the wagon?" she asked the first man she met up with. He was in his late fifties and had improvised a crutch from a tree branch to take the weight off his injured leg.

"No, ma'am. Those of us who've made it this far can most likely make it the rest of the way. Take this road almost to Westport, turn off at the big gnarled sycamore. There's a track there, and lots of bad-hurt soldiers in a clearing just south."

When Schooner and Katrin arrived at the clearing, they found that their hopes of helping were overoptimistic. There was precious little anyone could do for these men. The ones who had been slightly injured had gone on fighting. Those who were left behind were the very badly injured. Of the thirty who had been brought to the protected place in the woods, eight were already dead. Another seven were certainly going to die of shock and blood loss. Only a half-dozen were able to even sit up, and one man with no apparent injury except a bruise at his temple was plodding aimlessly in a small circle, singing a childhood song.

"My God! What can we do?" Schooner said after she had crawled down from her wagon and joined Katrin. The other wagons had taken different routes, and only the two of them had come to help these men.

Katrin unbuttoned her cuffs and pushed her sleeves up her forearms. "We do what we can," she said simply. "You get that ferhuddled one to help us," she added, pointing to the young man who was singing.

In a while they had both large wagons filled. It had been terribly hard work. Many of the men had involuntarily emptied their bowels and bladders when injured, and that stench was added to the smell of gunpowder and blood. This is what fear and despair smell like, Schooner thought, fighting down the bile that kept rising in her throat as she attempted to lift one man after another into the back of the wagons.

Only one of the thirty men was known to her: a man of twenty or so who was in James's regiment and had once visited Seventrees with him. But she could not ask him about her brother's whereabouts, for he was unconscious when they found him and died before they could put him on a wagon. She instructed the "ferhuddled" soldier to drive the wagon, and she rode with the men in the back, giving whatever small aid she could as the vehicle bounced along the eroded track. Katrin was directly behind, urging her horses in a tone so shrill and masterful that Schooner's horses obeyed her summons to hurry as well.

They reached Seventrees at the same time as two other wagons, and found that several others had already returned and discharged their sorrowful passengers. The makeshift hospital was filling up quickly. "Did you find . . . anyone?" Maggie asked, rushing out to meet her daughter and her friend. Her apron was soaked with blood.

Schooner shook her head. "Has anyone been brought back?"

"Adams is here."

"Where is he?" Katrin asked. "Is he badly hurt?"

"His rifle misfired, and broke his shoulder. There are burns, too. But he'll live, Katrin. He's up on the second floor. Addie is with him, and he's been asking for you. Beatrice is taking care of the children. She tried to help here, but she fainted after the first hour," Maggie added before Katrin dashed off.

Schooner helped empty the wagon and set out again. This time she and the others took a more southward route. The word was that an old farmer had shown the Union troops where there was a well-hidden "divide," a deep, wide gulch that led to the top of the hill where the Confederate troops were holding out. Union soldiers and civilians had poured through the twisted, well-protected pathway and surprised the enemy at the top, forcing them farther back. Now the worst of the fighting was just south of the ridge. Three hours fighting and dying for a half-mile victory, Schooner thought bitterly. What a precious, expensive half-mile! And there was no

373

assurance the line would hold. The Union might yet be forced back.

Schooner had taken the deranged soldier back with her to help. He had been useful and obedient to her commands before. But as they got closer to the sound of battle, he began to fidget and mumble to himself. "Don't worry," she told him. "We aren't going where the fighting is. We are here to help the hurt ones. You are going to help me," she said firmly. But she felt almost as whimpery and disoriented as he as she drove her wagon through woods strewn with the dead and dying.

She made five trips that day, never finding any of her family, seeing only a few men who were at all familiar. By late afternoon the Confederates had been pushed back several miles and were definitely in retreat. On her last trip she found that other houses in the path of the retreat had been set up as hospitals, and she was able to return to Seventrees with only half a wagon full of men. She found her mother sitting bent over on the bottom step of the school building. "Are you sick?" Schooner asked, scrambling down from her wagon seat with alarm.

"No. I'm fine," Maggie said, hurriedly getting up and calling for help to remove the soldiers from Schooner's wagon. "Your father has been brought in," she said.

As she said the words, Schooner noticed the tear paths down her cheeks. "Is he . . . is he alive?" Schooner asked.

"Yes, he is alive. A bullet grazed his head. He had bled profusely and must have been unconscious for quite some time."

"Will he be all right?"

"I think so. There doesn't seem to be any injury to his skull, but he's very weak. I think it's just the blood loss, but we won't know for days, maybe weeks."

"I'm sure he'll recover," Schooner tried to reassure her mother. "What about James? Does anyone know . . . ?"

"Woody was brought in an hour ago. He saw James and Quincy with Colonel Moonlight just before he came back. He said they were well then, and were with the forces pushing Price south."

"Woody said that? Then he's all right?"

Maggie answered, "No, I'm afraid he's not. He died a few minutes ago. He was shot through the stomach, and the bullet must have pierced his spine."

"Oh, Mother . . . no! Not Woody!"

"He was awake to the end, Schooner. He knew that if he lived, he would be utterly helpless and in terrible pain. His death was a merciful release. We must think of it that way."

Schooner knew then why her mother had been sitting on the porch with her head in her hands a few minutes earlier. Woody had been one of her first and dearest friends in Seventrees. Their joint memories went back to the very founding of the town, even before the Clays had come. They shared many years of hardships and happinesses. "Mother, I can't say how sorry I am," Schooner said, before her voice cracked and dissolved.

Through the long afternoon and evening, casualties continued to come to Seventrees; on wagons, on horseback, supported by friends, or hobbling by themselves, they came for help. But there was no sign of Quincy or James or Elgin Farrington. Maggie's cousin, Luther Halleck, came back, exhausted, and hungry, but unhurt. "Moonlight turned some of us back," he reported. "Said we ought to let the young men chase the rebs south. Only fair, I guess. Troops were harrying them all along the border as they fled. Reverend Whittacre is on his way in a wagon," he added.

"Hurt?" Maggie asked.

"Not exactly. He had a heart attack or a seizure of some sort. He's wobbly, but still full of vinegar."

By the time it was dark, the pain-filled pandemonium of the day began to subside. The able-bodied were up on the bluff, digging graves for the many men who had not survived their wounds. The women were either tending their own children or taking care of the patients who overflowed the schoolhouse. The odor of food cooking began to prevail over the odor of death. Schooner and Morning Wish fried an enormous platter of chicken and took it to the schoolhouse. Maggie was sitting with Gerald. Schooner was terribly alarmed at his gray color and slow, slurred speech, but Maggie, who had seen more of illness, swore that he was better and would recover in a short time. "Is there no word of James yet?" Gerald asked, carefully pulling himself into a sitting position so that he could eat a drumstick.

"Not yet," Maggie said, and Schooner ached at the sound of forced brightness in her mother's voice.

As soon as Gerald went to sleep, Schooner whispered to her mother, "I hear they have taken many of the soldiers to the Wornall house. Do you think we should go there tomorrow and see if they have enough medicine?"

"That would be a good idea," Maggie agreed. "We are well stocked."

Neither of them said what they were really talking about: that James, living or dead, might be there.

They set out at dawn and dispensed opiates and bandages to several houses along the way. There was an overwhelming number of dead and wounded. When they reached the Wornall house, a brick mansion a few miles south of Westport, they found themselves in the company of many other women who had come to find their missing husbands, sons, and brothers. There were bodies laid out in row after row on the wide, shady lawn. Their faces were all decently covered, but their torn and blood-spattered uniforms, both gray and blue mixed in death without regional prejudice, brought out the utter uselessness of the whole battle. History books would probably say the North had won the battle of Westport, Schooner thought, but nobody had won—only death had been given a grim victory.

Like the other women, Schooner and Maggie did not stop to look at the corpses, but went immediately to the house, assuming optimistically that their loved one, if there, was inside among the living. They handed their medical supplies over to a colonel in charge and then went through the house looking for James.

But he was not there. Mother and daughter exchanged a brief, stricken glance. "He must have gone farther south with Colonel Moonlight," Schooner said.

Maggie replied, "Yes, he must have."

Having dutifully said these platitudes, they stared at each other for a long moment. Finally Schooner broke the fly-buzzing silence. "Shall I look over here?" she asked, gesturing toward the rows of bodies on the south side of the walk. Maggie nodded and turned away to look on the other side.

Schooner moved along slowly. The first was not James; the body was clothed in a Confederate uniform. She did not have to look at the face. Nor the second, in civilian farm clothes, nor the third, dressed in Union jacket and trousers but wearing nonregulation boots. The fourth? No, far too tall and heavy to be James. The fifth and sixth were Confederates, but the seventh? It might be. She could not make herself look at the dead soldier's face—not yet. She stepped carefully between his body and the next. There was a calico handkerchief covering his face, and she was about to gingerly remove it when she realized that the hair was too dark to be James's.

With a long sigh she moved along the line. She was getting dizzy, and though it was a brisk, chilly morning, she was experiencing nauseating waves of heat from inside her body.

Suddenly she heard a low sob and whirled to see her mother kneeling beside a body. *Let her be wrong, God! Please let her be mistaken. Someone else. Someone else!* she thought frantically as she picked her way through the slaughter to Maggie's side.

But it was no mistake. Mercifully, his wounds had not damaged his head or features, and death must have been quick and painless, for his face, his poor dead young face, was serene and restful. His eyes were closed, remarkably long feminine lashes lying softly on his cheeks. His brow was smooth and his long, fair hair swept carelessly across his forehead as if he were merely sleeping. But he was not sleeping.

He was dead.

Dead.

Schooner knelt by her mother, and they clung to each other weeping. "Why?" Maggie sobbed. "Why did God do this to us? Why take James? He was so good, so kind and sensitive, so gentle . . ."

"Mother, don't! There was no reason. You know that."

"But you and James were my best, my most loved, and now I've lost him. I've outlived half of my children," Maggie said. And this tragic remark was to stay in Schooner's mind and haunt her for a long time.

16

The newspapers blazed accounts of the rout of Price's force across the country. The western arm of the Confederate army no longer existed. It would take years to rebuild it, and the South didn't have years. They were already calling the Battle of Westport "The Gettysburg of the West."

In Seventrees, they buried their dead. Woody; Reverend Whittacre, who'd had another seizure upon his return and died; and James, along with many others. Quincy returned unharmed after five days, and Beatrice collapsed with relief and accumulated tension. She was very ill and for a few days it was feared she would die. But she eventually recovered, though she was frailer than ever. Her spirits were lifted somewhat when mail delivery resumed and she received a letter from Jack Q. He and his father were well and were returning in the spring, he said. "I am grateful for one thing," she told Schooner, who had come to call on her as she did at least once a day. "If my father had been here, he'd have insisted on being in the middle of the battle. I'm sure of that."

"I think you are right. You see, Beatrice, there was a good purpose in his going to Europe. We just couldn't see it at the time," Schooner answered.

"And your Elgin came back safely, too," Beatrice said.

"He isn't 'my' Elgin," Schooner answered, but it lacked conviction. When the handsome Englishman had come strolling into Seventrees half a day behind Quincy, with his saddlebags slung over his shoulder, she had been astonished at how happy she was to see him. She had actually thrown herself into his open arms and made a spectacle of herself before her normal reserve asserted itself. Later, she made up all sorts of excuses for her unseemly behavior. She didn't really love him, she hardly knew him—that much was fact—but she did like him very much. And he was so attentive, seeming to take great interest in her every word.

There was something else about Elgin, something Schooner could not have even admitted to herself had she been more tightly swathed in the Victorian ideal of femininity. He had a tremendous physical appeal to her. He was tall, strong, healthy, and handsome. He always dressed beautifully and smelled good. The last two were rare qualities. She found herself wanting to touch him and be near him. She had known the physical love of a man, and she found herself craving it.

"Has he asked you to marry him, like I predicted?" Beatrice asked.

"Yes, he has. But I turned him down."

"Why?" her friend asked bluntly.

"Because I don't love him."

Beatrice traced the border of one of the squares of her lap robe. "Does that matter?" she asked. "I mean, you do *like* him. How many of the people we know here in Seventrees married for love? Most married for respect and necessity. Look at Charity Woodren. Remember the year of the gold rush, her husband died and she married Woody the next day to have a protector for her and her children? It was one of the happiest marriages in town. And Mrs. Smith down the road. She was a mail-order bride. She and Mr. Smith are a joy to one another. Love can come later, you know."

"But people should marry for love," Schooner objected. "My parents did."

"Yes, and look how unhappy they have made each other," Beatrice said.

Schooner would not have accepted this honest appraisal from anyone else, but she and Beatrice were too close and knew each other too well to pretend that Maggie and Gerald were ideally suited. "I know you must be right," Schooner said. "Still, I would feel like I was cheating if I married Elgin feeling the way I do."

"Does he know how you feel?"

"I've tried to tell him, but I don't think he really listens, not with his heart." Schooner stood up. "I'm tiring you, Bea. I'll come back tomorrow. Don't worry about me. I've got lots of time to make up my mind, and I'll let you know when I do."

Schooner bundled up in a warm cloak and hurried on with her errands. She had prepared some papers that had to be taken to the Freiler's Cures office in Kansas City, Missouri, and she welcomed the quiet time to think. As the horse clopped along the road (paved now with bricks—Schooner had liked it better as a dirt path), she thought about the one important fact that Beatrice had not marshaled in her effort to get Schooner married off. Children. Schooner had never forgotten the feeling of holding a baby in her arms, a baby of her own. In the few short months Nathan had lived, she'd been happier than any other time in her life. His every move, every precious baby coo, had been like the taste of honey to her soul. The first time he smiled at her had been so exciting that she still remembered every moment of the day—what she'd had for breakfast, which flowers were blooming, who came to call.

She kept thinking back to what her mother had said about outliving her children. *I've outlived mine, too,* Schooner thought. But she could still have a family. There was time yet. But not a lot of time, she realized. She was no longer a girl. In a few years she would be thirty. Thirty! Probably half her life over.

By the time she returned to Seventrees that evening, she had decided she would marry Elgin, but only if he truly understood and accepted her motives. She wanted children and would continue to work in the family business. She would also make sure that he knew she would not leave Seventrees. Never. If he intended to go back to England, he could not expect her to go along. Surely, she thought, he would not agree to all those rules. *I'm not worth it*, she thought with wry modesty.

She was astonished when Elgin not only agreed to her terms, but made a few of his own that were something of a relief. "I'm an artist, my dear. I intend to 'chronicle' this exciting new world. My, how pompous that sounds," he added with a laugh. "What I'm getting at is that I can't show the whole West from Seventrees. I'll have to travel like I did last summer. Sketch the things I see, and then do the final work here, during the winters. Perhaps it's been unfair of me to ask your hand without explaining that."

"I don't mind," she said, guiltily thinking how she could have all the benefits of being a wife this way and have the responsibilities of the condition only part of the time. What more could she ask? And yet she still felt a vague uneasiness. The decision seemed right on a practical, intellectual level, but her heart wasn't satisfied. *Nonsense!* she told herself. *If I keep dallying over making a decision, the choice will not be mine to make. I'll be too old and Elgin will lose interest in me.*

"Shall we tell your parents about our plans?" Elgin asked, taking her in a protective embrace that did much to allay her doubts.

"No, I think I should tell them by myself, if you don't mind," she replied. She was uncertain of how graciously her mother might receive the news.

"Very well, if you think it's best," he said, unoffended. If he had sensed Maggie's disapproval (and certainly he must have), he gave no indication that it bothered him.

"Where shall we live?" Schooner asked. "There's a nice house for sale on the mission road where we could live until we build our own house. It has nice windows, and you could have your studio there."

"Oh, no. I don't want that," he said.

"What do you mean?"

"Just that I like having my work shown when it's done, but I'm frantically secretive about it while I'm working. I'll keep my rooms at the boardinghouse for my work, and our home will be just that."

Schooner thought this strange. The Freilers' home and

work had always overlapped, but she supposed it was a minor difference in thinking and gave it no more thought.

She waited to talk to her mother until they were alone, suspecting that revealing her intentions to both her parents at once might result in unpleasantness. "Schooner! You can't really mean to marry the man!" Maggie exclaimed.

"Now, Mother," Schooner said, trying to remember that she was no longer a child and determined not to act like one. "You're not going to start that German business again, are you?"

"German? Whatever makes you say that? It's not the man's heritage that bothers me . . ."

"Then what is it? I know you have never liked him, and I think it's time to tell me why!"

"Because he's trivial and useless! He has no purpose. There is no real person under the facade."

"Perhaps it's just that you don't know the person underneath," Schooner snapped. She hadn't really meant to get in an argument with her mother, but neither had she expected such a vehement reaction from her.

"Do you?" Maggie replied.

"Oh, Mother, don't let's fight about this. I'm going to marry Elgin. I'm sorry you don't approve, but it's time I marry, and he's the best choice available."

Maggie was taken aback by her daughter's candor. "I'm sorry, dear," she said, taking Schooner's hand in a gesture of conciliation. "I was afraid you were trying to tell me you were really in love with him, and that frightened me."

"Why should it?" Schooner asked, her own temper cooling.

"Because I think it would be a tragedy for a person like you to love a person like him."

"I don't see why. What do you mean?"

"You are a doer. He is an observer. He will stroll through life, enjoying what appeals to him, and ignoring what does not. He has been raised without responsibility. He could never really understand the things that mean something to you. Things like duty and the pleasure of a difficult job well done."

Schooner suddenly realized what her mother was talking about. It was Elgin and it wasn't. Maggie was airing her own lifelong grievances against the man she loved. Gerald strolled through life, enjoying each new experience and hastening on to the next. It was his charm, the thing they all loved about him. And while he obviously loved Maggie and respected her constant striving to Do What Is Right, he did not share her compulsion to seek Right. If Right and Wrong came his way, he observed them impartially, made light table talk of their relative merits, and danced on to the next stage of life. Even his injury and experience in battle had become a matter of academic interest. The only recent exception to his light-hearted view of life had been James's death, which he had accepted in bitter silence and refused to discuss with anyone.

The irony of it all, Schooner thought. Her mother was warning her about Elgin because he was so much like Gerald. Years ago Gerald had warned her about Henry Grinnell because he was so much like Maggie. The sad part was, they loved each other as much as any couple could, and that very love had caused them both such pain that they wished to spare her. Did life really need to be this complicated?

"Don't worry, Mother. I haven't lost my heart. But I want a husband and I want children and I'm in grave danger of losing my chance for both."

Maggie smiled sadly. "You're wrong about that, but if you've made up your mind, you have my blessing. I'm sure you'll have your father's as well. *He* is very fond of Mr. Farrington."

"Mother, I understand what you're trying to tell me. But I know what I'm doing," Schooner said, refusing to listen to the voice of doubt in the back of her own mind.

17

The year 1865 was one of changes and great events. Abraham Lincoln was shot in April, and shortly after his death the war that had been planted in Kansas eleven years earlier came to a gasping end. Thousands upon thousands had died, families had been destroyed, and fortunes lost. But the Union had held together.

Schooner's life was marked by important changes that year, too, but of a happier nature. On New Year's Day she married Elgin Farrington, and by late March she was helping him prepare for his second trip into the western wilderness.

She hummed as she prepared a medical kit to pack for

him. Elgin himself, on this soft-scented morning, was at the boardinghouse putting his paints and canvases under wraps for the summer. Schooner was pasting the last of the carefully hand-labeled instructions on a bottle when she heard the knock at the front door of their rented house. Beatrice had promised to call, so Schooner hurried to open it. To her surprise, Beatrice had Jack Q with her.

"You're back!" Schooner exclaimed. "You weren't expected for another week. Oh, Jack Q, how fine you look!"

She almost hugged him, but there was something cool and forbidding in his expression that stopped her. "Hello, Mrs. Farrington," he said politely.

Schooner was thoroughly perplexed. "Jack Q, what has come over you?" she said. "Have you forgotten who I am? Come in, both of you. I've got a cake made, and I want to hear all about your trip. How is your father? Did you like France? What was the journey like?" Schooner shot questions while she took Beatrice's wrap.

By the time they were settled in the parlor with cakes and tea, Jack Q had relaxed and talked about the long trip he and his father had made. Torchy had thrived on a travel schedule that exhausted his son. "I think we must have seen every cathedral in France," Jack Q complained. "For a man who's never had the slightest interest in his Maker, he was certainly taken with the architecture of His houses."

"Just think of the sort of chicken coops he can devise now," Schooner said. "So he is really well?"

"Better than ever. The trip gave him back all his energy and interest in life. The only thing he didn't like was the language difference," Jack Q said.

"Language difference? But he speaks French—you all do."

Jack Q laughed. "I thought that too, but I found out we speak 'Kansas French.' It's a far remove from the real thing. The first month or so I thought the old man would have a stroke every time someone failed to grasp what he was saying. He kept claiming they'd changed the language since his father left."

They had a long chat about Torchy's adventures, linguistic and otherwise, before Jack Q finally said, "And what about you? I heard about James's death. I'm terribly sorry. I'm calling on your parents later this morning with my father. And you're married now . . ."

"Yes, for three months past," Schooner answered.

"Are you happy?" he asked sharply. The pleasant tone of a

moment before was gone. It was not a polite inquiry, but a demand. Beatrice fidgeted and made a half-gesture of warning toward her brother.

Schooner thought a moment before answering. "I'm very content."

Jack Q stood suddenly and paced the room with his familiar brisk stride. "You're willing to settle for 'content'?" he said. As he passed the window, a shaft of light caught his brilliant red hair and made it look like a match flaming up. "Schooner, you can't mean to tell me you love that—"

"Jacques!" Beatrice exclaimed. "What a way to behave!"

"Goddammit! The man's not worth the time it takes to say his name. I thought Schooner had better sense than to marry someone who regarded her as an oddity to be stuffed and mounted."

"Jacques!" Beatrice was almost in tears. Schooner was too surprised at his outburst to say anything.

"I've been in Europe for almost a year and a half. I know how they think of Americans. We're novelties. Something interesting to invite to dinner to make fun of. He'll take you back to England and keep you in sunbonnets and calicos to amuse his friends."

Schooner finally caught her breath and spoke. "I'm not going to England, Jack Q. That was our understanding. Elgin doesn't want to go back anyway. He likes it here."

"He'll get over that. The newness will wear off and he'll long for his castle and his hounds and Yorkshire puddings."

"Your travels have certainly broadened your scope of understanding," Schooner said coldly. "I'm glad you're back, for Beatrice's sake, but I don't recall asking for your opinion of my marriage!"

"Jacques, look what you've done," Beatrice lamented. "I wanted today to be such fun, and you've offended our best friend. Please take me home now."

"I think that would be best," Schooner said, fetching Beatrice's shawl.

"Oh, Schooner, I'm so sorry. I don't know what's come over him. I'm sure he's sorry—"

"I'm sorry, all right," Jack Q interrupted. "I'm as sorry for Schooner as I've ever been." With that parting shot, he marched out the door to await his sister at the gate.

Beatrice left in a flurry of tears and apologies, and Schooner closed the door behind them with a trembling hand. She was furious with Jack Q for his meddling outburst, and the thing that infuriated her most was that he was echoing her own misgivings exactly. His perception rankled more than his rudeness. She carried the tray of cake plates and cups to the kitchen and began to wash up. Her mind kept coming back to a portrait Elgin had done of her. She'd posed for it an hour every morning for two weeks in February, wearing her best dress, a dove gray wool with fine lace collar and a strand of pearls. He'd not let her see the work until it was finished. When she finally got to look, she was shocked. He'd captured her face, she supposed, but he'd painted her hair in windswept disarray and completely ignored her actual clothing and painted instead a dark gingham dress of the sort she would have worn to do the laundry.

"Elgin! Why did you change what I was wearing?" she had objected. "And my hair! I never let it get that messy."

"Schooner, you must understand about art—I'm not trying for a literal representation. These modern photo-image contraptions can do that. I'm trying to capture the 'essence' of Schooner." He gestured with pride to the completed painting.

"But that's *not* the 'essence' of me, whatever that means. I'm not untidy. You said you were sending this portrait back with the others for your London exhibition. I would be embarrassed to know my picture had gone off into the world this way!"

He'd just laughed affectionately at her distress and tried again to explain how he was trying to show the English the typical frontier woman, not an exact copy of an actual woman. But Schooner had remained upset about it without knowing quite why. She wasn't acquainted with anyone who might see it, and probably would care nothing for their opinion anyway. Nor was she particularly vain as a rule. She supposed it was because Elgin seemed to prefer to think of her as he'd painted her, not as she actually was. The whole unhappy incident had come back to the top of her thoughts since Jack Q's visit.

She'd been surprised when he asked so bluntly if she was happy. It was not a question she'd even put to herself until that moment. But she was satisfied with the answer she had given him. She was, for the most part, content. That was all she had expected of the marriage, and it was what she was getting. Elgin was gone for many hours every day. Except for the questionable portrait of her, he did all his work at his boardinghouse rooms, and it left Schooner free to spend her days as she always had, working with her mother in the business. In addition to the bookkeeping, they had been experimenting with some new combinations of drugs. Maggie had purchased some new books which they were studying avidly together.

At the end of the day Elgin and Schooner each returned to the house from their separate pursuits and spent long evenings together. Schooner would play the piano he had bought for her, while he struggled to master the flute Gerald had presented him. If the roads were clear, they often went to Kansas City and saw a play or an opera, and sometimes they had company in for evenings of cards. Beatrice and Quincy visited from time to time, and Schooner found, to her surprise, that her longing for Quincy had become less acute since her marriage.

Elgin was a charming escort, an excellent conversationalist, and best of all, an accomplished lover. So accomplished, in fact, that it would have upset her had she loved him more. She would have dwelt miserably on how he'd acquired such expertise. As it was, they could fully enjoy each other physically as people can when their hearts are not fully engaged. *Like the difference between playing cards for fun and playing for higher stakes than you can afford,* Schooner thought.

Content. Yes, that was the word for it. She was contented with her situation. Not excited with it, not always happy, but generally contented. Damn Jack Q, anyway! Why did he have to thrash his way back into the middle of her life and bring all her doubt back to the forefront of her mind? It would have been different if she didn't care for his opinion. But she *did* care. She valued his ideas. He'd been a good friend all her life, and had always (or so she thought) spoken his mind fully. She'd been grateful before, but she was only angry now. Not angry with him, but with herself.

That evening, before Elgin got home, she went to look out the front door and found a package on the steps. There was an envelope with a note.

Dear Schooner,
　I had no business behaving the way I did today. Please forgive me. I brought back something for you I hope you'll accept in the spirit of affection in which it is given.

Love,
Jack Q

Schooner took the package inside and removed the paper wrapping. Inside there was a beautifully carved walnut box about a foot square and four inches deep. Intricate designs in mother-of-pearl were set mosaic-style into the lid and sides. Opening the box, she found that it contained a delicately woven silk shawl. Thousands of threads, intricately looped and knotted, formed a fantasy garden of glossy pink roses on an ivory background. It was beyond doubt the most exquisite piece of work she'd ever seen. It was truly a gift for a bride, or a princess.

She held it to her face, feeling the luscious softness against her cheek, and suddenly found herself weeping.

18

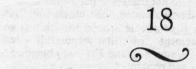

That fall when Elgin was scheduled to return from his trip west, Schooner was waiting at the riverfront docks in Kansas City. He'd sent a letter, giving the date of his probable arrival, but she'd had no way of writing back to him, so she'd been unable to tell him the news. She paced back and forth along the wooden sidewalk, looking in the windows of the shopfronts, but seeing herself rather than the wares on display. It didn't show yet. She wished it did. Five months along! Many women showed at four—women who didn't want to. Why did fine ladies go to so much trouble to conceal their pregnancies? She'd seen the most outrageous dresses, things with tucks and flounces and false waistlines, all of which looked like circus tents, on women who had nothing but a wonder of nature to conceal.

She smiled to herself, knowing that passersby must think her demented. Maybe she'd have twins, she thought. That way she'd have two babies for the price of one. She giggled to herself. Wouldn't that be fun! A boy and a girl. No, two girls and then a little brother for them later.

The shriek of a calliope whistle upstream interrupted her daydreams. She hurried to the dock, shaded her eyes, and rejoiced as the sidewheeler got close enough to identify. It was the boat Elgin had said he was taking. She got jostled by the crowd, but refused to submit her vantage point. Her spirits flagged as the boat drew nearer and she still couldn't see Elgin. But when the plank fell with a loud thud to the dock and the passengers started to disembark, she spotted him. They exchanged waves, Schooner nearly jumping up and down with excitement.

Finally he was beside her, sweeping her up in his arms. There were lines of fatigue or irritation in his face—she was too involved in her own news to analyze which. "How was your summer?" she asked.

"I'll tell you all about it later. You look wonderful, my dear. New dress, fancy hairdo—"

"Oh, Elgin, I've got something so wonderful to tell you," she gushed. "I was going to wait until later, but I can't."

"I could use an earful of something wonderful just now," he replied, failing to fall into her hysterical good spirits.

"I'm pregnant!" she almost shouted, then blushed and lowered her voice as she noticed people around her smiling and tittering at her announcement. "Isn't that wonderful? I realized it in the middle of the summer, and I've been bursting to tell you for three months and couldn't."

She knew he wouldn't behave as giddily as she was, she'd have been embarrassed if he had, but she was disappointed when he merely said, "Congratulations, darling. When is the happy event to be?"

"January sometime. Beatrice is expecting another child then, too. We'll have to get busy building a house. I've got a spot of land picked out. In fact, Mother owned it and is giving it to us. But I didn't want to start making definite plans until you were here. Oh, Elgin, get your trunks quickly and let's go home and talk. I have sketched some house plans. I know my artistic hand is awful, but you can fix them for me. Where are your trunks?"

"Well, there's a long and rather dismal answer to that. To sum it up, however, I think my trunks are now part of the furnishings in a tepee somewhere in the Dakotas."

"Oh, no! Not your drawings, too! What happened?"

"The last I saw of my wildlife sketches, they were rolled up and being smoked by some damn bloody squaw. She was getting a diabolical amount of enjoyment out of them," he answered. "They don't light as easily as Mr. Audubon's, but they have a nice fruity aftertaste," he mocked.

"But you have a good memory for what you've seen," Schooner tried to reassure him. He looked so utterly defeated as he made light of his loss. "You can go lock yourself in your rooms at the boardinghouse and redo them while you still remember. I won't bother you about the house. We'll just stay where we are until after the baby is born. We can build our house in the spring."

"By spring I have to have my exhibit ready to ship. I had a letter from my representative in London waiting in Omaha. He says he has a gallery booked for July, and everything has to be in London, uncrated, hung, and ready by late June."

"Well, summer then," Schooner said. She knew how terribly disappointed he was, and she was doing her best to understand, but she resented the fact that the conversation had veered so suddenly away from her main interest, the baby. "You look pale, Elgin. Are you well?" she asked as they gathered what few pieces of luggage hadn't been stolen by Indians.

"I am now, I think. I had some damn spotty fever most of the summer. Never really knew how many damn insects there are in this country waiting to chew you to bits if you stop moving for a moment. Mosquitoes the size of pigs!"

Schooner was alarmed by his tone, and without thinking, snapped, "I don't suppose you have insects in England!"

He laughed at her flash of temper. "Of course we do, but they know their place."

She laughed too. That was more like the lighthearted man she knew. "Come home, Elgin, and be happy with me," she said.

As autumn turned to winter and Elgin's health improved, he talked often of his misadventures during the summer. It seemed that nearly every variety of mishap that could strike a traveler to the wilds had struck the party he was with: an apparently unprovoked Indian attack, illness, injuries, unfriendly reception from the military posts where they stopped to provision, and greedy farmers who cheated them at every turn, not to mention a steamboat captain on the upper reaches of the Missouri who would not release their equipment without the payment of an additional fee far in excess of the agreed-upon price of passage.

Though Elgin told his friends and neighbors of these trials in a light, amusing way, Schooner could recognize the thundering undertone of dissatisfaction and always made an effort to divert the conversation. As the days grew shorter, Elgin seemed to talk more and more often about England—friends there, titled people whose remarks and experiences delighted

389

him and left Schooner confused and uncomfortable. He told her of foxhunts he'd been on, fine wines in his father's famous cellars, a private library more extensive than public libraries "over here."

"You're homesick," Schooner accused on one occasion.

"Not at all, my dear. I just thought you'd be interested. You said you've never been farther from here than Saint Louis, and England is so different, I thought you might like hearing about it," he said, his feelings obviously injured by her tone.

"I *am* interested, but it seems all you talk of these days."

"What do you want me to talk about?" he replied. "The exciting things that are happening here? I hear the blacksmith hurt his arm yesterday and Mrs. Johnson's oldest boy has mumps—"

"Elgin, don't turn your wit on me," Schooner protested.

"I'm sorry, darling," he replied contritely. "It's just been rather difficult for me lately."

"I'm afraid you don't like it here anymore," Schooner said.

"It's not that. It's just that I'm learning that there is a difference between being a visitor and being a resident. Visitors see just the best and most interesting of things. Residents have to adjust to the day-to-day failings of a place. I've been working such long hours and had trouble getting the right light and so forth. I suppose I'm just cranky. Don't let me worry you, my dear."

"How is your work going?" Schooner asked, anxious to keep him talking about a subject that pleased him.

"Quite well, on the whole."

"May I come see it someday?"

"No! I mean, you know how uneasy it makes me to have anyone see my paintings before they're done."

"What are they of?"

"Oh, different things," he said vaguely.

"You will let me see them before you send them off, won't you?"

"Oh, yes, certainly," he answered, but Schooner thought she detected something evasive in his tone. Why was he so reluctant? Her thoughts touched briefly on the unflattering portrait he had done of her.

Schooner and Beatrice were both due to give birth in January, but Beatrice's labor started early, a week before Christmas. Schooner, Katrin, and Maggie sat with her by turns while the doctor attended her. Schooner was frantic with worry for her friend. Beatrice was so frail and small-boned and had endured a long painful labor with Ned. This time she was older and in worse health. "Just as well she's early," the doctor confided outside the door of his patient's room. "It'll mean a smaller baby and easier passage. Don't worry about her, we'll pull her through this."

True to his word, ten hours into Beatrice's labor, the doctor announced that she'd given birth to a healthy baby girl and that the mother was doing fine, though she was very weak. Schooner stayed a few more hours, cuddling the infant, whom Beatrice named Lucy. She was vaguely aware that the weather was turning much colder outside and the night was falling quickly under overcast skies. She thought little of it, for it was the time of year one could expect a first good snow. She took reluctant leave of mother and new daughter and went home.

Elgin left quite early the next morning, as had become his habit. "There's so damn little daylight this time of year," he complained. "I've got to use every moment of it."

Schooner fixed his breakfast and got dressed. But it was an effort. Her back ached from the hours of sitting with Beatrice the day before, and she was terribly tired. After attempting an hour of housework, she decided to give up and go back to bed. Stepping to the door to check on the weather, an old habit, she discovered that it had warmed up a great deal from the sudden cold snap of the night before. The sky was a dark, rolling gray, and she thought what a lovely gloomy morning for a nap it was before crawling back into her high, soft bed.

She woke once during the morning, and gazing blearily out the window, noticed it was raining. A cold, sleety rain that was sticking to the trees and making what little light there was sparkle and reflect. When she awoke again near noon, she was astonished at the change in the landscape. The trees were thickly coated now with a heavy glaze of ice, and many of them were bending precariously. The ice rain had stopped, and it was beginning to snow—big, wet flakes. As she was dressing she heard something that sounded like the report of a gun. Rushing to the window, she saw that a large elm down the street had bent under the tremendous weight of ice and snow and a vast limb had snapped like a twig. It lay across the middle of the road, and a cart that had been sitting under it was smashed to kindling.

The phenomenon that had seemed a rare instance of

391

beauty moments before had now become a rare danger. Schooner hurriedly finished dressing and went from window to window. As she watched, several large limbs within her sight splintered and shattered before toppling to the ground. Her first thought was to go to a place of safety, but where was that? Everywhere a tree might fall was dangerous. Even if she knew of a structure that had no overhanging trees, how would she get there? One of the beauties of Seventrees was its luxurious growth of fine old trees. They'd always seemed a blessing; now suddenly they were a menace.

She watched the road in front as a few people struggled along. Everything was glazed with the ice, leaving neither foothold nor handhold. A wagon drawn by a pair of sturdy workhorses labored to get up the slight incline. The horses' heavy hooves slipped and skittered, and the wagon wheels turned uselessly. A few citizens minced carefully along the side of the roadway, clinging to sleet-slick fences and glancing up frequently at the overhanging limbs that seemed to be bending over them like a devil's embrace.

She opened the door a sliver and listened. The air was full of the sound of trees creaking under their load, an eerie, crackling whine punctuated occasionally by the clattering thud of heavy limbs striking the ground. Without venturing outside, Schooner took a mental inventory of the trees that shaded her own house. The big sycamore in back had several limbs that spread over the roof. In fact, the whole tree leaned toward the house. The elm in the side yard might be a danger as well. Glancing out the parlor window, she saw that the redbud had already fallen apart, broken limbs littering the ground, and a large, bushy pine farther back had simply collapsed in place, leaving a bare trunk where thick soft branches had once been.

There was a ripping crash and then the tinkle of glass as the elm flung the end of a shattered branch in the kitchen window. Where was Elgin? she thought frantically, then realized it was better that he stay where he was. He couldn't help her any, and probably couldn't fight his way from the boardinghouse studio anyway without great danger.

Very well, she thought, *I'm going to have to get through this by myself.* She was getting cold from the draft coming in the broken kitchen window. Wrapping up in her warmest coat, she went to the dining room. It was probably the safest place to be, considering the placement of trees around the house. She pushed the heavy table against the wall, making an additional bit of protection, then crawled under to wait it out.

She was miserably uncomfortable, huddled under the table trying to get her legs among its legs, but she felt relatively safe. She had been in her shelter for only a few moments when a tremendous, tearing explosion confirmed her worst fears. The house shuddered as the main trunk of the sycamore fell across the roof, hesitated a second, then crashed through. Schooner buried her face in her arms, tightened her whole body into a ball, and held her breath as the tree cut through the house. When the noise stopped and she dared to look, she could hardly believe it.

She was surrounded by ice-coated branches. The cold poured in through a vast hole in the roof, and the tree lay sprawled in the center of the house. One large, icy limb rested across the top of the table she was under. But she was safe. Peering cautiously out from under her shelter, she could see only sky. This, apparently, was the last of the tree. It had destroyed the house, but spared her; now it could do no more.

She was aware of shouts from somewhere. Elgin's voice and others. She called out, but knew her voice was being muffled by the surrounding rubble. She shouted again, louder, "I'm here. In the dining room."

"Schooner!" Elgin called. "Are you all right?"

"Fine. I'm fine," she called back. "But I'm trapped under a table."

Eventually Elgin and several of the neighbors managed to saw through and pull away enough limbs to get to her. "Careful, now," Elgin said, gently helping her out. "My God, Schooner. You really gave me a fright. I was just coming around the corner, practically on my hands and knees, when the tree came thrashing down. You showed remarkable ingenuity, getting under that table. You're not hurt, are you? The baby?"

"No, I'm really unhurt, and the baby is kicking me to bits," she replied, basking in his concern.

By the time they picked their way through the debris, the snow had stopped and the sun was beginning to shine through the clouds. "I think the worst of it is over," Elgin said. "But we better stay here for a while yet. Then we'll take you to your mother's house. I passed it on the way, and it was still intact."

"I suppose we'll have to live there the rest of the winter,"

Schooner said, concerned about inconveniencing her mother, but seeing no alternative.

"Live with your mother?" Elgin echoed dismally. "Do we really have to?"

"I don't see what else we can do," Schooner said. "Look around. Half the houses in town are damaged to some extent. Where else could we live?"

"But . . . live with your *mother*?" Elgin repeated as if the idea was so grim he couldn't quite grasp it.

"Don't worry," Schooner said, trying to sound bright and optimistic in spite of her own misgivings. "It won't be so bad. You'll see."

19

Victoria Freiler Farrington was born during a blizzard on January 29, 1866, the fifth anniversary of Kansas statehood. She came into the world shrieking, her little red face screwed into an enraged expression of dissatisfaction. She continued to voice her dissatisfaction for the next six weeks almost continually. It wasn't that she was "fussy" or "cranky"—she was just plain furious about something. "Pity we don't know what she's angry about," her mother said, trying to keep from screaming with frustration.

The entire household devoted itself to trying to please the baby. Morning Wish patted her and spoke in soothing tones. It didn't help.

Gerald tried rocking her and reading the classics in German. He played the flute and an old banjo from the attic and even sang. Victoria didn't appreciate his efforts either.

Maggie thumbed wildly through Grossmutter's hex book and her own accumulation of cures and tried everything that might help the colic. The child rejected it all, most frequently on her grandmother's shoulder.

Elgin paced and delivered lectures on the superior method with which children were handled in England. They were stashed away on the third floor with a nanny until they were socially acceptable, he claimed.

Victoria kept screaming.

Finally, the second week of March, she stopped. But by that time no one noticed. The tempers of the adults in the household were frayed beyond redemption. On one of the first mild days, Schooner tucked Victoria into her perambulator and walked to Beatrice's house. "Should you be out so soon? You look weary," Beatrice said when both babies were settled on a soft blanket for a midmorning nap. "Is Victoria stll crying so much?"

"No, it's not the baby, it's everyone else. Oh, Bea, it's almost like the old days with Addie. There are no conversations in the house anymore, only disputes conducted with varying degrees of heat. My mother is an exceptional person, very warm and caring to those she loves," Schooner said, prefacing her disloyalty, "but she can be perfectly awful in the nicest way to people she doesn't like."

"Elgin, you mean?"

Schooner nodded. "I knew she disliked him from the moment they met, and to be fair, I think she genuinely tries to be pleasant to him, but she just can't do it. She finds it unbearable that he doesn't 'work.' To her, art is not work, it is play—or worse."

"And Elgin doesn't recognize her good qualities either, I imagine," Beatrice said.

"Not at all. Besides everything else, I think he's a little afraid of her force of character, and he doesn't like being intimidated by a woman—and a German frontier woman at that!"

"What about your father?"

"Oh, he dashes into the middle and tries to gloss over any impending unpleasantness, and Mother most often turns on him, thinking he's taking Elgin's side. Usually he is. Bea, it's awful. They can get in nasty-nice disputes over the stupidest things. Last Sunday Mother and Elgin spent the whole day snipping at each other, ever so politely, about the right way to cook potatoes. Potatoes! As if God had sent the things from heaven with instructions written on the skins for the One Way to cook them."

Beatrice tried to keep a straight face, but couldn't. "Schooner, I'm sorry. I know it's not really funny, but . . ."

Schooner smiled too. "It would be, if they weren't making life so miserable for everyone—not just themselves. Mother ends up angry with Daddy, and Elgin turns around and blames me for the way Mother is. This morning was the worst! It was over accents."

"Accents?"

"Yes, Elgin had asked Mother if he could help with anything, and naturally, because he'd asked, she said no. So he got out a pad and started sketching a bird outside the window. Then she decided that she needed a bucket from the carriage house, though Lord knows she's got a half-dozen of them under the sink. That irritated *him*, and he commented airily on how interesting it was the way Germans always did such odd things with a hard 'g.' By way of illustration, he imitated the way she said carriage."

"What did your mother say?"

"Something terribly academic about the English habit of dropping them entirely off the end of words. I left the room and Elgin followed me to complain. I'm afraid I wasn't at my best either, and I said something childish about how he ignores the very existence of vowels . . ."

"Oh, dear!"

"He stormed out of the house, furious with me, and I can hardly blame him. Mother started slamming pots and Daddy got out his flute. Morning Wish had the good sense to simply disappear, so I followed her example and hurried over here, unannounced. I hope you don't mind."

"Of course I don't. I'm delighted to see you. I have a better idea, though. Why don't you leave the baby here for a little bit and go talk to Elgin?"

"He's at his studio. He doesn't like to be disturbed."

"I'm sure he'd welcome you."

Schooner didn't take much convincing. She was at the door of Elgin's rooms in a matter of minutes, apology poised on her lips.

"Schooner! What are you doing here? Is something wrong?" Elgin asked.

"No, I just wanted to tell you how sorry I am about this morning. I know it's been difficult for you, and I shouldn't have made it worse."

"You didn't, my dear. It was just a bad morning for everyone. Don't give it another thought," he said.

"May I come in? I'd like to see your work."

"Certainly. I'm just getting ready to start crating things. It's rather messy. Watch your step over that box."

Schooner came into the large unfurnished room, one of the two connecting rooms he rented at the boardinghouse. It was full of paintings, most of them quite large. They were stacked in profusion around the walls. But it was not their numbers, or their size, nor even their skill, that drew her attention. It was their theme.

Next to the window a large canvas showed a ragged group, civilians and soldiers, dashing up a hill through a steep ravine. A smaller canvas next to it portrayed a young soldier kneeling over his dead comrade. He clutched his friend's shirt in a desperate gesture, as if ordering him back to life. His expression was so desolate, so torturously rendered and lifelike, that Schooner had to look away. Another painting was of a stream, its natural beauty obliterated by the clouds of gunsmoke coming from both sides. Schooner tried to speak and couldn't. She walked to the door connecting the other room. It was the same. A large oil of a group of injured men helping each other to safety; a Confederate soldier sitting on the ground next to a small cannon, his face in his hands, weeping; an extraordinarily grand-looking commanding officer on horseback at the peak of a rise, looking down on the battle below.

Finally Schooner's gaze fell on one painting that took her breath away. A two-story brick house, seen from a little distance. The gardens had been trampled, and the lawn was covered with orderly ranks of bodies. "That's the Wornall house, isn't it?" she whispered. But she wasn't really talking to Elgin.

"Well?" he asked. "What do you think?"

Schooner stared at him as if he were a stranger, which, in fact, he had just become. "Think of this? How dare you ask me that? What do you suppose I think!"

He was surprised. "Schooner, whatever is wrong? They're good."

"They're all of the Battle of Westport," she accused.

"Yes, they are," he answered, still failing to understand her reaction.

"They are all of the Battle of Westport," she repeated.

"I know it isn't a pleasant memory to you," he said, "but it was an important battle, and the Europeans who will see the showing are interested in your Civil War battles. I've done them well, you can't deny that. What *is* the matter with you?"

She walked over to the painting of the Wornall house. Her throat was so dry she could hardly speak. "Which of these bodies is my brother?" she said harshly. "Or was he not dead, only dying, while you sat and sketched this?" She turned to the painting of the men charging up the ravine. "This is where my father was wounded. Did you stop to notice whether he was alive or dead before you got out your pencil? Did you fight in the battle at all? Did you help anyone?"

"Schooner, I'm an artist, not a soldier or a doctor."

"How many others you've shown might have lived if you'd helped them instead of drawing them? What of the boy kneeling over his dead friend? You might have comforted him—did you?"

"No, but—"

"No, you were too busy trying to capture his agony to give a thought to sparing him any of it! I understand something now I wondered about at the time. Why you struggled to carry back your saddlebags when your horse was gone. The preliminary sketches were in the saddlebags, weren't they?"

"Schooner, listen!"

"I don't want to."

He grasped her arm as she walked toward the door. Indicating the single chair in the room, he said, "Sit down. Please. You *must* listen to me!" He spoke slowly and carefully, as if giving an important lesson to a child. "You have had a hard life, Schooner, without as much time as some of us have for reflection, and you are bound to see some things differently. I also realize these scenes mean something more personal to you than to me—"

"I thought these people mattered to you, too."

"They do, but in a different way. Schooner, mankind tends to disregard the general in its day-to-day struggle with the specific. Like the old saying about not seeing the forest for the trees. You are concerned for the trees, by which I mean your friends and family. I'm trying to show the forest. A generalized representation of what this war is like to Americans. I've given a great deal of thought to this, and I've formed a theory. Do you want to hear it?"

Schooner just continued to stare at him coldly, so he went on. "I think the Almighty singles out an individual every now and then and gives him the ability to observe and record with insight what he sees in his fellowman. These are the artists—the painters and writers and poets. They are, in a sense, humanity's mirror by which it can see itself. Do you understand?"

"You think God has appointed you to show the rest of us what we are?" she said incredulously.

"Well, that sounds rather more glorified than I intended, but . . . yes, I suppose that is more or less what I mean."

"Does God approve of your work here, then? Or has he gotten around to looking at it yet?"

Elgin ran his hands through his hair. "Damnation, Schooner. How can I make you understand?"

"Let me help you understand something. A person doesn't have to have a rich, leisurely life in order to think about the meaning of it. Nor does he have to be a man or an artist to comprehend what is right and wrong. Sometimes it's very simple. *This* time it's very simple."

She stood and started to walk toward the door as she spoke. "The people of this community were in danger of losing their lives and property. They went out to protect their families. You went with them. You could have helped. You could have saved a life or given comfort. You did neither. Your paintings are very skillful, Elgin, but that doesn't matter—they are ghoulish and immoral. You are immoral!"

"There speaks Maggie Freiler's daughter! You declare me immoral. From your lofty plane of philosophy, *you* say I am immoral!"

"Yes, I say so. Who are you to suppose we know nothing of morality here? And where do you get the colossal nerve to think that God has told you to paint pictures!"

"We must all do what we are best able to do. There, that's an axiom that ought to please even your dreary, practical mother."

"Wouldn't that be nice—if we were all able to pick and choose and do just what we were best able to do. I'm sorry, Elgin, but your handy homemade axiom would not please my mother, nor does it please me. We do what we *must* do. That *is* dreary. Sometimes it's backbreakingly dreary. But it is also the truth."

"So now, having declared me immoral, you are going to teach me the truth. Teach away, frontier lady."

Tears came to her eyes. "That's what I am to you, isn't it? I've tried so hard to ignore it, and I knew from the beginning. I am one of the 'specifics' you are determined to generalize. Elgin, I'm *not* a 'frontier lady.' I am a particular person. I'm me! Schooner Freiler—"

"Schooner Farrington," he corrected. There was a glint of bitter victory in his eyes. "You see? You are, and always will be, part of your family—the Freilers. You even forget you bear my name. You belong to these people and this place, not to me. Never to me."

"I'm sorry. It was merely force of habit," Schooner said.

"But I wonder if perhaps you're right. There is one thing I do know, however. I shan't ever feel the way I used to about you. I thought you had gone to that battle with concern for the people who had accepted you into this community. I know now that you went out with your artist's eye to watch us spill our blood. As if we were some sort of noble experiment. I was wrong about you."

"We were both wrong about a great many things," Elgin said, regret replacing the anger in his voice.

"I'm afraid we were. Elgin, I have to go. Victoria will be hungry and screaming."

He cringed a little at the mention of his noisy daughter. "Schooner, I've been thinking about something . . ."

"Yes," she answered, hand on doorknob.

"I'm worried about the transportation for the exhibit. And there are some questions as to the framing and . . ." He stopped, looked at her questioningly.

"You are going to take the pictures back to England in person?"

She had confirmed what he was thinking. "I think perhaps I should, don't you?"

"I think you should—yes. When will you come back?"

"Oh, quite soon I should imagine. I'll stay for the duration of the show, of course. Then there are a few friends I'd like to have a spot of visit with. I will probably be back before the year is out."

"Probably," she echoed.

"Surely, then. We'll work this all out. I promise you. But I think it would be an excellent thing if we were to have this time apart, to think—you know, to try to see things from each other's viewpoint. Then next winter we'll get our own house and—"

"When will you be leaving?" she cut in. Part of her wanted to cry out: "Don't leave me! Don't run away and abandon me!" But another part—the part that was Maggie Freiler's daughter, she thought with a slight smile—was relieved. Perhaps they would fix their marriage. Perhaps when the searing heat of this conversation cooled, she could pick among the smoking ruins and find something worth piecing together.

But she doubted it.

"The paintings are to go next week," Elgin said. "I will arrange passage on the same vessel."

She started to ask why he thought there would be space available for another passenger, but thought better of it. She feared that he already had a ticket, and it was a truth she could not quite deal with today. Better to never know. "Very well," she said.

"I'm going to be very busy," he added hesitantly. "So much yet to do here. Would you mind if I just asked the landlady to bring up a bed and I'll stay here?"

"That would be very sensible," she replied. "I'll get your things at home packed and send them over."

"Schooner—"

"No, Elgin. Let's don't say anything more now. We'll just make it worse."

He nodded, gazed at her for a long moment, then opened the door. "I'll come see you and Victoria before I am ready to leave," he said.

"Yes, do that," she said distractedly before hurrying back to her daughter and family.

Schooner didn't tell anyone what had occurred between her and Elgin. Nor did she admit to having seen his paintings except to say she thought they were probably of the wildlife he was so interested in. To outward appearances, all was well with them, and she accompanied him to the docks in Kansas City to see him off on the first leg of his long journey. "Don't be so sad," Maggie said when she came home. "He'll be back before too long."

But Schooner suspected that she would never see him again.

20

Just before Christmas, while Victoria was learning to walk, Schooner received a letter from Elgin saying that his father and brother had been tragically killed in a railway accident. It would take some time to clear up the estate, he explained, thus delaying his return. Late the following spring another letter came saying that it was going to be impossible for him to return for some time, and that Schooner and Victoria should make ready to join him.

Schooner refused.

It took six months of letters to agree that a divorce was the only answer, and Schooner ended up, in November 1867, on a train bound for Saint Louis to consult with Elgin's American attorney. She left Seventrees with her emotions in a muddle of hurt, but when she walked out of the attorney's office, having officially severed the marriage, she found herself nearly dancing with relief. She'd made a terrible mistake, and now she'd corrected it. Divorce was a scandalous thing, of course, but she would weather it somehow. She was free!

Boarding the train home, she discovered she was to have welcome company for the rattling, cinder-strewn journey. "Jack Q!" she called excitedly when she saw his buckskin-clad figure swaying along the center aisle. She had not seen him for nearly a year, though they corresponded regularly on business matters and less often exchanged personal notes. A chemist Maggie had hired had come up with a new vitamin tonic sometime earlier, and Jack Q had gone abroad to act as salesman. He sent back orders, which Schooner was responsible for processing.

"Schooner! How nice to see you," he replied, dumping his bags and sitting down next to her.

"We weren't expecting you for another month. You're back early," she said.

"I got sick of England. I can only stand a month or two of predictable climate before I start longing for a storm or a drought or something interesting," he said lightly, not quite concealing his real homesickness.

"You were gone a long time. Bea and your father missed you. We all did."

"Far too long. Three months in England, then another five in Germany and France. I've got so many new orders for Freiler's Cures that it took an extra trunk," he said, laughing.

"I'm glad we ended up on the same train. We can catch up on everything," Schooner said.

"Start with what you were doing in Saint Louis," Jack Q said, trying to get his lanky legs comfortable under the seat in front. "Shopping?"

"No, signing papers freeing me from Elgin."

He had the good grace not to gloat or say "I told you so."

"Yes, he said you were getting divorced."

"You saw him?"

"Yes, I went to his exhibit in London. His paintings were the talk of the town. Quite impressive." He paused a moment, then went on. "It's a good thing he didn't show them to anyone in Seventrees. Did you see them?"

"I did," Schooner said softly. "I told him they were immoral."

Jack Q wasn't the least startled by this announcement. "They were, from our vantage point."

They sat together in companionable silence for a while, but Schooner's mind was working on something Jack Q said earlier. "Elgin told you we were getting a divorce?" she asked finally. "During the exhibition?"

Jack Q nodded.

She twisted her hands together angrily. "That was before the subject even came up. How dare he! I suppose I should count myself lucky that he got around to mentioning it to me at all."

"Schooner, put it out of your mind. It's over," Jack Q urged.

She smiled weakly. "You're right, of course. That's the most irritating thing about you. You're always right."

"Not always," he said, then quickly changed the subject. "How is Victoria?"

"She is still Victoria," Schooner said. "A law unto herself. She is sometimes so sweet I want to hug her to pieces, and she can turn right around and be so pigheaded I nearly scream."

"You said your mother was having trouble coping with her?"

"Oh, you got that letter? Yes, Mother has met her match. It was getting so difficult for everyone watching a grandmother and baby granddaughter constantly trying to 'out-stubborn' each other. I worked out a wonderful arrangement, however. Since Woody died, Charity has been so lonely. Their children are gone now—none stayed in Seventrees to raise their children. Charity asked us to move in with her. She adores Victoria and takes care of her when I work in the office or check on shipments at the warehouse."

"Are you going to marry again?" Jack Q asked unexpectedly.

"Marry again? Heavens, no. I've proved I'm absolutely no good at it. Why would you even ask?"

"Well, last time I'd been on an extended trip, I came home and found you wed. I thought, as attractive as you are, there were probably armies of young men asking for your hand."

"Armies? Nary a recruit." She laughed.

403

"How is Quincy?"

The significance of his name being brought up did not escape her. She suddenly sobered. "I suppose he is well. You'll have to ask Beatrice. I hardly see him."

"Is that deliberate?" Jack Q asked.

"Habit, I think," Schooner said honestly. "I'm delighted to see you, but stop prying in my affairs now and tell me what you saw in your travels."

"Fair enough, but all I saw was the inside of a couple hundred chemists' shops. I've yet to sell a single bottle of cures in a castle or cathedral or anyplace interesting."

They had a pleasant ride home, talking of friends and business and other harmless topics. Schooner had forgotten how very much she enjoyed Jack Q's company, and her spirits were high when they got off the train at the small stone building that served as Seventrees' train station. But her mother, waiting on the wooden platform, quickly changed her feelings. "Jack Q!" she said, rushing to meet them. "I'm glad you've come too. She's been asking for you, and we didn't think you'd be back for weeks yet."

"She who?" Schooner asked, alarmed at her mother's distracted manner.

"Beatrice. She's very ill. Hurry."

As they jolted along in Maggie's carriage, she explained. "It's a little difficult to sort out just what happened. Beatrice has been having faint spells lately, you know. She had the children down by the riverbank, collecting leaves or something for a school project of Ned's. She got dizzy and leaned against a tree for a minute, closing her eyes. She heard a splash, or claims she did, and assumed in a panic that one of the children had fallen in the water. Without even looking around to see if they were both there, which, of course, they were, she leaped into the water. Quincy was just coming down to meet them and saw the whole thing, though he was too far away and it happened too suddenly to stop her. He dragged her out of the icy water immediately. But she was crying and coughing, and she's been ill ever since."

"How long ago was this?" Jack Q asked.

Maggie cracked the whip over the horses, urging them to hurry. "Day before yesterday, but it seems much longer than that. I've done everything I can for her, and the doctor's hardly left her side, but I'm afraid . . ."

Jack Q leaped out of the carriage before it even came to a stop. Schooner followed along more slowly. Quincy met her at the door, his son, Ned, six years old now, hiding behind his father shyly. "Schooner, I'm so glad you've come," he said.

Schooner was shocked by his appearance. He looked like a man who had been ill or suffering for a long time. His face was pale and haggard with worry, and even his posture, usually so straight and proud, spelled despair. "I'm sorry I wasn't here when it happened," Schooner said. "Not that I could have done anything. But I'm here now. I'll stay with her as long as you both want me to."

"I don't know how much longer she has," he said.

Schooner hurried to the bedroom. Beatrice lay in the bed, her face as pale as milk and her thin body hardly making a ridge in the coverlet. Jack Q was in the chair beside her, leaning so close that their brilliant red hair meshed into one glorious cloud of color. He was whispering to her. She would have looked asleep except for the faint smile that touched the corners of her delicate mouth. Schooner stayed at the door until Jack Q motioned to her. "Here's Schooner, Bea. She came with me."

Schooner thought that a stranger, seeing him thus, hearing the gentle love in his voice, could never guess at the temper Jack Q sometimes displayed. Schooner put her head back so the tears could not spill over and went to the other side of the bed. She took Beatrice's hand in hers and said, "You must get well soon. I brought you a new hat from Saint Louis, and I want to see you wearing it."

Beatrice turned her head toward Schooner, and her eyelids fluttered open for a moment. "I'll try," she said so softly her voice could hardly be heard.

Schooner and Jack Q sat with her for a long time while Quincy got some needed rest in the other room. Late in the evening the doctor came in and ordered them out. Maggie took their place while Schooner ran home to change her clothes and look in on Victoria. "Don't worry about her, dear," Charity Woodren said. "Stay with Mrs. Clay as long as you need, and I'll take care of things here."

Schooner hurried back and found Jack Q pacing the parlor, his face almost as pale as Beatrice's had been earlier. "Jack Q, what's wrong? She's not . . . ?"

"No, not yet. But she had another coughing seizure while you were gone. God! It was awful." He sat down suddenly on a horsehair sofa, his usually sprightly movements abruptly stilled. "I wish I had the courage to kill her. Just to spare her the pain. And the fear. If you had seen the look in her eyes!"

Schooner wanted desperately to comfort him, but she didn't know how, so she just sat down beside him and took his hand. He clutched her fingers so hard it almost hurt. "How is your father?" she asked.

"Upset, of course. But holding up. He's tougher than any of us. I heard him putting Ned to bed a while ago. He was telling him about how Mommy was going to heaven and we'd all come to tell her good-bye. I don't think he believes a word of it himself—about heaven, I mean. But he's putting on a good front for the children."

"What about Quincy? And Ned?"

"They are being stoic and sensible. That boy is a copy of his father."

The doctor joined them. "She's resting now. I suggest you two do the same, in shifts, if you'd like."

"How long . . . ?" Schooner asked.

The doctor shrugged. "I can't guess. It could be minutes or it could be days. But she'll not recover this time. I don't mean to be cruel, but you mustn't get your hopes up."

They sat with her through the long, long night in turns. As the end drew closer, she became feverish and talked in her sleep. Once she called out for her mother, a woman she didn't remember when she was well. Often she called for Quincy, and he always hastened to assure her he was there. Once, when he was out of the room for a moment, she said very clearly, "He loves Schooner you know."

Schooner was startled, but Jack Q quickly leaned forward and said, "No, he doesn't, Beatrice. He told me so. He loves only you. Only you."

She smiled and stopped struggling against the bedclothes for a while after that.

Schooner felt sick inside.

Toward dawn, Beatrice began to shake, and her breathing became ever more labored. She suddenly began the horrible, racking coughing again, but it lasted only a moment. On one last shuddering exhalation, Beatrice died.

Schooner straightened her hair and clothes, and the doctor gently closed her staring eyes. Then Schooner slipped away, leaving Beatrice's men—father, brother, husband, and son—to bend under the first wave of grief without a woman's eyes to see. Heedless of the cold, Schooner walked out into the backyard, where she and Bea had often picked cherries in the spring, and sat in the welcome shade in the summer exchanging confidences.

406

But never again. Never again.

Wrapping her arms around one of the gnarled old trees and pressing her face against its bark, Schooner wept for Beatrice and for the past and for the future.

21

Mercifully, the first weeks after Beatrice's death were too busy to allow Schooner very much private time for reflection. There was the funeral to see to, and arrangements had to be made for the care of the children. Katrin Clay had recently injured her foot and wasn't able to keep up with them, so Schooner happily took charge. Every morning she went to the house and prepared breakfast for Quincy, Torchy, Jack Q, Ned, and little Lucy. Then, with Quincy and Jack Q on their way, she got Ned ready for school. Katrin came in later to keep Torchy company, as he had caught a bad chill at the funeral, but wouldn't stay indoors to recuperate unless guarded.

Schooner then took Lucy back to the house she shared with Charity Woodren, and the little girls, now almost two years old, played together. Schooner often found herself wondering why Lucy didn't object to being dominated by Victoria, but there were remarkably few arguments. Victoria led their games, decided who got which toys and when they would plague Charity for treats or a story. Lucy seemed perfectly content with the arrangement.

In the late afternoon, Schooner would return Lucy to her family, prepare dinner if Katrin had not already done so, and stay until the children were put to bed. It made for terribly long days, but sometimes Schooner would stay even later to sit in front of the fire with her friends and listen to Torchy reminisce about his trapping days or Jack Q talk about interesting things that had happened on his travels. Sometimes Quincy talked about childhood memories they all shared. Those evenings were such a source of contentment that it erased the fatigue.

On one such evening, not long after Christmas, Quincy went out to help a neighbor whose wagon was stuck in the snow, and Torchy retired early. Schooner and Jack Q were left alone. "There's something I'd like to talk to your mother about," he said, "but I'd like to discuss it with you first."

"Certainly. What is it? Is there something wrong?"

"Not really, but I want to make a change, and it will involve all of us, in a way. You see, I keep thinking how close I came to never seeing Beatrice again. It was an accident I returned when I did. And then I look at my father and I can't help but fear he won't be with us very much longer either. He's failing—he does his best to hide it, but time is catching up with him."

"You don't want to travel anymore?" Schooner asked.

"No, I don't. Even before this, I was thinking about it. I'm just not sure how your mother will feel. I would keep on all my life, if that's what she wanted. We have all become wealthy because of her and Freiler's Cures. I owe her a great deal."

"She feels the same way about you and Quincy. It would not have meant anything to have good products if she'd not had the two of you to convince people to buy them. I know she won't mind. We've got more orders than we can fill as it is."

"The name sells itself now, you know," Jack Q added. "I honestly think my going abroad on a regular basis is something of a waste. I've considered it well and kept a careful list of my contacts. I believe I could do as much good sending out advertising letters to the people I know as I could by continuing to visit."

"I'm sure you're right."

"I'll speak to Maggie, then. But, Schooner, I have another question. How do you feel about my staying here?"

"I think, if it would make you happier, you should," she replied.

"No, that's not what I asked. How do *you* feel?"

Schooner felt her face warming like a schoolgirl's. She hadn't blushed for years. "I would like for you to be here all the time, Jack Q," she answered, somewhat surprised at how appealing the idea really was.

"Good. I'll see what your mother has to say. It's gotten late. Let me drive you home."

As he spoke, Quincy came back in, shaking snow off his boots. "What are you doing? Don't drag out all your things, Jack Q. I'm already dressed for the weather. I'll take Schooner over."

Schooner bundled up and sat covered with a buffalo robe

while Quincy hitched the horses to the carriage. She'd been going through Beatrice's clothing that day, helping Katrin decide what to give away and what to keep for Lucy as mementos of her mother. Her mind was very much in the past, and she kept coming back to one particular memory. Jack Q had painted her a vivid word picture once of the future—a sad picture of thwarted longing and misguided love. She had been wondering all day if he was right. "I found the letters I wrote Bea when I lived in Lawrence," she said when Quincy climbed up beside her and clucked the horses into motion. "She'd kept them in a box. I'd have been far more eloquent if I'd realized they were being saved," she said.

"That seems a long time ago, doesn't it?" Quincy answered.

"In some ways, yes. It's odd, though—as the years go by, I find that I get smarter and more experienced, but I don't feel I get older. I can remember a time when I thought anyone over twenty-five must have their life completely mapped out and under control. But now that I'm past that age myself, I realize I'm still fifteen inside and eager to find out what is next. Do you suppose our parents still feel that way? Fifteen on the inside?"

"When you were fifteen—or not much older—you were in love with me. Are you still?"

The question took her by surprise, though she knew it shouldn't have. She looked away, embarrassed for the second time in one evening by a man's question.

"Schooner," he went on, "I know it's probably too soon, but we are both free now. We could marry when a decent mourning period has passed."

"Quincy, it *is* too soon. Please . . ."

"We were meant for each other. We've always known it. But if you can't talk about it now, we won't."

They pulled up in front of Schooner's house. Charity Woodren was at the window. "Victoria says she won't go to sleep until you tell her good night!" she called out, and Schooner was relieved to have a good reason to go straight inside. She thanked Quincy for the ride and hurried up the walk.

After giving her sleepy daughter a kiss and singing her a lullaby, Schooner went to her room. She blew out the candle by the bedside and undressed by the light of the moon. Sitting in the rocker by the window, brushing out her hair, Schooner tried to sort out her thoughts. Her mind was churning with confusion, but certain shocking truths were beginning to emerge in spite of her efforts to put them aside.

Earlier in the day, when she was sorting through Bea's belongings, and later, when they all talked of old times, she had realized that, though Beatrice was dead, the essence of her still lived in all their hearts. When a friend died, it was not as though she had simply never existed. She still felt the same love for Beatrice. The same caring pity. Most important, the same loyalty.

And it was her loyalty that had held her back all these years from the love she felt for Quincy. Or was it? That had been the reason she married Henry and moved away. But that was, as Quincy had said, a long time ago, and she had changed, in spite of what she'd said about still feeling fifteen.

Putting the brush down with a clatter, she rose and began to pace the room. She kept remembering Beatrice saying, "He loves Schooner." Those words would haunt her the rest of her life. Had she really guessed in spite of Schooner's efforts to hide it from her? Or was it just the disjointed thoughts of a sick woman? Either way, she would never be able to wipe those three words from her mind.

She stopped at the window and gazed down at the moon-washed snow below. She tried to imagine herself in Quincy's arms, in the bed he and Beatrice had shared. And she knew she could not love him without feeling every moment that she was being a traitor to her best friend.

But imagining making love to Quincy had made her realize something even more important. A concept so shocking it took her breath away.

She didn't love Quincy anymore.

Not the way she once had, anyway. Not with the dizzying passion she'd felt for him as a girl. The realization brought tears to her eyes. It was as though she had suddenly found out that her most treasured possession had been irrevocably lost. But this was not a tangible thing that had been wrenched away from her in a single moment. It was a part of the foundation of her life that had slipped away so stealthily she'd not even known until it was gone.

But it was gone. Truly gone.

She still loved him, in the way she had loved Beatrice and her family and other friends. But the passion of years ago was no more. Just as she was in the habit of looking out the window to check the weather every morning, her devastating love of Quincy had been a habit, not a real emotion. How long had it been so? she wondered, as she rested her head against the window frame and felt the ripples of cold air caress her face.

She suspected it had started to shrivel when she came back from Lawrence. When Jack Q had stayed with her that night in the cabin alongside the river. His presence had actually been more comfort to her than Quincy's, because he was a friend. A friend? Was that it? she wondered, remembering how happy she had been to see Jack Q boarding the train when she returned from Saint Louis.

She rubbed her eyes, pressed her fingers hard against her aching temples. Too many new ideas and understandings were sweeping over her. She felt she was losing her mind, her grip on her own feelings. She'd never felt so confused. Had she really been weeping over a phantom all these years while sprightly red-haired reality had been standing next to her all the time?

Dear God, I've made a mess of my life, she thought as she threw herself miserably into the cold, lonely bed. And the worst of it was, the years could not be called back to be fixed.

Jack Q had asked her only tonight if she wanted him to stay in Seventrees, and she'd given him a "Maggie-sensible" answer. Why hadn't she said "Yes, stay here. For God's sake—for *my* sake—stay!"

She must be mad, she thought as she tossed in bed, tangled in her nightshift. *I'll wait. I'll think this out and make sure it isn't just dead-of-winter insanity, and then . . . then I'll speak honestly to both of them. I'll certainly make a damned fool of myself and embarrass everyone, but I will have at least done the right thing—the honest thing for once in my life— and will have no more reason for regret. If I end up a dried-up, lonesome old maid, I'll at least know I was honest.*

Schooner had planned to stay home the next day with the girls because Charity was going to visit a friend in Westport. She went to Quincy's to get Lucy and was enormously relieved to find that both Quincy and Jack Q were gone. "Jack Q's over at your mother's," Katrin said. "And Quincy's probably at the cemetery. He ought to be back before long."

Schooner hurriedly dressed Lucy and escaped. She moved through the morning in a haze, playing games with the little girls and eventually fixing them their favorite lunch before putting them down for a nap. They were barely asleep when

411

she heard a forceful knock on the front door. It was Jack Q. She knew before she even opened the door.

"I've been talking to your mother," he said brusquely as he came in.

"Talking or arguing?" she asked.

"Talking. What do you mean?" He tossed his coonskin hat on a chair and struggled out of his coat as if it were a mortal enemy.

"You sound angry."

"Yes, but not at her. She was completely in agreement with me. We've got it all worked out. But I *am* angry and I'm going to tell you why. Sit down!"

"I'm sitting," she said calmly. She was accustomed to his temper, and almost welcomed it this time.

He didn't seem to notice her reaction. "Look here, Schooner," he said, practically dancing around the room with energy and anger. "There are some things you ought to know, and by damn I'm going to tell them to you, whether you like it or not. I don't know what went on between you and Quincy last night, and . . . No, don't say anything. I don't *want* to know. But he's going to talk to you about marriage sooner or later—"

"He told you that?"

"Of course he didn't tell me! But I've been watching the two of you giving each other melting looks for the last ten years. I know what's between you."

"Do you really?" Schooner said, thoroughly enjoying his tantrum.

"Yes, goddammit! But I don't think *you* know the whole truth of the matter, and you should. He goes to the cemetery every day, did you know?"

"No, I didn't," Schooner answered, suddenly less amused.

"Every day. Sometimes several times. I've found him there, crying like a child over her. Schooner, he loved her. I don't think the poor bastard realized it until she was gone, and now it's tearing him apart. But if I know him, he's still trying to believe he's in love with you too. Just because it would be dishonorable not to be. I mean . . ." He stopped a moment, his thoughts having raced ahead of his words.

"I know what you mean. I know exactly what you mean," Schooner assured him.

"I'm sorry to hurt you, but I'm trying to save you more hurt," he said. "He'll marry you now. And his love of my sister will always stand between you." He paused again, tact-

412

fully looking away and giving her a chance to absorb this. He tried to stuff some tobacco into a pipe and ended up spilling it all over the floor. Finally he threw the pipe on the hearth in frustration. "Schooner, I've been standing around like a damned useless I-don't-know-what, watching you marry the wrong men over and over again, and I haven't tried to stop you. This time I'm going to stop you if I have to carry you off physically and lock you up somewhere."

"Out of friendship?" she asked.

"Out of love, you simpleton!" he shouted.

"Shhh, you'll wake the girls."

"Damn! I wasn't going to say that!" he answered, only slightly more quietly. "It doesn't matter about me. What I'm trying to tell you is this: if you marry Quincy, you'll both be miserable. *Miserable!*"

Schooner stood and walked to where he stood fidgeting with the broken pieces of pipe by the fireplace. "What do you suggest I do instead of marrying him?" she asked.

He was disconcerted, but determined to keep up his tough stance. "If I had my way, you'd marry me!" he said belligerently.

Schooner took the pipe out of his hand and tossed it into the fire before stepping closer yet to him. "Is that a real proposal?"

Jack Q stared at her in amazement for a moment, completely unbalanced by this turn of events. "Of course it is," he finally said softly. "I've loved you for as long as I can remember."

"Why didn't you say so?"

"Because I didn't want to be a second-best choice. I still don't."

"A long time ago," Schooner said, "your sister told me she didn't think there was such a thing as 'falling in love.' She said it was something that took a long time to happen, and there was just a certain day when you realized how you felt." She put her hands to his face. "Jack Q, yesterday was the day. If you hadn't come to me, I'd have come to you."

"My God! You mean it, don't you?" he said, holding her tightly.

"I do! Yes, I do! For the first time in my life, I'm absolutely sure I'm doing the right thing. Why didn't you tell me sooner that you and I belonged together?"

"Because you wouldn't have believed me," he answered, his lips brushing hers.

Schooner clung to him, not knowing whether to laugh or weep. Suddenly she wasn't fifteen inside. She knew this was just the first of many kisses and the beginning of a love that would last her the rest of her life.

Part III

VICTORIA

Home

1

Dear Elgin,

I suppose this letter will surprise you, coming at a time other than Christmas, but there is something I would like to arrange. Victoria, as you know, will be sixteen this winter, and her studies at the girls' school in Saint Louis will be completed shortly after that. I'm sure she's told you about the school in the many letters she writes you. It is quite a good school, but in a way it has spoiled her. The deportment, languages, and fashion she has learned there have made her dissatisfied with the prospect of coming back to Seventrees. Though it is my dearest wish that she make her life here, I do not wish it to be a choice made simply from lack of alternatives.

So I am writing to ask if you would take responsibility for her for two years. I should like for her to take additional education in England and become acquainted first hand with the way you live. She is, after all, your daughter as well as mine. In many ways I feel she is *more* your daughter, inasmuch as taste and inclination are concerned.

Though we have corresponded but infrequently over the years, I think you know this is not a suggestion which truly appeals to me, nor do I ask for my own sake, but for Victoria's. It would please her greatly. She has a tremendous interest and fondness for you, and I think she should at least meet her father before her youth is over. I shall not, however, discuss this with her until I have your reply, in case there is some difficulty that makes this plan unworkable at the present.

As for other news, I suppose she has kept you informed, but you may not know about Morning Wish. We recently received a letter from my mother's old friend Black Feather. He has been gone for many years, and you did not meet him, but I'm sure you heard us mention him. He had moved away with the remnants of his tribe, and wrote Mother that he had started a school for Indian children in Wyoming. He asked her if Morning Wish could come and teach English there. We hated to see her go, of course, for we may not see her again for years, if ever. But I shall never forget the look of pleasure on her lovely face when she left.

My father and Quincy ask me to send you their regards. I look forward to hearing from you at your earliest convenience.

Respectfully yours,
Schooner

November 5, 1881

My dearest Schooner,

Regarding your excellent plan for Victoria, I'm afraid there is something of a problem. I would not in the normal way of things burden you with this, but under the circumstances, I feel I should explain. When my father and brother died years ago, I had the impression that the inheritance I was to receive was a large one. It was, but it was also encumbered with a great many debts and ongoing financial responsibilities. Besides Farrvale Manor, I have the houses in London and Bath and the shooting lodge in Scotland. Maintaining and staffing them is quite

418

a burden, and I have not been blessed with your family's uncanny affection for economy, and I'm afraid there is only enough left to maintain my own needs.

To entertain and educate Victoria in the proper style would be an expensive proposition, and I fear that I would be unable to do her justice. So, as much as I would love to see her, I'm afraid it's quite impossible.

Yours,
Elgin

It was not quite time for the Sunday-evening meal, and the sixteen students of the Winston Academy for Young Ladies were taking their evening walks in groups of two and three. Their normally subdued talk was a little noisier than usual, for it was spring and school was almost over. Lucy Clay and Victoria Farrington were the center of everyone's attention as groups of hoop-skirted girls began to drift toward the door in anticipation of dinner. "Tell me about it again," a plump girl with bunches of jonquil-yellow ringlets asked fawningly.

Victoria and Lucy turned to face her. Victoria was of less than average height, but her shapely figure and regal bearing often led people to think of her as a tall girl. She wore her hair, a rich topaz-blond mass, in a thick figure eight at the nape of her neck, a sophisticated style she'd seen in magazines from the Continent. She had a self-assurance verging on haughtiness that caused younger girls to have crushes on her and older girls to resent her. Her wide-set, tranquil eyes often flashed with anger, and her sensuous-looking lips tended, in repose, to curve into a vague smile that disconcerted people.

Victoria's adult appearance and manners made Lucy Clay, her constant companion, look all the more childish by comparison. Lucy's hair was the dark mahogany of her father's, but with her mother's tendency to frizz. She was small-boned, though strong, and her delicate features bore a perpetually wistful look. Her hands were small and often busy worrying some object. Her nails were never exactly bitten, just nibbled. Her voice was high-pitched, but breathy rather than shrill. Friends sometimes had to ask her to repeat things, though mere acquaintances usually discounted her and didn't bother to ask.

At the girl's question, Victoria's milky brow wrinkled. "Tell you about what?" she asked coolly.

"Why, your trip to England, of course," the plump girl said. "You and Lucy going to visit England, just imagine!"

"Not exactly a visit," Victoria explained. "It is to complete our education and prepare to join my father's circle of acquaintances. It is my proper place, you know. Not here."

"Oh, Vic, don't say that," Lucy said. She twisted her fan until one of the ribs splintered.

"Now, look what you've done," Victoria said affectionately. "I'll fix it for you."

Victoria Farrington's concern for Lucy was a source of curiosity to the other girls. In the four years Victoria had been at the Winston Academy, she had never been known to be friendly to, much less solicitous of, anyone but Lucy. Lucy was, or would have been, considered a poor little wet rag by the others, except for Victoria's concern. But because Victoria sponsored her, and Victoria's aloof friendship was so valued, Lucy too was treated as though she was special.

"More school! Oh, dear, I don't think I could bear it," another girl added as she joined the moths clustering around Victoria's light. "It's all I could endure to last this one out. I'm going to go back to Atchison and have parties till Papa runs out of money, then I'm going to marry and forget everything I've learned here."

This statement brought a ruffle of giggles until the girls realized how little amusement Victoria found in the remark. "That's very well, Liz, if you really think you can be happy rotting away in Atchison all your life. I've got other ideas, myself."

"I was just making a joke," the girl called Liz hastened to explain. "I really do envy you ever so much. And you, too, Lucy," she quickly added. They all knew the way to Victoria's heart (if, indeed, she had one) was through Lucy Clay.

"Envy us?" Lucy said, her customary meekness put aside. "Having to travel halfway around the world to live with a bunch of strangers?"

"You don't want to go?" the daffodil blond asked.

"Of course she does," Victoria assured them. "It's just such a new idea. We just got the letters explaining the plans yesterday. Lucy will accustom herself to the idea before long and be as pleased as I am that our parents have realized this is the best thing for young women of our age and station."

"Oh, Vic!" Lucy said, then quickly subsided.

"You're not going by yourselves, certainly," Liz said, trying to cover her former faux pas. "Will your mother take you over? Or your father—I mean, your stepfather," she corrected quickly, knowing how angry Victoria got when people inadvertently referred to Jacques LeSage as her father.

"My mother! Go to England?" Victoria scoffed. "Surely not, that's the whole reason my father divorced her—because she refused to go with him as her duty demanded. I suppose my stepfather might take us. After all, he is Lucy's uncle. But I rather hope not—I mean, those terrible clothes he wears would be an awful embarrassment. Now, Lucy, don't look offended. You know how silly we would look being escorted by a man who looks like . . ."

Lucy had been content to let Victoria dominate her most of her life, but however subordinate she was, she was not spineless. There was a line beyond which she would not be pushed. She knew precisely where the limit was; Victoria never quite caught on that there *was* a limit, and was surprised anew every time Lucy stood up for herself. Thus she turned astonished wide eyes on her friend when Lucy said, quite firmly, "Vic, Uncle Jack did business in Europe for many years, and never changed his manner of dress or behavior to do so. He was never an embarrassment to our parents and I think it's awful of you to talk about him like that. I would be perfectly glad to have anyone meet him and know he's my uncle." Her face was flushed and she looked uneasy about her outburst, but defiant, nonetheless.

Victoria drew herself up to her full five-foot-three and said, "Lucy, it's lovely of you to be so loyal. But having an eccentric uncle is something that can happen to anyone. Having the same man as a stepfather is a different matter altogether. Now, we'll say no more about it." This last remark was accompanied by a warning glance at the group of girls clustered around them. Speaking to them again, Victoria said, "The letter didn't say, but I should suppose that Lucy's father and stepmother will take us over. He does all the European end of the drug business now anyway and knows all about ships and hotels and such. Of course, his wife is from England and will probably want to visit."

"When are we to leave?" Lucy asked. "Father didn't mention a date in the letter he wrote."

"Neither did my mother," Victoria admitted. "But I suppose it will be soon. We'll need time to get ready—not that my mother or grandmother will want to part with enough money to outfit me properly." Victoria quickly realized this bitter remark might give the others the wrong impression, so she added, "Isn't it odd how people with a generous income can be so very stingy when it comes to their children's expenses?"

This was a frequent theme at the Winston Academy. The young women who attended, whose families represented a great deal of the wealth of Kansas and Missouri, were constantly lamenting the lack of adequate allowances for clothing and trinkets. The indignant chatter that followed the introduction of this familiar motif kept the girls occupied until the bell rang, signaling dinner. As the others hurried ahead, crinolines swaying, to get places at table next to their friends and as far from the watchful eye of authority as possible, Victoria and Lucy hung back. Victoria took her friend's hand. "Lucy, you mustn't be so cross and worried. We'll have a divine time, really we will. I promise you. If you truly don't like it after we're there awhile, we'll come back."

Lucy sighed. "Very well, Vic. I'll try to like the idea, but please . . . *please* don't continue to speak so badly of Uncle Jack and your mother. It's most distressing."

"I'll try. Now, let's go eat."

They arrived at Southampton in early September. Victoria was terribly disappointed that their route was not going to take them through London, but Quincy Clay insisted that there was not time. "Your father is expecting you. You'll have ample opportunities for travel. Hurry, ladies," he added, shepherding the girls and his wife toward another dock and the channel packet that would take them from Southampton to Dover. Victoria did her best not to gawk—she'd had a lot of practice these last few weeks. So many new sights and sounds and experiences.

The worst of it was, Lucy's father, of all people, acted as though it were all perfectly ordinary! He knew his way around New York; he knew how to find their suite of cabins aboard the luxurious steamship they took; at dinner he knew all about wines and French names for food; and now, here in England, he was handling strange money as if it were commonplace and was efficiently getting them from Southampton to the county of Kent without any apparent confusion. She was begrudgingly impressed. She'd always thought of him as just another boring, stay-at-home resident of Seventrees. Of course, he was gone a great deal, but she'd never given much thought to where he went or what he did, except that it was some part of the medicine business.

Why hadn't her mother set her cap for Mr. Clay instead of a temperamental woodsman like Jacques LeSage? She and Lucy could have been stepsisters. What a wonderful idea! Of course, they were closer than most sisters, anyway. She leaned back against the lush cushions of the first-class deck and thought about how different life might have been if she'd had the ordering of it. No Jack Q, no Eleanor Clay. Victoria had never been able to understand what Mr. Clay or Lucy had seen in the frail Englishwoman he'd brought back to Seventrees as his wife ten years ago. Lucy seemed to be genuinely fond of her, but Victoria didn't see why. Eleanor Clay was pale, shy, and vaguely "indisposed" most of the time. Utterly boring. But then, from what she'd heard, Lucy's real mother had been much the same way.

Another thought occurred to her. If her mother had married Mr. Clay, Ned would be her brother, too. That would have been such fun. She got along with Ned almost as well as she did with Lucy, which was somewhat odd, since Ned shared none of Victoria's pretensions. Unlike his sister, however, Ned was quiet in a completely confident way. There was nothing shy about him, no insecurities or uncertainties. He was merely reserved. Only those who knew him well were privileged to know what he thought, and even they seldom caught him talking about his passions: his family, friends, home, and business. He'd finished law school that spring and plunged straight into a job with Freiler's Cures. Victoria had thought this particularly foolish and wasted no time telling him so. "You could go anywhere in the world you wanted," she lamented.

"Yes, and I have," he answered quietly. They'd been sitting on the front porch of Maggie's house while last-minute preparations were made for loading Lucy and Victoria's trunks. Ned leaned comfortably against one of the porch pillars and sucked thoughtfully on a grass stem while Victoria ranted.

"I swear, Ned, you're wasted here."

Without looking at her or altering his smile, he said, "No, Vic, I'm useful here. I'm needed."

"Needed? Phoo! Who wants to be needed?" she scoffed.

"Everybody. You included. You just want right now to be needed by people you haven't yet met."

"Oh, Ned. That's stupid!" she said. She always seemed to

find herself arguing with him. Well . . . not arguing, because that took two people, and he utterly refused to be goaded. "Why aren't you coming with us?" she asked. "I wish you would. Your sister and father and stepmother are all going."

He turned and looked at her. "Then what do you want me along for?" He always seemed to be mocking her somehow, but in such a subtle and affectionate way she couldn't find fault. Ned made her question herself with his inquiries. Why did she want him to come?—for surely she *did* want it. She supposed it was because he and Lucy were her only real friends and she hated to let go of his companionship now that he was finally back from the years at college. She told him so.

"Well, Vic, I can't go running off the same month I start work, but I'll be right here when you get back."

"Back? Oh, I won't be back," she said with the light trilling laugh she'd been practicing for months. "No. Not me, unless to visit sometime. I'm going to England permanently. It's my . . . my 'spiritual home,' you see."

Ned made a choking noise like a laugh run amok. "Where in the world did you find a pretentious phrase like that, Vic?" he managed to ask between guffaws.

Victoria was offended. She'd thought it a lovely, deep thought. But it was hard to be haughty around Ned. "I don't see what's so amusing." She tried to say it very seriously, but a smile crept into her voice.

"You are, Vic," he said, coming over to sit by her and sling an arm around her shoulders.

She leaned against him for a moment. "Ned, I'll miss you."

"No, you won't. Not for a while, anyway," he replied.

"You'll come visit?"

Ned took his arm back and fitted the grass stem between his thumbs. Blowing between them, he created an ear-splitting squawk. Looking satisfied, he finally replied, "Oh, later perhaps. Father goes over every two years or so, and I might come along next time. We'll see how cravenly you beg me by then. I think that's the last trunk they're loading now. You better get ready," he had said. And he'd taken her arm, just like a gentleman was supposed to, for the first time ever.

Riding through the English countryside, so far from Ned, Victoria thought about it and must have smiled, for Lucy said, "You look happy, Vic. What are you thinking about?"

"I . . . oh, just how lovely everything is," Victoria answered. It was partly the truth. The small boat was hugging

424

the coast, giving them a sightseer's introduction to southern England. Everything was pretty and clean and "controlled." It was the only word she could think of to characterize the difference from the landscape she was used to. Even the undulating chalk cliffs looked as pristine as white satin curtains, and the sea was a soft blue-gray. Could it and the murky, churning brown fluid of the Kaw both be water? It seemed impossible.

In Kansas everything was wild and untamed outside the towns. It was always too hot or too cold, and when it rained, it rained too hard and washed big muddy gullies. But here there was a light mist falling that made everything look like a painting—soft, pasteled, and gentle. It was the sort of place where bad things couldn't happen. Refined. That was it, everything was delightfully refined. This was where she belonged.

When they got to Dover, they found a private coach waiting. A liveried servant sat atop, and it was drawn by a foursome of matched dappled gray horses. They were quite the most handsome animals Victoria had ever seen, and the coachman seemed like something out of a dream or a fairy story. He was arrayed in a splendid crimson-and-ivory uniform with yards and yards of gold braid. The carriage was painted the same deep red and polished to a mirror finish. The interior was ivory velvet and the door was ornamented with an elaborately medieval-looking coat of arms.

"'Afternoon, Mr. and Mrs. Clay," the coachman said, helping them into the carriage.

"How are you, Jarvis? New team, I see," Quincy replied.

"Yes, sir, just breaking them in. I thought you might like to show the young ladies the castle, sir, but with this fog . . ."

"They'll have adequate opportunities later," Quincy said. "Let's be off."

"Yes, sir."

"What about our trunks?" Victoria whispered.

Quincy smiled and discreetly pointed out a crimson-painted wagon parked farther along the quay. "That's your father's also. The footman will see to the bags. I've never figured out quite how it's done, but our things will get there before we do. See if they don't."

Victoria hugged Lucy, then hugged herself in glee. "Footmen, Lucy. Castles! Red carriages! Imagine!"

Lucy smiled wanly.

They rode through narrow, shady lanes alive with the

sweet songs of unfamiliar birds. Eleanor Clay sat forward in the seat, eagerly drinking in the sights and sounds of her home. She looked more lively and animated than Victoria had ever seen her. Victoria thought how fine it must be to feel that way about coming home. If it were the other way around and it was Victoria coming home to Seventrees, she thought she'd probably have her head on her knees, weeping.

Through gaps in the live hedgerows they caught glimpses of clean-looking black-faced sheep and well-kept cattle. Eventually they turned off a side road and drew up to a pair of enormous stone pillars, large enough to have small towerlike rooms inside. Two young men wearing uniforms that matched the coach driver's came out of small wooden doors in the pillars and pulled open the heavy iron gates. "Someone came out and opened those gates that way when Queen Elizabeth visited here," Quincy said as the girls sat staring.

"*The* Queen Elizabeth?" Victoria exclaimed. "This estate is that old?"

"Older," Quincy answered. "As I recall, Henry the Seventh granted the land to one of his friends after the Battle of Bosworth. The friend spent his entire fortune building the house, then had the bad luck to fall out with King Henry, who then took it back and bestowed it on an ancestor of your father's. They've held on to it ever since, somehow. Isn't that right, Eleanor?"

Victoria was awed by this information, not that she could remember what she'd been taught about all those Henrys when she was in school in Saint Louis, but she was certainly going to make a point of learning about them now. She kept craning her neck for a view of the house, but the ride seemed endless as the narrow lane wound through miles of forest. Finally they emerged from the trees at the top of a rise. Below them was a shallow scoop of green valley. In the middle sat the largest single structure Victoria had ever seen. She gasped with surprise, for it was immense. Built of yellowish-gray stone in a huge H shape, the house seemed to go on for miles. There were three stories with towers and turrets and crenellated battlements. There were hundreds of windows, set in deeply, attesting to the thickness of the walls. Here and there, the pattern of the stonework showed where a door or window had been, perhaps centuries before. Several faces of the building were cloaked in ivy, and a flag flew among a forest of chimneys on top. They were obviously later additions, constructed of brick laid in fantastic spiral patterns.

As they got closer, ornate stone carving and gargoyles became visible. "My father lives here?" she whispered.

"Oh, Vic . . ." Lucy's voice was almost inaudible. "Look. Arrow slits. It's a castle, a real castle!"

Victoria's heart was pounding so wildly she could hardly breathe. "Mr. Clay, why didn't you tell me?"

Quincy was smiling. "How could I? Would you have believed me? Actually, it's not a castle. It hasn't a curtain wall, just the remains of a moat on two sides. It's a fortified manor house."

As they approached the front door, the coach slowed. Victoria tried to assemble her wits enough so she wouldn't disgrace herself in front of the army of servants who were gathering on the front steps. There must have been a couple dozen of them. In their midst was a tall, middle-aged man; perhaps he was an uncle or something, waiting to escort her to meet her father. He would probably be inside, in the trophy room he'd told her about once in a letter. The coachman opened the door and offered her a hand. The strange man walked toward them. Yes, he might well be a relative. He had the same fair hair as the miniature painting she had of her father, though he was much older, heavier, and more tired-looking. His face had the pink flush of men in Seventrees who habitually drank too much. Victoria hoped he didn't live here, whoever he was. But then, he might be very nice. She warned herself not to judge too hastily.

As she stood waiting for the Clays to step down from the coach, the man came forward and took her hand. "Victoria," he said in a voice so fond it left no doubt.

"Elgin, let me introduce your daughter," Quincy said as the man embraced her carefully.

"You've all your mother's healthy beauty," he said, holding her back and looking her over. "Not so tall as either of us, but the color is exact. After we're better acquainted, I'll have to paint you. I've a painting of your mother in the Great Hall. She didn't approve of it, but I think it's one of the best things I did in America. My dear child, how glad I am to have you here. And, Eleanor . . . you haven't changed a bit. Still lovely. This must be your Lucy, Quincy. I haven't seen her since she was a baby, though Eleanor sends me pictures to keep me up on her progress. . . ."

He chatted on as he led them to the bank of servants, and Lucy whispered to Victoria, "What's wrong? You look like you swallowed something. Your father is very nice. He speaks so beautifully."

"But he's old!" Victoria answered. "I mean, he's not quite what I had pictured."

"Don't be silly, Vic, nothing is like we'd pictured. He's very pleasant."

But one of Victoria's dreams had shattered at her feet. Her father had been handsome and dashing in her mind. In fact, he was something else altogether. Just as the house had been more than she expected, her father was less. He was ordinary.

She put on a brave smile and was introduced to the servants. Fortunately only the chief house steward and head housekeeper were important enough to be introduced by name. The others merely bowed or curtsied *en masse*—footmen, valets, housemaids, laundresses, cook's assistants, and scullery maids all paid their respects to the new daughter of the master and hurried back to their jobs. These were, Elgin explained, only the indoor servants, and the girls' personal attendant, their lady's maid, would introduce herself later.

Taking Victoria's arm, Elgin escorted them into the house at last. The front doors were almost a story and a half tall and took two servants to push open. "We don't use this way often," Elgin said. "Only for official occasions." The front hall was the size of a small pasture, with an elaborate gallery on three sides, and up past it, a domed ceiling with a mural of angels and soldiers. "We'll go along to the library for a few moments," Elgin said, leading the way. "Then you may go to your rooms and wash away the journey."

The library seemed to be down a half-mile of corridors lined with old paintings and statuary and floored with exquisite marble. Their destination turned out to be an oak-paneled room, with banks of books on three walls. The room was cool and dim, and the ceiling was so high it was invisible. The fourth wall had a row of tall French windows opening onto a marble-balustraded terrace overlooking a small lake with swans floating regally on the water and sheep grazing contentedly on the banks. "Capability Brown did the view," Elgin said. Victoria had no idea what this remark meant, but Quincy Clay nodded as if it made sense.

The adults fell into a conversation about mutual friends. Quincy's wife, Eleanor, had often visited the house with her parents, and apparently this was where she first met Quincy. She and Elgin spoke brightly about people named Adelaide and Robert and Frederick while Lucy and Victoria looked out the windows. When they were finally comfortably seated, Elgin touched a bell on a side table and an immaculately gloved servant as stiff as a wooden Indian came in immediately with a silver tray bearing glasses and decanters. He poured brandy for the men and tiny crystal glasses of sherry for the women. Victoria sipped at the thimbleful of sweet liquid and cast a quick glance at Lucy. She, too, was trying hard not to make a face at the pungent taste. Victoria felt a giggle welling up and tried her best to stifle it, but when the corners of Lucy's mouth began to twitch, she couldn't hold it back.

Elgin rang the discreet little bell again, and the servant reappeared. "Summon Yvonne, if you will," he said, and a moment later a young woman in a severely tailored gray dress appeared. Elgin addressed her in a rapid spate of French, which Victoria couldn't understand except to catch the general idea that this was the personal maid for herself and Lucy. "Ladies, dinner is in two hours, if you feel like a rest first."

Victoria and Lucy trailed along after the maid. "I feel like I ought to be dropping crumbs so I can find my way back," Lucy whispered, and set Victoria's giggles off again.

They found they had a suite of luxurious rooms on the third floor, overlooking the same view as the library. There was a central sitting room with several groupings of sofas and tables, and by the windows, a piano. To one side there was a huge dressing room with mirrors and closets. Opening off the dressing room were their bedrooms, with a large private bathroom for each girl. Just as Quincy Clay had predicted, their luggage had arrived in advance. Their trunks had been unpacked, and Victoria found her own combs and brushes and perfume sitting out ready for her on the dressing table. Her favorite robe was laid out on the huge high bed. The maid offered to help them change their clothes.

"Oh, we can help each other," Lucy said.

"Nonsense, Lucy, that's what Yvonne is here for," Victoria said quickly. Then, to the maid she said, "Our ways are different in America. We have a great deal to learn about what is proper. I hope you are prepared to help us with what we must know. For instance, the schedule here in this house."

"Your papa, he will tell you all about such things. Now, if you will excuse me, mademoiselle, I will draw your bath."

When she had disappeared, Lucy and Victoria huddled together whispering excitedly. "Draw a bath?" Lucy said. "I'm not sure I like having people do things for me that I'm perfectly capable of doing for myself. But isn't it thrilling!"

"See, I told you it would be wonderful," Victoria said. "My mother must have been out of her mind! Imagine staying back in dreary old Seventrees when she could have come and lived here."

Lucy's smile faded. "Seventrees isn't dreary, Vic. This place is different—fancier and much bigger—but it's not *better* than home."

"Oh yes it is!" Victoria said with rare intensity. "It's much, much better and it's where I'm going to stay forever!"

Victoria quickly got over her initial disappointment in her father. Life at Farrvale Manor the first week was so exciting she could not have been unhappy about anything. Mornings she slept late and awakened only when a servant brought breakfast on a tray. And such a tray—several honeyed fruits, superb pastries, kippers, bacon, steaming jasmine-scented tea and porridge, all served on the most elegant of china and crystal.

She learned that it was best to be up and dressed by eleven o'clock, however, for that was when the staff began to invade the upstairs rooms, having finished with their jobs downstairs. The housemaid came in first to scour the firegrate and tools and to rekindle the dying embers of fire from the night before. Equipped with a basket of cleaning materials and rags, she worked furiously at her job, but would do no other. "Something has spilled on the floor here," Victoria said to her the second morning. "Could you wipe it up?"

The woman looked astonished and offended. "If you would ring your bell for the housekeeper, miss, she will see that someone attends to it."

The housekeeper, summoned from three floors and a quarter of a mile of hallways away, did not seem to find it odd that the housemaid, standing next to the offending stain with a basket of cleaning rags, had not simply bent over and wiped it up. Neither did she deign to correct the situation

430

herself. Examining the spill, she said politely, "I'll send Margy, miss."

A quarter of an hour later, Margy appeared, wiped up the spot, bobbed a curtsy, and disappeared. Victoria was left shaking her head in wonder.

After the housemaid finished her work with the fire and another servant had brought in a neat little basket of coal to replace what had been used, the waterman arrived. He was a giant of a man, dressed in a modified version of the red-and-white livery and carrying a yoke to which were attached two big canisters of boiling-hot water. With great care to prevent nicks to the porcelain, he dumped the scalding water into Victoria's bathtub and quickly disappeared for his next load. The bath had running water, but only cold, so he had to repeat this labor for each room.

Yvonne always followed hard on his heels to mix the bath to the proper temperature, pour in the scented salts, and then to do Victoria's hair when she was through bathing. These activities usually took until noon, at which time an ancient old man, shrunken and tottering, made his way down the halls tapping with a padded stick on the luncheon gong. This was obviously his retirement activity, for Yvonne explained that he used to be majordomo until his son was ready for the job, at which time he took over the light duties of roaming about the halls twice a day, ringing the gong. "So his son is the second generation to work here?" Victoria asked.

"No, miss. He is the seventh," the young woman answered, stunning Victoria into silence.

Lucy's father had business to conduct in London, and her stepmother had friends to visit, so they were going to stay only two days before moving on. Lucy stuck to them until the moment of departure, so Victoria had time alone to explore the house in the early afternoons. Her favorite—or, at least, the most impressive—was the Great Hall. It was the largest single enclosed space Victoria had ever seen. A long room on such enormous scale that it dwarfed even the huge cumbersome furnishings to dollhouse proportions. The hammer-beam ceiling, over thirty feet high, made her dizzy to contemplate. The lower parts of the walls were covered with paintings, most of them gigantic scenes of battles or classical themes. Even as little as Victoria knew about art, she could guess from the darkened condition and old-fashioned themes that they were not her father's work, but much older.

On the outside wall, there was a fireplace in which two or

three whole cows could have been roasted at once. Above the fireplace, set into niches, were life-size marble statues of what Victoria assumed were the twelve apostles. At the far north end of the Great Hall, slight partitions had been built out from the walls, and the semi-enclosed area thus created served as Elgin's own gallery. Golden oak paneling formed a background for a number of paintings. They were mostly portraits of people Victoria didn't recognize, but the central work was of her mother. Schooner, clad in gingham, her hair windswept, squinted into a searing yellow landscape.

On the opposite wall, there was an oversized scene of soldiers fighting their way up a ravine. Victoria was not impressed with this painting, nor did she realize the irony of her mother's picture facing one of those paintings that helped bring about the tattered end of her own marriage.

On the second afternoon, Victoria explored outside and discovered the stables. For a young woman from the American West, Victoria knew remarkably little about fine horses. In Seventrees horses were work animals, chosen for their ability to pull loads or plow fields, not for their beauty or speed. In fact, a beautiful horse was often suspect. "Looks like she's apt to be a finicky creature," farmers would say on those rare occasions that such a horse was seen in the streets.

In spite of her almost lifelong nagging for a show horse, her mother and grandmother had never even given her a serious answer on the subject. Always just an offhand remark about how expensive and impractical such a thing would be. Here at Farrvale Manor, Victoria's every dream was realized as far as horses were concerned—or so she thought at first. Her father raised racers, sleek, fidgety thoroughbreds with fancy stables and their own trainers. The only problem was, the grooms not only refused to let her ride her choice, they would not even let her near enough to touch the creatures. Victoria stomped back to the house angrily, determined to alert her father to this problem, but she could not find him and had temporarily forgotten it by dinner.

When Lucy's parents left, Victoria fully expected an outbreak of homesickness on her friend's part, but was pleasantly surprised. Lucy joined in her explorations with apparent enjoyment—at least at first. Every afternoon they would explore some new section of the house, much to the servants' distress. By the time the elderly servant rang the dinner gong, they were tired and hungry.

The evening meal was a luxurious repast of many courses

and several wines and took up most of the evening. At the end of each day, Victoria and Lucy would sit up late talking over the day. By the end of the first week, however, Lucy's viewpoint was becoming distressingly unlike Victoria's. She was enjoying herself, there was no denying that, but she regarded the first week as a temporary respite from real life. "When are we going to *do* something?" she inquired.

"Do what? Such a Seventrees attitude, Lucy! Young ladies of our class don't have to do anything but be decorative and amusing and enjoy life. That is what we're doing."

"Well, I don't feel either decorative or amusing. I'm just a tourist," Lucy replied. "I thought we were sent here to be educated. Lessons in how to be a lady, and all that sort of thing."

"But, Lucy, we *are* ladies. At any rate, my father must think so. He said nothing about shipping us off to a school."

That evening after dinner, Victoria found out she was wrong. She also met a woman she was to see often. "Girls, allow me to present Mrs. Wotton," Elgin said.

"How do you do?" Victoria and Lucy parroted politely.

"No, no, my darlings!" Mrs. Wotton exclaimed. "You absolutely must call me Adelaide, just as though we were old friends, for we will be soon."

Victoria could almost feel Lucy stiffening at her side, and her own reaction was much the same. She had an inborn distrust of women who gushed. Mrs. Wotton, or rather, Adelaide, was a big, bony woman who moved with exaggerated care, perhaps the result of a lifetime of trying not to knock things over. She had a rather attractive face, though her teeth were big and horsey-looking. Her hair color, a pale, almost pinkish blonde, could have been natural, but Victoria doubted it. And her eyes had a cold gleam of avarice that her gaudily cheerful demeanor could not hide.

Victoria wished there was some subtle way to find out just who this woman was. She seemed to be on extremely friendly terms with Elgin, making little moues of amusement at his every word and frequently touching his hand lightly or looking at him in a way Victoria could only think of as "intimate."

Victoria couldn't guess the woman's age. In her forties, she supposed, and her guess was partially confirmed when Elgin and she started discussing someone named Frederick. "Robert and Frederick are my sons, darlings," Adelaide explained. "I'm ever so anxious for you to meet them. But I think," she added with a gallingly understanding smile at Elgin, "I think it would be best if we waited just a while yet." With this cryptic remark she turned her full attention back to Elgin. "You did say you were getting Miss Wichett in, didn't you, dear?"

"She will be arriving with her staff in the morning," Elgin announced.

"Dear Miss Wichett," Adelaide said languidly. "I think perhaps I'll just hide away. She quite terrifies me this day."

"Who is Miss Wichett?" Victoria asked.

"She is to be your governess," Elgin said. "You see, your mother wanted you to be taught all the graces . . ." Victoria thought Adelaide had made a tiny sound of derision, but she wasn't sure. Elgin went on as if he'd noticed nothing. "But I'm afraid such things are not done in schools here as they are in your country. Not for people of our station, anyway. Young ladies learn at home."

"Then we're to have lessons?" Lucy asked eagerly.

"What sort of lessons?" Victoria was doubtful.

"Every sort," Adelaide said. "Miss Wichett is known for doing absolutely wonders with difficult cases. We had her in when my cousin from Scotland came to be made over. She's quite wonderful and will have you girls in shape in no time at all."

"Difficult cases? Whatever do you mean by that?" Victoria asked, quite certain now that she did not very much like this woman.

"Now, Victoria, don't be offended," Elgin said. "Adelaide just meant that you girls have so very much to learn in a short time."

Victoria went to bed unhappy. She didn't like Adelaide Wotton for her own sake, but most of all she didn't like her because she seemed to exert a great deal of influence at Farrvale Manor. Then there was this Miss Witchett person to consider, but Victoria felt sure she'd have no trouble there.

Victoria's introduction to Miss Wichett came as a rude awakening—literally. In seemed hardly past dawn when Yvonne timidly shook Victoria's shoulder. "Pardon, mademoiselle, but the teacher wishes to see you before breakfast. She waits in the Blue Parlor."

"Then she'll have to wait a little longer," Victoria said crankily. "I was up late and I don't plan to rise for several hours yet." With that she rolled over and buried her face in a goose-down pillow.

She was soundly asleep again when, without any warning, the covers were yanked off and a strident voice proclaimed, "My time is a valuable commodity, young woman. Far too precious to squander on stay-abeds. Get up!"

Victoria sat up, rubbing her eyes. "What . . . ? Who . . . ?"

"I am Miss Wichett, and until further notice every moment of your life belongs to me. You will not so much as yawn or look sideways without my instruction."

Victoria stared at her tormentor. She was an excruciatingly corseted woman of beefy proportions. She wore a dress and shoes that could only be characterized as "sensible," and her hair was hidden under an incongruously lacy cap. Her eyes were little and blue and close together. Her plump face was unlined, making it impossible to guess whether she was nearer thirty or eighty. "Miss Wichett, I was up quite late last night—" Victoria began.

"Well, there will be no more of that! Now, get up and let me look at you. Ah-hah, this must be the other young woman," she said, as Lucy staggered into the room, trying to get her dressing gown tied. "Miss Clay?"

"Yes, ma'am?" Lucy answered.

"Yes, Miss Wichett," the governess corrected. "Now ladies, you have a quarter of an hour to dress, and your breakfast will be waiting for you in the nursery—"

"The *nursery*!" the girls chorused in counterpoint anguish.

Ignoring their lamentations, she continued. "You may omit to put on your stays this morning, but it shall be the last time. Breakfast and lessons until eight, when the dressmaker arrives. Then we shall go through your wardrobe and prepare for riding in the afternoon. Hurry up, you've wasted a good ten minutes of my life as it is! It ill behooves a lady to be inconsiderate of other people's time."

The woman bustled out of the room, leaving the girls tossing about in her wake. Lucy, chastened by her first experience with Miss Wichett, hurried to present herself at the nursery—a grim suite of attic rooms. But Victoria was not intimidated, or at least she was determined not to let it show. The governess ushered them in and indicated their breakfast trays. Unsweetened tea, plain toast, and a boiled egg apiece. "I'm afraid I'm accustomed to a different sort of breakfast," Victoria said haughtily.

435

"That's the first habit you'll have to change, then," Miss Wichett snapped back.

"See here, I'll not be spoken to this way in my own home," Victoria persisted, her face mottling with anger.

"Such an unattractive accent," Miss Wichett observed, not the least cowed by Victoria's outburst. "We'll have a great deal of work to do there. As for the content of your speech, it shows a lack of understanding I would not have believed. Come along, we'll talk with your father—whose house this *is*, by the way."

"I think that's an excellent idea," Victoria said, turning on her heel and stomping off before Lucy could catch up. Unfortunately, she lost her way and had to grudgingly let Miss Wichett lead them to her father's smoking room, where he retired after breakfast.

"Sir Elgin," Miss Wichett said without introduction as she burst into his secret preserve, "we need to speak with you. It was my understanding that I was completely in charge of these young women. Is that correct?"

"Yes, yes, entirely so, madam," Elgin said, stubbing out his cigar and setting his first drink of the day in a place of partial concealment behind a gilt ostrich egg on a gold stand.

"I do hope so, for I will not remain in your employ otherwise."

"I understand that. Is there a problem?" Elgin was obviously uncomfortable with this domineering woman invading his privacy, and he was anxious to bring the discussion to a hasty conclusion.

"Father, you can't imagine . . . Could I speak to you privately?" Victoria asked.

Elgin pulled an ornate watch out of his vest pocket, flipped open the gold lid, and frowned. "I'm afraid I haven't much time. My coach will be here in a moment—"

"Coach? You're leaving?"

"Yes, yes, going shooting in Scotland, you know. Grouse season. I thought I'd stay on until Christmas. Servants can run the house, and Miss Wichett will be in charge of you girls."

"Fully in charge?" Miss Wichett persisted.

"Certainly! That's what I engaged you for. Now, Victoria, what was it you wanted to talk about? Oh, Ellis, have you packed my gray suit? I'll need it for the races, and ask Willie if he's sure Determination isn't having any more trouble with that leg. Don't want to set him back. Well, girls, have a nice

436

time while we're gone. Good-bye, my dear," he finished, dropping a badly aimed kiss on Victoria's forehead and hitting her hair instead.

When the dust of his departure had settled, Lucy and Victoria found themselves back in the nursery. Victoria felt like she'd been drifting along a peaceful stream and had suddenly found herself swept into the vortex of a whirlpool. She was muttering, but Lucy seemed to have accepted the situation. "You don't have any choice, Vic," she said. "She's probably not so bad when you get to know her."

"She's a horrible woman, and I won't have her dictating to me this way. They wouldn't have dared to treat us this way in our other school."

"Vic, we aren't there anymore," Lucy said softly. "We're here, and everything is different. You were the one who was so eager to come and learn how to be a fine lady. Why don't you just cooperate?"

"Lucy, you are the absolutely worst goose! You're just scared of that hideous woman. Just let yourself be bullied, then, but I won't have it. I won't!"

Lucy just shrugged and applied herself to her now-cold tea and soggy toast. Victoria gathered her skirts and swept out of the nursery before Miss Wichett could return. Walking hard on her heels, her wide eyes flashing with anger, she went back to her room, shed her dress, and crawled back into bed. "Outrageous!" she muttered, punching her pillow into a comfortable shape. Before long she heard someone outside her door. A light tap, then Yvonne's voice. "The men—they are here to put the new hardware," she said.

Victoria leaped out of bed and dragged the covers along as a robe. "What men? What hardware?"

"I do not know, mademoiselle. Miss Wichett, she ordered a new doorknob."

"Oh, very well," Victoria said. If Miss Wichett was going to concern herself with doorknobs, so much the better. *It will keep her from bothering me*, Victoria thought. "See that luncheon is laid for me," Victoria ordered. "Then help me do my hair."

She found, however, when she got to the small dining room where luncheon was usually served, that she was eating alone among a roomful of dust covers. Looking around at the shrouded chairs, she asked of the maid who served her, "What is this? Why is everything covered up?"

"Housekeeper's orders, miss. No guests until Sir Elgin

comes back. The furniture is always covered when he's gone."

"But *I'm* here. It's not as though the house is empty."

"I'm sorry, miss. You'll have to talk to the housekeeper about that."

"Never mind, I'll take care of it later," Victoria said. She stabbed at her boiled sole and braised potatoes and thought over her grievances. She'd never felt so irritated in all her life. Everything had gone out of control, and she didn't like it. She was in the habit of keeping a firm grip on the reins of her own life, as much so as a girl her age could, anyway. Now her own father had abandoned her to the clutches of witchy Miss Wichett. The servants had shut the house down as if no one were home, and Lucy had gone over to the enemy. Everything was going as wrong as wrong could be. And there was no alternative except to go home to Seventrees, and that was completely unthinkable.

After her solitary meal, she went back to her room for a nap. By the time she awoke, there was still no sign of Lucy having returned. She was going to go looking for her when she realized the significance of the new doorknob. She was locked into her rooms!

"Let me out!" she shouted, pounding on the solid oak door with her fists. "Lucy! Let me out!"

"I'm sorry, Vic, I can't," Lucy said, her voice muffled by the thick wood. "Miss Wichett has the only key."

"Get her!" Victoria screamed. She was nearly speechless with rage. The woman had really gone too far!

After what seemed like years, Miss Wichett's voice came through the door. "You wanted to talk to me, Miss Farrington?" she asked innocently.

"No, I don't want to talk to you. I want out! Now, open this door!"

"I'm afraid that's impossible with the attitude you have now. With an apology and a pledge to follow my instructions—"

"Apology! Pledge! Why, I . . ." Victoria sputtered. "I'll stay in here until I starve. See what my father thinks of you then!" she announced finally, flinging a paper weight at the door.

"Very well," Miss Wichett answered with poisonous sweetness, "but I warn you, I've never lost a girl yet this way. Let me know when you're hungry enough to apologize."

"Never!"

438

Victoria stormed around the room for a while until she heard Lucy's voice again. "Vic, why don't you stop being so angry and come out. Miss Wichett isn't so bad. She told me all sorts of interesting things about which spoons and forks to use today. Do you know what that tiny little fork on the end is for?"

"No, and I don't care a fig! You're just frightened of her and you're behaving like a spineless mouse!"

There was a complete silence from the other side of the door. Victoria waited a long while, then said, "Lucy, I'm sorry. I didn't mean that."

"Oh, Vic," Lucy said. She was trying not to cry. "Why do you make things so difficult? You're the one who wanted to come here, now you're locked in your room, shouting insults at me. I don't like this. I want to go home. I'm sending a message to my father to come back for me."

"No, Lucy! Don't do that. I said I'm sorry. I shouldn't have spoken rudely to you. It's not your fault. Please don't say you're going away. It's just that I hate that awful woman."

"You don't have to like her," Lucy said, her voice stronger now. "I'm sorry, Vic, but I've got to go to the nursery for dinner now. She told me not to be late. It shows a lack of refinement. Please just apologize and come out."

"I will not!" Victoria said, but she was getting hungry enough that she lacked some of her former conviction.

Lucy did not return. *Miss Wichett probably locked her in a closet someplace,* Victoria thought bitterly. Fortunately, she still had access to her bathroom and the balcony outside her window. Bored and hungry, Victoria used up an hour taking a cold bath and gazing out at the view while she brushed her hair. As it got dark, however, she kept thinking of the picturesque sheep as mutton and the lush green lawns as potential salad. Her stomach rumbled loudly. It was getting chilly, and she thought about lighting the logs laid in the grate in her small fireplace. Unhappily, the housemaid could not get in to tend to it with the door locked. Victoria scrabbled around with the ornaments on the mantle, hoping to find matches, but there were none.

The lack of light also prevented the possibility of reading to pass the time. Not that there was anything worth reading in the room anyway. Victoria kept pacing around until it got distinctly cold, and finally gave up and went to bed. It was not yet nine o'clock, and she had no intention of sleeping, but

439

there was nothing else to do. She considered another bath, but she'd have to take it in the dark, and she'd be even colder afterward. Snuggling down into the covers, she went to sleep out of pure boredom.

But she could not stay asleep. Her stomach kept making awful noises, and her dreams were fitful nightmares. By dawn she was fully awake and ready to nibble on the soap in the bathroom, had she not been too chilled to get out of bed. Even though she was fully a city block from the kitchens of the huge house, she imagined she could smell food cooking. The meager breakfast offered her the morning before came back to haunt her. It had seemed like food unfit for anyone then. Today strong tea and plain toast sounded like a king's repast. Perhaps Lucy could slide a piece of bread under the door. Victoria steeled herself against the cold and hopped nimbly over to look at the door. No, it fit too tightly to slide so much as a piece of paper under. Why did this stupid great museum of a house have to be so well made?

She scurried to the bathroom and got a large drink of cold water. But her stomach was empty and it made her feel nauseated. Victoria Farrington had never been truly hungry in her life, and she found it a terrible experience. She was having to fight off the urge to cry.

Back in bed, she started thinking about what Lucy had said about going home. Dear God, she couldn't let that happen. With hunger guiding her thoughts, Victoria began to rationalize what she would be depriving Lucy of if she persisted in defying Miss Wichett. After all, Lucy would never have another opportunity like this. Lucy was shy and needed confidence. If knowing what the funny little fork on the end was for, why, who was she to deprive her friend of such information? It would be frightfully easy for Lucy to throw away her chances and go back to dreary old Seventrees if she was unhappy here. And she will be unhappy here, unless I'm around to keep her happy. *I certainly can't do that, if I'm locked up in here all the time,* Victoria thought. Poor Lucy. Perhaps she would have to swallow her pride. Not for her own sake, of course, but for Lucy's sake. She owed it to her friend to apologize to Miss Wichett.

Victoria went to the door again and pounded until Yvonne came. "Yes, mademoiselle?" she mumbled through the barrier.

Victoria swallowed hard, threw back her head, and said, "Would you please *ask* Miss Wichett if I could have a word with her?"

3

Victoria rolled over, bruising her joints on the hard bed Miss Wichett made the girls sleep on in the nursery. Yawning, she reached over and shook Lucy. "Rise and shine, my dear," she said, mocking Miss Wichett's cheerful tones. "It ill behooves a lady to sleep past the first cock's crow. I should think it also 'ill behooves' a lady to go around with black-and-blue marks from sleeping on a slab of granite like this. When do you suppose she'll let us back in our real rooms? I've spent a week trying to sleep on this thing, and it will take me years to recover."

Lucy rose, wincing. "Miss Wichett says it will improve our posture."

"Miss Wichett says, Miss Wichett says . . ." Victoria complained, but not as bitterly as she might have a week earlier. She had not changed her mind about the governess—she would go to her grave loathing the woman—but she had come to realize there was no point in locking horns with her hourly. Not while they were virtually her prisoners.

So far they had spent most of their time in the attic schoolrooms with the instructors Miss Wichett brought along. Their French, the girls had learned, was unforgivable, and the tutor, an effeminate little man with curled mustaches, had leaped about most entertainingly trying to impress upon them the correct pronunciations. *"Bon jour,"* he intoned, sounding like a funeral bell.

"Bon jour," the girls repeated in their flattest Kansas English.

"Mais, non, non, NON!" he shrieked. *"Bon jour!"*

"Bon jour."

"EEEEEEAH!" he screamed, pulling his hair at the sides until it stood out as if lightning had struck him.

Victoria and Lucy collapsed in fits of giggles.

441

"It ill behooves a lady to laugh boisterously," Miss Wichett had informed them later.

It was, surprisingly, Lucy who objected to their French lessons. "All we're learning is the words for food and clothes, Miss Wichett," she said. "I'd like to be able to read French books."

"Whatever for?" Miss Wichett exclaimed in such shocked tones that Lucy let the subject drop.

After they had tortured the French teacher's ears for a few hours each morning, the history teacher arrived. He, too, was an older man, so old in fact that the girls believed he had lived in the reigns of most, if not all, of the ancient English kings he made them memorize. "What is the point of learning all this old, dead history?" Victoria had complained to Miss Wichett. "It can't make very interesting table talk."

"Table talk! Good heavens, Miss Farrington, one would never discuss what you are learning in mixed company."

"Why not? Is there something indecent about it?" Victoria asked, thinking perhaps she'd missed something interesting.

"No, but one would not like for the gentlemen of a company to know how knowledgeable you are."

"You mean," Lucy said in amazement, "we are to act stupid?"

"Not stupid, just above such things."

"I'm above them already," Victoria mumbled.

"No, you are not, Miss Farrington. One must know about something before one can be above it."

"But—"

Miss Wichett folded her hands. "It ill behooves a lady to belabor a point," she declared, effectively putting an end to any further discussion.

After their initial introduction to the English kings, the girls began what was, to Miss Wichett, the true purpose of history lessons—the study of the family relationships among the upper classes. They learned when each dukedom was established and, more important, who held it now and who was to inherit. "What difference can this make to us?" Victoria grumbled.

"You are expected to marry one of them, of course," Lucy explained.

"I'll marry whomever I please," Victoria replied.

Lucy said nothing to this, feeling there was no point in belaboring the obvious. Victoria would realize sooner or later what her fate was to be.

After history lessons the girls were allowed to eat luncheon—a Spartan meal eaten, as were all their meals, in the nursery. Hardly a bite of food passed their lips without Miss Wichett's scrutiny. "Do not gulp your food. It makes you appear hungry," she declared. "It ill behooves a lady to appear hungry."

"But I *am* hungry," Victoria said. "I could eat a horse."

Miss Wichett's hand flew to her generous bosom as if to stop the palpitations of her heart by force. "Such a vulgarity! Miss Farrington. You must work on eradicating these terrible Americanisms from your vocabulary! A lady is never hungry. Miss Clay, put that carrot back and cut it into at least three pieces and chew each piece fifteen times. A lady must always appear to be eating merely to keep up a little strength. One never comments adversely on the food, but still one picks daintily."

Victoria found herself longing desperately for the cherries or apples at home that they simply pulled off a tree and popped into their mouths in one motion. There was one memory in particular that touched a fond chord in her. A hot summer day when she and Lucy and Ned invaded a strawberry patch and gorged themselves. Ned had been punished, for he was old enough to have known better, but she and Lucy were merely admonished against future raids.

Afternoons the entire first month were spent painting. Landscapes and flower arrangements only, for Miss Wichett declared it unbecoming to ladies to do portraits. She found Victoria's early attempts to paint disconcerting. "Such vivid colors, Miss Farrington, are unladylike," she declared.

Unfortunately, Miss Wichett had been unable to find a suitably elderly instructor and had been forced to employ a reasonably attractive young man. This, she knew, was dangerous business, but there was nothing to be done about it. She hovered so protectively that it nearly drove them all wild. She would not allow Mr. Newby close enough to the girls to get a good view of what they were working on. After the first month, he quit. "We will have more instruction in the spring," Miss Wichett said, vastly relieved that the terror of a possible sexual attraction had passed. "When we travel."

"We're to travel?" Victoria asked brightly.

"Yes, we will discuss it in more detail later."

"Oh, where are we to go? And when?"

"It ill behooves a lady to be inquisitive," Miss Wichett said.

"My father is a painter," Victoria said, knowing there was no point in persisting in her questions.

"My *dear* Miss Farrington, one says, 'My father paints,' not 'My father is a painter.' The first way implies an interest or talent, the second implies an occupation." The very word "occupation" seemed to offend her, and she grimaced slightly as if caught in something slightly improper.

"Sir Elgin painted that portrait of Victoria's mother in the Great Hall," Lucy volunteered.

Miss Wichett cocked her head in the coy way she had been trying to teach the girls. "Painting in the Great Hall? I don't think I remember seeing it. The only picture I recall there is that ragged pioneer woman with the funny name under it—Conestoga or something."

Victoria had often lamented the fact that her mother went by such a terrible name, and had herself thought the portrait ragged and embarrassing, but to hear her thoughts through Miss Wichett's lips was crushing. Blinking back tears, she stood and riveted Miss Wichett with an eagle glare. "My mother is well-groomed, intelligent, and very kind. She is called 'Schooner,' not 'Conestoga.' If *you* are to speak of her at all, you should refer to her as Mrs. LeSage." With that, she turned and walked quickly away before the tears spilled over. For the first time since she'd left home, she found herself missing her mother. The feeling was strange to her and made a painful hollow in her chest. Imagine a silly frump like Miss Wichett daring to speak lightly of her mother. Grandmother Maggie would have made short work of Miss Wichett, Victoria thought, not realizing that Maggie Freiler would probably have done precisely what Victoria herself had.

Miss Wichett was hard on her charges when they made mistakes. To her credit, she was just as hard on herself. She found Victoria later the same afternoon and said, "It ill behooves a lady to grovel, Miss Farrington, but when she has made a serious and harmful mistake, she must admit it and take the consequences. It was tactless of me to speak so rudely about your mother. I did so out of ignorance, but that is no excuse."

"It was understandable," Victoria said, with rare graciousness, and was rewarded with the first genuine smile she'd ever seen on the older woman's face.

Knowing that Miss Wichett could apologize when she was genuinely in the wrong made a great difference in their relationship. From that day on, Victoria applied herself to learning what Miss Wichett had to teach, and even found that remarks she would previously have regarded as insults simply flowed over her without leaving a mark.

With the departure of the art teacher, afternoons were given over to clothing and dancing. Miss Wichett went through Victoria and Lucy's wardrobe like a hot hatchet through butter—another American vulgarism that shocked her to the core. "These outrageous crinoline skirts and hoops might have been acceptable twenty years ago," she pronounced. "And even then they would have been inappropriate to girls who have not yet made their debut into society. I'll have the seamstress run up some suitable dresses with a slight bustle for now. We will go into the question of your wardrobe in more detail later."

"But we are old enough to have made our debut," Lucy said, trying to remove her favorite pink dress from Miss Wichett's clutches.

"It is not purely a matter of age, it is a matter of having the necessary grace in the social accomplishments. It will take at least another year. Now, we must work with the dressmaker on reducing your midsections."

Victoria and Lucy exchanged a confused glance. "You mean, pull in our stomachs?" Lucy asked.

Miss Wichett's eyes rolled heavenward. "It ill behooves a lady to name bodily parts, Miss Clay. I thought we had this clear when we discussed lower limbs. The dressmaker will begin her fittings this afternoon, and I want you both in the nursery in suitable undergarments and dressing gowns. Until she arrives, we shall work on your hair."

Victoria had a naughty look in her eye that should have warned Miss Wichett. "Isn't hair a rather vulgar word? Should we not rather work on our cranial accoutrements?"

"Really, Miss Farrington, it ill behooves a lady . . ."

A dance mistress was called in to perfect their waltz, and they spent a happy time in the schoolroom for an hour every afternoon. "Really, ladies," Miss Wichett exclaimed. "You must not gallop about with such abandon!"

"But this is how we learned at home," Victoria protested.

"No doubt," Miss Wichett proclaimed dryly.

After a brief bout with the "language of flowers," during which time Miss Wichett endeavored to convince the girls that certain blossoms had an almost innate meaning—lilies for purity, roses a rather more passionate and not quite nice connotation—they moved on to matters a bit more practical.

"You will someday run a household, very probably a grand household like this one. You must know everything that is done and who is to do it. You must be able to recognize whether it is done properly," Miss Wichett said. "Now, most young ladies of your age would have absorbed this information from birth, but you must learn it in a short time. I have enlisted Housekeeper's help with this."

Accordingly, the girls spent several weeks trailing the nameless woman known only as Housekeeper and her minions around the huge house, learning the precise division of labor at Farrvale Manor. They indulged in the only mathematical study they were to have—that which involved looking over the household books, which were always presented to the lady of the house for her approval on the first week of the month. "Many ladies give only the most cursory attention to such matters," Miss Wichett said. "This is not only careless, but betrays their husbands' trust."

This led Miss Wichett into her next subject—the marital relationship. Miss Wichett summed it up in a single phrase quoted from Milton: "He for God only, she for God in him."

"Once you are married, you will exist for your husband," she said. "Your dress and behavior will reflect on him." Victoria said nothing to this, but she thought of her mother and grandmother. Their behavior reflected on no one but themselves. People tended to like or dislike them for their own merits, not their husbands. How different things were here, she realized. She must work at changing her thinking. "You see, Miss Farrington, your obedience to your parents, and later to others such as myself, is merely a practice exercise for your lifelong obedience to your husband. This is why I say you have been at a disadvantage, living in America."

During this same time, they began what Victoria had looked forward to most—the accumulation of a proper wardrobe. It was necessary for a lady to change her clothes for each different activity of the day. She would have a gown for morning wear. This should be a fairly simple dress, suitable for attending to such details as correspondence and taking care of domestic activities like planning menus and checking accounts. A selection of ten such dresses was necessary to begin adult life. There would be another dress, slightly more elaborate, for luncheon at home. Fancier versions of the luncheon dress must be ready for days when

446

there were guests. Midafternoon tea called for a wardrobe of its own. Since tea was a daily occasion that almost always involved guests, a lady must have at least fifteen such gowns. Dinner at home and dinner with guests or as a guest had special requirements, and a lady must have three or four ball gowns on hand, though of course she would order a new one for every occasion, if possible.

A lady must have three different sets of riding habits, each worn according to the social status of the company with whom one was riding. There were also special garments that must be ready for other occasions. A tennis dress, for instance, had to have a modest bustle, no trailing skirts, and an embroidered apron to go over it. It could be in two pieces, bodice and skirt separate—as could outfits designed for boating excursions.

If her mother had only been able to understand that this was the sort of thing money was meant to be used for, Victoria thought. But then, her mother never seemed to really appreciate what wealth was for, only the dubious joy of accumulating it. What a pity for her, Victoria mused as she stood on a stool while the dressmaker pinned a hem.

The only drawback to the burgeoning wardrobe was that Miss Wichett wouldn't allow the girls to wear any of it, except to try it on for fittings. "The Blue Bedroom is almost filled with dresses," Victoria complained, brushing her hand along the skirt of the rose Ottoman satin gown she was trying on. "Why can't we wear them?"

"They will be ready when I decide you are ready," Miss Wichett said. "You don't even know how to walk in a trailing skirt without tripping over it."

"But when will we be up to the standards of the dresses?" Lucy asked.

The irony in her voice was wasted on the governess. "I do not know," she answered feelingly.

By the time Elgin Farrington returned from hunting in Scotland and settled in to enjoy Christmas at home, the indefatigable Miss Wichett declared the girls fit to be present downstairs—but only as girls, not as ladies.

One of the first guests to arrive was Adelaide Wotton. "What do you think of Miss Wichett's work?" Elgin asked her as she surveyed the girls.

"Well, there is an improvement," she said.

Lucy and Victoria stood in the middle of the room feeling like resentful dressmaker's dolls. Apparently they had to have

447

this woman's approval before they could pass Elgin's approval. Who the devil was she anyway? Victoria wondered angrily.

"What do you think?" Adelaide asked of Miss Wichett, rare deference shading her normally domineering voice.

"Girls, you are dismissed," Miss Wichett said before going any further.

Victoria and Lucy did not get to hear her opinion, but it soon became evident, for as the house began filling with holiday guests, the girls found that they were to be briefly presented to Elgin's friends, then whisked away to the confines of the nursery again. "I was sent here in order to meet my father's friends," Victoria wailed.

"You are not ready to move among them," Miss Wichett said. "Perhaps by next fall—"

"Next fall? I'll grow old and die before then!"

"In that case, you have a great deal to learn in a very short time," Miss Wichett replied without a trace of humor. "Now, put on your gray dress. It's almost time for your dancing lesson."

All during Christmas, Victoria and Lucy watched from their nursery windows as elegant carriages arrived at the big front doors of the house and deposited beautiful strangers. The sounds of revelry wafted up the steps, and portions of the dinners being consumed in the dining hall found their way upstairs on trays for the outcasts. Several times one of Elgin's acquaintances expressed a mild interest in meeting his daughter and her friend. On such occasions Miss Wichett got her charges into their plain, prim dark dresses and herded them downstairs for inspection. These were not pleasant experiences. Victoria always went back to the schoolroom flushed and angry and feeling like a slab of pork at market.

At New Year's there was to be a ball. Miss Wichett, infected at last by a shadow of holiday spirit, allowed the girls to have spiced eggnog with their dinner. By some error in housekeeping procedure, Miss Wichett got a portion laced with brandy, and she retired early complaining of dizziness. Lucy and Victoria took full advantage of this opportunity for freedom to creep away from the nursery. Nightgown-clad, they tiptoed down to the second floor, made their way along the long west hall, and found a concealed place from which to look down on the ball. Huddled together in their dark, secret nook, they gazed down raptly on the party. There were other young women, certainly no older than themselves, dancing and flirting and balancing tiny crystal plates of dainty pastries and sipping from long-stemmed glasses. "We should be down there!" Victoria said indignantly.

Lucy wasn't so sure. "But, Victoria, they all seem so sure of themselves. I don't think I'll ever be comfortable among them. There's that woman—Adelaide—and your father," she said. "Who's that young man with him?"

The object of their attention was a sullen-looking youth in his middle twenties. His blond hair was a trifle overlong for fashion and he had a sort of swagger to his walk that made Victoria instinctively dislike him, even from this distance. "I don't know, but I bet he's one of those 'dear boys' of hers she's always talking about," she answered. She was disappointed to see that her father seemed to take a proprietary interest in him, smiling, nodding at his words, and clapping him on the back in a fatherly manner that Victoria mistrusted without knowing quite why.

"Oh, Vic," Lucy said reverently, "look over there. Aren't they the most handsome men you've ever, ever seen?"

Victoria's gaze followed Lucy's pointing finger. Standing by a pillar at the opposite end of the ballroom were two perfectly wonderful men. The taller of the two had the dark, curling hair and pale skin Victoria always thought of when she heard the term "Black Douglas." She was sure he had pale blue eyes—he would have to. The perfect cut of his formal attire enhanced rather than hid his broad-shouldered, strong-limbed physique. He reminded her of a bear. Strong and raw beneath a thin coating of Victorian good manners. He looked as though he might suddenly whirl and roar.

The other man had straight chestnut-colored hair and was more slightly built, but seemed—even standing still—to have uncanny grace. He held his head up with fine, somewhat petulant dignity. He made Victoria think of her father's fine racing horses. Lean, proud, bred for elegant motion. It didn't cross her mind that he might have a personality, any more than she thought of beautiful horses as being creatures of character. He was simply a handsome being to be admired. "Who are they?" she whispered. "Do you suppose they're married to any of the beautiful women down there?"

"I don't know. I've never seen them before. They can't be married. They can't! Oh, look! The black-haired one pointed up here. You don't think they can see us, do you?" She cringed back into the shadows, but did not take her eyes off the men.

449

Victoria was stunned. She'd never seen Lucy behave this way. She'd never shown any interest in men at all, certainly not in particular men. Granted, those two seemed to have an almost electric aura about them, but imagine Lucy being susceptible! "He's quite good-looking, isn't he? The dark-haired one, I mean," she said experimentally.

"Is he? Oh, yes, I suppose. But the other one—my goodness, he reminds me of a god in a story. Narcissus, maybe. If I were a man and looked like that, I'd never be without a mirror. Oh, Vic! They do see us, I know it. Hurry, let's go back to the nursery."

Victoria hesitated a moment, then put one hand out between the newels and wiggled her fingers.

Lucy yanked her arm back. "What are you doing! My God, they saw you. They waved back! Miss Wichett will have a fit. Oh, Vic . . . I think I shall die!"

"Miss Wichett won't know unless you tell her, you goose. Do you suppose they're going to go up to that awful little prison of ours and say, 'Pardon me, but have you anyone who might have waved at us, miss?' She isn't going to know and you aren't going to die and I predict that the racehorse and the Black Douglas are going to fall madly in love with us when we make our debut. Have you ever known my predictions to be wrong, Lucy dear?"

Lucy started to giggle. "I've never known you to *make* predictions, Vic."

"See?" Victoria answered, as if it were all settled. "Now, wait until no one is in the hallway, and we'll make a dash for the stairs."

As soon as Christmas was over, Elgin disappeared again. This time he went to the south of France in search of sunshine. The girls spent three more months preparing to emerge from their American cocoons. Now, however, they were both interested in hurrying the process. Even Lucy felt she had been in the schoolroom long enough. In April they departed on a round of visits. "Not very important people, really," Miss Wichett declared, "or they'd be in London. But nice enough, and they will provide an opportunity to try out all you have learned. It will also give you the ability to speak knowledgeably about the places people go—Bath, for instance."

Elgin was supposed to return before their departure, but sent a message saying he'd be delayed. Victoria wanted to wait, but Miss Wichett would have none of it. "But, Miss Wichett, I came here to see my father, and I don't think I've spoken to him more than four or five times yet," Victoria complained.

But they set out on schedule, nonetheless. Taking a southern route, they worked their way along the coast, stopping at every historic spot on the way. It was chilly yet, and rained continuously. Not the exciting kind of rain like in Kansas, where the sky turned yellow-green and exploded with slices of lightning and bass concussions of thunder, but a perpetual, gentle English rain. Timid, nagging stuff that never let up. The scenery consisted almost entirely of winding lanes through thick woods that occasionally opened onto a view of gently rolling hills and the gray sea beyond. "Isn't it lovely?" Lucy said the first six or seven times such a view was offered them.

But Victoria found the landscape soporific. "Oh, Lucy, stop saying that," she finally said. "It is lovely, but it's boring, boring, boring!"

"But we'd never see anything like this at home. Look at that adorable little thatched cottage—"

"Probably full of bugs and mice," Victoria snapped. "And it doesn't look one whit better than a nice sturdy sod house."

The people they stayed with were no more interesting than the weather or the landscape. Most of them were doddering old things who remembered her father as a boy and seemingly had missed everything that had gone on since then. The girls spent endless evenings in drafty great houses, trying to make polite conversation with rich, elderly strangers.

One memorable visit was with an ancient harridan who had once flirted with the prince regent in 1820. Apparently she'd thought and spoken of nothing else in the intervening sixty-two years. Her husband was a monstrously fat man who spoke infrequently and even then managed to confine his thoughts to sentences of no more than four words. "Saw Henry today," he told the girls (who had no idea who Henry was). "Looking well. Touch of lumbago. Bad thing, lumbago. Hurts like bloody hell! Har, har, har."

Their departure from that household had been nothing less than a pell-mell escape. Even Miss Wichett seemed rattled. "It ill behooves a lady to speak badly of her elders, but I had no idea what Lord and Lady Bremer had come to. Shocking!"

"Miss Wichett, won't we meet anyone under the age of seventy?" Victoria lamented.

"Certainly, when we return to Farrvale."

"But when will that be?" Lucy asked. "Can't we go back now?"

To the girls' surprise, Miss Wichett seemed to be considering it. "I don't suppose I could have devised a better test of your manners than this past weekend. You were both quite remarkably well-behaved, you know."

Lucy and Victoria stared at her, fearing to believe their ears, fearing even to breathe. "Then you think we're ready?" Victoria finally said in delicately careful tones.

Miss Wichett continued to brood over her thoughts for a moment, then said, "Yes, I believe you're ready. I'll speak to Sir Elgin about it as soon as we can get back. But first, there's a perfectly charming little ruin just a few miles up the road. It would be a shame to miss it. Miss Farrington! Miss Clay! It ill behooves a lady to grin so broadly!"

4

Victoria tried to stand still while Yvonne worked at fastening the long row of tiny shell buttons up the back of her dress. "Please to not move," Yvonne said as Victoria began to readjust her long gloves. They were white with green embroidered flowers to match the pattern in the cream-colored dress, and they came almost to her shoulders. Victoria kept craning her neck to see the mirror. She loved the lines of the dress. Having finally given up the idea of crinolines, she had decided that current fashion suited her better. The long narrow-fronted skirt had a loop of draped fabric over it that dipped down in front and pulled together at the back of the waist into a huge, loose bow over a slight bustle. The padded pillow that was worn beneath it made sitting down difficult, but the girls had finally learned to perch on the front of chairs when wearing this style. It was not much more difficult than learning to maneuver a hoop through a doorway, just different.

"You look lovely," Lucy said from where she sat at the

window seat observing the final touches being put on her friend.

"So do you," Victoria said. "Just like a princess." It was true. Lucy's dress, too, was cream silk, but instead of a bow at the back, there was a cascade of ruffles trimmed in chocolate brown. Her russet hair was pulled up into a tiara of braids that wrapped around her head, then fell in fat, bouncy curls beside her face.

They were preparing to go downstairs to their first formal dinner. Elgin and Miss Wichett had agreed that the time had come for the fledglings to leave the nest, and tonight was their first real trial. "Are we ready?" Victoria said when Yvonne finally stepped back. Surprisingly, Victoria was more nervous than Lucy and was glad she had gloves to hide the fact that her hands were as cold as fish. They swept along the hall, and down the wide marble staircase. Elgin, waiting below, was visibly impressed. Even Adelaide Wotton, standing next to him with her arm looped through his, allowed her eyes to widen with surprise. "My goodness! They are true gems. Miss Wichett seems to have taken some lumps of glass and turned them into diamonds."

"Thank you," Victoria said, not sure this was wholly a compliment, but feeling that it called for a reply of some sort.

"Oh, my dear, here's Frederick!" Adelaide said as the surly-looking young man Victoria had seen with her father at the New Year's ball strolled into the room.

Victoria felt a resurgence of the vague dislike she'd felt upon first seeing him. He had a pinched expression, a long thin nose, and oversize teeth like his mother's. His skin was so fair as to appear sickly. His overlong hair was lank and didn't appear to be quite scrupulously clean. He wore a floppy bow at his neck, a pretentious style that did not suit him well. The whole artistic effect was spoiled by his hands, which were square and sturdy and looked like they belonged to a farmer or a bricklayer. "How do you do, Miss Farrington, Miss Clay," he said in a nasal whine.

Victoria almost laughed, for she had suddenly thought of Ned Clay and what that sensible, humorous young man would have made of a silly, superior fop like this. Controlling her features with great difficulty, Victoria said, "How do you do, Mr. Wotton."

"So you are Freiler's Cures," Frederick said.

"I beg your pardon?" Victoria said stiffly.

453

"Frederick!" Adelaide exclaimed.

"Well, Mama, that's what *you* said," Frederick drawled.

Adelaide looked genuinely shaken, but recovered quickly enough to say, "Poor Frederick, blessed and cursed both with his dear late father's frankness."

So that explains why there's never a husband around, Victoria thought. *But if she's after my father, as she appears to be, why hasn't she caught him yet? He seems to like her well enough, though heaven alone knows why.* She exchanged a quick, understanding look with Lucy, who nodded her recognition of the answer to a question they had often discussed.

"Nonsense, Mama," Frederick was saying. "Papa had nothing to do with my honesty. I just happen to believe that we should all be much better off if we spoke our minds truthfully. Miss Farrington comes from a family with a well-known name and a great deal of wealth. I'm sure there's no reason to disguise the fact or pretend we don't all know it. Anyway, Americans have a way of being refreshingly vulgar about such things."

"Do you know many Americans," Lucy asked in a voice as cold and pointed as an icicle. Victoria nearly cheered. It was seldom that Lucy really got her back up about something, and when she did, it was a wonder to behold.

"Oh, two or three," Frederick answered, oblivious of the fact that he'd been rude.

Lucy stepped closer to him and said with menacing sweetness, "I wonder if you'd like to find out just how refreshingly vulgar we can be?"

Victoria smiled behind her fan, eagerly awaiting Lucy's example, but apparently Adelaide didn't feel up to it. "There, now, Frederick, you've offended Miss Clay. How positively naughty of you. Just for that you'll have to escort your poor old mother in to dinner."

They were spared further examples of Frederick's inclinations to honesty by the arrival of the rest of the guests, who were a mixture of Elgin's old friends. There was a hawk-nosed man from London who had something to do with art sales and who had brought along his dumpling wife and a daughter who looked like the feminine equivalent of Frederick. Apparently she recognized the similarity too, for she spent the evening gawking at him with adoration. Victoria found it a spectacle to ruin the appetite.

There was also a family who owned the neighboring estate. They had along a daughter, too, a sweet, sleepy-looking girl named Alicia. Every time anyone addressed a polite question to her, she answered with, "My betrothed, the Honorable Wilton Smythe, says . . ."

Victoria finally said to her, after one of these replies, "But what do *you* think, Lady Alicia?" The girl had simply stared at Victoria as if such a concept had never occurred to her.

The rest of the party consisted of acquaintances of Elgin's who had to do with racing. Another duke, whose sentences were punctuated with nervous throat clearings that sounded a great deal like whinnies, and his wife and son looked like peasants dressed up for the day. They were all more concerned with horse talk than the food or the present company.

The party was completed by a young couple with a Scottish name Victoria didn't catch. He was "in trade," a great social disgrace, Victoria had learned, unless the "trade" in question was enormously successful.

When they sat down to the formal dinner, Victoria began to understand why Miss Wichett had warned them to eat daintily. The first course was a choice of soup, clear or cream turtle for the hot, cucumber or consommé for the cold choice. Next the white-gloved servants offered each guest a choice of two fish, Dover sole or crab with lobster sauce. This was cleared and replaced with an intermediate dessert of cheese and truffles in champagne. Finally, after half an hour of culinary preliminaries, the main course was served. There was boar's head in aspic, turkey stuffed with herb-and-mushroom dressing, a saddle of mutton with mint sauce, and pork smothered in apples and rosemary. There was a choice of four vegetables in addition to potatoes or wild rice.

Feeling so full she thought she might burst, Victoria endeavored to find a way to lean back slightly in spite of the bustle. She'd been trying to eat only a bite or two of each offering, but everything was prepared so excellently, it was hard to pace herself. The plates having been cleared away, an iced goblet of lemon sorbet with tiny star-shaped puff pastries was put before each place; then the game course was offered. Each guest was given a roasted quail as well as servings of partridge, duck, woodcock, and a share of pheasant mousse.

After this there was another salad course, this time lobster salad and cheese with tiny squares of bread with maraschino jelly.

Victoria, almost gagging with satiation by this point, looked around the table. No one else seemed the least impressed by the mountains of food. The men—most of whom were on the hearty side of slimness, she noticed for the first time—were all still polishing off everything that came their way. Even the ladies (except for Lucy, who looked distinctly distressed) were all nibbling at each course as if they might go on forever this way. Except for her physical discomfort, Victoria was so happy she felt like singing. All these beautiful, rich people at her father's table, all the silver and gold and fine china and crystal, were a setting for a queen or a princess in a fairy tale. It was what she had dreamed about in school back in Saint Louis. Except she'd not even been able to imagine it accurately. She wondered if her mother had an idea what she'd missed by not coming back to England. Victoria tried to picture Schooner at this table. She'd look well enough, that was true. In fact, she was really far more attractive than any of the women here, but she'd not have been willing to lace herself into underwear that made it impossible to eat the food before her. She would have been too busy to spend hours and hours just getting her hair done and her dress donned.

Nor would she have been able to stand the sight of all the food that was returned uneaten. She and Grandmother would have been scraping it into covered bowls to put in the springhouse to keep cool for the next meal. And they both would have leaped up long ago and fled the leisurely discussions of horses and gossip to go work on their account ledgers or formula books.

"What are you thinking about, Vic?" Lucy asked in a low voice. "You look so far away."

"What? Oh, nothing. Isn't this just everything you ever dreamed, Lucy?" she said quietly enough that no one else would hear her.

The servants, operating as quietly and efficiently as well-oiled machines, were clearing away all the silver and plates. Even the tablecloth was removed, revealing another one underneath. Then clean plates, glasses, silver, and napkins were set before each guest, and dessert was served. Several puddings, all done in fancy molds, were offered, as well as a selection of fruits.

When at last the food was consumed, the plates cleared away for the last time, the servants set a silver-and-mother-of-pearl wagon at the head of the table in front of Elgin; then they departed, to enjoy, no doubt, the leftovers before the massive cleanup started. Elgin served himself from one of the three crystal decanters on the caddy, and the next gentleman pulled the ornate little wagon along so that he could serve himself claret and the lady to his right some sherry. When the little wagon got to the other end of the long table and everyone was served, Elgin rose and gained their attention. Raising his glass he said, "I would like to propose a toast to the most gracious and beautiful young women it has ever been my pleasure to have at my table . . . my daughter, Victoria, and her friend Miss Clay."

With a muted shuffling of chair legs, the gentlemen stood and the ladies held their glasses high. "Hear, hear!" someone said before they all drank.

Victoria felt tears stinging her eyes as she smiled acknowledgment. "Thank you," she murmured.

The art dealer stood and regarded the guests with hawk-hooded eyes. "To our host," he said, raising his glass again, "who has, through the pleasures of matrimony, provided himself with the most lovely model in this fair isle!" A titter of shocked amusement greeted this toast.

Frederick Wooton stood quickly and said, "I propose a toast to truth, compared to which beauty is but a frail ornament." No one knew quite how to take this, except the art dealer's daughter, who gazed at him as if he'd just explained the real meaning of life.

Several toasts later, Victoria rose just as Miss Wichett had laborously instructed her and glanced around the table, "catching eyes." "Ladies, I think perhaps we should retire and leave the gentlemen to their port," she said, and led the other women from the dining room to the drawing room adjoining. It was a lovely room for relaxing after a meal. The walls were all done in a white-and-gilt-wood paneling, the floor was dark walnut polished to a glassy finish. The deep rose draperies picked up the ruby hues in the scattered Persian rugs that formed islands upon which groupings of delicate Empire sofas, tables, and chairs stood.

It was not the largest room in the house, nor the most impressive in ornamentation, but it was by far the most attractive. Victoria discreetly signaled to a servant to open the draperies, and as the fabric was looped back from the French doors, the last shimmers of sunset glittered on the vast, shallow fish pool outside and bathed the ladies in a flattering rosy glow.

"You conducted yourself very well, my dear," Adelaide whispered as she passed Victoria.

Victoria stiffened, irritated by the compliment. She did not need, or want, the older woman's approval. There was something overpoweringly condescending about it. Trying to put aside her annoyance, she noticed that Lucy had taken to her role as "assistant" hostess and had shepherded some of the ladies to a chair grouping around a fragile table upon which were the pieces of a "dissected picture." "You see, each piece fits alongside some other piece," she was saying. "When you get them all together properly, they form a picture." The art dealer's daughter and Lady Alicia fell upon the novelty with enthusiasm while their mothers and Adelaide Wotton settled into a comfortable discussion on the difficulties of getting good help these days. The women of the horse set gathered by the window to discuss the weather in regard to a hunt that was planned for the next day.

Victoria moved from group to group as the governess had instructed. As the last of the sunlight faded, servants discreetly appeared to light the candles, and refuel the fires at either end of the room. Before too long, the men, bluff with drink and carrying faint clouds of tobacco smoke, joined them. The conversational groupings scattered, reassembled, and scattered again, to come together for talk or cards or music. The art dealer's wife was prevailed upon to play the piano, which she did with grace and charm, while her daughter made an attempt to engage Frederick in a board game. But Adelaide had different ideas. "Elgin's gardener has done some nice things with the plantings around the pool. Why don't you get Victoria to show you, Frederick?"

Gritting her teeth a little, Victoria allowed herself to be taken for a stroll around the fish pool. Sitting on a little ledge at the near end and dangling her fingers in the cool water, Victoria said, "I'm afraid I know little of gardening. Is it an interest of yours?"

"Heavens, no. That was just my mother's way of getting us off together. Surely you recognized the ploy? I wonder," he went on, "when it will be? Autumn is nice for weddings."

"I beg your pardon? Is someone getting married?" Victoria asked, unaccountably afraid he meant his mother and her father.

"You dissemble well for an American," he said. "I meant our wedding, naturally."

Victoria was stunned beyond speech for a moment; then she said as calmly as she could manage, "Our wedding? Yours and mine?"

"Why, of course. You mean they didn't tell you?"

"No," Victoria said, "though I should have guessed."

"To be quite honest, I was prepared for the worst—in you, I mean. But I'm quite pleased. A rich wife is a necessity, a beautiful one is a pleasure. I think we'll suit well enough."

"If you'll excuse me, I feel rather faint," Victoria said, working very hard at not shouting or stamping her feet in outrage.

"Faint? Are you really? You look flushed, actually."

"Mr. Wotton, I prefer not to discuss this subject any longer—marriage, I mean. Excuse me."

As she turned away, he took her arm lightly, but there was an unmistakable air of command in the gesture. "Discuss it or not, it is a fact. It would be more pleasant for both of us if you would accept the arrangement gracefully."

"I do not care to be lectured to!" Victoria said, shaking free of his grasp.

She walked as sedately as she could back to the drawing room, when she wanted most of all to run to her father and shout at him to straighten out this horrible misunderstanding. *Damn Frederick Wotton!* she thought. He'd ruined the whole mood of this wonderful day for her.

When at last everyone had gone, she found herself alone in the drawing room with her father. "I need to talk to you," she said softly. "Your friend Adelaide's son spoke to me in the garden about marriage," she said, trying to make her voice light and disguise the panic she actually felt.

"Oh, he did? Silly ass! I asked Adelaide to muzzle him," Elgin said. He sounded no more concerned than if she'd told him someone had broken something of slight importance. As though it were a pity, but not to be regarded seriously.

"But, Father, you *knew* he had this idea?"

"Oh, it's not his idea," Elgin assured her. "He's never had an idea in his life. You'd probably read about it in the papers if an original thought ever came to his mind."

"Then whose idea is it?" Victoria demanded. Her panic was turning to confusion and anger.

"Adelaide's and mine, of course. But he really shouldn't have mentioned it yet."

"Father, I don't want to marry him. He's a fool. You know that."

"Of course he is, but he is also the heir to an impressive fortune and a great deal of land that adjoins ours and gives us access to the riverfront. His uncle is a duke and childless. Someday you will be a duchess."

459

"But I don't like him!" Victoria said, aware that her voice was rising shrilly and unable to help it.

"Like him? You don't have to like him. In fact, I'd lose faith in your judgment if you did. Don't worry, my dear, no one is rushing you. I told Adelaide you were to be allowed a full season to enjoy yourself before any engagement was announced. By that time you'll have gotten used to the idea." He strolled to the walnut table next to the piano and poured himself a generous portion of brandy. "Don't worry, dear. It will sort itself out."

"No, Father," Victoria said with deadly calm. "I will not marry him."

She regarded him levelly for a moment. Elgin put a hand to his eyes, removed it immediately. "My God, for a moment there, you looked and sounded just like your grandmother. Gave me a bit of a start."

"Father, do you understand how strongly I feel about this? I would throw myself into the sea before I'd turn my life over to that pretentious oaf!"

"Now, Victoria, no need to be dramatic. We'll say no more about it for the time being. I'm sure by next fall you'll feel differently—"

"I shall not. Good night, Father," she said before turning on her heel and leaving him to enjoy his drink alone.

5

To Victoria's surprise, nothing more was said about Frederick Wotton. She had prepared for a true battle of wills and was relieved, yet vaguely disappointed, when it didn't happen. She had learned enough about the English upper class to realize that a matter like land and water rights formed an important consideration in marriages, and she felt sure her father had not given up the idea of marrying her off to Frederick so easily. He didn't really know her well enough to understand what it meant when she was firmly set against something.

But Victoria herself knew. Her remark about throwing herself into the sea *had* been melodrama. She would never sacrifice her own interests. But she would gladly see Frederick thrown into any body of water close at hand. Frederick and his mother. Especially his mother. It was all very clear now why the not-so-fair Adelaide had taken such an interest in Victoria's progress. She was being made ready to be offered to Frederick. Well, she would thwart Adelaide and her father, and Frederick could spend his life airing his vapid opinions to someone else.

It wasn't until her anger cooled that the chill of disappointment began to set in. Her father had been willing to barter her away for a piece of river frontage. "I'm sure you misunderstood," Lucy had assured her when she tearfully confessed the whole unhappy situation. "He's just trying to look out for your interests and make a good match financially."

"But I don't need it. A husband to bring more money," Victoria said. "I'm my mother's only child, and my father's as well, and they've both got money I'll inherit someday. Of course, Mother will have to be in her grave before I'll get any of it," she added, reverting to her old grievance. "But my father's generous and well-off."

"How do you know that?" Lucy asked. At Victoria's surprised expression, she said, "I mean it. Think what it must cost to operate this household alone. A fortune, year after year."

"Which he does quite nicely, year after year. Don't be so grim, Lucy. This is all beside the point. Would you let yourself be married off to a horrible person like Frederick? For any amount of money or security?"

"Of course not. I'm not saying you should either, I'm just suggesting that you might not have your feelings so hurt if you tried to consider why your father tried to set this up. Good heavens, Vic, I'd die if you wed him! He's quite the nastiest man I've ever met."

"Well, I won't, and I'll just keep telling my father that until he accepts it."

But Victoria didn't have the opportunity to discuss it again, for the subject didn't come up. She assumed that her father and Adelaide had decided to let the subject drop for the time being, probably in the hopes that she'd change her mind. Neither was there any sign of Frederick in Farrvale Manor. Adelaide imparted the information later in the week that he was planning to tour the Continent for the summer and fall. "Italy, in particular," she said, assuming that Victoria was vitally interested in where he was. "He's ever so interested in Roman culture. I suppose that's where he gets his shocking philosophies. The Latin temperament is so very different from ours. So vulgar, I've always thought, though they did make lovely pottery for all that. Some friends of mine have a pair of delightful urns on their terrace that came from some old Italian city or another."

Once the imminent threat of Frederick's appearance was disposed of, Victoria found that she could go back to enjoying herself. The summer turned into a constant round of parties. The thirty-two guest bedrooms at Farrvale Manor were filled almost all the time. Wealthy, amusing people played endless games of croquet and tennis and laughed and flirted their way from one luxurious meal to the next. The time in between was filled with changing clothes. This was what Victoria had expected when she first came to England, and after nearly a year of Miss Wichett's care, she felt like she had earned it.

There were drawbacks, of course. Frederick's eventual return loomed on the horizon like a menacing cloud that would eventually have to be dealt with, and there was getting to be a slight problem with Lucy. She wasn't altogether happy, and Victoria could neither understand nor alleviate her distress. "Do you realize, Vic, that not a single person at the party last night has ever done a moment of work? Not a single one of them!" she complained one morning.

"Naturally they haven't. They don't have to; they're rich."

"But how can they fill whole lifetimes with utter idleness?"

"They travel, they visit friends, and paint and dance and shop and talk. That's not idleness. It's what we've spent the last year learning to do. What's really the matter with you, Lucy? I'll wager I know. It's that young man at the New Year's ball. I've been wondering, too, why we haven't met him and his friend yet. But I think I have it figured out. Earnest Blakely said a group of his friends went on a tour of Egypt this summer. I bet the Black Douglas and the racehorse are with that party. Too bad we don't know their names. But we'll meet them sooner or later. Don't worry."

Victoria convinced herself that this had cheered Lucy, and she therefore went back to her own pleasures with a clear conscience.

Both girls were at first amused and later vaguely irritated at how little their new acquaintances knew about America. "Kansas?" they would say, rolling it about on their tongues as if it were a foreign phrase. "Is that near San Francisco? I had an ancestor killed near San Francisco, I believe. Think it was called Boston." Another frequent guest, the dim-witted Lady Alicia, repeated the same question nearly every time she visited. "You must know my cousins in New Hampshire, being American and all, don't you?"

"What do you do when red Indians attack you?" an elderly woman asked once. "I forget now, is it the whites or the Indians who live in those quaint little triangular-shaped things? Tebees or something?"

"Indians don't attack us," Victoria answered simply.

"No," Lucy added. "In fact, Victoria's aunt—"

"Lucy!"

"Victoria's aunt once saw an Indian," Lucy amended lamely, glaring at Victoria. "Are you ashamed of Morning Wish?" she asked later when they were alone. "Like you're ashamed of your mother's picture."

The accusation made Victoria uncomfortable. "You know I'm not ashamed of them, but even my mother doesn't like that portrait. She told me about it before I even came here. It makes her look like a sloppy farmer's wife. If I were her, I'd buy the thing away from Father and burn it. But she wouldn't part with the money, I don't imagine."

"Vic, that's not fair. You act like your mother had starved you to death before you came here."

"Well, she might as well have, compared to my father. Just think of how generous he's been to us. All these new clothes must have cost a king's ransom. And the coach he had made for us to go visiting in and the way he had our rooms made over and bought all the new furniture we wanted—"

"*You* wanted," Lucy corrected.

"Lucy, don't be so prim and gloomy. Can't you just enjoy yourself? I vow, you could hire yourself out as a professional mourner."

This brought a reluctant smile to Lucy's lips. "I just keep waiting for something to happen or hoping I'll find something to do! This all seems so endless and pointless. It's like knitting a scarf that someone keeps secretly unraveling from the other end at night. Each day's pattern is pretty and interesting and serves no purpose. Don't you ever feel that way?"

"No, never. I'm taking a positively indecent amount of enjoyment in every single day, now that we've gotten out of Miss Wichett's clutches. Lucy, your problem is that you've learned all the rules of society, but you haven't gotten the Seventrees mentality out of your head."

"What do you mean?"

"You know, work, work, work. Make things, do things, accumulate money. That's all they're interested in. My family and yours as well. They're all wrapped up in Freiler's Cures, like it was the only thing in the world."

"I disagree. They have other interests—"

"Not many. Look, even Ned got his law degree and could have gone anywhere, done anything, but he came back to Seventrees and started working for the company."

"What's wrong with that?" Lucy asked indignantly.

"Absolutely nothing, Lucy, if that's what he really wanted to do, and I think it was. I just want you to realize *we* don't have to be like that. In the meantime, I have an idea for something we can do. Father's invited an absolutely huge number of people down for a Midsummer's Eve ball, and we've got to decide on what sort of dresses we need made. Come, now, smile again, Lucy. I have a wonderful idea of something for us to wear."

Sir Elgin's Midsummer's Eve ball was *the* social event of the season. It was to be the formal unveiling of his daughter and her friend to society at large, and because of this he spared no expense. The ballroom was draped with boughs of fragrant greenery, orange trees from the manor's extensive greenhouses bloomed in gilt tubs around the perimeter of the dance floor, and bouquets of exotic flowers alternated with the food on the long tables of the buffet. The ladies, too, were caught up in the horticultural atmosphere. Most of the gowns the maids scooted back and forth to the pressing rooms with were in flowery pastel shades—orchid, fuchsia, lavender, rose, and mint.

Victoria and Lucy had decided it would be fun to have dresses made alike, but in different colors, and had spent many hours with the dressmaker. Lucy's dress was a pale, icy apricot with light persimmon-colored roses stitched in satin around the deep V-shaped neckline and wide waistband as well as the sweeping hem. The color brought out the mahogany highlights in her elaborately arranged hair and her excitement brought a flattering pink to her cheeks. She wore a long strand of fat pearls and matching earrings that Elgin had happily lent her from the Farrington family jewel collection.

Victoria's dress, made the same way except that it had more tucks in the bodice to flatter her more generous bosom and a slightly longer train as befitted the nominal hostess, was in powder blue with ivory overstitching. She wore her blond hair pulled to the top of her head, from whence an intricate arrangement of satiny golden curls cascaded down the sides. Nearly a dozen dizzily fragrant gardenias were interwoven. "Lucy, look at us," Victoria said, pointing to their images in the dressing-room mirror when they were ready to go downstairs. "We're beautiful!"

"I know it 'ill behooves a lady' to say so, but, *yes*, we are!" Lucy answered. "I only wish my father and Eleanor could have seen me tonight. I think they'd be pleased. Just imagine if the girls in Saint Louis could see us this way. Or our neighbors in Seventrees."

"If I wore this dress in Seventrees, my grandmother would probably take it away from me, cut it up, and use it for packing medicine bottles."

"Is the prince coming, do you think?" Lucy asked, twirling around to look at the back of her gown.

"No. He'd accepted, you know, but Father got a note from him this afternoon saying his grandmama, the queen, had some ribbon cutting or another she wanted him to do for her tomorrow someplace way up north."

"That's a pity, but I'm not sure I really wanted to meet him, except to be able to say I'd met a man who will someday be King of England. I hear Prince "Eddy" is not really very pleasant."

"Well, it doesn't matter now if he's coming or not. The point is, a lot of people thought he was coming and they're here because of that. It's going to be such a grand crush that nobody will notice he's missing. Not after they see us. Say, Lucy"—Victoria lowered her voice—"did you meet that woman in the west wing—the one who has such dark hair and a single white streak running through it?"

"Baroness Ramsey-Something-or-Other? I was introduced to her this afternoon in the garden. Why?"

"Well . . ." Victoria glanced around to see if any of the servants were listening. "Come sit by the window so no one will overhear us. There. I heard my father reminding Adelaide to tell the housekeeper that Baroness Ramsey-Essex was to be given a room 'within walking distance' of that strange poet who carries the silver cane. You know the one? Anyway, he said that, and then he and Adelaide exchanged knowing smiles. Do you know what I think? I think they are"—she lowered her voice to the merest whisper—"lovers."

Lucy looked shocked. "Oh, Vic, do you really! You mean

your father wanted it arranged so that the poet could go to her room at night?"

"Exactly. I've been thinking about it, Lucy. Have you noticed how certain people are always placed in certain arrangements here? For instance, Lord and Lady Rowbotham always have separate rooms, but Ernest Blakely always has the room next to hers. It doesn't matter where in the house they are, it always works out that way. It's the same with that orange-haired widow who plays the harp and Sir John, though he's so old, I wonder . . ."

"Vic, do you realize what you're saying? That your father actually encourages such shameful behavior."

Victoria leaned closer. "I'll bet everyone does, Lucy. We'll be invited to other house parties after this, and I'll wager we'll find the same arrangements."

Lucy's shock had faded and was being replaced by bright-eyed curiosity. "Do you really think the halls are full of men tiptoeing about all night?" She giggled in an extremely unladylike manner that Miss Wichett would have deplored.

"Let's find out," Victoria said.

"Oh, Vic! We couldn't. What if we were caught?"

"What if *we* were caught? Come on, Lucy. It would be great sport. Remember that place where we hid and watched the ball last year? We could slip in there and just see who went by and where they were going. It would be a lark. Nobody could see us, and even if they did, they wouldn't dare make a fuss. After all, we live here. We're allowed to be anywhere we like."

"Oh, I don't know. Well . . . yes, all right. It would be fun, but I still think you're just imagining all this sneaking about."

Victoria held her hand up. "A pledge?"

Lucy smiled, put her hand up, and laced her fingers with Victoria's—their lifelong secret sign. "A pledge."

"Now, let's go downstairs and let everybody see what Miss Wichett did with her 'difficult' cases."

As they were descending the staircase, Victoria took Lucy's arm suddenly and said, "You don't suppose my father and Adelaide are . . . you know?"

Lucy looked surprised, but considered it a moment. "I don't know, Vic. I suppose they might be."

Victoria thought for a moment, then said, "Why do you imagine they don't just marry? Oddly enough, he seems to like the old harridan. He invites her here all the time and lets her act like mistress of the manor."

"Maybe she doesn't want to marry him," Lucy speculated.

"Well, I do think it's a mystery," Victoria said, "but just now I'm more concerned about our romantic future, not theirs. Perhaps we'll meet the richest, most handsome men in the world tonight, and they'll carry us off to castles in the sky."

"Sometimes, Vic, I think you almost believe yourself," Lucy said with a laugh.

After two hours of introductions and dancing, Victoria and Lucy found themselves near one of the French doors to the balcony. A draft of seductively fresh air was coming in. "Let's sneak away for a moment," Victoria suggested. "Nobody will miss us."

Glancing around to make sure no one was watching them, the young women slipped out of the ballroom and found a quiet place on the balcony where they could relax for a few minutes. Victoria draped herself over the cool stone of the balustrade. "Oh, Lucy, I never had any idea that dancing in this gown would be such hot work. It reminds me of being in Seventrees and canning in August. I'm melting."

"You mustn't melt before we've had a chance to meet you," came a strange male voice from the shadows.

Victoria straightened instantly, mortified at having been caught in such an unladylike posture. She regarded the men appearing from the shadows farther along the balcony. "Why, it's the Black Douglas and the racehorse," she said with a smile.

The dark-haired man stepped forward and took her hand to kiss. "I believe I've seen this hand before," he said with a twinkle in his winter-blue eyes. "I couldn't have imagined what beauty was attached to it, however. You must be Miss Farrington, and I must be the Black Douglas."

Victoria felt an apology trying to force its way out, but squelched it. She sensed instinctively that to apologize to this man would be to put herself in his power. And he had a substantial power, a magnetism that defied definition. "I am Victoria Farrington, sir, and this is my friend Lucy Clay."

"I'm afraid I'm not a Black Douglas, but you were close. The Black Douglases are the legitimate line of the Earls of Angus. The Reds are the illegitimate line, and I do have an extremely remote connection with them. I am James Lithgow and this is my friend Howard Wilton."

"If we had known what exquisite blossoms Farrvale Manor's hothouses grew, we'd have come down from London sooner," Howard Wilton said, kissing Victoria's hand briefly and Lucy's more lingeringly. "Imagine Sir Elgin hiding such roses of elegance away like this."

"Hiding them from the likes of rakes like you," Sir Elgin's voice cut in amiably. "Ladies, we are about to open the buffet, and you and I should begin the procession. If you gentlemen will excuse us?" he added, leading Lucy and Victoria away.

The young women drifted through the rest of the evening in a pleasant haze. They saw little more of the two men, but that was not surprising, as there were a great many people present. Toward the end of the evening, they asked for a dance, but Lucy and Victoria's cards were already full. "You will be staying here, won't you?" Victoria asked.

"Most certainly. Until your father throws us out, most likely," James Lithgow replied. "Perhaps a card game or a ride tomorrow?"

"Perhaps," Victoria said coolly. It wasn't anything learned, but rather a buried wellspring of feminine logic that told her it would not be wise to be entirely agreeable to this man. He was the sort who would want a woman to be a challenge. Victoria was a little surprised at herself for knowing this, but she was quite sure she was right, nonetheless.

The ball was not over when Elgin insisted that his charges get along to bed. "It would not do for you to stay about until the last dogs had died," he said, and his request was met with little resistance. Lucy and Victoria were exhausted and eager to get out of their confining dresses and to bed. Their earlier plan for watching the hallway forgotten, they exchanged a few yawned confidences. Victoria was glad Lucy had found someone who took her fancy, but she was a little alarmed as well. "Now, Lucy, keep in mind you don't know a thing about Howard Wilton. He might even be married."

"I know he would have said so," Lucy said. "He is sensitive and honest. You can tell just to look at him. I'm sure he's just the most wonderful person."

"I hope you're right."

"What about Mr. Lithgow? What do you think of him?"

"I'm not sure. I think I'm afraid of him. Well, not exactly afraid. But it's as though I know all about him and nothing about him at the same time."

Lucy looked at her oddly. "I don't think I understand what you mean."

"I'm not sure I do either. It's rather exciting, but I'm not certain I like it."

6

The next day they went riding with James and Howard. Victoria found Howard boring and mopish, but Lucy was obviously more besotted with him by the moment. James Lithgow turned out to be a masterful horseman, riding with skill and energy. Victoria found herself cursing the ridiculous sidesaddle that fashion declared that ladies must use. There was a spirit of competition built into their budding relationship, and she wished she could show him how really well she could ride had she been allowed to sit astride like she did at Seventrees.

The same competitive spirit entered into their conversation. James had a dry, critical wit that matched Victoria's, and most of their talks turned into "matches," which were far more interesting than the overblown compliments that made up Howard's conversations.

"Your father showed me the portrait of your mother in the Great Hall," he said as they waited for Lucy and Howard to catch up with them during a ride. "She's a stunning woman. I see where you get your beauty."

"That's a terrible portrait. It makes me angry that Father shows it to everyone," Victoria said.

"Terrible? I think it's superb. She looks so strong and independent. So American. You have that look about you, too."

"I do not!"

"Why should you wish to deny it? I've met a number of Americans here in England, and they all seem to do just what you're doing. Spend all their time and energy denying their best traits. Why should you come here and worship a crusty shell of a dead society when what you've left is so vital and exciting?"

"Vital? Exciting? I assure you, Mr. Lithgow, you have a mistaken impression. It is merely harsh and crude."

469

He smiled. "I imagine you're up to it." There was a trace of languid sarcasm in his voice.

"I think you're insulting me," Victoria said, trying not to lose her temper.

"Not at all. It was a compliment," he answered with the same mocking smile.

As the week went on, the four were always together. They went for walks, played cards, and talked until late into the evenings. When Sir Elgin started dropping hints that they were on the verge of overstaying their welcome, James and Howard reluctantly left. As their carriage disappeared around the last bend of the long front drive, Lucy said, "Isn't it wonderful, being in love?"

Victoria didn't answer. She wasn't sure she was in love, but she knew that this was the only man she'd ever met whose spirit matched her own. Was that love? she wondered.

"My little girl, eighteen years old! Doesn't seem possible," Sir Elgin said to the assembled dinner party. A light, steady snow had been falling since the previous day, and the halls of Farrvale were cold, though the rooms in use all had roaring blazes in the fireplaces. It gave the illusion of coziness to the huge house as long as one kept near the little islands of warmth and light. The ladies around the long table all wore wool dresses and stockings and elaborately knitted shawls. "Eighteen," Elgin repeated. He'd had a little too much to drink, as he seemed to be doing more and more often, and was feeling sentimental. "To think, she almost wasn't born at all."

"What do you mean, Sir Elgin?" the woman to his right asked.

"Just that she had a typically Wild West adventure even before she was born."

Victoria, at the far end of the table, perked up. Much as she disliked it when her father talked in front of others about Seventrees, she'd not heard of any such "adventure" and was curious.

"Yes, it was an ice storm," Elgin went on. "An extraordinary phenomenon. I've tried a hundred times since then to capture the essence of it on canvas, and I can't. Everything became coated with inches of ice. Each twig and leaf imprisoned, as if in amber, but in sparkling, smooth ice. So smooth it seemed almost greasy to the touch. Was working at my studios when the trees started collapsing under the unusual weight. Made my way home, had to actually crawl part of the way. No foothold at all. When I got there, I found that a big tree had fallen on the house. Dead center. Sliced the house right in half." He stopped and took a long drink of port. "Yes, the tree just threw itself right in the middle. We found Victoria's mother in what had been the dining room. All surrounded by branches and snow, but she'd gotten under a heavy table."

His voice was lowered as if he'd forgotten there was anyone else there. "Prettiest thing I ever saw—Schooner crawling out of that rubble. Her hair—pretty, fair hair like Victoria's—all come loose around her shoulders, with snow spangles in it. If she hadn't been large with Victoria, she'd have looked like a wood nymph coming shyly out of an enchanted hideaway." He was lost in thought for a moment; then he laughed and added, "Too sad. She had the mind of a clerk, the determination of a rhino, and the conscience of a middle-class saint to go with all that beauty."

The guests had fallen silent while he talked. Now it was an uncomfortable silence. Lucy broke it. "She still is very pretty, Sir Elgin."

This had the desired effect of snapping him back to the present. "Certain she is. Beautiful woman. Victoria's got her coloring. Have you all seen the portrait I did of her—"

"Father, please!" Victoria warned. "Not now." She could barely hear James Lithgow's deep, muffled chuckle from her left.

"Yes, yes. Suppose you're right," Elgin said. "Let's get on with the gifts, shall we?"

A discreet signal to the servants got the table cleared in a matter of moments. The table behind Victoria was piled high with packages. "Do open mine first, Victoria," Frederick Wotton said.

He'd just returned from his travels, and Victoria so far had avoided having so much as a word with him. In fact, the only thought she'd given him was to wonder how anyone could spend that much time in the south of Europe and still look like he'd been born and raised in a lightless cave. She opened the small, sloppily wrapped square and found a small volume of Italian essays—written in Italian, which she did not read. It was not, she noted, even bound attractively. "Thank you, Frederick," she said with an icy smile.

"I shall be glad to begin reading them to you this week," Frederick offered.

Victoria glanced at her father, and he was smiling vaguely. This apparently suited him, Frederick's resuming his doomed courtship. Victoria had hoped desperately she'd made her point and that Elgin and Adelaide had given up their plans. "Thank you, Frederick," Victoria answered. "But I'm thinking of taking up the study of Italian, and reading them myself will be most instructive."

One by one, the rest of the gifts were brought to the table. An ivory-and-gold-lace fan from Adelaide, a book of sonnets from Lucy, a tiny crystal perfume glass from the staff. Finally there were only two gifts left on the table—a huge box and a tiny one. One had to be from her father and the other from James Lithgow. "Open the large one next," Elgin said. Then, to the other guests he added, "It's from her mother. Been here for weeks, hidden in a closet. Been wondering what was in it. Letter said there were two gifts, one for Victoria and one for Miss Clay."

Victoria felt deflated. If the big box was from Seventrees, that meant James Lithgow had not given her anything at all. How embarrassing and disappointing.

Victoria unwrapped the large but lightweight box. As she lifted the last layer of tissue, Lucy exclaimed, "Oh, Vic, how lovely. Quilts. Your grandmother must have worked them— that's an old German pattern."

Victoria started to hastily put the tissue back, but Lucy reached faster and pulled one of the quilts out of the box. "Look, everyone. Isn't this pretty? See the flowered blue pieces? They are from matching dresses Victoria and I had when we were little girls. And this green is from that coat you had when we first went to Saint Louis to school."

"How quaint," Adelaide said condescendingly. "I once had a tenant on my Yorkshire land make me one of those. Charming things, but what does one do with them?" She laughed, a superior little waterfall of a laugh.

"Lucy, put it back in the box!" Victoria whispered.

Lucy looked hurt and angry. She flung a look of such loathing at Adelaide Wotton that Victoria would have been alarmed, had she not been so wrapped in her own concerns at the moment. "You put yours back in the box, I'm going to look at mine," she said defiantly.

Victoria was miserable. It was a pretty quilt, but they didn't use such things in England. At least, stylish people didn't. And it was such a damnably "homespun" sort of gift. Quite embarrassing. "Here's mine, my dear," Elgin said handing her the last package, a long flat box that spoke of jewelry.

Victoria lifted the lid and gasped at the sight of the necklace. It was delicately carved ivory roses, each about an inch in diameter. Linking them together were tiny clusters of jade leaves. "Oh, Father! It's the most beautiful thing," Victoria exclaimed, rushing over to kiss him. The quilt was forgotten in the flurry over the necklace.

Finally the servants began picking up the discarded wrappings, and Victoria, being very careful not to look at James, said, "Thank you all so much for your lovely thoughts. It's an important date in my life, and you've made it all the more memorable—"

"But you're not finished opening gifts yet," James said. With an amused smile he pulled a small box from his breast pocket and handed it to Victoria.

"Oh, James!" Victoria said. She felt relief come over her in almost tangible waves. He hadn't forgotten after all. He'd just waited till last. When she opened the tiny box, she found a pair of ivory-and-jade earrings that matched her father's gift. "How did you know?" she asked breathlessly.

"He showed me the necklace weeks ago," James explained. "I went to the same jeweler."

The only member of the party who was not impressed with Lithgow's gift was Sir Elgin. It had stolen some of his own thunder, but more than that, it suggested a sort of family intimacy he was loath to see. "Well, if that's all, perhaps you ladies would excuse the gentlemen to enjoy their port now," he said, effectively breaking up the knot of guests admiring the earrings.

Later in the evening Victoria went to the drafty library to find a novel to read before retiring. James found her there. "How nice that necklace will look around your neck," he said, taking her in his arms and dotting light kisses around her throat. Victoria shivered delightfully and tried to pull away. "James, please, someone will see us."

But she didn't really care, and he knew it. "And the earrings," he continued, nibbling on her earlobes. "I'm going to ask your father for your hand tomorrow," he said.

She pulled away. Walking to the fireplace, she said, "Hadn't you better ask first what I think?"

He laughed. "My dear, I know what you think. It's your father I'm worried about. I'm not sure he'll want to turn

473

loose of you. You've made an extraordinary change in him, you know."

"I have?"

"Yes, he was always slouching about, crying poor, and complaining about expenses. Always the guest, never the host, you know. Then you came and he broke down and started enjoying himself. Quite a miracle you've worked on the old fellow."

"Stop talking about my father," Victoria said. "I haven't agreed to marry you."

"But you will. Think of it, combining all that wonderful money, yours and mine."

"Money? Is that all you want of me?" Victoria said in her best coquettish manner.

He laughed again. "Why else would a man give up his freedom?"

Victoria never knew when he was being outrageous to shock her and when he was serious. It was part of the mysterious power he had over her, the power that both frightened and thrilled her. It was so much more exciting than a conversation with, say, Ned Clay. "Lots of young women have substantial dowries," she said. "Why haven't you married one of them?"

"Because they were not you. I've been waiting for you," he answered in an unusually gentle voice as he took her into his arms again. "Howard is going to propose to Lucy as well. We'll have a double wedding and take a nice long trip all over Europe together. Howard and I want you both to see Egypt."

"But—" Victoria said, before he smothered her in a kiss. She supposed, dizzily, that she was engaged. "But my father still thinks I'm going to marry Frederick Wotton," she said.

"Wotton? That ass!" James said. "Why would he want a thing like that?"

"Just what you said earlier," Victoria replied. "It's financially advantageous. Something about river frontage."

She expected James to laugh at the foolishness of this, but he did not. Instead, he stepped away and began to look for a suitable cigar in a tooled leather case. "Hmmm."

"James! You're behaving as though that makes sense!" Victoria said.

"Well, it does, you know. These rich old families like your haven't stayed that way by accident. The best way to gai money and power is to marry more of it. I just hadn't thought Elgin cared——"

"It doesn't matter if he does," Victoria said quickly. James sounded almost as if he might retract his proposal. "He can't make me marry that pompous ninny! This is not the Dark Ages, when you could drag a girl to the altar and make her take vows against her will. Sooner or later Father will realize I will not accept Frederick. If we tell him we wish to marry, it will hurry the process."

"You think so?" James said. He sounded genuinely unsure, but he had his customary mocking smile that Victoria could never interpret.

Because of her prodding more than a passionate inclination (Victoria feared), James approached her father the next day with his request, and was politely but firmly turned down.

Within five minutes of hearing this, Victoria was in her father's den. "Father, I am *going* to marry James Lithgow," she said in a sweet but forceful tone.

Sir Elgin supposed otherwise, however, and was not as intimidated as Victoria had expected. "Won't have you marrying yet," he declared. "You're too young."

"I'm not. I'm eighteen, Father."

"Your mother wouldn't approve," he added.

"Mother doesn't have to approve," Victoria said. "You just don't like James. That's it, isn't it?"

"Not at all!" Elgin said, pacing about his smoking room and taking long swigs from a glass of pale amber liquid. "Just don't think you know enough about him." Suddenly he looked at her with a desperate, maudlin look. "I don't want to lose you, Victoria. I need you here."

It was the first time he'd ever indicated any genuine fondness for her, and Victoria was touched. "Very well, Father. We'll wait awhile for the actual wedding, but I am engaged to James, and I wish you to announce it formally at dinner tonight."

"And you'll wait to marry? A year, at least."

"A whole year?"

"That's a proper length of time," Elgin said. There was a pleading note in his voice that broke her heart. Imagine him caring so much and never showing it before.

"Very well, a year, but not a day longer." Victoria would not have admitted to anyone, not even herself, that a small part of her was grateful to have an excuse to put off the wedding date. Life with James Lithgow was going to be exciting, of that she was sure, but she had some doubts. They were as insignificant as gnats, but they never ceased to whisper and buzz at the back of her mind.

"You'll announce our engagement at dinner, then?" she asked.

Elgin paced the room. "Well, about that—let's wait just a bit to make the announcement. Adelaide has her heart so set on you and Frederick marrying, you know. I will have to have a little time to . . . to, ah . . . prepare her. Only courteous, don't you know?"

"How much time?" Victoria asked.

"Oh, let's say a month or two?"

"Father! You are hedging. You could break it to her in a matter of a few seconds."

"Please, Victoria . . ."

"Oh, very well. But don't start thinking I'm going to change my mind. I won't!"

"Just think, in less than a year we'll be married women," Lucy said as she brushed out her hair. "Why don't we run up to London next week and see about dresses? We're only a few miles now. We could shop before we go back to Farrvale."

They were at the third of the many house parties they'd been invited to already, and though the homes were all quite grand, Victoria had been pleased to note that none of them was on the scale of Farrvale Manor. Joining Lucy by the window and looking out at the moon-bathed walks and gardens below, Victoria said, "Lucy, I keep telling you there is no reason *you* should wait so long."

"Don't start being silly again," Lucy said. "I told you I want us to go on our wedding trip together. I don't really mind. Well, maybe I do," she added, blushing noticeably even in the dim light. "But it will be worth the wait. We'll have such a wonderful time, the four of us. Howard is looking forward to making the trip together. He and James are never apart. I don't think I could get him away without the two of you."

"Yes, I have a picture of you and me sitting together in one hotel after another while the two of them go off and do whatever it is they do. Say, Lucy, have you been noticing the room arrangements? Remember when we talked about it once before?"

Lucy put down her hairbrush. "I have. You've noticed, too,

that no one ever puts us anywhere near James and Howard," she added with a smile.

"Lucy, I'm not tired, are you?" Victoria said.

"No, not really, but . . . Oh, no, Victoria. We couldn't. Not in someone else's house."

"You pledged," Victoria reminded her.

"No. I won't do it."

"Of course you will. There's that window alcove just between the two bedroom wings, remember? It's got heavy draperies, and we could see everything that went on without anyone seeing us. It would be fun. Please, Lucy. It's so boring here, and it would be ever so informative."

"What if someone saw us?"

"Nobody is going to stop and have a rendezvous in the alcove. Besides, anyone who was out roaming about and saw us would have more reason to keep it quiet than we would. Come on, Lucy. Put on that dark dressing gown."

Reluctantly Lucy let herself be dragged into Victoria's adventure. They made their way to the window enclosure without being seen, and hid there behind the heavy green draperies. Lucy knelt, Victoria stood over her, and they peered through the slit where the fabric met. For a long time nothing stirred; then Victoria whispered, "I hear something. Look, there in the shadows. Isn't that Major Weybarton?" She stifled a giggle. "If he came to my room for an assignation, I think I'd die! Shhh, he went into Mrs. Arbuthnot's room. Oh, Lucy, I'd never have guessed, would you?"

But Lucy didn't answer. The slit in the draperies suddenly snapped shut. Victoria looked down into the darkness. "What's the matter, Lucy?"

"Howard . . ." she whispered, stricken.

"What!" Victoria pulled the fabric apart slightly and looked down the hall. Surely Lucy was mistaken. But no, the graceful figure sliding along the dark hall was certainly Howard. "He's probably just unable to sleep and going out for some air," Victoria said, trying to voice a reassurance she didn't feel.

"He has an assignation with some woman," Lucy said grimly.

Victoria didn't answer for a moment, then said, "No, he hasn't, Lucy. He just went into James's room. See, it's just like us. He couldn't sleep, so he went to visit with James. You shouldn't have doubted him."

Lucy was trembling with relief. She rose and took Victoria's hand in her own cold one. "Vic, this isn't fun. Let's go back to our rooms. Please."

"Very well. I guess it wasn't such a good idea. I'm sorry I led you into something that upset you."

They hurriedly tiptoed along, but just as they neared the door to James's room, they heard someone coming toward them around the bend. "Dear God!" Lucy whispered.

"Quick! In here!" Victoria said with her hand on the doorknob.

"No, James and Howard are there. What will they think of us if we go barging in—"

There wasn't time to argue or to explain to Lucy how much more embarrassing it would be to be caught standing in the hall in their nightshifts and dressing gowns. Victoria quietly opened the door, pushed Lucy through ahead of her, and carefully closed the door again behind them. Suddenly Lucy grasped her arm in a painful grip. "Lucy! What's . . . ?" The words died.

There was little light in the room—only the dying embers of a fire in the grate and one single candle next to the bed. But that one candle was behind the two men, silhouetting them as perfectly as if they'd been cut from black paper by an obscene artist. The warm yellow light bathed the outlines of their naked bodies. Frozen in surprise, they remained where they stood, locked in a lovers' embrace. James's arms were around Howard's lithe body.

At Victoria's shocked intake of breath, they turned. Howard put out a hand as if to ward off a blow. James took a step forward. "Victoria—" he began. But his words were cut off by Lucy's shrill scream.

Victoria whirled and yanked the door open. Pulling on Lucy's arm, she tried to take her away. But Lucy screamed once more and collapsed. Victoria tried to catch her, and ended up falling to the floor in the hallway with her.

Doors opened, slippered feet scurried on the carpeted hall. "What the devil . . . ?"

"Someone is hurt."

"Who screamed?"

A crowd of sleep-blurred features looked down on them. "What has happened? What are you young ladies doing here?" the hostess asked.

"Get smelling salts, and our maid!" Victoria answered, trying to disentangle herself from Lucy's recumbent figure. Even in the dim hall, Lucy was so pale it was alarming.

478

Howard Wilton, a hastily thrown-on dressing gown sweeping the floor, bent over her. "Lucy. Please wake up. . . ."

Victoria drew back her arm and delivered a stinging slap. It was not a gesture of disapproval. It was a strong, badly aimed blow at someone who had dared to hurt Lucy. That she, too, had cause for offense did not then occur to her. "Get away from her! Don't you dare touch her, you . . . you beastly—"

"Here, here! Get a hold on yourself, Victoria," James said.

She glared up at him, unaware of the tears running down her cheeks. She wanted to fling acid insults at him, but she did not have the words. She'd never even contemplated the possibility of such a thing as she'd just seen. She felt herself growing hot, and waves of nausea swept over her. "Leave us alone," she said weakly. "Leave us alone. Forever."

"A lovers' tiff," someone in the background said, tittering.

Victoria buried her face in her hands and wept. Not for herself as much as for Lucy and a lost innocence for both of them that would never be recovered.

7

Victoria reined in her horse at the top of the rise. She had ridden as if demon-pursued, back and forth across the breadth of Farrvale's long pasture. Instead of a proper riding habit, she wore one of the simple dresses Miss Wichett had made them wear during their "schooldays." She had the full gray skirts tucked up most improperly so that she could ride astraddle instead of sidesaddle. Several months earlier it would have been social disaster to be seen this way, but this summer she wouldn't *be* seen, and the social disaster had already happened. She'd been all but ostracized. After that horrible night and subsequent dawn departure, the invitations had suddenly dried up. She and Lucy had broken the rules. They had made a scene. They had let emotion overcome etiquette.

The night had been filled with nosy solicitude. At first, Victoria refused to explain what had happened because of shock and a lack of adequate vocabulary to even describe what they had witnessed. Later, when the whispers and speculation grew louder and more derogatory to Victoria and Lucy's morals, she had refused to explain out of pride. Elgin had asked just enough questions to ascertain that Victoria no longer intended to marry James Lithgow; then he had subsided with the sage advice that they take their maid and some elderly woman as escort and travel on the Continent. "It will all be forgotten sooner or later," he'd said. Fortunately he had the wit to leave out any mention of Frederick.

Victoria hoped he was right, but she refused his offer of a journey. It would not suit Lucy, and her primary concern was Lucy's welfare. Victoria grasped a strand of hair that had escaped her hat and wound it back into the bun at the back of her neck. In turning, she noticed a coach coming along the drive. She spurred her horse forward, wanting to get a look at who was calling. If it was someone who might disturb Lucy, she could take a shortcut back to the house and take Lucy off to hide. Concealing herself among the bushes at a turn, she waited until the coach was even with her.

The occupant was a young man. Good heavens! It was Lucy's brother, Ned. "Hold!" she shouted to the coachman, spurring her horse forward. "Stop."

As the vehicle clattered to a halt, Victoria slid from her horse and Ned Clay leaped from the coach. He caught her up in a hearty embrace. "My God, Vic, it *is* you. When I heard that voice and saw you tearing out of the shrubbery, I couldn't believe it. I thought I'd find you in diamonds and ball gowns. You've changed, all right. But not like I expected," he added, his frank sun-browned face alight with a friendly smile.

"Oh, I've changed, Ned. More than you know. Send the coach ahead and come with me. Can you ride double like we used to when we were children?"

He laughed. "Why would you think I'd forgotten how to ride?"

"I don't know," Victoria said, suddenly feeling oddly shy. "You just seem so . . . so adult."

"All because I'm wearing business clothes," Ned said. He pulled his tie loose, hitched one trouser leg up an inch at the knee, and sprang into the saddle, pulling Victoria up in front of him a moment later. Gesturing the astonished coach driver to go on, he said, "Which way, milady?"

They rode back to the rise where Victoria had first sighted

the coach. Looking down at the vast house, Ned sighed. "My God, it's enormous! How do you find your way around?"

"I don't," Victoria said. "There are whole wings of it I've never been in. Ned, did you get my letter, or are you here by coincidence?" She sank into a lush, grassy place in the shade of an oak and gestured to him to join her.

"Yes, I got your letter," he said, suddenly serious.

"You didn't tell your father? I promised—"

"No. I didn't tell him. He was coming anyway, to surprise Lucy. Your letter came just two days before he was due to leave, and I told him I'd had a sudden change of heart and would like to come along. He doesn't know there's anything wrong, but he might suspect. Your letter didn't make much sense, really. Tell me what happened and how Lucy is."

"You know she was engaged . . ."

"You both were, or are?"

"We both *were*. No longer. It's difficult to explain. I don't know the words. . . . Remember that spotted dog that Torchy had when we were little? The one was was always trying to . . . to 'do things' with other male dogs?"

Ned nodded. "Yes, I see. Lucy's betrothed . . . ?"

"Yes, and mine. We saw them together. *Really* together!"

"Oh, no," Ned said feelingly.

"It was perfectly horrible for a great many reasons, but you know how even the most awful things don't seem quite so terrible or important after a while? Well, it hasn't been that way with Lucy."

"And you?" Ned leaned forward and plucked a long strand of grass.

"Me? Oh, I don't know. It was embarrassing, and I was as mad as a surprised skunk for a while, but I didn't care as much, somehow. I suppose I'd never truly meant to marry James. I mean, I'd said I would, and thought I was going to, but I didn't stay awake nights counting how many days or trying to picture life with him. Lucy did. She was very much in love with Howard, though I can't see why. He was about as interesting as a guttering candle. Dim and weak."

"It doesn't sound like he was the right man for her, even if his sexual inclinations had been normal," Ned said.

"I don't suppose so, but none of that matters. She had loved him enough to give up going back to Seventrees, and she cried steadily for a week after. She made herself sick with it. Vomiting and fainting."

Ned frowned. "Even Freiler's doesn't have a cure for that. Poor Lucy."

"She finally stopped the crying. Now she sits. Just *sits!* She answers politely when you talk to her, but that's all. The last two weeks she's been pleading a headache and not even coming down for meals. I'm frightened for her, Ned. She's acting like an invalid. Like those silly women you hear about who take to their beds and never get up again."

"And you say she's not recovering?"

"No, she's getting worse every day. She reminds me of those decorated eggs you see that someone's blown the inside out and left it empty."

"And what do you think the solution is?" Ned asked, getting directly to the point, as was his habit.

"I don't know, but I think the first thing is to take her home."

"I think so too. You'll come along?"

Victoria hadn't considered the possibility, but she answered promptly, "No. I'll stay here. Things are a little difficult for the time, but Father assures me it will pass. Come see the house and visit with Lucy. It will do wonders for her to have you to talk to."

Lucy did improve when her brother, and later her father, came to Farrvale, but she still was unhappy. "You must cheer up, Lucy," Victoria said. "Ned and your father are taking you home. That pleases you, doesn't it?"

"Ned and my father? Aren't you coming?" Lucy said, a slight alarm being the first emotional reaction she'd shown to anything in weeks.

"No. I'm staying here. You don't need me."

Lucy reached out and clutched Victoria's arm. "I can't face everyone by myself, Vic! Come with me."

"Face everyone? What do you mean? You haven't done anything wrong."

"I've been made a fool of. I'll be going home in disgrace, and I won't have you . . ." She began to cry again like she had at first, great uncontrolled sobs.

Victoria put her arms around her friend. "Now, Lucy, don't start crying again. I don't want you to be ill. Please stop. . . ." Patting Lucy's shoulder, Victoria thought quickly about her situation. Disinclined to put anyone's interests above her own, Victoria had often made exception where Lucy was concerned. It was silly of Lucy to want her to come along, but obviously Lucy thought it was vitally important. Victoria realized she had to do as her friend wished if she was ever to respect herself. Lucy asked very little of her, and Victoria felt a certain responsibility for the situation. Lucy had never wanted to come to England in the first place. Besides, if she was ever to visit Seventrees, this would be a good time, Victoria thought. Her father had told her that she should simply stay away from social functions for a while and let the furor die of its own accord. She could accompany Lucy, and when she returned in a few months, everyone would have fastened on a new bit of gossip and the scene in the hallway outside James Lithgow's bedroom would be forgotten. "Very well," Victoria said. "But I won't stay more than a month, you understand."

Surprisingly, it was Elgin who made the strongest objection to Victoria's plan. "No sense in it at all," he said angrily.

"It doesn't have to make sense, Father. My friend needs me," she said. "Besides, it is exactly what you suggested. Staying away for a while until the vultures fasten on a new victim to gossip about."

"I didn't say 'vultures' and I certainly didn't intend for you to go so far away. What about Frederick?"

"Oh, Father! Not Frederick again."

It was late in the evening, and Elgin had indulged in even more brandy than usual. Slurring his words a little, he said, "I want you to marry Frederick. It will be an excellent arrangement and would please both Adelaide and me."

"I would dearly love to please you, Father. I'm more grateful than I can say for your generosity to me, but I cannot go that far. Frederick is a pretentious idiot, and the worst of it is, you know that and would still let me ruin my life by marrying him. I would certainly be the most miserable woman on earth."

Elgin swung around quickly, swayed, and said, "Victoria, I cannot get along without you here."

Victoria was awake until quite late, thinking over this statement. Elgin had spoken with such desperation, and she knew it was not feigned. But when she faced the naked truth, she was forced to admit he'd never seemed to genuinely care about her. It hurt her pride to think it, but nevertheless, she believed it to be true. He never sought her company. He traveled often, never inviting her along. When he was home, she saw little of him. When he had guests, she was only occasionally asked to join them, and then it was most frequently when the guests were the Wottons.

483

Adding up her mental ledger, Victoria thought he was proud of her appearance and "post-Wichett" deportment. But on the rare evenings when they dined alone, he seemed to have very little to say to her, and even less interest in what she had to say. Victoria tried to rationalize that he simply did not show his feelings like the other side of her family. But she could not make that idea hold up. He was quite obviously fond of Adelaide, and there was no mistaking his affection. He had friends he liked well, including Quincy Clay, and he had no trouble making known his feelings.

Victoria was left with a snarl of facts and opinions she could not unravel. Her father didn't seem to especially like her, and yet he became almost maudlin every time he thought he might lose her—except when it came to nasty Frederick, and he was desperately eager to throw her into his arms. It was like one of the dissected pictures. Clearly defined individual pieces which presumably fit together. But Victoria had neither the experience nor the patience to make them into a single picture.

The next day she informed the Clays that she would accompany them and told her father she was leaving within the fortnight. Elgin tried several delaying tactics—parties they simply must attend, people they must meet, a certain ship they should take that didn't leave for two months. He even prevailed upon Adelaide to talk to Victoria—an interview that was doomed from the beginning. But Victoria was not the only one who was unwilling to put off the journey. Ned and Quincy were both worried about Lucy and anxious to get her home. With varying degrees of courtesy they turned down the invitations and advice and insisted they must leave.

The day before they were to leave, Elgin changed his approach. "You must let me sketch you one last time," he told Victoria sadly.

"One *last* time," Victoria said in a matter-of-fact tone much like her grandmother's. "You've never yet sketched me, though you've talked about it often enough."

Elgin ignored this. He sighed. "I would like to have it to remember you by when I'm an old man."

"Father, I haven't time to sit still for an hour today. Let's do it when I get back."

"Get back. No, you'll never come back to me. I can feel it in the very marrow of my bones."

Victoria was too concerned with her packing to be touched

by this maudlin appeal. She kissed his cheek and dashed away, calling over her shoulder, "Later, Father."

That evening Victoria was alarmed, very nearly disgusted, with the amount of drink Elgin was indulging in. The Wottons, as usual, had come to the farewell dinner. Ned, who didn't drink at all, and Frederick, who did, but badly, exchanged unpleasant remarks over the dinner. At least Frederick was openly unpleasant. Ned treated him as one might a five-legged cow trying to dance. *Amusing,* his attitude seemed to suggest, *but somewhat pitiful.* Victoria was delighted with the way Ned kept relentlessly puncturing Frederick's asinine remarks with his own gentle wit. Unaware that he was making a fool of himself, Frederick finished a long, loose verbal essay with the remark, "I have always said that society must abandon its search for physical perfection and instead bend all its efforts toward the solution of the universal moral question, that is to say, What is truth? Don't you think so?"

Ned regarded him steadily over a forkful of quail and said, "Actually, what *I* always say is: The more you stir a stink, the louder it smells."

Quincy Clay choked on his wine. Lucy buried her smile in her napkin. But Victoria could not contain herself and burst out laughing. Ned went right on eating as if he didn't notice, except to glance once at Lucy and wink. Frederick gaped, entirely unable to comprehend Ned's statement or the Americans' reaction to it. Adelaide glared at the four of them in turn and nudged Elgin, who was too drunk to have much interest in what was going on.

Finally, wiping her eyes and feeling a case of hiccups coming on, Victoria rose and excused herself and Lucy, pleading last-minute packing that still remained. It wasn't until an hour later that she remembered she'd neglected to tell Cook some special instructions for breakfast. Hurrying through the dark hallway, she met up with Ned coming out of Elgin's smoking room. "Dear Ned," she whispered. "I've never been so delighted. Silly Frederick!"

"What? Oh, at dinner . . ." he said, but he was clearly preoccupied. He glanced over his shoulder and pulled the smoking-room door shut tightly.

"Ned, what's the matter?"

He walked along the hall a little ways with her. "Victoria, you wouldn't really consider marrying him, would you?"

"Ned! Of course not. He's a fool—"

"He's worse than a fool," Ned said softly.

"What do you mean? Oh, no, not him too!"

Ned smiled. "No, Vic. He didn't try to get me into a corner and kiss me!"

"Then what do you mean?"

"Oh, nothing. We'll talk about it later. Hadn't you better get to bed? We have a long day tomorrow." He put a hand on her shoulder and kissed her cheek lightly.

Victoria astonished herself by standing on her toes and kissing him back—but on the lips. It was over in a second, and she was genuinely shocked and embarrassed at what she'd done. "Oh, my, I'm sorry, I . . . I . . ." she said before fleeing.

"Good night, Vic," he called softly after her, and she could hear the smile in his voice.

Departure the next day was a carnival of disorganization. Victoria and Lucy kept counting and recounting trunks, suitcases, parcels, and hampers. Elgin made no attempt to hide his distress, but Victoria was unmoved by it because she was too busy and because Lucy seemed so pleased to be going. While not cheerful by any definition, she was at least less morose than she had been in the preceding months. And as the journey progressed, she improved. On the steam liner crossing the Atlantic, she began talking of her own accord, not just when a question was addressed her, and later, on the long trip down the Ohio River, Victoria heard her humming to herself as she stood at the rail watching the riverbank slide by.

That was when Victoria first realized that while her efforts to help Lucy were apparently working, her own normal state of confidence and high spirits had changed. She was vaguely unhappy and didn't know quite why. It wasn't that she was nearing home. After all, it was only for a short visit. No, it was something else. She joined Lucy at the rail. Lucy turned to her with a soft smile that seemed almost serene. "I've been awful," she said.

"Don't be a goose," Victoria replied.

"Thank you for putting up with me. Vic, why do you suppose they proposed to us at all?"

Victoria said, "Are you sure you want to talk about this?"

"Yes, there are enough miles between me and the problem now."

Victoria followed the flight of a crane while she chose her words carefully. "James came to talk to me the next day. He didn't really admit it right out, but it was primarily our money. He claimed that they liked us 'well enough' but that they'd assumed all rich American girls were desperately anxious for the prestige of marrying into the English aristocracy. So anxious that we would have handed over our inheritances and turned a blind eye on their relationship. Lucy, he was genuinely surprised to find out he was wrong." She glanced at Lucy, afraid she might have set off a new cycle of tears.

But Lucy was still smiling. "I imagine you made quite clear how wrong he *was*."

Victoria grinned. "I used some perfectly obscene American vulgarities and enjoyed saying every one of them."

"I think it must be the hardest thing in the world," Lucy said, "finding out that someone you thought loved you, doesn't."

Suddenly Victoria's discontent crystallized into a single lump of unhappiness. She knew as surely as if it had been proclaimed from the treetops. Her father had said he wanted her to stay in England, that he needed her to stay, that he feared she might not be back. But never had he said he loved her . . . and there was a very good reason he hadn't. "Oh, Lucy," she said in sudden despair. "He doesn't love me!"

"James Lithgow?" Lucy said, surprised.

"No, my father."

"Now you're being the goose," Lucy said. "Why would he have done so much for you otherwise? Think of the money he's spent on you. That must be the way he expresses his affection."

Victoria thought about it for a long time and finally said, "I don't think so."

The excitement at their homecoming was muted by an anxiety that pervaded the entire community. Several weeks before, Maggie Freiler had taken the carriage to Kansas City to check on a drug shipment. On the way back a cat had run under the horse's hooves. Unfortunately, the cat was being pursued by a small dog, which caught up with it under the horse. In the ensuing fight, the horse had become terrified and bolted. He raced wildly over the edge of the road and through several front yards before overturning the carriage.

Maggie had walked away from the wreckage and seemed merely shaken by the incident, but that night she began to cough. The coughing had become more violent overnight, and in the morning the doctor diagnosed a broken rib, which had apparently punctured the right lung. He'd prescribed bed rest and a number of different medicines, but she had slowly grown worse.

"Have you called in anyone else?" Quincy Clay asked Schooner as they all sat around the big scarred kitchen table at Maggie's house.

Schooner was red-eyed and incredibly weary-looking, but composed. "I haven't had to. The word has spread, and she has many friends across both Kansas and Missouri. We've had legions of doctors stop by to offer their services. They are all in agreement. Victoria, I'm sorry you had to come home to such an unhappy circumstance, but I'm glad you're here. Your grandmother will be pleased to see you. As soon as she wakes, you can visit with her; then you can start telling me all about England." She was careful not to ask why Victoria had come or how long she was staying, and Victoria appreciated her tact.

Victoria was shocked when she saw her grandmother. Even ill and in pain, Maggie had her usual ramrod dignity. Her hair, which had gracefully gone from blond to white, was wrapped around her head in sleek braids, and she wore a neatly pleated, almost tailored bed jacket. But she was alabaster-pale and there were creases of suffering crossing her forehead.

"Victoria? You're back?" she said when her granddaughter came into her bedroom.

Oddly enough, Victoria found a sense of familiarity and comfort in the slight German accent that had previously annoyed and embarrassed her. "Lucy wanted to return, and I decided to come along for a visit," she said, pulling a chair forward to sit beside Maggie's bed. "You must hurry and get well, though. I saw some new buildings as we drove through town. You'll have to give me a tour before I go back."

"You'll have to get your grandfather to show you. I'm not going to get well. I am dying," Maggie said.

"Grandmother, you must not say such a thing."

"Why not? It is the truth. Victoria, do me the honor of not speaking to me as though I were a frightened child to reassure. To waste the last of our time together pretending is not worthy of you or me." Her voice was beginning to fail. "You talk," she said bluntly.

Victoria was shocked for a moment by Maggie's frankness, yet she realized she shouldn't have been. For the first time since leaving Farrvale, Frederick Wotton came to mind. He

488

was always yammering about truth in lofty terms, and yet this old woman was the only individual Victoria knew who had no trouble identifying truth and no fear of facing it. How ironic. Frederick, with all his breeding, his money, his aristocratic friends and fancy education, knew so little. But this plain, uneducated, eccentric German frontier woman could cut through all pretense and say, "I am dying."

Victoria talked for a while about her travels. She told her grandmother about some of the places she had seen, and before very long Maggie dropped back into a light sleep. Victoria tucked the covers around her and slipped out the door. She found Gerald sitting in the hall outside. "Grandpa, I'm sorry," she said, hugging him.

"Now, now. Don't be upset. We might yet pull her through this," Gerald said with forced cheer. "Your mother tried to wait to talk to with you, but she fell asleep in the back bedroom. She's exhausted."

"I know. I'll just do some unpacking and come back in an hour or two to relieve you. Let's let her get some rest."

"That's a good girl," Gerald said, but he sounded remote. His attention was obviously not on the conversation. Victoria watched as he turned away and went to his wife's side. His glossy black curls had long since gone to a silvery gray, making him look even more dashing and distinguished than ever, but his normally gay, charming demeanor had deserted him, leaving him looking haunted and terrified. Victoria found herself reflecting for the first time in her life on how strangely mismatched Maggie and Gerald were. Grandpa was the one she'd always gone to when she felt the need of advice, because his advice was always so easy to follow. *Enjoy yourself,* the gist of his recommendations always seemed to be. *Pluck the sweetest, ripest pieces of life available and taste every delectable bit of juice you can.* He was entertaining and lovable except for his rare black, despairing moods. But his wife was the spine of the family. Serious, almost grim, Maggie Preiler was the opposite of her husband in every way. Yet, they'd made a life together and had both seemed happy in their own ways.

Victoria went back to her mother's house, scuffing the leaves that were beginning to fall as she walked. Autumn was pretty time here, she realized. She'd never really noticed that before. Her mother and Jack Q's house was only three blocks from Maggie's, but it was getting dark and the air was turning brisk. "You look cold," Jack Q said as she came in the front door. "I've got a fire going. Come sit down."

Victoria surveyed the trunks and boxes in the front hall. "I see the carter brought my things. Oh, dear, I think one of those matched blue trunks my father gave me is missing. There are only four of them."

"Probably just got mixed up with Lucy's things. How is your grandmother doing?" he asked as she joined him by the fireplace.

"No better than when you were over this afternoon, I'm afraid. I'm worried about Mother, though. She was so tired she fell asleep before it even got dark. I've never known her to do that."

"It will be over soon," Jack Q said sadly. "Until then, there is no power on earth that could move Schooner from that house."

Victoria rubbed her hands in front of the warmth of the fire. "Why is it that everyone, except perhaps Grandpa, so matter-of-factly accepts the fact that Grandmother's dying? If I didn't know better, I'd think no one cared. I'm angry about it, aren't you?"

Jack Q carefully put some tobacco into his pipe and considered it. "Your grandfather doesn't accept it because that's the way he is. As for the rest of us, well, I suppose it's because we all grew up here. Most of us were just formed in the days when we had to fight something every day just to survive. The weather, the river, wild animals sometimes, and the war. I guess we just learned that there is no sense in attempting to fight the inevitable as well."

Victoria stared into the flames, thinking over his words. How strange that she'd never heard him say anything quite so sensible before. But then, in all fairness, when had she ever asked him a serious question and truly listened to his answer. Had Jack Q changed in the time she was gone, or had she?

"You mustn't look upon our attitude as uncaring, though," he added after a long, companionable silence. "There is not a single person in Seventrees who has not had their life touched by your grandmother. In fact, there would not be a town not for her." He went on, talking more to himself than Victoria. "My earliest memory is of Maggie Freiler. Getting off raft with my sister and grandmother and father. You remember my father, don't you? He and Katrin Clay died within a week of each other when you were about seven. Bea and I had lost our mother, and our father was wild with grief and

490

drink. We came here and your grandmother came down to the riverbank. She talked to us and took us to her house for cookies and a nap. Not the house she lives in now, of course, but the one that washed away in the flood. I don't remember much about that day except her leaning down to talk to us. We didn't speak English then, so I don't know what she said, but she had the prettiest blond hair and she knelt right down on the ground to speak to us on our own level. I remember that. She made us feel like we were home."

Victoria said nothing. His words had stirred something in her she'd never felt before, a feeling she could not define, which both worried and warmed her. Finally Jack Q spoke again. "We've been invited to go over and have dinner with the Clays. You don't mind, do you? My cooking is unforgivable . . ."

Victoria laughed. "Your cooking isn't bad, but you're afraid I might offer to fix dinner, and I *am* terrible at it."

Jack Q didn't trouble to deny it, merely smiled as he got his worn leather jacket out of the closet.

Dinner at the Clays' was a subdued affair, all of them obviously deep in their own thoughts about Maggie. Eventually, as dinner was being cleared, Jack Q said, "Victoria, Lucy tells me the two of you made a trip to Bath while you were in England. I've always meant to go there. What did you think of it?"

"I'm afraid I found it rather boring," Victoria began, but mention of traveling brought something else to mind. "Lucy, I'm missing one of those blue trunks. Did it get delivered here by mistake?"

"No. I've had all my things taken upstairs, and it wasn't with them."

Victoria frowned. "I hope it hasn't really been lost. It must have been very expensive, though I didn't have anything terribly important in it."

Ned was reaching for a second piece of pie. "Oh, well, your mother will certainly get you another."

It was a remark that Victoria would never have paid attention to except for the reaction it got from the others. Quincy Clay set his water glass down with a thud and looked up sharply. "Ned!"

Ned looked perplexed, then stricken. "Damn!" he said.

Victoria gazed first at Ned, then at Quincy. What was the matter with them?

"Perhaps you didn't have a proper tour of Bath. I've heard

so many people say how interesting it is," Jack Q said hurriedly. "I don't think anything could be more interesting than Dover, myself. Certainly you visited there. So close to Farrvale and—"

Victoria cut in. "Jack, you're babbling! I've never known you to do that. What on earth is wrong with all of you?"

A complete silence fell over the table. Lucy looked as confused as Victoria. The rest of them had the appearance of bank robbers who'd accidentally locked themselves in the vault. Eventually Ned spoke to his father. "I didn't mean to say it, you know. But I've always maintained she should be told."

"Told what?" Victoria demanded.

Quincy stared at her for a moment, then at Jack Q. "What do you think?"

Jack Q said, "She was bound to find out sooner or later, now that it's come up." He took Victoria's hand and said, "My dear, your mother bought that trunk. She bought the contents. All the dresses and jewelry and gifts. Every penny that was spent on you in England was hers."

8

"What do you mean?" Victoria whispered.

"Just what he said," Ned said. "Your mother financed your visit with your father. Everything he spent on you came from her. And more."

"Ned! You've said too much," Quincy said.

"What do you mean, 'and more'?" Victoria said. She felt cold and sick.

Ned ignored his father's warnings and went on. "She paid him a generous allowance as well."

"She had to *pay* him to have me in England?" Victoria said incredulously. "Jack, is this true? Lucy, did you know?"

Lucy got up and hurried around to Victoria's side. "Of course I didn't know. Naturally my father reimbursed your father for his expenses on my behalf, but you . . . ? I didn't know. I swear it! Oh, Vic, I'm so sorry."

All the sharp, loose bits of the puzzle were flying about in

Victoria's mind, relentlessly matching up and forming into a picture at last. But it was a terrible picture. Victoria was swamped with emotion. Shock, anger, embarrassment that it all fit so neatly, so obviously. Why hadn't she figured it out? He said he needed her there. That he couldn't get along without her. And all the time he'd meant her money. Not her. Her money. *Her mother's money!*

And he'd been so damnably generous with it! Hideous! The extravagant dresses and jewels and parties. The new racehorse! Schooner bought him a new racehorse. The redecorating at Farrvale Manor. The new furnishings in her rooms. His trips to the south of France. He'd mentioned that it had been a long time since he'd traveled. That was why. She'd paid for those trips. The trips he didn't take his daughter on! He had cheated her mother out of a small fortune. *Robbed* her. She had a sudden recollection of James Lithgow saying how her father used to cry poor all the time and had become a new man since her arrival. Of course he had. Oh, why hadn't she seen it? It all fit together—except one thing.

She made herself speak. "Why did he want to marry me off to Frederick?" Her voice was almost inaudible.

It was Ned who answered. "Remember the night before we left? I'd been in the smoking room with the men. They'd all been drinking too much, talking too freely—"

"Ned! There is no reason—"

"Sorry, Father, but she *should* know." Turning back to Victoria, he went on. "Adelaide apparently has a great fortune which she would not share with Elgin until one or the other of them had permanent control over your inheritance. She refused to marry him until you and Frederick were married. Believe it or not, Frederick has a woman. He lives with her in London, and it was assumed by all of them that he would continue to keep her. You were a pawn in a financial scheme—"

Victoria covered her eyes with one hand and raised the other for silence. "Don't go on, Ned. I understand."

Jack Q put his hand on her arm. "Your mother must never know that *you* know, Victoria. It would break her heart that you found this out. We all argued with her about the wisdom of it, but she was adamant."

"I . . . I wanted s-s-so much for him to l-l-love me!" Victoria wept.

"Schooner knew that. That's why she did it. She wanted

493

you to be happy, and thought by buying your father's attentions, she could make you happy."

Trembling and with tears pouring down her cheeks, Victoria rose shakily. She squeezed Lucy's shoulder, took a deep, shuddering breath, and said, "I'll never tell her I know. I promise you that. Now, you must excuse me."

"I'll take you home," Ned said, jumping to his feet.

"No, Ned. I need to walk."

No one argued with her. Jack Q got her coat, and Ned saw her to the door. He stood on the porch in the darkness with her for a long, quiet moment. Finally Victoria said, "This has been the worst night of my life. There was nothing I wanted to hear less or needed to hear more. You were right, Ned, to tell me."

"I hope so. I betrayed a confidence and made you unhappy. It's hard to believe I did the right thing." He sounded almost as miserable as she felt.

"You did," she said simply, and walked away, toward her grandmother's house.

When she got there, she was relieved to find that her mother was still sleeping. She tapped lightly at Maggie's bedroom door. Gerald opened it. "Grandfather, there was a hamper of food on the front step when I came in. Someone must have left it while I was gone. I unpacked it. Go down and have your dinner. I want to talk to Grandmother. Is she awake?"

"Yes, she is—"

"The girl's right, Gerald." Maggie's voice came strained and soft from the bed. "You must eat."

"I'll be right back," Gerald promised.

Victoria went to Maggie's bedside and took the old woman's hand in hers. "Grandmother, there is something I must tell you before it is too late."

"Then say it now."

Leaning closer and lowering her voice, Victoria said, "I know about Mother and my father and the money."

Maggie sighed, coughed slightly. "Your mother didn't want you to know."

"I shan't tell her—ever. But I wanted *you* to know that I'm grateful and I love her very dearly. It must have been awful for her, paying for extravagant frivolities and knowing that I thought they were proof of *his* love. I've been terribly wrong about her, all my life. I am a fool."

494

"No. When you can say that, you no longer are one," Maggie said.

Victoria heard the door swing open. Schooner came in and smiled at the sight of her mother and daughter holding hands. Victoria leaped up and hugged her, but couldn't find words to say.

It was almost dawn when Victoria awoke. At first she couldn't figure out what had disturbed her; then she heard the music. Broken bits of melody, played on a flute. She knew instinctively that her grandfather was crying as he played, and she knew what it meant.

Everyone said it was a fine day for a funeral. Clear, sunny, warm for autumn. A light breeze swept across the top of the bluff, bringing the scent of the prairies and the soft rustle of the dried sunflower heads nodding farewell. Maggie's grave was at the north end of the cemetery, closest to the edge of the bluff and next to the road leading down to the town. The headstone said:

MAGGIE FREILER

1810-1884

Founder and Beloved Citizen

Gerald Freiler stood with his left hand on the gray granite monument and his back to the mound of fresh earth. He was looking out over the Kaw Valley. Schooner was beside him, and Victoria and her Aunt Addie next to her. "She picked the site herself," Gerald said, though they all knew it. "We stopped the wagon just here the first time we saw the place. I watched her face light up as she looked down the hill. There was nothing then but the mission and a dirt trail and Woody's ferry crossing, but a change came over her. I should have known then what it meant to her . . ." His voice cracked.

Addie, as plump and placid as an old cow, said, "Papa, you're tired. Come home with me now."

Bowing his head, Gerald let his once-favorite daughter lead him away. Victoria stayed with her mother as friends passed, laying flowers on the grave and speaking a few words of condolence. They were all the same theme. A woman named

Nancy said, "I came up here and sat while the water came up. I didn't have anything but my babies and my grandmother's quilt. She saved our lives."

A bent old man took Schooner's hand in his gnarled one and said, "I heard she was poorly and I came from Wichita to thank her one more time. We came through here in '46 with a wagon train. She gave us a packet of cures. We couldn't even afford to pay for them, but they saved my youngest when he took the fever along the trail."

"She gave us her best horse when ours was lost crossing the river. God bless her."

"She paid our rent the year my man broke his back. When we tried to repay her, she told us to send the money to that Indian place in Wyoming where the other daughter teaches."

A fussy-looking little old man said, "I attended your birth, Mrs. LeSage. I never knew a finer person, man or woman, than your mother."

"Do you recollect me, ma'am? Your ma took me in after the Battle of Westport. Kept me right there in your house and cared for me just like I was her own boy she lost."

"I was burned bad in Lawrence. Mrs. Freiler brought us medicines. Nary a bill. She was highly regarded, yes ma'am, she was."

Eventually they all went down the hill. Schooner sighed, rubbed her eyes, and said, "I'm going to Addie's to check on Father. Are you coming, Victoria?"

"In a few minutes."

Schooner rearranged a few of the flowers that formed a vast pile on the grave, then laid her hand briefly on the headstone before leaving. Victoria watched her go, shading her eyes against the bright Kansas sunshine. Then she went to the edge of the bluff and sat down in the long, dry grass. "Ned, come sit with me," she said.

Ned had been standing in the shade of an elm, keeping his distance. "I didn't want to intrude," he said as he came over and sat down next to her.

"I spent a long time trying to learn how to be a fine English lady," Victoria said without preamble. "I wanted to know how to adhere to all the dusty, old, meaningless traditions. I didn't realize that my own grandmother was a tradition herself. A living, energetic one. I'm prouder of being part of her than I am of being a duke's daughter. I've learned more in the last week than all the time I was at Farrvale."

She moved closer to Ned, and he put his arm around her. "What else did you learn this week, Vic?" he said softly.

She slipped her arm around his waist. "I learned that I'm a strong woman like my mother and grandmother. I'd rather be part of making traditions than slavishly following them. I've learned that I belong here. I think Mother and Grandmother have been trying to tell me all my life that 'home' is more than a place. I'm rooted here as firmly as those seven trees around Grandmother's house. There's something else, too . . ." she said.

"What else?"

She looked down, tongue-tied for once, and picked a burr off her black skirt. "I can't tell you," she said quietly.

"Would it be easier to tell me if I said I've always wanted to marry one of those strong-minded Freiler women who love this place?" Ned said, smiling.

She turned to face him. "Oh, Ned, I'm so glad to be home at last . . . with you. Let's stay here together forever."

"You're sure that's what you want?"

"I'm sure. I'm home now. *Home.*"

Author's Note

For readers like myself who like to have the fact and the fiction sorted out at the end, I offer the following:

The town of Seventrees did not exist, but is a combination of three places in the Kansas City area that *were* real: Grinter's Ferry, crossing the Kaw in Bonner Springs; the Shawnee Methodist Mission (located in the suburb of Fairway); and a tiny trading settlement in Kansas City, Kansas, called Choteau's Four Houses. Because the loop in the Kaw River does not swing as far south as I have indicated on my map, it did not border the Sante Fe Trail, but paralleled it at a distance of several miles.

Of the three actual places, the one that means the most to me is the mission since I have lived all my life within three blocks of it and my house is shaded by a gigantic oak which is said to have been planted by the minister of the mission as a windbreak. Several older residents, including my own father, remember playing in the wagon ruts of the Santa Fe Trail as children. I walked in them myself while researching this book near Baldwin, Kansas, the site of the Battle of Black Jack (where Adams and Ernest are injured in the story).

The devastating flood that figures in the book really happened in 1844, and I took the liberty of putting it off three years for the sake of my story. The first territorial legislature did meet at the mission and was hastily adjourned by an outbreak of cholera.

I had a great deal of fun researching the windwagon. Accounts of it and its inventor, Captain Smith, occur in tantalizing bits in several sources. But the dates, the captain's last name, and the precise location of the "maiden voyage" are so changeable that I've formed the opinion that it was very possibly a practical joke perpetrated by a local paper. More knowledgeable historians than I might disagree, but there seems to be a distinctly tongue-in-cheek tone to the accounts.

There are copious and heartbreakingly vivid eyewitness accounts of Quantrill's raid on Lawrence. Everything in that scene actually happened to someone, including the fact that the raiders tried to help General Lane's wife get her piano out of the burning house, and the "rug rescue."

I have tried to portray the Battle of Westport and the events leading up to it accurately, and had an interesting experience while studying it. The Westport Historical Society sponsors a very fine tour of the battle sites each fall on the anniversary of the battle. When I took the tour, the guide got on the bus wearing a Confederate hat and said, as part of his jovial introductory patter, that we were going to see the battle from the Confederate point of view. At that, three people got up, marched down the aisle of the bus, and demanded their money back. I was astonished to discover that they were *not* joking. The bloody rivalry of the Bleeding Kansas period of our history is still felt almost a hundred and twenty years later in some circles.

Janice Young Brooks

Shawnee Mission, Kansas

ABOUT THE AUTHOR

A native Kansan, Janice Young Brooks lives in Shawnee Mission, Kansas, a suburb of Kansas City. *Seventrees* is set in her own back yard—literally, as her home is on land once belonging to the Indian missions she fictionalized for this book.

Janice is married, has two children, and is a member of Mensa. The Brooks have three cats who graciously allow them to share the house and open cat food cans.